the tutu ballet

story and illustrations
by Sally O. Lee

The Tutu Ballet

I would like to thank Stephanie Robinson-Craine,
and the staff at BookSurge
for helping me to publish this book.

I would also like to thank my family and friends
for their love and support.

Library of Congress Control Number: 2008907897
Publisher: BookSurge Publishing
North Charleston, South Carolina

www.booksurge.com

For more information: visit www.leepublishing.net

Lee, Sally O.
The Tutu Ballet / Sally O. Lee

Summary: Ms. Berry, the ballet teacher, is given a talented
group of students. The students do not always do what Ms. Berry instructs
them to do. A ballet emerges that suits the talents of her students and
it is the best ballet ever. It is a story about tolerance, patience,
creativity, teamwork, and love.

ISBN :1-4392-0917-0

This book is typeset in "snowman" created by Sally O. Lee
The illustrations are rendered in watercolor and pen and ink on paper.

Printed in the U.S.A.

First Edition

To: Cindy

Every Saturday, all the mothers who lived in the forest brought their children to the local ballet class that was held in a small field under some very tall trees.

One by one, the mothers arrived with their children dressed in their proper ballet attire.

The ballet teacher, Ms. Berry, would
wait patiently for her students to arrive.
Ms. Berry had been a prima ballerina
and knew everything there was to
know about ballet.

in her class were Belinda the bear,
Mirabel the mouse, Harriett the Hare,
and Fillippo the Fox.

The mothers were very proud
of their children and each and
every week they would stand on
the side and watch as their
children twirled and plied,
jumped and spun.

Each
ballet position more
spectacular than
the last.

They cheered
and hollered,
quietly of course.
as they did not
want to disturb Ms. Berry
and her teaching.

Although Belinda the bear worked very hard
in the class, all she really liked to do was
kick her leg high in the air.

She did this over and over, and
she performed
it perfectly.

And Ms. Berry praised
her favorite kick.

Harriett the hare was especially adept at twirling round and round until she got so dizzy that she could barely stand.

She made the most wonderful twirls in the world.

Fillippo the fox was especially good at jumping. He could jump and jump across the field, and he did the highest jumps of any of them.

He didn't care so much about twirls or plies.

And Finally. Mirabel loved to plie
more than anyone else in the class.

She would plie for her mother.
she would plie for her friends.

and finally she would plie
for Ms. Berry.

Mirabel could do a perfect plie
for the whole world.

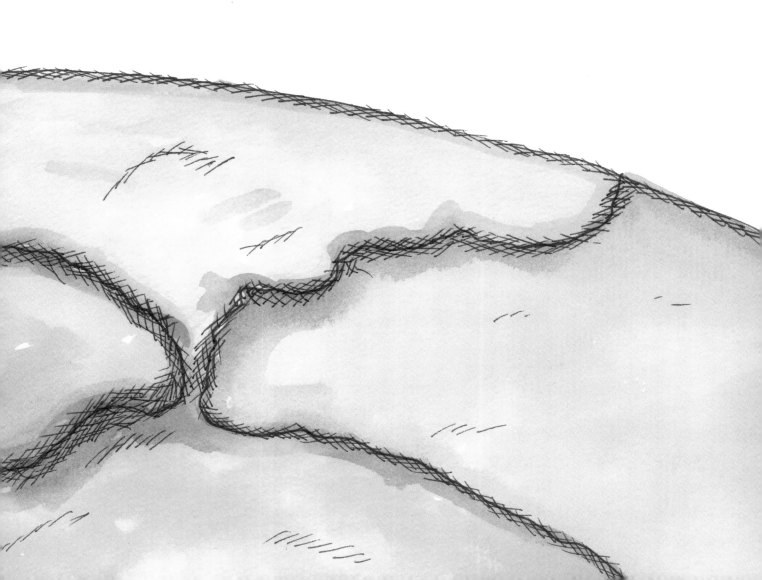

Ms. Berry had her hands full with this class. She tried very hard to get all her students to plie at the same time, or jump at the same time, but they would all fall back to their favorite dance steps and it would result in mayhem.

Fillippo would bump into Harriett with his jumps and Belinda would accidently kick Mirabel with her famous left kicks.

Sometimes it looked more like a boxing match
as opposed to a ballet class.

It started to
look like
things were not
going to go
as planned
for Ms. Berry.

So, she decided to design a ballet recital that would suit all the steps of the students in her ballet class.

If Belinda only liked to kick her left leg high in the air, then she could begin the ballet and Harriett could appear from behind Belinda and twirl and twirl until....

she bumped into Fillippo who could jump and jump
across the stage and then Mirabel could
appear at the end
with her perfect plie.

The night of the recital came and
all the students in Ms. Berry's
class were ready
for their first ballet recital.

They were a little nervous, and
they could see all the people
in the audience
including their families.

Belinda started when she heard the
music and kicked to her
heart's content.

Harriett suddenly appeared and
twirled and twirled
until she disappeared off the stage.

Fillippo then appeared jumping and
jumping as high as he could go.

And then little Mirabel quietly
appeared and gave one of
her fabulous plies.

The audience cheered,
and it was the best ballet ever.

The author has committed to providing students and faculty with technology updates monthly for the text. These enhance students' learning by relating the topic in the text to real-world, current events and serve to keep the text up-to-date in an increasingly complex, fast-moving discipline.

Links to all the companies introduced in the text's end-of-chapter Real-world Cases and the in-chapter Bookmarks features are included on the site, with questions and exercises that can again be e-mailed to the instructor.

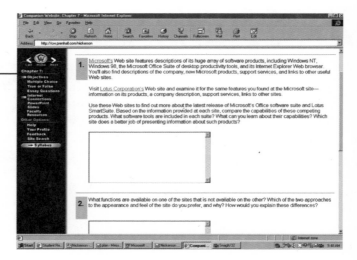

In addition to the PowerPoint slides provided for students' and instructors' classroom use, instructors can also download the Instructor's Manual in Word format.

Business and Information Systems

2

Business and Information Systems

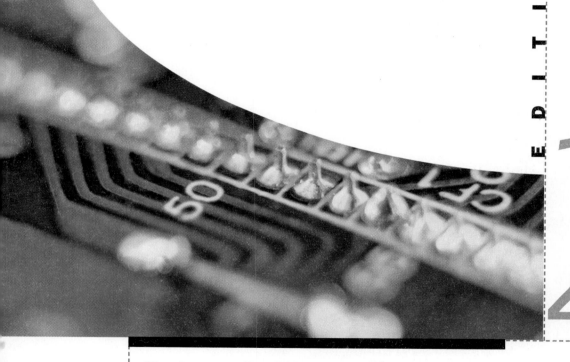

E D I T I O N

2

Robert C. Nickerson
San Francisco State University

Prentice Hall, Upper Saddle River, New Jersey 07458

Acquisitions Editor: David Alexander
Editor-in-Chief: Mickey Cox
Developmental Editor: Rebecca Johnson
Editorial Assistant: Erika Rusnak
Director Strategic Marketing: Nancy Evans
Senior Marketing Manager: Kris King
Managing Editor/Production: Sondra Greenfield
Manufacturing Buyer: Lisa Babin
Senior Manufacturing Supervisor: Paul Smolenski
Manufacturing Manager: Vincent Scelta
Senior Designer: Cheryl Asherman
Design Director: Patricia Smythe
Interior Design: Amanda Kavanagh
Photo Researcher: Teri Stratford
Cover Design: Cheryl Asherman
Illustrator (Interior): Tech Graphics
Photo Illustration: Guy Crittendon © SIS
Senior Print/Media Production Manager: Karen Goldsmith
Print Production Manager: Christina Mahon
Production Services: UG / GGS Information Services, Inc.

Photo and screen capture credits appear before the index.

Library of Congress Cataloging-in-Publication Data

Nickerson, Robert C.
    Business and information systems/Robert C. Nickerson.—2nd ed.
      p. cm.
    Includes index.
    ISBN 0-13-089496-6
    1. Management information systems—Case studies. I. Title.

HD30.2.N53 2000
658.4′038—dc21   00-038514

Prentice-Hall International (UK) Limited, *London*
Prentice-Hall of Australia Pty. Limited, *Sydney*
Prentice-Hall Canada Inc., *Toronto*
Prentice-Hall Hispanoamericana, S.A., *Mexico*
Prentice-Hall of India Private Limited, *New Delhi*
Prentice-Hall of Japan, Inc., *Tokyo*
Prentice-Hall Pte Ltd., *Singapore*
Editora Prentice-Hall do Brasil, Ltda., *Rio de Janeiro*

10 9 8 7 6 5 4 3 2 1
ISBN: 0-13-089496-6

BRIEF CONTENTS

Preface   xix

PART I   INTRODUCTION   1

Chapter 1   Information Systems in Business   2

Chapter 2   Business Fundamentals   31

Chapter 3   Information System Fundamentals   62

PART II   INFORMATION TECHNOLOGY   90

Chapter 4   Information System Hardware   91

Chapter 5   Information System Software   134

Chapter 6   Information System Networks and the
Internet   167

Chapter 7   Information System Data Management   200

PART III   BUSINESS INFORMATION SYSTEMS   236

Chapter 8   Personal Productivity and Problem Solving   237

Chapter 9   Group Collaboration   275

Chapter 10 Business Operations   304

Chapter 11 Management Decision Making   336

Chapter 12 Electronic Commerce and the Strategic Impact of Information
Systems   371

**PART IV   DEVELOPING AND MANAGING INFORMATION
SYSTEMS   406**

Chapter 13 Information System Development   407

Chapter 14 Managing Information Systems and Technology   439

Glossary   467
Photo Credits   480
Acknowledgments   481
Index   484

CONTENTS

Preface   xix

PART I   INTRODUCTION   1

Chapter 1   Information Systems in Business   2

Basic information system concepts   4
What is an information system?   4
Examples of information systems   4
Bookmark: *Inventory management at 7-Eleven*   5
Information system functions   8
Information system components   9
Data versus information   11
Types of information systems   12
Individual information systems   12
Workgroup information systems   13
Organizational information systems   15
Interorganizational information systems   16
Global information systems   16
Information system users   17
How users use information systems   17
The ethical use of information systems   18
Connecting users to information technology   19
Networks   19
The Internet and the World Wide Web   19
Electronic commerce   21
Bookmark: *Electronic Commerce at Michelin North America*   22
Benefits of information systems   22
Better information   23
Improved service   23
Increased productivity   23
Competitive advantage   24
An approach to the study of information systems   24
Chapter summary   25
Key terms   26
Review questions   26
Discussion questions   27
Ethics questions   27
Problem-solving projects   27
Internet and electronic commerce projects   28
Real world case: *The Benetton Group, Italy*   29

Chapter 2   Business Fundamentals   31

The nature of business   32

Types of businesses   33

Manufacturers 33

Wholesalers 34

Retailers 34

Service businesses 34

Bookmark: *Internet connections for native Canadian tribes*   35

Not-for-profit organizations 36

Government 36

Business trends   36

Business functions   37

Accounting 37

Finance 37

Marketing 38

Production 38

Human resource management 38

Other business functions 39

The organization of a business   39

Information and business operations   40

Information and business management   43

Basic business information processing   44

Entering customer orders 45

Billing customers 45

Bookmark: *Order processing at The Sharper Image*   46

Collecting customer payments 48

Keeping track of inventory 48

Purchasing stock and materials 51

Paying bills 52

Paying employees 53

Reporting financial information 55

Information systems and business   55

Chapter summary   57

Key terms   58

Review questions   58

Discussion questions   58

Ethics questions   59

Problem-solving projects   59

Internet and electronic commerce projects   59

Real world case: *Coca-Cola*   60

Chapter 3   Information System Fundamentals   62

Hardware for information systems   63

Computer and communications hardware 63

The need for computer hardware in information systems 64
The need for communications hardware in information
systems 65
Computer and network systems 65
**Bookmark: *Handheld computers at Sodexho Marriott
Services* 68**
Software for information systems 71
Types of software 71
The need for software in information systems 72
Sources of software 72
Stored data for information systems 73
Data organization 73
The need for stored data in information systems 75
Personnel for information systems 75
Users and operating personnel 75
The need for personnel in information systems 76
Procedures for information systems 76
Types of procedures 76
The need for procedures in information systems 77
Ethical issues for information systems 77
Ethical decision making 77
Ethical issues 78
Bookmark: *Web site for HarlemLive* 79
Applying ethics 83
Chapter summary 84
Key terms 85
Review questions 85
Discussion questions 86
Ethics questions 86
Problem-solving projects 86
Internet and electronic commerce projects 87
Real world case: *Beamscope Canada* 88

PART II   INFORMATION TECHNOLOGY 90

Chapter 4   Information System Hardware 91

Computer organization 92
Input and output devices 94
Keyboards 94
Pointing devices 95
Other input devices 96
Screens 99
Printers 100
Other output devices 103
Terminals 104

Devices for people with disabilities 105
Multimedia input and output 106
Virtual reality input and output 107
Bookmark: *Virtual reality at the Education Center in Alvdalen, Sweden* 108
Primary storage 109
Primary storage structure 109
Data representation 110
Primary storage organization 112
Primary storage capacity 112
The central processing unit 113
CPU structure 113
CPU compatibility 115
CPU speed 116
Common CPUs 116
Bookmark: *Massively parallel processing at United Airlines* 118
Secondary storage 119
Magnetic disk storage 119
Optical disk storage 123
Magnetic tape storage 125
Chapter summary 126
Key terms 128
Review questions 128
Discussion questions 129
Ethics questions 129
Problem-solving projects 130
Internet and electronic commerce projects 131
Real world case: *Chevron* 132

Chapter 5   Information System Software   134

Software concepts 135
Application software 135
Individual application software 136
Workgroup application software 137
Organizational application software 137
Interorganizational application software 138
System software 139
Operating system concepts 139
Common operating systems 145
Bookmark: *Linux at the City of Medina, Washington* 146
Other system software 148
Software development 149
Programming language concepts 149

Traditional programming languages 153

Object-oriented programming languages 156

Internet programming languages 158

Bookmark: *A Java inventory ordering system at Motor Spares & Staff* 160

Chapter summary 161

Key terms 162

Review questions 162

Discussion questions 163

Ethics questions 163

Problem-solving projects 164

Internet and electronic commerce projects 164

Real world case: *BMG* 165

Chapter 6   Information System Networks and the Internet   167

Communications concepts 168

Communications hardware 169

Communications channel characteristics 169

Communications channel media 170

Bookmark: *Wireless communications at Illinois Power* 172

Communications channel sources 174

Communications processors 175

Communications protocols 176

Communications security 178

Communications software 178

Personal computer communications software 178

Multiple-user computer communications software 179

Network communications software 179

Network concepts 179

Network organization 180

Types of networks 182

Local area networks 183

Local area network structure 183

Business uses of local area networks 183

Client/server commuting 184

Wide area networks 185

Wide area network structure 185

Bookmark: *A wide area network for Designer Shoe Warehouse* 186

Business uses of wide area networks 187

Internetworks 187

The Internet 188

Internet communication 188

Internet services 189
Intranets 191
Extranets 191
Electronic commerce 192
Hardware and software for electronic commerce 192
Electronic commerce use 193
Chapter summary 194
Key terms 195
Review questions 195
Discussion questions 195
Ethics questions 196
Problem-solving projects 196
Internet and electronic commerce projects 197
Real world case: *CDNOW* 198

Chapter 7 Information System Data Management 200

File processing 201
File organization 202
File management 204
Advantages of file processing 205
Disadvantages of file processing 205
Database processing 206
What is a database? 207
Database management 207
Advantages of database processing 209
Disadvantages of database processing 209
Database organization 210
Data relationships 210
Early databases 213
Relational databases 214
Object-oriented databases 216
Common database software 216
Bookmark: *The affinity database for the Carolina Mudcats* 217
Personal computer database software 218
Multiple-user computer database software 218
Networked computer database software 218
Using database software 219
Query languages 219
Application programs 221
Web access 222
Database use in information systems 223

Data warehouses   224
  Data mining 224
Multidimensional databases   225
  On-line analytical processing 227
Bookmark: *Multidimensional data analysis at Aqua-Chem* 228
Database administration   229
Chapter summary   229
Key terms   230
Review questions   231
Discussion questions   231
Ethics questions   232
Problem-solving projects   232
Internet and electronic commerce projects   233
Real world case: *Proctor & Gamble*   234

PART III   BUSINESS INFORMATION SYSTEMS   236

Chapter 8   Personal Productivity and Problem Solving   237

Improving personal productivity   238
Managing stored data   239
  Using database software to manage data 239
  A case study of data management 241
Analyzing data   245
  Using spreadsheet software to analyze data 245
  A case study of data analysis 246
  Combining data management and data analysis 247
Presenting information   248
  Presenting information in text form 248
  A case study of text information presentation 248
  Presenting information in graphical form 249
  A case study of graphical information presentation 253
  Combining other applications and information presentation 253
  Presenting information in published form 255
  Presenting information in multimedia form 256
Bookmark: *Multimedia presentation at Orient-Express Trains & Cruises*   257
Locating and retrieving information by using the Internet   258
  Searching the World Wide Web 259
Bookmark: *Web searching at Sparks.com*   260
  Evaluating information from the World Wide Web 261
Solving problems with personal applications   262
  Problems, solutions, and solution procedures 262

End-user computing 263

The problem-solving process 263

Problem definition 264

Solution procedure design 265

Software implementation 266

Implementation testing 266

Documentation 267

Chapter summary 268

Key terms 269

Review questions 269

Discussion questions 270

Ethics questions 270

Problem-solving projects 271

Internet and electronic commerce projects 272

Real world case: *Haworth Inc.* 273

Chapter 9   Group Collaboration   275

Encouraging group collaboration 276

Characteristics of group collaboration 277

The time and place of collaboration 277

The form of communication 279

Types of workgroup applications 279

Electronic messaging 280

Information sharing 282

Bookmark: *Group collaboration for the Sable Offshore Energy Project* 283

Document conferencing 284

Audioconferencing 286

Videoconferencing 287

Bookmark: *Collaborative applications for a Web site at Reebok International* 289

Electronic conferencing 290

Electronic meeting support 291

Group calendaring and scheduling 292

Workflow management 293

Summary of workgroup applications 294

Office automation 296

The virtual work environment 297

Telecommuting 297

Virtual offices 297

Virtual meetings 297

Virtual companies 298

Chapter summary 298

Key terms 299

Review questions 299
Discussion questions 300
Ethics questions 300
Problem-solving projects 301
Internet and electronic commerce projects 301
Real world case: *Saab* 302

Chapter 10 Business Operations 304

Increasing business operations efficiency 305
Transaction processing systems 306
Transaction processing system structure 306
Transaction processing system functions 307
Controlling transaction processing systems 311
Processing data in transaction processing systems 312
Basic business information systems 313
Order entry system 314
Billing system 316
Accounts receivable system 317
Inventory control system 318
Bookmark: *Warehouse management at Owens & Minor* 319
Purchasing system 320
Accounts payable system 321
Payroll system 322
General ledger system 323
Other business information systems 324
Accounting information systems 324
Financial information systems 324
Marketing information systems 325
Manufacturing information systems 326
Bookmark: *Supply chain management at Miller SQA* 327
Human resource information systems 328
Enterprise resource planning systems 328
Chapter summary 330
Key terms 331
Review questions 331
Discussion questions 332
Ethics questions 332
Problem-solving projects 332
Internet and electronic commerce projects 333
Real world case: *Kozmo.com* 334

Chapter 11 Management Decision Making 336

Improving management decision-making effectiveness 337

Management decisions 338
Levels of management decisions 338
Characteristics of management decisions 339
Information needs for management decisions 340
Information systems for management support 341
Management information systems 342
Management information system structure 342
Management information system functions 343
Management information system software 347
Decision support systems 348
Management decision support 348
Decision support system structure 348
Decision support system functions 349
Decision support system software 350
Group decision support systems 351
Geographic information systems 351
Executive support systems 352
Executive information needs 352
Bookmark: *Geographic information system at the City of Oakland* 353
Executive support system structure 355
Executive support system functions 356
Executive support system software 357
Expert systems 357
Expert advice 358
Expert system structure 358
Expert system functions 360
Expert system software 360
Other artificial intelligence applications 360
Knowledge management systems 362
Organizational knowledge 362
Knowledge management 362
Bookmark: *A knowledge management system at Shell Oil* 363
Knowledge management systems 364
Chapter summary 365
Key terms 366
Review questions 366
Discussion questions 366
Ethics questions 367
Problem-solving projects 367
Internet and electronic commerce projects 368
Real world case: *Grand & Toy, Canada* 369

Chapter 12   Electronic Commerce and the Strategic Impact of Information Systems   371

Providing a strategic impact   372
Cost leadership   372
Differentiation   372
Focus   373
Innovation   373
Growth   374
Business alliances   374
Electronic commerce systems   374
The strategic impact of electronic commerce   374
Types of electronic commerce   375
Characteristics of electronic commerce systems   377
Bookmark: *Business-to-business e-commerce at Adolph Coors*   380
Electronic business   380
Interorganizational information systems   381
Business alliances   381
The strategic impact of interoganizational systems   382
Characteristics of interorganizational systems   383
Electronic data interchange systems   384
Global information systems   386
International business   386
The strategic impact of global information systems   388
Characteristics of global information systems   389
Global electronic commerce   392
Bookmark: *A global information system at Avon*   393
Strategic information systems   394
Characteristics of strategic information systems   394
Identifying strategic information system opportunities   397
Chapter summary   399
Key terms   400
Review questions   401
Discussion questions   401
Ethics questions   401
Problem-solving projects   402
Internet and electronic commerce projects   403
Real world case: *1-800-Flowers*   404

PART IV   **DEVELOPING AND MANAGING INFORMATION SYSTEMS   406**

Chapter 13   Information System Development   407

People in information system development   408

The system development process   408
  System planning 409
  System analysis 411
  System design 413
  System implementation 414
  System maintenance 415
Bookmark: *System conversion at Carlson Hospitality Worldwide*   416
System development tools   417
  Data flow diagrams 417
  Entity-relationship diagrams 418
  CASE tools 420
A case study of information system development   421
  System planning 421
  System analysis 422
  System design 424
  System implementation 424
  System maintenance 425
Other system development approaches   426
  Prototyping 426
  Rapid application development 426
  Object-oriented analysis and design 427
Individual information system development   428
Electronic commerce system development   429
Bookmark: *E-commerce system development at AutoNation,*   431
Business processes reengineering   431
  Chapter summary 432
  Key terms 434
  Review questions 434
  Discussion questions 435
  Ethics questions 435
  Problem-solving projects 435
  Internet and electronic commerce projects 436
  Real world case: *Pinnacol assurance* 437

Chapter 14   Managing Information Systems and Technology   439

Planning for information systems and technology   440
  Determining the planning horizon 440
  Evaluating risk 441
  Selecting the application portfolio 441
Acquiring information technology   443
  Hardware 443

Software 444
Network technology 444
Data management technology 445
Personnel and training 445
Organizing information systems activities 445
Centralized versus decentralized management 445
Information systems organizational structure 447
World Wide Web and electronic commerce support 448
Bookmark: *Internet technology strategist at Sprint Paranet* 449
Controlling and securing information systems 450
Information system controls 450
Information system security 452
Preventing computer crime 453
Bookmark: *Security at MasterCard International 455*
The effects of information technology on employment 458
Displaced employees 459
Changing patterns of work 459
Employee health 459
Ethical management of information systems and technology 460
Chapter summary 461
Key terms 462
Review questions 462
Discussion questions 463
Ethics questions 463
Problem-solving projects 463
Internet and electronic commerce projects 464
Real world case: eBay 465

Glossary 467
Photo Credits 480
Acknowledgments 481
Index 484

Information systems are essential to the operations and management of businesses today. To become effective business professionals, students must be educated in information systems and technology, and in the integration of information systems into business activities. A student's understanding of business is limited without an understanding of information systems. But how can a student understand information systems without *first* understanding business?

This question prompted the writing of the first edition of this book. The question is even more important today, as businesses increasingly rely on information systems. The second edition of *Business and Information Systems* continues to take the unique approach of covering both business fundamentals and information systems. The book views information systems and businesses as intricately intertwined. It presents not only the traditional information systems and technology topics, but also the fundamental business background that students need in order to understand the relevance of these topics. The book describes how businesses operate and are managed, and shows how information systems support business operations and management. It discusses the importance of competitive advantage to businesses and explains how information systems can help provide that advantage. The book covers the technical foundations of information systems and shows how the technology is critical to the success of businesses.

Students taking an information systems course often find the approach followed by other books unsatisfactory. Although most books explain information systems and technology adequately, they do not provide a sufficient foundation in business functions for students to fully understand the importance of the technical topics. As a result, students often complete the information systems course without knowing how the course material relates to other areas of business, such as accounting, finance, marketing, production, and human resource management. When they take other business courses, they are not able to use information systems concepts in those courses.

This book overcomes these difficulties by integrating business topics with information systems concepts. For example, the second chapter of the book explains business fundamentals. It describes the functions and organization of a business, explains the flow of information in a business, and examines the use of information in business management. This background serves as a basis for understanding the need for and structure of information systems. This approach is carried through in other chapters. For example, the chapter on information system fundamentals (Chapter 3) discusses the need that businesses have for information technology, and the chapters on specific technologies (Chapters 4 through 7) emphasize the role of each type of technology in businesses. Similarly, each chapter on business information systems (Chapters 8 through 12) discusses the advantages businesses gain from the systems described in the chapter. These chapters also cover such topics as management decision making and competitive advantage to provide a basis for understanding the role of management information and strategic information systems.

Students taking an information systems course may also find that some books provide a narrow view, focusing primarily on personal computers and applications. This book presents a broad view of information systems, showing how systems function at many levels within an organization and between organizations. It describes how individuals, workgroups, and organizations as a whole use information systems. It examines systems that operate within a business and between businesses—including

electronic commerce systems—and that function at local, national, and global levels. All these perspectives, from the individual to the interorganizational and global, are covered completely in the book.

Content and Organization

The book is organized into four parts. Part I introduces business and information systems concepts and examples. Chapter 1 motivates the students by showing that they will be involved with information systems as end users in their jobs and careers. Chapter 2 covers basic business concepts that students need to know in order to understand information systems. More advanced business concepts appear in later chapters, where they relate to different types of information systems. Chapter 3 examines the basic structure of information systems, emphasizing the need for each component of the system. This chapter also discusses ethical decision making and ethical issues for information systems in detail. With the background in Part I, the other parts of the book can be covered in any order.

Part II examines the information technology that forms a foundation for information systems. Chapter 4 covers information system hardware that is relevant to the user. Chapter 5 describes information system software, again emphasizing concepts that are most relevant to the user. Chapter 6 discusses networks used in information systems, including local area networks, wide area networks, internetworks, and the Internet. Chapter 7 covers data management for information systems, including database organization and processing.

Part III of the book examines information systems in businesses. Chapter 8 discusses the need for improving personal productivity in the workplace, explains how people use common end-user software to improve their productivity, and shows how users solve business problems using this software. Chapter 9 examines the importance of group collaboration in businesses and describes the groupware tools that encourage such collaboration. Chapter 10 covers basic business operations and explains how information systems can increase the efficiency of these operations. Chapter 11 examines management decision making, the information and analysis that can improve the effectiveness of decision making, and the information systems that provide the necessary support. Chapter 12 explains how information systems can have a strategic impact on a business and examines the types of systems that can have such an impact, with particular emphasis on electronic commerce systems. Numerous examples are used throughout this part of the book to illustrate the information systems that are described.

Part IV of the book discusses the development and management of information systems. Chapter 13 covers the development of information systems, with an emphasis on end-user involvement in the development process. Chapter 14 examines the management of information systems.

Changes in the Second Edition

A number of changes, including the following, have been made in the second edition based on the experiences of users of the first edition.

- Chapter 3 has been almost entirely rewritten to eliminate redundancy with other chapters. The emphasis in this chapter is on the business need for the technological and other components of the information system.
- The material on individual problem solving in Chapter 13 of the first edition has been moved to Chapter 8 and rewritten to increase its relevance. Other material

in Chapter 13 that overlapped with Chapter 14 of the first edition has been eliminated.

- New material on electronic commerce has been incorporated throughout the book. Chapter 1 introduces electronic commerce, Chapter 6 covers information technology for electronic commerce, Chapter 12 discusses electronic commerce from an organizational perspective, Chapter 13 examines the development of electronic commerce systems, and case studies throughout the book examine applications of electronic commerce.
- Ethics in information systems has been moved to Part I, and the material has been expanded. Chapter 1 introduces ethics and the problem of evaluating ethical questions, and Chapter 3 covers ethical issues for information systems in detail. In addition, each chapter has a separate set of ethical questions in the end-of-chapter material.
- Coverage of the Internet and the World Wide Web has been expanded throughout the book. In addition, more cases emphasizing the Internet have been included, and separate end-of-chapter projects on the Internet, the Web, and e-commerce have been added to each chapter.
- All chapters have been updated to ensure that the material is current. A few examples of the many new topics are rewritable compact disk (Chapter 4), XML (Chapter 5), DSL (Chapter 6), multidimensional databases (Chapter 7), portals (Chapter 8), instant messaging (Chapter 9), ERP (Chapter 10), and knowledge management (Chapter 11).
- Almost all in-chapter boxed cases and end-of-chapter real-world cases have been replaced with newer cases. More electronic commerce and Internet/World Wide Web cases have been added.

Key Features

The importance of information systems to end users is emphasized throughout the book. Starting with the first chapter, examples show how end users are involved in information systems. Part II discusses only the information technology topics that are immediately useful to end users or that provide a foundation for understanding important concepts. Part III discusses personal productivity for end users and end-user involvement in workgroup, organizational, interorganizational, and global information systems. Part IV shows how end users are involved with others in the development of organizational information systems.

Three fictitious businesses are presented in Chapter 1 and used as examples in various chapters. These businesses—a campus sports shop, an athletic clothing wholesaler, and an athletic shoe manufacturer—were selected because they are easy for students to understand and represent a range of business types. Examples of information systems for these businesses are used in different chapters to illustrate basic concepts.

In addition to fictitious businesses, a wide range of real businesses and organizations are used for examples of information systems in case studies throughout the book. Systems in small, local businesses, those in regional and national companies, and systems in multinational corporations are all presented. Systems in not-for-profit organizations and government agencies also are described. Many of the examples come from businesses and organizations that are based outside the United States, including businesses in Canada, Europe, and Asia.

The book takes the view that the Internet and the World Wide Web are essential to information systems in businesses and organizations. Consequently, these topics are covered throughout the book, not just presented in a single chapter. The goal is for students to see how the Internet and the Web help support business operations and management at different levels and in different ways. Chapter 1 introduces the Internet and the World Wide Web, and other chapters expand on these topics as appropriate. Technical descriptions of the Internet, the World Wide Web, intranets, and extranets are provided in Chapter 6, but students do not need the technical background to use the Internet and the Web.

Electronic commerce is also viewed as essential to businesses today. The topic is introduced in Chapter 1, expanded on in other chapters, and discussed in cases throughout the book. Chapter 6 covers the technical background necessary for electronic commerce but, again, the technical topics are not necessary to understand the use of electronic commerce in businesses. Chapter 12 covers electronic commerce in detail from the organizational point of view, including business-to-consumer and business-to-business e-commerce. Chapter 13 examines the process of developing electronic commerce systems.

Each chapter in the book begins with the chapter outline and a list of learning objectives. Within each chapter are two boxed cases, called Bookmarks, that describe applications and systems in real businesses. These cases, taken from professional publications, show how the topics in the chapter apply in the real world. Each case includes questions to challenge the students. Each case also includes one or more URLs of relevant Web sites. Many of the cases involve either non-U.S. companies or U.S. companies engaged in international business.

Each chapter in the book ends with a chapter summary, a list of key terms introduced in the chapter, review questions, discussion questions, ethics questions, problem-solving projects, and Internet and electronic commerce projects. The discussion questions are designed to challenge the students to think more deeply about the chapter's topics. The ethics questions ask the students to examine ethical issues for information systems. The problem-solving projects, which are designed to encourage the application of the chapter's material, present problems that the students must solve, often using personal computer software such as spreadsheet and database software. The Internet and electronic commerce projects mostly require the use of the World Wide Web to locate and analyze information related to chapter topics or to the application of chapter topics in electronic commerce. Finally, each chapter concludes with a real-world case taken from a professional publication or similar source. The case integrates many of the chapter's topics and includes questions that require the students to apply chapter material in analyzing the case.

Instructor Support Materials

A complete set of instructor support materials is available to adopters of the book. The materials are designed to improve instructor effectiveness and enhance the learning experience for the students. Included in the materials are the following:

- Instructor's Resource CD-ROM. The Instructor's Resource CD-ROM contains the instructor's manual, test item file, Windows PII Test Manager, PowerPoint slides, and image library.
- Instructor's Manual with Test Item File. A full and complete instructor's manual, written by Robert C. Nickerson and Robert Kachur, is available in print, on the Instructor's Resource CD-ROM, and through the book's Web site. The manual includes teaching suggestions, answers to review and discussion questions, answers to Bookmark and Real-world Case questions, and other items to help the instructor prepare the course. The test item file, written by Arthur Rasher, features multiple-choice, true/false, fill-in-the-blank and essay questions. It is printed in the back

of the instructor's manual and is available on the Instructor's Resource CD-ROM; it is not available on the Web site.

- Windows PH Test Manager. The Windows PH Test Manager, also found on the Instructor's Resource CD-ROM, is an excellent suite of tools for testing and assessment. The questions used in the Test Manager are the same as those found in the test item file.
- PowerPoint Slides. PowerPoint slides, created by T. Warren Harding, delivered on the Instructor's Resource CD-ROM and through the book's Web site, feature key concepts from the book.
- Image Library. The image library is an excellent resource to help instructors create vibrant lecture presentations. Almost every figure and photo found in the book is provided and organized by chapter for the instructor's convenience. A complete listing of the images, their copyright information, and page references is also provided. These images can easily be imported into Microsoft PowerPoint to create new presentations, or to add to existing sets.
- Videotapes. Commercially produced videotapes can be used to enhance lectures on concepts presented in the book. The videotapes are available free of charge to qualified adopters.

Companion Web Site

The companion Web site for the book (www.prenhall.com/nickerson) was designed specifically to provide support for students in the course. The site features an Interactive Study Guide with numerous items to enhance the students' learning experiences. Included in the Interactive Study Guide are the following:

- Links to general business and information systems Web sites.
- Links to Bookmark and Real-world Case Web sites.
- Updates to the material in the book.
- Study Guide questions in which students receive automatic feedback and can print or e-mail their results to their instructor.

A secure Faculty Resource section of the Web site is also available where adopters can download the Instructor's Manual and PowerPoint slides.

Acknowledgments

Many of the ideas for the second edition of *Business and Information Systems* came from comments and reviews by users of the first edition. I greatly appreciate their input. The manuscript reviewers did a thorough job, and their comments were especially useful. My colleagues at San Francisco State University provided much useful advice. David Chao, Sam Gill, Bonnie Homan, Jim Glenn, and Art Kuhn were especially helpful, but many other colleagues contributed in some way. Finally, I could not have completed this book without the help and support of my family.

Reviewers

The following reviewers provided valuable input in the development of the second edition of *Business and Information Systems,* I greatly appreciate their efforts:

Boris Baran
Concordia University

Louise Darcey
Texas A&M University

Brian R. Kovar
Kansas State University

Trevor H. Jones
Duquesne University

Stephen L. Loy
Eastern Kentucky University

John Melrose
University of Wisconsin–Eau Claire

Ali A. Nazemi
Roanoke College

Merrill Parker
Chattanooga State Technical Community College

Laurette Poulos Simmons
Loyola College in Maryland

Jayne Stasser
Miami University

L. Richard Ye
California State University–Northridge

Alfred Zimermann
Hawaii Pacific University

The following individuals reviewed the first edition of the book:

Beverly Amer
Northern Arizona University

Gary Armstrong
Shippensburg University

Michael Atherton
Mankato State University

Robert Behling
Bryant College

Eli Cohen
Grand Valley State University

John Eatman
University of North Carolina at Greensboro

Terry Evans
Jackson State Community College

Dan Flynn
Shoreline Community College

Terribeth Gordon-Moore
University of Toledo

Rassule Hadidi
University of Illinois–Springfield

Constanza Hagmann
Kansas State University

Binshan Lin
Louisiana State University–Shreveport

Thom Luce
Ohio University

Gerald F. Mackey
Georgia Institute of Technology

Michael L. Mick
Purdue University–Calumet

John Palipchak
Pennsylvania State University

James Payne
Kellogg Community College

John V. Quigley
East Tennessee State University

David Russell
Western New England College

Janice Sipier
Villanova University

Janet Urlaub
Sinclair Community College

Bruce A. White
Dakota State University

Robert C. Nickerson
San Francisco State University

Part
one

Introduction

Information Systems
IN BUSINESS

1   Explain what an information system is and describe the functions of an information system.

2   Identify the components of an information system.

3   Explain the difference between data and information.

4   List several types of information systems and give an example of each type.

5   Explain who information system users are and describe how users use information systems.

6   Explain what ethics are and why it is important to use information systems ethically.

7   Describe how users are connected to information technology locally, nationally, and internationally.

8   Describe several benefits of information systems.

CHAPTER OUTLINE

Basic Information System Concepts
Types of Information Systems
Information System Users
Connecting Users to Information Technology
Benefits of Information Systems
An Approach to the Study of Information Systems

An essential element in the operations and management of every business today is information. Employees in all positions and at all levels of a business need information to do their jobs. For example, consider the employees of a supermarket. A checkout clerk in the supermarket needs information about prices for certain products, such as produce, to help check out customers. The supervisor in the supermarket's warehouse needs information about how much stock is available on the shelves and in the warehouse to decide when to reorder. An advertising manager for the supermarket needs information about which products are selling well and which are selling poorly to help develop advertising programs and promotions. The supermarket's general manager needs information about revenues and expenses to evaluate the profitability of the store. All employees of the supermarket need information related to the business to help them do their jobs.

How do the employees of a business get the information they need? They use *information systems*. Put simply, an information system provides information to help employees operate and manage a business. Figure 1.1 shows some of the information systems in a supermarket. The checkout clerk uses an information system called a *point-of-sale (POS) system* to find prices of products. The warehouse supervisor uses an information system called an *inventory control system* to keep track of stock availability. The advertising manager uses an information system called a *sales analysis system* to find out how well different products are selling. The supermarket's general manager uses an information system called a *general ledger system* to get reports on the income produced by the store.

This book is about how businesses and other organizations use information and information systems. Since many information systems include computers, some of this book is devoted to computers and related technology. But this is *not* a computer book. It is a book about businesses and their use of information systems. After reading this book, you should understand *why* information systems are important, *how* information systems function and are developed, and *what* your role in information systems is likely to be in the future.

This chapter starts by introducing several basic concepts about information systems. It surveys types of information systems and gives examples of each type. It

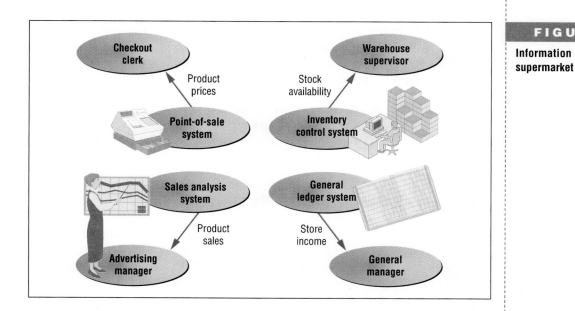

FIGURE 1.1

Information systems in a supermarket

examines the critical role of people—*users*—in information systems and discusses the ethical use of information systems. It explains the importance of connecting users to the technology of information systems and discusses the benefits of information systems to people and organizations. Finally, the chapter outlines the approach that this book takes to the study of information systems.

Basic Information System Concepts

This book covers many topics and ideas about information systems. To get started, this section presents several basic concepts you need to know.

What Is an Information System?

An information system is not one thing, but a group of things that work together. These things are called the *components* of the system, and they include equipment such as computers, instructions for the equipment, facts stored in the system, people to operate the system, and procedures for the people to follow. Later in this section we describe these components of an information system in more detail, but for now it is sufficient just to know that an information system is a group of components. The components work together to provide information that is used in the daily operations and in the management of an organization. Put succinctly, an **information system (IS)** is a collection of components that work together to provide information to help in the operations and management of an organization.

An information system may include computers, but it does not have to; people use manual information systems all the time. For example, an address book is part of an information system used in completing letters and making telephone calls. Many information systems, however, do include computers. Such a system may be called a **computer information system (CIS)**, although often people just use the term *information system* when they mean one that includes computers. This book uses the terms *information system* and *computer information system* interchangeably.

In addition to computers, information systems use other types of technology, including communication equipment such as telephone lines and satellites and various devices such as fax machines, video cameras, and audio speakers. Taken together, the computers, communications equipment, and other technology used in information systems are called **information technology (IT)**.

Often people use the term *computer application* when referring to an information system. A **computer application** is a use of a computer. For example, using computers to prepare written documents, to project revenues and expenses, and to keep track of customer names and addresses are computer applications. An information system may involve a single application or it may include several applications. Sometimes *computer application* is used when referring to a small system that is not too complex, and *information system* is used for a large, comprehensive system. This book often uses these terms interchangeably.

Examples of Information Systems

This book shows many examples of information systems in different types of businesses. To illustrate some basic ideas in this and other chapters, the book uses several simplified examples taken from businesses that manufacture, distribute, and sell athletic shoes and clothing. Examples of well-known athletic shoe manufacturers are Nike and Reebok, and many stores sell shoes, including national chains such as Footlocker. Athletic shoe and clothing distributors are less common.

Inventory Management at 7-Eleven

Dallas-based 7-Eleven has an inventory management/sales data system that not only makes the most of its limited shelf space and product assortment, but also moves new products into its stores and improves its position with its suppliers.

To make it all happen, all 5,600 franchisee- and company-owned 7-Eleven stores nationwide got an information technology overhaul that transformed the minimarts into data marts. The system encompasses software and hardware for each store's checkout counter and office, as well as a corporate data warehouse, and a network to connect them all.

Analysts say the system is a major technological leap for the 95,000-store convenience-store industry. "I don't know anybody who is doing more," says Jonathan Ziegler, an analyst at Salomon Smith Barney Holdings in San Francisco.

Because convenience stores are small and generate little revenue—the average 7-Eleven gets 1,100 visitors per day, but generates only $1.2 million in sales per year—companies have avoided throwing expensive technology at them, Ziegler says, but "technology is going down in price."

The 7-Eleven system probably cost at least $50 million, or about $9,000 per store, says Dennis Telzrow, an analyst at Hoak Breedlove Wesneski in Dallas. "They'll get the return on their investment," he predicts.

7-Eleven is the nation's number-one convenience-store chain in sales, with $7.3 billion last year. The company's earnings have been dropping in the past few years, though, partly because of information technology investments, according to 7-Eleven's annual report.

The new system lets store managers take control of the 2,500 or so products in a typical 3,000-square-foot store. With reports based on item-by-item sales data, managers can determine what hot merchandise deserves better displays and which duds should be pushed aside or discontinued to open up precious space. The system also alerts managers to upcoming weather events and other news that could affect which items will be in demand.

Franchisee Greg Kaloustian, who owns four stores on Long Island, New York, says the system showed him he should dedicate more shelf space to nutritional snack bars, and customers are making that decision pay-off. Kaloustian says, "it has meant a dramatic increase in cases where we've made changes like that."

Without the ability to gather and analyze the data, 7-Eleven knew only what it was buying from suppliers, not what consumers were buying from its stores, says Tom Ingram, retail information systems manager.

At the store level, suppliers would often push products to satisfy their own quotas, even though they weren't the best use of his shelf space, Kaloustian says. "We were being driven by the vendor," he says. "We're being driven now by sales."

Using sales data, 7-Eleven suggests about two dozen new products to store managers weekly, as well as which products to get rid of, says Margaret Chabris, a 7-Eleven spokesperson. The chain has also been trying to extend its fresh and perishable offerings, which makes optimizing sales and managing inventory more urgent.

The data may also help with sales forecasting and collaborative product development with suppliers, Chabris says. But a more immediate benefit of the system is a component that connects each store to suppliers and regional warehouses to manage ordering and fulfillment, she says.

Questions

1. Why have convenience stores not used information technology in the past?
2. How do 7-Eleven stores benefit from the inventory management/sales data system?

Web Site

7-Eleven: www.7eleven.com

Source: *Adapted from* David Orenstein, "Sales Data Helps 7-Eleven Maximize Space, Selection," *Computerworld*, July 5, 1999, p. 38.

To get started, consider three fictitious businesses:

Campus Sport Shop. An athletic shoe store near a medium-sized university. The store also sells athletic clothing.

Sportswear Enterprises. A business that sells and distributes athletic clothing to individual stores. The business purchases the clothing from a number of domestic and foreign manufacturers.

Victory Shoes. A company that manufactures a wide range of athletic shoes domestically and abroad. The company sells shoes to stores and businesses worldwide.

To illustrate the basic information systems concepts presented in this chapter, we take a look at a system in each of these businesses.

An Inventory Control System.   As a first example of an information system, consider an *inventory control system* at Campus Sport Shop, the athletic shoe store (Figure 1.2). In general, *inventory* is the stock of goods that a business has on hand; in a shoe store, it is the stock of shoes that the store has. Each style of shoe that the store stocks is called an *item* in the store's inventory. An inventory control system keeps track of information about the items that the business stocks. The quantity of each item that the business has on hand is an example of the information it tracks. Campus Sport records the quantity on hand of each shoe style it stocks in its inventory control system.

Every time Campus Sport sells a pair of shoes, the inventory control system reduces the quantity recorded in the system of that style of shoe. Each time Campus Sport adds items to stock, usually because it receives a shipment of new shoes from a manufacturer, the system increases the quantity of each style recorded in the system.

The inventory control system provides information for the daily operations of Campus Sport. For example, a salesperson can check the system to see if shoes of a particular style are available in stock. The system also provides information to help in the management of the store. For example, periodically the system reports on the quantity on hand of each style of shoe. This information helps the store's manager decide whether to increase inventory by ordering more shoes (if stock is low) or to reduce inventory, perhaps by having a sale (if stock is high). Thus, the inventory control system at Campus Sport helps in both the operations and management of the store.

FIGURE 1.2

Inventory control at an athletic shoe store

FIGURE 1.3

Order entry at an athletic
clothing distributor

An Order Entry System. Another example of an information system is an *order entry system* at Sportswear Enterprises, the distributor of athletic clothing (Figure 1.3). Customers of Sportswear, such as stores like Campus Sport, place orders that include the customer's name, the descriptions of the items ordered, and the quantity of each item ordered. This information is entered into an order entry system, which keeps track of the orders from all of Sportswear's customers. The order entry system provides information to Sportswear's warehouse employees about orders to be filled. If there is adequate stock in the warehouse, Sportswear immediately ships the items to the customers. If the items are not available, Sportswear checks with the manufacturers of the items to determine when they will be delivered. Eventually, when Sportswear receives the items from the manufacturers, it ships them to the customer.

The order entry system helps Sportswear in its daily operation of filling customer orders by providing information about customer orders to the warehouse. This information helps the warehouse ship orders as quickly as possible. The system also provides information to management. For example, management can determine how quickly orders are being filled, and decide whether action, such as using different manufacturers, should be taken. Thus, the order entry system at Sportswear helps in the operations and management of the business.

A Production Scheduling System. A final example of an information system is a *production scheduling system* at Victory Shoes, the athletic shoe manufacturer (Figure 1.4). Production scheduling involves determining what items the manufacturer should produce at what times. One factor that affects the production schedule is the demand for different items, which can vary over time. For example, the demand for basketball shoes increases just before and during basketball season, and the demand for running shoes increases during the summer Olympic Games. Another factor is the production facility's capacity to manufacture shoes. Only a certain number of shoes can be produced in a period of time.

Victory Shoes enters information about the expected demand for different types of shoes into its production scheduling system. This information includes what types of shoes to produce, what quantities to produce, and when the shoes will be needed. The system uses this information, along with production capacity information, to prepare schedules for the production of different shoes at different times. The production schedules tell the production facility what to do.

As with the other examples described in this chapter, the production scheduling system assists in the operations and management of the business. The system provides information about what shoes to produce at what times, and the production

FIGURE 1.4

▲ Production scheduling at an
athletic shoe manufacturer

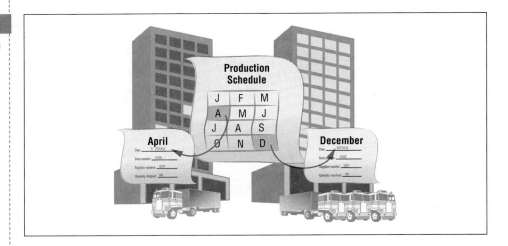

facility uses this information in its operations. The system also helps management
plan for production. If, for example, the production facility is not adequate to meet
the required production needs, management can determine whether new facilities
should be built.

Information System Functions

The information system examples described so far illustrate the main activities that
take place in an information system. Put briefly, an information system accepts facts
from outside the system, stores and processes the facts, and produces the results of
processing for use outside the system. These activities are performed by four *functions*
of an information system: the input function, the storage function, the processing
function, and the output function. Figure 1.5 summarizes these functions.

The facts that go into the system are **input data**. The **input function** accepts the
input data from outside the system. The **storage function** of the system retains the
input data along with other stored data, and retrieves stored data when it is needed by
the system. The **processing function** of the system calculates and in other ways
manipulates the input and stored data. Finally, the **output function** of the system
produces the results of processing for use outside the system. These results are called
information, or **output data**.

The inventory control system at Campus Sport Shop illustrates these functions
(Figure 1.6). The input data consists of numbers representing changes in inventory—

FIGURE 1.5

▲ The functions of an information system

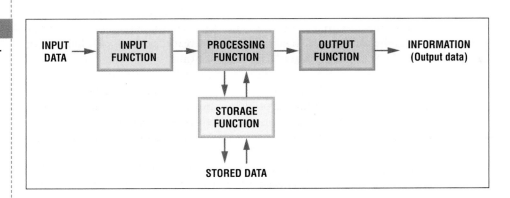

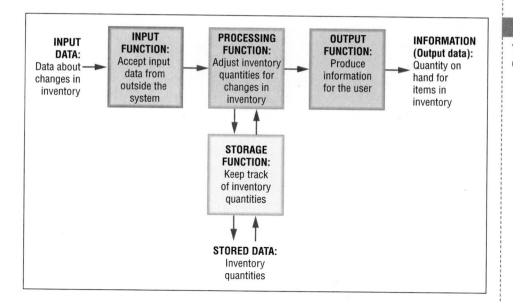

FIGURE 1.6

The functions of an inventory control system

that is, items removed from stock and items added to stock. The input function accepts this input data when it is entered into the system. The storage function keeps track of stored inventory data, including inventory quantities. The processing function adjusts the inventory quantities for changes in inventory. Finally, the output function produces information from the system, including the current quantity on hand. This information is used by the salesperson to check inventory availability and by the store's manager to determine whether more stock should be ordered or whether prices should be reduced.

Information System Components

The input, storage, processing, and output functions of an information system are performed by the system's components. These components are:

- Hardware
- Software
- Stored data
- Personnel
- Procedures

Figure 1.7 summarizes these components. Hardware and software are the *information technology* in the system, and personnel and procedures are the *human resources* of the system. The stored data ties together the information technology and the human resources.

Hardware. The first component of an information system is **hardware**, which consists of the computers, communications equipment, and other devices used in a system. An information system can use any type or size of computer. Many information systems include several types of computers and more than one of each type all connected together, using communications equipment such as wire or fiber-optic cables and special circuit boards. Other hardware devices such as digital cameras, microphones, and circuit boards for sending faxes are used in information systems.

FIGURE 1.7

The components of an information system

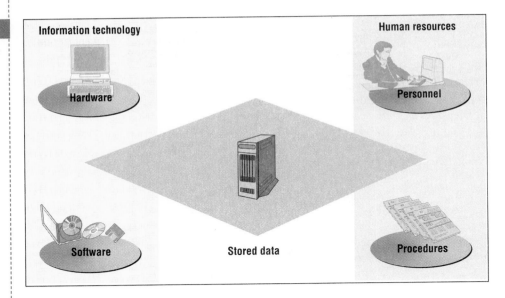

All the computers, communications equipment, and other devices used in an information system form the hardware component of the system.

The inventory control information system for Campus Sport Shop needs hardware to function. This hardware includes devices to accept input data about stock removed from and added to inventory, hardware to store the data about the quantity of each item on hand, hardware to calculate values for the new quantities on hand and identify which items have low or high inventory, and devices to produce information in a form understandable to humans. In addition, this system needs communications hardware to provide communication between different parts of the system.

Software. **Software** is another component of an information system. Software consists of instructions that tell hardware what to do. Computers and computer-controlled hardware, such as communications equipment, cannot function without software; they *must* have instructions to tell them what to do. Many types of software are needed in information systems. Some software tells computers to solve specific business problems, such as computing payroll, whereas other software manages the computer system to make it usable. Still other software controls communications equipment to provide communication between computers.

For Campus Sport's inventory control system, software is needed for several functions. Some software instructs a computer to accept input data about items that have been added to and removed from stock. Other software tells a computer to make changes in the stored data about the quantity on hand so that this data is up to date. Still other software tells a computer how to produce output with information about which items are low in stock and which are high. Finally, additional software provides instructions to control communication between computers in the system.

Stored Data. The third component of an information system is the data that is retained in the hardware and processed by the software. The **stored data** component of an information system consists of all the data that is kept in computers in the system and that is used by the software of the system.

In Campus Sport's inventory control system, the stored data component includes data about each item that the business stocks. The system uses an item number to identify each item. The stored data consists of this data, along with the description of each item, how much each item costs the business to purchase or manufacture, how much the business sells each item for, and the quantity of each item that the business has on hand.

The stored data component of an information system includes only data that the system stores, not input and output data. Users enter input data into the system and receive output data, or information, from the system. In a sense, the input and output flow through the system, but they are not part of the system because they do not contribute to the purpose of the system. Thus, input and output data, while critical for the use of an information system, are not components of the system.

Personnel.   An information system does not operate by itself; people are needed to make it run. People have to supply input data to the system, receive output information from the system, operate the hardware in the system, and run the software that is part of the system. These people, or **personnel**, are the fourth essential component of an information system.

The inventory control system at Campus Sport Shop includes personnel. Some of the personnel are users of the system. These include salespeople, clerical personnel, and the store's manager. Other personnel operate the hardware and software in the system.

Procedures.   The final component of an information system consists of **procedures**, which are instructions that tell people how to use and operate the system. Just as hardware cannot function without software, people do not know what to do unless they have procedures to follow.

Campus Sport's inventory control system needs procedures for the personnel to follow. Some procedures describe how to enter input data and what output information to expect from the system. Other procedures describe how to operate the hardware and software.

Data Versus Information

Although we have used the terms *data* and *information* almost interchangeably, there is a difference between them. **Data**[1] is a representation of a fact, a number, a word, an image, a picture, or a sound. For example, the number 10 is data; it might represent the fact that 10 cartons of shoes arrived. Data is entered into the system, stored in the system, and processed by the system. **Information**, on the other hand, is data that is meaningful or useful to someone. For example, the statement "There are 10 pairs of running shoes left in inventory" is information. Information comes out of the system, so it is sometimes called *output data*. Information is used to help operate and manage the organization.

Data for one person may be information for another. For example, if an employee's job is to decide when to buy more shoes for inventory, he or she needs information about the current stock of goods. But that employee does not need data about which shoes were sold today. On the other hand, an employee whose job is to restock store shelves from supplies in a warehouse would need information about the items sold today. Thus, whether something is information or data depends on how it is used.

---

[1] The word *data* is used most correctly as a plural noun. The singular of data is *datum*. A common practice, however, is to used the word *data* in a singular as well as a plural sense.

Types of Information Systems

One way of categorizing information systems is in terms of the number of people in an organization whose work is affected by the system. Some systems affect the work of only one individual, some affect several people who work closely in a group, others affect the work of many people throughout an organization, and still others affect people in several organizations. In this section we look at each of these types of information systems.

Individual Information Systems

Many information systems affect the work of only a single person, so they are called **individual**, or **personal**, **information systems**. Usually, these types of systems operate on *personal computers* used by one person at a time.

An example of an individual information system is one used to prepare legal documents, such as wills and contracts, in a law office. A legal secretary, under direction of a lawyer, would use a *word processing system*, consisting of a personal computer and *word processing software*, to put together a legal document from standard paragraphs stored in the computer and new material dictated by the lawyer.

Another example of an individual system is a *financial analysis system* that uses *spreadsheet software* on a personal computer to do financial projections for Campus Sport Shop. A *spreadsheet* is an arrangement of data into rows and columns (Figure 1.8). Calculations can be done with the data in the spreadsheet, and the results can be displayed on a screen. An employee at Campus Sport Shop could use a spreadsheet to project the store's revenues and expenses for several periods in the future, trying different options for certain items such as advertising expense to see what option is likely to produce the greatest income.

Many individual information systems are used to store and retrieve data on a personal computer using *database software*. A *database* is a collection of related data

FIGURE 1.8

▲ A spreadsheet

	A	B	C	D
1		PROJECTED NET INCOME		
2				
3		January	February	March
4				
5	Revenue	$ 180,000	$ 198,000	$ 217,800
6				
7	Expenses			
8	Cost of goods sold	$ 68,500	$ 75,350	$ 82,885
9	Salaries	32,800	36,080	39,688
10	Rent	24,200	26,620	29,282
11	Advertising	12,500	13,750	15,125
12	Other expenses	21,800	23,980	26,378
13	Total expenses	$ 159,800	$ 175,780	$ 193,358
14				
15	Net Income	$ 20,200	$ 22,220	$ 24,442

FIGURE 1.9

Computer graphics ▲

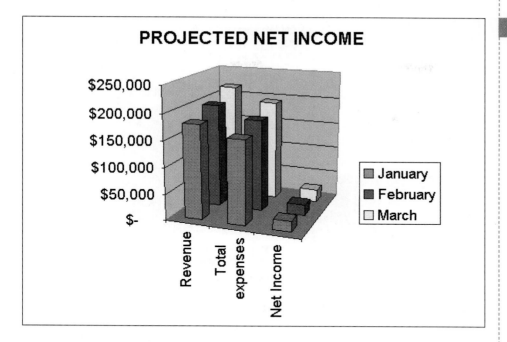

stored in a computer. For example, a sales representative for Sportswear Enterprises could keep a list of customers in a database on a personal computer. The representative would have an individual *customer database system* that he or she could use to periodically check to see which customers to contact next.

A final example of an individual information system is a *graphics system* used to prepare graphic images, either for including in a document or for showing at a presentation (Figure 1.9). *Graphics software* is used to create the images on a personal computer, and then word processing software can be used to include the images in a document. A type of graphics software called *presentation graphics software* is used to create images for presentations.

Workgroup Information Systems

Information systems often affect groups of individuals who work together, such as the employees on a team or in a department of a business. Such **workgroup**, or **group**, **information systems** often operate on nearby personal computers that are connected in a *local area network* (*LAN*) so that people at different computers can work with each other (Figure 1.10).

An example of a workgroup information system is one that allows individuals in the group to communicate electronically using an **electronic mail** (**e-mail**) system (Figure 1.11). With e-mail, letters and memos that normally would be sent on paper are transmitted electronically from one computer in the network to another. This type of system lets members of a workgroup easily communicate with each other from different locations and at different times.

Another example of a workgroup information system is an *information sharing system* in the sales department of Sportswear Enterprises. Such a system allows employees to share information about projects they are working on together. For example, employees in the sales department may be working on a brochure. With an informa-

FIGURE 1.10

▲ **A local area network (LAN)**

FIGURE 1.11

▲ **Electronic mail (e-mail)**

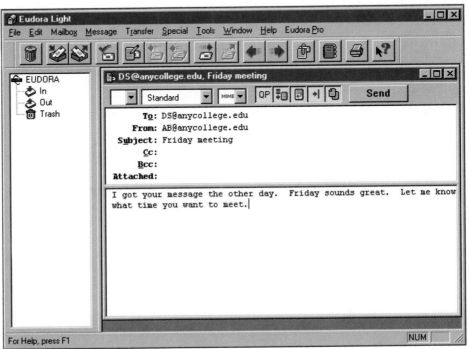

FIGURE 1.12

Information sharing ▲

tion sharing system, group members can view and comment on the brochure through their personal computers connected to a network (Figure 1.12). Periodically, one person in the group can summarize individual team members' comments and revise the sales brochure.

Organizational Information Systems

An information system that affects many people throughout a business or organization, not just an individual or the people in a single group, is called an **organizational**, or **enterprise**, **information system**. These systems usually operate either on *mainframe computers* used by many people at a time, or on groups of computers connected over a long distance to form a *wide area network* (*WAN*) (Figure 1.13).

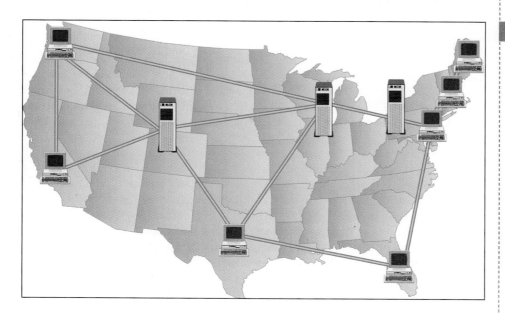

FIGURE 1.13

A wide area network (WAN) ▲

One of the most common examples of an organizational information system is a *payroll system*, which keeps track of when employees work and periodically prepares paychecks for the employees. At Victory Shoes, this system prepares paychecks for employees who get paid by the hour as well as for those who receive a monthly salary. The system also prepares quarterly and annual reports necessary for tax reporting, and other reports used by the business to keep track of expenses.

Another example of an organizational information system is an *automated teller machine*, or *ATM system*, used by banks. An ATM, which allows a customer to perform various banking transactions, is not a computer, but is connected to a computer at the bank's office that performs the tasks requested by the customer. The computer looks up the customer's account in its records, keeps track of transactions requested by the customer, and adjusts its records to reflect these transactions. The computer is connected electronically to many ATMs that may be located some distance from the computer.

Interorganizational Information Systems

The information systems described so far in this chapter function only within a single business or organization. Some information systems, however, function among several organizations. Such **interorganizational information systems** operate on groups of computers located in different organizations and connected in an *interorganizational network*. These systems allow the organizations to use computers to transact business among themselves.

An example of an interorganizational information system is an **electronic data interchange (EDI)** system, which allows businesses to exchange data electronically, such as purchase information and bills. For example, Sportswear Enterprises can electronically place an order to purchase shoes from Victory Shoes. Victory can then, in turn, electronically bill Sportswear for the shoes it ships.

Banks and other financial institutions use interorganizational **electronic funds transfer (EFT)** systems, which allow funds to be electronically transferred between financial institutions. For example, when you withdraw cash from an ATM associated with a bank other than your own, your bank electronically transfers the funds from your bank account to the bank issuing the cash. Another example of an interorganizational EFT system is one that directly deposits paychecks issued by one bank into employee accounts in other banks.

Global Information Systems

If a business operates only within a single country, then its information systems are confined to that country. Many businesses, however, have facilities in more than one country. Such *international businesses* often have information systems that span national borders. These systems are called **global**, or **international**, **information systems**. Often, global information systems are connected by means of a global WAN (Figure 1.14).

An example of a global information system is one used by Victory Shoes. Victory has facilities for manufacturing shoes in several countries and uses a global *production scheduling system* to schedule shoe production at different facilities. Production data and schedules are transmitted between Victory's headquarters and different foreign locations using the business's global WAN.

Interorganizational information systems may also be global. An international EDI system may be used to transmit orders for merchandise to foreign suppliers. An ATM at a bank in one country can be used to withdraw cash in the local currency, deducting the appropriate amount from an account at a bank in another country.

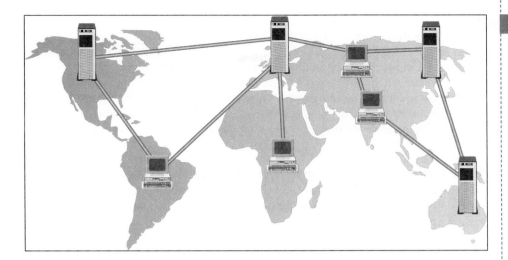

FIGURE 1.14

A global wide area network ▲

An international EFT system then transfers the funds electronically between the banks.

Information System Users

Many examples throughout this book illustrate people using information systems. These people are not computer professionals such as computer programmers and operators; they are other people who gain some benefit from using computer information systems in their personal or work lives. We call these people **users**.

A user performs a task in his or her personal or work life with the aid of a computer information system. For example, a person using an ATM is a user because he or she performs various banking transactions by using an ATM system. Similarly, a person using a computer with word processing software is a user because he or she prepares letters or reports with the help of a word processing system.

Computer professionals also use computers. For example, computer programmers and operators use computers in their technical jobs. We do not think of these people, however, as users, as we have defined the term here. In this book, a user is always a person who uses a computer information system to help with some noncomputer activity in his or her personal or work life. Sometimes this type of user is called an **end user** to distinguish him or her from computer professionals.

How Users Use Information Systems

A user uses an information system by entering input data and receiving output information. Many users use an information system *directly* by pressing keys on a computer keyboard or by operating a piece of equipment that sends input data to a computer. The computer receives the data, does the required processing, and then sends the output information back to the user, often displaying it on a screen or printing it on paper. A person using spreadsheet software to do financial projections at Campus Sport Shop and a person checking inventory availability on a computer screen at Sportswear Enterprises are examples of direct users.

A user may also use an information system *indirectly*. In this case, the user may have someone else enter the input data and receive the output information, which is then given to the user. A sales manager at Sportswear Enterprises who receives periodic, printed sales reports is an indirect user.

One person may use an information system directly, and another may use the same system indirectly. For example, some sales managers could use a sales reporting system directly when they review sales information on a screen, and others could use it indirectly when they receive printed sales reports. Sometimes many users use a system at the same time, such as when many people use an ATM system to do their banking. Often, however, only one user uses a system at a time. For example, a word processing system is used by only one person at a time.

The Ethical Use of Information Systems

Sometimes users use information systems inappropriately. For example, a user may use an information system to gain access to personal data not intended for that user, such as employee salary data. As another example, a user may use the software of an information system without permission on his or her personal computer at home. Users may also use an information system to steal money from a business or even steal or destroy the hardware used in an information system. Information system security measures, discussed in Chapter 14, are designed to make a system more secure and to minimize the likelihood of some of these activities. Still, they do occur.

Ultimately, the behavior of the individual determines how a system is used. **Ethics** has to do with the standards of behavior that people follow: what is right and what is wrong. For example, people act ethically when they tell the truth even when lying is not against the law. Information system users must be ethical in their uses of the system, for without such ethical behavior, system use would be so strictly controlled that only a few people would be able to use them.

Ethics does not provide simple answers to all questions. The answers to many ethical questions are complex and contradictory. In some cases there is no right answer because doing something that is right may also involve doing something that is wrong, a situation called an *ethical dilemma*. In this situation, it is important not to make a quick decision, but instead to consider carefully all sides to the question before deciding what to do.

To illustrate the role of ethics in information systems, consider the following scenario. Assume that you have been using a spreadsheet to do sales forecasts for your company. Your forecasts show that the company can expect considerable growth in sales in the next few years. Based on your forecasts, the company has hired several new sales representatives who have just finished their training and are beginning to make sales calls.

In making modifications to your spreadsheet one day, you discover that you did several calculations in the spreadsheet incorrectly. You correct the calculations and redo your sales forecasts, but this time the forecasts indicate that the sales are likely to be level for the next few years. What do you do?

This is an ethical dilemma because you feel you should admit your error so the company does not spend money on new sales representatives, but if you do, the new people will be terminated. You do not want people to lose their jobs, but you do not want to hurt the company, either. To further complicate the situation, you run the risk of being terminated now, if you admit your error, or later, if you do not admit your error and sales do not improve as you had incorrectly forecasted. Deciding what to do in this situation involves carefully considering a number of ethical factors.

The ethical use of information systems involves many issues. These issues arise in questions of confidentiality of information, copying of software, use of someone else's computer, and ownership of information, to name a few. Even though many ethical questions have no clear answer, users need to understand and think about them anyway. We discuss ethics for information systems in detail in Chapter 3, but for now it is enough to recognize that there are ethical issues in the use of information systems.

Connecting Users to Information Technology

Most users use information systems directly: They enter input data through a keyboard and see output data on a computer screen. In an individual information system, a user uses a personal computer for this interaction. For other types of information systems, the user often uses a personal computer connected to other information technology that is located some distance from the user. Such distant connectivity of users and technology is a critical part of most information systems.

Networks

Typically, users are connected to information technology through a network. In general, a **network** is a collection of computers and related equipment connected using communications equipment so that they can communicate with each other. Networks can cover a small area such as a building (a *LAN*), or a large area such as a city, region, country, or several countries (a *WAN*).

Users at different computers in a network may use a network to work with others in a group by means of a workgroup information system. Users may also use a network to enter input data into and receive output information from an organizational information system. In some organizations, users may use a network to transact business with other organizations through an interorganizational information system. Finally, users may use a network to process data at locations around the world using a global information system.

The global nature of networks has become increasingly important in recent years. Global connectivity means that businesses are able to operate around the world without concern for where input, processing, storage, and output take place. Business facilities can be separated by considerable distance and many time zones, and still have access to information systems and technology at other business locations. As more businesses globalize their operations, the benefits of global networks will be increasingly important.

The Internet and the World Wide Web

Users need to be connected to information technology in both their work lives and their personal lives. Businesses provide networks for their employees to use. For personal use, as well as for much business use, many users use the Internet to access information technology. Put simply, the **Internet** is a worldwide collection of interconnected networks. We say more about what the Internet is and how it works in Chapter 6, but you do not need to know the technical details to use the Internet.

The Internet can be used for a variety of business and personal activities. One of the most common uses is for transmitting e-mail. Using the Internet, e-mail can be sent to any computer in the world that is connected to the Internet.

Another important use of the Internet is for locating information from various computer sites around the world. The **World Wide Web (WWW)**, usually just called

FIGURE 1.15

▲ Using the World Wide Web

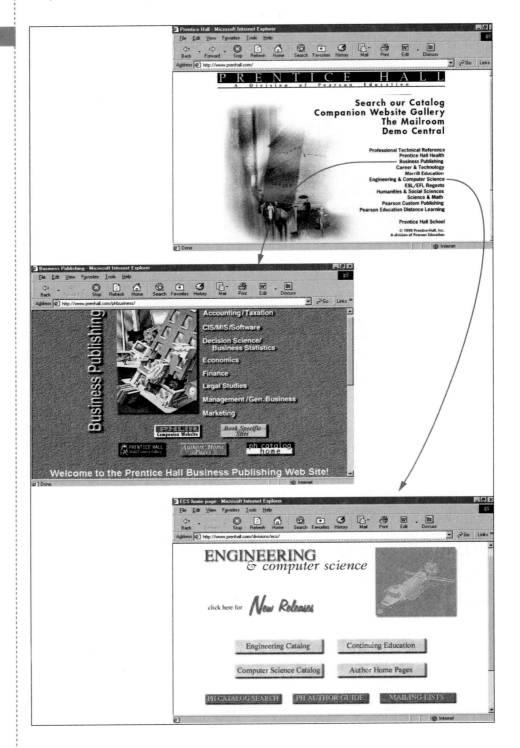

the **Web**, is a service on the Internet that links information stored on different computers. By following the links, users can locate information at businesses, universities, libraries, research institutes, government agencies, and so on (Figure 1.15). The Web and the Internet have become essential to the global connectivity of users and information technology.

Electronic Commerce

The ease with which users can connect to information technology by means of the Internet and the Web has resulted in a significant new application. This application, called **electronic commerce (e-commerce)**, allows businesses to use networks, including the Internet, to promote and sell products and services. With e-commerce, consumers can purchase products from businesses through the Web. Consumers can locate items of interest on the Web, review their characteristics and features in advertisements and product literature viewed on the Web, place orders electronically, and pay for their purchases through the Web (Figure 1.16). Many types of businesses provide some form of e-commerce for their customers through the Web.

Consumers are not the only ones who use e-commerce. Businesses also purchase products and services from other businesses electronically. In fact, more business-to-business commerce takes place electronically than does business-to-consumer commerce. Electronic commerce between businesses may use networks other than the Internet, but increasingly the Internet and the Web are being used for this purpose.

In addition to business-to-consumer and business-to-business e-commerce, consumer-to-consumer e-commerce is increasingly common. This type of e-commerce involves an individual using the Web to offer to sell something to other individuals. Often the sale takes place by means of an auction on the Web.

The use of e-commerce is growing rapidly, both for businesses and for consumers. In the future, more commerce may take place electronically than by traditional means. Chapter 12 discusses e-commerce in depth.

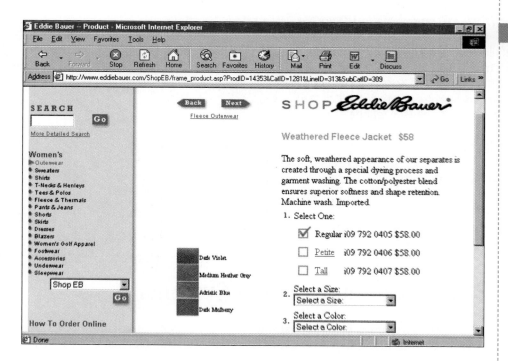

FIGURE 1.16

Electronic commerce
(e-commerce)

BOOK
M A R K

Electronic Commerce at Michelin North America

Michelin North America realized that many of its 1,700 independent tire dealers held the perception that Michelin was difficult to do business with. In some cases, delivery receipts from dealers were languishing for three or four weeks before being processed.

Hiring more customer service representatives and getting them to work in teams was one way the Greenville, South Carolina, tire maker addressed the problem. Web-based technology was another.

Dealers can now access Michelin's Bib Net Web site—named for the 100-year-old inflated "Bibendum" Michelin man—to order products, schedule deliveries, check order status, make real-time inventory inquiries, receive advance shipment notices, create claims, scan pricing, and see a national account directory.

A dealer only needs a personal computer, a Web browser, and a phone connection. Michelin doesn't have to worry about dealers' disparate hardware and software platforms and widely varying technological savvy. A total of 286 dealers—90% of the 318 the company initially targeted—are using the system so far, says Lynn Melvin, manager of electronic-commerce application development at Michelin.

Less technologically inclined customers have let Michelin know that they don't want to see the customer service phone lines go away.

All told, Michelin has spent more than $5 million on its Bib Net since May 1995, when the project team commenced planning, Melvin says. Some savings have been realized in printing materials, reduced order errors, and, to a small degree, customer service. But the Bib Net site hasn't paid for itself yet. "We didn't really go into this to save money," Melvin says. "Basically, we wanted to create close partnerships [with customers]."

The tire dealers also benefit. Leo Zannetti, director of purchasing at Belle Tire, a chain headquartered in Allen Park, Michigan, says the reduction in order errors alone is worth it. His company is also using a more extensive tire inventory management system that Michelin installed on Zannetti's PC.

To develop the Bib Net site, Michelin put together a cross-functional team from its marketing, sales, customer service, and information technology departments. The team also enlisted independent tire dealers, visiting 55 of them and bringing 15 to 20 dealers to South Carolina to brainstorm a technical wish list and help design the user interfaces.

"They gave us carte blanche to draw up what we wanted," Zannetti says. "They did a great job taking in our input. Most companies would say, 'Here's what we have.' I guess corporate America's changing every day."

Questions

1. What benefits do Michelin tire dealers receive from using Bib Net?
2. What is the main benefit Michelin North America receives from Bib Net?
3. Why is Bib Net an example of electronic commerce?

Web Site
Michelin North America:
www.michelin.com

Source: *Adapted from* Carol Sliwa, "Michelin Links Dealers," *Computerworld*, November 30, 1998, pp. 44–45.

Benefits of Information Systems

Information systems provide several important benefits to an organization. These benefits stem from the system as a whole, not just from the fact that computers are used in the system. Computers are fast and accurate, and they process large volumes of data. Although these characteristics make computer information systems very useful, the real benefits of information systems are much more involved.

Better Information

One of the main benefits of using information systems is *better information*. Information systems store and process data, but they produce information, which is the basis for good decision making. When a business person makes a decision, he or she selects one of several alternative courses of action. Almost always the person is uncertain about what exactly will happen with each alternative. Information helps reduce the person's uncertainty, and so with better information a business person is more certain about the outcome of the decision.

To illustrate this idea, let's look at an example of a personal decision that you may need to make. Assume that you want to buy a new car. You have to make a decision: Which car should you buy? You could go to several car dealerships, select one car that you like, and buy it. But is it the best car for you? Are there other models with the qualities you want—more power, more space, better fuel economy, and more reliability—for less money? With more information you might save money and get a better car. So instead of making your decision hastily with incomplete information, you can gather the information you need to help with your decision. For example, you can use a computerized library system to search for articles and reviews of the cars that interest you. You could also use the Web to find information about cars. With this information, you can make a decision that is more likely to result in selecting a better car.

Better information is the principal benefit of many information systems in businesses. For example, a customer database system provides better information to a sales representative for deciding when to contact customers. Similarly, a sales reporting system provides better information to a sales manager for making decisions to help improve sales. Many other examples throughout this book illustrate the benefit of better information provided by information systems.

Improved Service

Another benefit of information systems is *improved service*. Computer information systems operate at any time of the day or night and process data faster than humans. Thus, organizations and businesses serve their customers and clients more conveniently and efficiently with computer information systems than without them.

Customers see the effect of improved service from information systems when they use an ATM system for their banking transactions, or when they purchase groceries or merchandise from a store that uses a POS system. These systems provide service that the customer would not otherwise have. Consequently, customers are able to complete their transactions and do their shopping conveniently and quickly.

Improved service means that customers may be attracted to a certain business because of its service. In fact, many people have come to expect computerized services, and some types of businesses cannot compete without them. For example, many gas stations have a computerized system that allows customers to pay at the pump with a credit card. Gas stations that do not offer this service may not attract as many customers.

Increased Productivity

A third benefit of information systems is *increased productivity*. Productivity has to do with how much people can accomplish in a given period. With computer information systems, people can do more work in a period of time than they would be able to do if they did not have such systems.

For example, a typist using a word processing system can revise and print a long document faster than if he or she had to retype the document completely on a typewriter. Hence, the typist's productivity is increased with such a system. A person working in an office with an e-mail system is more productive because it is easy and quick for the person to communicate with other workers. Similarly, a clerk using a POS system instead of a standard cash register can check out more customers, and a bank with an ATM system can handle more customers without increasing the number of human tellers.

Increased productivity means that it costs less for a business to provide its goods and services. These cost savings may be passed on to the customer in reduced prices. Such savings also result in increased profits for the business.

Competitive Advantage

A final benefit of information systems is that they can provide a *competitive advantage* for a business. A business has a competitive advantage when customers clearly prefer its products over those of other businesses. Some businesses gain a competitive advantage by being the least expensive seller of particular products. Others gain it by having products that are different from those of its competitors. Still other businesses concentrate on special or unique products for a small section of the market to gain a competitive advantage.

Information systems can help a business gain a competitive advantage. For example, information systems can help reduce the cost of production so that a business can have the least expensive product. Information systems can also help a business determine how a product should be different from those of its competitors. Information systems can also help a business identify small segments of a market that are looking for special or unique products. In all these examples information systems can help give businesses an advantage over their competitors. Chapter 12 discusses the competitive advantages provided by information systems in detail.

An Approach to the Study of Information Systems

To understand information systems in business, you first need to understand business. You may already have worked in certain types of businesses and have an understanding of how some aspects of a business function. But information systems are found in *all* types of businesses and encompass *all* aspects of a business. To fully understand information systems, you need a broad overview of business and business functions.

This book approaches the study of information systems by first examining businesses and their use of information. Chapter 2 explains what a business does, how a business is organized, and how a business uses information in its operations and management. Chapter 2 also examines some of the basic business information processing activities that are common to many types of businesses. With this background you will be well prepared to understand how information systems support the operations and management of a business.

Chapter 3 discusses the components of an information system, emphasizing the need for each component. It also examines ethical issues for information systems. After completing this chapter you will be prepared to move on to more in-depth study of different aspects of information systems.

Part Two of the book explains the technology used in information systems, which includes computer hardware and software. This part also describes how computers are interconnected in networks and how data is organized for storage and processing in information systems.

Part Three examines common types of information systems used in business and gives examples of each type. This part describes information systems that improve personal productivity, encourage group collaboration, increase the efficiency of business operations, improve the effectiveness of management decision making, and provide a strategic impact on the business. The understanding you gain will help you utilize information systems in your job.

Part Four completes the study of information systems by examining their development and management. This part shows how information systems are developed by computer professionals and what role the user plays in their development. In addition, this part explains how information systems and technology are managed in organizations.

You can use information systems on your job with little understanding of how the systems function. But to be an *effective* user of information systems, you need a more in-depth understanding of information systems. An effective user is one who is able to make the best use of information systems by knowing how and when to use them. This book is designed to provide you with the understanding necessary to be an effective information system user in businesses and other organizations.

CHAPTER SUMMARY

1   An **information system (IS)** is a collection of components that work together to provide information to help in the operations and management of an organization. The functions of an information system are the **input function**, which accepts data from outside the system; the **storage function**, which stores data in the system until needed; the **processing function**, which manipulates data in the system; and the **output function**, which produces information resulting from processing. (pp. 4–9)

2   The components of an information system are **hardware**, which are the computers, communications equipment, and other devices used in the system; **software**, which are the instructions that tell the hardware in the system what to do; **stored data**, which is the data stored in the system and used by the software; **personnel**, which are the people who use and operate the system; and **procedures**, which are the instructions that tell the people what to do. Hardware and software are the **information technology (IT)** in the system, and personnel and procedures are the human resources of the system. The stored data ties together the

information technology and the human resources. (pp. 9–11)

3   **Data** is a representation of a fact, a number, a word, an image, a picture, or a sound. **Information** is data that is meaningful or useful to someone. Data for one person may be information for another. (p. 11)

4   An information system that affects a single person is called an **individual information system**. Examples include a system to prepare written documents using word processing software, a system to do financial projections using spreadsheet software, a system to store and retrieve data using database software, and a system to prepare graphic images using graphics software. An information system that affects a group of individuals who work together is called a **workgroup information system**. Examples are an **electronic mail (e-mail)** system and an information sharing system. An information system that affects people throughout a business or an organization is called an **organizational information system**. Examples include a payroll system and an automated teller machine (ATM) system. An information system that func-

tions among several organizations is called an **interorganizational information system**. Examples are an **electronic data interchange (EDI)** system and an **electronic funds transfer (EFT)** system. Finally, a **global information system** is one that spans international borders. An example is a global production scheduling system. (pp. 12–16)

5 A **user**, or an **end user**, is a person who gains some benefit from using a computer information system in his or her personal or work life. A user enters input data into the system and receives output information from the system. Some users use information systems directly by pressing keys on a computer keyboard or operating a piece of equipment that sends data to a computer. Other users use information systems indirectly; they receive output information from the system without operating any computer equipment. (p. 17)

6 **Ethics** involves the standards that people follow in determining right and wrong behavior. Information systems must be used in an ethical way, or their use will be restricted to only a few people. The ethical use of information systems involves many issues, including confidentiality of information, copying of software, use of someone else's computer, and ownership of information. (p. 18)

7 Users are often connected to information technology through a **network**, which is a collection of computers and related equipment connected electronically so that they can communicate with each other. A network may cover a small area, such as a building, or a large area, such as a city, region, country, or several countries. The **Internet** is a worldwide collection of interconnected networks that allows users to access information technology. One important use of the Internet is for locating information through the **World Wide Web (WWW)**. Networks, including the Internet, are often used for **electronic commerce (e-commerce)**, in which businesses promote and sell products and services electronically. (pp. 19–21)

8 One benefit of information systems is better information, which helps people make decisions. Another benefit is improved service, which means customers and clients of businesses and organizations get faster and more convenient service. A third benefit is improved productivity, which means people can accomplish more in a period of time. A final benefit of information systems is that they can provide a competitive advantage for a business. (pp. 22–24)

KEY TERMS

Computer Application (p. 4)
Computer Information System (CIS) (p. 4)
Data (p. 11)
Electronic Commerce (E-commerce) (p. 21)
Electronic Data Interchange (EDI) (p. 16)
Electronic Funds Transfer (EFT) (p. 16)
Electronic Mail (E-mail) (p. 13)
Ethics (p. 18)
Global (International) Information System (p. 16)

Hardware (p. 9)
Individual (Personal) Information System (p. 12)
Information (p. 11)
Information System (IS) (p. 4)
Information Technology (IT) (p. 4)
Input Data (p. 8)
Input Function (p. 8)
Internet (p. 19)
Interorganizational Information System (p. 16)
Network (p. 19)
Organizational (Enterprise) Information System (p. 15)

Output Data (p. 8)
Output Function (p. 8)
Personnel (p. 11)
Procedures (p. 11)
Processing Function (p. 8)
Software (p. 10)
Storage Function (p. 8)
Stored Data (p. 10)
User (End User) (p. 17)
Workgroup (Group) Information System (p. 13)
World Wide Web (WWW, Web) (p. 19)

REVIEW QUESTIONS

1 What is an information system?

2 Do all information systems use computers? Explain your answer.

3 What are the four functions of an information system?

4 What are the components of an information system?

5 What is the difference between data and information?

6 Give several examples of individual information systems.

7 What people in a business are affected by a workgroup information system?

8 Give several examples of organizational information systems.

9 What type of information system is an EDI or EFT system?

10 What is an information system user?

11 What is the difference between using an information system directly and using one indirectly?

12 How are business and personal users connected to information technology?

13 What is electronic commerce?

14 How do businesses benefit from information systems?

15 What does it mean to be an effective information system user?

DISCUSSION QUESTIONS

1 Think of a business other than a supermarket and list several types of employees in that business. What information does each of the employees you listed need in his or her job?

2 Think about the course registration system at your college or university. Describe as much as you can the components and functions of that system.

3 Identify several examples of information systems, other than those described in this chapter, that might be used in Campus Sport Shop, Sportswear Enterprises, and Victory Shoes. For each system, decide whether it is an individual, a workgroup, or an organizational information system. Explain your decision.

4 What interorganizational information systems might be used between Campus Sport Shop, Sportswear Enterprises, and Victory Shoes?

5 Think of the outputs produced by your college or university class registration system. For what users of the system (such as students, faculty, advisors, administrators, etc.) are each of these outputs information, and not just data?

6 In the global economy, everyone in the world is a user of information systems. Do you agree or disagree with this statement? Why?

ETHICS QUESTIONS

1 What are some of the things that could happen if people did not behave ethically in their use of information systems?

2 Do ethical standards in the use of information systems differ in different countries? In what ways do you think that ethics might vary in other countries?

PROBLEM-SOLVING PROJECTS

1 Write a description of a manual information system that uses an address book to assist in completing letters. What are the input data, stored data, and output information of the system? Briefly describe how the system functions.

2 Contact a business that will give you information about its information systems. Write a brief description of one information system for that business, including a summary of the components and functions of that system. Using graphics software, draw a diagram similar to the one in Figure 1.6 for that system.

3 Using appropriate software, set up a table with the following headings:

System name	Users	Inputs	Outputs	Stored data	Processing

Fill in one row of the table for each system described in this chapter. Under *System name* give the name of the system (for example, Inventory Control). Under *Users* list the users by job (for example, salesperson, manager). Below *Inputs* list the input data (for example, data about changes in inventory) and below *Outputs* list the output information (for example, quantity on hand for items in inventory). Under *Stored data* list data stored in the system (for example, inventory quantities). Below *Processing*, briefly describe the processing done in the system (for example, adjust inventory quantities for changes in inventory). Complete the table for all the systems discussed in the chapter.

As you read about other information systems in other chapters, add entries to the table.

4 Develop a spreadsheet to help decide which car to buy. The columns should be characteristics of the car that are important to you, such as the safety, mileage, and so on. The rows should be different cars you are considering. If some characteristics can be quantified (such as mileage), use the spreadsheet to find the maximum, minimum, and average of those characteristics for all cars you are considering.

INTERNET AND ELECTRONIC COMMERCE PROJECTS

1 Software that is used in workgroup information systems often is called *groupware*. Use the Web to find several examples of groupware. For each example, write a brief summary of how it can be used by a group of employees in a business.

2 Decision making involves selecting among alternatives. The basis for good decision making is information about the alternatives. Select a personal or business decision you need to make and identify three alternatives. For example, if you are trying to decide where to go on vacation, you could select three different destinations. Then use the Web to gather information about each alternative. Gather information from several sites on the Web. When you have enough information to make a decision,

write a brief summary of your alternatives, the information you gathered about each alternative, the source of the information on the Web, and your decision. Justify your decision based on the information you gathered.

3 Find three e-commerce sites on the Web for products that you could buy at a store. Evaluate each site in terms of how purchasing a product through it compares with buying the same product at a physical store. What can you conclude about the types of products that are better sold through e-commerce and the types that are better sold in a physical store? Write a summary of your evaluation and the conclusion you reach.

The Benetton Group, Italy

Founded in 1965, the Benetton Group consists of a number of companies that design, manufacture, and distribute Benetton products in 120 countries. In a recent year, it recorded revenue exceeding 3,800 billion lira (over $2 billion). With the acquisition of Benetton Sportsystem, the Benetton Group combined its own strengths in the textile and clothing sector (United Colors of Benetton, Sisley, and 012) with prestigious brands, including Prince, Rollerblade, Nordica, Asolo, Kastle, and Killer Loop. This success is based on several factors, ranging from the creation of an avant-garde sales network to the decentralization of certain nonstrategic stages of the manufacturing process to medium-sized Italian companies—in addition to the key role information technology has always played.

Benetton sees information technology as key to its operations and is constantly seeking new ways to capitalize on the competitive power of properly used, technology-based business systems; the philosophy is to use information technology to make complex things simple.

In the Benetton Group, each company manages its own processing environment with autonomy in the operations and system development, but they all have a common architecture and infrastructure. The headquarters in Ponzano, Italy, operates on large mainframe computers to which more than 800 workstations are connected through a local area network; typically, other companies of the Benetton Group run smaller mainframe computers, and the 84 agent offices, which represent the sales organization in the world, use personal computers.

All the companies involved in design, manufacturing, and distribution of the products sold by Benetton shops are connected through a network to the agent offices. All the companies use an information system called Global that is developed and supported centrally to manage the database and the communications. Each agent office runs a computer application, in a different language, developed and supported by the central information technology staff. This application,

installed in more than 30 countries around the world, manages databases of customers, styles, and prices, keeping them aligned with the databases of the companies. The application also provides for commercial functions, including order collection and management, order forwarding to the companies, shop management, and sales analysis.

Orders are taken by the companies three times per day and processed at night to be sure that they are available for production the next day. All the production processes—from programming and material requirements to packaging—are managed by computers using highly sophisticated custom-developed application systems. For example, Benetton's Apparel Bill of Material system is the most advanced in Italy.

After the products are packed by a highly automated packing system, the approximately 15,000 boxes per day enter an automated warehouse from which they are forwarded to shops around the world, according to the delivery programs managed by the central computer. When the forward starts, EDI messages with the box numbers and their contents are sent through the network to the computers of Benetton agents to keep them updated and allow the forwarding agents to prepare the custom clearance documents. The computers of the shops that will receive the goods also receive EDI messages. The agents are continuously updated on the state of the customer orders and they can see, through their computers, what is available in inventory for restocking. When an agent enters an order for restocking, the shop receives the goods in an average of 8 days in Europe and 12 days in the United States. For shops, an efficient restocking process means improved business in terms of increased sales volumes and profits, with fewer items sold at reduced price.

Agents are also continuously updated through the network on the credit status of each retail store. This is made possible by the fact that almost all the payments by the stores in the world are done using cash management systems connected though networks to Benetton computers.

The results of applying information technology

to the business are essentially due to the capability to integrate the systems with the overall business purposes, the changing business environment, and the corporate culture and processes of the company.

Questions

1   What type of information system is described in this case? Explain your answer.
2   Who are the users of the information system?
3   What information do the users receive through the information system?

4   How is a network used in the information system?
5   What benefits does Benetton receive from the information system?

Web Site
Benetton: www.benetton.com

Source: Adapted from "'Millennium Bug': Benetton Case History," www.benetton.com/wwd/how/production/file2128.html, copyright 1999/2000 Benetton. "Information Technology," www.benetton.com/ wwd/how/distribution/file1882.html, copyright 1999/2000 Benetton.

Business
FUNDAMENTALS

CHAPTER OUTLINE

The Nature of Business
Types of Businesses
Business Trends
Business Functions
The Organization of a Business
Information and Business Operations
Information and Business Management
Basic Business Information Processing
Information Systems and Business

After completing this chapter, you should be able to

1 Explain the purpose of a business and describe the main types of businesses.

2 Describe several trends that affect businesses today.

3 Describe the major business functions and explain how a business is organized.

4 Diagram typical flows of information in business operations.

5 Explain how information is used in the management of a business.

6 Describe several basic business information processing activities used in businesses.

7 Explain how information systems support information needs in all functions of all types of businesses and organizations.

nformation systems provide information to support the operations and management of businesses and other organizations. To understand information systems, it is first necessary to understand how businesses and other types of organizations operate and are managed. It is also important to know how businesses use information in their various functions, and how common business activities process information. Although you already may have worked for certain types of businesses and know some things about how they function, you need a broad understanding of business and its use of information to fully comprehend the role of information systems.

This chapter first explains what businesses do and describes different types of businesses. Then it outlines business functions and examines how businesses are organized. Next it shows how information flows within a business to support business operations, and explains how information helps in the management of a business. Then it describes several basic business information processing activities. Finally, this chapter explains how information systems support information needs in all aspects of all types of businesses.[1]

The Nature of Business

The purpose of a business is to provide products—goods and services—for its customers. For example, an athletic shoe store sells running, tennis, basketball, and other types of athletic shoes (goods), and a shoe repair shop repairs shoes (services). The money received from the customers for its products is the business's *revenue*. To provide its products, the business has certain *expenses*. For example, a shoe store must buy shoes to sell, and a repair shop must pay service people to repair shoes. The difference between the revenue and expenses is called the *net income*. If the net income is greater than zero, then the business makes a *profit* for the owners of the business.[2]

Some businesses sell goods and services to individual consumers, and some businesses sell to other businesses. For example, an athletic shoe manufacturer sells shoes to shoe stores, which in turn sell shoes to consumers. It does not matter, however, whether a business sells to individuals or to other businesses. In either case it receives revenue, has expenses, and makes a profit.

Not all businesses operate for a profit. Some *not-for-profit organizations* do not give any income to the owners, but instead use all net income to improve the organization. Examples include hospitals, churches, schools, and community service organizations. Government agencies also are not-for-profit organizations. Although this book mainly uses examples from for-profit businesses, the concepts and principles apply equally well to not-for-profit organizations.

Businesses do not operate in a vacuum, but rather exist within a *business environment* that includes economic, legal, cultural, and competitive factors. Economic factors affect businesses by influencing what and how many goods and services consumers buy. Laws and regulations have an impact on many activities in a business. Cultural and social factors influence the characteristics of the goods and services sold by businesses. Competition affects what products and services a business offers, and the prices it charges.

---

[1] If you have already taken an introduction to business course or other courses in business, you may find that this chapter repeats some of what you know. Still, it would be a good idea to read the chapter for a review and summary.

[2] Some of the net income may be used to improve the business, and some of it may be given to the owners of the business.

The business environment is not limited to the effect of these factors in a single country. Many businesses operate on a global scale. These *international businesses* have to be concerned with world economic factors, laws in many countries, cultural differences between countries, and competition from foreign businesses. As more businesses produce and sell goods and offer services internationally, these factors will become increasingly important.

Types of Businesses

The goods sold by businesses typically flow from raw materials to the final consumer as shown in Figure 2.1. Raw materials, such as oil and iron, are manufactured into products such as gasoline and automobiles. These products are sold to other businesses at *wholesale*—that is, in large quantities. The products then are resold at *retail*—that is, in smaller quantities—to the final consumer.[3]

Three main types of businesses are involved in this flow from raw materials to the consumer: manufacturers, wholesalers or distributors, and retailers. In addition, service businesses provide services to other businesses or to individual consumers.

Manufacturers

A **manufacturer** produces goods that are sold to other businesses or to individual consumers. The goods that the manufacturer produces may be final products, such as automobiles, or they may be components, such as engines and transmissions, that other businesses use in the manufacturing of the final product. The manufacturer produces goods out of basic materials, such as rubber and steel, or from parts and components purchased from other manufacturers.

Athletic shoe production illustrates the role of manufacturers. A business that manufactures athletic shoes may produce some parts of a shoe from basic materials

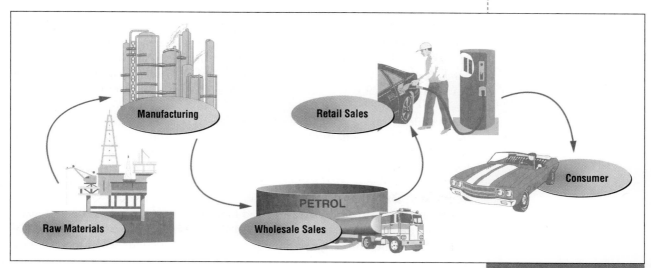

FIGURE 2.1

The flow of goods from raw materials to the consumer

[3]The flow of goods from raw materials to the consumer is often called a *supply chain*.

and purchase other parts from other businesses. For example, a shoe manufacturer may purchase raw fabric and leather from which it makes the upper part of a shoe. In addition, it may purchase finished rubber soles from another manufacturer, which it then combines with the other materials to produce the final shoe.

Many businesses manufacture some or all their products, or components for their products, in foreign countries. For example, a shoe manufacturer may manufacture some of its shoes in its own production facility in a foreign country and then ship the finished shoes to other countries, where they are sold. A shoe manufacturer may also contract with a foreign manufacturer to produce products to its specifications for sale elsewhere. As another example, some U.S. companies manufacture automobiles sold in the United States in other countries. In these examples of foreign manufacturing, the business is an *importer* of goods to the country where they will be sold. Some manufacturers produce their products domestically and then sell them in other countries, in which case the manufacturer is an *exporter* of goods.

Wholesalers

A manufacturer may sell its goods to a **wholesaler**, or **distributor**, which purchases large quantities of the goods and stores them in warehouses. It then sells smaller quantities to retailers (discussed in the next section), and ships or distributes these quantities to the retailers. Sometimes the manufacturer is also a wholesaler/distributor in which case the manufacturer sells and distributes directly to retailers.

A wholesaler may purchase large quantities of athletic clothing from several manufacturers. If the clothing were manufactured in other countries, the wholesaler would also be an importer of clothing. The wholesaler would store the clothing it purchases in one or more warehouses until it sells and distributes the clothing to retailers.

Retailers

A **retailer** purchases quantities of goods from wholesalers or directly from manufacturers. The retailer keeps the goods at a store or other retail location and resells them one at a time or in small quantities to individual consumers. If the manufacturer is in another country and the retailer purchases goods directly from the manufacturer, then the retailer is an importer. Sometimes the retailer purchases large quantities for its own warehouse and then distributes smaller quantities to its retail shops, in which case the retailer is acting as a distributor. In some instances the retailer is also a manufacturer. For example, some mail-order businesses manufacture their own goods.

An athletic shoe store is a retailer. It purchases several of each type of shoe it plans to sell from shoe manufacturers and keeps these shoes in the store. It also purchases athletic clothing from a clothing wholesaler. Customers come to the store, try on the shoes and clothing, and purchase the items they want.

Service Businesses

A **service business** is not directly involved in manufacturing, wholesaling, and retailing products, but instead provides services needed by other businesses and individual consumers. Some businesses provide services related to goods sold by other businesses, such as repair and delivery services; sometimes manufacturers, wholesalers, and retailers furnish these services. Other businesses provide services unrelated to such goods; these services include communications (telephone), transportation (airline), utilities (gas and electricity), hospitality (food and lodging), and health (medical and dental) services. Still other businesses furnish financial services such as banking and insurance.

Internet Connections for Native Canadian Tribes

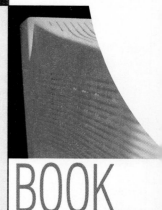

BOOK
M A R K

When your construction season is only five months long, getting documents for government funding processed in a timely fashion is essential to launching water, sewer, and building projects.

"Once it hits 30 below, we don't do anything," says George Mouldo, executive director of the Gitksan Government Commission. "If we get late approval or a late contract, it will cost more and take longer."

That's one of the reasons Mouldo is looking forward to getting an Internet connection for his commission, which represents five bands, or tribes, of native Canadians and three school districts in the northwestern section of British Columbia.

The government officials that Gitksan needs to deal with—whether in Ottawa; Vancouver, British Columbia; Victoria, British Columbia; or Edmonton, Alberta—are all far away. When the Gitksan Government Commission queries Canadian officials in writing, it can take a month to get a paper-based response.

Cognizant of the need for timelier communications, the Canadian government is making up to $10,000 available to any of the country's 626 bands to become enabled for the electronic exchange of data relating to housing, population, social assistance, education, and capital projects.

Paper reduction and data quality improvement will be added benefits, says Robert St. Germain, manager of corporate databases at British Columbia's Department of Indian Affairs and Northern Development (DIAND) unit, which works with the province's 197 bands. He said 95 have submitted applications for funding.

"By the time they provided us with the information and hard copy and it was inputted and processed, it was almost time for the next reporting period, so they never got any feedback," St. Germain says. "We're just trying to get into the 20th century." The eventual goal is to streamline the system so that the data can be dumped directly into DIAND's databases for processing.

For some bands, the new initiative will mean getting a computer and sending information via disk. For others, it will mean getting an Internet connection, and that's not always the simplest task in some of the more remote regions of Canada.

For instance, Takla Lake First Nation has 553 members in British Columbia: 255 don't live on the reserve, and 298 do. The band's financial center, in Prince George, British Columbia, will have no problem hooking in to the Internet because there are at least eight local providers in town, says Joe Bowers, the group's accountant and manager. But some Takla Lake members live about 350 miles to the northwest, in a logging community served by a road that is rough gravel for the last 150 miles. They already have two-line satellite-based phone service, and they will need a new satellite connection to get online, Bowers says.

"There will be an Internet connection at Takla Lake, but it is very expensive and definitely involves the federal government in a larger way," Bowers says. The band will get the school hooked up through a different government program.

Gitksan is outsourcing its Internet setup to two Canadian business partners—HLVD Interactive Systems in Regina, Saskatchewan, and Clan Raven Systems in Kamloops, British Columbia. Clan Raven is run by Gerald Couldwell, a First Nation's businessman who knows the region well, having grown up in Kitimat (which translates roughly to "valley of the snows"), where some winters see 30 feet of snow.

Questions

1. What benefits will the Gitksan Government Commission receive from an Internet connection?
2. What difficulty is there in setting up Internet connections for bands in remote regions of Canada?

Web Sites

Indian and Northern Affairs Canada: www.inac.gc.ca

Source: *Adapted from* Carol Sliwa, "Canada Hooks Native Tribes to Internet," *Computerworld*, September 7, 1998, pp. 37–38.

A shoe repair shop is an example of a service business. Another example is a business that replaces worn-out soles on athletic shoes. A business that provides shipping and delivery services for shoe manufacturers and clothing wholesalers is also a service business.

Not-for-profit Organizations

Manufacturers, wholesalers, retailers, and service businesses usually operate for a profit. Not-for-profit organizations, on the other hand, provide goods and services without the intent of making a profit. Most not-for-profit organizations provide services, such as medical care, education, cultural activities, and religious services. Some not-for-profit organizations are involved in manufacturing, wholesaling, or retailing. For example, Goodwill Industries refurbishes goods donated to it and sells them in retail stores.

Used athletic shoes and clothing often end up being donated to not-for-profit organizations. Churches and charitable organizations collect used clothing for distribution to the poor and homeless. Various organizations sell used shoes and clothing donated to them and use the income to provide community services.

Government

Government is a special type of not-for-profit service business. Government makes laws and regulations that affect businesses and individuals. It also provides some basic services such as police and fire protection. People pay for these services through taxes and fees charged for the services.

An example of the government's effect on athletic shoe and clothing businesses is government regulations regarding product labeling. Other examples are jogging paths, bicycle lanes, and tennis courts built by local governments. These facilities encourage the purchase of athletic clothing and equipment.

Business Trends

Businesses today are being affected by several important trends. One trend is *globalization* of businesses. No longer do many businesses operate only in a single country. Instead businesses manufacture, distribute, and sell goods in many countries or provide services worldwide. One effect of this trend is that businesses may have to operate differently in different countries because of variations in laws and customs.

Another important trend is toward *consolidation* of businesses. Companies are buying other companies to increase their share of the market or to move into new markets. Businesses are becoming bigger and more complex, and smaller businesses are finding it harder to compete. Distributors are not common in some industries because manufacturers distribute their products themselves. Some businesses do everything: manufacture their products, distribute them to their own stores, sell them at retail, and service them. This trend toward larger businesses is also part of globalization, as domestic companies buy foreign companies to compete with other large international businesses.

A third trend in some countries is a shift away from manufacturing and toward service businesses. This trend is especially prevalent in the United States, where many businesses no longer manufacture their products domestically, but instead purchase them from foreign suppliers. Service businesses have replaced manufacturers in many parts of the country. Some service businesses provide services globally; examples are banks and other financial service businesses that operate on an international scale.

Business Functions

To accomplish its purpose, a business or an organization must perform certain functions. For example, a business must buy and sell goods, manufacture products, pay employees, and so forth. Businesses group these functions into general categories, often called *functional areas* (Figure 2.2). This section describes the main business functions and discusses how these functions vary for different types of businesses.

Accounting

The **accounting** function is responsible for recording and reporting financial information about the business. The function records data about the business's assets, which are the items the business owns, such as cash, equipment, and buildings, and its liabilities, which are its debts. It also records data about the business's revenues and expenses. Periodically the accounting function produces reports on the financial state of the business.

All types of businesses require an accounting function. The details, however, vary somewhat for different types of businesses. For example, manufacturers have to account for production equipment, but wholesalers, retailers, and service businesses usually do not. A wholesaler, however, may have shipping expenses that a manufacturer does not have. A retailer has to account for store space that other types of businesses do not have. Finally, a service business, such as a repair business, may have to account for spare parts expenses, whereas other businesses may not.

Finance

The **finance** function of a business is responsible for obtaining money needed by the business and for planning the use of that money. Money for a business comes from the sale of goods and services, from investments made by the business, and from banks and other institutions that loan money to the business. When a business obtains money, it can use it for the day-to-day operations of the business or it can

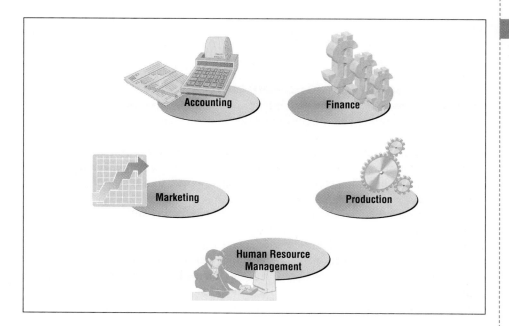

FIGURE 2.2

The main functional areas of a business

invest it for future use. The finance function plans what money is needed, determines the best way to obtain the money, and decides how the money should be used. The finance function is closely related to the accounting function; in some businesses accounting is part of the finance function.

All types of businesses need a finance function, but some do more financial work than others. For example, financial services companies such as banks have extensive finance functions. Other businesses, such as retail stores, may have comparatively small finance functions.

Marketing

The **marketing** function sells the goods and services of a business. To do so it must determine what products to sell and at what price. Then it must promote the products by advertising and other means. Finally, it must make the actual sale and distribute the products it sells.

All businesses have some form of marketing function, although the size varies significantly. Retail and many service businesses have very large marketing functions because they must sell to many customers. Wholesalers also may have fairly large marketing functions because they must sell to many retail businesses. Manufacturers often have comparatively small marketing functions because they may sell to only a few wholesalers.

Production

The **production** function is responsible for producing or manufacturing the goods that the business sells. The production function must acquire the materials or parts that go into the goods being manufactured. It must keep track of the goods as they are manufactured and after they are completed. It must control the manufacturing process to be sure it runs smoothly and cost-effectively.

In a manufacturing business, the production function is very large and important. In other types of businesses, however, this function usually does not exist. Instead there may be a related function, sometimes called **operations**, that performs various activities. For example, in a wholesale business the operations function would be responsible for running the warehouse where goods are stored. In a service business the operations function would involve activities that provide services to the customers.

Human Resource Management

The **human resource management** function, sometimes called **personnel**, is responsible for hiring, training, compensating, and terminating employees. This function must recruit and select employees, assess the skills of employees, and determine the appropriate jobs for employees. In addition, it must provide for the continual education and development of employees; determine appropriate compensation, including benefits; and provide procedures for termination due to resignation, retirement, or dismissal.

All types of businesses require human resource management. Businesses that have many employees with specialized skills, such as some manufacturers, need an extensive human resource management function for employee skill assessment and training. Businesses in which many employees perform similar types of work, such as some retail businesses, may not have such an extensive human resource management function.

Other Business Functions

The business functions just described are the most common ones in businesses. Other functions, however, may be performed in certain businesses. One is the **research and development** function, which is responsible for developing new products to be manufactured by the business. Another is the **information services** function, which is responsible for providing computer information systems support for the business. Yet other functions are present in certain types of businesses.

The Organization of a Business

The employees of a business are often grouped by the general functions they perform. Within each functional area may be smaller groups of people, often called **departments**, which have specific responsibilities related to the function. For example, in the marketing area there may be a Sales Department that is responsible for making sales, and an Advertising Department that prepares promotional material. The employees of a department form one or more **workgroups** to perform specific tasks or activities. For example, several employees in the Sales Department may form a workgroup to sell a particular line of products. In many situations, the entire department forms one workgroup. Workgroups are not, however, restricted to departments, but may exist across departmental and functional area boundaries. For example, a product-line workgroup may include several employees from both the Sales Department and the Advertising Department.

Each department is headed by a *manager* who is in charge of the people working in the department. Thus, the Sales Department has a sales manager and the Advertising Department has an advertising manager. All the managers of the departments in a functional area report to the manager of the area. The functional area managers are often called *vice presidents*. Thus there would be a vice president of marketing, a vice president of finance, and so forth. (The vice president of accounting is often called the controller.) In smaller businesses, functional areas may be called departments, and the person in charge may be called a manager instead of a vice president. In any case, all the functional area managers or vice presidents report to the manager of the whole business, who is usually the *president* or *chief executive officer* (*CEO*).

This arrangement of people who work for a business is often shown in a diagram called an **organization chart**. Figure 2.3 shows the organization chart for an athletic-clothing wholesaler. Each box represents a person or a workgroup with several people. The boxes are connected by lines that show who manages what part of the business.

The organizational structure of a business varies for different types of businesses. For example, whereas a manufacturer would have a production functional area, a wholesaler, retailer, or service business would not. Some businesses combine finance and accounting into one area, and some businesses have other areas, such as research and development and information services.

The organizational structure illustrated in Figure 2.3 is common in many businesses. Some businesses, however, have other types of organizational structures not based on business functions and not organized in a vertical hierarchy. For example, some businesses group employees by product line or by geographic area, and some businesses organize employees across functions into workgroups. Variations of these organizational structures are used in different businesses.

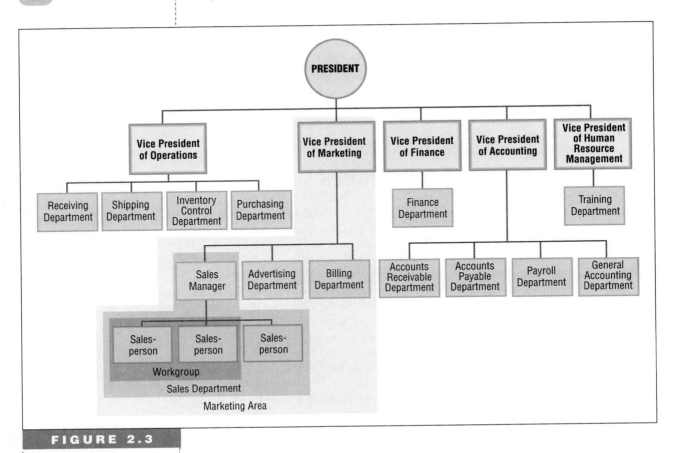

FIGURE 2.3

▲ An organization chart

Information and Business Operations

Business operations are those activities that provide the goods and services of the business and that ensure that the business makes a profit. Manufacturing products, processing customer orders, billing customers, keeping track of inventory, purchasing raw materials, and many more activities are all part of business operations. Information is needed for these operations to function efficiently. Information about what products to manufacture, what items have been ordered, how much a customer owes, when inventory is low, and from where to purchase raw materials are a few examples.

The information used in business operations flows between people within a workgroup or a department, and from one workgroup or department to another. The information may be sent by voice, on paper, or by computer. We will discuss several examples of the information flow that might be found in the operations of the athletic-clothing wholesale business whose organization chart is shown in Figure 2.3.

Figure 2.4 shows how information related to the sale of goods and the payment for the sale flows in a business. When a customer, which in this case is another business, wants to purchase something, the customer transmits information about what it wants to order. The Sales Department receives the customer order information and sends information about what is being sold to the Shipping Department, which packages the goods and sends them to the customer. The Shipping Department sends information about what it shipped to the Billing Department, which prepares billing information indicating how much the customer owes. The Billing Department sends this information to the customer and to the Accounts Receivable Department, which keeps track of customer bills and sends reminders to customers who have not paid their bills. After receiving the billing information, the customer sends payment to the Accounts Receivable Department.

Figure 2.5 depicts the information flow related to inventory control. Recall that inventory is the stock of goods that the business has on hand. The Shipping Department sends information to the Inventory Control Department about what goods it has shipped from the inventory in the warehouse. The Receiving Department receives goods sent to the business and stores them in inventory in the warehouse. It sends information to the Inventory Control Department about what goods it has

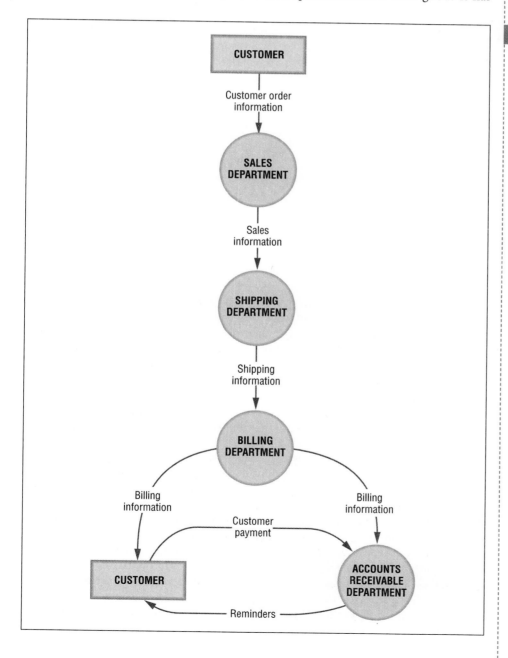

FIGURE 2.4

Information flow related to sales

FIGURE 2.5

Information flow related to
inventory control

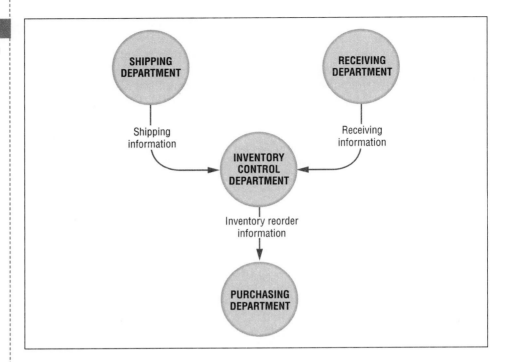

received. The Inventory Control Department keeps track of the inventory quantity,
subtracting goods shipped and adding goods received. Periodically it determines
what goods should be reordered and sends this information to the Purchasing
Department.

Figure 2.6 shows the flow of information related to purchasing goods. The Inventory Control Department gives information about the goods to reorder to the Purchasing Department. The Purchasing Department prepares purchasing information and sends it to the supplier that sells the goods. The Purchasing Department also sends purchasing information to the Accounts Payable Department, which keeps track of bills owed by the business. The supplier sends billing information for the goods purchased to the Accounts Payable Department. This department also gets information from the Receiving Department about which goods were received from the supplier. It then sends payment to the supplier for the goods that were billed and received.

The flow of information in business operations described here may be different in other types of businesses. For example, a manufacturing business does not replace inventory for items the business sells by purchasing new stock, but by producing the items. Thus, in this type of business, inventory information would flow to the Production Department to start the manufacturing process. In a retail business, the customer is a person and the customer "order" is a sale, which the business normally fills immediately. Thus, no shipping information flows from the Sales Department to the Shipping Department. Furthermore, billing information in a retail business is necessary only if the customer charges the purchase. Finally, some service businesses need information to keep track of customer service requests. This information may flow from the customer to the Service Department

FIGURE 2.6

Information flow related to
purchasing

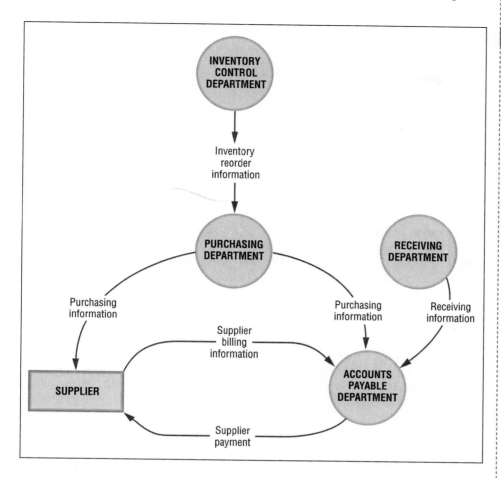

and on to the Billing Department. Chapter 10 describes information systems that
support business operations.

Information and Business Management

In addition to supporting business operations, information is used in the management of the business. *Management* is all the activities related to deciding how a business functions. Managers decide on a day-to-day basis who should be allowed to purchase from the business on credit, how much should be ordered for inventory, and
which suppliers should be used for purchases. Managers decide on a longer-term
basis what items should be stocked next season and even whether the business should
change to a whole new product line.

All managers make decisions. In general, a *decision* is a selection among different
courses of action. For example, in a credit-granting decision, a manager must choose
between granting credit and not granting credit to a customer. To make a decision, a
manager needs information. Thus, to decide whether to grant credit, the manager
needs information about the customer's previous credit history. The information
reduces uncertainty for the manager and, as a consequence, reduces risk for the business. Credit-history information reduces uncertainty about whether the customer

will pay its bill. With less uncertainty, granting credit is less risky for the business. The information has value to the decision maker and to the business because of the reduction of uncertainty and risk.

Much of the information managers need is produced from the information that flows in the business. To illustrate, consider a manager's inventory reordering decision. Figure 2.5 shows that inventory shipping and receiving information flows to the Inventory Control Department. This department keeps track of the quantity of inventory that the business currently has in stock and detects when the inventory level is too low. The Sales Department receives customer order information (see Figure 2.4) and uses this information to help forecast sales. When the manager receives information that the inventory level is low, he or she can use the sales forecast information to help determine how much new stock to reorder. Thus, information flows to the manager so that he or she can make appropriate decisions.

Decisions are made at different levels of a business. The highest-level decisions, called *strategic decisions*, are made by top managers such as the president or vice president. These decisions affect the business for a long time. For example, deciding whether the business should change to a new product line is a strategic decision. Middle-level decisions, called *tactical decisions*, are made by departmental managers or workgroup leaders and affect the business for an intermediate time. Deciding what items should be stocked next season is an example of a tactical decision. The lowest-level decisions, called *operational decisions*, are made by individuals at the bottom of the management hierarchy, such as credit evaluators, inventory supervisors, and purchasing personnel. These decisions affect the business for a short time. The credit-granting decision is an example of an operational decision. Chapter 11 describes information systems that support management decision making.

Basic Business Information Processing

The use of information in business operations and management is made possible by various information processing activities. These activities involve people (and computers, if the activities are computerized) that receive data for processing, process the data as required, store the data for future processing, and produce information resulting from the processing.

Although businesses perform many information processing activities, eight basic ones are common:

- Entering customer orders
- Billing customers
- Collecting customer payments
- Keeping track of inventory
- Purchasing stock and materials
- Paying bills
- Paying employees
- Reporting financial information

This section describes these eight activities. The descriptions are general and do not assume that the activities are done with or without the aid of computers. Each

FIGURE 2.7

A customer order

SPORTSWEAR ENTERPRISES
Customer Order Form

Customer name Campus Sport Shop   Number 12345

Salesperson Jim   Date 9/18/XXXX

Item number	Item description	Quantity ordered
1537	Shorts	12
2719	T-shirt	30
4205	Socks	24
5172	Sweatshirt	6

activity is illustrated with an example of how it would be used in an athletic-clothing wholesale business.

Entering Customer Orders

The first business information processing activity is entering customer orders. The purpose of this activity is to accept customer orders for goods or services and to prepare them in a form that the business can use. This activity is part of the marketing function and is performed by the Sales Department.

The input to this activity is the *customer order*, which may be received by the business in several forms. A customer may phone in an order to a salesperson, who writes the order on a form (Figure 2.7), or the customer may fill out the order form and mail it to the business. The customer also may order by sending in a purchase order prepared in a format the customer uses. The purchase order may be sent by mail, by fax, or by computer, if an electronic data interchange system (discussed in Chapter 1) is used. In any case, the Sales Department receives the order.

When processing an order, the Sales Department must determine whether there is sufficient inventory to fill the order and whether credit should be extended to the customer. If both conditions are met, the Sales Department prepares a *sales order* (Figure 2.8), which is the output from this activity. This document, which is also called a *shipping order*, contains customer information, such as customer name and address, and inventory information, such as the item ordered. The Sales Department sends the sales order to the Shipping Department.

Billing Customers

The Shipping Department uses the sales order to determine what items should be shipped to the customer. In some cases the quantity shipped is different from the quantity ordered because of inadequate stock on hand. Therefore, the Shipping Department must mark a copy of the sales order with the actual quantity shipped (Figure 2.9) and send this copy to the Billing Department. The Billing Department uses its copy of the sales order to prepare the customer's bill, which is called the *invoice*. The Billing Department may be part of the marketing function or the accounting function.

Order Processing at The Sharper Image

Building on the strength of its order-processing system, The Sharper Image developed an updated Web site, capitalizing on several new features, to prepare not only for the rush of online shoppers during the holiday season, but also for the company's expectations of growing online commerce.

A purveyor of gadgets, gizmos, and handy products ranging from in-shower CD players and Ionic Breeze air purifiers to model cars, The Sharper Image was an early entrant into the world of e-commerce, launching its original Web site in 1995.

According to Greg Alexander, senior vice president of information systems at The Sharper Image, the move from retail and catalog sales to online sales—and the continuing additions to online services—would have been difficult without an accommodating order-processing system to handle all those orders.

"It would have been far more expensive to get out onto the Web [without the order system already in place]," Alexander says. "This is definitely a homegrown system that is very tailorable. It doesn't end up requiring a lot of change because it was designed and written in such a way as to provide maximum flexibility for whatever sales channels might come down the road."

With the order-processing system as a solid foundation, The Sharper Image prepared for anticipated increased online traffic by making sure site features were ready for the holiday shopping season.

An auction room and 3D product viewing were added to the company's Web site, both of which were spruced up for holiday shoppers. SharperImage.com auctions include refurbished and returned products certified to be in working order and with the same return privileges as their nonauction counter-parts, a feature Alexander considers attractive for buyers used to retail stores.

3D viewing brings selected products to life. "The idea was to give the customer the closest experience to actually being in our stores," Alexander says. "It's a great service to a customer to pick up a product, so to speak, and turn it around and open it up, push the buttons, and be able to utilize the functions of the product."

Alexander says that thanks to the preparations made before the holiday rush, everything ran very smoothly: "Traffic was tremendous, sales were excellent, and [the system] handled the situation well." In fact, The Sharper Image saw online sales jump almost five times in one year.

The company expects to remain on the cutting edge with its products and Web site, thanks in part to the solid order-processing system that keeps track of copious product orders from The Sharper Image's catalogs, retail stores, and Web site.

"We don't want to just be flashy," Alexander says. "We want to be flashy and functional at the same time."

Questions

1. Why was it important that The Sharper Image had an order-processing system before it added features to attract customers to its Web site?
2. What would The Sharper Image have had to do if it had not had an order-processing system that worked with the Web site?

Web Site

The Shaper Image:
www.sharperimage.com

Source: *Adapted from* Stephanie Sanborn, "The Sharper Image Hones in on I-commerce," *Infoworld*, January 24, 2000, p. 37.

FIGURE 2.8

A sales order

The sales order (see Figure 2.9) is the input to the billing activity. The output is the invoice (Figure 2.10), which contains the information about how much the customer owes for the items ordered. To prepare the invoice from the sales order, the Billing Department must look up the customer's billing address so that this information can be included on the invoice. It must also look up the price of each item shipped and calculate the amount due by multiplying the quantity shipped by the price per item. This information is part of the invoice, as is the total amount due for all items purchased. The Billing Department sends a copy of the invoice to the customer and another copy to the Accounts Receivable Department.

FIGURE 2.9

The sales order from the Shipping Department

FIGURE 2.10

▲ **An invoice**

SPORTSWEAR ENTERPRISES

Invoice

Sold to
Campus Sport Shop
123 South Avenue
P.O. Box 543
Portland, OR 97208

Customer number
12345

Date
9/23/XXXX

Item number	Item description	Quantity ordered	Quantity shipped	Unit price	Amount
1537	Shorts	12	12	11.50	138.00
2719	T-shirt	30	24	9.75	234.00
4205	Socks	24	24	3.25	78.00
5172	Sweatshirt	6	6	18.75	112.50
				Total	562.50

Collecting Customer Payments

The Accounts Receivable Department uses the copy of the invoice received from the Billing Department to keep track of money customers owe to the business, which is called *accounts receivable*, and to record customer payments for invoices. In addition, this department sends reminders of overdue invoices to customers, sends summaries of invoice charges and payments to customers, and provides reports of accounts receivable to other business functions. The Accounts Receivable Department is part of the accounting function.

The inputs to this activity are the copy of the invoice received from the Billing Department (see Figure 2.10) and the customer payment. One of the outputs is a *statement*, which summarizes the invoice charges and payments and gives the current balance due (Figure 2.11). The Accounts Receivable Department prepares statements once per month and sends them to the customers. (Some businesses do not prepare statements.) Another output is *overdue notices*, which the Accounts Receivable Department sends to customers who have not paid their invoices. (Sometimes the statements include notices for overdue customers.) A final output is an *accounts receivable report* summarizing charges and payments for the month (Figure 2.12). This report contains the total invoice charges and total customer payments for all customers. The Accounts Receivable Department sends this report to the General Accounting Department.

Processing in this activity involves several tasks. One task is to record the balance due for each customer, along with the current month's invoice amount and payments. Another task is to compute the new balance due each month by adding the customer's previous balance due and the total of the current month's invoices, and then subtracting the total of the current month's payments.

Keeping Track of Inventory

To be sure that there is adequate stock on hand to meet customer demand, a business must keep track of its inventory and report when inventory is low so that it can order more stock. The Inventory Control Department performs this information pro-

FIGURE 2.11

A statement ▲

SPORTSWEAR ENTERPRISES

Statement

Customer name
 Campus Sport Shop
 123 South Avenue
 P.O. Box 543
 Portland, OR 97208

Customer number
 12345

Date
 9/30/XXXX

Date	Description	Amount
	Previous balance	**1,205.75**
9/15/XXXX	**Invoice**	**742.00**
9/17/XXXX	**Payment**	**1,205.75–**
9/23/XXXX	**Invoice**	**562.50**
	New balance	**1,304.50**

cessing activity. In some businesses this department is part of the production or operations function, and in other businesses it is part of the marketing or accounting function.

The inputs to this activity are the sales order from the Shipping Department, indicating the quantity of each item shipped (see Figure 2.9) and the *receiving notice* from the Receiving Department, giving the quantity of items received from suppliers or other sources (Figure 2.13). One output is the *inventory reorder report*, which lists the items that should be reordered because stock is low (Figure 2.14). The Inventory Control Department sends this report to the Purchasing Department. Another output is the *inventory value report*, which gives the value of the items in stock (Figure 2.15). This report goes to the General Accounting Department.

FIGURE 2.12

An accounts receivable report ▲

ACCOUNTS RECEIVABLE REPORT
9/30/XXXX

Customer number	Date	Invoice charge	Payment
12345	9/15/XXXX	742.00	
12345	9/17/XXXX		1,205.75
12345	9/23/XXXX	562.50	
48721	9/11/XXXX		2,135.00
48721	9/15/XXXX	1,079.25	
⋮			
93142	9/12/XXXX	425.00	
93142	9/25/XXXX		975.25
Total		72,213.50	63,409.00

FIGURE 2.13

▲ A receiving notice

RECEIVING NOTICE

Date _____9/17/XXXX_____

Item number _____4205_____

Supplier number _____6214_____

Quantity received _____180_____

FIGURE 2.14

▲ An inventory reorder report

INVENTORY REORDER REPORT
9/30/XXXX

Item number	Item description	Quantity on hand	Reorder point	Quantity to order
2719	T-shirt	0	10	30
3804	Tennis shirt	8	12	25
5173	Sweatpants	18	18	44
6318	Swimsuit	12	20	36

FIGURE 2.15

▲ An inventory value report

INVENTORY VALUE REPORT
11/30/XXXX

Item number	Item description	Inventory value
1537	Shorts	4,232.00
1609	Jacket	960.00
2719	T-shirt	2,340.00
3512	Tennis shorts	690.00
3804	Tennis shirt	1,904.40
4205	Socks	480.20
	⋮	
5172	Sweatshirt	3,515.75
5173	Sweatpants	4,002.00
5501	Cap	874.00
6318	Swimsuit	1,197.00
Total value		85,352.00

Processing in this activity involves keeping track of the quantity on hand for each item in inventory. The Inventory Control Department updates this quantity from data in the sales orders and receiving notices. It calculates the new quantity on hand for an item by subtracting the quantity shipped of an item found on each sales order from the item's old quantity on hand, and adding the quantity received for the item on each receiving notice.

The type of inventory described here is called *finished goods inventory* because it deals with final products ready for sale. Manufacturing, wholesaling, retailing, and some service businesses use this type of inventory. Manufacturers, however, do not prepare the inventory reorder report. Instead, they produce a report indicating what items should be manufactured. Manufacturers usually have two other types of inventory: *Raw materials inventory* consists of the materials and parts used in manufacturing, and *work-in-process inventory* involves partially manufactured items. Manufacturers need inventory control systems for these other types of inventory.

Purchasing Stock and Materials

When a business purchases items for inventory, it must first determine the best suppliers of the items and then prepare documents, called *purchase orders*, which indicate to the suppliers what items the business wants to purchase. The Purchasing Department, which is usually part of the production or operations function but may be part of the accounting function, performs this activity.

The input to this activity is the inventory reorder report (see Figure 2.14), which comes from the Inventory Control Department. This report indicates what items and what quantity of each item to reorder. The output is the purchase order (Figure 2.16), which lists the items the business wants to purchase. The Purchasing Department sends a copy of the purchase order to the supplier and another copy to the Accounts Payable Department.

To produce the purchase order, the Purchasing Department must decide from which supplier to purchase the item. It analyzes different suppliers' sales policies and performance information to determine the best supplier for each item. The Purchasing Department bases its determination of the best supplier not only on price, but also on sales terms, delivery time, or other factors the business considers important. To prepare a purchase order, the Purchasing Department looks up the preferred sup-

FIGURE 2.16

A purchase order

SPORTSWEAR ENTERPRISES

Purchase Order

Date   9/5/XXXX

Supplier
Eastern Clothing Co.
125 Central Rd.
Newark, NJ 07101

Ship to
482 North Street
San Francisco, CA 94108

Item number	Item description	Quantity
148720	T-shirts	30
290461	Sweatpants	44

plier's name and address. It includes this information on the purchase order, along with information about the item ordered.

The activity described here is characteristic of purchasing for finished goods inventory in a wholesale, retail, or service business. In a manufacturing business, purchasing is necessary for raw materials inventory, but not for finished goods inventory. Instead, manufacturers do production scheduling to determine, based on inventory needs, what items to produce.

Paying Bills

The Accounts Payable Department uses its copy of the purchase order, received from the Purchasing Department, to keep track of money owed by the business for purchases, which is called *accounts payable*, and to pay suppliers for the items purchased. The Accounts Payable Department is part of the accounting function.

The inputs to this activity are the copy of the purchase order from the Purchasing Department indicating what items were ordered (see Figure 2.16), the invoice from the supplier showing what items the supplier shipped and the charges for the items, and a copy of the receiving notice from the Receiving Department indicating what items were received (see Figure 2.13). The outputs include the supplier payment, which is a check sent to the supplier, and an *accounts payable report* summarizing the supplier charges and payments for the month (Figure 2.17). The report contains the total charges and payments for all suppliers. The Accounts Payable Department sends this report to the General Accounting Department.

Processing in this activity includes several tasks. The Accounts Payable Department compares the purchase order with the supplier's invoice to determine whether the supplier shipped the items ordered. It also compares the supplier's invoice with the receiving notice to see whether the business received the items shipped. If the supplier's invoice correctly states what items were ordered and received, then the Accounts Payable Department makes a record of the data on the invoice. Included in this data is the due date for the payment of the invoice. Frequently, perhaps every day, the Accounts Payable Department checks this data to see if any invoice payments are due soon. When a payment is almost due, the department prepares a check. Once each month, the department prepares the accounts payable report.

FIGURE 2.17

▲ An accounts payable report

ACCOUNTS PAYABLE REPORT
9/30/XX

Supplier number	Invoice date	Invoice charge	Payment
2147	9/3/XXXX	10,132.50	10,132.50
2895	9/7/XXXX	15,911.00	
3245	9/12/XXXX	780.75	
3513	9/13/XXXX	9,470.00	9,470.00
7409	9/27/XXXX	425.00	
7723	9/28/XXXX	2,630.00	
Totals		68,425.00	52,095.50

TIME SHEET

WEEK OF 9/14/XXXX
EMPLOYEE NUMBER 68431
EMPLOYEE NAME J. Jones
MONDAY HOURS 7½
TUESDAY HOURS 8
WEDNESDAY HOURS 6
THURSDAY HOURS 8
FRIDAY HOURS 8
TOTAL HOURS 37½

FIGURE 2.18

A time sheet

Paying Employees

An essential information processing activity in all businesses involves paying employees and providing payroll reports for other business functions. The Payroll Department performs this activity. In many businesses this department is part of the accounting function, but in some businesses it is part of the human resource management function.

The input to this activity is the employee work report. For an employee whom the business pays on an hourly basis, this report is a time sheet that shows how many hours the employee has worked each day (Figure 2.18). For an employee to whom the business pays a fixed salary, the report indicates whether the employee was present for all workdays, and, if he or she was absent, for what reason. The outputs include the paycheck the employee receives and the *payroll report*. The payroll report (Figure 2.19) lists the gross earnings for each employee, which is the amount earned by the employee, the amount deducted for taxes and for other reasons, and the net pay, which is the difference between the gross earnings and deductions; it also gives the

PAYROLL REPORT
11/30/XXXX

Employee number	Employee name	Gross earnings	Federal tax	Soc. Sec. tax	Other deduct.	Net pay
23890	S. Smith	1,305.50	180.83	93.34	.00	1,031.33
25008	M. Andrews	1,162.00	106.80	83.08	15.00	957.12
31942	R. Gonzales	2,443.75	276.56	174.73	7.50	1,984.96
37926	J. Franklin	988.00	80.70	70.64	.00	836.66
			⋮			
87435	L. Wong	1,352.00	229.84	96.69	.00	1,025.47
88207	F. Richardson	872.00	148.24	62.35	18.00	643.41
92371	A. Baker	460.25	78.24	32.91	.00	349.10
	Totals	40,305.00	6,859.50	2,885.03	507.50	33,097.97

FIGURE 2.19

A payroll report

total of the gross earnings, deductions, and net pay for all employees. The Payroll Department sends this report to the General Accounting Department.

Payroll processing involves using the employee work data and the data from the employee records, such as pay rate or salary, to calculate the pay for each employee. If the business pays the employee on an hourly basis, the Payroll Department multiplies the hours worked listed on the time sheet by the pay rate to calculate the gross earnings. For a salaried employee, the gross earnings is the employee's salary, unless he or she worked less than a full pay period. In addition, the Payroll Department calculates the tax and other deductions and the net pay.

FIGURE 2.20

▲ Financial statements

SPORTSWEAR ENTERPRISES
Income Statement, September XXXX

Revenue:		
Sales		$232,458
Expenses:		
Cost of goods sold	$88,231	
Salaries	40,305	
Rent	33,250	
Advertising	15,140	
Delivery	13,518	
Supplies	1,519	
Depreciation	12,350	
Total expenses		204,313
Net income:		$28,145

(a) Income statement

SPORTSWEAR ENTERPRISES
Balance Sheet, September 30, XXXX

Assets:		
Cash	$46,219	
Accounts receivable	52,436	
Inventory	85,352	
Equipment	36,750	
Total assets		$220,757
Liabilities:		
Loans payable	$111,500	
Accounts payable	44,216	
Total liabilities		155,716
Owner's equity:		65,041
Total liabilities & owner's equity		$220,757

(b) Balance sheet

Reporting Financial Information

The last business information processing activity we will discuss here is found in all businesses. Its purpose is to provide reports of financial information for the management and owners of the business. To accomplish this activity, a business keeps financial accounts for each form of revenue it receives and each expense it pays. A business receives revenue from sales and other sources such as investments. It pays expenses for the cost of the goods it sells and for salaries, rent, advertising, office supplies, and so forth. A business also keeps an account of each of its assets and liabilities. *Assets* are items the business owns, such as cash, equipment, and buildings. Inventory and accounts receivable are also assets. *Liabilities* are obligations the business has to pay money, including loans and accounts payable. This activity records revenues and expenses, as well as changes in assets and liabilities, and it prepares reports, called *financial statements*, that summarize the business's accounts. The General Accounting Department, which is part of the accounting function, performs this activity.

The inputs to this activity are reports on revenue, expenses, assets, and liabilities. The accounts receivable report (see Figure 2.12) provides information about accounts receivable (an asset). The inventory value report (see Figure 2.15) gives the total value of the inventory (an asset). The accounts payable report (see Figure 2.17) provides information about accounts payable (a liability). The payroll report (see Figure 2.19) gives payroll expense information. Other reports provide information about other accounts.

The outputs from this activity are financial statements; the two most common are the income statement and the balance sheet (Figure 2.20). The *income statement* lists all revenues and expenses for a specific period (such as a month) and the difference between the total revenue and total expenses, which is the net income if positive, or loss if negative. The *balance sheet* lists all assets and liabilities and the difference between the total assets and total liabilities, which is called the owner's equity. This activity may include producing other financial statements as well.

Processing in this activity involves recording data about revenues, expenses, assets, and liabilities. Periodically, the General Accounting Department prepares the financial statements from the recorded data.

Information Systems and Business

So far this chapter has shown how information flows in business operations, how managers use information in decision making, and how businesses perform basic information processing. Although a business could handle this flow, use, and processing of information without the aid of computers and related technology, using computer information systems for these activities can greatly increase a business's efficiency and effectiveness.

Information systems and technology can control the information flow in business operations. Computers and networks can transmit data from one department to another. For example, a computer can send sales information through a network from the Sales Department to the Shipping Department, then send shipping information to the Billing Department, and finally transmit billing information to the Accounts Receivable Department. Controlling the flow of information between departments using computers and networks increases the efficiency of the business operations involved.

Information systems and technology also increase the effectiveness of management decision making. Managers use information systems to get information to help in their decision making. For example, when deciding whether to grant credit to a customer, a manager can use an information system to examine the customer's credit history. With relevant and readily available information from computer information systems, managers can make better decisions.

Finally, almost all information processing activities are more efficient and effective when computer information systems perform them than when they are performed without computers. Entering customer orders is faster and more accurate with computers. Preparing customer bills is quicker using a computer information system. Collecting customer payments is more effective with an information system. Keeping track of inventory is more accurate using information technology. Businesses perform all the information processing activities discussed in this chapter, as well as many more, with the aid of information systems and technology.

Information systems provide the methods and technology to support information needs and processing for every function in all types of businesses. Information systems are used in accounting, finance, marketing, production, and human resource management. Information systems also provide for communication of information between the functions of a business and for processing that involves several functions. One way to envision information systems is that they form a layer that floats over the functions of a business, connecting the functions and providing information services to them and among them (Figure 2.21).

Information systems are not limited to just certain types of businesses. Manufacturers, wholesalers, retailers, service businesses, not-for-profit organizations, and government agencies all use information systems. The size of a business does not affect the need for information systems either. Small businesses, national companies, and multinational corporations all need information systems. No matter

FIGURE 2.21

Information system support for all functions of a business

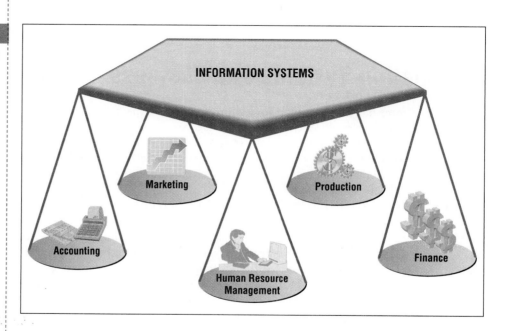

what the function, or the type or size of the business, information systems play essential roles.

CHAPTER SUMMARY

1 A business provides goods and services for its customers. A **manufacturer** produces goods that are sold to other businesses or to individual customers. A **wholesaler** purchases large quantities of goods, and then sells smaller quantities to retailers, and ships or distributes the goods to the retailers. A **retailer** purchases quantities of goods from wholesalers or manufacturers and resells them, one at a time or in small quantities, to individual consumers. A **service business** provides services to other businesses or to individuals. (pp. 33–34)

2 One trend affecting businesses today is globalization. Increasingly, businesses manufacture, distribute, and sell their products in many countries and provide their services worldwide. Another trend is consolidation of businesses. Companies buy other companies, domestically and globally, to increase their market share or to move into new markets. A third trend in some countries is a shift away from manufacturing and toward service businesses. (p. 36)

3 The **accounting** function of a business records and reports financial information about the business. The **finance** function obtains money needed by a business and plans the use of that money. The **marketing** function sells the goods and services of the business. The **production** function produces the goods sold by the business. The **human resource management** function hires, trains, compensates, and terminates employees of the business. Many businesses are organized according to the main functions of the business. Within each function may be **departments** that have specific responsibilities related to the function. Within each department or across departmental lines may be **workgroups** that perform specific tasks or activities. (pp. 37–39)

4 Information flows between people within a workgroup or a department, and from one workgroup or department to another. Figure 2.4 shows the flow of information related to the sale of goods and the payment for the sale. Figure 2.5 de-picts the flow of information related to inventory control. Figure 2.6 shows the flow of information related to purchasing goods. (pp. 40–43)

5 The managers of a business use information to help in decision making. A decision involves selecting among different courses of action. To make a decision, a manager needs information, which reduces uncertainty for the manager and risk for the business. The information has value to the decision maker and to the business because of the reduction of uncertainty and risk. (pp. 43–44)

6 Entering customer orders requires accepting customer orders for goods or services and preparing them in a form that can be used by the business. Billing customers involves preparing customers' bills or invoices. Collecting customers payments requires keeping track of money owed to the business by its customers (accounts receivable) and recording customer payments. Keeping track of a business's inventory is important so that customer demand is met and inventory can be reordered when it is low. Purchasing stock and materials involves determining the best suppliers from which to purchase items and preparing purchase orders. Paying bills requires keeping track of money owed by the business (accounts payable) and paying suppliers for items purchased. Paying employees involves preparing paychecks for employees and providing reports of payroll. Reporting financial information consists of maintaining the business's financial accounts and preparing financial statements. (pp. 44–55)

7 Information systems provide the methods and technology to support information needs and processing in businesses. Information systems control the flow of information in business operations. They make information readily available to help in management decision making. They improve the efficiency and effectiveness of information processing activities. They are used in all functions of all types and sizes of businesses and organizations. (pp. 55–57)

K E Y   T E R M S

Accounting (p. 37)
Department (p. 39)
Finance (p. 37)
Human Resource Management
    (Personnel) (p. 38)
Information Services (p. 39)

Manufacturer (p. 33)
Marketing (p. 38)
Operations (p. 38)
Organization Chart (p. 39)
Production (p. 38)
Research and Development (p. 39)

Retailer (p. 34)
Service Business (p. 34)
Wholesaler (Distributor) (p. 34)
Workgroup (p. 39)

R E V I E W   Q U E S T I O N S

1 What is the purpose of a business?

2 How do goods flow from raw materials to the final consumer?

3 What does a wholesaler do?

4 List three trends that affect businesses today.

5 What does the finance function of a business do?

6 What things are done by the marketing function of a business?

7 What is the purpose of the human resource management function of a business?

8 What is a workgroup?

9 How does the Shipping Department know what goods it should ship to a customer?

10 What does the Accounts Receivable Department of a business do?

11 What information does the Inventory Control Department need in order to keep track of inventory?

12 How does the Purchasing Department know when to purchase more goods?

13 What information does the Accounts Payable Department need to make payments to suppliers?

14 How does the management of a business use information?

15 What must the Sales Department determine when processing customer orders?

16 For what business information processing activities is a sales order an input?

17 What are the outputs from the information processing activity that collects customer payments?

18 Which information processing activity discussed in this chapter affects all employees of a business?

D I S C U S S I O N   Q U E S T I O N S

1 In some industries, wholesalers are not used; the retailer buys directly from the manufacturer. In other industries, wholesalers are used extensively. Why would a manufacturer want to use a wholesaler to sell and distribute its products instead of selling directly to a retailer? Why would a retailer want to purchase goods from a wholesaler rather than directly from a manufacturer?

2 This chapter discusses globalization, consolidation, and a shift to service businesses as important trends. What other trends affect businesses? What effect do they have on businesses?

3 In which function of a business do you plan to work? What job do you hope to have in that function? What information do you think you will receive in the course of doing that job? What decisions will you have to make in the job? What information will you need to make these decisions?

4 Identify several business information processing activities other than those described in this chapter. What are the inputs and outputs for each activity?

5 To reduce manufacturing costs, many businesses produce products in foreign countries or purchase products from foreign manufacturers. Also, many businesses sell their products worldwide. What problems do international production and international marketing create for the business information processing activities discussed in this chapter?

ETHICS QUESTIONS

1 Would ethical issues and standards be different in a not-for-profit business than in a for-profit business? In what ways? Would they be different in government agencies? How?

2 Information can be used in many ways in a business, including unethical ways. What are some unethical uses of information within a business? How can these uses be prevented?

PROBLEM-SOLVING PROJECTS

1 Draw an organization chart of a business or an organization with which you are familiar. Use graphics software to prepare the chart.

2 Using graphics software, draw a diagram like the ones in Figures 2.4, 2.5, or 2.6 for the flow of information related to some activity in a business or an organization with which you are familiar.

3 Using spreadsheet software, set up a table in which the columns are the eight business information processing activities discussed in this chapter, and the rows are the various reports and documents that are inputs and outputs for these activities. At the intersection of a row and column, put an *I* if the report or document is an input into the system, an *O* if it is an output, and nothing if it is neither an input nor an output. Use the spreadsheet software to count the number of inputs and the number of outputs for each activity. Also use the software to count the number of times each input or output is used. What pattern can you see in this data?

4 Using database software, develop an inventory database. Each record in the database should have fields for the item number, item description, unit price, and quantities on hand. Supply 20 to 30 records of data for a business of your choice. Then prepare a report that lists all items in inventory that have a quantity on hand less than a certain value that you decide on.

5 Contact a company in which you are interested and get its most recent annual report with financial statements. Then transfer the information from the financial statements to a spreadsheet and, using the spreadsheet software, compute the following:

$$\text{Working capital} = \frac{\text{Total current}}{\text{assets}} - \frac{\text{Total current}}{\text{liabilities}}$$

$$\text{Current ratio} = \frac{\text{Total current assets}}{\text{Total current liabilities}}$$

$$\text{Acid-test ratio} = \frac{\text{Cash} + \text{Accounts receivable}}{\text{Total current liabilities}}$$

$$\frac{\text{Rate of return}}{\text{on equity}} = \frac{\text{Net income}}{\text{Owner's equity}}$$

$$\text{Earnings per share} = \frac{\text{Net income}}{\text{Shares of stock outstanding}}$$

INTERNET AND ELECTRONIC COMMERCE PROJECTS

1 Select a category of consumer products other than athletic shoes and clothing. Identify several major manufacturers, wholesalers (if used for these products), and retailers of these products. Use the Web to gather information about these businesses and how products are manufactured, distributed, and sold to consumers. Write a brief report summarizing the information you gathered.

2 Select a category of consumer products in which you are interested. (If you did the preceding project, this category can be the same one you selected in that project.) Identify a manufacturer, a distributor, and a retailer that use electronic commerce to sell these products. Evaluate their Web sites in terms of the similarities and differences in the way they sell their products electronically. Write a summary of your evaluation.

3 Use the Web to find financial statements for a company in which you are interested. Then transfer the information from the financial statements to a spreadsheet and use the spreadsheet software to do the calculations in Problem-solving Project 5.

real world case

Coca-Cola

The Coca-Cola Company has used a handful of expert programmers and more than 100 years of marketing expertise to come up with a free program that's helping its retailers bring more customers into their stores and sell more of everything.

With Coca-Cola's help, retailers are translating frequent-shopper data into sales. Take Gerland's Food Fair in Houston, Texas: The 16-store supermarket chain increased sales 9.8% to its core customers, who account for 88% of dollars spent. "We found this program simple and easy to work with, and they understood the business, so that was a tremendous help to us," says Kevin Doris, chief executive officer of Gerland's.

Coca-Cola benefits from increased sales at the checkout counter, but it also positions itself as a true marketing partner to its retailers. It uses their retail space as real-world laboratories for large-scale, long-term marketing experiments, such as the one at Gerland's.

In the initiative's three-year history, Don Hodson, senior manager for category management information, has worked with more than 40 retailers, from gas stations to supermarkets—any business that sells a significant volume of Coca-Cola products.

And Coke doesn't preach. It gets down in the trenches and draws up strategies with its retailers. "We diagrammed each store, set up mandatory end caps in every store, and gave stores lists of all the items and highlighted the ones they should promote," Doris says.

Virtually every retailer with a scanner collects huge amounts of data on customer purchases, including universal product codes, number of items, price, time, and store. Retailers with frequent-shopper card programs can also tie a transaction to specific households and track purchasing patterns. Some even know how many children, adults, and pets are in a household.

Retailers are already doing some analysis of customer data themselves, but their capabilities vary, Hodson says, and not necessarily by company size. Some are sophisticated, but most can do only fairly basic analyses, such as identifying the top 10% of shoppers.

For those companies, Coke can offer much more. Retailers in the program pass huge transaction files of information gathered during several months (stripped of any customer identifiers) to Coke's Atlanta headquarters. At Gerland's, for example, Coke analyzed more than 400,000 transactions involving 5.7 million items, 32,000 shoppers, and $10.7 million in sales.

Because businesses collect information in different formats, the data goes through a painstaking cleaning process to prepare it to be run through Coke's proprietary analysis software, which runs on a dedicated server. Then it is fed to modules built in-house, using statistical data analysis software. The modules segment shoppers by such factors as frequency of shopping, time, day, average basket size, total spending, profit generated, category, and brand preferences. With that information, the other modules in the system can analyze the data in various ways. "We have over 30 different applications that we can run," Hodson says.

The initiative is a garden of delights for Hodson, a statistician. "We quantify what it means in dollars if they put one additional item in the basket, or if you're able to get shoppers in your store one more time," he says.

Hodson stresses that this isn't just about soft drinks. "We identify opportunities to grow that total business," Hodson says. "That's the fun part." All kinds of manufacturers would like to be in on the fun, says Bryan Spillane, an analyst at Warburg Dillon Read, a Wall Street research firm. "The retailer has the information, and anybody who's selling into a supermarket wants it," he explains. "They all try to buddy up and say, 'If you share that, we can help you sell more.'" But

Spillane says he views Coke's role as a total business partner with some skepticism. "How much do you really think Coke knows about selling Hellman's mayonnaise?" he asks.

Coke seems to know more than the competition, and that may be enough for its customers. Unlike third-party marketing vendors, its services are free. And unlike other grocery vendors, Coke addresses the whole store rather than just its product categories. "Pepsi doesn't have any approach similar to what we're doing," Hodson says. "We've consistently heard from retailers that we are unique."

"A lot of manufacturers offer to help retailers, but they don't seem as advanced as Coke," says Scott Ukrop, vice president of marketing at Ukrop's Supermarkets in Richmond, Virginia: "Coke's got a lot more resources behind it."

One of those resources is Glenn Stoops, managing director for market research and category management, who's been analyzing that kind of data for more than a decade. "The others just started a year or two ago," Stoops says. "They haven't invested in the data mining capabilities, the infrastructure, the analysts. Unless you understand how to put it all together, it's just a bunch of pieces."

In the course of the program, Coke gives its customers advice on specific ways to grow their businesses. At Gerland's, for example, the displays at the ends of each aisle had been largely given over to snack and convenience items—the targets of fill-in and occasional shoppers. The Coke study suggested that if the stores replaced them with stock-up items such as pasta, soup, and tissues sought by core customers, the increased visibility would boost the average basket size for core shoppers and turn fill-in shoppers into core shoppers by reminding them to stock up on essentials.

It worked. "It converted some secondary shoppers into primary shoppers," Doris says. "We made a big jump in sales and have maintained that. In fact, we're at the highest level we've ever experienced."

But Spillane says Coke probably isn't telling retailers anything they don't already know. "All supermarkets know the centers of their stores are dying," he says. "So Coke tries to put products along the perimeter, trying to get people to buy more."

Even so, some retailers like the program so much that they participate indefinitely, allowing Coke to manipulate displays, product placement, and signage to test new strategies. Others work with Coke intermittently. At Gerland's, for example, sales have reached a plateau, and Doris says he may go another round with the program to tweak sales. The program also builds relationships. "When we're able to help them grow their business, it positively affects the relationship," Hodson says.

"We've always had an excellent relationship with Coke," Doris says, "and we appreciated the fact that they did this. The buzzword is you're supposed to partner up with suppliers, but we do consider them a partner."

Questions

1 How does the relationship between the manufacturer in this case (Coca-Cola) and the retailer (Gerland's) help both companies?
2 What data do retailers with scanners and frequent-shopper cards collect?
3 What information do retailers receive from the Coca-Cola program?
4 What information does Coca-Cola receive from the program?
5 Other than the information it receives, how does Coca-Cola benefit from the program?

Web Site
Coca-Cola: www.cocacola.com

Source: *Adapted from* Kathleen Melymuka, "Coca-Cola: Marketing Partner," *Computerworld*, June 21, 1999, pp. 70–71.

Information System
FUNDAMENTALS

After completing this chapter, you should be able to

1 Explain why businesses need computer and communications hardware in information systems.

2 Distinguish between the three main types of computer systems.

3 Explain the difference between application software and system software, and give an example of each.

4 Explain why businesses need software in information systems.

5 Describe the way stored business data is commonly organized in information systems.

6 Explain why businesses need stored data in information systems.

7 Identify the types of personnel in information systems and explain why businesses need personnel in information systems.

8 Identify the types of procedures used in information systems and explain why businesses need procedures in information systems.

9 Describe different approaches to ethical decision making.

10 Explain several ethical issues for information systems.

CHAPTER OUTLINE

Hardware for Information Systems
Software for Information Systems
Stored Data for Information Systems
Personnel for Information Systems
Procedures for Information Systems
Ethical Issues for Information Systems

nformation systems, computer systems, educational systems, and transportation systems are different types of systems, but they all have a basic characteristic in common: Each is a collection of parts or *components* that work together for a purpose. For example, an automobile is a system. Its components are an engine, a body, a drive train, and so forth. These components work together for the purpose of providing transportation. As explained in Chapter 1, an *information system* is a collection of components that work together for the purpose of providing information to help in the operations and management of an organization. The components of an information system are hardware, software, stored data, personnel, and procedures.

This chapter describes the components of an information system. First, it examines the information technology components of the system: hardware and software. Next, it describes the system's stored data component. Then the chapter explains how people and procedures, the human resources components, are involved in information systems. Finally, because information systems are used by and affect people in various ways, this chapter examines ethical issues for information systems.

Hardware for Information Systems

The hardware component of an information system consists of computers and communications equipment. Computers perform the input, storage, processing, and output functions of the information system. Communications equipment provides the connections between computers to form a network.

Computer and Communications Hardware

The physical equipment that makes up a computer is called **computer hardware**. This hardware consists of a number of interconnected devices. Some devices, called *input devices*, accept input data from outside the computer. Other devices, called *output devices*, produce output data or information for use outside the computer. Still other devices, called *primary storage* and *secondary storage*, store data within the computer. Finally, a device called the *central processing unit* processes data within the computer. Chapter 4 describes these computer hardware devices in detail.

Computers and computer devices need ways of communicating with each other. Computer devices are usually connected by electronic cables when they are located near each other. Often, however, computer hardware needs to be connected over some distance. For example, a computer at one location may need to communicate with a computer at another location. Such distant communication requires **communications hardware**, which is as much a part of the hardware component of information systems as are computers.

Usually, a number of computers are connected to each other to form a network. As explained in Chapter 1, a *network* is a configuration of computers connected electronically so that they can all communicate with each other. A network may be located in a single building or a group of nearby buildings, in which case it uses communications hardware consisting of cables and special circuit boards to connect computers. A network may also be spread over a large geographic area, such as a region or a country. In this case it often uses long-distance telephone lines and other devices as communications hardware to connect the computers in the network. The Internet is a worldwide collection of interconnected networks that uses various types of communications hardware to connect computers. Chapter 6 describes communications hardware, networks, and the Internet in detail.

The Need for Computer Hardware in Information Systems

Businesses need computer hardware in information systems so that the systems can operate quickly and accurately, and can handle large amounts of data (Figure 3.1). *Speed* is important in information systems, and computers provide speed for the system by processing data and producing information rapidly. Businesses benefit from rapid processing by providing better service at a reduced cost. For example, an automated teller machine (ATM) system in a bank can process customer withdrawals, deposits, and transfers faster and less expensively than a human teller because it uses computer hardware.

Accuracy is also important in information systems, and computers ensure that the results of processing are correct by not making mistakes as people do. Without accurate processing, a business's costs would be greater and its information less reliable. For example, a point-of-sale (POS) system in a supermarket is more accurate than a human clerk in recording the prices of items purchased by a customer because it uses computers. Thus, the system reduces the cost of selling a product at an incorrect price. A POS system also keeps an accurate count of stock because of its use of computer hardware, and therefore the system provides better information about inventory. You sometimes hear about computer errors, but usually these result from mistakes made by humans, not by computers.

Finally, *capacity* is important in information systems, and computers provide the capacity to handle large amounts of data. Businesses benefit from this capability by being able to process volumes of data easily. For example, a sales analysis system in the marketing department of a business can examine data about thousands of sales because it uses computer hardware. The results of the analysis help managers draw conclusions about sales trends. A computer can handle these large amounts of data more easily than a human.

All these benefits gained from the use of computer hardware in information systems allow a business to compete effectively with other businesses. Without the use of hardware in information systems, a business would not be able to process data as quickly and accurately, and in the same volume, as its competitors. The business's costs would be greater, its customer service poorer, and the information it needs for decision making less reliable. In the long run, without the necessary computer hardware, the business might not be able to survive against competitors who have the appropriate hardware in their information systems.

Sometimes a business can gain an advantage over another business by being the first to use new computer hardware. For example, the first supermarkets to use POS hardware gained an advantage over other supermarkets by being able to check out customers quickly and more accurately. This type of advantage, however, often disappears in a short time as other businesses acquire the hardware. Hardware development proceeds very rapidly, and businesses need to be constantly on the lookout for hardware that will give them or maintain for them a competitive advantage.

FIGURE 3.1

▲ The need for computer hardware in information systems

Need for computer hardware	Importance in information systems
Speed	Ability to process data and produce information rapidly
Accuracy	Assurance that results of processing are correct
Capacity	Ability to handle large amounts of data

The Need for Communications Hardware in Information Systems

In addition to computer hardware, businesses need communications hardware in information systems. There are four main reasons for this need (Figure 3.2). The first reason is for *remote access* to information and processing. Often a user with a computer at one location needs to use a computer at another, remote location to store, retrieve, and process data. To access the capabilities of the remote computer, the user's computer and the remote computer must be connected so that they can communicate with each other. Communications hardware provides the capabilities needed for remote access.

A second reason businesses need communications hardware is for *information sharing*. Users in an organization often need to share information related to the operations and management of the business. The information may be shared by using electronic mail (e-mail); by transmitting documents, spreadsheets, data, images, sound, and so forth; and by accessing common data. Communications hardware provides the capabilities for sharing such information.

The third reason businesses need communications hardware is for *resource sharing*. Often businesses have certain expensive and scarce computer resources such as high-volume output devices, large-capacity storage devices, high-speed computers, and special software. These resources may need to be available to many users for specialized processing. By using communications hardware, users can easily share resources.

A final reason businesses need communications hardware is for *interorganizational communication*. Computers in different businesses need to communicate with one another in order for interorganizational systems to function. Electronic data interchange and electronic funds transfer systems are examples of systems that require interorganizational communication. Interorganizational communications hardware provides the capabilities needed for such communication.

Computer and Network Systems

Computers vary considerably in a number of ways, including capacity, speed, and cost. In addition, computers can be used alone or connected to other computers using communications hardware to form networks. All the variations produce three main hardware configurations used in information systems: personal computer systems, multiple-user computer systems, and networked computer systems. These configurations are shown in Figure 3.3.

Personal Computer Systems. A *personal computer system* consists of a single computer used by one person at a time. Most personal computer systems are **micro-**

Need for communications hardware	Importance in information systems
Remote access	Access to information and processing at remote locations
Information sharing	Sharing of information related to business operations and management
Resource sharing	Sharing of expensive and scarce computer resources
Interorganizational communication	Communication between computers in different businesses

FIGURE 3.2

The need for communications hardware in information systems

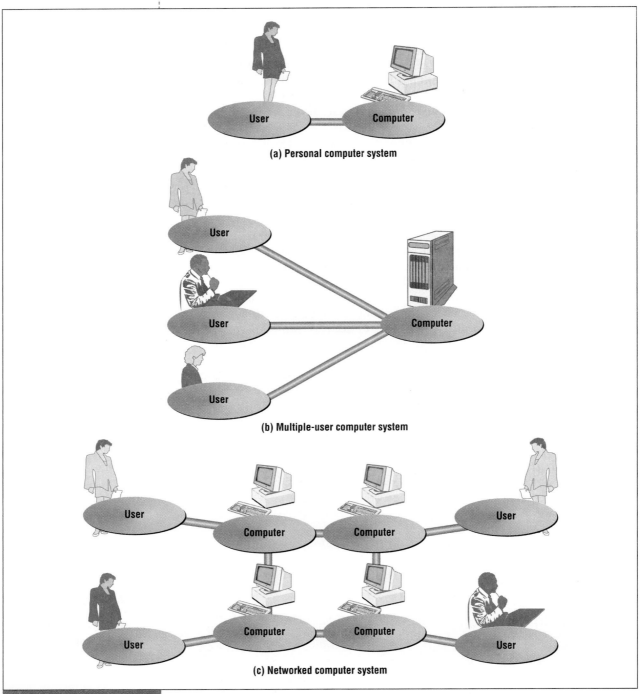

(a) Personal computer system

(b) Multiple-user computer system

(c) Networked computer system

FIGURE 3.3

Hardware configurations for
▲ information systems

computers, which are small computers costing a few thousand dollars or less. Because only one person at a time can use most microcomputers, they are *personal* computer systems. In fact, the term **personal computer** (**PC**) is often used to mean a microcomputer. Individual information systems in all types of organizations and businesses use microcomputers.

The most widely recognized microcomputers follow designs introduced by International Business Machines (IBM) and Apple Computer. IBM's first microcomputer was called the IBM Personal Computer or PC, and often people use the term *PC* to refer to any IBM-like microcomputer. IBM microcomputers evolved over time, but, in many ways, current models are very similar to the original IBM PC. Apple's first microcomputer was the Apple II, which is no longer manufactured. Apple currently produces the Macintosh, or Mac, microcomputer, which is available in several models.

Companies that make computers that act just like IBM personal computers produce most microcomputers in use today; people sometimes call these computers IBM *clones*. Some examples of the many companies that make IBM clones are Compaq Computer, Gateway, and Dell Computer.

Microcomputers come in various sizes (Figure 3.4). Microcomputers that are designed to sit on a desk and not be moved are called **desktop computers**. IBM,

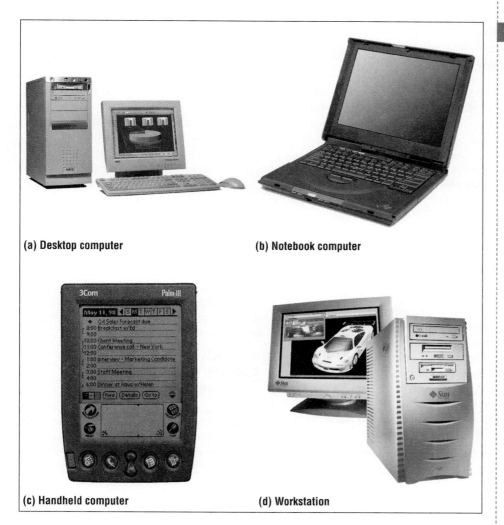

(a) Desktop computer

(b) Notebook computer

(c) Handheld computer

(d) Workstation

FIGURE 3.4

Microcomputers

Handheld Computers at Sodexho Marriott Services

When auditors from Sodexho Marriott Services traipse through kitchens and boiler rooms to conduct surprise inspections for food and fire safety, they carry the Clio, a handheld computer from Vadem, San Jose, California.

Auditors can use the 3-pound device like a tablet, using a stylus or a finger to answer dozens of questions on the 9.4-inch color screen. Or they can enter longer comments through a near-standard-size keyboard when the screen is flipped up.

The food-service vendor said it chose the $999 Clio over other handheld computers costing half as much because its larger screen is easier to read.

The Gaithersburg, Maryland, company uses 22 of the Clios to conduct more than 500 audits nationwide, says Frank Romeo, senior manager of loss prevention. Previously, auditors carried paper forms, which had to be duplicated and faxed to dozens of locations.

Results are now e-mailed quickly and are easily compiled to create monthly reports. The Clios run Mobile Auditor software from Steton Technology Group in Santa Clara, Utah, Romeo says.

"It used to take about six hours with paper, and I can [now] do [an audit] in less than four hours," says Katie Hoagland, a loss-prevention analyst at Sodexho Marriott.

The company chose the Clio over several other handhelds, including Apple Computer's Newton, which is no longer sold, the Phillips Nino, and a prototype of the Jornada 420 from Hewlett-Packard. "At first, I thought smaller was better," Romeo says. "But we had two guys wearing glasses who thought the [Nino's] screen was hard to read."

Upon finishing audits, Sodexho Marriott wanted to immediately share the results with dining hall managers, who favor the Clio because its screen can be seen by several people at once when the system is in easel mode.

When a manager accepts the audit, he simply signs his approval on the screen, and the signature is captured for corporate records, Romeo says.

On the downside, Romeo says he doesn't use the Clio as his only computer on the road; he prefers a full-size laptop for editing presentations. The Clio software has limited editing capabilities, a problem shared by other applications, analysts say.

Since so-called Jupiter-class machines (computers smaller than notebook computers but larger than palmtop computers) such as Clio debuted, "some people thought they'd take the world by storm, but they have been surprised at how slow Jupiter has taken off," says Jill House, an analyst at International Data Corp. in Framingham, Massachusetts.

Vadem and analysts say that the most promising market for such systems will be in vertical industry applications where a machine is chosen to solve a specific need, as at Sodexho Marriott, rather than general business use.

Questions

1. Why does Sodexho Marriott use handheld computers instead of desktop computers?
2. Why did Sodexho Marriott choose the Clio over other handheld computers?
3. What benefits do handheld computers provide Sodexho Marriott auditors?

Web Site
Sodexho Marriott Services:
www.sodexhomarriott.com

Source: *Adapted from* Matt Hamblen, "Smaller Isn't Better for Some Handheld Users," *Computerworld*, August 2, 1999, p. 52.

Apple, and all the other companies named previously, as well as many others, make desktop computers. Small microcomputers that fold up to the size of a notebook so they can be easily carried are called **notebook**, or **laptop**, **computers**. Most companies that make desktop computers also make notebook computers. Still smaller microcomputers that are designed to be held in a hand are called **handheld**, or **palmtop**, **computers**. They are also called **personal digital assistants** (**PDAs**) because they provide capabilities to assist an individual in his or her work. Several companies make handheld computers, including 3Com and Hewlett-Packard (HP). Very powerful desktop microcomputers are commonly called **workstations**. Workstations have capabilities beyond those of ordinary microcomputers, especially regarding producing graphic diagrams and pictures on the screen. Examples are computers made by Sun Microsystems and Silicon Graphics.

Multiple-user Computer Systems. A *multiple-user computer system* is a single computer used by many people at one time. Most microcomputers are not multiple-user computers because they are not designed to be used by more than one person at a time. Instead, minicomputers, mainframe computers, and supercomputers are used for this purpose (Figure 3.5).

A **minicomputer** is a medium-size computer, typically costing between $5,000 and $200,000. Minicomputers can be used simultaneously by just a few people to as many as several hundred people. Small- to medium-size organizations and businesses sometimes use minicomputers for organizational information systems. Larger businesses may use them for special applications, such as for controlling computerized checkout stands in a supermarket or for workgroup information systems.

A number of companies, including HP and IBM, make minicomputers. Each of these companies makes several models of minicomputers that range in size from small systems that are close to being microcomputers to large computers that are almost mainframe computers. Because it is often hard to identify whether a com-

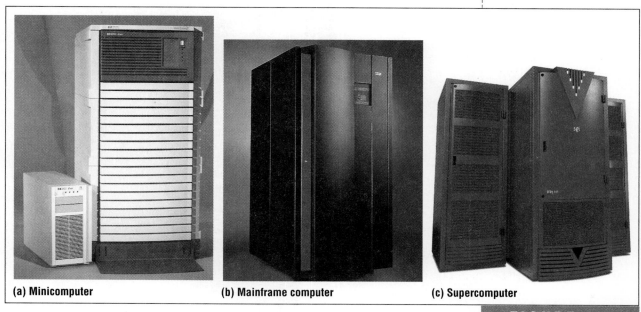

(a) Minicomputer   (b) Mainframe computer   (c) Supercomputer

FIGURE 3.5

Multiple-user computers

puter is a minicomputer, this type of computer is sometimes called a *midrange computer*.

A **mainframe computer** is a large computer usually costing between $100,000 and $10 million. A mainframe computer can be used by several hundred to several thousand people at one time. Mainframe computers are sometimes used by medium- and large-size organizations and businesses for their organizational information systems. For example, the computer used by a bank to process data from ATMs may be a mainframe computer.

IBM makes the most widely known mainframe computers. Some companies, such as Amdahl, make mainframe computers that are similar to IBM's. Other companies, including Unisys, make mainframe computers different from IBM's.

The most powerful multiple-user computers are called **supercomputers** and can cost between $5 million and $20 million, or even more. These computers are specifically designed for very fast processing speeds. Supercomputers are mainly used for complex mathematical calculations, such as those needed in scientific research.

Cray Research developed the first supercomputers that were commercially successful. Several other companies also make supercomputers.

Networked Computer Systems.   A *networked computer system* consists of many computers connected in a network used by many people at one time. The network may be located in a single building or several nearby buildings, or it may span a large geographic area such as a state, country, or several countries. Microcomputers, minicomputers, mainframe computers, and supercomputers may all be used in a network. The trend, however, is toward more use of microcomputers and less use of larger computers.

FIGURE 3.6

▲ **A server**

All sizes of organizations and businesses use networked computer systems for workgroup and organizational information systems. Many businesses have replaced their multiple-user minicomputers and mainframe computers with networked computer systems. Interorganizational information systems also use networks, as do global information systems.

Networks usually include one or more computers, called **servers**, that provide services to other computers in the network (Figure 3.6). For example, a server may be used to store data so that the data is available to all computers in the network. A server may also be used to print output from any computer in the network, and for other purposes. Servers are also used to store information for Internet users. Any type of computer can be used as a server, including microcomputers, minicomputers, mainframe computers, and even supercomputers.

Many information systems are designed so that some parts of the system use a server in a network and other parts use personal computers attached to the network. These personal computers, with which users interact directly, are called **clients**. For example, a server may store data for use by all client computers. The client computers allow any user to retrieve the data. This approach is called **client/server computing**, and it is becoming increasingly common in businesses.

Software for Information Systems

The software component of an information system consists of all the computer instructions used in the system. A computer can do nothing without software. For example, to calculate the payroll for a business, the computer must have software that tells it how to do the calculations. Even to do word processing, a computer needs software to tell it what to do. There must be an instruction in computer software for every step that the computer goes through. The computer will do whatever it is told, even if it leads to an incorrect result.

Types of Software

Two main types of software are application software and system software. **Application software** is software designed for specific computer applications for a business or an organization. For example, software that prepares the payroll for a business is application software. Other examples of application software include software that analyzes sales and software that keeps track of inventory. Word processing software and spreadsheet software are also application software. Application software is used in all types of information systems, including individual, workgroup, organizational, interorganizational, and global information systems.

System software is general software designed to make computers usable. System software does not solve a problem for a specific application, but instead makes it easier to use the necessary application software. System software helps the computer function, whereas application software helps the business or organization function.

An example of system software is an **operating system**, which is software that controls the basic operation of the computer. The operating system does many things, such as determine where application software is stored in the computer. The operating system is always in control of the computer when some other software (such as application software or other system software) is not in control. Examples of operating systems are Windows, MacOS, and UNIX. Operating systems are needed in personal, multiple-user, and networked computer systems, although their characteristics are different for different types of systems.

Another example of system software is **communications software**, which is used to provide communications between computers. When computers are connected using communications hardware, communications software is needed to control the communications between the computers. In a network, communications software is necessary to transfer data between computers connected to the network.

The Need for Software in Information Systems

Businesses need both application software and system software in information systems (Figure 3.7). They need application software to perform specific *information system functions*. Chapter 1 explains that an information system has four main functions: the *input function*, the *storage function*, the *processing function*, and the *output function*. The input function accepts data from outside the system; the storage function stores and retrieves data in the system; the processing function manipulates data within the system; and the output function produces the results of processing for use outside the system. The application software of an information system tells the hardware how to perform these functions.

Businesses also need system software in information systems so that systems will be *easy to use*. For example, an operating system, which is system software, is needed because without it the computer would require very complex procedures to perform even simple tasks. Other system software besides an operating system is also needed, including communications software and software to help develop other software.

The operating system software together with the computer and communications hardware creates the environment, or **platform**, on which the application software of an information system runs. For example, a personal computer system with a specific operating system is one platform, and a networked computer system with its operating system is a different platform. The application software for these two platforms would be different because the hardware and the operating systems are different.

A business needs to select the platform used for its information systems. Personal computers with their operating systems, multiple-user computers with their operating systems, and networked computers with their operating systems are all different platforms with different characteristics. The choice of platform and the specific hardware and system software selected affect the form the application software takes and the functioning of the information system.

Sources of Software

If a business needs software for a particular purpose, it has two main ways of getting it. One is to purchase existing application or system software. Purchased software, which is often called **packaged software**, is available for personal, multiple-user, and networked computer systems.

The other way a business can get software is to create it from scratch. Software acquired in this way often is called **custom software**. A business can prepare custom software using its own personnel, or it can have a software company prepare it. Custom software can be prepared for all types of computer systems. A business can also purchase packaged software and customize it so that it better meets the business's needs.

Need for software	Importance in information systems
Information system functions	Performance of input, storage, processing, and output functions
Ease of use	Provisions that make system easy to use

Businesses most often purchase system software, but they may purchase application software or create it from scratch. Individual and workgroup information systems usually use packaged software. For example, for a word processing system on a personal computer a business would purchase word processing software, and for an e-mail system on a network a business would purchase e-mail software. A business can also prepare custom software for individual and workgroup information systems, although this is done less often than using packaged software. Businesses use both packaged and custom software for organizational, interorganizational, and global information systems.

Stored Data for Information Systems

The stored data component of an information system consists of all data used by the system that is stored in the system's computers. Stored data can represent facts, numbers, words, images, pictures, or sounds. In business information systems, stored data most often represents numbers, words, or other written forms.

Data Organization

Stored data must be properly organized in information systems so that it can be processed easily. Figure 3.8 shows the common way information systems organize stored business data. At the most basic level, business data in information systems is composed of **characters**—that is, letters, numerals, and special symbols, such as periods, commas, and dollar signs. A blank space is also a character.

Although a single character can represent data, information systems usually use groups of characters for this purpose. A group of related characters, representing some piece of information, is called a **field**. For example, a person's name could be a field; it is a group of characters that represents specific information. A Social Security number could also be a field, as could a person's address, pay rate, and age. A field usually contains several characters, but can consist of a single character. For example, a one-character code field can be used to represent a person's marital status (where *M* stands for *married*, and *S* for *single*).

An information system groups fields together to provide information about a single entity such as a person or an event. Such a group of related fields is called a **record**. For example, all the fields containing payroll information about a single employee (such as the employee's name, address, Social Security number, and pay rate) form an employee payroll record.

All the records that are used together for one purpose are called a **data file**, or simply a **file**.[1] For example, all the employee payroll records for a business make up the employee payroll file. The file contains one record for each employee in the business.

Finally, related groups of data, such as related data files, can be combined to form a **database**. For example, an employee database may contain employee payroll data, employee job skill data, and employee work history data. All these types of data are related because they contain information about employees who work for the same business, and therefore they form a database of employee information.

To summarize, data is often composed of characters. A group of related characters is a field. A record is a group of related fields, and a data file is a group of related records. Finally, a database is formed from related groups of data.

---

[1] The term *file* is used to refer to any collection of related items stored in the computer, including documents, spreadsheets, and graphs. The term *data file* is used for a collection of related data organized into records. Many people, however, use the term *file* when they mean *data file*.

FIGURE 3.8

Data organization for information systems ▲

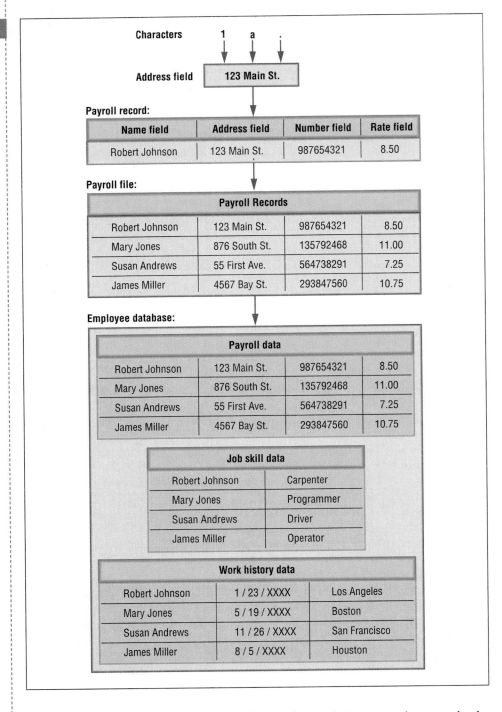

Although we have concentrated on data made up of characters, data can also be in other forms such as images, moving pictures, and sound. This type of data is often referred to as **multimedia** data because it is in more than one form. For example, a business may store multimedia data consisting of images, pictures, and sounds, along with words and numbers, to describe a new product it has developed. Organizing stored multimedia data requires more complex techniques than those described here.

Need for stored data	Importance of information systems
Data availability	Ease of locating and retrieving data for processing
Data modifiability	Ease of updating data for changes in the business
Data controllability	Assurance that data is accurate and secure

FIGURE 3.9

The need for stored data in information systems ▲

The Need for Stored Data in Information Systems

Businesses need stored data in their information systems for three main reasons (Figure 3.9). The first is so that the *data is available* for the system to process. The data needs to be available so that the information system can easily locate and retrieve the data it needs for processing. To make the data available, it must be organized in such a way that the required data can be easily located and retrieved. Data can be organized as data files or databases, or in other ways. Well-organized stored data is readily available for the information system to process.

The second reason businesses need stored data in their information systems is so that the *data is modifiable*. Stored data reflects the state of a business, such as how many items are in inventory or how much money is available for paying bills. The state of the business changes constantly, however; for example, inventory items are sold and money is paid out. The stored data needs to be changed, or *updated*, regularly so that it correctly reflects the current state of the business. Keeping stored data up-to-date is important in information systems.

A third reason businesses need stored data in information systems is so that the *data is controllable*. Stored data is an important asset of a business and it must be kept under control. One aspect of stored data control is ensuring that incorrect data is not stored in the information system. Input data cannot simply be entered into the system and stored; it must first be checked for errors and inconsistencies. A well-known acronym in information systems is GIGO, which stands for *garbage in, garbage out*. This means that if you put bad data (garbage) into the system, you will get bad data (garbage) out of the system. Checking data for errors before storing it in the system is one aspect of data control. Another aspect is making sure that the data is secure from loss, destruction, or theft. Proper control of stored data helps prevent such situations.

Personnel for Information Systems

The personnel component of an information system consists of all people who are involved with the system. Because an information system is used and run by people, personnel is an essential component of the system.

Users and Operating Personnel

One type of person who is part of an information system is the *user*. As explained in Chapter 1, users are people who gain some benefit from using the information system. Users supply input data to the system and receive output data from the system. The output provides information that the user needs in his or her job. A user may use the system directly or indirectly. In any case, the user is not separate from the information system, but is part of the personnel component of the system.

Need for personnel	Importance in information systems
Information use	Use of information in operations and management of the business
System operation	Operation of hardware and software in system and correction of problems that arise

Other people who are part of an information system are *operating personnel*, who perform technical functions to operate the hardware and software in the system. These people prepare input data received from the user, enter the data into the system, operate computers, manage networks, run software, and pass the output to the user. If the system is an individual or a workgroup information system, the user may operate the system; but with organizational information systems, specially trained computer and network operators are needed.

The Need for Personnel in Information Systems

Personnel are needed in information systems for two reasons (Figure 3.10). One reason is to *use information* from the system. Information systems exist to provide information for people in businesses. People operate and manage businesses and they need information to perform their jobs. Information systems provide that information for the users of the system. Without people to use the information provided by the system, there would be no reason for most systems to exist.

The second reason personnel are needed in information systems is that these systems require that humans *operate the system*. While some uses of computers do not need humans (except to start and stop the computers), computers in information systems in businesses need people to operate them. People are needed to run the hardware and software, and to fix problems that arise during processing.

Procedures for Information Systems

The final component of an information system consists of all the procedures that personnel follow to use and operate the system. The procedures are the instructions to the personnel, just as the software is the instructions to the hardware.

Types of Procedures

Two main types of procedures are used in information systems. The first type tells people how to use and operate the system under normal circumstances. Among other things, these procedures explain how to operate the hardware, run the software, enter input data, and receive output information. An example of this type of procedure is one that tells users what option to select to begin running particular software.

The second type of procedures is the type that tell people what to do if the system does not function normally. These include procedures for correcting errors and recovering lost data. An example of this type of procedure is a backup recovery procedure that tells the user how to retrieve stored data from a backup copy of the data.

Procedures need to be written so that personnel can refer to them. This is the purpose of system **documentation**, which is written instructions on the use and operation of an information system. Personnel must be trained in the procedures so that

FIGURE 3.11

The need for procedures in
information systems   ▲

Need for procedures	Importance in information systems
Use of system	Knowledge of how to start system, interact with system, and stop system
Correction of system	Knowledge of problem correction process

they will know what to do. Thus, when we say personnel is a component of the system, we mean personnel who are trained in the use of the procedures.

The Need for Procedures in Information Systems

People do not know instinctively how to use or operate complex systems. They need to have instructions and training to tell them what to do. For example, a person using an automobile needs procedures for driving the car and for repairing the car if it does not work.

Personnel in information systems need procedures for two main reasons (Figure 3.11). The first reason is because people need to know how to *use the system*. People need to know what steps to take to start the system, how to interact with the system as it functions, and how to stop the system when they are done.

The second reason personnel in information systems need procedures is to tell them how to *correct the system* if something goes wrong. Information systems are complex, and problems sometimes arise. People need to know what to do if a problem occurs with the system.

Ethical Issues for Information Systems

As you have seen in this chapter, information systems are more than hardware and software; they also involve people who use and operate them. Unfortunately, people can use information systems in ways that are not ethical. To avoid unethical use of information systems, it is important to examine ethical issues when making decisions about the use of systems and technology. This section looks at ethical decision making and ethical issues related to information systems.

Ethical Decision Making

Chapter 1 introduces the concept of ethics—the standards that govern right and wrong behavior—and the problem of contradictory answers to many ethical questions. Decision-making situations often involve ethical questions with conflicting alternatives. To deal with these situations, many approaches to ethical decision making have been proposed over the years. The following are some of the approaches:

- *The Golden Rule.* This is the ethical approach based on the rule "Do unto others as you would have them do unto you." In other words, you should not do anything that would harm someone else.

- *Utilitarianism.* Utilitarianism is an ethical approach that says you should do what is best for the greatest number of people; that is, follow the principal "the greatest good for the greatest number."

- *Categorical imperative.* This ethical approach says you should do only that which you feel should be adopted as a rule for everyone, that is, as a universal law.

- *Ethical egoism.* This ethical approach says you should do what is best for yourself. A variation of this approach says you should do what is best for the organization.

In the case of a for-profit business, this approach means you should do what has the greatest impact on the profit of the business.

There are arguments for and against each of these approaches to ethical decision making. In addition, there are many other approaches besides these. Ethical decisions can also be made without applying a formal approach—by using your own feelings about what is right and wrong. The individual must decide what approach to use in an ethical decision-making situation.

Many businesses have a **code of ethics**, which is a set of ethical standards or rules (usually written) that the employees are supposed to follow in making decisions in their jobs. Such a code may be based on philosophy, religion, customs, laws, or a combination of these. These codes often include penalties for failure to follow the rules in the code, ranging from reprimand to termination.

Professional information systems organizations also have codes of ethics for their members. For example, the Association for Computing Machinery (ACM) and the Association of Information Technology Professionals (AITP), two prominent professional organizations in the computing and information systems field, have detailed codes of ethics. Members of these organizations often manage or develop information systems, and the codes serve as guidelines for ethical behavior in their professional work.

Ethical Issues

Many ethical issues arise in information systems, but four are most prevalent: privacy, accuracy, property, and access, which together are known by the acronym PAPA.[2]

Privacy. Privacy has to do with keeping information about yourself to yourself. People need privacy so that they feel free to do what they want. If people do not have privacy and the things they do are recorded somewhere, they may feel threatened and inhibited. (Read George Orwell's *1984* for some idea about what the world would be like without privacy.)

Information systems reduce people's privacy by recording information about people. Many government agencies have computer files and databases that include personal information. For example, the Social Security Administration has files on practically everyone who has worked in the United States. The Internal Revenue Service has computerized versions of tax returns.

Nongovernment organizations and businesses also have computerized information about people. For example, credit reporting companies in the United States have computerized credit histories for millions of people. Firms that sell mailing lists have large files listing personal characteristics and preferences so that mailings can be targeted at certain types of individuals. Many electronic commerce companies maintain large databases with personal information about their customers.

There are legitimate uses and benefits of computerized information about people. No one would receive Social Security checks without the Social Security Administration's system. Credit would be harder to get without computerized credit bureaus. But such information can also be abused. For example, should Social Security information about you be available to any business that wants to check on your work history? Should credit information about you be available to anyone without your permission? To many people, the answer to questions such as these is no.

---

[2] This section is based on a paper by Richard O. Mason, titled "Four Ethical Issues of the Information Age," *MIS Quarterly*, March 1986, pp. 5–12.

Web Site for HarlemLive

When Richard Calton left a 10-year teaching career to work as a computer coordinator at the Harlem public school district in New York, he found he missed the kids. So he got hold of a laptop, a digital camera, a server, and a handful of former students, and he used his Web skills to bring HarlemLive to life.

HarlemLive is a mosaic of life in that African-American community produced by Harlem high school students and delivered as a Web magazine. Calton says it was his kind of project from the start. "There were no committees, no forms, no permissions [needed], no bureaucracy," he recalls. But there was also no money and no place to work. So Calton persuaded the Institute for Learning Technologies (ILT) at Columbia University in New York to host the site on its server and provide some unused office space, phone lines, and computers. Eventually, the project moved to a community technology center in Harlem, called Playing 2 Win.

The staff is all-volunteer, including Calton, who by his own example has induced two dozen adult advisers from the community to join in. "Everyone sees he is volunteering his time, so they say, 'I guess I can do that too,'" says Mara Rose, director of Playing 2 Win. "He's very devoted and true, and that spreads to everyone who gets involved."

Although several years old, HarlemLive still has the vibrancy of a new idea. "So many sites have a brief period of creative fervor and then stagnate," says Robbie McClintock, co-director at the ILT. "But HarlemLive keeps changing."

A recent issue included a visit with U.S. Representative Charles Rangel (D–NY), a look at how three new businesses will affect the community, reporting on a protest over the imprisonment of a former Black Panther accused of murder, and reaction to the Littleton, Colorado, high school shootings. There were also book, theater, and movie reviews; poetry; editorials; and lots of excellent photographs.

"It keeps growing, and we have more and more ideas, but we still haven't received funding, so it's hard to keep it together," says Calton, who pays expenses out of his own pocket. "There are times when it gets frustrating," he concedes. "People say, 'Oh, you're so fundable! You're so fundable!' So give us some money!" A couple of the project's advisers are writing grant proposals, and Calton says he hopes that eventually he can hire some full-time staff, including himself. The student staff has grown to about 75, half of whom are regulars like Kerly Suffren, a two-year veteran and a junior at Martin Luther King Jr. High School. Suffren, a poet, reporter, and spokesperson for the project, says HarlemLive makes learning fun. "My communications skills went up dramatically," he says. "I've applied what I learn to my schoolwork, and my grades have gone up."

"I've also learned to deal with people," Suffren adds. "As a reporter, sometimes you talk to people and you know right away you don't like them, but you have to deal with these things." He credits Calton with much of what he's learned. "He's a very good teacher," Suffren says. "He's very giving and willing to listen, and he cares about us."

"It's an excellent example of a fully authentic education," McClintock says. "They learn because they want to make an excellent site that tells the world what's going on in Harlem. They feel they're doing their own community a significant service. It's a wonderful framework for education." Observers call Calton the glue that holds the staff together. "He loves working with the kids," Rose says. "He comes right from work and is here till 10, 11, or 12 every night. And the kids know it."

Clearly, Calton is teaching more than academics. "The biggest thing is not necessarily the computer skills, though those are a big plus for getting into college and getting better jobs," Calton says. "And it's not just the writing skills, though that's good to have as

well. It's the exposure they get. It's going into situations and meeting people—particularly people of color—they would have no way of doing otherwise and communicating and realizing there are opportunities open to them as well."

"He's very inspirational," Suffren says. "Sometimes I question how he does it because he has a real job, then he comes in and deals with us kids. We're fortunate to have him on our side."

(The project reported in this case is one of the 1999 *Computerworld* Smithsonian Award winners. The Smithsonian Awards honor information technology projects that benefit society.)

Questions

1. What aspect of access to information does the HarlemLive Web site address, and what aspect does it not address?
2. What ethical issues other than access to information could arise with the Harlem-Live Web site?
3. Why has HarlemLive had difficulty getting funding?

Web Site

HarlemLive: www.harlemlive.org

Source: *Adapted from* Kathleen Melymuka, "Mentor Helps Students Bring Harlem to Life on the Web," *Computerworld*, June 7, 1999, pp. 40–41.

One way computerized information can be abused is through **matching**, which is a process in which data in one file or database is compared with data in another. Computers can match data in large files or databases very rapidly. Matching can be useful; for example, matching welfare recipient data with Social Security data can detect welfare fraud. But it can also be used to further reduce people's privacy. For example, matching credit files, mailing list files, work history files, and medical databases would provide detailed descriptions of people, thus reducing their privacy.

As information systems become larger and more comprehensive, and as information technology becomes more sophisticated, it becomes easier to match information about people from many sources. How would you feel if all the computerized information about you were stored in one central computer and made available to anyone who requested it? This may be a far-fetched idea, but it shows the abuse that is possible with large computerized files and databases.

Fortunately, legal safeguards exist to help prevent the misuse of computerized information. Various laws limit the use and access of computerized information about individuals. Some of the major laws in the United States are listed in Figure 3.12. Other countries have their own privacy laws. Although laws cannot prevent all misuses of computerized information, they can help minimize the problem and thus provide more assurance of privacy to people.

Accuracy. Accuracy of the information produced by information systems is critical. Whenever you use information, you need assurance that it is correct. Without correct information, decisions based on the information may result in negative impacts on you, your company, and other people. In the worst-case situation, incorrect information can affect the outcomes of life-and-death situations.

Consider credit information used to evaluate applications for bank loans. If that information, which comes from the credit bureau's information system, is not accurate, a risky loan may be approved when it should not be or a desirable loan may not be approved when it should be. Both alternatives affect not only the bank, but also

FIGURE 3.12

Major U.S. privacy laws ▲

- **Freedom of Information Act of 1970**

  Lets people find out what information government agencies store about them.
- **Fair Credit Reporting Act of 1970**

  Allows people to inspect and challenge information in their credit records.
- **Privacy Act of 1974**

  Prohibits government agencies from collecting information about individuals for illegitimate purposes.
- **Right to Financial Privacy Act of 1978**

  Gives procedures that the government must follow to examine information about individuals in financial institutions.
- **Electronic Communications Privacy Act of 1986**

  Provides protection from unauthorized interception of electronic communications.
- **Computer Matching and Privacy Act of 1988**

  Regulates the use of matching of files and databases by the government.

the loan applicant, which could be an individual or a business. In addition, the loan officer who made the decision based on faulty information is affected because his or her job performance falls.

Life-and-death situations can be a serious result of inaccurate information coming from an information system. For example, if a system in a hospital that monitors patient care provides incorrect information—such as information that an important medication was administered to a patient when it was not—the consequences can be fatal. Another example is a system used in a production process, such as oil refining, where people are part of the process; incorrect information from such systems can lead to personal injury or death.

Inaccurate information in information systems comes from two sources. One is incorrect input data. Remember the acronym GIGO, for garbage in, garbage out? This means that if incorrect data goes into an information system, only incorrect data can come out. It is critical that input data be checked carefully to be sure it is correct and complete before it is entered into the system.

The other source of inaccurate information from information systems is the software used in the system. Software often has errors, called **bugs**, in it. Some bugs in software are not serious, such as when a feature in word processing software does not work correctly. But some software bugs can be very serious. If erroneous software is used to calculate financial information in a business, inaccurate information from the system can affect the functioning of the business. It is important that all software be carefully checked for errors. Even if you are just setting up a spreadsheet for sales forecasting, it is critical that you ensure that there are no errors in it.

Erroneous functioning of some software can endanger human life. For example, software that controls airplanes must be error free, or there is a chance that inaccurate information produced by the software could lead to a serious accident. Many critical systems, such as those on airplanes, have several versions of the software, developed by different companies, each producing the same type of information. Then the output from each version can be compared to see if there is the possibility of inaccurate information being produced by the system.

Property.   The ethical issue of property in information systems involves a number of dimensions. One is the ownership of information. Who owns information about people, things, and events? Is it the originator of the information, the owner of the thing, or the sponsor of the event? Or is it the organization that gathers, stores, and disseminates the information? What rights does the originator of the information have after the information has been obtained by an organization? These and similar questions need to be addressed in making decisions about the ownership of information.

Another property dimension is the ownership of the pathways over which information is transmitted. Communications equipment uses various means for transmitting information, including electronic signals, such as radio signals, in different frequencies. The pathways conveying these signals have become clogged not only with data signals, but also with signals carrying sound (e.g., telephone) and images (e.g., television). Who owns the pathways? Who controls them? What rights do those who wish to send information over the pathways have? It is important to examine these and similar questions when thinking about the transmission of information.

Perhaps the most complex property dimension, however, is the ownership of the knowledge that goes into an information system. Information systems contain the knowledge of employees who work for a business as well as others who are involved in the development of the system. For example, an information system to evaluate credit applications contains the knowledge of those who do credit evaluation. Such a system could replace credit evaluators in some businesses. Should the evaluators be compensated for giving their knowledge to the business?

The dimension of knowledge ownership revolves around *intellectual property*, which is the things that we know and express in various ways, such as through writing, engineering, designing, and other creative activities. There are various ways to protect intellectual property, including copyrights and patents, but these methods are imperfect. In addition, when the expression of intellectual property is stored in an information system, it is very easy to copy it or transmit it to another location. The easy availability of information, much of it copyrighted, on the World Wide Web is an example of this problem. How to protect intellectual property is an important issue in information systems.

The property issue is not only a matter of ownership, but also a matter of protecting information and intellectual property from theft or inappropriate access. Electronic information is so easy to copy and transmit that it is difficult to ensure that it is not acquired inappropriately. Copyrighting or otherwise legally protecting intellectual property does not guarantee that it will not be used without the owner's permission. Chapter 14 has more to say about information system security measures designed to help prevent inappropriate access to information or intellectual property.

Access.   Access to information technology and the information it provides has become an essential aspect of today's society. No business in the industrialized world can compete effectively without information systems. Individuals may not be able to flourish without access to information through technology.

There are two aspects to access. First, the technology must be available. Computers and networks must be provided so that organizations and individuals can use them. Software must be provided to produce the information needed by organizations and individuals. Second, the necessary information must be available through use of the technology. Information must be gathered, stored, and made accessible to those who need it.

The problem with providing the required access is that it can be expensive. Information technology—hardware and software—is costly. Although the cost of much of the technology has decreased over time, more complex technology is always needed. For example, the price of computers continually drops, but more powerful, and thus more expensive, computers are needed to provide access to information. In addition, computers need to be connected to the networks in which the information exists, which increases cost.

Technology is not the only cost. Another significant cost is the information itself. Much information, especially that which has real value to an organization or individual, is not free. It is necessary to pay the supplier of the information for what is provided. This payment could be for connection to the Web by an individual or for developing a complex information system for a business.

One consequence of the cost of access to information is that some are able to pay for it and some are not. This applies to individuals, organizations, and whole societies. Those who can afford the expense pay to be assured of having access to the information they need. Those who cannot afford to pay are left behind.

Applying Ethics

In your work you may confront a number of ethical questions revolving around information systems and technology. Many of these questions may deal with privacy, accuracy, property, or access issues. For example, you might find out that a coworker accesses the company's database to learn salary information about managers (a privacy issue). You might discover that another coworker enters data that he makes up into an information system to save time when he does not have the correct data immediately available (an accuracy issue). A good friend might ask you to make a copy of software your company uses so that he or she can try it out at home (a property issue). A local charity for which you volunteer might ask you to use your company's network to locate information that the charity cannot afford to purchase (an access issue). What would you do in each of these situations? Although these may seem like harmless situations, they involve questions of ethics with which you have to deal.

There are common rules for the ethical use of information technology. Figure 3.13 shows one list of rules. In addition, your company may have a code of ethics, as

1. Do not use a computer to harm other people.

2. Do not interfere with other people's computer work.

3. Do not look in other people's computer files.

4. Do not use a computer to steal.

5. Do not use a computer to bear false witness.

6. Do not copy or use proprietary software for which you have not paid.

7. Do not use other people's computer resources without authorization or proper compensation.

8. Do not appropriate other people's intellectual output.

9. Think about the social consequences of the program you are writing or the system you are designing.

10. Always use a computer in ways that ensure consideration and respect for your fellow humans.

FIGURE 3.13

Rules for the ethical use of computers

may a professional organization to which you belong. You should adhere to the rules and codes that apply to you. But ethical behavior goes beyond lists of rules and professional codes. Individuals must decide for themselves what is ethical. Businesses and their employees must understand and address ethical questions in the use of information systems and technology.

CHAPTER SUMMARY

1 Businesses need **computer hardware** in information systems for three main reasons. The first is for speed so that the system processes data and produces information rapidly. The second is for accuracy so that the system does not make mistakes. The third is for capacity so that the system can handle a large amount of data. Businesses need **communications hardware** in information systems for four main reasons. The first is to provide remote access to information and processing for users. The second is to allow users to share information related to the operations and management of the business. The third is to allow users to share expensive and scarce computer resources. The fourth is to provide interorganizational communication so that different businesses can communicate with each other. (p. 63)

2 The three main types of computer systems are personal computer systems, multiple-user computer systems, and networked computer systems. A personal computer system consists of a single computer, usually a **microcomputer**, used by one person at a time. A multiple-user computer system consists of a single computer, usually a **minicomputer, mainframe computer,** or **supercomputer**, used by many people at a time. A networked computer system consists of many computers of any type, connected in a network used by many people at a time. Networks usually include computers, called **servers,** to provide service to other computers, called **clients**, in the network. This approach is called **client/server computing**. (pp. 65–71)

3 **Application software** is any software designed for a specific computer application. An example is software that prepares payroll for a business. **System software** is any general software designed to make the computer usable. Examples are an **operating system** and **communications software**. (pp. 71–72)

4 Businesses need application software in information systems to perform the input, storage, processing, and output functions of the system. They need system software, such as an operating system, so that the system will be easy to use. The operating system together with the computer and communications hardware create the **platform** upon which the application software of an information system runs. (p. 72)

5 Stored business data in information systems is composed of **characters**–that is, letters, numerals and special symbols. A group of related characters, representing some piece of information, is called a **field**. A **record** is a group of related fields, and a **data file**, or simply a **file**, is a group of related records. Related groups of data can be combined to form a **database**. (p. 73)

6 Businesses need stored data in information systems for three main reasons. The first is so that data is available for processing by the system. The second is so that data can be modified to ensure that it is current. The third is so that data can be controlled to ensure that it is accurate and secure. (p. 75)

7 Personnel in an information system include users and operating personnel. Users supply input data to the system and receive output data or information from the system. Operating personnel operate hardware and software in the system. Businesses need personnel in information systems to use information from the system in the operations and management of the business and to operate the hardware and software and fix problems that arise during processing. (p. 76)

8 Procedures in an information system tell people how to use and operate the system under normal circumstances. These include procedures for operating the hardware, running the software, entering input data, and receiving output information. Procedures also tell people what to do if the system does not function normally. These include procedures for correcting errors and recovering lost data. Businesses need procedures in information

systems to tell people how to use the system and how to correct the system if something goes wrong. (pp. 76–77)

9 Some approaches to ethical decision making are The Golden Rule, which says you should act toward others in the same way that you would want others to act toward you; utilitarianism, which says you should do what is best for the greatest number of people; categorical imperative, which says you should do only that which you feel should be adopted as a rule for everyone; and ethical egoism, which says you should do what is best for yourself. (p. 77)

10 Four ethical issues for information systems are privacy, accuracy, property, and access. Information systems reduce people's privacy by recording information about them. Accuracy relates to ensuring that information from the information systems is correct. Property deals with the ownership of the information in information systems, the pathways over which information is transmitted, and the knowledge that goes into information systems. Access has to do with making information technology available and ensuring that the necessary information is available through use of the technology. (pp. 78–83)

KEY TERMS

Application Software (p. 71)
Bug (p. 81)
Character (p. 73)
Client (p. 71)
Client/Server Computing (p. 71)
Code of Ethics (p. 78)
Communications Hardware (p. 63)
Communications Software (p. 72)
Computer Hardware (p. 63)
Custom Software (p. 72)
Database (p. 73)
Data File (p. 73)

Desktop Computer (p. 67)
Documentation (p. 76)
Field (p. 73)
File (p. 73)
Handheld (Palmtop) Computer (p. 69)
Mainframe Computer (p. 70)
Matching (p. 80)
Microcomputer (p. 65)
Minicomputer (p. 69)
Multimedia (p. 74)
Notebook (Laptop) Computer (p. 69)

Operating System (p. 71)
Packaged Software (p. 72)
Personal Computer (PC) (p. 67)
Personal Digital Assistant (PDA) (p 69)
Platform (p. 72)
Record (p. 73)
Server (p. 71)
Supercomputer (p. 70)
System Software (p. 71)
Workstation (p. 69)

REVIEW QUESTIONS

1 What is the purpose of computer and communications hardware in information systems?

2 Why do businesses need computer hardware in information systems?

3 What are four reasons businesses need communications hardware in information systems?

4 What are the three main types of computer systems, and how do they differ from one another?

5 What are three types of multiple-user computer systems?

6 What is a server? What is a client?

7 What is the difference between application software and system software?

8 Why do businesses need software in information systems?

9 What are the differences between fields, records, and data files?

10 Why do businesses need stored data in information systems?

11 What are two types of personnel involved with information systems?

12 Why do businesses need personnel in information systems?

13 What are two general types of procedures personnel need in an information system?

14 What is documentation in an information system?

15 Why do businesses need procedures in information systems?

16 What are four approaches to ethical decision making?

17 Why is privacy an important ethical issue for information systems?

18 Why is it important that information systems are accurate?

19 What ethical aspects of property are important in information systems?

20 What difficulties are there in providing access to information in information systems?

DISCUSSION QUESTIONS

1 An international business has decided to purchase the same IBM clones for all its offices around the world. What problems could this decision create?

2 A trend in business is to replace multiple-user computer systems with networked computer systems. What reasons can you give for why a business would do this?

3 Computer applications that involve the storage, retrieval, and display of data often use database software. This software, however, will not operate as needed without the user first providing special instructions to the software about how the application is to function. Is this an example of system or application software? Why?

4 What could happen if personnel and procedures are ignored when a new information system is developed for a business?

ETHICS QUESTIONS

1 Which of the four approaches to ethical decision making discussed in the chapter is closest to your approach and why? If none fit well, what is your approach to ethical decision making?

2 Choose one of the four ethical issues discussed in the chapter (privacy, accuracy, property, or access) and describe a situation in your life related to that issue. What did you do in that situation and why?

3 Some companies read some of their employees' e-mail. What ethical issues does this policy raise?

If you were the chief executive of a company, would you have such a policy? Why?

4 Assume that a fellow employee has printed out information about a celebrity client of your company and is passing it around the office. What would you do in this situation?

5 Besides privacy, accuracy, property, and access, what other ethical issues do you think might arise in information systems?

PROBLEM-SOLVING PROJECTS

1 Set up a spreadsheet to analyze the stock price of a company over a five-year period. Because five years provides a lot of data, design the spreadsheet so that you only need to enter the closing stock price at the end of each month. Pick a company in the computer industry, such as a computer hardware company, a communications hardware company, or a software company. Locate the company's stock prices for the past five years, enter this data into the spreadsheet, and plot the stock price of the company over the five-year period. Use the spreadsheet to calculate how much your stock would be worth now if you had invested $2,500 in the company at the beginning of the five-year period. (Do not consider dividends.) Also use the spreadsheet to calculate the percentage increase or decrease in your investment over the five years.

2 Contact a business that will give you information about its information systems. Choose one information system in that business and identify the components of the system. Interview someone involved in the management of this information system to find out how the needs for the different components discussed in the chapter apply to that system. (Refer to Figures 3.1, 3.2, 3.7, 3.9, 3.10, and 3.11.) Are there other needs besides those listed in the chapter that the components satisfy? Write a report summarizing your findings.

3 Locate a business that has recently changed from using a multiple-user computer system to using a networked computer system for one or more of its information systems. Find out why the business made the change and what advantages and disadvantages the business sees in the networked computer system compared to the multiple-user computer system. Write a report about what you learn.

4 Think of the procedures you follow when you use an ATM. Write these procedures in a form that would be understandable to someone who has never used an ATM. Use graphics software to prepare a diagram showing the procedures.

INTERNET AND ELECTRONIC COMMERCE PROJECTS

1 Find information on the Web about the computers produced by several mainframe computer manufacturers. Try to find information from non-U.S. companies as well as U.S. companies. What models of computers does each company manufacture? Write a report summarizing what you find.

2 Use the Web to gather historical data on stock prices of a microcomputer manufacturer (e.g., Apple), a minicomputer manufacturer (e.g., HP), and a mainframe computer manufacturer (e.g., IBM). Enter each company's stock price data into the spreadsheet you created for Problem-solving Project 1. (You will have to modify the spreadsheet to handle three companies at once.) On a single graph, plot the stock prices of the three companies.

3 Find information about the code of ethics for a professional organization in your field by using the Web. Write a summary of this code of ethics.

4 Examine several electronic commerce Web sites to see what they say about protecting the privacy of their customers. Write a summary of what you find.

Beamscope Canada

You can't blame Danny Gurizzan for being a little bit delighted with his company's new computer system, especially when he considers how things used to work. "When I say it was manual, I mean manual," says Gurizzan, director of operational services at Beamscope Canada, a Scarborough, Ontario, electronics distributor. "When a customer called to place an order, the clerk would scribble it down, run down the hall to the credit check guys, and flip through the files and folders to see if their credit was okay." The clerk would then run to see whether Beamscope actually had the item in stock and then go back to the telephone to confirm the order. "I think we had two PCs in here, and we were doing $93 million (Canadian) worth of business," he says.

In recent years, though, the company has gone from the *Flintstones* to *Star Trek*, thanks to Gurizzan, Ephram Chaplick (vice president and general manager), and Jim Jameson (chief operating officer). The three were instrumental in designing Beamscope's new system, which not only takes on order entry, but also features a radio frequency bar-code system for inventory control, electronic data interchange, and a data warehouse (database) for decision support.

Today, when Beamscope's largest customers call to purchase PCs, printers, software, or the latest game, they connect over a Datapac line (a toll-free, data-only service), where they can browse 120,000 square feet of shelves holding 8,500 different products in the company's two warehouses. Customers can place orders themselves, check the status of previous orders, and download product literature. If an item is temporarily out of stock, the system suggests a substitute or puts the customer on a list for backorders.

At the heart of the system is the Cantoc Business Systems's Censys database, which resides on an IBM AS/400 computer. Beamscope Online, a graphical front end for customers, was jointly developed with Canadian software developer Ironside Technologies.

The database holds data on Beamscope's products, orders, and inventory. By way of a net-work, it connects to a bank of IBM and HP servers and warehouses in Toronto and Vancouver.

All incoming shipments are bar coded and scanned. "When a new order comes in," Gurizzan explains, "our runners go out, pick the order, and send it down a conveyor belt and shoot it before and after with the RF gun. Then the order gets dropped, boxed, and put on the truck." The system is directly tied to UPS's electronic shipping service.

Under the old system, phone orders were manually routed to the warehouse, where they would sit for at least a week. Plus, it was hard to know what was actually in the warehouse and where it was. Now that orders are placed electronically, they show up at the warehouse every 14 minutes. Warehouse clerks pick up the order ticket, which tells them exactly where the item is, and send the order down to a waiting UPS truck. The RF gun picks up the bar code, which sends electronic alerts to the order processing system and to UPS.

It used to take Beamscope five to seven days to ship an order. "Now we can take an order up to 5 p.m., and it will be delivered to your shop the very next day," Chaplick claims.

Since the system went online, business has soared from $93 million to $300 million (Canadian). "We don't make mistakes with orders anymore, unless they were incorrectly placed to begin with," Gurizzan says.

Customers concur. Beamscope fulfills most of Radio Shack Canada's software inventory, for example, including 450 stores and dealers across Canada. "They're connected to our system right through to the point-of-sale terminals in our stores to replenish our software," says Bob Mayes, vice president of merchandising at Radio Shack. Thanks to Beamscope, Radio Shack carries no software inventory at all in its warehouses. This is very important, Mayes explains, because software titles go out of date quickly.

Products aren't collecting dust at Beamscope's physical warehouse, either, thanks to a data warehouse. The warehouse database is an extraction of the Censys database, which is then overlayed with Cognos's PowerPlay to enable multidimensional analysis. To make the warehouse manageable, Beamscope pulls out only necessary data, such as information on shipments of individual products or product types, customer buying habits, gross margins, and so forth. Through Microsoft's FoxPro and Wall Data's Rumba queries, users can analyze shipments of any product on any given day or can generate charts showing trends by product type.

The success of Beamscope's data warehouse, Gurizzan says, is its ease of use. "There's a [PC] on our president's desk, and he loves his reports. If the president or CEO of the company is using your product, you're doing something right."

Beamscope's system has become quite a showpiece. Representatives from pharmaceutical companies to distributorships have been coming in to view the system. Beamscope worked with Ironside Technologies to create an Internet version of the graphical front end.

Questions

1 What is included in the hardware component of the information system described in this case?
2 What is included in the software component?
3 What is included in the stored data component?
4 What procedure is used with the new information system to fill orders in the warehouse?
5 What benefits does Beamscope Canada receive from the information system?

Web Site

**Beamscope Canada:
www.beamscope.com**

Source: *Adapted from* Chris Staiti, "Beamscope Canada, Inc.", *Computerworld Client/Server Journal*, August 1996, pp. 49–50.

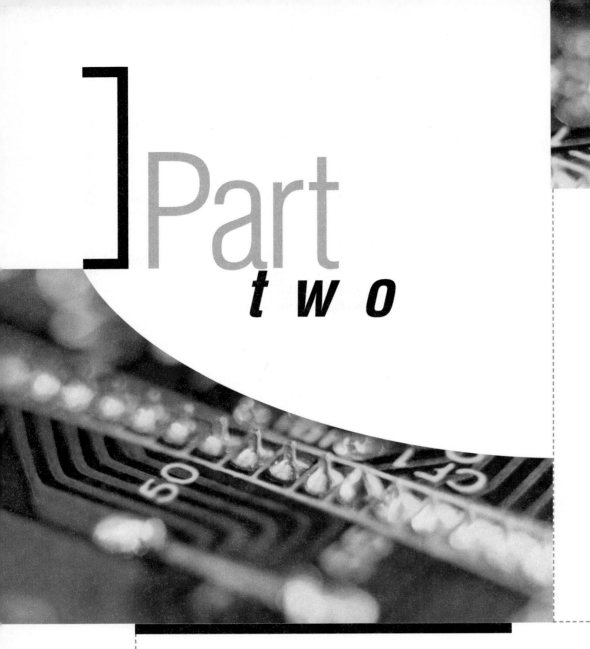

Part
two

Information
Technology

Information System
HARDWARE

F O U R

CHAPTER OUTLINE

Computer Organization
Input and Output Devices
Primary Storage
The Central Processing Unit
Secondary Storage

After completing this chapter, you should be able to

1 Describe the main components of a computer.

2 List common input and output devices.

3 Explain how data is represented in a computer.

4 Describe how primary storage is organized.

5 Describe the structure and function of the central processing unit.

6 Explain how data is stored and retrieved using common forms of secondary storage.

The hardware component of an information system consists of all the equipment used to process, store, and communicate data. For computer information systems, the topic of this book, hardware consists of computers and communications equipment. Information systems that do not use computers, however, also have "hardware." For example, a manual information system may use a calculator to process data, a file cabinet to store data, and a telephone to communicate data. In a sense, all this equipment is hardware—just not computer hardware. This book, however, focuses on computer-related hardware.

This chapter takes a detailed look at computer hardware used in information systems. First, it explains the overall organization of a computer. Then it describes the hardware used for data input and output, data storage, and data processing. Chapter 6 covers hardware for data communications.

Computer Organization

This book has used the word *computer* many times without defining it because most people have a general understanding of computers. But what exactly *is* a computer? Many simple devices, such as pocket calculators, perform computation of some sort and could be called computers. When we use the word *computer*, however, we do not mean one of these devices; instead we mean a device that has certain distinguishing characteristics. Specifically, a **computer** is a device that (1) is electronic, (2) can store data, and (3) can store and follow a set of software instructions, called a **program**, that tells the computer what to do. Its electronic characteristic means it can do processing quickly. The fact that it can store data means that data is available for processing when needed. The computer's capability to follow the stored instructions in a program means that it can perform processing without human intervention.

The actual hardware of a computer is more complex than this definition implies. A computer consists of several interconnected devices or components, as shown in Figure 4.1. In this diagram, symbols represent the components of the computer, and arrows show the paths taken within the computer by data and program instructions. A computer has five basic hardware components: the input device, the output device, primary storage, the central processing unit, and secondary storage.

An **input device** accepts data from outside the computer and converts it into an electronic form that the computer can understand. The data it accepts is the input data. For example, if a computer is going to compute the pay for each employee in a business, the input data would include the employees' names, pay rates, and hours worked. An input device would accept this data from the user and transfer it into the computer. Common input devices are a keyboard and a mouse.

An **output device** performs the opposite function of an input device. It converts data from an electronic form inside the computer to a form that can be used outside the computer. This converted data is the output data or information. For example, the output from a payroll computation would include paychecks with the employees' names and pay. An output device would produce this data in a form understandable to the user. Common output devices are a screen, or monitor, and a printer.

Most computers have several input and output (I/O) devices attached at one time. For example, a multiple-user computer may have many keyboards and screens, as well as several printers. A personal computer usually has two input devices (a keyboard and a mouse) and two output devices (a screen and a printer).

The **primary storage**, also called **internal storage**, is the "memory" of the computer. An input device converts input data into an electronic form and sends the data

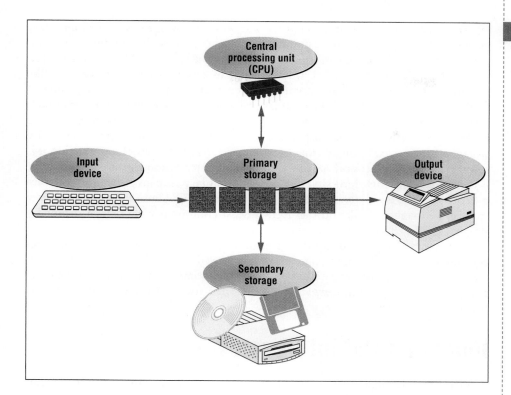

FIGURE 4.1

The organization of a computer ▲

to the primary storage, where the data is stored. The computer then uses the data in calculations and for other types of processing. For example, a computer would store input data for payroll computations, such as employees' pay rates and hours worked, in the primary storage and use it to calculate each employee's pay. After completing the processing, the computer would send the results from primary storage to an output device, where the data would appear as the final output. The primary storage also stores instructions in the program currently being performed. For example, in a payroll computation, the computer would store the instructions necessary to calculate an employee's pay in the primary storage.

The **central processing unit** (**CPU**), which is also called the **processor**, carries out the instructions in the program.[1] Among other things, the CPU contains electronic circuits that perform arithmetic and logical operations. Data is brought from primary storage to the CPU, where it is processed by these circuits, and the results of processing are sent back to primary storage. In a payroll computation, basic arithmetic and logical operations are needed. For example, computing an employee's pay involves the arithmetic operation of multiplying the hours worked by the pay rate. Determining how much income tax each employee should pay involves logical operations.

The CPU also contains electronic circuits that control the other parts of the computer. These circuits perform their functions by following the instructions in the program, which the computer stores in its primary storage. In a payroll computation, many program instructions are needed to tell the computer what steps to follow.

---

[1]Some people consider primary storage to be part of the central processing unit rather than a separate component. Other people use the terms as they appear in the text.

The final component of a computer is **secondary storage**, also called **auxiliary storage**, which stores data not currently being processed by the computer and programs not currently being performed. Its function differs from that of primary storage, which stores the data and instructions that are currently being processed by the computer. For example, if the computer is currently doing payroll processing, it stores the employee data and the payroll computation program in its primary storage. The computer stores other data and programs that are not currently being used, such as those needed for sales analysis, in secondary storage and brings them into primary storage when needed. Primary storage is *temporary storage*, and anything stored in it is lost when someone turns off the power to the computer. Secondary storage, however, is *permanent storage*; anything stored in secondary storage remains there until the computer changes it, even if someone turns off the power. Common types of secondary storage are magnetic disk and CD-ROM. Most computers have several secondary storage devices attached to them at one time.

Secondary storage and input and output devices are often called **peripheral equipment** because they are located outside the central part of the computer, that is, the CPU and primary storage. The word *computer* is sometimes used just for the CPU and primary storage, and *computer system* is often used for the computer with its peripheral equipment.

Input and Output Devices

The hardware that affects users of an information system the most is input and output hardware. A user communicates with computers in an information system through input and output devices. The user enters input data into the system through input devices and receives output information through output devices. It is important that a business select the right input and output hardware for its information system so that the hardware will be appropriate for the system and easy for the users to use. This section describes the characteristics of common input and output devices.

Keyboards

The most widely used input device is a **keyboard**. Keyboards are used for input because most input data consists of letters and numbers. In addition, people are usually familiar with how to use keyboards and with the layout of the keys. Thus, little training is required for users to become familiar with keyboards.

General-purpose computer keyboards usually have keys in the same basic layout. Many special-purpose keyboards are also used. For example, the keyboard on an automated teller machine (ATM) or on a point-of-sale (POS) system usually only consists of the 10 digits and a few special keys such as an Enter key. Despite their limited capabilities, these keyboards are still considered input devices.

Extensive use of a keyboard can lead to physical problems called *repetitive strain injuries*, an example of which is a painful condition called *carpal tunnel syndrome*. These problems may occur when a user performs the same task, such as keying data, over and over again. Taking regular breaks and performing certain exercises may reduce the risk of such injuries, as can having proper seating position and using a wrist support.

Special keyboards have been designed to make keying more comfortable. For example, some keyboards are hinged in the middle or curved with keys set at different angles (Figure 4.2). In general, the study of how to design machines for effective human use is called **ergonomics**. Ergonomically designed keyboards may improve user comfort and efficiency and reduce the risk of injury. Businesses

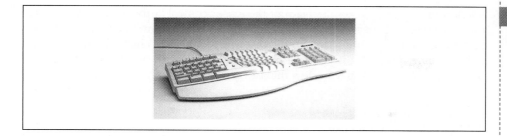

FIGURE 4.2

An ergonomically designed
keyboard ▲

should consider using these keyboards, although they are more expensive than
standard keyboards.

Pointing Devices

After keyboards, the most common input devices are pointing devices. A **mouse** is a
pointing device with a ball on the bottom and one or more buttons on top. Figure
4.3 shows other pointing devices. One is a **trackball**, which is like an upside-down
mouse. A trackball has a ball on the top, which is rolled by a hand or finger, and buttons around the ball. The advantage of a trackball over a mouse is that the user does
not need as much table space to use it. Another pointing device is a small stick, sometimes called a **trackpoint**, that often protrudes between the letters of the keyboard
and that the user moves with a finger. Still another pointer device is a small pad,
often called a **trackpad** (also called a *touchpad*), over which the user runs a finger.
Trackballs, trackpoints, and trackpads are commonly used on notebook computers
because they require little space to use.

Pointing devices have two purposes. The first is to move the **cursor**, which is a
mark, arrow, or highlighted area, on the screen. As the user moves the mouse on a
table, rolls the ball on a trackball, moves a trackpoint, or runs a finger over a trackpad,
the cursor moves to point at different words or symbols on the screen. The second
purpose is to select what the computer does next. The user points the cursor at a
word or symbol on the screen that indicates what the computer is to do and then
presses one of the buttons on the device, a process called *clicking*. This action sends a
signal to the computer that tells it to perform the task.

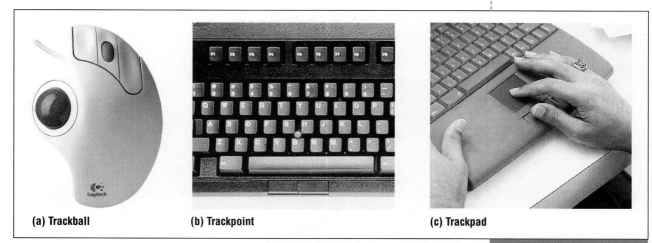

(a) Trackball   (b) Trackpoint   (c) Trackpad

FIGURE 4.3

Pointing devices ▲

A pointing device takes the place of the cursor control (arrow) keys and the function (F1, F2, etc.) keys on a keyboard. The advantage of a pointing device over keys is that using it is like pointing, something that everybody knows how to do. Thus, little training is necessary. Most pointing devices require the user to take a hand off the keyboard, however, which can slow the user down.

Other Input Devices

Keyboards and pointing devices are the input devices most commonly encountered by users. Many other input devices are used, however.

Touch Input Devices.   Several types of devices allow users to enter input by touching something with either a finger or another device (Figure 4.4). One common touch input device is a **touch screen,** which is a screen with the capability of sensing where it is touched by a person's finger. A touch screen can be used to control the functioning of the computer. The screen shows a list of the tasks the computer can do, and the user touches one of the tasks in the list to indicate what is to be done next. A touch screen can also be used for data input. One reason businesses use touch screens is they take little or no training to use. Another reason is that touch screens work well in places, such as production areas, where dirt or contaminants could cause a keyboard or mouse not to function.

Another touch input device uses a screen that is sensitive to the touch of a special pen, a method called **pen input.**   The user can touch points on the screen with the pen to select computer functions. The user can also write on the screen with the pen, and the writing becomes input to the computer. With pen input, a keyboard is not necessary for certain types of input data. Many handheld computers use pen input.

Other types of touch input devices include a *graphics tablet*, which is a rectangular pad that the user touches with a pen called a stylus to draw graphic images; a *light pen*, which is a penlike device that the user touches to the screen and that can sense where it touches the screen; and a *digitizer tablet*, which is a large pad that the user touches with a stylus or a mouse-like device to convert an image on the pad into a computerized form. Touch input devices have the advantage of being used by pointing and touching, actions familiar to users. A disadvantage, however, is that the user must take a hand off the keyboard, which can slow down the work.

FIGURE 4.4

▲ **Touch input devices**

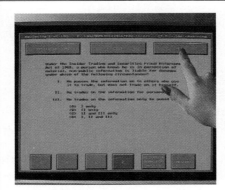

(a) Touch screen   **(b) Pen input**

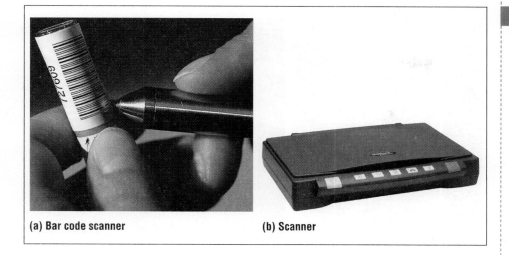

FIGURE 4.5

Optical scanning input devices

(a) Bar code scanner   (b) Scanner

Optical Scanning Input Devices. Some input devices recognize data by scanning symbols or codes with light (sometimes with laser light). Because the symbols or codes are "read" much as you read data with your eyes, these devices are called *optical scanning input devices* (Figure 4.5).

One of the most common optical scanning input devices is a **bar-code scanner.** This device recognizes a *bar code*, which is the series of bars of different widths found on grocery and other items. The width and placement of the bars represent a code that identifies the item. The bar code used on grocery merchandise is called the *Universal Product Code* (*UPC*), but other bar codes are also used. A bar-code scanner, which may be either handheld or fixed, is a device that recognizes the code represented by a bar code and sends the code to the computer.

Businesses use bar-code scanners because with them the user does not have to enter the code through a keyboard. As a result, the user can enter the code into the computer quickly and accurately. A disadvantage of these types of devices is that each item to be scanned must have a bar code on it.

Another optical scanning input device is simply called a **scanner** (or, sometimes an *image scanner* or a *page scanner*). This device uses light to sense an image on paper. Any type of image can be scanned, including text, graphics, pictures, artwork, color images, and photographs. Businesses use scanners to transfer documents and images into a computer, where they can be changed, stored for future use, or used in screen or printed output.

Other optical scanning input devices include *optical character recognition* (*OCR*) devices, which recognize certain printed characters; and *mark-sense readers*, which sense marks made on forms such as those used to take multiple-choice tests. All scanning input devices sense the input—whether it's bars, images, characters, or marks—and transfer the input to the computer.

Magnetic Scanning Input Devices. Another type of scanning input device recognizes magnetic patterns. Data, recorded in a magnetic form, is sensed by a *magnetic scanning input device* (Figure 4.6).

One example of a magnetic scanning input device is a **magnetic strip reader**. This device recognizes data recorded in small magnetic strips that are used on credit and ATM cards to store the card number and on some price tags to store information about an item. The magnetic strip reader senses the data as the strip is passed through

(a) Magnetic strip reader   **(b) MICR character reading device**

the reader or as it is scanned by a wand. Sales clerks sometimes use one magnetic strip reader to scan price tags and another to check customer credit cards. For a business, the advantages of magnetic strip readers are that few errors are made in entering data and the data can be entered very quickly. A disadvantage is that the magnetic strip can be easily damaged.

Another example of magnetic scanning is **magnetic ink character recognition** (**MICR**) which is an input technique used in the banking industry to process checks. MICR characters are the special characters printed at the bottom of checks. These characters indicate the bank, the check number, and the customer's account number. The amount of the check is printed on the check in MICR characters after it is received by the bank. MICR characters are processed by devices that first magnetize the characters, and then read the magnetized characters and send the data to the computer for checking-account processing. Use of this technology in the banking industry is essential because of the high volume of checks that are processed every day.

Voice Input Devices.   A type of input that is becoming more common is voice input. In this form of input, the user speaks into a microphone that is attached to the computer. Special computer hardware and software are needed to convert a person's voice into a form that the computer can understand, a process called *voice recognition.*

To use voice input, voice recognition software often must first be trained to recognize the user's voice. The user speaks words several times so that the software can learn how the user says the words. Then, when using voice input, the user must be careful to speak each word in a fashion similar to the way in which the software was trained.

Some voice recognition systems are designed to recognize only a few words and do not need to be trained. For example, some telephone systems can recognize a spoken number so that the user does not have to press a key. Other voice recognition systems can recognize thousands of different words and can be used for general input, but they require extensive training.

Because voice input is the easiest form of communication for most people, businesses find it very attractive. Even with software that must be trained, however, voice input is not perfectly accurate in recognizing words. Someday, when it is perfected, voice input may be the most common form of input.

Camera Input Devices. Photographic images can be entered into a computer by being scanned, using a scanner. An alternative is to directly enter the image from a camera. This process requires a digital camera that records the images in a form the computer can use. Digital still cameras can be used to enter single images into a computer and digital video cameras can be used to enter moving images. Someday, digital cameras may be used for all types of "vision" input to computers.

Screens

The most widely used output device is a **screen**, which displays the output as a video image. Screens are used for output because most people can easily read them, and their display can be changed quickly.

Character output is formed on a screen from individual dots, called picture elements, or **pixels**, arranged in the patterns of the characters. For example, Figure 4.7 shows how pixels can be arranged to form the letter *S*. Graphic output—diagrams, charts, pictures, and other images—are also formed from pixels arranged in a pattern that represents the image.

The more pixels that are used and the closer they are together, the more the display on the screen looks like a character or a graphic image. The number of pixels that can be displayed at one time is called the **screen resolution**. The higher the resolution, the more the image on the screen looks like the desired output. For example, a screen with 1,280 pixels horizontally by 1,024 pixels vertically has a higher resolution and produces a better image than a screen with a resolution of 640 by 480 pixels.

Several types of screens are used with computers (Figure 4.8). The most common type uses a **CRT**, which stands for *cathode ray tube*. A CRT is a tube similar to that used in a television. A CRT screen designed for computer use is called a **monitor**. Monitors sold today display images in color and vary in size from 14 inches, measured diagonally, to 21 or more inches. (Some older monitors, called *monochrome monitors*, display images in one color.)

CRTs, although very good for displaying output, have a serious disadvantage: They are bulky. To display the image on the screen, a CRT must be deep. The larger the screen, the deeper the CRT, which makes CRTs big and heavy. Although size is usually not a serious problem with desktop computers, it is a problem with portable computers. To overcome the problem of CRT bulk, **flat-panel screens**, which are

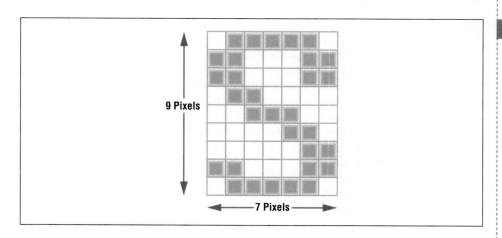

9 Pixels

7 Pixels

FIGURE 4.7

The letter *S* formed from pixels

FIGURE 4.8

▲ Screens

(a) CRT screen   **(b) Flat panel (LCD) screen**

thin and lightweight, are used. They are incorporated into portable computers or used on desktops where space is limited.

The most common type of flat panel screen uses a *liquid crystal display* (*LCD*). LCD screens are thin and lightweight, but they can be harder to read in low light or at an angle than CRT screens. They are also more expensive than CRT screens, but because of their size and weight, they are commonly used on portable computers.

Screens are generally designed to be viewed by only one person at a time. In situations where several people need to view a computer screen simultaneously, a **screen projector** can be used. This type of projector uses LCD technology together with a lens and a light source to display computer output on a viewing screen some distance away. Screen projectors work best when the room is darkened so the image is easier to see.

As with keyboards, ergonomic considerations are important with the design and use of screens. Screens normally have brightness and contrast controls that provide for adjustment for different light conditions. The surface of a screen may be designed to minimize glare. Monitors often have stands that allow them to be rotated and tilted for the best viewing angle. These and other ergonomic factors may improve user comfort and efficiency, and should be considered by businesses in selecting screens.

Printers

Although screens are the most widely used output device, they do not provide a permanent record of the output. **Printers** produce output as printed symbols on paper and thus create a permanent copy of the output.

Many types of printers are used with computers. Some are relatively fast and designed for situations in which a high volume of output is produced, and others are comparatively slow and used when the volume of output is low. Personal computer systems and many networked computer systems use relatively slow, low-volume printers, called *desktop printers*, because they are small enough to fit on the top of a desk or table. Multiple-user computer systems usually use fast, *high-volume printers*, also called *production printers*.

Printer Classifications.   Computer printers can be classified in several ways. One is by how they impact the paper. An **impact printer** makes an image on paper by striking the paper hard with a metal or plastic mechanism. A **nonimpact printer** makes an image in some way other than by a hard strike on the paper. (An example of a nonimpact printing device is a copier, such as those made by Xerox.) Impact printers tend to be noisier than nonimpact printers, which can be an important consideration in an office environment.

Computer printers can also be classified by how many characters are printed at one time. Printers that print one character at a time are called **serial printers**. The speed of a serial printer is measured in *characters per second* (*cps*). Printers that print one line at a time are called **line printers**. Their speed is measured in *lines per minute* (*lpm*). Finally, printers that print an entire page at a time, like a copier, are called **page printers**. Their speed is measured in *pages per minute* (*ppm*).

A final way of classifying printers is in terms of the quality of the images they produce. The printers that produce the best images are called **letter-quality printers**. The output from these printers is the quality you would expect in a business letter. At the other extreme are **draft-quality printers**, which produce output that, although readable, is not of the quality that would normally be acceptable for a business letter. Letter-quality printers should be used for correspondence or documents that go to individuals or organizations outside the business, but draft quality can often be used for documents or reports that are only circulated within a business.

Desktop Printers.   The most common types of desktop printers are ink-jet printers, laser printers, and dot-matrix printers (Figure 4.9).

An **ink-jet printer** is a nonimpact printer that creates an image by spraying drops of ink on the paper. The drops form characters from dots, much the way pixels on a screen form characters. Ink-jet printers are serial printers with typical speeds of 200 to 300 characters per second, although their speed is normally stated in pages per minute. Ink-jet printers produce letter-quality output or output that is nearly letter quality. Most ink-jet printers can print in color, as well as black and white.

A **laser printer** is a nonimpact printer that prints by using technology similar to that of a copier. First, an image of the page to be printed is recorded on the surface of a metal drum by a laser. Then ink called toner is spread on the drum and adheres to the image. Next, the toner is transferred from the drum to paper. Finally, the toner is fixed to the paper, using the same technique as with a copier. A laser printer prints one page at a time, so it is a page printer. Speeds typically range between 4 and 24 pages per minute. The image on a laser printer is made up of dots, like an ink-jet printer, but the dots usually produce a slightly better image. Laser printers print letter-quality output. Although they are more expensive than ink-jet printers, a busi-

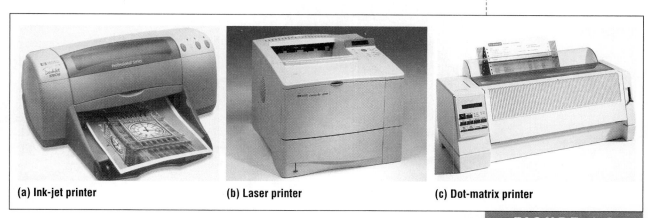

(a) Ink-jet printer   **(b) Laser printer**   **(c) Dot-matrix printer**

FIGURE 4.9

Desktop printers   ▲

ness usually selects a laser printer over an ink-jet printer because the quality of the output is better. Color laser printers are also available, but they are very expensive.

A **dot-matrix printer** is an impact printer that prints each character by striking a ribbon and the paper with a group of pins that cause dots, arranged in a rectangular pattern or matrix, to be printed on the paper. To form a character, some pins are raised and others are not, so that only certain dots in the matrix are printed. Dot-matrix desktop printers are serial printers with speeds typically ranging from 200 to 300 characters per second. They print draft-quality output. Although dot-matrix printers are not as popular as ink-jet and laser printers, they are still used because they are inexpensive and can print on multipart paper, which consists of several sheets of paper with carbon paper between them. They are about the same price as ink-jet printers.

Some printers can do more than just print computer output. These **multifunction printers** can also send and receive faxes, scan images, and make copies. Multifunction printers use either laser or ink-jet technology to create an image. They are useful in small businesses or departments of a business that do not have the need or space for separate machines.

High-volume Printers.   Printers designed for high volumes of output are used mainly with multiple-user or large networked computer systems. These printers require special training to operate and are almost always operated by computer professionals. The two main types of high-volume printers are line printers and page printers (Figure 4.10).

Line printers are impact printers that use several techniques to print output. In one common technique, a band containing forms of all the characters moves rapidly past a ribbon and the paper. As characters on the band pass positions to be printed, hammers in the printer strike the band, causing the character to be printed. The band

FIGURE 4.10

▲ **High-volume printers**

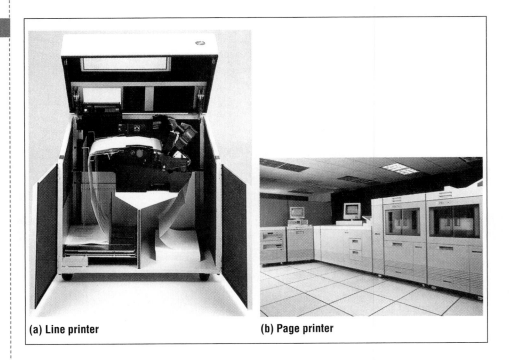

(a) Line printer   (b) Page printer

moves so quickly that it appears as if the entire line is printed at one time. Some line printers print as much as 3,600 lines per minute. They produce draft-quality output and can cost as much as $50,000.

High-volume page printers are nonimpact laser printers that use a printing technique similar to desktop laser printers. The difference is that they are much faster and much more expensive than desktop models. High-volume page printers can print more than 200 pages per minute and can cost over $100,000. These printers print letter-quality output. Businesses use high-volume page printers when large amounts of printed output are needed, such as in utility companies that print millions of bills each month.

Other Output Devices

The output devices described so far—screens and printers—are most commonly encountered by users. Several other types of output devices are also used.

Plotters. A **plotter** creates graphic output on paper (Figure 4.11). Some plotters use one or more ink pens to draw a graphic image, and other plotters spray drops of ink (like an ink-jet printer) in a graphic pattern. Although most printers can create graphic output, plotters produce better-quality graphic images. Some plotters draw with one color (usually black), and other plotters can draw with several colors.

Plotters usually plot on large sheets of paper, as wide as 50 inches. They are most commonly used for producing engineering and architectural drawings.

Voice Output Devices. In voice output, a human-sounding voice speaks the output to the user through a speaker or an earphone. An example of voice output is telephone directory assistance. In this system, a human operator takes the request for a telephone number, but the required number is spoken by a computer-generated voice.

FIGURE 4.11

A plotter

Voice output is produced in two ways. One way is for the computer to play recorded words stored in secondary storage. The second way is to create the voice with special computer circuitry, a process called *speech synthesis*.

The advantage of voice output over other forms of output is that it is in a form with which people are most familiar. Voice output, however, is not permanent, as is paper output. Generally, voice output is best for small amounts of output.

Sound Output Devices.   Computers often have speakers to produce sound output, which could be recorded voices, music, or simple beeps and tones. The speakers are attached to circuits in the computer that supply the electronic impulses for the sounds to the speakers. Often the speakers require separate power to amplify the sound so that it can be heard.

Terminals

An input device combined with an output device, such as a keyboard and a screen, forms a **terminal**. Large multiple-user computers often use many terminals as input and output devices.

The most common type of terminal is a **video display terminal** (**VDT**), which consists of a keyboard and a screen (Figure 4.12). Some VDTs (called *dumb terminals*) can only send input to the computer and receive output from the computer, but others (called *intelligent terminals*) can also perform some basic data processing such as identifying errors in input data.

Microcomputers can also be used as video display terminals. To do so requires data communication technology, as discussed in Chapter 6. The result, however, is that the microcomputer can do much of the data processing normally done by the larger computer, and it can act as a terminal for the other computer. Because of these advantages, microcomputers have replaced terminals in many businesses.

FIGURE 4.12

▲ **A video display terminal**

Numerous other devices are also terminals. For example, an ATM is a terminal connected to a distant computer operated by the bank. An ATM has several input and output devices. For input it has a magnetic strip reader to sense the magnetic strip on the back of the ATM card, a keyboard, and sometimes a touch screen. For output it has a printer to print receipts, a screen, and a money dispenser.

Devices for People with Disabilities

People with visual, hearing, or motion impairments may need special input and output devices to use computers, or they may be able to use common devices with enhanced features. The particular device needed depends on the extent and type of the person's disability.

Visually impaired people can benefit from a number of devices, many of which have already been described. For individuals with some visual ability, screen displays can be enhanced to show text in a large typeface or images in an enlarged format, often with easily viewed colors and high contrast. If a keyboard is difficult for a visually impaired person to use, a speech input device can be used to allow voice communication with a computer. For people with severe visual disabilities, speech output devices can synthesize spoken words as they are displayed on the screen. Coupled with a scanner to scan a document into a computer, a speech output device can "read" a document to the user. Speech output devices can also be used to read e-mail sent to the user. **Braille display devices** can be used to display text output as a series of raised pins (Figure 4.13). Printers are also available that can print output in Braille. The user, of course, must know how to read Braille to use either of these devices.

Individuals with hearing impairments can have the computer display special images or words on the screen when the computer makes a sound, thus alerting the user to the sound. For people with some hearing ability, headphones with volume controls can be used to provide an adequate sound level for the user, without disturbing others in the room.

For people with disabilities that limit motion, special keyboards and pointing devices are available. For example, one keyboard device has images of letters, numbers, and other keys that the user can tap (Figure 4.14). Another device is available that the user sucks on ("sips") or blows into ("puffs") to enter input into the computer. Still another device senses where the user is looking on the screen. With this device the user can control the cursor movement and select computer functions with

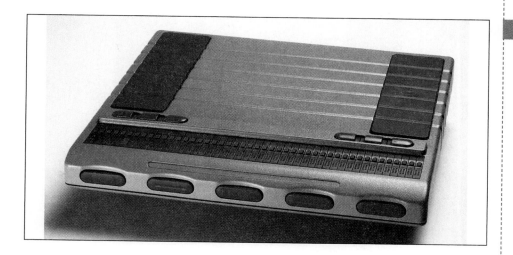

FIGURE 4.13

A Braille display device

FIGURE 4.14

A keyboard for people with
▲ disabilities

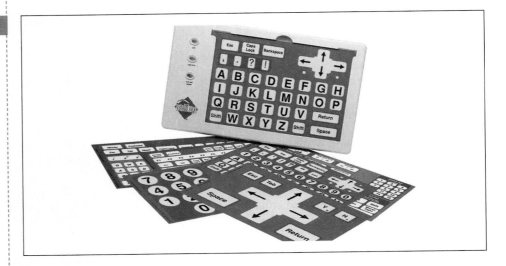

his or her eyes. Although limited in their functions, these types of devices can make computers accessible to people with disabilities.

Multimedia Input and Output

Multimedia input and output consists of data in more than one form. Multimedia input can include still pictures, moving images, and sound. Multimedia output can include graphic images that are still or moving pictures or animation, and sound that is voice, music, or any other sound. In the future, multimedia input and output may include other forms, such as that sensed through touch or smell.

Multimedia output is often used in highly interactive presentations to users. The user can select what he or she wants to see or hear, and can move through the presen-

FIGURE 4.15

▲ A multimedia kiosk

tation in sequence or jump from one point in the presentation to another. Because of its characteristics, multimedia is useful in education and training, in product presentations to customers, in reference works such as encyclopedias, and in entertainment.

To produce multimedia output, appropriate output devices must be available, including a high-resolution screen and speakers or headphones. Because multimedia is interactive, printers are not normally needed unless certain output can be printed.

Input devices for multimedia depend on whether the presentation is to be used or created. To *use* multimedia, a keyboard and a pointing device such as a mouse are necessary so that the user can interact with the presentation. A touch screen may also be used, and some multimedia kiosks in public locations such as shopping centers are used entirely through a touch screen (Figure 4.15).

To *create* a multimedia presentation, however, additional input devices are necessary. These include digital cameras that can take still images or moving pictures and convert them to a form that can be stored in the computer. This process is called *digitizing* because the image is converted to the digits 1 and 0. Sound input devices are also needed, and they include microphones, tape recorders, music keyboards, and other audio devices. These devices must be connected to special digitizing circuits to convert the sound input into a form that can be stored in the computer.

Virtual Reality Input and Output

Virtual reality is the use of a computer to produce realistic images and sounds in such a way that the user senses that he or she is a part of the scene. In effect, virtual reality creates a nonreal, or *virtual*, world and puts the user in the world through sight and sound.

Special input and output devices are needed to use virtual reality (Figure 4.16). The user usually wears a headset connected to a computer. The headset contains two

FIGURE 4.16

Virtual reality input and output devices ▲

Virtual Reality at the Education Center in Alvdalen, Sweden

Eventually, forestry students at the Education Center in Alvdalen, Sweden, have to train in a real tree harvester, but experiencing some hours in a virtual reality simulator is proving to be a popular choice for safe and cost-effective training.

When teacher Tomas Wiklund experimented with virtual reality as a teaching tool, he found that students who first used a simulator were more confident and productive when they started driving the real machine. Students who jumped right into operating the intimidating machine, which cuts down and carries 90-foot pine trees with a 33-foot arm, were more nervous and thus more dangerous.

Long a staple in aviation and the military, virtual reality training is only now catching on in other industries, says Roy Latham, editor of the "Real Time Graphics" newsletter and president of Mountain View, California-based CGSD, a virtual reality research and applications firm.

After some premature enthusiasm about virtual reality technology a few years ago, many companies became disillusioned with mediocre technology that simply didn't simulate reality well enough, Latham says. The industry has had to win back credibility as its technology has improved. "We are early in that phase," he says.

Although several universities are actively researching virtual reality training applications, most companies that have invested in virtual reality are more interested in prototyping manufacturing concepts, Latham says. Caterpillar is one of them, having worked with the University of Illinois for more than four years on virtual reality systems that model products.

According to the journal *I/S Analyzer*, Chicago-based Amoco has used virtual reality for truck-driver training, and Bethel, Connecticut-based Duracell has used it for improving workers' skills on the factory floor.

Wiklund says the logging simulator is a bit slow and offers only a frontal view, but is a worthwhile asset. Experienced operators can find nuances that don't feel right, giving the simulator limited value for more advanced loggers, he adds.

But the simulator, made by Partek (Pargas, Finland) accounts for terrain, weather conditions, and the size of each tree and log, to simulate both normal and dangerous working conditions. The simulator is based on a Silicon Graphics Onyx2 server and software developed by Montreal-based Lateral Logic. It costs about $100,000 less than a $400,000 harvester, and its 65-in. screen can be used to teach several students at a time.

Wiklund says the machine also simulates a harvester's onboard computer systems, which calculate where to cut a tree to maximize the value of each log.

Questions

1. What benefit is there to using a virtual reality simulator in training students to drive a tree harvester?
2. What are some other uses of virtual reality for training?
3. Why has virtual reality not been accepted more by businesses?

Web Site
Partek Corporation, Finland: www.partek.fi

Source: *Adapted from* David Orenstein, "Virtual Reality Saves on Training," *Computerworld*, March 8, 1999, p. 44.

small screens, one for each eye, that project three-dimensional images for the user. The headset also contains headphones for sound output.

The headset is not only an output device, but also an input device. As the user moves his or her head, the movement is sensed and the image is adjusted to where the user is looking. Another input device that may be used is a glove that senses hand movement so that the user can point to things in the virtual world. Instead of a glove, some virtual reality systems use a joystick, which is a stick that can be moved to control the virtual world.

Virtual reality has many uses. An obvious one is for entertainment. Users can experience fantasy worlds and play games using virtual reality. Another important use is to train doctors in sophisticated medical procedures. Virtual reality is also used in architecture and design to allow the user to "walk" through a building or room to see how it will look after it has been constructed.

Primary Storage

Input data is stored in primary storage (memory) after it is received from an input device, and output data is stored in primary storage before it is sent to an output device. Data from secondary storage and programs that are executing are also stored in primary storage. It is important that a computer used in an information system have adequate primary storage so that it can store the data and program instructions needed for current processing. Without enough primary storage, it may not be possible to execute certain programs or use certain data. Even if there is enough primary storage, more storage may result in faster processing. Thus, businesses need to select computers with adequate primary storage to meet their needs. This section describes the structure and function of primary storage.

Primary Storage Structure

Primary storage is composed of silicon **chips** (integrated circuits) containing millions of electronic circuits. Silicon, a substance found in sand, is formed into pieces about ¼-inch square into which electronic circuits are etched (Figure 4.17). A computer's primary storage usually consists of a number of memory chips.

Each circuit on a chip can be in only one of two states: on or off. In a way, a circuit is like a lightbulb, which can be only on or off. You can think of primary storage as being composed of millions of lightbulbs, each of which is either on or off. The computer stores data in primary storage by turning some circuits on and others off, in a pattern that represents the data. For example, Figure 4.18 uses the lightbulb anal-

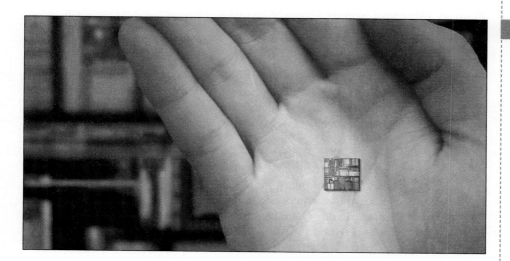

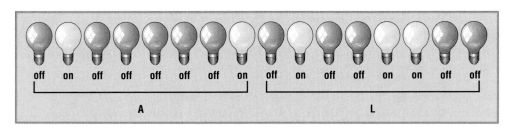

FIGURE 4.18

▲ Storing a name in primary
storage: the lightbulb analogy

ogy to show a pattern that represents a person's name. Later you will see the types of patterns that computers use to represent data.

When data is stored in primary storage, it stays there until the computer changes it. To change the data, the computer changes the pattern in the circuits by turning some circuits on and others off. When the computer changes the data, the original data is destroyed and replaced by the new data. To retrieve data from primary storage, the computer senses the on/off pattern in the circuits. It can transfer this pattern to another part of the computer such as the CPU, an output device, or secondary storage. When data is retrieved, the old data is *not* destroyed; it remains in primary storage and can be retrieved again.

Primary storage circuits, like lightbulbs, need electricity to stay on. If the power to the computer is turned off, all the circuits will turn off, and all data in primary storage will be lost. When the computer is turned back on, the data will not reappear; the data is lost forever (unless it is stored in some other form). Because of this characteristic, primary storage is called **volatile storage**.

The type of primary storage described so far is called **random access memory (RAM)**. *Random access* means that data in any part of the primary storage can be retrieved (accessed) in any order (i.e., randomly). RAM is the main type of primary storage used with computers and, as you know, it is volatile. Computers also have a type of primary storage called **read-only memory (ROM)**. ROM is **nonvolatile storage**, which means that when the power to the computer is turned off, anything stored in ROM is not lost. ROM, however, can store only preset programs and data put in ROM by the computer manufacturer. Programs and data in ROM can be retrieved (read) as many times as needed, but new programs and data cannot be stored in ROM. ROM is used to store special programs and data needed for the basic operation of the computer.

Data Representation

Data appears in several forms, including graphic images, pictures, and sound. Most common data, however, is made up of characters. People represent data by using a group of characters, such as a group of letters for a name, or a group of numerals for a quantity. Computers, however, cannot represent this data in the same form that people use.

There are more than 100 common characters, such as letters, numerals, and symbols like periods, commas, and spaces. If a computer circuit were used to represent any character, that circuit would need more than 100 states, one for each character. But as you have seen, each computer circuit has only two states: on and off. Thus, it is not possible to represent any character with a single circuit.

Computers represent data by using different patterns of on/off states in a series of electronic circuits. A computer stores data by converting the data to this two-state representation, which is called *binary representation*. To show data in binary representation on paper, people use the digit 1 for the on state and the digit 0 for the off state. The digits 1 and 0 are called **binary digits**, or **bits**. For example, the bits that represent the data in Figure 4.18 are

0100000101001100

All data is stored in the computer as patterns of bits.

Characters are stored in a binary representation by using a code for each character. Although over the years many codes have been developed, two common codes—ASCII and EBCDIC—are used today.

The name **ASCII** is pronounced "as-key" and stands for *American Standard Code for Information Interchange*. An industry group composed of many computer manufacturers developed this code as a standard code to be used on all computers. In ASCII, each character is represented by 7 bits, and because there are 128 combinations of 7 bits, 128 characters can be represented in the code. For example, the name JOHN in ASCII is

Notice that 28 bits are needed for the name, 7 bits for each character. Although ASCII is a 7-bit code, computers normally use an 8-bit version of ASCII, which allows for 256 characters. ASCII is used in all microcomputers, including those made by IBM and Apple, and in many minicomputers, mainframe computers, and supercomputers.

Although ASCII is an industry-standard code, it is not used in all computers. IBM mainframe computers, and some mainframe computers that are similar to IBM's, use the **EBCDIC** code. The name of this code is pronounced "eb-si-dick" and stands for *Extended Binary Coded Decimal Interchange Code*. It was developed by IBM for use in its computers. In EBCDIC, each character is represented by 8 bits. Because there are 256 combinations of 8 bits, 256 characters can be represented in EBCDIC. The name JOHN in EBCDIC is

Notice that 32 bits are needed for the name, 8 bits for each character.

When computers use different codes to represent data, a problem arises if the computers need to communicate with each other. For example, a microcomputer using ASCII cannot communicate with an IBM mainframe that uses EBCDIC without special hardware or software to convert between the codes. Although the necessary hardware and software is readily available, businesses must be aware of this problem so they can acquire what they need.

As computers are used for more and more international information systems, limitations in the ASCII and EBCDIC codes become evident. These codes can represent only 256 characters, but there are many more characters found in the alphabets and writing systems used around the world. For example, the Russian alphabet has 31 characters and the Greek alphabet has 24. In addition, systems such as those used in

China and Japan have thousands of characters. An 8-bit code such as ASCII or EBCDIC is not adequate to represent all possible characters.

In an effort to create a single code for all characters, a 16-bit code called **Unicode**, for Universal Code, has been developed. With 16 bits, Unicode has 65,536 combinations, which is enough for all the characters used in all the alphabets and writing systems in the world. Although not widely used yet, it may some day be the standard code on all computers.

Primary Storage Organization

Recall that each circuit in primary storage can be either on or off, and hence each circuit can store 1 bit. The bits in primary storage must be organized so that they can be used to store characters and so that the stored data can be retrieved. This organization is accomplished by arranging the bits into groups called **storage locations**.

The number of bits in each storage location depends on the type of computer being used. Most computers have 8 or 9 bits per storage location. Computers with 8- or 9-bit storage locations use either 8-bit ASCII or EBCDIC and store one character in each location. In addition, computers often add a ninth bit, called a *parity bit*, which is used to check if there are any errors in the other bits. A group of bits that are used to store one character is called a **byte**. Usually, a byte is 8 or 9 bits. Computers organize primary storage so that each storage location is 1 byte.

The computer keeps track of storage locations by giving each location a unique number called an **address**. A simple analogy is post office box addresses. Think of primary storage as being organized into boxes just like the boxes in a post office. For example, Figure 4.19 shows part of primary storage organized into 12 boxes, or storage locations. Each storage location in primary storage, like each post office box, has an address to identify it. The contents of each storage location in the computer is data, just like the contents of each post office box is mail. To locate a specific post office box, you search through the boxes until you locate the one with the desired address. You can store mail in the box or retrieve mail from the box. Similarly, the computer locates a specific storage location by its address and stores data in or retrieves data from that location.

Primary Storage Capacity

A computer's storage capacity is measured in terms of the number of bytes in primary storage. In older computers, the capacity is stated in **kilobytes**, or **K bytes (KB)**. One kilobyte is 1,024 bytes (2^{10} bytes), but most people round this number to 1,000

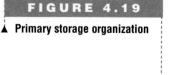

FIGURE 4.19

▲ **Primary storage organization**

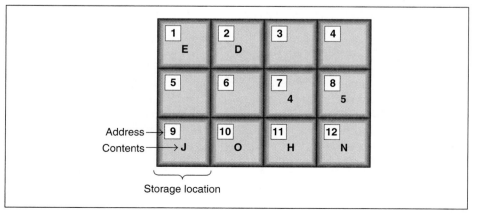

Storage location

bytes. The primary storage of most current computers is measured in terms of **megabytes**, or **M bytes** (**MB**). One megabyte is 1,048,576 bytes (2^{20} bytes), but again, people round this number to 1 million bytes. Thus, 128 megabytes of primary storage would be about 128 million bytes. An even larger measure than megabyte is **gigabyte**, or **G byte**, (**GB**), which is approximately 1 billion bytes (2^{30} bytes). Some mainframe computers have gigabyte primary storage capacity. A still larger capacity is **terabyte**, or **T byte** (**TB**), which is about 1 trillion bytes (2^{40} bytes). Someday, computers may have terabyte primary storage capacities.

The Central Processing Unit

The central processing unit (CPU) does arithmetic and makes logical decisions using data in primary storage. In addition, the CPU controls the computer by following instructions in a stored program, sending signals to other parts of the computer to tell them what to do.

From a business's point of view, the CPU is important because it determines to a large extent the speed at which processing is done. Businesses need to be aware of this fact when purchasing computers so that processing will be completed at an acceptable rate. In addition, not all CPUs are the same, so programs for some computers will not work on other computers. This compatibility problem must also be considered by businesses when selecting computers. This section describes how the CPU functions, and explains the speed and compatibility characteristics of CPUs.

CPU Structure

The CPU is composed of one or more silicon chips, each containing millions of electronic circuits. The circuits in the CPU are organized into two main units, called the **arithmetic-logic unit** (**ALU**) and the **control unit** (Figure 4.20).

The ALU contains circuits that perform arithmetic and logical operations. The arithmetic circuits can add, subtract, multiply, and divide two numbers. More complex operations, such as finding the square root of a number, are done by using sequences of these basic operations. The logic circuits in the ALU can compare two values to determine whether they are equal or whether one is greater than or less than the other.

To perform an arithmetic or logical operation, numbers are transferred from primary storage to the ALU. These numbers are then sent to the appropriate arithmetic or logic circuit in the ALU for processing. Finally, the result is sent back to primary storage.

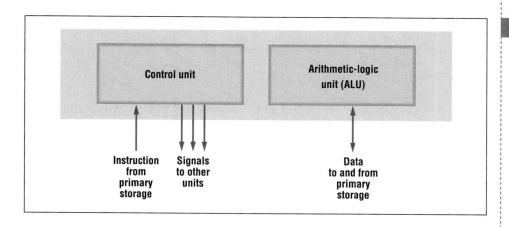

FIGURE 4.20

The structure of the central processing unit ▲

The control unit contains circuits that analyze and execute instructions in a program. Instructions are brought one at a time from primary storage to the control unit. In the control unit, circuits analyze the instruction to determine what type of instruction it is. Then other circuits in the control unit execute the instruction by sending signals to the ALU, primary storage, I/O devices, and secondary storage, that cause the actions required by the instructions to be performed. These steps are repeated for each instruction in the program, until all instructions have been executed.

To illustrate how the control unit analyzes and executes instructions in a program, assume that it is necessary to find the sum of two numbers using a computer. To solve this problem, the computer must go through a sequence of steps. First, the computer must use an input device such as a keyboard to get the two numbers from the user. Then, the computer must add the numbers in the ALU to find their sum. Finally, the computer must send the sum to an output device such as a screen so that the user can see the result. Thus, to solve this problem, a computer program would contain three instructions:

1 Get two numbers from the input device.

2 Add the numbers to find the sum.

3 Send the sum to the output device.

To execute a program, the instructions in the program must be in the computer's primary storage. Before execution, the program is usually stored in secondary storage. Then, to execute the program, the computer first must transfer the program from secondary storage to primary storage, a process called *loading* the program (Figure 4.21).

When the program is in primary storage, the computer executes it by going through the instructions in sequence. The computer brings each instruction in the program, one at a time, to the control unit, analyzes it, and executes it. The execution sequence for the instructions in the example program to find the sum of two numbers would proceed as follows (Figure 4.22):

1 *Get two numbers.* The control unit sends a signal to the input device that causes two numbers (input data) to be transferred to primary storage.

2 *Add the numbers.* The control unit sends a signal to primary storage that causes the two numbers to be sent from primary storage to the ALU in the CPU. Then the ALU adds the numbers and sends the sum to primary storage.

FIGURE 4.21

Loading a program into primary storage

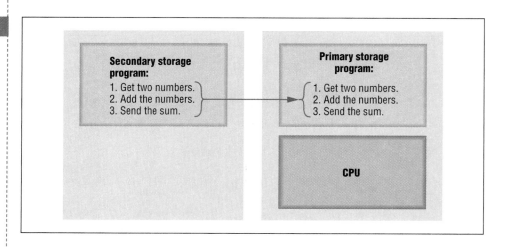

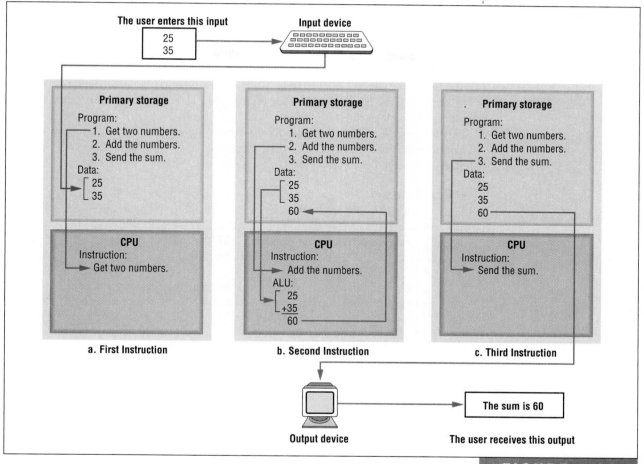

a. First Instruction

b. Second Instruction

c. Third Instruction

FIGURE 4.22

Executing a program ▲

3 *Send the sum.* The control unit sends a signal to primary storage to transfer the sum to the output device. Then the output device displays the sum (output data).

This example illustrates the point that primary storage stores both program instructions and data. The computer stores the instructions in the program in primary storage as it executes the instructions. The computer brings data into primary storage as it executes the program.

The example also shows that the computer executes the instructions in a program in the sequence in which they are stored (unless an instruction is included to change the sequence). The sequence must be in an order that, when executed, solves the problem. For example, if someone switched the first two instructions in the previous example, the program would not solve the problem. If the instructions are out of order, the computer cannot figure out what the right sequence should be. The computer would simply follow the instructions in the order in which they are given and produce an incorrect result.

CPU Compatibility

The CPU functions by executing instructions in a program. The instructions are in a very basic form called **machine language**. Each instruction in a machine language program consists of a code that indicates the operation to perform (e.g., add, subtract) and the location of the data on which to perform the operation. The instructions are in a binary form (i.e., a sequence of 1s and 0s).

Different CPUs use different machine language instructions for their programs. Each type of CPU has its own set of instructions, which may be different from that of other CPUs. The instruction sets may differ in the types of operations that can be performed, which codes are used for each operation, and how the location of the data to be processed is identified in an instruction. This incompatibility means that a machine language program for one CPU may not be executed on a different CPU. Two different CPUs are *compatible* if the machine language instructions for one are identical to those of the other. Thus, a machine language program for one CPU can be executed on a compatible CPU and vice versa.

CPU Speed

The way a CPU is designed affects its speed. One factor is the number of bits that can be processed in the CPU at one time. Early CPUs could process only 8 or 16 bits at a time (1 or 2 bytes), whereas current CPUs process 32, 64, and even 128 bits at a time. In general, the more bits that can be processed in the CPU, the faster the computer.

Another factor is the amount of data that can be transferred between the CPU and primary storage at one time. Data is transferred between these and other components of the computer over a set of wires called a *bus*. Older computers could transfer only 8 or 16 bits (1 or 2 bytes) at a time, but current computers can transfer 32 bits (4 bytes) or 64 bits (8 bytes) at a time. In general, the more data that can be transferred between the CPU and primary storage at a time, the faster the computer.

The speed at which a computer can transfer data is measured in fractions of a second. The first computers could transfer data to and from primary storage in **milliseconds**. One millisecond is one-thousandth of a second. Later computers stored and retrieved data in **microseconds**. One microsecond is one-millionth of a second. Today's computers transfer data between primary storage and the CPU in **nanoseconds**. One nanosecond is one-billionth of a second.

Another factor that affects CPU speed is *clock speed*. CPUs are synchronized to run at the speed of an internal clock. With each tick of the clock, the CPU performs one step in executing an instruction. If the clock ticks faster, then the CPU runs faster. Clock speed is measured in **megahertz (MHz)** or **gigahertz (GHz).** One megahertz is one million cycles (ticks) per second and one gigahertz is one billion cycles per second. For example, the CPU in the original IBM PC ran at 4.77 MHz, or 4,770,000 cycles per second. The CPUs in many microcomputers today run at 700 MHz or faster, which means that many more operations can be performed in a second on these computers than on early IBM PCs. Some high speed CPUs run at over 1 GHz.

In recent years, new types of CPUs have been developed that are designed to be faster and less expensive than older ones. These types are called *reduced instruction set computer* (*RISC*) processors. A RISC processor has a smaller set of instructions than an older type of processor, which makes it less expensive, but it can execute its instructions very rapidly. Older types of processors are called *complex instruction set computer* (*CISC*) processors.

Common CPUs

CPUs in all computers have basically the same structure: a control unit and an ALU. CPUs differ, however, in the machine language instructions they can execute and in characteristics that determine their speed.

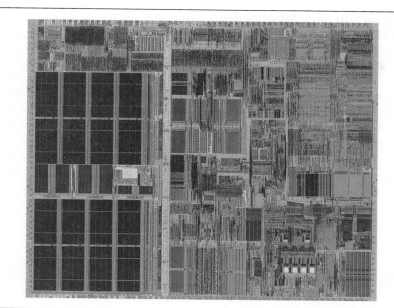

FIGURE 4.23

A microprocessor

Microcomputer CPUs. A microcomputer uses a single-chip CPU, called a **microprocessor** (Figure 4.23). The first microprocessor was developed by Intel in the early 1970s and was called the Intel 4004. It was a slow processor used in calculators. Over the years, Intel has developed faster and better microprocessors, including the 8088, which was used as the CPU in the original IBM PC; the 8086; the 80286, usually just called the 286; the 80386, or simply the 386; and the 80486, or 486. After the 486, Intel changed the way it named processors, and called the next model the Pentium. Then came the Pentium Pro, the Pentium II, and the Pentium III. All the Intel microprocessors use the same machine language instructions so they are compatible. Each new model, however, is faster and more powerful than the previous one. They are used in IBM microcomputers and IBM clones.

The original Apple Macintosh used a microprocessor for its CPU developed by Motorola, called the 68000. This microprocessor is not compatible with the Intel microprocessors. Faster Motorola microprocessors—called the 68020, 68030, and 68040—were used in later models of the Macintosh. Even faster is the most recent Motorola microprocessor, called the PowerPC, which was developed jointly by Motorola, Apple, and IBM. It comes in various models, including the G4, which is used in many Macintosh models.

As you can see, microcomputer companies, such as IBM and Apple, use microprocessors developed by other companies, such as Intel and Motorola. Different microcomputers may use the same microprocessor and thus the computers are compatible with one another. For example, all IBM clones using the Intel Pentium III are compatible. A microcomputer that uses a different microprocessor, however, is not compatible. Thus a Macintosh using a PowerPC is not compatible with an IBM clone.

New microprocessors are always being developed by Intel, Motorola, and other companies. These new microprocessors are faster than previous ones, and may offer improved capabilities. You can expect this trend to continue. In a few years, all the microprocessors in use today will be obsolete.

Minicomputer and Mainframe Computer CPUs. Minicomputers and mainframe computers often use CPUs developed by the computer manufacturers. The CPUs developed by one company often are not compatible with those of another company. Within a line of computers manufactured by a company, however, the CPUs are usually compatible. For example, HP 3000 minicomputers are compatible through all models in the line. Similarly, all IBM System/390 mainframe computers are compatible. IBM mainframe computers, however, are not compatible with HP minicomputers. Thus, a machine language program for an IBM System/390 cannot be executed on an HP 3000.

Some CPUs developed by computer manufacturers for their computers are used by other companies for their machines. For example, the CPU developed by DEC (now owned by Compaq) for its Alpha minicomputer is sold to several other companies and used in those other companies' computers.

BOOK

M A R K

Massively Parallel Processing at United Airlines

United Airlines has an $18 million massively parallel processing system that could eventually bring in as much as $100 million more in annual profits.

The system helps the airline allocate seat reservations for its 4,000 daily flights. This maximizes revenue by letting United better plan how many seats to hold for last-minute business travelers, how many seats in each flight to overbook, and how to best manage connecting flight seating.

At first 4,000 flights may not sound like an unmanageable amount of data, but when you split each of those into as many as seven different fares per flight and take into account that United accepts reservations 331 days in advance, you start to realize just how large the problem is.

United uses a massively parallel processing system based on a 24-node IBM RS/6000 SP (in which each node has several CPUs) using Orchestrate software from Torrent Systems in Cambridge, Massachusetts. Orchestrate is a development tool that lets United build massively parallel applications for the SP. "Our old mainframe couldn't handle that size load," recalls Bob Bongiorno, director of information systems research and development at United.

Orchestrate lets developers program an application for a single node, and then simulate and test it across several CPUs. It also automatically partitions data into subsets and distributes it across the CPUs, instead of making the user manually decide what the distribution pattern should be, as some other software tools do.

Because each day's flights could be processed as a self-contained set, the massively parallel processing system breaks up queries into small pieces and spreads them out among the system's processors for quick handling.

United isn't the only company using massively parallel processing. The Fingerhut catalog retailer, based in Minnetonka, Minnesota, has built a massively parallel processing system for optimizing its 400 million mailings.

Questions

1. Why does United Airlines use a massively parallel processing system?
2. How does the massively parallel processing system handle queries?

Web Site

United Airlines: www.ual.com

Source: *Adapted from* Stewart Deck, "United Taps Massively Parallel Application," *Computerworld*, June 28, 1999.

Supercomputer CPUs. Like minicomputer and mainframe computer CPUs, supercomputer CPUs are often developed by the computer manufacturer. As a result, the CPU used in one supercomputer is usually not compatible with that of other supercomputers.

To obtain great processing speeds, supercomputers often use CPUs that can process 64 or 128 bits at a time. In addition, special chips that are designed for high-speed processing are used. For example, supercomputers often use special high-speed chips for arithmetic calculations. Another technique used to increase speed is **multiprocessing**, which involves using several CPUs in the computer. For example, a supercomputer may have 8 CPUs, which means 8 operations can be performed at one time, making the computer 8 times as fast as a computer that has only a single CPU. (This multiprocessing technique is also used in some less powerful computers, including some microcomputers, minicomputers, and mainframe computers.)

Some supercomputers do not use specially developed CPUs, but instead use many standard CPUs, such as those made by Intel. These supercomputers may have several hundred to several thousand CPUs, allowing hundreds to thousands of operations to be performed simultaneously. This approach is called **massively parallel processing**, and it may be the direction that most supercomputers go in the future.

Server CPUs. Servers in networks are often microcomputers and thus use the same microprocessor CPUs found in microcomputers, including those made by Intel and Motorola. Because servers provide services to many computers in a network, only the most powerful microprocessors are used. Sometimes servers have several microprocessors, similar to multiprocessing in supercomputers, to provide enough processing capability.

Servers can also be minicomputers, mainframe computers, and even supercomputers. In this case the server's CPU is the one supplied by the computer manufacturer.

Secondary Storage

A computer in an information system stores not only data and programs currently being processed, but also data and programs for future processing. Primary storage, as you know, stores data and programs currently needed by the computer. Data and programs that are not being processed, but that may be needed in the future, cannot be stored in primary storage because primary storage is volatile. Secondary storage, on the other hand, is nonvolatile, and so it is used to store data and programs needed in the future.

Secondary storage has several characteristics that affect information systems in businesses. One characteristic is the capacity of secondary storage for storing data and programs. Different types of secondary storage have different maximum capacities. Another characteristic is the speed at which data can be retrieved from secondary storage. Different forms of secondary storage can retrieve data at different rates. Businesses need to be aware of these characteristics when selecting secondary storage for computers used in information systems.

Magnetic Disk Storage

The most widely used form of secondary storage is magnetic disk, or simply *disk*. Magnetic disk storage is used on all types of computers, from microcomputers to supercomputers.

Magnetic Disks. A **magnetic disk** is a flat, round platter made of metal or plastic and covered with a metallic coating, which can be magnetized at different spots. You probably remember that a magnet has a north end and a south end. When a spot

FIGURE 4.24

▲ **Tracks on a magnetic disk**

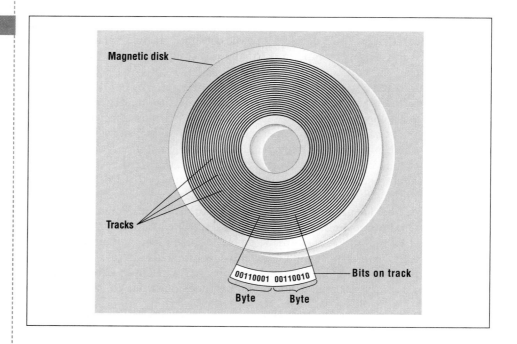

on a disk is magnetized, imagine that a magnet is placed there. The magnet may be aligned with the north end up or with the south end up. To store data on the disk, let one way of aligning the magnet (north end up) represent the digit 1 and the other way (south end up) represent the digit 0. Thus, each spot of magnetism stores a binary digit, or bit, on the surface of the disk.

Millions of bits (magnets) can be recorded on a magnetic disk. The bits are organized into concentric circles called **tracks** (Figure 4.24). The number of tracks on the surfaces of disks vary with different types of disks; some have as few as 40, and others have more than 500 tracks.

The bits along tracks are grouped to form bytes in the same way that the bits in primary storage form bytes. Each byte stores the code for one character of data. The code, such as ASCII or EBCDIC, is the same code used to store data in the primary storage of the computer.

The capacity of a magnetic disk depends on the number of bytes per track and the number of tracks. Early disks could store only a few hundred thousand bytes. For example, the disk used with the original IBM PC stored 360 kilobytes. Current disks can store millions, billions, and even trillions of bytes. For example, disks on most microcomputers can store many gigabytes. Minicomputers and mainframe computers have hard disks that can store hundreds of gigabytes or even many terabytes.

Because data is stored magnetically on a disk, the data remains on the disk even when the power to the computer is turned off. This characteristic explains why data is permanent on a disk, unlike data in primary storage. The data can be changed, however, by realigning the magnetic spots.

Magnetic disks come in various forms and sizes. A **floppy disk** is made of plastic with a metallic coating. The most common floppy disk is 3½ inches in diameter. A **hard disk** is made of rigid metal and ranges in size from less than 2 inches to 14 inches across. Sometimes a single hard disk is used, and at other times several disks are stacked on top of each other, with space between the disks. This latter arrangement is called a **disk pack**. Because both sides of a disk are used to record data, a disk pack with three disks, for example, has six surfaces on which data can be recorded.

FIGURE 4.25

A magnetic disk drive ▲

Magnetic Disk Drives.   A magnetic disk is a medium on which data is stored. To use the disk, it must be in a **magnetic disk drive**, usually just called a *disk drive* (Figure 4.25). This device stores data on a disk and retrieves data from a disk. The disk drive rotates the disk at a speed ranging from 300 to 7,000 revolutions per minute, depending on the type of disk. While the disk is rotating, an access arm comes out of the side of the disk drive; at the end of the arm is a read/write head (Figure 4.26). The access arm can position the read/write head over any track on the disk. As the disk rotates, data can be stored on the track by sending electronic signals to the read/write head; that is, the read/write head can *write* data on the disk. Similarly, as the disk rotates, the data stored on a track can be retrieved by the read/write head; that is, the read/write head can *read* data from the disk. When data is written on a disk, any data

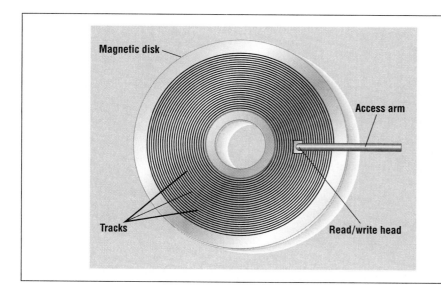

FIGURE 4.26

A magnetic disk in a disk drive ▲

in the same place is destroyed, but when data is read from a disk, the data is not destroyed.

A disk drive has one access arm and read/write head for each side of a disk. Thus, a floppy disk drive has two access arms and a hard disk drive for a disk pack with three disks has six access arms. All arms move back and forth in unison.

The speed at which data can be retrieved from a magnetic disk depends on how fast the disk rotates and how quickly the access arm moves. Floppy disk drives are the slowest. The average time to retrieve data from a floppy disk and transfer it to primary storage can be as slow as one-third of a second. A hard disk drive is much faster. The average time to retrieve data from a hard disk and transfer it to primary storage can be as fast as one-hundredth of a second.

Floppy disks can always be removed from the disk drive, but hard disks may be removable or nonremovable. An advantage of removable disks is that they allow unlimited storage capacity; if you use all the space on a disk, you just remove it and insert another disk. Nonremovable disks have the advantages of being more reliable, being faster at transferring data, and having greater storage capacity.[2]

Some disk systems include many disks or disk packs on which data is stored. These systems, called **RAID**, for *redundant array of inexpensive disks*, allow data to be duplicated on other disks or spread across a number of disks. The advantage of this approach is that if any disk or disk pack fails, the data can be recovered from the other disks. Thus, RAID systems provide a high level of reliability for storing important business data.

Magnetic Disk Access. Recall from Chapter 3 that business data in secondary storage is stored in files. A file consists of many records, each record has many fields, and each field consists of one or more characters. On a magnetic disk, each byte on a track stores one character (Figure 4.27). The bytes are grouped to form fields, and all

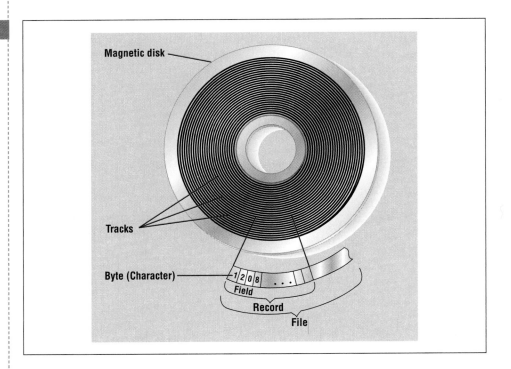

FIGURE 4.27

Magnetic disk data organization

▲

Magnetic disk

Tracks

Byte (Character)

Field

Record

File

[2]Sometimes people use the term *hard drive* for the disk drive with a nonremovable hard disk on a personal computer.

the fields in a record are grouped together on a track. One record is stored after another along a track, and each track can usually hold several records. When a track is full, another track is used, and so a file may occupy many tracks.

Data is written on or read from a disk one record at a time. To write a record on a disk, instructions in a computer program tell the computer to send the data for the record from primary storage to the disk drive, which then records the data on the disk. Any data in the space where the record is written is destroyed when new data is written on the disk. To read a record from a disk, program instructions tell the computer to retrieve the data in the record from the disk and bring it into primary storage. When data in a record is read, the original data in that record on the disk is not destroyed.

When the disk drive reads or writes a record in a file, the drive can position the read/write head at the first track of the file and read or write the data in sequence, one record at a time, moving the read/write head from track to track. This method is called **sequential access** because the disk drive goes through the records in the file in sequence. It is also possible for the disk drive to move the read/write head to any track in a file, and read or write a specific record on that track without going through other records in the file. This method is called **random**, or **direct**, **access**. The records in the file are read or written in random order by moving the read/write head forward and backward to any track in the file.

Magnetic Disk Usage.   Magnetic disk is the main form of secondary storage on most computers because it enables large volumes of data to be stored or retrieved rapidly. In addition, data can be accessed randomly or sequentially. Because of these characteristics, many computers use magnetic disk as their sole form of secondary storage.

Microcomputers usually have one or two floppy disk drives and a nonremovable hard disk. Larger computers usually have one or more removable hard disks. Some mainframe computers have dozens of hard disk drives. Some minicomputers and mainframe computers also have nonremovable hard disks.

Optical Disk Storage

Another form of secondary storage that was developed more recently than magnetic disk and that has become extremely common is optical disk. Optical disks are used with all types of computers.

Optical Disks.   An **optical disk** is a round metal platter on which small holes or pits are used to store data (Figure 4.28). A pit represents the binary digit 1; the absence of a pit represents the binary digit 0. Thus, the surface of an optical disk is covered with pits that represent data in the same way that magnetic spots on a magnetic disk represent data. This system of storing data is similar to that used for storing music on compact disks.

Data is recorded on an optical disk along a single track that spirals into the center of the disk. The bits along a track are grouped to form bytes, just as on a magnetic disk.

Optical disks come in several sizes, but the most common, called **compact disks (CDs)**, is about 5 inches in diameter. Because the bits can be placed very close together, a single CD can store more than 600 megabytes of data. This large capacity is one of the main reasons CDs are used. Even higher-capacity optical disks, called **DVDs**, for *digital video disks* or *digital versatile disks*, can store much more data, between 4.7 gigabytes and 17 gigabytes depending on how it is used.

FIGURE 4.28

▲ Optical disk storage

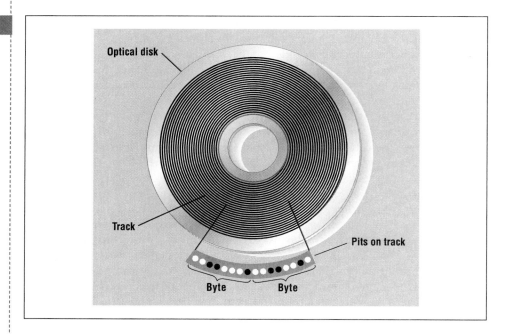

Optical Disk Drives.   To record data on an optical disk, the disk is put into an **optical disk drive**. In the drive, a high-powered laser burns pits into the disk's surface as it turns the disk. Data can be recorded only once because there is no way of erasing the pits after they are burned into the disk. To retrieve data from the disk, a low-powered laser is used to sense the pits on the disk's surface. The data can be retrieved as many times as needed. The speed at which data can be retrieved from an optical disk falls between that of a floppy disk and that of a hard disk.

Most optical disk drives only retrieve–that is, read–data from disks. For CDs, this type of disk drive is called a **CD-ROM**, which stands for *compact disk-read only memory*, and for DVDs, this type is called a **DVD-ROM**, for *digital video (versatile) disk-read only memory*. The disks used with CD-ROMs and DVD-ROMs contain prerecorded data such as a computerized encyclopedia or a movie video. CD-ROMs and DVD-ROMs are used mainly with microcomputers.

Some optical disk drives can store, or *write*, data once and read the data many times. In general, this type is called a *WORM* drive, which stands for *write once, read many*. WORM drives can be used to store data that is not likely to change in the future, such as old business records. After the data is stored, it can be retrieved repeatedly. WORM drives are found on all sizes of computers. A WORM drive for a CD is called a **CD-R**, for *compact disk-recordable*.

Optical Disk Access.   Data on optical disks can be accessed sequentially or randomly. Sequential access is accomplished by using the laser to read data in sequence along the track on the disk. In random access, the laser is moved to the part of the disk where the data is stored. Then, as the disk rotates, data is retrieved from that part of the disk.

Optical Disk Usage.   Optical disks have several common uses. One is for storing large amounts of prerecorded information sold to consumers, which is the common use of CDs and DVDs. Encyclopedias, dictionaries, cookbooks, and other reference works are available on optical disks. Works of literature, such as the complete works of Shakespeare, are also available. Many computer programs and games are sold on optical disks.

Another use of optical disk is for recording multimedia material. Because optical disks use the same technology used in music and video disks, optical disks can store music, pictures, and video, as well as words and diagrams, which makes them ideal for storing multimedia presentations. Many multimedia titles are available on CD and DVD. Many full-length motion pictures are available on DVD.

Optical disks are also used to store data for *archival* purposes. Data appropriate for such storage is not normally changed in the future, such as old tax records for a business and transcripts of students who have graduated from a college. Data storage requires a writable optical disk drive such as a WORM drive. Because archival data normally is not changed in the future, the fact that the data cannot be erased is not important.

Rewritable Optical Disks.   Several types of optical disk drives are available that can erase data on an optical disk and write new data on the disk. One type, called **CD-RW**, for *compact disk-rewritable*, is a CD drive that uses a laser to create spots on a CD surface that appear to be pits when read back. The spots can be erased, however, so that new data can be recorded on the disk.

Another type of rewritable optical disk drive records data in a magnetic form, like a magnetic disk drive. Consequently, the data can easily be erased and changed. To record data, however, the optical disk drive uses a laser. To retrieve data from the disk, another laser is used. Because this type of optical disk drive uses both magnetic and laser (optical) techniques, it is called a *magneto-optical*, or *MO, disk* drive.

Magnetic Tape Storage

The last common form of secondary storage is magnetic tape, or simply *tape*. Developed before magnetic or optical disk, magnetic tape is much less common than the other forms of storage. Although tape can be used on all types of computers, including microcomputers, it is most commonly found on minicomputers and mainframe computers.

Magnetic Tapes.   A **magnetic tape** is made of a plastic material covered with a metallic coating, which can be magnetized at different spots, much like audio recording tape. The spots of magnetism on magnetic tape are similar to those on a magnetic disk and represent bits on the surface of the tape.

Several approaches are used to record data on a tape. In one approach, the bits on a tape are recorded along parallel tracks. Bytes are stored on the tape by recording 1 bit of the byte in each track across the tape. The capacity of tape ranges from 200 megabytes to over 40 gigabytes.

As with magnetic disks, data stored on a tape remains there when the power to the computer is turned off, because the data is stored magnetically. The data can be changed, however, by changing the magnetic spots on the tape and thus changing the bits that are stored.

Tapes come in various forms and sizes. One form is open-reel tape, which is $\frac{1}{2}$-inch wide and usually comes on reels that are $10\frac{1}{2}$ inches in diameter. Another form is cartridge tape, which is $\frac{1}{2}$-inch or $\frac{1}{4}$-inch wide.

Magnetic Tape Drives.   Data is stored on and retrieved from a magnetic tape by using a **magnetic tape drive**, often just called a *tape drive* (Figure 4.29). In the tape drive, the tape is fed past a read/write head. Data can be stored (written) on the tape

FIGURE 4.29

▲ A magnetic tape drive

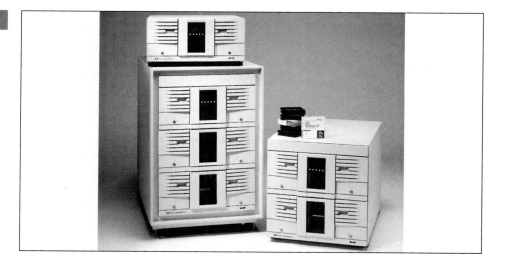

by sending electronic signals to the read/write head. Similarly, data stored on the tape can be retrieved (read) by the read/write head. As with magnetic disks, writing data destroys existing data, but reading data does not.

Magnetic tape can always be removed from the tape drive. Thus, tape provides unlimited storage capacity. When a tape is full, it can be removed and replaced by another tape. Some organizations have thousands of tapes in a *tape library.*

Magnetic Tape Access. Data on magnetic tape can only be accessed sequentially. When reading or writing data on a tape, the tape drive starts at the beginning of the tape and reads or writes the data in sequence. It is not possible to go forward without reading or writing data along the way, and it is not possible to go backward, except back to the beginning of the tape. Thus, unlike magnetic and optical disks, data on a tape cannot be accessed in random order.

The speed at which data can be retrieved from a magnetic tape depends on where the data is located. If the data is at the beginning of the tape, it can be retrieved quickly, maybe as quickly as retrieving data from a floppy disk. On the other hand, if the data is in the middle or at the end of a tape, it can take minutes or even hours to retrieve the data.

Magnetic Tape Usage. Magnetic tape is not used as the main form of secondary storage on a computer because tape data can only be accessed sequentially, and usually an information system needs to access some data randomly. Normally, tape is used along with magnetic disk on a computer. Tapes are much less expensive, however, than disks, so when data needs only to be accessed sequentially, tape could be used. Tape is most often used for storing copies of disk data, called **backup copies**, in case the original data is lost or destroyed.

CHAPTER SUMMARY

1 The main components of a computer are the **input device**, the **output device**, **primary storage**, the **central processing unit** (**CPU**), and **secondary** storage. An input device accepts data from outside the computer and converts it to an electronic form understandable to the computer. An output device converts data from an electronic form inside the computer to a form that can be used outside the computer. Primary storage stores data and program instructions currently being processed. The CPU carries out instructions in the program. Secondary storage stores data and programs not currently being processed. (pp. 92–94)

2 Common input devices are **keyboards**, and pointing devices, such as **mouse, trackball, trackpoint**, and **trackpad** devices. Other types of input devices are touch input devices (**touch screens, pen input** devices, graphics tablets, light pens, and digitizer tablets), optical scanning input devices (**bar-code scanners**, image or page **scanners**, optical character recognition [OCR] devices, and mark-sense readers), magnetic scanning input devices (**magnetic strip readers** and **MICR** devices), voice input devices, and camera input devices. Common output devices are **screens** and **printers**. Screens can be either **CRT monitors** or **flat-panel screens**. Printers can be **impact** or **non-impact printers; serial, line,** or **page printers**; and **letter-quality** or **draft-quality printers**. Desktop printers include **ink-jet, laser,** and **dot-matrix printers**. High-volume printers include line printers and page printers. Other types of output devices are **plotters**, voice output devices, and sound output devices. A **terminal** is a combination input and output device. A common type of terminal is a **video display terminal** (**VDT**), which consists of a keyboard and a screen. People with disabilities may need special input and output devices, such as Braille displays, to use computers, or they may be able to use common devices with enhanced features, such as screen displays with large type. Input and output devices used for multimedia presentation include keyboards, pointing devices, high-resolution screens, and speakers or headphones. **Virtual reality** input and output devices include headsets and gloves that sense hand movement. (pp. 94–109)

3 Data is represented in a computer in a binary form—that is, as patterns of **binary digits**, or **bits**, which are the digits 1 and 0. Characters are represented by using a code for each character. Examples of codes are **ASCII, EBCDIC,** and **Unicode**. Computers using different codes cannot communicate with each other without hardware or software to convert between the codes. (pp. 111–112)

4 Primary storage consists of many electronic circuits, each capable of storing 1 bit. The bits are organized into groups called **storage locations**. Each storage location is a **byte**, which is a group of bits capable of storing one character of data. The storage capacity of computers is measured in terms of **kilobytes** (thousands of bytes), **megabytes** (millions of bytes), **gigabytes** (billions of bytes), and **terabytes** (trillions of bytes). It is important that a computer have enough primary storage to store the data and programs needed for current processing. (pp. 112–113)

5 The central processing unit consists of the **arithmetic-logic unit** (**ALU**) and the **control unit**. The ALU performs arithmetic operations and makes logical comparisons. The control unit analyzes and executes instructions in a program. The instructions are in a basic form called **machine language**. Different computers use different types of machine language instructions, and so machine language programs for different computers may be incompatible. (pp. 113–116)

6 Data is recorded on a **magnetic disk** by spots of magnetism representing bits along concentric circles on the disk's surface, called **tracks**. A **magnetic disk drive** stores data on a disk by moving the read/write head at the end of the access arm to the appropriate track, and writing the data on the track as the disk rotates. A magnetic disk drive retrieves data from a disk by moving the read/write head to the appropriate track and reading the data recorded there as the disk rotates. Data can be retrieved in sequence from a series of tracks, which is called **sequential access**, or from a specific track not in sequence, which is called **random access**. Data is recorded on **optical disks** by pits that represent bits recorded along a track on the disk's surface. The pits are created by a high-powered laser in an **optical disk drive**. After the data is recorded in this manner, it cannot be changed because the pits cannot be erased. The data can be retrieved by sensing the pits with a low-powered laser in an optical disk drive. Data can be accessed sequentially or randomly on an optical disk. Types of optical disks are **CDs** and **DVDs**. Data is recorded on **magnetic tape** by spots of magnetism representing bits recorded along tracks on the tape's surface. A **magnetic tape drive** stores data on a tape by moving the tape past a read/write head and writing the data on the tape.

A tape drive retrieves data from a tape by moving the tape past a read/write head and reading the data recorded on the tape. Data can be accessed only sequentially on magnetic tape. (pp. 119–126)

KEY TERMS

Address (p. 112)
Arithmetic-Logic Unit (ALU) (p. 113)
ASCII (p. 111)
Backup Copy (p. 126)
Bar-Code Scanner (p. 97)
Binary Digit (Bit) (p. 111)
Byte (p. 112)
CD-R (p. 124)
CD-ROM (p. 124)
CD-RW (p. 125)
Central Processing Unit (CPU) (p. 93)
Chip (p. 109)
Compact Disk (CD) (p. 123)
Computer (p. 92)
Control Unit (p. 113)
CRT (p. 99)
Cursor (p. 95)
Disk Pack (p. 120)
Dot-Matrix Printer (p. 102)
Draft-Quality Printer (p. 101)
DVD (p. 123)
DVD-ROM (p. 124)
EBCDIC (p. 111)
Ergonomics (p. 94)
Flat-Panel Screen (p. 99)
Floppy Disk (p. 120)
Gigabyte (G byte, GB) (p. 113)
Gigahertz (GHz) (p. 116)
Hard Disk (p. 120)
Impact Printer (p. 100)
Ink-Jet Printer (p. 101)
Input Device (p. 92)

Keyboard (p. 94)
Kilobyte (K byte, KB) (p. 112)
Laser Printer (p. 101)
Letter-Quality Printer (p. 101)
Line Printer (p. 101)
Machine Language (p. 115)
Magnetic Disk (p. 119)
Magnetic Disk Drive (p. 121)
Magnetic Ink Character Recognition (MICR) (p. 98)
Magnetic Strip Reader (p. 97)
Magnetic Tape (p. 125)
Magnetic Tape Drive (p. 125)
Massively Parallel Processing (p. 119)
Megabyte (M byte, MB) (p. 113)
Megahertz (MHz) (p. 116)
Microprocessor (p. 117)
Microsecond (p. 116)
Millisecond (p. 116)
Monitor (p. 99)
Mouse (p. 95)
Multifunction Printer (p. 102)
Multimedia (p. 106)
Multiprocessing (p. 119)
Nanosecond (p. 116)
Nonimpact Printer (p. 100)
Nonvolatile Storage (p. 110)
Optical Disk (p. 123)
Optical Disk Drive (p. 124)
Output Device (p. 92)
Page Printer (p. 101)
Pen Input (p. 96)
Peripheral Equipment (p. 94)

Pixel (p. 99)
Plotter (p. 103)
Primary (Internal) Storage (p. 92)
Printer (p. 100)
Processor (p. 93)
Program (p. 92)
RAID (p. 122)
Random Access Memory (RAM) (p. 110)
Random (Direct) Access (p. 123)
Read-Only Memory (ROM) (p. 110)
Scanner (p. 97)
Screen (p. 99)
Screen Projector (p. 100)
Screen Resolution (p. 99)
Secondary (Auxiliary) Storage (p. 94)
Sequential Access (p. 123)
Serial Printer (p. 101)
Storage Location (p. 112)
Terabyte (T byte, TB) (p. 113)
Terminal (p. 104)
Touch Screen (p. 96)
Track (p. 120)
Trackball (p. 95)
Trackpad (p. 95)
Trackpoint (p. 95)
Unicode (p. 112)
Video Display Terminal (VDT) (p. 104)
Virtual Reality (p. 107)
Volatile Storage (p. 110)

REVIEW QUESTIONS

1 What are the five basic components of a computer?

2 What is ergonomics and why is it important in computer information systems?

3 What are two purposes of a pointing device?

4 What are two touch input devices?

5 What is meant by screen resolution?

6 What is the difference between impact and nonimpact printers?

7 How are the speeds of different types of printers measured?

8 What are the two main types of high-volume printers?

9 What is a video display terminal, and what is it used for?

10 What special I/O devices are used for virtual reality?

11 What is the difference between volatile and non-volatile storage?

12 What is the difference between RAM and ROM?

13 What do we mean when we say data is stored in binary representation in a computer?

14 What are two codes for representing data in computers?

15 What is a gigabyte? What is a nanosecond?

16 What are the main units in the CPU, and what does each do?

17 What do we mean when we say two CPUs are compatible?

18 If a computer salesperson tells you that one microcomputer has a 600 MHz CPU and another has a 700 MHz CPU, what does this mean?

19 What is parallel processing, and why is it used?

20 How is data recorded on a magnetic disk?

21 How does a magnetic disk drive store and retrieve data on a magnetic disk?

22 What is the difference between sequential access and random access?

23 Can data on an optical disk be changed? Explain.

24 How does a tape drive store and retrieve data on a magnetic tape?

DISCUSSION QUESTIONS

1 Identify several computational devices that are not computers (e.g., abacus, pocket calculator). Explain why each is not a computer as defined in the chapter.

2 Many colleges and universities use a telephone system for course registration. What input and output devices does a student use with this system? What input and output devices does the college's or university's administrators use?

3 Computer speed and storage capacity increase with each new model. Why do you think this is true? Is this necessary? Why or why not?

4 How do the components of a computer other than the CPU affect the speed of the computer?

5 Why does a computer have two forms of storage, primary storage and secondary storage? Why does it not have just one, large form of storage?

6 Why do computers often have several different forms of secondary storage?

ETHICS QUESTIONS

1 Assume that the business you work for has decided not to get ergonomically designed keyboards for its data entry clerks who use a keyboard up to 8 hours per day. Instead, the business has decided to pay medical bills for any employees who suffer repetitive strain injuries, arguing that this approach will be less expensive. What ethical issues does this decision raise?

2 Assume that you have to decide which of two applicants to hire for a job that involves extensive computer use. One applicant has a disability and the other does not. The applicant with the disability is somewhat more qualified for the job, but your company would have to buy several thousand dollars' worth of special computer equipment for the person to use. What ethical issues does this situation raise? How would you make your decision?

3 The speed of computers continually increases. As a result, more output is produced faster. Some people feel they cannot keep up with computers or the output they produce. They feel as though they are being left behind by the "information age." If you were a manager in a business and had an employee who felt this way, what options would you have for dealing with this employee, and what are the ethical issues involved in evaluating the options?

PROBLEM-SOLVING PROJECTS

1 If you have a computer or have access to one, find out everything you can about it. What input and output devices does it have? How much primary storage capacity does it have? What CPU does it use? What forms of secondary storage does it have? Write a brief description of the computer.

2 Visit computer stores to gather information about several personal computers that you might be interested in buying. Develop a spreadsheet in which the columns are the different personal computers and the rows are characteristics of the computers. The characteristics might include, among others, the types of input and output devices, the amount of primary storage, the type of CPU, the number and type of secondary storage devices, the software included, and the price.

3 The total cost of a printer includes not only the purchase price, but also the cost of operation. Operating costs include the cost of paper, ribbons, ink, and so on. Set up a spreadsheet to determine the total cost and the cost per printed page of an ink-jet, laser, and dot-matrix printer. Include in your spreadsheet the purchase price and the operating costs. Assume that the printer will have a useful life of three years and that you can sell it for 25% of its purchase price after three years. Assume that you print an average of 5,000 pages per year. Use the following data in the spreadsheet or get real data for printers from a computer store:

Type of printer	Ink-jet	Laser	Dot-matrix
Purchase price	$220	$450	$180
Paper cost	$2/500 pages	$2/500 pages	$15/2,500 pages
Ribbon/ink cost	$30/1,000 pages	$80/3,000 pages	$12/2,500 pages

4 New models of microprocessors are introduced regularly. Using appropriate software, set up a table that lists information about microprocessors. Have columns for the manufacturer, model, clock speed, computers in which the microprocessor is used, and any other information you want to include. Research information about current microprocessors using whatever method you want, including the Web. Enter the information into your table about the microprocessors. As new models are introduced, add information about them to your table.

5 Personal computers sold at retail stores need to have characteristics that appeal to consumers. Market research is often used to gather information about consumer preference. Some questions that might be asked in a questionnaire about consumer taste in computers are the following:

- Do you prefer computers that are putty (light beige), black, or another color?
- Do you prefer a standard keyboard or an ergonomic keyboard?
- Do you prefer a mouse, a trackball, or some other pointing device?
- Do you prefer speakers that are attached to the monitor or separate from the monitor?
- Do you prefer a monitor that is separate from the CPU box or combined with the CPU box?

Prepare a questionnaire based on these questions and others that you think of. Include a "no preference" answer for each question. Give the questionnaire to at least 15 people. (You might want to have everyone in your class complete the questionnaire.) Then use a spreadsheet to analyze the results. Enter the response from the questionnaires into the spreadsheet. For each question, compute and plot on a graph the response percentages. For example, for the first question, compute and graph the percentage of people who prefer putty, the percentage who prefer black, the percentage who prefer another color, and the percentage who have no preference.

INTERNET AND ELECTRONIC COMMERCE PROJECTS

1 Use the Web to find information on several input or output devices not covered in this chapter. Write a brief report summarizing your findings.

2 In 1965 Gordon Moore, one of the cofounders of Intel, made an observation about how the number of circuits on a silicon chip changes over time. This relationship has become known as "Moore's Law." Use the Web to find information about Moore's Law. What is the law? Has it held until now? Do people think it will hold in the future? Write a report on what you find.

3 Find a Web site through which you can order computers for home delivery. Use the site to find the cost of several different configurations of computer systems. How easy is the site to use? What would make the site easier to use? Write a summary of what you find. Include with your summary a printout of the configuration and the price of each computer system you check.

real world case

Chevron

Imagine users at a giant global corporation not being able to perform a routine computing task, such as opening a Word document. This was exactly the problem that Chevron faced recently. Because of desktop platform differences and memory constraints on PCs and applications used by the tens of thousands of end users from Nigeria to California, simple desktop tasks became impossible. That caused Chevron's information technology managers to realize something had to change.

Over a nine-month period, all the existing hardware was removed, and at a cost of $20 million, Chevron implemented its new information technology strategy—GIL (Global Information Link)—which started with standardizing desktop and mobile computers for all Chevron users.

Chevron's push to adopt a standard across its massive desktop infrastructure reduced the San Francisco-based company's annual operating expense by $35 million. The GIL initiative has also allowed Chevron to roll out standard LAN and WAN technologies around the world and provide Internet access for everyone in the company.

"We wanted to make sure that we were using technology to achieve a competitive advantage," says Sheila Taylor, general manager of shared services with Chevron Information Technology, in San Ramon, California.

"Part of that is enabling Chevron users to take advantage of the network world," Taylor says. "We said that every employee in Chevron must have access to the Chevron [internal network] and the ability to not only collaborate internally but also with customers."

That's not a small task when many users are at oil camps in remote regions of the world. Sites located on oil rigs in the Caspian Sea and Papua New Guinea were to be given the same access as those at corporate headquarters in San Francisco, which meant setting up satellite connections along with the new WAN infrastructure.

To help put this infrastructure in place, Chevron looked for a single PC vendor that could offer a wide variety of system configurations and

has a global presence to provide service worldwide. Chevron's choice: Hewlett-Packard (HP).

Today, Chevron's end users are each equipped with Pentium II-based machines. Its desktop systems, numbering about 24,000 worldwide, are HP Vectra VL 6 machines. Each of these 266 MHz Pentium II computers includes 64 MB of RAM, a 4 GB hard disk drive, a CD-ROM drive, a 3.5-inch floppy drive, a 17-inch monitor, a sound card, headphones, and network interface hardware.

Another 4,000 Chevron users have 166 MHz Pentium II HP OmniBook 5700 notebooks. 4P OmniBook 7100 notebooks serve as Chevron's scientific, in-the-field notebook for about 50 users. These 266 MHz Pentium II-based machines include 14-inch displays, three-dimensional video acceleration capabilities, and 8 GB hard disk drives.

Chevron does not use HP exclusively, however. Chevron selected IBM for its lighter notebook. Chevron bought about 1,000 IBM ThinkPad 560X notebook computers with 233 MHz Pentium II processors for users who travel frequently and need a featherweight solution.

Now, with the help of HP, Chevron allows universal access to corporate data. "If you are traveling to the Caspian Sea and take your laptop, you can plug it into the network and work just like you are sitting in San Francisco," says Bob Araldi, HP's client business manager responsible for the Chevron account.

Chevron also benefits from the widespread Internet access, which includes connecting external customers through several e-commerce initiatives. One of the business-to-business e-commerce projects is the Chevron Retailer Alliance, an Internet-based system that connects Chevron service stations with corporate headquarters. The system allows Chevron gas stations to access information, purchase fuel and items for their convenience stores, and track invoices. As part of the e-commerce initiative, Chevron service stations are also upgrading to the HP desktop hardware.

Chevron's corporate users have universal access to more than 4,000 desktop applications via the company internal network. In addition to Microsoft's Office, including Internet Explorer, which is used on each desktop for communications and general functions, Chevron's internal network provides access to thousands of programs for various businesses and departments. "Any employee can go on the [network] and download any application," Taylor says.

The GIL infrastructure, including desktop, notebook, server, and network devices, is managed by 80 central design and support staffers and 250 field support staffers. In fact, the desktop upgrade was partly driven by a need to centrally manage computers. It was also done to provide ubiquitous access to applications, including everything from a companywide financial system to a reservoir simulation program used in Nigeria.

Accompanying these applications are collaboration tools such as Microsoft NetMeeting, which helps Chevron bring together employees who may be oceans apart. For example, if a Chevron machine operator in Nigeria requires technical help, a year ago that would have required calling a U.S. office, describing the problem, and possibly waiting for an expert to be flown in. But Net-Meeting allows the operator in Nigeria to share oil well data over the company internal network to solve the problem.

Chevron's information technology group credits all the standardization aspects of GIL with streamlining operations companywide. Ironically, in Chevron's case, standardization has led to innovation because Chevron officials now recognize how they can do business better, Taylor says.

Questions

1. What problems did Chevron have that prompted the company to standardize desktop and mobile computer hardware?
2. What type of desktop computer did Chevron select, and what are its specifications?
3. What notebook computers did Chevron select, and for what types of users is each intended?
4. What is the Chevron Retailer Alliance, and what is it used for?
5. What benefits did Chevron receive from standardizing hardware?

Web Site
Chevron: www.chevron.com

Source: *Adapted from* Kristina B. Sullivan, "Chevron Hits the Gas on PC Standardization," *PC Week*, June 21, 1999, p 82.

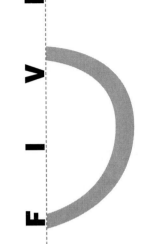

Information System
SOFTWARE

FIVE

After completing this chapter, you should be able to

1 Explain in detail what programs and software are.

2 Identify the common application software used in information systems.

3 Describe some ways users can tell an operating system what to do.

4 Describe some of the capabilities of operating systems.

5 Explain the main differences between the five types, or generations, of programming languages.

6 Explain the difference between object-oriented programming and traditional programming, and identify one traditional and one object-oriented programming language.

7 Identify programming languages that are used with the Internet and the World Wide Web.

CHAPTER OUTLINE

Software Concepts
Application Software
System Software
Software Development

The software component of an information system consists of all the programs used in the system. Software is needed because hardware cannot function without it; computers and computer-controlled equipment must have programs to tell them what to do. Information system software tells the hardware in the system how to perform the functions required of the system.

This chapter examines computer software used in information systems. First, it describes software in general. Then it explains different types of application software. Next it looks into system software, especially operating systems. Finally, the chapter describes how software is developed.

Software Concepts

The words *program* and *software* are often used interchangeably. A *program* is a set of instructions that tells the computer what to do. *Software* can be a single program, or it can be a group of programs needed to perform several functions. For example, for payroll processing several programs are needed, including a program to print paychecks each week, one to produce reports for the government every few months, and another to prepare tax forms for employees at the end of the year. Each program by itself is software, but all the programs together are also software—payroll software.

Programs must have instructions that tell the computer the step-by-step process necessary to perform the required tasks. No instruction can be left out, for if it is, the computer will not know what to do. Similarly, no instruction can be out of place. The computer follows the instructions as they appear in the program, whether they are right or wrong.

The instructions in a program are executed in sequence by the central processing unit (CPU), as described in Chapter 4. The sequence can be changed by including special types of instructions. For example, one type of instruction tells the computer to do one of two sets of other instructions based on the value of certain data. (This pattern is called a *decision*.) This type of instruction would be used in a payroll program to decide whether to do a regular time or an overtime payroll calculation, based on the number of hours the employee has worked. Another type of instruction tells the computer to repeat a group of instructions as long as some condition is true. (This pattern is called a *loop*.) In a payroll program, this type of instruction would be used to tell the computer to repeat the payroll calculation as long as there are employees left to be paid.

Simple programs can contain just a few hundred instructions, but most programs have tens or hundreds of thousands or even millions of instructions. A word processing program, for example, typically has several million instructions. Later this chapter describes the forms instructions in a program take and how software is developed.

Application Software

Application software is the software that performs the functions of an information system. The user interacts with the application software when entering input into an application program and receiving output from the program. The application program also performs the processing and storage functions required by the information system.

Because most of this book is devoted to information systems and the application software used in these systems, this section only summarizes the common applica-

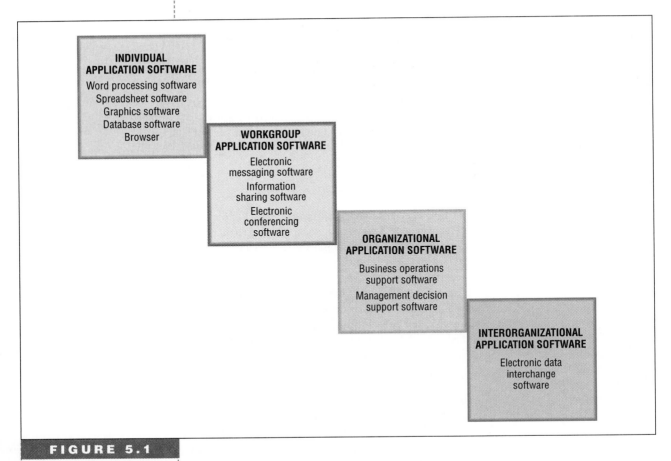

FIGURE 5.1

▲ **Common application software**

tion software. Figure 5.1 lists some of the common application software used in businesses.

Individual Application Software

The application software with which many users are most familiar is individual, or personal, application software, which is software used by a single person for an individual purpose. This type of software is usually used on a personal computer system, which may be connected to a network.

Word processing software is probably the most widely used type of individual application software. With word processing software, a user can enter the text of a document—such as a letter or report—into the computer, make changes in the document, and print one or more copies of the document. The user can save the document in secondary storage and return to it in the future, perhaps to make changes and print another copy.

Spreadsheet software is also a widely used type of individual application software. With spreadsheet software, the user can create an *electronic spreadsheet*, which is a computerized arrangement, in rows and columns, of data and formulas for calculating spreadsheet values. The electronic spreadsheet can be used to analyze data such as budgets and income projections. The user can change values or formulas in the spreadsheet to see the effect of the change, and can print copies of the spreadsheet for presentation to others.

Another type of individual application software is **graphics software**. This type of software allows the user to create various types of graphic output on a screen or on paper. Graphs, charts, diagrams, designs, art, and other forms of visual images can be created with graphics software. Several types of graphics software are available. For example, some graphics software lets users create images for use in a presentation, and other graphics software lets users create engineering designs. Software that is not graphics software sometimes include graphic capabilities. An example is spreadsheet software that includes features for creating graphs or charts from the data in a spreadsheet.

Database software is another common type of individual application software. With database software, the user can store large amounts of data in a database in secondary storage, change data in the database when necessary, and retrieve data from the database to find useful information. For example, a salesperson can store customer data in a database; modify the data when information about a customer, such as the phone number, changes; and retrieve data about a customer, such as when the last sales contact was made and what was purchased.

Another type of software used for individual applications is a **browser**. With a browser, a user can view screens, called **pages**, on the Web, and go from one page to another. This capability allows a user easy access to information on the Web.

Although there are other types of individual application software, word processing, spreadsheet, graphics, database, and browser software are the most common. The principal benefit of individual application software is that it helps people improve their productivity. Chapter 8 discusses personal productivity and individual application software in detail.

Workgroup Application Software

Users often work in groups and use workgroup application software called **groupware**. This type of software allows users to collaborate with each other without having to be in the same place at the same time. Groupware is used on networked computer systems.

The most widely used form of groupware is e-mail software, which allows a user to send letters and memos electronically to other users. E-mail software is a type of **electronic messaging software**. In general, electronic messaging software provides e-mail capabilities and other capabilities, such as the ability to send work assignments or reminder notes to others.

Another type of groupware is **information sharing software**. With this type of software, users in a group can share ideas by putting notes and comments in a common database that can be viewed by other users. This approach is not the same as using e-mail, in which a message is sent from one person to another, but is more like using a bulletin board that all users can view.

A third type of groupware is **electronic conferencing software**, which lets users talk to and see each other while also viewing a common document on a computer screen (Figure 5.2). This type of software requires a computer with a microphone, speakers, and a video camera, as well as special software. Electronic conferencing is very useful when group members are located some distance apart.

There are a number of other types of groupware, but in general, all workgroup application software is designed to encourage collaboration between group members. Chapter 9 discusses group collaboration and workgroup application software in detail.

Organizational Application Software

Much application software used in a business is designed to provide applications that affect more than an individual or a workgroup. The most all-encompassing information systems in a business use such organizational application software, which can be run on networked or multiple-user computer systems.

FIGURE 5.2

▲ Electronic conferencing

Some organizational application software is designed to support the day-to-day operations of a business. This type of software, which usually processes basic business transactions such as the sale of products or the purchase of items for inventory, increases the efficiency of business operations. Chapter 10 discusses business operations and the organizational application software used in basic operations.

Other organizational application software supports management decision making in a business. This type of software supplies information to managers to help in decision making. It can also provide ways of analyzing data used in decision making, special support for the highest level of decision making in a business, and expert advice to decision makers. Chapter 11 discusses management decision making and the organization application software used in decision making.

Interorganizational Application Software

Transactions between two businesses can often be done electronically, using interorganizational application software. This type of software, which allows one business's computer to transmit data to another business's computer, is used on networks that operate between two or more businesses.

An example of interorganizational application software is *electronic data interchange (EDI) software*. This type of software lets businesses electronically exchange data about business transactions, such as a request to purchase items or a bill for items purchased. The business does not have to send a paper copy of the request or bill to another business; computers and networks, with the necessary interorganizational application software, provide all the capabilities needed to exchange data.

Interorganizational application software can give a business an advantage over another business by reducing costs and increasing transaction speed. Other types of application software, including those used in organizational and international applications, can affect a business in a similar way. Chapter 12 discusses the types of application software that can have such an impact, including interorganizational application software.

System Software

Application software, which performs the functions of the information system that the user needs, does not work without system software. System software provides capabilities that make computers usable.

The most important system software is the operating system because without it computers would be extremely difficult to use. Operating systems were introduced in Chapter 3. This section takes a look at operating systems in detail and describes other types of system software.

Operating System Concepts

An operating system is a group of programs that manages the operation of the computer. The operating system controls the computer whenever another program, such as another system program or an application program, is not executing. As soon as one program stops executing, the operating system takes control of the computer. It then begins execution of the next program. During the execution of a program, parts of the operating system may be used by the program to perform certain functions.

Figure 5.3 illustrates the role of the operating system in a series of layers. The inner layer is the hardware. Around this layer is the operating system, which communicates with the hardware and manages its operation. If the operating system is in control of the computer, the user can communicate directly with it to perform various functions, as shown in the top half of Figure 5.3. For example, if the user wants to display the contents of a disk, the user gives the operating system an instruction to do so. Then the operating system tells the hardware what to do to display the disk contents. If an application program is executing, the user communicates with that program, as shown in the bottom half of Figure 5.3. The application program may use parts of the operating system to perform certain functions. For example, if the user wants an application program to print certain output, the user tells the program to do so. Then the program gives the operating system an instruction to print, which in turn tells the hardware what to do to print the output.

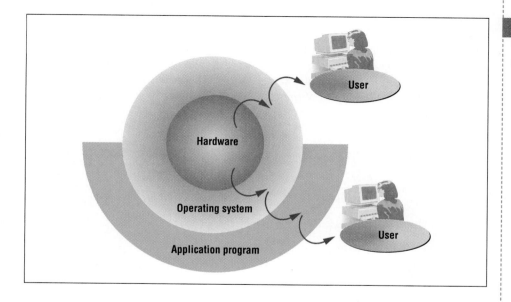

FIGURE 5.3

The role of an operating system

Functions of an Operating System. An operating system has three main functions: process management, resource management, and data management. To understand the first function, *process management*, think of the execution of a program as a process that the computer performs. The operating system keeps track of all processes—that is, all program executions. It schedules programs for execution, starts the execution of programs when needed, and monitors the execution of a program in case an error occurs.

The second main function of an operating system is *resource management*. A computer has many resources, including primary storage, input and output devices, and secondary storage. The operating system assigns the required resources to each process. The operating system determines where in primary storage programs and data are stored, what input and output devices are used by the program, and where in secondary storage program and data files are stored.

The final main function of an operating system is *data management*. The operating system manages the movement of data between the main components of the computer. Any time input data is entered or output data is produced, a part of the operating system controls the transfer of the data between primary storage and the appropriate input or output device. Any transfer of data between primary storage and a data file in secondary storage is handled by another part of the operating system.

Organization of an Operating System. An operating system is made up of many programs. Most of the programs in the operating system are stored in secondary storage, but one program in the operating system is stored in a section of primary storage whenever the computer is running. This program goes by different names, depending on the operating system, but for simplicity we will call it the *supervisor* because it supervises the rest of the operating system. It is the part of the operating system that controls the computer when another program (such as an application program) is not executing.

The part of primary storage not occupied by the supervisor is used to store one or more other programs. To start the execution of a program, the supervisor passes the control of the computer to the program in primary storage (Figure 5.4a). When the program finishes executing, it returns control of the computer to the supervisor. Then the supervisor can start the execution of another program by passing the control of the computer to that program (Figure 5.4b). This process continues for all the programs to be executed.

The supervisor brings programs into primary storage when they are needed. Nonexecuting programs are stored in secondary storage. When a program is needed, the supervisor *loads* it into primary storage. After the supervisor has loaded the program, it can start the execution of the program.

FIGURE 5.4

Operating system control of the execution of programs

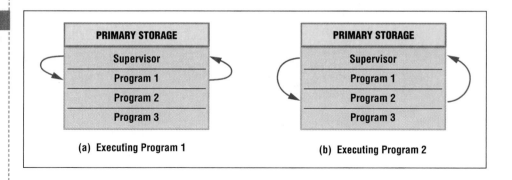

(a) Executing Program 1   (b) Executing Program 2

The supervisor loads the other programs in the operating system into primary storage from secondary storage when they are needed. These other programs perform functions that are used less frequently than those of the supervisor. An example is a program that copies the contents of one disk to another disk. Because this program is not often used, it is stored in secondary storage and loaded only when it is needed.

Using an Operating System.   Although the supervisor is in primary storage whenever the computer is running, it, as well as everything else in primary storage, is lost when the computer is turned off. Thus, when the computer is turned on again, there is nothing in primary storage—not even a program to load the supervisor. How, then, does the supervisor get into primary storage when the computer is turned on?

The process of loading the supervisor into primary storage is called **booting**; someone "boots the computer" or the computer "boots up." The supervisor is stored permanently in secondary storage. A special program for loading the supervisor into primary storage is stored in nonvolatile, read-only memory (ROM). When the switch for the computer is turned on, a circuit is activated that causes the program in ROM to execute. This program then loads the supervisor into primary storage and transfers control of the computer to it.

A user can use a personal computer's operating system immediately after the computer has finished booting. With multiple-user computers, however, a user normally has to go through a process called *logging in* before using the operating system. This process, which connects the user's terminal to the operating system, is needed because multiple-user computers are used by more than one person at a time, and the operating system must have a way of distinguishing the users. After using the computer, the user must disconnect his or her computer or terminal by following a procedure called *logging out*. With networks, a procedure similar to logging in may be necessary to connect the user's computer to the network.

When using an operating system, the user needs to be able to tell it what to do. The way this is accomplished depends on the **user interface**, which is the link between the user and the software (Figure 5.5). Some operating systems have a user interface in which the user keys in words or phrases called **commands** after a **prompt** on the screen, which is a word or symbol indicating that the software is ready for the next input. Many operating systems have a user interface in which the user selects a command from a list, or **menu**, shown on the screen by pointing at it with a mouse and then clicking the mouse. The user interface of most operating systems shows some commands on the screen by using small pictures called **icons**, which the user selects by pointing at an icon with a mouse and then clicking the mouse. Icons or other symbols enclosed in shapes that look like keys on a keyboard are often called **buttons**. In any of these cases, the supervisor interprets the command and performs the requested function for the user.

Operating systems, as well as other software, that use buttons, icons, menus, and other features are said to have a **graphical user interface (GUI)** (Figure 5.6). The user uses the system through the GUI by selecting icons and menu options, and by providing input requested by the system in small boxes called **dialog boxes**. A GUI is also divided into sections surrounded by borders, called **windows**, within which different functions can be performed. The user can change the size and position of windows, and create (open) new windows and delete (close) old ones. Using windows allows the user to customize the graphical user interface.

FIGURE 5.5

Operating system user interfaces

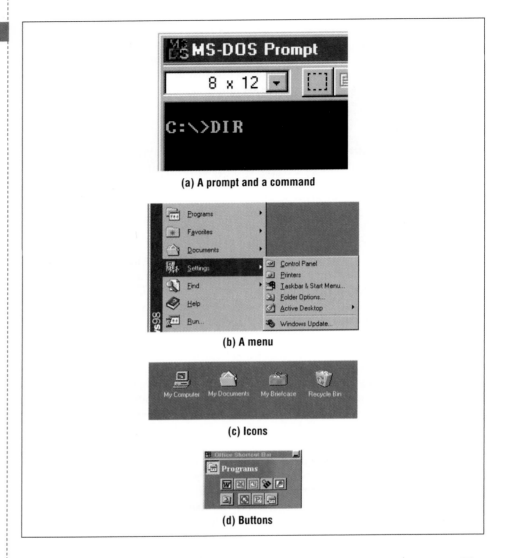

(a) A prompt and a command

(b) A menu

(c) Icons

(d) Buttons

Capabilities of Operating Systems.   Not all operating systems are alike. Different operating systems have different capabilities. Some of the capabilities of operating systems are discussed here.

MULTITASKING.   Some operating systems allow only one program to be executed at a time. The operating system will not begin the execution of the next program until the current program is finished. You can think of this process as *single-tasking* because only one task (program) is done at a time. With a single-tasking operating system only one program (and the supervisor) is in primary storage (Figure 5.7a).

Most operating systems allow **multitasking**, which means that more than one program can execute at a time. With these operating systems all programs being executed are in primary storage at the same time[1] (Figure 5.7b). Although the CPU can execute instructions from only one program at a time, the operating system can jump

---

[1] If the operating system uses virtual memory, which is discussed later, this statement may not be entirely correct.

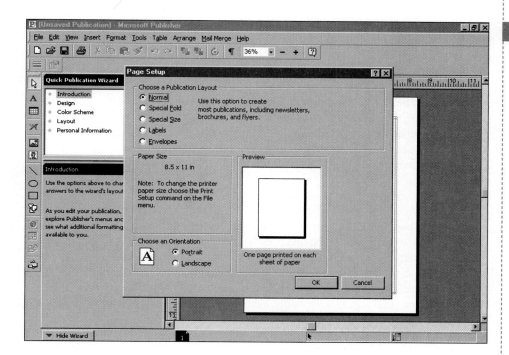

FIGURE 5.6

A graphical user interface (GUI)

from one program to the next without waiting for the first program to finish. Thus, the computer can execute a few instructions in the first program, then a few instructions in the second program, then some in the third program, and so forth.

One reason multitasking is used is that a user often wants to go from one program to another without losing the work done by the first program. A user may begin executing one program, decide to execute another program, and later go back to the first program. Multitasking is accomplished in this situation by letting the user interrupt the execution of a program whenever he or she wants to execute another program, usually by selecting the other program with the mouse. The operating system remembers where the first program was interrupted so that the user can go back to where he or she left off in that program and continue execution.

Another reason multitasking is used is that programs often have to wait for some other process to take place in the computer. For example, a program may have to wait for a user to enter input data or for output to be printed. During the wait, another program can be executing. Multitasking in this case is accomplished by giving each program a priority level. When a program with a higher priority has to wait for some

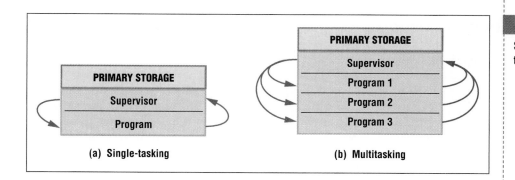

FIGURE 5.7

Single-tasking and multi-tasking

other process such as input or output, the operating system executes a lower-priority program. When the higher-priority program needs to execute, however, the operating system interrupts the lower-priority program and gives control back to the higher-priority program.

MULTIPLE-USER.   Some operating systems allow only one user to use the computer at a time; they are *single-user operating systems*. A user can decide which program he or she wants to execute, and no other users can execute a program at the same time. These operating systems may allow the user to execute only one program at a time or may be multitasking systems so the user can have several programs executing simultaneously.

Other operating systems allow more than one user to use the computer at a time; they are *multiple-user operating systems*. These operating systems are multitasking because each user could be executing a different program. A technique that is used with multiple-user operating systems is called **time-sharing**. With this technique the operating system allows each user a small amount of time to execute his or her program before going on to the next user. After all users have had a small amount of time to execute, the computer returns to the first user. This process is accomplished so fast, however, that the user probably never knows that his or her program was not executing for a period of time.

INTERACTIVE.   The first operating systems were *batch operating systems*, which meant that a program and its data had to be prepared in a batch before it could be processed on the computer. The computer executed the first program and processed all its data in a batch, and then went to the next program and processed its data, and so on. These operating systems did not allow the user to enter data as the program executed.

Current systems are *interactive operating systems*, which means they allow interaction with the users as programs execute. A user can enter input data and get the results of processing that data before going on to the next input. Interactive operating systems also allow programs and data to be prepared in a batch and processed without user interaction. Thus, current operating systems provide both interactive and batch processing.

When an operating system interacts with multiple users, each user sometimes has to wait a few seconds for a response. Some systems, called *real-time operating systems*, respond immediately to high-priority requests for processing. The "users" of these operating systems usually are machines or equipment that must get a response immediately—that is, in real time. For example, an operating system for a computer that controls equipment monitoring patients in an intensive care unit of a hospital must respond immediately to any abnormal change in a patient's condition.

VIRTUAL MEMORY.   One of the limitations of computers is the amount of primary storage available for storing programs. A program may be too large for primary storage, or several programs that need to be in primary storage at one time may require more space than is available. Some operating systems can execute only programs that can fit into the available primary storage, or *real memory*. Most operating systems, however, can execute programs that are too big for primary storage by using secondary storage to make the computer appear as if it has more memory than the real memory. The memory the computer appears to have with these operating systems is called **virtual memory**. For example, a computer may have real memory of 64 megabytes and virtual memory of 512 megabytes. Thus, programs larger than 64

FIGURE 5.8

Virtual memory

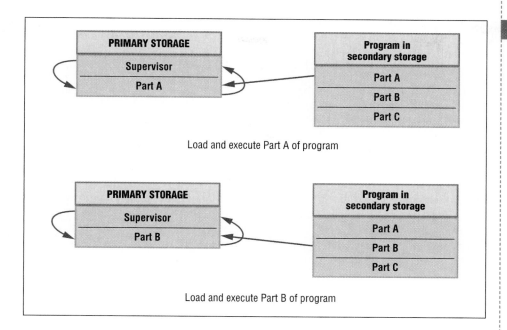

Load and execute Part A of program

Load and execute Part B of program

megabytes can be executed. If the operating system is multitasking, several programs that together requiring more than 64 megabytes can be executed.

A virtual-memory operating system executes large programs by dividing the program into parts in secondary storage and loading into primary storage only one part at a time (Figure 5.8). When a part of the program that is not in primary storage is needed, the operating system loads it from secondary storage, replacing another part of the program already in primary storage. This process is handled automatically by the operating system, without the user knowing it is going on. The disadvantage of virtual memory is that execution of the program is slower than with real memory because parts of the program must be loaded into primary storage when they are needed.

Common Operating Systems

Many operating systems are currently in use. For some computers, only one operating system is available, but for many computers several different operating systems can be used.

Personal Computer Operating Systems.   Several common operating systems for personal computer systems are available. Because personal computers are used by one person at a time, they all use single-user operating systems. Other characteristics of these operating systems vary, however.

WINDOWS.   Windows refers to one of several programs from Microsoft for IBM personal computers and clones. The first versions of Windows (up to version 3.1) were not operating systems, but rather **operating environments**, which are programs that provide a special interface between the user and the operating system. These versions of Windows required an older operating system called Disk Operating System (DOS). DOS is a single-tasking, real-memory operating system that the user controls by entering commands after a prompt. Thus, it is difficult to use. The first versions of Windows provided a graphical user interface for DOS so that the operating system

Linux at the City of Medina, Washington

An operating system at no charge? In the cost-conscious world of enterprise business automation, you'd think a free or nearly free operating system might be a really attractive proposition. But the situation is more complex than you might think, and the answer often doesn't point to Linux. However, a few enterprising organizations are piloting the use of Linux, and some are already using it for critical run-the-business applications.

Enterprises giving Linux a try include Amerada Hess, Burlington Coat Factory, Cendant, BFGoodrich, the *Los Angeles Times*, and the city of Medina, Washington. For these organizations, the opportunity to save money is important. Characteristics such as performance and reliability are also high on the list of Linux attractions.

The reasons for and against using Linux in an enterprise are many. On the one hand, it's inexpensive, and for many applications, it runs more efficiently than other operating systems, which makes it possible to use less expensive hardware. Linux is also based on open standards and thus is highly vendor neutral. On the other hand, Linux has almost no track record as a serious business platform, and its ongoing administrative costs are pretty much the same as those of any other UNIX-like system. And adopting Linux requires that the organization give some additional training to administrators, developers, and users who are already well-versed in UNIX or Windows.

Linux was the choice of the City of Medina, Washington, for its document management system. Like most city halls across the nation, the government of Medina is quietly drowning in paper. Its tight budget for capital improvements is also typical. Medina couldn't afford one of the popular document management systems costing $75,000 or more. It chose to automate the storage of city records, which includes anything in a City Hall file cabinet, with a Linux-based system costing about $27,000.

The city contracted with Archive Retrieval Systems, headed by President Bill Campbell, to install and configure the document management system. Recently the system went into production, and Campbell says the city is already realizing considerable savings.

The document imaging system is the only application running on Linux now, but the city plans to use Linux for file and print serving in the not-too-distant future. Eventually, the same Linux machines will also handle Internet routing and e-mail serving.

The new system scans paper records and stores the results on write-once CD-ROMs. A Linux server holds the digital documents, and a Linux client manages the image-scanning device. Campbell says the scanning device client initially ran on an Intel version of Solaris (a UNIX-like operating system), but software vendor ViviData was able to port its scanning utility to Linux in a week instead of its projected six to eight weeks of development time. Campbell says the system runs almost twice as fast on Linux as on Solaris, and adds that it's now more robust and easier to configure.

Persuading ViviData to port its software to Linux was his biggest problem, Campbell says. Minor problems have included some glitches between Linux and the hardware, such as occasional errors in Linux's management of the document-feeder unit, but Campbell was able to go into the Linux software and fixed the problem himself.

Campbell says he appreciates the speed, size, and reliability of Linux, but he hastens to add that a "university mind-set" regarding changes to the operating system is a risk that Linux users face every day. He says he believes value-added resellers and other vendors should shield customers from the vagaries of multiple, geographically dispersed programmers making changes to the operating system. Businesses shouldn't be subject to a lack of programming consistency and quality, and Cambell is glad Linux

was easier to use. They also made available a simple form of multitasking, not available with DOS, that allowed the user to switch between programs.

A current version of Windows, called Windows 98, is a complete operating system and does not require DOS. It has a different graphical user interface than previous versions of Windows. It also provides a more sophisticated form of multitasking than was available previously, but it is still a real-memory operating system (although it has a feature that provides some capabilities similar to virtual memory).

Another version of Windows, called Windows CE, is used on handheld computers. It has features specifically designed for small, portable computers, including the ability to recognize handwritten pen input. Although many handheld computers use Windows CE, some use other operating systems developed specially for them. For example, the Palm handheld computers from 3Com use an operating system called Palm OS.

The most recent version of Windows is called Windows 2000 Professional. (This operating system was originally called Windows NT Workstation.) It is a sophisticated operating system designed for powerful microcomputers that usually are connected in a network. It provides multitasking and virtual-memory capabilities. Windows 2000 Professional can be used on standalone personal computers—that is, those not connected to a network—but it is most often found in networked computer systems.

OS/2. OS/2 is an operating system from IBM for IBM personal computers and clones. It has a graphical user interface similar to that of Windows. OS/2 has multitasking capabilities and is a virtual-memory operating system. Some large businesses that have IBM mainframe or server computers use OS/2 for their personal computers.

MAC OS. The operating system for the Apple Macintosh is called Mac OS. (Originally it was called System, followed by a number, such as System 7.) This operating system provides a graphical user interface similar to that of Windows. It has a simple form of multitasking so that a user can switch from one program to another. It also provides virtual-memory capability.

UNIX. Some powerful microcomputers use an operating system called UNIX. This operating system was developed for minicomputers in the early 1970s by Bell Laboratories. Since its original development, it has undergone many revisions. Today, versions of UNIX are available for some microcomputers.

UNIX is a sophisticated multitasking, virtual-memory operating system. It is also a multiple-user operating system, although on personal computers it is only used by a single user. The user can, however, have multiple programs executing at the same time and can execute programs larger than primary storage can hold. UNIX has a number of special features, but some people find it difficult to use.

LINUX.   Linux is an operating system that is similar to UNIX. It provides the same multitasking, virtual-memory, multiple-user capabilities as UNIX, as well as other UNIX features. Unlike UNIX, however, Linux can be obtained free and thus it has become very popular by those who want a UNIX-like operating system on their personal computers.

Multiple-User Computer Operating Systems.   The first operating systems for large computers were single-tasking, batch, real-memory systems. As computers became more powerful, their operating systems became more sophisticated. Today, multiple-user computers such as minicomputers and mainframe computers use operating systems that are multitasking, time-sharing, interactive, virtual-memory systems. These operating systems have many more features than personal computer operating systems. For example, they often have complex security features to prevent unauthorized use of the computer. They are also more complex to use than personal computer operating systems. Two examples are OS/390 for IBM mainframe computers and MPE (which stands for Multiprogramming Executive) for HP minicomputers.

Most operating systems for minicomputers and mainframe computers, such as those listed in the previous paragraph, are designed to be used on a specific computer. For example, OS/390 can be used only on IBM mainframe computers. Versions of UNIX, however, are available for many minicomputers and mainframe computers. As discussed earlier, UNIX is also available for some microcomputers. It is a multiple-user, multitasking, virtual-memory operating system.

Networked Computer Operating Systems.   Computers connected to a network require special operating systems to handle communications between them. Recall from Chapter 3 that in a network, computers used by end users are called *clients*, and computers that provide service to many clients in the network are called *servers*. Client computers can use any of the personal computer operating systems discussed previously: Windows 98, Windows 2000 Professional, OS/2, Mac OS, UNIX, and Linux.

Server computers, however, require special operating systems to manage multiple clients and to provide communication between clients and server computers. Often, this type of operating system is called a **network operating system** (**NOS**). An example is Windows 2000 Server, which is like Windows 2000 Professional, except that it has the necessary features for a server. Another example is NetWare from Novell. UNIX and Linux are also used as server operating systems. In general, network operating systems provide capabilities for handling significant software malfunctions and security features to prevent unauthorized use of the network.

Other System Software

Operating systems are just one type of system software. Several other types are also used. One type is **utility programs**, which perform common functions. Examples are a *sort utility*, which rearranges data in a file into a specified order, and a *merge utility*, which merges two files into one. Other utility programs are a *print utility*, for printing the contents of a file, and a *copy utility*, for copying data from one device to another, such as from a disk to a tape. Sometimes utility programs are included with the operating system. Businesses use utility programs because these programs make it easy to perform common processing functions on a computer.

Other system software includes *communication software*, which is used for communication between computers (discussed in Chapter 6), and *database management sys-*

tems, which are used for managing databases (described in Chapter 7). Finally, some system software is used to help develop programs. The next section discusses this software.

Software Development

Software is developed by people called **programmers** who prepare the instructions in computer programs. The process they go through, called **programming**, involves a number of steps, including writing the instructions in a form that a computer can understand. The form that the instructions take depends on the **programming language**, which is a set of rules for preparing a computer program. This section takes a look at common programming languages used to develop application and system software.

Programming Language Concepts

What is a programming language? Why are there many programming languages? How do you select a programming language? What are the types of programming languages? These are some common questions about programming languages that we answer here.

What Is a Programming Language?   English is a *natural language*. It has words, symbols, and a set of grammatical rules for combining the words and symbols into sentences. When you form a grammatically correct sentence, it means something. You can make grammatical errors in a sentence, however, and a person might still be able to understand it.

A programming language is like a natural language in many ways. It has words, symbols, and rules of grammar. The grammatical rules are called the *syntax* of the language. A programmer forms an instruction by combining the words and symbols according to the syntax rules. The instruction formed by the programmer has some meaning; that is, it tells the computer to do something.

Unlike in a natural language, if a programmer makes an error in writing an instruction in a programming language, the instruction does not mean anything; the computer is not able to understand it. To write a program, a programmer must know the syntax rules of the language he or she is using. If the programmer does not abide by those rules, the program has errors and the computer is not be able to execute it.

Each programming language has a different set of syntax rules. When a new language is invented, the designer of the language determines its syntax rules and the meaning of each instruction. To use a new language, a programmer must learn the syntax and meaning of each instruction.

Why Are There Many Programming Languages?   There are two answers to this question. First, programming languages have evolved over time as researchers have found better ways of designing them. The first languages were developed in the 1950s and, by today's standards, were poorly designed. Today, researchers know much more about what makes a good language, so current languages are quite a bit different from the early languages.

Second, different programming languages are designed for different types of programs. Some languages are designed for writing system programs, and some for application programs. In addition, there are two major types of application programs: business application programs, which are used in information systems for business data processing, and scientific application programs, which are used to solve problems in science and engineering. Some languages are designed for business application programs, and some for scientific application programs. Because a computer can be used for many types of programs, there are many programming languages.

How Do You Select a Programming Language?   Several factors must be considered when selecting a programming language for a particular program. One factor is whether the language is designed for the type of program that needs to be written. Different languages are appropriate for different types of programs. Another factor is the availability of languages on the computer being used. Not all languages can be used on all computers. A third factor is the availability of trained programmers to write and maintain the programs using the language. Some languages, although excellent for certain programs, are known by so few programmers that it may be very difficult to find someone qualified to write or modify the program. Another factor to consider is the ease of writing programs in the language. Writing programs in some languages is easier and takes less time than in others. The final factor in selecting a programming language is the efficiency of the program written in the language. Some languages produce programs that are faster and take less primary storage space than do programs in other languages.

What Are the Types of Programming Languages?   Programming languages have evolved over time. As a result, languages fall into five generations.

MACHINE LANGUAGES (FIRST GENERATION).   In Chapter 4 we introduced machine language, which is the basic language of a computer. When computers were first invented, this was the only type of programming language available. Hence, machine language forms the first generation of programming languages.

A machine language instruction consists of an *operation code* for operations such as addition and subtraction, and one or more *operands* that identify data to be processed. Instructions are represented in a binary form, so they appear as strings of 1s and 0s. For example, Figure 5.9 shows a machine language instruction to add one number to another number.

Each type of computer has its own machine language that may be different from the machine language of other types of computers. Hence, programs written for one computer may not be compatible with another computer; we say machine language is *machine dependent*. Machine language is the only language a computer can understand. Any program for a computer must either be written in the machine language of the computer or in some other language and then translated into machine language, a process that is discussed later in this section.

With machine language the programmer has control over everything the computer can do and so can write very efficient programs. Writing programs in machine language is very difficult, however, because the programmer must remember binary codes and numbers. Hence, machine languages are normally not used today.

A machine language instruc-
▲ tion

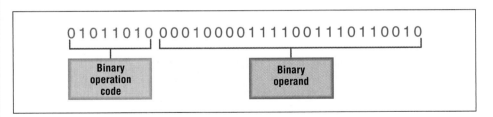

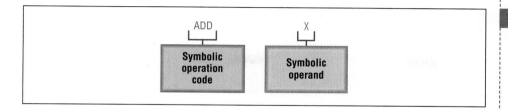

FIGURE 5.10

An assembly language instruction

ASSEMBLY LANGUAGES (SECOND GENERATION). Early in the history of computers, computer professionals thought there must be an easier way of writing programs than by using machine language. Their idea was to replace instructions represented in a binary form with words and symbols. Binary operation codes were replaced by symbolic codes that stood for the operation. Thus, instead of using the binary operation code 01011010 for the addition operation, the word ADD was used. In addition, instead of using a binary operand, a symbol such as X was used to stand for the data to be processed by the instruction. Thus, an instruction to add one number to another number would be written as in Figure 5.10 instead of the form shown in Figure 5.9. Languages using this form became the second generation of programming languages.

Because programs written this way are not in machine language, they have to be translated into machine language before they can be executed. The translation process involves converting each symbol into its equivalent binary form. This translation process is called *assembly*, and therefore these languages are called **assembly languages**. In the assembly process, each assembly language instruction is translated into one machine language instruction.

Originally, assembly was done by hand; a person would manually translate each assembly language instruction into its equivalent machine language instruction. Then, computer professionals realized that because the translation process was largely mechanical, a computer could do it. People wrote computer programs in machine language to translate assembly language programs (called *source programs*) into equivalent machine language programs (called *object programs*). An assembly language translation program is a system program called an **assembler**.

Because each type of computer has its own machine language, each has its own assembly language, which may be incompatible with the assembly languages of other computers. Hence, assembly language is machine dependent. In addition, each type of computer needs its own assembler to translate its assembly language into its machine language.

As with machine language, the programmer has control over everything the computer can do with assembly language, and programs written in assembly language are usually as efficient as those in machine language. Programming in assembly language is easier than it is in machine language, however, because symbolic codes are easier to remember than binary codes. Still, assembly language is not used much because other languages are even easier to use. Only in certain situations, such as when the program has to control special parts of the computer, is assembly language used to write system and other types of programs.

THIRD-GENERATION LANGUAGES. Although assembly language is easier to use than machine language, it is not very close to human language because each assembly language instruction is equivalent to one machine language instruction. In the mid-1950s computer professionals started to develop languages that were closer to human language. In these languages, each instruction was equivalent to several

X = Y – Z

FORTRAN

SUBTRACT TAX FROM GROSS-PAY GIVING NET-PAY

COBOL

x = y – z

C

machine language instructions. Hence, fewer instructions were required in programs written in these languages than in assembly languages. They became the third generation of languages.

The first third-generation languages were similar to simple mathematical notation. Later third-generation languages were closer to English. Still later languages were closer to other notations, such as those used in advanced mathematics. Figure 5.11 shows examples of instructions in FORTRAN, COBOL, and C, which are common third-generation languages.

Programs written in third-generation languages (*source programs*) have to be translated into equivalent machine language programs (*object programs*) before they can be executed. Several processes are used for the translation. One process is called *compilation*, and it is done by a machine language system program called a **compiler**. Sometimes third-generation languages are called *compiler languages*. In the compilation process each third-generation language instruction is translated into several machine language instructions. An alternative to compilation is *interpretation*, which is done by a system program called an **interpreter**. The difference is that in compilation the entire program is translated into machine language before any instruction is executed, whereas in interpretation each instruction is translated and executed before going on to the next instruction.

Third-generation languages are not tied to particular computers as are assembly and machine languages; we say they are *machine independent*. If a programmer wants to use a third-generation language on a different computer, he or she just needs a compiler or an interpreter to translate programs in the third-generation language into programs in the machine language of the computer.

With third-generation languages, the programmer has less control over what the computer can do than with assembly or machine languages, and third-generation language programs usually are less efficient than assembly or machine language programs. Third-generation languages, however, are easier to learn and have features that make writing programs easier than assembly or machine language. Many people are familiar with one or more third-generation languages. Many common third-generation languages are in use, including C, C++, COBOL, Visual Basic, and FORTRAN.

FOURTH-GENERATION LANGUAGES.   The fourth generation of programming languages is not so clearly defined as the earlier generations. Most people feel that a **fourth-generation language**, commonly referred to as a **4GL**, is a high-level language

FIGURE 5.12

A fourth-generation (query)
language instruction ▲

```
SELECT ADDRESS
FROM PERSONNEL
WHERE NAME = "JONES"
```

that requires significantly fewer instructions to accomplish a particular task than a third-generation language requires. Thus, a programmer should be able to write a program faster in a 4GL than in a third-generation language.

Many 4GLs are used to retrieve information from files and databases. These 4GLs contain a *query language*, which is used to answer queries with data from a database. For example, Figure 5.12 shows an instruction in SQL, a common query language. (Query languages are discussed further in Chapter 7.) Some 4GLs include special *report generators* that make it easy to produce complex printed reports. Other 4GLs include *forms designers*, which are used for creating forms for data input and output on screens. Still other 4GLs have *application generators* that produce complex programs for computer applications. The programmer specifies the queries, reports, and forms needed, and the application generator creates the necessary program.

Fourth-generation languages are mostly machine independent; usually they can be used on more than one type of computer. Some 4GLs are designed to be learned easily and used by end users. With these languages, the user can create programs without the aid of a programmer.

FIFTH-GENERATION LANGUAGES. What is the fifth generation of computer languages? There is no clear answer to this question right now. Some people feel that human languages, that is, *natural languages*, are fifth-generation languages. There have been some attempts to create computer programs that understand natural languages such as English. These programs, however, are very limited in their capabilities. Someday we will probably have programs that can understand natural languages. When that happens, we might be able to say what fifth-generation languages are.

Traditional Programming Languages

Hundreds, perhaps thousands, of programming languages exist today, but only a few are commonly used. The most widely used languages are third-generation languages, although some 4GLs are used often. Third-generation languages fall into two groups: traditional programming languages and object-oriented programming languages. This section takes a look at some of the common traditional programming languages. The next section examines object-oriented programming languages.

FORTRAN. The first widely used third-generation language was **FORTRAN**, which stands for FORmula TRANslation. It was developed by researchers at IBM in the mid-1950s and has undergone a number of modifications and improvements since that time. As its name implies, FORTRAN is designed to make it easy to write programs that include many mathematical formulas. Because scientific application programs have numerous formulas, FORTRAN is commonly used for these types of programs. In fact, FORTRAN may be the most common third-generation language used today by scientists and engineers. Figure 5.13 shows an example of a simple FORTRAN program.

FIGURE 5.13

▲ **A FORTRAN program**

```
C   TEST SCORE AVERAGING PROGRAM
        CHARACTER*18 NAME
        REAL SCORE1,SCORE2,SCORE3,TOTAL,AVE
        PRINT *, 'ENTER STUDENT NAME OR TYPE END TO STOP:&'
        READ (*,300) NAME
100  IF (NAME .EQ. 'END') GO TO 200
            PRINT *, 'ENTER THREE TEST SCORES:'
            READ *,SCORE1,SCORE2,SCORE3
            TOTAL = SCORE1 + SCORE2 + SCORE3
            AVE = TOTAL / 3.0
            PRINT *
            PRINT *, 'STUDENT NAME ',NAME
            PRINT *,'TOTAL SCORE ',TOTAL
            PRINT *,'AVERAGE SCORE ',AVE
            PRINT *
            PRINT *, 'ENTER STUDENT NAME OR TYPE END TO STOP:'
            READ (*,300) NAME
        GO TO 100
200  STOP
300  FORMAT (A18)
        END
```

COBOL. The second widely used third-generation language was **COBOL**. It was developed by a group of computer professionals in 1959 and has evolved through a number of versions since then. COBOL stands for COmmon Business Oriented Language. As the name implies, the language is designed to be common to many different computers. In addition, it is used most effectively for business application programs, not for scientific programs. Today COBOL is one of the most widely used third-generation language for business data processing.

COBOL is available on almost all computers, including personal computers. However, it is most often used on mainframe and minicomputers, although COBOL programs are often developed on personal computers for later execution on larger computers. Many businesses use it as the only language for business application program development. Figure 5.14 shows an example of part of a simple COBOL program.

BASIC. **BASIC**, which stands for Beginner's All-purpose Symbolic Instruction Code, was developed in the mid-1960s at Dartmouth College. At that time the main languages, FORTRAN and COBOL, were used for programs that processed batches of data; it was not easy to use these languages to write programs that interacted with the user. The designers of BASIC wanted a simple language for students to write programs with which they could interact through terminals.

BASIC, like FORTRAN and COBOL, has evolved through a number of versions over the years. Recent versions for IBM personal computers are *QBasic* and *Quick-BASIC*. Another version, called *Visual Basic*, which is an object-oriented programming language, is discussed later. Most versions of BASIC are good for quickly writing programs to solve simple problems, although Visual Basic is used for writing sophisticated programs with complex graphical interfaces. Figure 5.15 shows an example of a simple program in QBasic.

C. **C** was developed by Bell Laboratories in the early 1970s. It includes features that provide the control and efficiency of assembly language (second generation) but at the same time has third-generation language features. C is used extensively for system

FIGURE 5.14

Part of a COBOL program

```
        PROCEDURE DIVISION.
*
        A000-MAIN-CONTROL.
            OPEN INPUT STUDENT-FILE
                OUTPUT REPORT-FILE.
            PERFORM B010-WRITE-HEADING.
            MOVE "N" TO WS-EOF-FLAG.
            PERFORM B020-READ-INPUT.
            PERFORM B030-PRODUCE-REPORT-BODY
                UNTIL WS-EOF-FLAG IS EQUAL TO "Y".
            CLOSE STUDENT-FILE, REPORT-FILE.
            STOP RUN.
*
        B010-WRITE-HEADING.
            WRITE REPORT-DATA FROM HEADING-LINE
                AFTER ADVANCING PAGE.
            MOVE SPACES TO REPORT-DATA.
            WRITE REPORT-DATA
                AFTER ADVANCING 1 LINE.
*
        B020-READ-INPUT.
            READ STUDENT-FILE INTO STUDENT-RECORD
                AT END MOVE "Y" TO WS-EOF-FLAG.
*
        B030-PRODUCE-REPORT-BODY.
            PERFORM C010-CALCULATE-TOTAL-AVERAGE.
            PERFORM C020-WRITE-DETAIL-OUTPUT.
            PERFORM B020-READ-INPUT.
*
        C010-CALCULATE-TOTAL-AVERAGE.
            ADD ST-SCORE1, ST-SCORE2, ST-SCORE3
                GIVING WS-TOTAL.
            DIVIDE WS-TOTAL BY 3
                GIVING WS-AVERAGE ROUNDED.
*
        C020-WRITE-DETAIL-OUTPUT.
            MOVE ST-NAME TO DL-NAME.
            MOVE WS-TOTAL TO DL-TOTAL.
            MOVE WS-AVERAGE TO DL-AVERAGE.
            WRITE REPORT-DATA FROM DETAIL-LINE
                AFTER ADVANCING 1 LINE.
```

FIGURE 5.15

A QBasic program

```
REM - TEST SCORE AVERAGING PROGRAM
INPUT "ENTER STUDENT NAME OR TYPE END TO STOP: ", StuName$
DO WHILE StuName$ <> "END"
    INPUT "ENTER THREE TEST SCORES: ", Score1, Score2, Score3
    LET Total = Score1 + Score2 + Score3
    LET Ave = Total / 3
    PRINT
    PRINT "STUDENT NAME "; StuName$
    PRINT "TOTAL SCORE"; Total
    PRINT "AVERAGE SCORE"; Ave
    PRINT
    INPUT "ENTER STUDENT NAME OR TYPE END TO STOP: ", StuName$
LOOP
END
```

FIGURE 5.16

▲ **A C program**

```
main ()    /*Test score averaging program*/
{
    char name[19];
    float score1,score2,score3,total,ave;
    printf ("Enter student name or type end to stop: ");
    scanf ("%s",name);
    while (strcmp (name,"end") != 0)
    {
        printf ("Enter three test scores: ");
        scanf ("%f%f%f",&score1,&score2,&score3);
        total = score1 + score2 + score3;
        ave = total / 3;
        printf ("\n");
        printf ("Student name %s\n",name);
        printf ("Total score %4.0f\n",total);
        printf ("Average score %5.1f\n",ave);
        printf ("\n");
        printf ("Enter student name or type end to stop: ");
        scanf ("%s",name);
    }
}
```

programs. For example, the UNIX operating system, discussed earlier, is written in C. Many personal computer application programs, such as word processing, spreadsheet, and database programs, are also written in C. C is used for complex system and application programs that require control of the computer and that must execute rapidly and use primary storage efficiently. Figure 5.16 shows an example of a simple C program.

Object-oriented Programming Languages

Programs written in traditional programming languages consist of sequences of instructions that tell the computer how to process data. The data processed by the program is separate from the program, perhaps stored in a file or a database. Another approach to programming uses languages in which the instructions for processing the data and the data are not separate, but instead are combined to form an **object**. This approach, called **object-oriented programming**, has become common in recent years.

To illustrate the idea of object-oriented programming, consider data consisting of a bank customer's account number and balance, and instructions for adding to the account balance (depositing), subtracting from the account balance (withdrawing), and displaying the account balance. In traditional programming, the customer number and account balance would be stored in a customer account file, and the instructions for depositing, withdrawing, and displaying the balance would be in a program separate from the data (Figure 5.17a). In object-oriented programming, a customer account object would be created with the customer number and account balance, along with the instructions for the different forms of processing (Figure 5.17b).

The advantage of object-oriented programming is that after an object has been created, it can be reused in many programs. Thus the customer account object just described could be used in a checking account program and in any other program that uses the same data and procedures. As a result, object-oriented programs can be

FIGURE 5.17

Traditional and object-oriented programming ▲

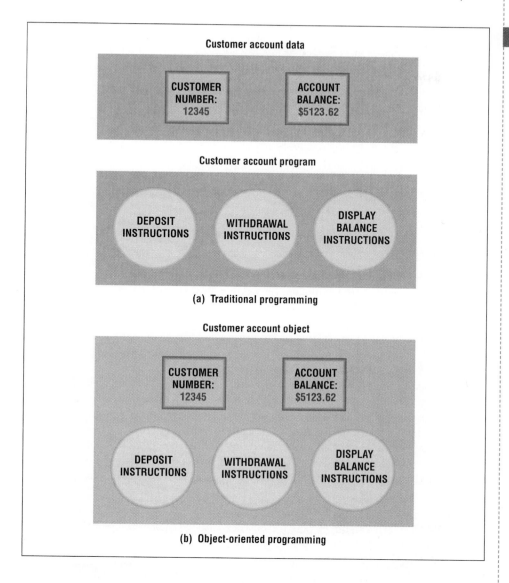

Customer account data

CUSTOMER NUMBER: 12345

ACCOUNT BALANCE: $5123.62

Customer account program

DEPOSIT INSTRUCTIONS

WITHDRAWAL INSTRUCTIONS

DISPLAY BALANCE INSTRUCTIONS

(a) Traditional programming

Customer account object

CUSTOMER NUMBER: 12345

ACCOUNT BALANCE: $5123.62

DEPOSIT INSTRUCTIONS

WITHDRAWAL INSTRUCTIONS

DISPLAY BALANCE INSTRUCTIONS

(b) Object-oriented programming

easier to develop than traditional programs. Objects are especially good for storing sound, pictures, and video, and object-oriented programs are commonly used for processing this type of data.

A number of object-oriented programming languages have been developed over the years. One of the first was *Smalltalk*, which was developed in the mid-1970s by Xerox. It is still in use today on some computers. The most widely used object-oriented programming language is **C++**, which is a version of C with additional features for object-oriented programming. It is widely used today for developing system and application software. Figure 5.18 shows an example of a simple C++ program.

A number of object-oriented languages provide the ability to easily develop graphical user interfaces. Items displayed in a graphical user interface such as icons, menus, and windows are representations of objects. Languages for developing such interfaces are sometimes called *visual programming languages* because the programmer

FIGURE 5.18

▲ A C++ program

```
// Filename: acctmain.cpp
#include "account.h"
#include <iostream.h>
int main()
{
    cout << endl;
    cout << "Starting project";
    Account myAccount;
    myAccount.deposit(199.99);
    cout << endl;
    cout << "My Account has $" <<  myAccount.retrieveBalance();
    cout << endl;
    cout << "Ending project";
    return 0;
}
```

develops a program in the language by using a mouse and a screen that displays graphical images for icons, menus, windows, and so forth. (See Figure 5.19.) An example of such a language is *Visual Basic*. Object-oriented and visual programming languages have replaced traditional programming languages in many organizations.

Internet Programming Languages

Special programming languages are used with the Internet and the Web. The main language used to create pages on the Web is **HTML**, which stands for Hypertext Markup Language. With HTML, a Web page developer can lay out the form of a page, with text, graphics, and connections called *hyperlinks* to other pages. The developer does this by putting brief codes called *tags* in the page to indicate how the page should be formatted (Figure 5.20). When viewed with a browser, the page appears in its formatted form, without the tags. Software is also available for developing Web

FIGURE 5.19

A visual programming lan-
▲ guage screen

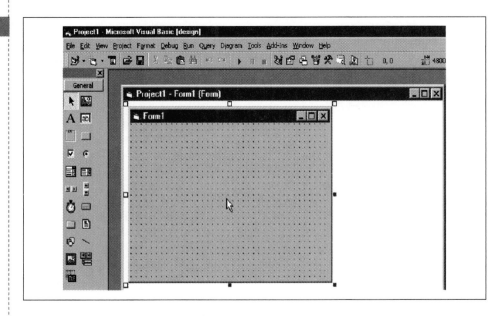

```
<HTML><HEAD><TITLE>Business Publishing</TITLE>
<META content="text/html; charset=windows-1252" http-equiv=Content-Type>
<META content="MSHTML 5.00.2314.1000" name=GENERATOR></HEAD>
<BODY background="Business Publishing_files/bkgd.gif" bgColor=#13724e
text=#4f3e51>
<CENTER>
<TABLE border=0 cellPadding=0 cellSpacing=0>
 <TBODY>
 <TR align=middle vAlign=top>
  <TD align=middle rowSpan=2 vAlign=top><IMG alt="Business Publishing"
   border=0 height=323 hspace=20 src="Business Publishing_files/title.gif"
   width=54> </TD>
  <TD align=middle vAlign=top><IMG border=0 height=278
   src="Business Publishing_files/picture.jpg" width=209 VALIGN="TOP"> </TD>
  <TD align=middle vAlign=top>
   <TABLE border=0 cellPadding=5 cellSpacing=0>
    <TBODY>
    <TR align=middle vAlign=top>
     <TD align=left vAlign=center><A
      href="http://www.prenhall.com/phbusiness/html/account.html"><IMG
      alt=Accounting/Taxation border=0 height=22
      src="Business Publishing_files/cat1.gif" width=181></A> </TD></TR>
    <TR align=middle vAlign=top>
     <TD align=left vAlign=center><A
      href="http://www.prenhall.com/phbusiness/html/cismis.html"><IMG
      alt=CIS/MIS/Software border=0 height=21
      src="Business Publishing_files/cat7n.gif" width=149></A> </TD></TR>
    <TR align=middle vAlign=top>
     <TD align=left vAlign=center><A
      href="http://www.prenhall.com/phbusiness/html/descience.html"><IMG
      alt="Decision Science/Business Statistics" border=0 height=36
      src="Business Publishing_files/cat8.gif" width=185></A> </TD></TR>
    <TR align=middle vAlign=top>
     <TD align=left vAlign=center><A
      href="http://www.prenhall.com/phbusiness/html/economics.html"><IMG
      alt=Economics border=0 height=20
      src="Business Publishing_files/cat2.gif" width=96></A> </TD></TR>
```

FIGURE 5.20

HTML for a World Wide Web page ▲

pages without having to use HTML directly. This type of software automatically puts the necessary tags in the page.

XML, which stands for Extensible Markup Language, is another language used with the Internet and the Web. XML is actually a language for defining other languages. With XML, languages can be created for describing specialized types of documents for the Internet and the Web. For example, a language can be created in XML for describing customer orders that are sent over the Internet.

Another language used with the Web is **Java**. Java is an object-oriented programming language similar to C++ that allows a Web page developer to create programs for applications (called *applets*) that can be used through a browser. For example, a Web page for a bank could have a Java program that calculates mortgage payments from input entered by the user. Using Java, developers can create Web pages that do more than just display words and images.

As use of the Internet and the Web increases, more applications will be written using HTML, XML, Java, and similar languages. Someday, the majority of applications may be developed in Internet programming languages.

A Java Inventory Ordering System at Motor Spares & Staff

A Java-enabled inventory ordering system developed in Australia is making deep inroads into the car spare parts trade in New Zealand. The product, called Catalogue and Ordering System, is used by companies in the highly competitive motor trade to order spare parts for cars, simultaneously reducing costs, lifting profits, and improving service.

The system allows engine reconditioning companies to dispense with static parts catalogues by calling up an electronic catalog either with a PC or via an Internet site called MotorWeb, using a standard Web browser.

Using Java applets (small programs) as communication agents to access a legacy COBOL database, clients of component supplier Motor Spares & Staff, New Zealand, are able to locate required components, determine availability, arrange delivery details, and authorize payment for the products. Orders are shipped upon receipt of a bank transfer payment.

Both the desktop version, developed using IBM's VisualAge for Smalltalk, and the Internet version, developed with Java, function in the same way and offer the user an almost identical look and feel.

The innovative system has delivered commerce as a competitive advantage in a cutthroat market where an overabundance of component suppliers has forced down margins and, in many cases, undermined the ability of companies to provide a high quality of service.

Jointly developed by Motor Spares and software developer Internet Age (Sydney, Australia), Catalogue and Ordering System has enabled Motor Spares to reduce its telephone ordering staff by 60%, while improving profitability and turnaround times for orders.

Besides producing a more orderly flow of orders during the day (previously, 60% of daily orders were placed via the telephone between 2:30 p.m. and 5:30 p.m.), the system has reduced printing and advertising costs by diminishing the need for printed catalogs: Sales bulletins are sent electronically.

The company's strategy has been to deploy the Smalltalk desktop version with its New Zealand customers and to use the Internet version for customers in southeast Asia, the Pacific, and the United States.

Although New Zealand's engine reconditioning industry is not highly computerized, with only one quarter using installed accounting packages, the Motor Spares Catalogue has met with resounding success. Customers who previously saw no need for computerization immediately recognized the benefits of access to a large database of models and engines, information about parts availability, up-to-date pricing, and precise identification of parts changes within an engine.

Catalogue and Ordering System identifies 1,900 vehicles, which can be selected by manufacturer, model, type, size, or bore. There is a Catalogue Page for each of 590 different models, and there are currently 11,800 component parts from which to build orders. The catalogue contains more than 800 text bulletins and 3,000 pictures.

Internet Age adopted Java to use for the client part of the application, with Java client applets connecting to VisualAge for Smalltalk server on the server.

Internet Age's Doug Marker, director of research and development, says the company selected Java for the Catalogue system because early prototypes of the Internet version using only HTML pages and CGI scripts required too much Web traffic. "It was Java applets' ability to provide interactive Web page windows that turned the promise into reality," he says.

This system is a good demonstration of how e-commerce has come of age in a business sense. The use of Smalltalk for PC

access and Java components via the Internet has transformed legacy corporate data
into a valuable competitive resource for both
Motor Spares and its clients.

Questions

1. For what parts of the Catalogue and
Ordering System were different programming languages used?
2. Why was Java used in the system?

3. What benefits has Motor Spares received
from the system?

Web Site
MotorSpares:
www.internetage.com.au/
motorweb/

Source: *Adapted from* "Motor Spares," www-4.ibm.com/
software/developer/casestudies/story-motor-spares.html,
copyright © 1994–1999 IBM Corporation.

BOOK
M A R K

CHAPTER SUMMARY

1 A program is a set of instructions that tells the computer what to do. The instructions in a program must describe the step-by-step process necessary for a computer to perform its tasks. The instructions are executed in sequence by the CPU, unless a special type of instruction changes the sequence. A program can contain hundreds of thousands—and even millions—of instructions. The term *software* is often used interchangeably with *program*. Software can be a single program or it can be a group of programs needed to perform several functions. (p. 135)

2 Individual application software is used by a single person for an individual purpose. It includes **word processing software, spreadsheet software, graphics software, database software**, and Web **browsers**. Workgroup application software, or **groupware**, is used by members of a workgroup to collaborate with each other. It includes **electronic messaging software, information sharing software**, and **electronic conferencing software**. Organizational application software provides applications that encompass much of the business, not just an individual or a workgroup. It can be used to support day-to-day business operations and management decision making. Interorganizational application software allows one business's computer to transmit data to another business's computer. (pp. 136–137)

3 Some operating systems are told what to do by the user keying in instructions called **commands** fol-

lowing **prompts** displayed by the operating system. Other operating systems allow the user to select commands, using a mouse, from a **menu** displayed on the screen. Many operating systems display available commands as **icons** or **buttons**, which the user selects with a mouse. Operating systems that display icons, menus, **dialog boxes**, and **windows** are said to have a **graphical user interface (GUI)**. (p. 141)

4 Some operating systems can execute only one program at a time, and others are **multitasking**, which means they can execute more than one program at a time. Some systems can be used by only one user at a time, and others can be used by multiple users simultaneously through a technique called **time-sharing**. Early systems were batch operating systems, which meant that all data had to be prepared in advance in a batch. Current operating systems are interactive, which means they allow interaction with the users as programs execute, but they also provide for batch processing. Finally, some operating systems are capable of executing only programs as large as the actual primary storage or real memory of the computer, and other operating systems allow programs to be larger than real memory by using secondary storage to store parts of programs. With these operating systems the computer has **virtual memory** that is larger than the real memory. (pp. 142–145)

5 Machine languages (first generation) have instructions with operation codes and operands in a binary form. **Assembly languages** (second generation) use symbolic operation codes and operands, but each instruction is still equivalent to one machine language instruction. In third-generation languages, each instruction is equivalent to several machine language instructions. Programs in these languages require fewer instructions than are needed in assembly language programs. Programs in **fourth-generation languages (4GLs)** require even fewer instructions than third-generation language programs. Thus, a programmer can write a program faster in a 4GL than in a third-generation language. Fifth-generation languages may turn out to be natural languages like English. (pp. 151–153)

6 In traditional programming the data processed by the program is separate from the program instruc-

tions. In **object-oriented programming** the data and the instructions for processing the data are combined to form an **object**. FORTRAN, **COBOL, BASIC,** and **C** are traditional programming languages. Smalltalk and **C++** are object-oriented programming languages. (pp. 153–156)

7 **HTML** is used to create pages on the Web. Using HTML, a page developer puts codes, or tags, in the page to indicate how the page should be formatted. **XML** is used to define other languages for describing documents for the Internet and the Web. **Java** is an object-oriented programming language that allows page developers to create programs for applications that can be used through a browser. (pp. 158–159)

KEY TERMS

Assembler (p. 151)
Assembly Language (p. 151)
BASIC (p. 154)
Booting (p. 141)
Browser (p. 137)
Button (p. 141)
C (p. 154)
C++ (p. 157)
COBOL (p. 154)
Command (p. 141)
Compiler (p. 152)
Database Software (p. 137)
Dialog Box (p. 141)
Electronic Conferencing Software (p. 137)
Electronic Messaging Software (p. 137)
FORTRAN (p. 153)

Fourth-Generation Language (4GL) (p. 152)
Graphical User Interface (GUI) (p. 141)
Graphics Software (p. 136)
Groupware (p. 137)
HTML (p. 158)
Icon (p. 141)
Information Sharing Software (p. 137)
Interpreter (p. 152)
Java (p. 159)
Menu (p. 141)
Multitasking (p. 142)
Network Operating System (NOS) (p. 148)
Object (p. 156)

Object-Oriented Programming (p. 156)
Operating Environment (p. 145)
Page (p. 137)
Programmer (p. 149)
Programming (p. 149)
Programming Language (p. 149)
Prompt (p. 141)
Spreadsheet Software (p. 136)
Time-Sharing (p. 144)
User Interface (p. 141)
Utility Program (p. 148)
Virtual Memory (p. 144)
Window (p. 141)
Word Processing Software (p. 136)
XML (p. 159)

REVIEW QUESTIONS

1 Are programs and software the same thing? Explain your answer.

2 What are three examples of individual application software?

3 What is workgroup application software called, and what is an example of this type of software?

4 Does organizational application software support only the day-to-day operations of a business? Explain your answer.

5 What is an example of interorganizational application software?

6 What are the three main functions of an operating system?

7 What does the supervisor of an operating system do?

8 What are some of the ways users can tell an operating system what to do?

9 What is a graphical user interface?

10 Why do users use multitasking?

11 What is time-sharing used for?

12 Why is virtual memory useful?

13 What are some common personal computer operating systems?

14 What is the name of an operating system that can be used on some personal computers as well as on some networked computer systems?

15 Why is there not just one programming language that can be used for all programs?

16 What are several factors that should be considered in selecting a programming language?

17 What is the difference between assembly and machine language?

18 What must be done to a third-generation language program before it can be executed?

19 What is a fourth-generation language, or 4GL?

20 What are several traditional third-generation languages?

21 What is an object, and what languages are used for object-oriented programming?

22 What programming languages are used with the Internet and the Web?

DISCUSSION QUESTIONS

1 Sometimes it is hard to decide whether a program is application software or system software. For example, some application programs, such as spreadsheet programs, are not capable of solving a business problem until they are customized, and some operating systems come with applications such as simple word processing and graphics capabilities. Why is it important to distinguish between application and system software?

2 Some people complain that graphical user interfaces, although easier to use than other interfaces, are still difficult to use. In what ways do you think a user interface can be improved to make it easier to use?

3 Much software for personal computers comes with documentation on CD-ROM rather than in printed form. What are the advantages and disadvantages of having documentation in each form? Which form do you prefer and why?

4 What is an example of an individual application in which multitasking would be useful?

5 Why is there not just one operating system for all computers?

6 Think of an application in a business with which you are familiar, other than an individual application. What programming language would you select for that application? Why?

7 Some people feel that third-generation programming languages are no longer needed because of fourth-generation languages. On the other hand, languages like C, COBOL, and FORTRAN are still used extensively. What do you think is the future of programming languages?

8 What problems besides natural language differences do software companies have in developing application and system software for sale around the world?

ETHICS QUESTIONS

1 Software, especially that used on personal computers, is easily copied. Most software, however, is copyrighted, so it is usually illegal to copy software without the developer's permission. What would you do if a coworker gave you a copy of a program and asked you to try it out to see if you liked it?

2 Sometimes programmers like to include personal things in programs they are preparing. For example, a programmer may include a computer game in a program that has nothing to do with games. What would you do if you accidentally discovered a computer game in an application program that your business uses?

PROBLEM-SOLVING PROJECTS

1 Go to a computer store and look at the software available on the shelves. Write down five different types of software (e.g., word processing software) that the store sells. Also write down the name and price of each software package of each type sold. Enter the information into a spreadsheet, and use the spreadsheet software to find the minimum, maximum, and average price of each type of software sold by the store. Plot the averages in a graph using the spreadsheet software so you can compare the prices of different types of software.

2 Analyze the graphical user interfaces of several software packages. Identify the elements found in each (e.g., menus, icons, buttons) and determine what they are used for. If possible, print copies of sample screens. Prepare a report in which you summarize the results of your analysis and comment on the ease of use of each interface. Conclude the report by outlining the characteristics you feel are the most important in a user interface.

3 Using appropriate software, set up a table that includes information about different personal computer operating systems. Include columns for the name of the operating system, the company that developed it, the current version, the price,

the capabilities of the operating system (e.g., multitasking, virtual memory), and any other information you want to include. Fill in the table with information about the operating systems listed in the chapter. You will have to research some information, such as the current version and price. Identify several other operating systems not listed in the chapter, and add information about them to the table. As new operating systems or new versions of existing operating systems become available, update the table.

4 Set up a table that includes information about programming languages. List the name of the language, the generation, whether it is machine dependent or machine independent, and the types of programs for which it is used. Include machine language, assembly language, all the third-generation languages listed in the chapter, and fourth-generation languages. Find several other third-generation languages not listed in the chapter to include in the table. Use appropriate software to prepare the table.

5 Interview a programmer and find out what programming languages he or she uses. Find out what the programmer likes and dislikes about the languages. Write a summary of the interview.

INTERNET AND ELECTRONIC COMMERCE PROJECTS

1 Use the Internet to investigate the legal requirements for copyrighting software in the United States. Start at the Web site for the U.S. Copyright Office. Also use a search engine to explore other sites that have information. Prepare a brief summary of what a business must do to copyright a program it has developed.

2 Pick a personal computer software company. (Microsoft is the largest, but you might want to pick a smaller company.) Use the Web to find out what you can about the software products sold by that company. Write a summary of the company's software.

3 Find three Web sites that provide software on-line. One site should sell software that the user downloads from the Web site after paying for it (usually by credit card). Another site should allow the user to download software from the Web site and pay for it later, after trying it out for a period of time. (This type of software is called *shareware*.) The third site should allow the user to download software from the Web site for no charge. (Usually this type of software is not copyrighted and is called *public domain software*.) How do the three Web sites compare in terms of providing software? Write a summary of the three Web sites.

BMG

Scientists often make lousy business people. The scientific method isn't an easy companion to the gambling nature of business or the emotional character of the market.

There is, however, one business any mathematician could love. It's called direct marketing. The only thing more scientifically calibrated than the direct marketing business is a closed ecological system such as Biosphere II. An exaggeration? On the contrary: At the top of the direct marketing pyramid, the BMG music house probably does Mother Nature one better. From the millions of pieces of mail offering "12 CDs for 1 penny!" to the automatic monthly product orders received by 8 million BMG members, the executives of BMG know exactly what is going out and what will be coming in.

Unfortunately for BMG, even a perfectly balanced ecology must eventually face a change in weather. BMG's storm came in the form of a new market threat that if responded to correctly, could be a new market opportunity: e-commerce.

New York-based BMG first began to communicate with its customers via the Internet in 1996, with a modest Web site. Within a year, however, it became apparent that a simple informational Web site was an inadequate marketing vehicle at best, and a crippling competitive disadvantage at worst. Competitors such as CDNOW were entering the market with slick multimedia Web sites that were able to reach customers more inexpensively than BMG could by using the U.S. Postal Service.

BMG knew it would have to set up its own e-commerce site. But in a business with otherwise little uncertainty, such a project pushed the company headlong into the unknown. The new notion of transactions via the Internet wasn't the problem. BMG executives don't suffer from a lack of imagination. Rather, the problem was technological: The company had to find a way to adapt its extensive legacy systems to its Web site, in order to create an elegant, intelligent customer interface while preserving security. It was a challenging mandate.

The first order of business was recruiting Elizabeth Rose, a McKinsey consultant, to manage the project. As the senior director of strategic planning and new business development, Rose's job when she came on board with BMG was to determine the company's overall Internet strategy and specifically how the site should look. She wanted an attractive user interface that could accommodate BMG's complex pricing structure.

"The business problem was how do you take a paper-based business that at any point in time has 50 different versions going out to 8 million people, and have that experience online reflect that level of differentiation?" Rose says. "One member coming on the site might have mailing No. 1, while a different member might have mailing No. 18."

Adds Chris Mollis, technical project manager at BMG, "The site had to reflect a 30-year-old paper business model that says the user has a very personalized experience. We had to build a unique site because it's in real time. Meaning, you're actually looking at exactly what our legacy system says is the status of your account. It's pretty remarkable."

To create a real-time exchange of information, BMG needed a Web site that could interact with the company's mainframe in Indianapolis.

"So many of the companies doing e-commerce on the Web are Internet-centric companies," Rose points out. "A lot of the real challenge—and frankly where the hype and disappointment is on the Internet—is in companies with existing businesses trying to adapt to the Internet. What real-time accounting did in particular is take these huge legacy issues and move it forward to the Web site."

"While the [user interface] was extremely critical, you also simply had to have performance," Mollis says. The front end was jazzed up with a RealAudio server from RealNetworks, in Seattle. The back-end database was Oracle, and the application server chosen was Sun Enterprise 2.

To implement all this technology, Rose outsourced the Web development and deployment to Renaissance Solutions, a systems integrator, and Art Technology Group, a Boston-based Java developer and professional services organization. The two shared the system integration work, leaving Mollis as the only full-time dedicated staffer at BMG facilitating the project.

Art Technology Group brought its Dynamo Java-based Web application development framework to the table. The BMG site used the Dynamo Application Server to create a dynamic HTML page-generation engine, which had to be extremely scalable. Currently, the site is handling peak loads of 1,500 concurrent users. But with more than 8 million customers, the potential for exceeding that capacity looms large.

A second piece of the BMG solution was the Dynamo Profile Station, which is a personalization layer. Sitting on top of the dynamically generated pages, it tracks what people are doing on the site, while generating prices for individual users. In one fell swoop, the software, a set of Java Database Connectivity-compliant Java APIs that maps to a back-end database, addressed Rose's complex pricing headache.

The final module was the commerce engine, Dynamo Retail Station, which creates the front end to the commerce engine—the ordering display that users see. Renaissance Solutions and Art Technology used Retail Station to create a shopping basket metaphor for the site.

Although Rose and Mollis say Java as a standard wasn't a criterion for selecting Dynamo, Joe Chung, chief technology officer at Art Technology Group (Cambridge, Massachusetts), believes Java played a crucial, if cloaked, role in the success of the site.

"[BMG] may not be seeing Java right away because they're trying to get a solution out this quarter, but I think it has already played a large role in the success of the site," Chung says. "They had so many business rules; you would not necessarily design an online club like this if it weren't for the many legacy issues."

"Creating all that logic in C++ would have been tremendously time consuming. I think we shaved 50 percent off the development time," Chung says. "Also really important is Java's openness: Virtually every back-end piece of software has an integrated Java plug-in. One reason this project is working is because it's so extensible. I would say 50 percent of extensibility is from our product, but 50 percent is Java itself."

The Web site is off to what Rose assesses as a very good start. With good planning, which she attributes to keeping both the decision-making team and the initial technology ambitions small, it has been successful. BMG has played its first e-commerce game and even carried the ball a little further down the field.

"If you are going to be there, you've got to take advantage of the capabilities e-commerce offers, like an artist search—the full product catalog, the 'what's new' feature of the site, and real-time account history," Rose says.

Questions

1 Why did BMG decide to set up an e-commerce Web site?
2 What technical problem did BMG have to solve in creating its e-commerce site?
3 What business problem did BMG have to solve in creating its e-commerce site?
4 What software tools were used to develop the BMG Web site?
5 What role did Java play in the development of the BMG Web site?

Web Site
BMG Music Services:
www.bmgmusicservice.com

Source: *Adapted from* Ilan Greenberg, "BMG Site Hits the Right Notes," *InfoWorld*, May 4, 1998, p. 79.

Information System

NETWORKS AND THE INTERNET

CHAPTER OUTLINE

Communications Concepts
Communications Hardware
Communications Software
Network Concepts
Local Area Networks
Wide Area Networks
Internetworks
The Internet
Electronic Commerce

After completing this chapter, you should be able to

1 Summarize the communications hardware and software needed for computers to communicate with other computers.

2 Describe the main characteristics of communications channels.

3 Describe the main types of communications processors and give several examples.

4 Describe the main functions of communications software.

5 Explain how local area networks are organized and list the special hardware and software used in them.

6 Describe the structure of wide area networks.

7 Explain how and why networks are interconnected.

8 Explain what the Internet, intranets, and extranets are.

9 Describe the special hardware and software needed for electronic commerce.

etworks in information systems provide communication between computers. The communication may be between two computers or thousands. It may be over a short distance, such as within a single building, or over a long distance, such as throughout a country or between countries. It may use a single network or it may use many interconnected networks. It may involve a private network, which can be used only by the employees of a specific business, or it may involve the Internet, which can be used by anyone.

To make communication possible, networks use special communications hardware and software, which is often called *telecommunications*, or *data communications*,[1] hardware and software. This chapter covers communications hardware and software, and explains how this hardware and software is used in networks that function within a business, between businesses, and between businesses and consumers. First, this chapter presents basic concepts about communications. Then it examines communications hardware and software in detail. Next, it explains basic network concepts including network organization. Then it describes the main types of networks. Finally, this chapter discusses the technology used in the Internet and for electronic commerce.

Communications Concepts

Communications hardware and software allow computers to communicate with other computers. Two main types of communications hardware are needed (Figure 6.1). The first type is a **communications channel**, which is the link over which data is sent. An example of a medium that is used for a communications channel is a telephone line, but other media are used for channels. The second type of communications hardware is **communications processors**, which provide processing capabilities between the computer and the channel. An example of a communications processor is a *modem*, but there are other types of communications processors.

Communications software provides the capabilities for computers to communicate using communications processors and channels. This software sends data from a computer to communications processors, which provide special processing of the data before sending it over a channel. Communications software also receives data for a computer from communications processors after the data has been received

FIGURE 6.1

▲ **Communications hardware**

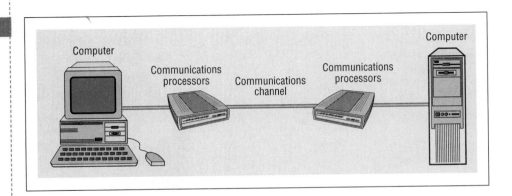

---

[1] Sometimes the term *telecommunications* is used to refer to all forms of electronic communication, including telephone and fax, and the term *data communications* is used just to refer to transmission of data. Often, however, these terms are used interchangeably.

from a channel and processed by the processors. An example of communications software is a network operating system (discussed in Chapter 5) that provides communications capabilities over a network.

Two computers can communicate with each other using a single channel, a minimal number of communications processors, and relatively simple communications software. This approach is called *point-to-point communication*. More often, however, many computers communicate with each other by using one or more channels, many communications processors, and sophisticated communications software. This approach is *network communication*, and it is the main topic of this chapter.

Communications Hardware

Before examining networks in detail, you need to understand some of the characteristics of communications hardware and software. This section describes communications hardware—communications channels and communications processors—and the next section looks at communications software.

Communications Channel Characteristics

A communications channel is the link over which data is transmitted when using data communications. Data is transmitted over a channel as bits; each bit is sent after the other over the channel (Figure 6.2). The bits are grouped to form bytes that represent characters using ASCII, EBCDIC, Unicode, or some other code. The way in which the bits are sent determines two main characteristics of the channel: signal type and data rate.

Signal Type. One characteristic of channels is the type of signal sent over the channel. Bits can be sent as either a **digital signal** or an **analog signal** (Figure 6.3). A digital signal is one that transmits bits as high and low pulses. In a digital signal, a high pulse represents a 1 bit and a low pulse represents a 0 bit. An analog signal, on the other hand, transmits data by a wave pattern that varies continuously. A human voice is an analog signal because it varies continuously from high to low. In an analog channel, different wave patterns represent bits.

Some channels can transmit digital signals, some can transmit analog signals, and some can transmit both digital and analog signals. A computer uses digital signals to send data between its components. Thus, a computer can transmit data over a digital channel without changing the signal type. The wire from most telephones is an analog channel, so to transmit computer data over a telephone line, the data usually must be converted from a digital to an analog form, a process that is discussed later in this chapter.

Data Rate. Another characteristic of channels is the rate at which data is sent over the channel. Data rate is measured in *bits per second* (*bps*). Each type of channel has a maximum data rate, varying from a low of several hundred bps for very slow-

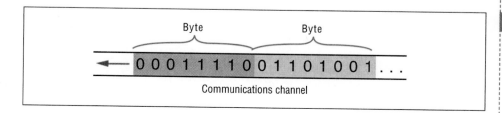

FIGURE 6.2

Sending bits over a communications channel

FIGURE 6.3

▲ **Signal types**

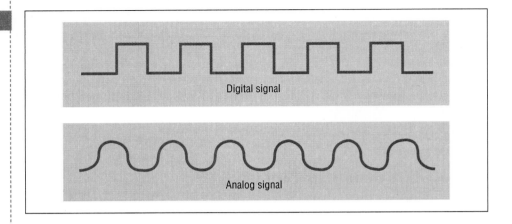

speed channels to billions of bps (gigabits per second, or Gbps) for high-speed channels. In between are channels that transmit thousands of bps (kilobits per second, or Kbps) and millions of bps (megabits per second, or Mbps). It is always possible to transmit at a slower rate than the maximum allowed by the channel.

Sometimes the term **baud rate** is used to express the data rate. For example, someone might say he or she is transmitting at 9,600 baud, meaning 9,600 bps. This term is not exactly correct, however. Baud rate refers to the number of times per second that the signal on a channel changes—for example, changing from a high to a low pulse. Depending on the channel, each signal change can represent 1, 2, or more bits. If the channel is such that each signal change represents 1 bit, the baud rate and bps are the same. But if the channel is such that each signal change represents more than 1 bit, then the baud rate is less than the bps. Hence, baud rate and bps may or may not be the same. To be safe, the data rate should always be stated in bps.

Because data is transmitted on a channel in a code, each character requires a certain number of bits (7 or 8 bits for ASCII, 8 bits for EBCDIC, 16 bits for Unicode). In addition to the code for the character, other bits are sent with the character bits. These bits are used to separate characters and to check for errors. As a rough rule of thumb, you can assume that each character requires 10 bits (or 20 bits, if Unicode is used). Hence, you can estimate the data rate in characters per second by dividing the bps by 10 (or 20, for Unicode). For example, a 33,600 bps channel can transmit approximately 3,360 characters per second.

The term **bandwidth** is also used when discussing data rate. Bandwidth has to do with how much data can be transmitted over a channel. "Higher bandwidth" means more data can be transmitted. The technical definition of bandwidth is not important here—only the concept that higher bandwidth means more data can be sent. Bandwidth becomes especially important when transmitting graphics, sound, video, and other nontext data because this type of data uses large numbers of bits.

Communications Channel Media

Different media can be used for communications channels. In fact, a channel may consist of several different media, connected in sequence. The choice of the media affects the speed and the cost of communications.

Wire Cables.   Wire cables are the oldest media used for electronic communications. They have been used since the first telegraph machines in the 1800s. Data is transmitted over a wire cable by sending an electrical signal along the wire. Data may

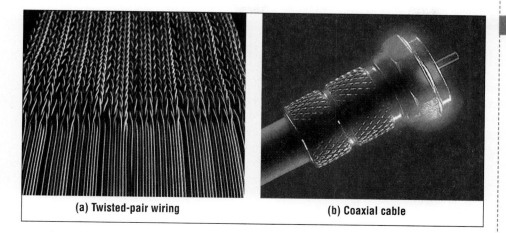

FIGURE 6.4

Wire cables ▲

| (a) Twisted-pair wiring | (b) Coaxial cable |

be sent in an analog or a digital form over a wire cable. Today, two main forms of wire cables are used for data communications: twisted-pair wiring and coaxial cable (Figure 6.4).

Twisted-pair wiring consists of two wires twisted together. Most telephone lines use this medium for local voice communications, but it can also be used for data communications. It is relatively inexpensive, but its data transmission rate is slow compared to other media. *Coaxial cable* consists of copper wire heavily insulated with rubber and plastic. It is the type of cable used with cable television systems and is more expensive than twisted-pair wiring, but can transmit data at a greater rate.

Fiber-optic Cables.   An alternative to wire cable is *fiber-optic cable* (Figure 6.5). A fiber-optic cable consists of bundles of glass or plastic fibers. Each fiber is 1/2,000 inch thick—about the size of a human hair. Data is transmitted by a laser that pulses light through the fiber. Each pulse represents a bit, so data is transmitted in a digital form. The laser can pulse more than one billion times per second, meaning data can be transmitted at more than 1Gbps, a very fast rate. For long-distance communications, fiber-optic cables are preferred over wire cables.

Most telephone companies use fiber-optic cables for some voice communications. Because a voice is an analog signal, the voice must be converted to digital form (bits) for transmission over a fiber-optic cable and then converted back to analog

FIGURE 6.5

Fiber-optic cable ▲

Wireless Communications at Illinois Power

Illinois Power is plugging wireless technology into its customer service activities in a bid to improve its field operations and help retain customers as Illinois opens its electric marketplace to competition.

Illinois Power, a subsidiary of $2.4 billion Illinova in Decatur, Illinois provides gas and electric services to nearly 1 million customers, mainly in central Illinois.

After years of planning and implementation, Illinois Power completed a wireless land-antenna-based system that connects 500 service trucks equipped with laptops to a central computer-aided dispatching system, says Roger Koester, supervisor of energy delivery technology. The system has reduced the utility's dispatching and service costs and allows customers to schedule service more reliably.

Koester says the project has cost millions, but declined to elaborate for competitive reasons. Spending began in 1997, and Illinois Power expects to see a return on its investment soon. For example, the project has generated thousands of dollars per month in fixed-cost savings because dispatching is now done centrally, said Koester. Still, he stresses that the main improvement has been in customer service. "A few years ago, there weren't that many competitors," said Koester, adding that since then, the competition "has just exploded."

Utilities nationwide are looking for ways to apply a variety of new technologies, including wireless networks and pagers, to gain a competitive edge as deregulation takes root, says David Burks, a financial analyst at J. J. B. Hilliard, W. L. Lyons in Louisville, Kentucky.

Burks adds that Illinois Power's customer service project has helped the company increase its stock price during the past year, at a time when the stock prices of 30 other utilities he follows have dropped.

Before Illinois Power upgraded its dispatching system with technology from Bell-South Wireless Data LP in Atlanta, the utility's 26 field offices would take phone requests from customers for services or repairs. The customers' calls would be written down by a customer service agent, who would then forward them to dispatchers to coordinate work orders with repair crews.

Now, says Koester "the driver gets in his truck and instead of searching through paper, his day's work is loaded on the laptop." Many drivers now start their routes from home, eliminating trips to a central dispatcher. That's saving the company thousands of dollars in gas and making its repair crew more productive.

Because the trucks are also equipped with global positioning system (GPS) locators tied to a central computer, Illinois Power can easily find a truck to respond to an emergency.

Koester says some crew members have balked at learning to use the laptop system, but the majority likes using it, partly because they can take the laptops from the truck docking stations to a meter or switch, where they can type in updated information.

Kevin Bennett, the business manager of Local 1306 of the International Brotherhood of Electrical Workers in Decatur, says some crew members initially complained about communications when their trucks were in dead radio zones in the service territory. When that happened, he says, the repairmen had to leave the job and find a phone to contact a dispatcher.

Koester says Illinois Power at the outset created a partnership with BellSouth to build 27 wireless base stations throughout central Illinois to keep dead zones to a minimum. In fact, he says, the wireless laptop project is so successful that it will be used as a model by Dynegy, a Houston-based power company Illinova is merging with.

Questions

1. Why did Illinois Power decide to use wireless technology to connect laptop com-

puters in its service trucks to a central computer-aided dispatching system?

2. How has Illinois Power benefited from the wireless system?

3. How have service truck drivers benefited from the wireless system?

Web Site
Illinois Power:
www.illinoispower.com

Source: *Adapted from* Matt Hamblen, "Wireless Net Helps Utility Improve Customer Service," *Computerworld*, January 24, 2000, p. 36.

form at the receiving end. (This conversion is done by a device called a *codec*, which stands for coder-decoder.) Computer communication using fiber optics, however, does not require conversion because computer signals are already in digital form.

Microwave Communication.   *Microwaves* are special types of radio signals that are sent from one microwave antenna to another. Microwave transmission is *line-of-sight*, which means that there must be nothing between the antennas because microwaves cannot bend around objects. Both voice and data can be transmitted by microwaves, and the signal can be in analog or digital form. Microwave systems are very expensive, but they do not require direct cables, and they can transmit data very rapidly.

Two types of microwave systems are used (Figure 6.6). The first is a land-based system, in which data is sent from one microwave antenna to the next. Because microwave transmission is line-of-sight and because of the curvature of the earth, land-based microwave antennas must be no more than about 30 miles apart. The second type of microwave system is satellite based. In this system, data is sent from an earth microwave antenna up to a satellite and then down to another earth antenna. The satellite is about 22,300 miles in space. At that altitude, the satellite revolves around the earth at the same velocity as the earth rotates, so it appears to be in a fixed position in the sky. Satellite-based microwave systems can transmit data over a much greater distance than can land-based systems.

Wireless Communication.   Microwaves are a form of wireless transmission that is used for long-distance communication. For shorter-distance communication other wireless systems are used. There are two main categories of these wireless sys-

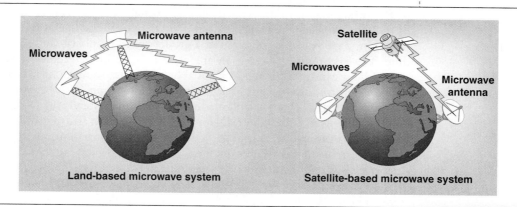

FIGURE 6.6

Microwave systems

tems. One category is designed for wireless communication within a small area such as a room or a building. These systems use two common approaches. One is radio waves similar to those used in cordless telephones. Another is infrared light beams, which are like those used in television remote controls. Infrared light is line-of-sight, transmission, so infrared systems must be placed such that the beam cannot be broken.

The other category of wireless systems is designed for communication from a computer that is moved often, a situation sometimes called *mobile computing*. In this situation, the computer needs to be connected to a network from almost anyplace, including a moving automobile, a factory floor, or an agricultural field. These wireless systems usually use cellular telephone communication, which is a type of radio communication.

Communications Channel Sources

Communications channels are provided in two main ways. One is by purchasing and installing the necessary hardware, which forms a *private communications system*. The other is by purchasing access to hardware owned by another company, which is called a *public communications system*.

Any organization can purchase the necessary hardware to set up a private communications system. This approach is common when the communication is limited to a small geographic area, such as a building or a group of nearby buildings. Private systems are rare, however, for long-distance communications. Stringing long-distance wire or fiber-optic cables, setting up a system of microwave antennas, or launching a satellite is very expensive. Such expense is warranted only when the organization has significant communication needs.

Most organizations use public communications systems for long-distance communications. These systems are called *public* because anyone who is willing to pay the fee can use them. The main public system is the telephone network, which is owned by many companies called *common carriers*. In the United States, local telephone companies, such as Pacific Bell in California, handle short-distance communications, and other companies, such as AT&T, Sprint, and MCI, handle long-distance communications. In many other countries, telephone communication is handled by government-owned systems.

Telephone networks from common carriers usually send an analog signal over the telephone line connected to the customer's telephone. An alternative approach is to use a system that sends a digital signal over the telephone line. One system for this is **ISDN**, which stands for Integrated Services Digital Network. The advantage of ISDN is that both voice and data can be sent over the telephone line at the same time. In addition, data can be transmitted at a greater speed than with an analog telephone line. The maximum speed for an analog telephone line currently is 56 Kbps, but ISDN lines can transmit at 128 Kbps. The main disadvantage of ISDN is that it is more expensive than standard telephone communication. Another system for sending a digital signal over a telephone line is **DSL**, which stands for Digital Subscriber Line. DSL is even faster than ISDN, up to 6 Mbps, but it is also more expensive.

Instead of using the telephone network for communication, the cable television network can be used. This network uses coaxial cable, which can send data faster than the twisted-pair wiring used in the telephone network, up to 5 Mbps, and even faster in some cases. In addition, cable can carry voice, television, and radio signals at the same time it is sending data. The disadvantage of cable TV communications is that it is not available everywhere. Currently, cable TV communication is analog, although in the future it may be digital.

Communications Processors

A computer cannot communicate over a channel by itself; it needs special communications processors between it and the channel. These devices provide various functions so that the computer can send and receive data over the channel. Two main types of communications processors are channel interface devices and communications control units.

Channel Interface Devices.   A channel cannot be plugged directly into a computer; a **channel interface device** is needed to provide the connection between the computer and the channel. Depending on the type of channel, different devices are used for this purpose.

When a computer is connected to an analog channel, a **modem** is needed to provide the connection. Computers transmit data using digital signals. To send data over an analog channel, the digital signals from the computer must be converted to an analog form for transmission, a process called *modulation*. The analog data, when it reaches the other end of the channel, must be converted back to digital form, which is called *demodulation*. Modulation and demodulation are performed by a modem, which stands for modulator-demodulator. There must be a modem at each end of the channel—one to modulate the signal and one to demodulate it (Figure 6.7).

Because the most common source of analog communications channels is the telephone network, most modems are designed to connect computers to telephone lines and to modulate and demodulate signals sent over those lines. Usually with a personal computer, a modem is a circuit board in the computer and has a jack into which the telephone line is plugged. It is called an *internal modem* because it is inside the computer. Sometimes an *external modem*, which is outside the computer, is used with a personal computer, connected to it by a cable. With larger computers, modems are usually external. Most personal computer modems also include facsimile, or fax, capability, which allows the computer to send and receive faxes by using the modem. This type of modem often is called a *fax modem*.

In addition to providing conversion between digital and analog signals for a channel, modems determine the data rate of the transmission. Modems for telephone lines can be purchased with different data rates. For example, 33 Kbps and 56 Kbps modems are common. In general, the faster the modem, the more expensive it is. The speed of the modem must be less than or equal to the maximum speed allowed by the channel. In addition, the modems at each end of the channel must transmit data at the same speed.

For a cable television channel, a special **cable modem** is needed. This modem provides modulation and demodulation like a modem for a telephone line, but also does other processing necessary to send and receive data over cable.

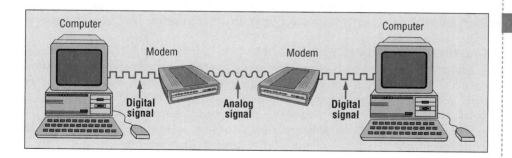

FIGURE 6.7

Use of modems

Modems are used to connect computers to analog telephone lines. To connect a computer to a digital telephone line, such as an ISDN or a DSL line, a **terminal adapter** is needed. Because the channel is digital, the adapter does not have to modulate and demodulate the signal as does a modem. Instead, the adapter adjusts the form of the digital signal from the computer to the form required by the digital line.

Different adapters are needed for different types of lines. For an ISDN line, an *ISDN terminal adapter* is needed, and for a DSL line, a *DSL terminal adapter* is used. Often people refer to these adapters as "modems." For example, someone may refer to an "ISDN modem" or a "DSL modem." These devices do not do modulation and demodulation as we have described them here, so this terminology is not correct, although it is common.

Communications Control Units.   Two computers may be connected over a channel with no other devices sharing the channel. In this simple situation, only channel interface devices such as modems are needed to connect the computer to the channel. An alternative is to have several computers share a channel. When this situation occurs, special **communications control units** are needed. These units control the communications traffic over channels much like traffic police control automobile traffic on city streets. For example, when several terminals share a channel, a device is needed to keep the communications from getting mixed up.

There are several types of communications control units. One is a *multiplexer*, which takes the signals from several slow-speed devices and combines them for transmission over a high-speed channel. At the other end of the channel another multiplexer breaks the high-speed signal from the channel into the separate signals from each device. Another type of communications control unit is a *controller*. This unit allows several devices to communicate over a channel by storing signals from each device and forwarding them when appropriate.

Many computer systems have a separate computer, often a minicomputer, that handles communications control. This computer is called a *front-end processor* because it operates between the channel and the main computer. It performs all communications functions for the main computer, thus reducing the workload of that computer.

Figure 6.8 shows how communications control units might be used for data communications. In this figure, several terminals at the user's local site are managed by a controller. This controller, along with personal computers at the local site, send signals to a multiplexer, which combines the signals and forwards them to a modem. The modem modulates the signal from the multiplexer for transmission over a high-speed communications channel. At the remote site, where the main computer is located, another modem demodulates the signal and sends it to the front-end processor, which breaks the multiplexed signal into separate signals. Also at the remote site, the front-end processor receives signals directly from other personal computers and from another controller. The front-end processor sends signals from all sources to the main computer, which is sometimes called the *host computer*. To send signals back to the terminals and personal computers from the computer, this process is reversed.

Communications Protocols

When people talk with each other, they follow unstated rules about how to communicate. For example, they agree to talk in the same language, they say *hello* when they meet and *good-bye* when they part, and when one person talks, the other person is quiet. These rules are necessary to ensure proper communication.

When computers communicate, they also must follow rules. These rules are called **protocols**. The protocol states what language the communication will be in

FIGURE 6.8

Use of communications control units

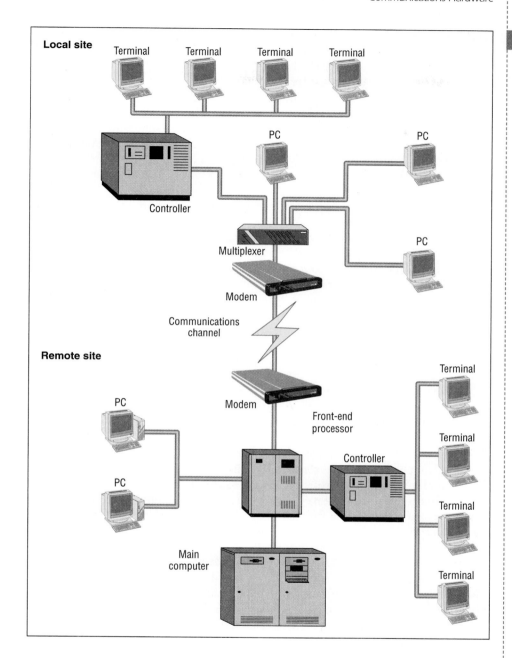

Local site

Terminal Terminal Terminal Terminal

PC PC

Controller

PC

Multiplexer

Modem

Communications channel

Remote site

PC

PC

Modem

Front-end processor

Controller

Main computer

Terminal

Terminal

Terminal

Terminal

(ASCII, EBCDIC, Unicode), what signal will start the communication and what signal will end it, and how one device will know whether the other is communicating so that it does not try to communicate at the same time.

Unfortunately, not all computers use the same protocols. Often, computers manufactured by different companies use different protocols. If two computers with incompatible protocols are to communicate, some way of converting the protocols of one computer to those of the other is needed. This function is performed by a communications processor called a **protocol converter**. The converter connects one computer with the channel that goes to the other computer. With the appropriate type of protocol converter, a computer that uses one set of protocols can communicate with one that uses different protocols.

Communications Security

One problem with data communications is the lack of security of the data transmitted over a channel. It is sometimes possible to tap into a communications channel and intercept data sent over it. This is especially a problem with wireless communications, such as microwaves, which can easily be intercepted by anyone with the appropriate equipment. If the data is transmitted in a common code, such as ASCII, then the data is easy to interpret. In most cases, personal and business data must be keep secure from interception.

One way of solving this problem is to code the data in an unintelligible form before it is transmitted. This process is called **data encryption**, and it can be done by a special data encryption device. The data is coded by the device and then sent over the channel. The code is not a simple code such as ASCII, but rather a complex code that cannot be interpreted without a special *key*. The key, which is a long number, is entered into the data encryption device, and the device encodes the data using the key. At the other end of the channel, a similar device is used to decode the data after it is received. The key must be entered into the receiving data encryption device so that the data is decoded correctly. If the channel is tapped and the key is not known, the coded data cannot be interpreted correctly. The key is changed periodically so that if an unauthorized person gets access to the key, it will not work after the key has been changed.

Communications Software

Communications software is needed to control communications between computers. Each computer must have communications software. This software receives data from communications processors connected to the channel and passes the data to other software in the computer for processing. The communications software also gets the results of processing from software in the computer and sends this data to communications processors for transmission over the channel.

Personal Computer Communications Software

A personal computer can be used in two ways when communicating with another computer: as a terminal and as a client computer for client/server computing. To use a personal computer as a terminal, communications software called **terminal emulation software** is needed. This software makes the personal computer act like a terminal so that the other computer thinks it is communicating with a terminal, not with another computer. Then a user can use the personal computer exactly as if he or she were using a terminal connected directly to the other computer. Because different types of terminals have different characteristics, personal computer terminal emulation software allows the user to select which type of terminal he or she wants the software to emulate.

To use a personal computer as a client for client/server computing, communications software that provides communication for **client software** is needed. Recall from Chapter 3 that client/server computing involves personal client computers communicating with a server computer that provides services to the clients. The client computers need special client software so that they can process and display data from the server. To send data to and receive data from the server, the client soft-

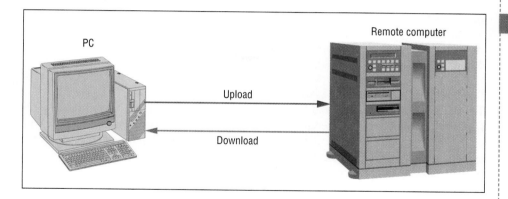

FIGURE 6.9

File transferring

ware uses communications software. This software often is included in the client software. Examples of client software are Web browsers and many e-mail programs. These types of software usually include the necessary communications software.

Personal computer communications software often provides **file transfer** capability, which allows the user to send data from a file at the personal computer to the other computer and vice versa. When data is sent from a personal computer to a remote computer, the process is called **uploading**. When data is sent from a remote computer to a personal computer the process is called **downloading** (Figure 6.9). Personal computer communications software allows a user to both upload and download files with another computer.

Multiple-user Computer Communications Software

Multiple-user computer communications software provides the ability for minicomputers and mainframe computers to communicate with many terminals (or personal computers with terminal emulation software). This type of software, which is sometimes called a *telecommunications monitor*, keeps track of which terminal sent which data and decides to which terminal the results of processing should be sent. The telecommunications monitor also provides security. When the user logs in, it checks to see if the user's identification number and password are valid. The telecommunications monitor or other software in the computer may provide certain functions, sometimes done by hardware, including protocol conversion, code conversion (e.g., conversion between ASCII and EBCDIC), and data encryption. If the system has a front-end processor, the telecommunications monitor runs in that computer so that the main computer does not have to do communications processing.

Network Communications Software

With a network, software is needed on server computers to provide communications over the network. This software is the *network operating system (NOS)*, as discussed in Chapter 5. The network operating system allows multiple client and server computers in a network to send and receive data over the network. It also provides security features so that unauthorized users cannot use the network.

Network Concepts

Although two computers can communicate using point-to-point communication, most often many computers communicate using network communication. Network communication involves the transmission of data between computers and servers connected to a network. The network may include just a few computers and one server, or it may involve thousands of computers and many servers. In the case of the Internet, millions of computers and thousands of servers communicate with each other.

Network Organization

To accomplish network communications, the network must be organized in a logical way. Each computer connected to a network is called a *node* in the network. One way of organizing the nodes in a network is for each node to be connected to all other nodes in the network, an arrangement sometimes called a *mesh* (Figure 6.10). The problem with this arrangement is that as more nodes are added to the network, many more connections are needed. (With 5 nodes, 10 connections are needed; with 6 nodes, 15 connections are needed; with 7 nodes, 21 connections are needed, and so forth.) To solve this problem, several common organizations are used for networks (Figure 6.11).

In a **star network** each node is connected to a central computer node. For two nodes to communicate, data must be sent from one node to the central computer, and then the central computer sends the data on to the other node. The primary advantage of this approach is that the "distance" that data has to travel is short; data has to travel only through the central computer to get from one node to another. The main disadvantage is that if the central computer fails, the entire network cannot function.

A **hierarchical network** consists of nodes organized like a family tree. The top node is a central computer that is connected to several nodes. Each of these nodes is connected to several other nodes, and so forth. Two nodes can communicate by sending data from the first node "up" the hierarchy to a common node, which then sends the data "down" to the second node. This approach is more reliable than a star network because failure of any one node does not mean the entire network cannot function. It is more complex than a star network, however, and data may have to travel a greater "distance" to get from one node to another.

In a **bus network**, each node is connected to a single, common communications channel called a *bus*. To transmit data from one node to another, the first node sends

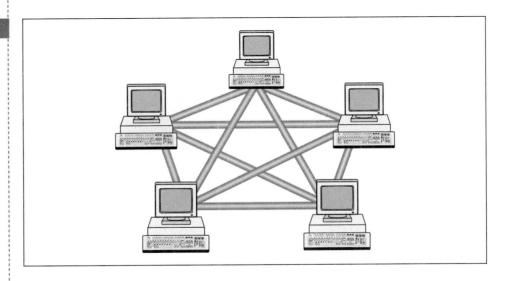

FIGURE 6.11

Network organizations ▲

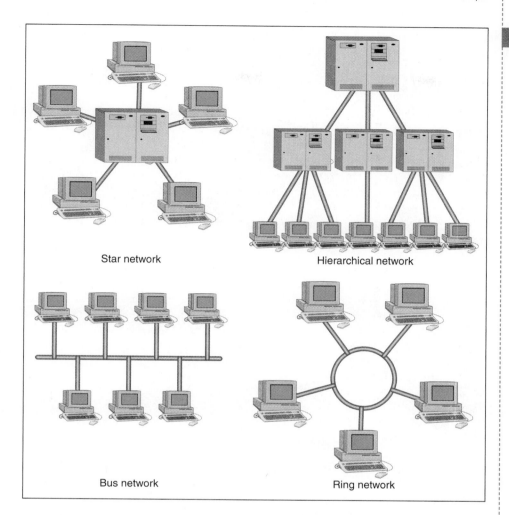

Star network   Hierarchical network

Bus network   Ring network

the data and information that identifies the node that is to receive the data in both directions over the bus. Each node on the bus examines the identifying information and, if it is the receiving node, takes the data from the bus. This approach is very reliable because there is no central computer, and failure of any node does not affect the function of the network. Communication speed can be slower than in other types of networks, however.

A **ring network** consists of nodes connected to form a loop. Data travels from node to node in the ring, usually in one direction only. To send data from one node to another, the first node sends the data and information about which node is to receive the data to the next node in the ring. This node either keeps the data if it is the receiving node or forwards the data on to the next node. This process continues until the data reaches the receiving node. Most ring networks are as reliable as bus networks because if a node fails, the data can be sent past the failed node and hence the function of the network is not affected. Like a bus network, communication can be slower on a ring network than on other types of networks.

Finally, many networks are **hybrid networks**, which means they are combinations of the network organizations described so far. Thus, a network may have some nodes

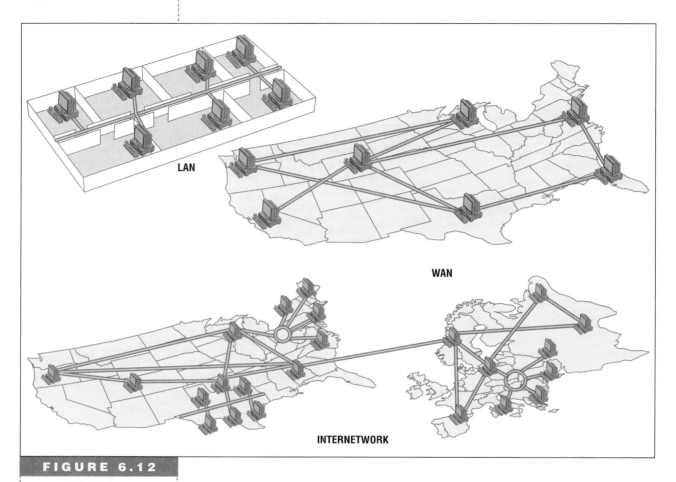

FIGURE 6.12

▲ **Types of networks**

connected in no particular pattern, others connected in a star or a hierarchy, and still others that form a bus or a ring. A hybrid network provides the greatest versatility in network organization.

Types of Networks

A network can span any area from a single room to the entire globe. Networks fall into two main types—local area networks and wide area networks—depending on the area covered by the network. In addition, networks can be interconnected to form a third type of network—internetworks (Figure 6.12).

If a network occupies a room, a building, or a group of nearby buildings, such as a business park or a college campus, it is called a **local area network** (**LAN**). LANs can contain just a few computers or hundreds of computers. When a network covers a large geographic area, such as a city, a country, or several countries, it is called a **wide area network** (**WAN**). A WAN can have hundreds or thousands of computers. (A WAN that just covers a city is sometimes called a *metropolitan area networks* [*MAN*].) Finally, several networks can be connected together to form an **internetwork**. An internetwork can be made up of interconnected LANs and WANs. For example, two WANs can be interconnected along with three LANs in different locations to form an internetwork. As we will discuss later in this chapter, the Internet is a special internetwork.

Local Area Networks

Local area networks are used in many businesses. Their simple structure and important business uses make them very popular. Many businesses with operations and offices in different locations have a LAN at each location.

Local Area Network Structure

LANs are usually organized as bus or ring networks, using coaxial cable, twisted-pair wiring, or fiber-optic cable as a communications channel medium. LANs may also use wireless communication channels such as radio waves and infrared beams. Local area bus networks are usually a type of network called an *Ethernet*, which is a networking approach developed by Xerox. Ring networks, on the other hand, are often a type of network called a *Token Ring*, which is a networking approach developed by IBM.

Wireless communication is used for **wireless LANs**, which are local area networks that communicate without wires. Wireless LANs are used in situations where it is difficult to connect computers directly with wires. For example, a wireless LAN might be used in a production area where wiring a LAN would be difficult, or in a situation where portable computers are used and frequently moved to different locations.

Users most often use a LAN through client personal computers that communicate with server computers in the network. Figure 6.13 summarizes the hardware and software needed for LAN communications. To connect a personal computer to a LAN channel, a channel interface device called a **network interface card** (**NIC**) is needed. The NIC is a circuit board in the computer into which the LAN cable or wire is plugged. A personal computer also needs communications software to allow it to send and receive data over the network's channel. This software is normally part of the operating system of the personal computer. A server computer is also connected to the LAN channel by a NIC. A server needs a network operating system to provide communication with client computers.

A LAN may contain several types of servers with resources that can be used by any of the client computers. A **print server** is a server with a printer that can be used for printing by other computers connected to the LAN. A **file server** is a server with a secondary storage device, usually a large hard disk drive, that can be used for file storage by other computers in the LAN. (Often one server is used as both a print server and a file server.) A **database server** is a server with secondary storage that can be used for database processing by other LAN computers.

LANs always use private communications systems because a business or an organization purchases the necessary hardware and software to set up the LAN. The business must buy cable for the LAN channel (unless it is wireless, in which case other hardware is required to send and receive the wireless signals), the servers needed in the LAN, a NIC for each computer, and the necessary software for all computers. In addition to installing the NICs and software, the business has to run the LAN cable to each location with a computer that is to be connected to the LAN. This process can be very expensive because of the need to run cable through walls between rooms and between buildings.

Business Uses of Local Area Networks

A user can use any of the resources in a LAN. For example, when the user needs to print output, he or she can send the output data to the print server. To store or retrieve common data, the user can communicate with the file or database server. The user can use any of the shared resources in the LAN by sending data over the LAN.

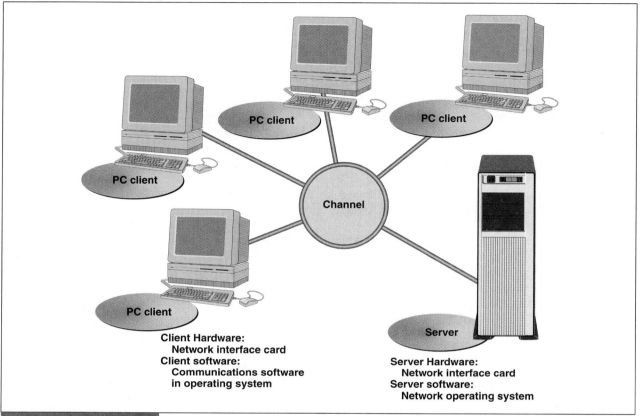

FIGURE 6.13

Communications hardware
and software needs for local
▲ area network communications

A LAN also provides convenient information sharing. Data can be stored on a file or database server, where it is available to all users. Word processing documents, spreadsheets, graphic images, and other items can also be stored on a file server for access by different users. A LAN usually has an e-mail system that stores electronic messages on a file server. All these techniques make LANs very useful for sharing information.

Client/Server Computing

LANs are often used for client/server computing (Figure 6.14). In this approach, a database server computer in the LAN stores databases for use by many client computers. The server has database software for storing and accessing data on the server. The client computers are usually the users' personal computers with application software that processes data and provides a user interface.

Client/server computing might be used as follows: A user enters a request for data processing through the user interface on the client computer. The client software determines what data is needed and sends a request for the data over the LAN to the database server. The server's database software then locates the requested data and sends it back to the client over the LAN. The client software processes the data and presents the results of processing through the user interface to the user.

Businesses use client/server computing extensively in information systems. For example, a business may do inventory control using client/server computing. The inventory database would be on the database server in the network, and the client computers in the network would have access to the inventory data, processing it and presenting the results to the user.

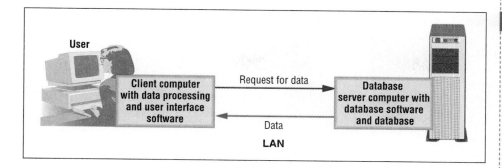

FIGURE 6.14

Client/server computing ▲

Client/server computing has several advantages over multiple-user computer processing. One advantage is that the shared database server computer only does database management, not data processing or user interface control. With multiple-user computer processing, however, the central computer must do database management, data processing, and user interface control, which requires a much larger computer than a database server. Another advantage to client/server computing is that it is relatively easy to add capabilities for more users. More client personal computers with the required software can easily be added to the network without changing the server. With multiple-user computer processing, however, it is often necessary to acquire a new main computer in order to add more users. Because of these advantages, networks using client/server computing have replaced multiple-user computers in many businesses.

Wide Area Networks

Wide area networks are used in many businesses that have operations or offices at distant locations. Although their structure is more complex than that of LANs, the business uses of WANs provide many benefits. Some businesses have more than one WAN, with different WANs covering different parts of the operations.

Wide Area Network Structure

WANs sometimes are organized as star or hierarchical networks, but more often are organized as hybrid networks. WANs can use any channel media, including fiber-optic cable and microwaves, for communications. Often, the channel is a combination of media. For example, a channel may start as a twisted-pair wire that connects to a fiber-optic cable, that then connects to a land-based microwave system, and eventually connects to a satellite system.

WANs often include many different types of computers, from personal computers to supercomputers. Users usually use a WAN through personal computers. The user's computer can be connected to the WAN using the communications processors described earlier, such as channel interface devices and communications control units. Multiple-user computers in WANs also need various communications processors. Servers in WANs can be similar to those used in LANs, or they can be minicomputers, mainframe computers, or even supercomputers. All computers in WANs require communications software.

WANs may use private or public communications systems. A business can set up a private communications system for its WAN by purchasing the necessary cables and installing a microwave system for communication among its locations. If a WAN spans a significant area, however, it is usually more economical to use a public communications system for the WAN. In this case, a business can lease long-distance

A Wide Area Network for Designer Shoe Warehouse

After passing on more expensive wide area network services, Designer Shoe Warehouse (DSW) replaced the rudimentary system it uses to poll (access) stores for sales data with a relatively inexpensive dial-up virtual private network (VPN).

The VPN, which uses AT&T's Internet backbone (communications channel), is far cheaper, faster, and more secure than using what had largely been 9.6 Kbps dial-up connections to DSW's 50 stores nationwide.

"What we're creating is a pseudo wide area network that's available around the clock for our stores," says Fred Bunell, management of information services director at the shoe retailer's parent company, Shonac Corporation in Columbus, Ohio. "It's very inexpensive, offers a great degree of flexibility, and provides a foundation for us to deploy new systems for our stores."

Using a VPN based on one Internet service provider's (ISP's) backbone is a popular approach, but it's less common to move directly from simple polling to using a VPN for real-time communications and applications such as e-mail, according to Tom Nolle, president of CIMI, a consultancy firm in Voorhees, New Jersey.

Nolle says DSW's approach is a relatively inexpensive way for customers to make such a move. It's also flexible because individual stores can use leased lines to the network if their transmission needs increase, he says.

Bunell says he considered a frame relay network and a dial-up frame relay network. The former would have provided guaranteed speeds of 56 Kbps to 64 Kbps, but would have cost $25,000 to $30,000 per month. The latter would have cost $13,000 to $15,000 per month. The VPN implementation DSW selected offers speeds of 56 Kbps at best, but costs only $1,200 to $1,500 per month.

The company considered building a VPN using the services of multiple ISPs, but Bunell wanted one that offered points of presence, or entry points to the backbone, close to each DSW store. "A single [ISP] providing a VPN on its own infrastructure can provide service-quality assurances, whereas all you get is best-effort performance with the Internet," Nolle says. But customers can still be subject to problems on the backbone, such as congestion and security, he adds.

With the VPN, a DSW employee is first authenticated against a list in a special server running at a DSW location. If the user is approved, a 56 Kbps modem connects him to the closest AT&T entry point. Then a 3Com router at the DSW site establishes a connection to the destination and applies encryption to the data for transmission. That data is then decrypted by the router at the receiving site.

After the VPN is completed, DSW stores will be able to communicate with headquarters online in real-time, allowing e-mail to replace heavy faxing and phone calls to headquarters, Bunell says.

Questions

1. Why did DSW choose to use a VPN for its wide area network instead of another approach?
2. What can DSW do if its transmission needs increase in the future?
3. What do routers do in the system?

Web Site

Shoes on the Net:
www.shoesonthenet.com

Source: Adapted from Bob Wallace, "Shoe Chain Likes Fit of Dial-up for Its VPN," Computerworld, May 3, 1999, p. 66

channels from a common carrier for its WAN. The business has to provide hardware and the software for WAN communication using the common carrier channel. Alternatively, a business can contract with a special type of communications company for the long-distance links. This communications company provides a **value added network (VAN)** for use by the business. The VAN usually uses communications channels from common carriers, but the communications company provides additional hardware, software, and services needed for the WAN—the "value added" to the network—thus relieving the business using the WAN of this responsibility.

An alternative to using a common carrier channel or a value added network for a WAN is to use the Internet. One problem with using the Internet for this purpose is that it is not very secure; it is sometimes possible to intercept data sent over the Internet. To solve this problem some businesses contract with a company that sets up a type of network called a **virtual private network (VPN)** that uses the Internet for communications. The VPN uses special technology, including data encryption, to ensure the security of the data sent over the Internet.

Business Uses of Wide Area Networks

WANs are set up by businesses that have offices and other facilities at distant locations. For example, airlines use WANs for their reservation systems so that reservation clerks at airports and travel agents in their offices can communicate with central computers. Another example is banks, which use WANs to connect automated teller machines (ATMs) with the bank's computers.

WANs provide long-distance remote access to information and processing. When data is stored on a computer in the WAN, it can be accessed by any other computer connected to the WAN. Processing can be done at remote computers in the WAN by signaling the computer to execute a particular program.

As with LANs, WANs allow easy sharing of information. Data stored in a computer in a WAN is available to any other WAN computer. Many organizations use WANs for sending and receiving e-mail over long distances.

WANs make it easy to share resources. A WAN may contain special computers, printers, storage devices, software, and other resources that can be shared among all WAN users. For example, a business may have a supercomputer connected to a WAN that can be used by anyone in the business. WANs provide such resource sharing over long distances.

WANs make global connectivity a reality for businesses. Through international WANs, global businesses are able to keep track of distant operations. For example, a business with headquarters in San Francisco can communicate with its operations in South America, Europe, and Asia, and share information with offices in New York and London. Such international communication is made possible by WANs.

WANs, like LANs, are used for client/server computing. Users at client computers, which are usually personal computers, can access data stored on server computers in the WAN. The only difference between client/server computing on LANs and WANs is the distance over which the data has to travel between the server and the client.

Internetworks

One of the major trends in communications is toward interconnecting different networks to create an internetwork. For example, a business may have LANs in each office that are connected to a national WAN, which in turn is connected to an international WAN. Internetworks provide the ability for any user connected to any network in the business to share information and resources, or have access to remote information or processing throughout all the networks in the business.

Internetworks use various devices to connect different networks. A *bridge* is a hardware device that is used to connect two similar networks, such as two similar LANs. A *gateway* is a device used to connect two different types of networks, such as a LAN with a WAN. A *router* is a device that routes messages through various networks. Sophisticated communications software is required with these and other devices to interconnect networks.

Internetworks are often used in organizational information systems that span significant distances. For example, a business may have a customer order system in which orders are entered at computers connected to LANs in several distant locations. The remote LANs are connected by a WAN to another LAN at a central location where access to customer and product databases is provided. The internetwork may cross national borders so that different parts of it are in different countries, in which case it would be an *international network*. The customer order system would then be an international information system. The order system functions smoothly because of the ability to interconnect the different networks.

Internetworks are also used for interorganizational information systems. These systems, discussed in Chapter 1, allow organizations to use computers to transact business among themselves. Examples of interorganizational information systems are electronic data interchange (EDI) systems that allow businesses to exchange data such as purchase orders and bills, and electronic funds transfer (EFT) systems that allow funds to be transferred electronically between financial institutions. These systems require networks in different businesses to be interconnected in *interorganizational networks* so that information can be electronically exchanged between the businesses.

The Internet

The most well-known internetwork is the **Internet**. The Internet is the name of a public, international collection of interconnected WANs and LANs. It is a public network because anyone who is willing to pay the necessary access fee can use it. It is international because it is available in practically every location in the world. It is an internetwork because it consists of many interconnected WANs and LANs.

The Internet grew out of several military, academic, and research networks. Today its exact size is unknown, but it includes several million computers and many millions of users around the world. The Internet is part of the **information superhighway**, which is a concept for allowing any computer to be connected to a national or an international network, just as any telephone can be connected to a telephone network.

Internet Communication

The Internet is not one network, but many networks connected together. The networks are connected to high-speed communications channels, called *backbones*, that are used to transmit data between networks. Routers are used in the network to route data from one location to another.

In order for the Internet to function, computers in the network must use the same rules, or protocols, for communication. The Internet uses two protocols: *Transmission Control Protocol* (*TCP*) and *Internet Protocol* (*IP*). Together these are referred to as *TCP/IP*. Using these protocols, any computer connected to the Internet can communicate with any other computer.

To connect to the Internet a business must have the necessary communications hardware and software to provide a link between the business's computer and the Internet. The business's computer must use TCP/IP to communicate over the Internet. A user may connect to the Internet through his or her company's computer or may use an **Internet service provider** (**ISP**), which is a company that provides Internet access for its customers. Users usually connect to an ISP over a telephone line, using a modem or terminal adapter. The ISP maintains computers that have hardware and software connections to the Internet.

Internet Services

The Internet provides a number of services, the most widely used of which are electronic mail and the World Wide Web. Any user of the Internet can send **electronic mail** (**e-mail**) to any other user of the Internet, provided they each have an *e-mail address* (for example, myname@anycollege.edu). E-mail addresses are provided by businesses for their employees, schools for their students, and Internet service providers for their customers.

The **World Wide Web** (**WWW**), usually just called the **Web**, provides easy access to many types of information found on the Internet. The Web is a *hypertext* system, which means that information on the Web is linked so that the user can easily go from one page of information to another, related page by using a browser. A Web page is identified by a **uniform resource locator** (**URL**; for example, www.anycollege.edu) and the user enters the URL into a browser to go to a page. Through the Web the user can access many types of information from universities, businesses, libraries, research institutes, government agencies, and so on, all of which maintain numerous pages of information on the Web. Web information includes not only text, but also graphic images, pictures, video, and sound.

The Internet includes a number of other services besides electronic mail and the Web, including

- *Telnet*. This service connects one computer on the Internet to another computer on the Internet so that a user at the first computer can use the other computer as if he or she were directly connected to it.

- *FTP* (*File Transfer Protocol*). This service transfers a file from one computer to another and is used for uploading and downloading files.

- *Gopher*. This menu-driven service provides easy access to information on the Internet.

- *Usenet or NetNews*. This service allows users to share information about a wide range of topics.

- *Chat*. This service allows users to carry on conversations by keying comments and receiving responses from other users, all within a few seconds.

The Internet is an international network. Any Internet information or service almost anywhere in the world is available to almost any computer anywhere else in the world. Such easy access to Internet information and services has been part of the reason for its very rapid rise in popularity. The popularity of the Internet, however, has resulted in heavy use and slow response at times. Currently, a research effort is under way to develop a faster successor to the Internet, often called *Internet II*.

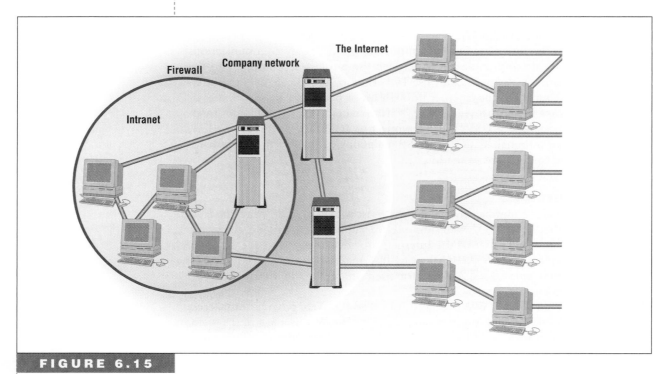

FIGURE 6.15

▲ **An intranet with a firewall**

FIGURE 6.16

▲ **A network computer**

Intranets

The popularity and ease of use of the Internet has resulted in businesses establishing Internet-type networks entirely within the business. Such a network, which uses TCP/IP, is called an **intranet**. An intranet is used in the same way as the Internet, but only by users within the business.

Users outside a business cannot access the business's intranet. To prevent such access, a hardware and software system called a **firewall** is used (Figure 6.15). Users from outside the business have access to public company information, such as pages with descriptions of products and services, but the firewall prevents them from accessing the private company data in the intranet.

In general, users do not need sophisticated personal computers to use intranets or the Internet. All that is needed is a computer that can run a browser and has the necessary communications capability. A computer with capabilities limited to intranet and Internet access is called a **network computer** (or a *thin client*) (Figure 6.16). Network computers sell for one-third to one-half the price of other personal computers. Some businesses have eliminated many of their personal computers and replaced them with network computers, resulting in a considerable cost savings.

Extranets

Some businesses have set up intranets that they let certain companies or individuals outside the business access. For example, a business may have an intranet with inventory data that a supplier can use to check inventory levels for automatic restocking. Connection to the intranet is allowed by means of codes and passwords so that only certain companies or individuals have access to it through the firewall. This type of externally accessible intranet is called an **extranet**. For example, Figure 6.17 shows an intranet at ABC Company that is accessible from XYZ Company, thus forming an extranet.

The use of intranets and extranets is likely to increase in the future. Businesses are finding that intranets and extranets, along with the Internet, provide a common net-

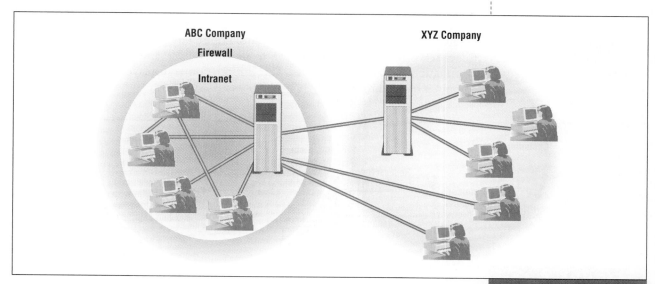

FIGURE 6.17

An extranet ▲

work system that can handle many of their needs. Someday, businesses may use intranets, extranets, and the Internet for most of their networks.

Electronic Commerce

Businesses use the Internet and the Web for **electronic commerce** (**e-commerce**). E-commerce involves promoting and selling the products or services of a business through networks. Although businesses can use various types of networks for e-commerce, most often they use the Internet.

Hardware and Software for Electronic Commerce

To engage in e-commerce using the Internet, a business must establish a **Web site**, which is the set of Web pages with information about the business's products or services. The Web site may also provide capabilities for purchasing the products or services.

Figure 6.18 shows the hardware and software needed for e-commerce.[2] The computer that stores the pages of a Web site is called a **Web server**. The Web server has special e-commerce software that provides electronic commerce functions. A business may have its own Web server, or it may use a Web server provided by another company, such as an ISP. The Web server must be connected to the Internet using communications hardware so that customers can access it. Communications software is needed in the Web server to provide access from the Internet to the server.

Usually the Web server is connected through a LAN to a database server that contains data about the business's products or services. For example, a database server may contain inventory data about the business's products. When a customer requests information about products that he or she is considering purchasing, the Web server sends a request for data about the products to the database server. The database server looks up the availability and price of each product, and sends this data back to the Web server. Then the Web server calculates the amount of the customer's purchase and forwards this information to the customer.

A customer communicates with the business's Web server through a personal computer connected to the Internet. This computer only needs a Web browser because it just displays Web pages and does not do any processing of data. The customer sends requests for information to the Web server, and receives the requested information back from the server. This information is displayed on the customer's computer by the browser.

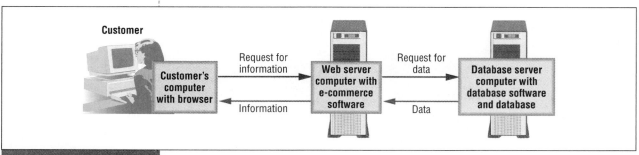

FIGURE 6.18

▲ Hardware and software for electronic commerce

[2] The approach shown in Figure 6.18 is sometimes called *three-tiered* client/server computing, in contrast to the approach shown in Figure 6.14, which is sometimes called *two-tiered* client/server computing.

Electronic Commerce Use

A customer engages in e-commerce by using a browser to locate the business's *home page*, which is the beginning page for information at the business's Web site (Figure 6.19). The customer enters the URL of the business's home page into his or her browser, and the network software locates the Web server with the home page on the Internet. This process can be quite involved because reaching the Web server over the Internet may require going through a number of networks to get to the server's location. When the page is located, the Web server retrieves the home page from its secondary storage and sends it over the Internet to the customer's computer, where it is displayed by the browser.

After the business's home page is displayed, the customer can select other pages from the Web site to see details about products or services available from the business. The Web server retrieves each requested page from its secondary storage and sends it over the Internet to the customer's computer for display by the browser. The customer can often request additional information about the products or services to be sent by regular mail. If the customer wants availability or price data, the Web server sends a request for the data to the database server. To purchase a product or service, the customer fills in an order form displayed by the browser and enters credit card or other payment information. The purchasing process requires the use of special security measures to ensure that important information such as a credit card number is not used inappropriately.

Most businesses have Web sites for their products or services and use the Internet for e-commerce. Businesses may also use an intranet for e-commerce within the business, such as selling to other divisions of the business, or an extranet for e-commerce with other businesses. The use of e-commerce is increasing rapidly, and someday most commerce may be electronic. Chapter 12 discusses in detail how businesses use e-commerce.

FIGURE 6.19

A home page

CHAPTER SUMMARY

1   The communications hardware needed for computers to communicate with other computers consists of **communications channels**, which are the links over which data is sent, and **communications processors**, which provide processing capabilities between computers and channels. Communications software is needed to send data from a computer to communications processors, which then transmit the data over a channel, and to receive data for a computer from communications processors after the data has been received from a channel. (pp. 168–169)

2   The main characteristics of a communications channel are signal type and data rate. A channel can transmit data using a **digital signal**, which is a series of pulses, or an **analog signal**, which is a wave pattern. The data rate of a channel is the speed at which bits are sent over the channel and is measured in bits per second (bps). (p. 169)

3   Communications processors consist of **channel interface devices** and **communications control units**. A channel interface device provides the link between the computer and the channel. Examples are **modems**, which convert digital signals to analog signals (modulation) and convert analog signals to digital signals (demodulation), and **terminal adapters**, which connect digital lines such as **ISDN** and **DSL** lines to computers. Communications control units allow several computers to share a channel. Examples are multiplexers, controllers, and front-end processors. (pp. 174–176)

4   Communications software controls communications between computers. For personal computers, communications software includes **terminal emulation software**, which makes a personal computer act like a terminal, and software that provides communication for **client software**. For multiple-user computers, communications software keeps track of which terminal sent which data and where to send the results of processing. For server computers in a network, communications software, which is the network operating system, provides communications over the network. (pp. 178–179)

5   A **local area network** (**LAN**) is usually organized as a **bus** or **ring network**. Each computer in a LAN must have a **network interface card** (**NIC**) to connect it to the LAN channel. A LAN may contain several servers, including **print servers**, **file**

servers, and **database servers**. Each client personal computer in a LAN needs communications software. A server computer in a LAN needs a network operating system. (pp. 180–182)

6   A **wide area network** (**WAN**) is sometimes organized as a **star** or **hierarchical network**, but more often as a **hybrid network**. All types of computers are found in WANs, from personal computers to supercomputers. Various communications processors are used in WANs, including channel interface devices and communications control units. All computers in WANs require communications software. (pp. 180–182)

7   Networks are interconnected to form **internetworks** by using devices such as *bridges*, *gateways*, and *routers*, along with special communications software. Internetworks allow businesses to connect different networks within the business to support organizational information systems. They are also used for interorganizational information systems such as electronic data interchange and electronic funds transfer systems. (pp. 188–189)

8   The **Internet** is a public, international collection of interconnected WANs and LANs that provides a number of special services, including **electronic mail (e-mail)** and the **World Wide Web (WWW)**. An **intranet** is an Internet-type network that is contained entirely within a business. An **extranet** is an intranet that is accessible from outside the business by certain companies and individuals. (p. 191)

9   To engage in **electronic commerce (e-commerce)** a business must establish a **Web site**, which is the set of Web pages with information about the business's products or services. A computer that stores the pages of a Web site is called a **Web server**. The Web server has special e-commerce software that provides e-commerce functions. The Web server must be connected to the Internet by using communications hardware. Communications software is needed in the Web server to provide access from the Internet to the server. Usually the Web server is connected through a LAN to a database server that contains data about the business's products or services. A customer communicates with the business's Web server through a personal computer connected to the Internet. This computer needs a Web browser. (p. 192)

KEY TERMS

Analog Signal (p. 169)
Bandwidth (p. 170)
Baud Rate (p. 170)
Bus Network (p. 180)
Cable Modem (p. 175)
Channel Interface Device (p. 175)
Client Software (p. 178)
Communications Channel (p. 168)
Communications Control Unit (p. 176)
Communications Processor (p. 168)
Database Server (p. 183)
Data Encryption (p. 178)
Digital Signal (p. 169)
Downloading (p. 179)
DSL (p. 174)
Electronic Commerce (e-commerce) (p. 192)
Electronic Mail (e-mail) (p. 189)

Extranet (p. 191)
File Server (p. 183)
File Transfer (p. 179)
Firewall (p. 191)
Hierarchical Network (p. 180)
Hybrid Network (p. 181)
Information Superhighway (p. 188)
Internet (p. 188)
Internet Service Provider (ISP) (p. 189)
Internetwork (p. 182)
Intranet (p. 191)
ISDN (p. 174)
Local Area Network (LAN) (p. 182)
Modem (p. 175)
Network Computer (p. 191)
Network Interface Card (NIC) (p. 183)
Print Server (p. 183)
Protocol (p. 176)

Protocol Converter (p. 177)
Ring Network (p. 181)
Star Network (p. 180)
Terminal Adapter (p. 176)
Terminal Emulation Software (p. 178)
Uniform Resource Locator (URL) (p. 189)
Uploading (p. 179)
Value Added Network (VAN) (p. 187)
Virtual Private Network (VPN) (p. 187)
Web Server (p. 192)
Web Site (p. 192)
Wide Area Network (WAN) (p. 182)
Wireless LAN (p. 183)
World Wide Web (WWW, Web) (p. 189)

REVIEW QUESTIONS

1 What hardware is needed for computers to communicate with other computers?

2 What is the difference between a digital signal and an analog signal?

3 How is the rate at which data is sent over a communications channel measured?

4 What are several common media used for communications channels?

5 What does a modem do? What is used instead of a modem for ISDN or DSL communication?

6 What do communications control units do?

7 What are protocols?

8 How can data sent over a communications channel be kept secure?

9 What does terminal emulation software do?

10 What are several ways networks can be organized?

11 What is the difference between a LAN and a WAN?

12 How are LANs usually organized?

13 What communications hardware and software are needed with a personal computer so it can be used on a LAN?

14 What types of servers are used in a LAN?

15 Why do businesses have LANs?

16 What is client/server computing?

17 What communications hardware and software are used in a WAN?

18 What is a VPN?

19 Is it possible to do client/server computing on a WAN? Explain your answer.

20 What are internetworks and why are they important?

21 What is the Internet?

22 List several services on the Internet.

23 What is an intranet, and what is an extranet?

24 What special hardware and software are needed for e-commerce?

DISCUSSION QUESTIONS

1 What communications methods do businesses use, other than computer networks?

2 With notebook and personal computer communications, it is possible to do some types of work almost anywhere. What advantages and disadvantages does this provide a business?

3 Imagine a college or university with no desktop computers for students to use. Instead, the school would be wired with a large LAN. Jacks to plug into the network would be provided almost everywhere—in the library, in all classrooms, in the student lounge, in dorm rooms, everywhere students can go—and wireless access to the network would also be provided. Each student would have a note-book computer that could be plugged into the network at anytime. How would this system change the educational process?

4 The Internet is an international network. Why would an international business want to have its own international WAN instead of using the Internet?

5 Sun Microsystems has a trademarked slogan: "The network is the computer." What does this mean, and do you agree or disagree with it? Why?

ETHICS QUESTIONS

1 Data encryption is common in businesses today, but you must have the key to encrypt and decrypt the data. Assume that your boss has asked you to encrypt some data he wants sent and has given you the key. What measures would you take to protect the key from others seeing it?

2 Networks, and especially the Internet, make access to information very easy. Businesses and govern-ments often want to limit access to certain information, however. Assume that you work for a business and you have found some information showing that one of your company's products has a defect. Would you ask to have that information put on the company's Web site?

PROBLEM-SOLVING PROJECTS

1 If you are using a LAN or have access to one, find out everything you can about the network. What type of network is it? How is the network organized? What medium is used for the network channel? At what rate is data sent over the channel? What client and server computers are connected to the network? Write a summary of what you find out.

2 Assume that you want to set up a LAN in your house. You want the network to connect a computer in the kitchen, one in the living room, one in each bedroom, and one in any other room you want. Assume that you already have the computers, and now you need the communications hardware and software. Set up a spreadsheet to estimate the cost of the network. You will have to go to a computer store to find out the price of NICs, cables, and software. The amount of cable you will need depends on how far apart the computers are. Be sure to estimate the cost of installing the cables. Design your spreadsheet so that you can change the number of rooms with computers connected to the network. Use the spreadsheet to calculate the total cost and the cost per computer.

3 Contact several ISPs or other companies that provide Internet access, and find out what services they have and how much the services cost. Prepare a spreadsheet that summarizes the services provided by each ISP and how much they cost. Most ISPs have several rate plans. Some charge a flat monthly fee, and some charge a fee plus a variable amount, depending on use. Include formulas in your spreadsheet to compute the total monthly cost of using each ISP with each of its different rate plans. Try several different scenarios for monthly use to see how much each ISP would cost to use. Plot the results by using the graphics capabilities of spreadsheet software.

4 Web sites are put together and managed by people who often have the title "Webmaster." Interview the Webmaster at your college or university, or at another organization to which you have access. Find out how the Webmaster decides what pages are put on the Web site and how the pages should be linked. Also find out what computer or computers are used as Web servers. Write a summary of your interview.

INTERNET AND ELECTRONIC COMMERCE PROJECTS

1 Use the Web to find information about jobs and careers in your field of interest. Locate an announcement for a job that you might be interested in applying for someday. Keep track of how you found the information, such as what Web sites you visited. Write a summary of how you found the information and what you learned.

2 Use the Web to identify several software products that are used for e-commerce Web sites. Identify the features of each product. Construct a table comparing the features of the products.

3 E-commerce can be used for a number of things. It can be used for advertising by displaying promotional material for products and services. It can be used to gather information about consumer preferences by collecting responses to a questionnaire. It can be used for selling products by providing customer order entry forms. Find e-commerce Web sites that include each of these uses. (Try to find one site that has all three uses.) Write an assessment of how effective this approach is for marketing products compared to traditional forms of marketing.

CDNOW

CDNOW, which currently ranks as the top music retailer on the Internet, used to regularly shut down its e-commerce site for maintenance and upgrades. But as the online music business has become increasingly competitive, CDNOW has found it imperative to remain available around the clock.

For Mike Krupit, vice president of technology, the guiding mantra in managing CDNOW's infrastructure is "Capacity is king." He says, "When I started in April of 1997, we would have key periods of unavailability—we would literally have to close the site down. But now we are focused on capacity and availability, which means we never want more than 60 percent of our network's capacity to be used." Krupit says the CDNOW site could handle a 300% to 600% increase in traffic without modifying the current infrastructure at all.

CDNOW, located in Jenkintown, Pennsylvania, offers more than 250,000 items for sale, including 200,000 music CDs, as well as CD-ROMs, videos, books, and T-shirts. The publicly held company recently reported 165,000 average daily visits to its site for one month.

The design of the network that runs the CDNOW site is very simple, Krupit says. It is split into three networks—one handles Web traffic, one handles database and file sharing, and one handles data backups.

At the core of CDNOW's operations are its Sun Enterprise 4000 servers running Solaris (a version of UNIX), each of which has a specific role as either Web server, application server, or database server. Citing competitive concerns, Krupit cannot discuss the exact number or configurations of servers, but he says the Web servers run Apache software.

The site also has two Sun Ultra 2s that serve banner ads using NetGravity's AdServer software. However, ad serving isn't a tremendous concern operationally, as CDNOW currently doesn't accept any outside advertising; house banner ads announcing CDNOW promotions are the only ones run on the site. "None of the ads take you off the site, and that's key," says Krupit.

For Internet connectivity, CDNOW uses Savvis Communications and Digex, with 45 Mbps channels connecting it to each Internet servic provider. Currently, Krupit has no plans to increase the capacity of those connections. CDNOW uses Cisco routers at its data center, and runs Border Gateway Protocol between the two ISPs for fault tolerance.

CDNOW does have some vulnerabilities, Krupit says. "The Internet connection is a point of [potential] failure for us, as is our power supply," he says. "If either of those goes down, they can knock us out of business."

CDNOW has investigated whether to establish multiple data centers to deal with these issues, he says. Part of what has prevented CDNOW from establishing multiple data centers is the need for a centralized order-transaction database that processes credit card information, Krupit says.

"Replicating transactions across multiple data centers is a real challenge," he says. "Sites like Yahoo and Lycos already have multiple data centers, but they're content sites, where we're a transaction site. I've told the vendors that the first ones who can come up with the solution for this problem, we'll buy it."

Since it was founded in 1994, CDNOW has seen vast increases in traffic. Although Krupit cannot say how much bandwidth CDNOW uses—again citing competitive reasons—he says that over a recent nine-month period CDNOW's traffic increased fourfold, placing heavy demands on the servers.

"Still, while overall bandwidth needs have quadrupled, day-to-day bandwidth patterns have tended to hold steady. "Our traffic patterns are typically very predictable—for example, during the Grammys we knew we would have a big spike," Krupit says. "Right now, 2 to 9 p.m. are our peak hours, but nine months ago the peak came at around 1 to 4 p.m."

For balancing the load among the servers, CDNOW developed its own systems. This do-it-yourself attitude reflects CDNOW's approach to solving most of the site's technical challenges. With a team of around 27 engineers, CDNOW has an intense focus on developing solutions to manage its growth. In addition to load balancing, the site's commerce and transaction server applications are homegrown as well.

CDNOW's content, which is aggregated from several sources, is also served by internally developed applications. The dynamic search-driven pages are built in a proprietary search language that pulls the information from the Oracle databases where it is housed. Data from CDNOW's partners is loaded into its databases through back-end electronic data interchange processes.

CDNOW's credit card transactions are handled by dedicated servers running proprietary software. Confidential information, such as credit card numbers and their expiration dates, is stored on a separate database server. Yet another proprietary application pulls the information, which is transmitted securely via encryption, from the Web-based forms to the database server after customers enter it. This server is accessible only via CDNOW's network, which cannot be reached from the public Internet.

Although homegrown solutions are central to CDNOW's ethos, the company has chosen to outsource some elements of its operations. All the RealAudio sound clips on the site—which give prospective CD purchasers 30-second previews of selected songs—are provided by Enso Audio Imaging, a division of Muzak, and are hosted on Enso's audio servers. Meanwhile, song track listings and album-cover images on the site are served from Muze, a Web content supplier located in New York City.

Besides offloading CDNOW's infrastructure, the content provided by Muzak and Muze have the added benefit that those companies have already secured the licensing rights and have digitally converted the content for the Web.

"We considered handling this ourselves, but we're focused on retail," says Krupit. "We said, 'Let someone else build the infrastructure for multimedia.'"

Questions

1. Why is it important that CDNOW have adequate capacity in its e-commerce site so the site can be available around the clock?
2. What servers are used in the CDNOW e-commerce site?
3. How is the CDNOW e-commerce site connected to the Internet?
4. Why does CDNOW not have multiple data centers?
5. What applications for the e-commerce site were developed by CDNOW engineers?

Web Site

CDNOW: www.cdnow.com

Source: *Adapted from* Sarah L. Roberts-Witt, "When Sales Are Tied to a Site's Capacity," *Internet Week*, June 1, 1998, pp. 28–29.

Information System

DATA
MANAGEMENT

After completing this chapter, you should be able to

1 List advantages and disadvantages of file processing.

2 Explain what a database is and what a database management system does.

3 List advantages and disadvantages of database processing.

4 Identify the main types of relationships in database processing.

5 Explain the organization of relational databases.

6 Describe differences between database software for personal computers, multiple-user computers, and networked computers.

7 Describe several ways of using database software.

8 Describe the use of databases in different types of information systems.

9 Explain what a data warehouse is and what is meant by data mining.

10 Describe multidimensional databases and explain on-line analytical processing.

CHAPTER OUTLINE

File Processing
Database Processing
Database Organization
Common Database Software
Using Database Software
Database Use in Information Systems
Data Warehouses
Multidimensional Databases
Database Administration

The stored data component in an information system consists of all data stored in the system's hardware and processed by its software. This data must be managed so that it will be usable by the system. Data management involves making the data available for processing, keeping the data up-to-date, and maintaining control of the data to be sure it is correct and secure from loss or destruction.

This chapter examines data management in information systems. Because stored data in information systems is usually organized as data files and databases in secondary storage, this chapter concentrates on file and database processing. First, the chapter presents file processing concepts. Then it covers database processing, including database organization, database software, and database use. Next it describes some of the recent developments in data management, including data warehouses and multidimensional databases. Finally, this chapter looks at database administration.

File Processing

The simplest way to manage data in an information system is to store the data as a *data file* in secondary storage. Recall from Chapter 3 that a data file, or simply a *file*, consists of a group of related *records*. (Refer to Figure 3.8.) Each record in the file contains a group of related *fields*, and each field consists of one or more related *characters*. Data is read from or written to a file in secondary storage one record at a time.

To illustrate the idea of a file, Figure 7.1 shows a file of inventory data in an athletic-clothing wholesale business. Each row in this figure represents a record in the inventory file. Each record contains fields with data about one item stocked in inventory. The fields are the columns in the figure. The first field is the item number, the second field is the item description, the third field is the unit price (how much the business sells one item for), and the last field is the quantity of the item on hand.

	Item number field	Item description field	Unit price field	Quantity on hand field
	1537	SHORTS	11.50	136
	1609	JACKET	24.85	40
	2719	T-SHIRT	9.75	24
	3512	TENNIS SHORTS	18.90	35
Inventory records	3804	TENNIS SHIRT	17.45	118
	4205	SOCKS	3.25	160
	5172	SWEATSHIRT	18.75	225
	5173	SWEATPANTS	14.70	322
	5501	CAP	7.20	90
	6318	SWIMSUIT	21.50	52

FIGURE 7.1

An inventory file

The records in a file should be identified in some way, usually by including a field that uniquely determines the record. Such a field is called a **key field**, or simply a **key**. In the inventory records, the key field is the item number. Each record in the inventory file has a different value in its key field. Then, if the value of the key field is given, the corresponding record can be located in the file.

Key fields are usually code fields consisting of numbers or combinations of numbers and letters. Thus, item number, customer number, Social Security number, and similar fields are used as key fields. The reason codes and not names or descriptions are used for key fields is that codes can be assigned that are unique. Name and description fields, although easier to remember, are often duplicated in a file and thus cannot be used as key fields.

File Organization

A file can be organized in secondary storage in several ways, and its organization determines how a key field is used to locate a record in a file (Figure 7.2). In a **sequential file**, the records are organized in sequence, one after the other, in the order in which they are placed in the file. For example, Figure 7.2a shows the inventory file stored as a sequential file, with one record coming immediately after the previous one, in the order in which they were put in the file. (Records in this figure are numbered in the order in which they appear in the file.) The records in a sequential file can be retrieved only in the order in which they are stored. The computer must first retrieve Record Number 1, then Record Number 2, and so on. As explained in Chapter 4, this method is called *sequential access*. A sequential file can only be accessed sequentially. A sequential file can be stored on any type of secondary storage—magnetic disk, optical disk, or magnetic tape.

The key field in the records in a sequential file identifies which record was retrieved. When the computer retrieves a record, it simply gets the next record in sequence, not a record with a particular key field value. After a record has been retrieved, the computer can examine the value of the key field in that record to see exactly which record it is.

In a **direct file**, which is also called a **random file**, the records are not necessarily stored in sequence. For example, Figure 7.2b shows part of the inventory file stored as a direct file. Notice that the records are in random order and that there are spaces in the file with no data. Where a record is stored in a direct file is determined directly by the value of the record's key field. Several different methods are used to determine where a record is stored. For the direct inventory file in Figure 7.2b, the computer uses the last two digits of the item number (the key field) as the record number where the item's record is stored.[1] Thus, the record for item 1609 is stored as Record Number 9, the record for item 3804 is stored as Record Number 4, and so on. Notice that this approach can waste storage space in the file and can lead to conflicts when two records have the same last two digits in their key fields.

A computer can retrieve records in a direct file in any order. Recall from Chapter 4 that this approach is called *random* or *direct access*. Given the value of the key field, the computer can find the corresponding record. For example, to retrieve the data for item 1609 from the direct inventory file, the computer would determine from the last two digits of the key field that the data is found at Record Number 9. Then, the computer would retrieve that record directly, without going through the other records in the file in sequence. Because a direct file can be accessed randomly, it can only be

---

[1] Usually a much more sophisticated technique is used to determine where a record is stored in a direct file, but the concept is the same.

Record number

1	1537	SHORTS	11.50	136
2	1609	JACKET	24.85	40
3	2719	T-SHIRT	9.75	24
4	3512	TENNIS SHORTS	18.90	35
5	3804	TENNIS SHIRT	17.45	118
6	4205	SOCKS	3.25	160
7	5172	SWEATSHIRT	18.75	225
8	5173	SWEATPANTS	14.70	322
9	5501	CAP	7.20	90
10	6318	SWIMSUIT	21.50	52

(a) A sequential inventory file

Record number

1	5501	CAP	7.20	90
2				
3				
4	3804	TENNIS SHIRT	17.45	118
5	4205	SOCKS	3.25	160
6				
7				
8				
9	1609	JACKET	24.85	40
10				

(b) A direct inventory file

Index file

Key field	Record number
1537	1
1609	2
2719	3
3512	4
3804	5
4205	6
5172	7
5173	8
5501	9
6318	10

Data file

Record number

1	1537	SHORTS	11.50	136
2	1609	JACKET	24.85	40
3	2719	T-SHIRT	9.75	24
4	3512	TENNIS SHORTS	18.90	35
5	3804	TENNIS SHIRT	17.45	118
6	4205	SOCKS	3.25	160
7	5172	SWEATSHIRT	18.75	225
8	5173	SWEATPANTS	14.70	322
9	5501	CAP	7.20	90
10	6318	SWIMSUIT	21.50	52

(c) An indexed inventory file

FIGURE 7.2

File organizations

stored on secondary storage devices that provide random access, such as magnetic disks and optical disks. It cannot be stored on magnetic tape.

An **indexed file**,[2] is actually two files: a data file and an index file. The *data file* is organized as a sequential file, with the records in increasing order by key field. The *index file*, or simply the *index*, is a file that has one record for each record in the data file. Each index record contains the value of the key field of a record in the data file and the location of that record in the file.[3] Figure 7.2c illustrates the idea of an indexed file. The inventory file is stored as a sequential file, with its records in increasing order by key field, which is the item number. The index contains the key field and the number of the corresponding record for each record in the data file.

The records in an indexed file can be accessed either sequentially or randomly. For sequential access, the computer retrieves the records in the data file one at a time, in the order in which they are stored. To access the records randomly, the computer locates the key field of the desired record in the index, which can be done faster than searching the data file for the record because the index is much smaller than the file. After the key field is found, the corresponding record number in the index indicates where the record is stored in the data file. The computer retrieves the record directly, without retrieving any other records in the data file. (This process is like using an index of a book to locate a subject rather than reading the book in sequence to find the subject.) Like direct files, an indexed file can only be stored on a random access device such as magnetic disk or optical disk, but never on magnetic tape.

File Management

To manage stored data, the data must be made available for processing, kept up-to-date, and controlled to be sure it is correct and secure. With file processing, data is made available by organizing the data in one of the three ways described here. A computer program can then access the data. If the file is a sequential file, the program accesses the data sequentially. For a direct file, the program accesses the data randomly. If the file is an indexed file, the program can access the data either sequentially or randomly.

File data is kept up-to-date by modifying it regularly. Modifying, or *updating*, data can involve any of three activities: *adding* records to a file, *deleting* records from a file, or *changing* data in records in a file. A computer program does the updating. If the data is organized as a sequential file, the program creates an entirely new updated file because it is normally not possible to change an existing sequential file. If the data is organized as a direct or an indexed file, however, a program can update the file itself; it is not necessary to create a new file.

Maintaining control of the file data involves ensuring that the data is accurate and secure. Accuracy of the data is ensured by checking the data to be stored in the file as it is entered into the system. This process is called **data validation**, and it is done by a computer program. This program accepts the data from outside the system (usually the data is entered at a terminal or personal computer) and checks the data for errors. Examples of data validation checks include checking to be sure that the correct type of data has been entered (e.g., that only letters and no numbers have been entered for a person's name), that acceptable values have been entered (e.g., that only an *M* or an *F* has been entered for a person's sex), and that the data is within reasonable limits (e.g., that a person's pay rate is less than $50 per hour). If a record con-

---

[2] Some types of indexed files are also called *indexed sequential access method (ISAM)* files.
[3] The index is usually more complex than described here, but the concept is the same.

tains any data that has errors, the record is not stored in the data file. Only records that pass all data validation checks are included in the file.

Security of the data in a file involves preventing the loss or destruction of the data, or the unauthorized access or updating of the data. Loss or destruction of the data is secured by a procedure for backing up the data on a regular basis. Backup copies of all data files should be made periodically. The copies normally are kept in a special fireproof vault or at a separate location. Another procedure is needed for recovering the data from the backup copy if the original data is damaged. Security against unauthorized accessing or updating of the data involves procedures that prevent the data files from being removed from the business and that prevent programs that process the data from being executed by unauthorized personnel.

Advantages of File Processing

Data files are used in information systems because they are simple to use. Many information systems do not need anything more complex because they use only a single file of data. For example, an inventory control system may need only a single inventory file to store all data. In situations such as this, a data file is the easiest way to organize the data.

Because of their ease of use, data files are used extensively in information systems. Sequential files are used in simple situations where only sequential access is needed. Direct or indexed files are used where random access is needed. Direct files are more complex to use than indexed files, so they are not as common.

Disadvantages of File Processing

The main disadvantages of file processing appear when it is necessary to process data in more than one related file. For example, assume that the athletic-clothing wholesale business needs to do inventory control, order entry, and customer billing. With file processing, the business would need three files in secondary storage to store the data: an inventory file, an order file, and a billing file (Figure 7.3). Application programs for inventory control would access the inventory file, programs to enter customer orders would access the order file, and programs to bill customers would access the billing file.

One of the main problems with this situation is that some data may be duplicated in several files. For example, the customer's name and address may appear in both the order file and the billing file. Duplicated data requires extra storage space. More significantly, if duplicated data changes, someone must make sure it is updated everyplace it is stored. Thus, if a customer moves, his or her address must be updated in all files in which the address is stored. Ensuring that all duplicated data is updated can be a difficult task.

Another problem in this situation is that it is difficult to access data from more than one file at a time. If, for example, the order entry program needs to process data in both the inventory file and the order file, complex programming is required. If a program needs to access three files, the programming is even more complicated.

A final problem with file processing is that there is a dependency between programs and data. Each program must have instructions that tell it how the data in the files it processes is organized. Each program must identify what fields are in the records of each file and how the files are organized. If the fields in the records or file organization are changed, every program that processes that file must be modified. Such modification can be time-consuming and expensive.

FIGURE 7.3

▲ **File processing**

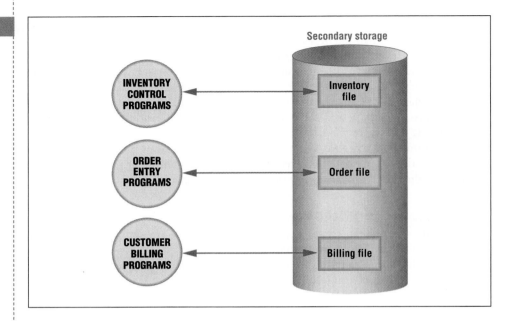

FIGURE 7.3

▲ **File processing**

Database Processing

To overcome some of the disadvantages of file processing, database processing is used. In database processing, related data is not stored as separate files. Instead, all data is stored together in a *database* in secondary storage. In our athletic-clothing wholesale business example, the database would contain inventory, order, and billing data (Figure 7.4). To process the data in the database, special database software is needed. This software is called a **database management system (DBMS)**. (On personal computers, this software is usually called *database software*. On networks and multiple-user computers it is normally called a DBMS.) The DBMS provides capabilities for creating, accessing, and updating data in a database. In fact, the DBMS

FIGURE 7.4

▲ **Database processing**

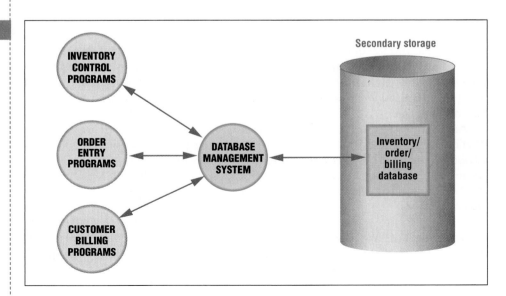

handles all interaction with the database. If a user or an application program, such as an order entry program, needs to process data in the database, the program sends instructions to the DBMS, which then carries out the actions requested by the program.

What Is a Database?

To understand database processing, you first need to know exactly what a database is. Chapter 3 explains that related data is sometimes grouped to form a database. This definition is adequate for a basic understanding of databases, but a complete definition is needed for a thorough knowledge of database processing.

A **database** is a collection of *data* and *relationships* between the data stored in secondary storage. The data in a database may be stored in several separate files or in one large file. The way the data is stored depends on the database software. The user, however, views the database as a single set of stored data. The data in the database is arranged into related groups, similar to records, each containing several fields. Groups of data are related to other groups of data, meaning that the groups have something in common. The ways in which the groups of data are related are called **relationships**, and they are part of the database.

To illustrate the idea of a database, consider how data used for inventory control, order entry, and customer billing in an athletic-clothing wholesale business can be stored in a database. Figure 7.5 shows a database with the required data. Notice that inventory data, order data, and billing data are arranged separately in the database. The relationships between the data are shown by lines connecting the groups of data. There is a relationship between inventory data and order data if an item in inventory has been ordered. An inventory item can be ordered one or more times or not at all. There is a relationship between billing data and order data if a customer needs to be billed for items ordered. Each customer can order one or more items.

Databases are not stored in secondary storage the same way as data files are stored. A database must store not only data, but also the relationships between the data. Consequently, special storage organizations are used for databases, although techniques similar to those used in direct file organization and indexed file organization are often found in database storage. How the data and relationships are stored depends on which of several database organizations is used, a topic that is covered later in this chapter.

Database Management

With database management, data is made available by accessing the data in the database with the database software. Accessing may involve retrieving data from a single group of data or from several related groups of data. For example, in the database shown in Figure 7.5, inventory data could be retrieved alone, or inventory and order data could be retrieved together. To retrieve inventory and order data together, the relationship between the data is used by the database software. Thus, to answer the question "What are the descriptions of the items ordered by customer number 48721?" the database software uses the relationship that links together the order data containing the customer number with the related inventory data to get the item descriptions.

Database data is kept up-to-date by modifying the data in the database. The database software handles the updating, which may involve *adding* data or relationships, *deleting* data or relationships, or *changing* data or relationships. A single group of data can be updated, or several related groups of data can be updated. For example, assume that the database in Figure 7.5 needs to be updated when a customer orders

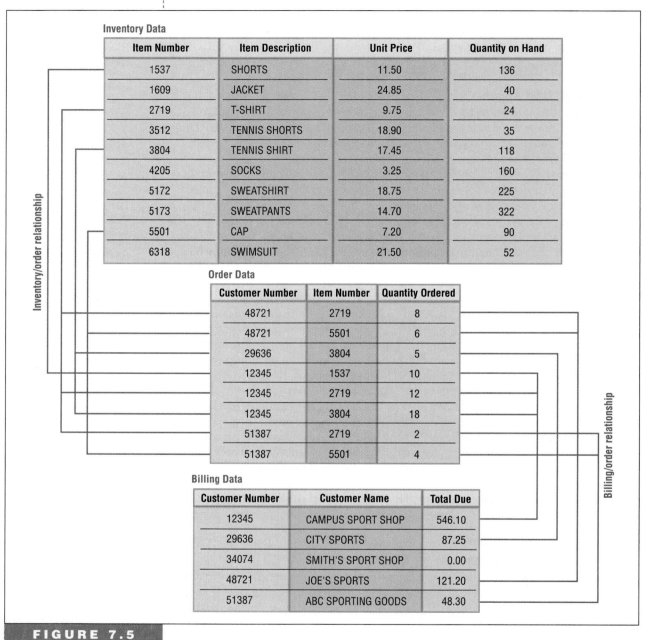

Inventory Data

Item Number	Item Description	Unit Price	Quantity on Hand
1537	SHORTS	11.50	136
1609	JACKET	24.85	40
2719	T-SHIRT	9.75	24
3512	TENNIS SHORTS	18.90	35
3804	TENNIS SHIRT	17.45	118
4205	SOCKS	3.25	160
5172	SWEATSHIRT	18.75	225
5173	SWEATPANTS	14.70	322
5501	CAP	7.20	90
6318	SWIMSUIT	21.50	52

Order Data

Customer Number	Item Number	Quantity Ordered
48721	2719	8
48721	5501	6
29636	3804	5
12345	1537	10
12345	2719	12
12345	3804	18
51387	2719	2
51387	5501	4

Billing Data

Customer Number	Customer Name	Total Due
12345	CAMPUS SPORT SHOP	546.10
29636	CITY SPORTS	87.25
34074	SMITH'S SPORT SHOP	0.00
48721	JOE'S SPORTS	121.20
51387	ABC SPORTING GOODS	48.30

Inventory/order relationship

Billing/order relationship

FIGURE 7.5

▲ **A database**

another item. That customer's order must be added to the order data, a relationship to the item in the inventory data must be established, and the total due in the billing data must be changed. All this updating is handled by the database software.

Control of the data in the database is maintained by ensuring the accuracy and security of the data. The accuracy of the data in a database is ensured by data validation, as with file processing. In database processing, however, the database software often does the validation. Thus, it is not necessary to have a special computer program to validate the data. The database software not only checks the data for errors, but also checks the relationships to be sure they are valid.

Security of the data in a database is handled in a manner similar to that in file processing. Security from data loss or destruction is accomplished by a procedure for regularly backing up the database and keeping the backup copy in a safe location. If the database is damaged, a recovery procedure is followed to restore the data from the backup. Securing against unauthorized accessing or updating of the data usually is handled by the database software. Often, the software can be set to require special passwords or codes before data can be accessed or changed. The software may also be set so that different users have different privileges. For example, some users may be able to access the data but may not be able to update it, and other users may be able to both access and update the data.

Advantages of Database Processing

Database processing has important advantages over file processing. First, duplication of data is reduced. Most data values need to be stored only once in the database because the data is treated as one collection of data rather than as separate files. Thus, in our athletic-clothing wholesale business example, each customer's address needs to be stored only once in the database. This characteristic means that extra storage space is not required for duplicate data. More importantly, updating of data needs to be done only once, thus improving the likelihood that the data is correct.

A second advantage of database processing is that it makes it easier to process different groups of data—that is, data that in file processing would be stored in separate files. Because the data in a database is stored as one collection of data, the database software can process any data in the database with minimal difficulty. Thus, in our example, if a program needs to process inventory data and order data, it sends instructions to the database software to tell it what to do, and the software handles all details of processing the data.

A final advantage of database processing is that programs are not dependent on the organization of the data in the database. The database can be changed without changing every program that uses the database. For example, if fields or records are added to the database, it is necessary to change only those programs that use those fields or records. All other programs can be left unchanged. This characteristic results from the fact that the database software handles all database interaction. Because programs do not have to be changed as much, less time and expense are required for programming.

Disadvantages of Database Processing

There are several disadvantages of database processing. First, it can be expensive. One source of expense is the cost of the database software. On personal computers this software typically costs $100 to $500, but on multiple-user computers and networks the DBMS can cost $25,000 to over $100,000. Another source of expense is that usually a faster computer with more primary and secondary storage is needed for database processing to get the same performance as in file processing. Such a computer is more expensive than one needed for file processing. Finally, programmers' salaries are usually higher with database processing because the programmers are more skilled than those who know only file processing.

Another disadvantage of database processing is that data is more vulnerable than it is in file processing. If several files are used in file processing, each file can be stored on a different disk. If one disk is accidentally destroyed, the files on other disks are not damaged. In database processing, however, all data must be stored on the same disk. Damage to that disk means all data is lost.

A final disadvantage of database processing is that information systems that use this approach can be complex to develop. Such systems often involve several applications, all using the same database. The development of these information systems usually requires more careful planning and is more time-consuming than in file processing systems.

You can see from this discussion that database processing has advantages and disadvantages over file processing. In general, file processing should be used for simpler systems that involve few programs and a single file. Database processing is best for systems that have numerous programs and that use multiple files. In between are many information systems in which the best approach may be either file processing or database processing.

Database Organization

A database is a collection of data and relationships between the data. The data is organized much like data in a file: Characters are grouped to form fields, and fields are grouped to form records (although the terms *field* and *record* may not be used). The key to database organization, however, is not the data, but the relationships between the data. Different types of relationships can be used in databases, and using them results in different types of databases.

Data Relationships

Three main types of relationships are used in databases: one-to-one relationships, one-to-many relationships, and many-to-many relationships. In a **one-to-one relationship**, one group of data is related to only one other group of data, and vice versa. For example, assume that a database contains records of customer data, each with the customer's number and name, and records of accounts receivable data, each with the balance owed by the customer and the date due. There is one customer record for each customer, and one accounts receivable record for each customer. Then, each customer record is related to one accounts receivable record, and vice versa. Thus, there is a one-to-one relationship between customer records and accounts receivable records.

Figure 7.6 shows a one-to-one relationship between two records. Figure 7.6a shows the *structure* of the records and the relationship between the records. The record structures are shown by the long boxes with smaller boxes for the fields in each record. The relationship structure is indicated by the line connecting the records. This line means that there is a one-to-one relationship between the records. Figure 7.6b shows data for the fields in two records. These records are connected by a line, meaning that they are related. This diagram gives an *occurrence* of the records and the relationship between them. In this occurrence, customer number 12345 has a balance due of $1789.60.

The second type of relationship is called a **one-to-many relationship**. In this type, one group of data is related to one or more other groups of data, but not vice versa. For example, assume that a database contains customer records and invoice records, each with an invoice date and amount. Each customer can have any number of invoices, but each invoice can be associated with only one customer. Thus, the relationship between customer records and invoice records is one-to-many.

Figure 7.7a shows the structure of the customer and invoice records and the one-to-many relationship between them. As before, the record structures are shown by boxes, and the relationship structure is indicated by a line connecting the records. The line, however, spreads out at one end (sometimes called a *crow's foot*). The spread-out part of the line points to the "many" record and the other end of the line points

FIGURE 7.6

A one-to-one relationship ▲

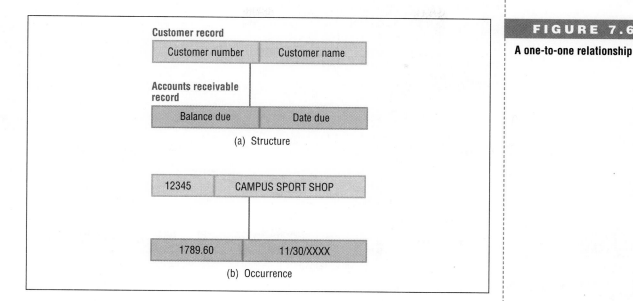

Customer record

Customer number	Customer name

Accounts receivable record

Balance due	Date due

(a) Structure

12345	CAMPUS SPORT SHOP

1789.60	11/30/XXXX

(b) Occurrence

to the "one" record. Thus, the relationship is one-to-many. Figure 7.7b gives an occurrence of these records and the relationship between them. In this occurrence, customer number 12345 has three invoices.

The last type of relationship is a **many-to-many relationship**. In this relationship, one or more groups of data are related to one or more other groups, and vice versa. For example, assume that a database contains supplier records, each with a supplier's number and name, and inventory records, each with an item number, an item description, a unit price, and a quantity on hand. Each supplier can supply several inventory items, and each item can be supplied by several suppliers. Thus, the relationship between supplier records and inventory records is many-to-many.

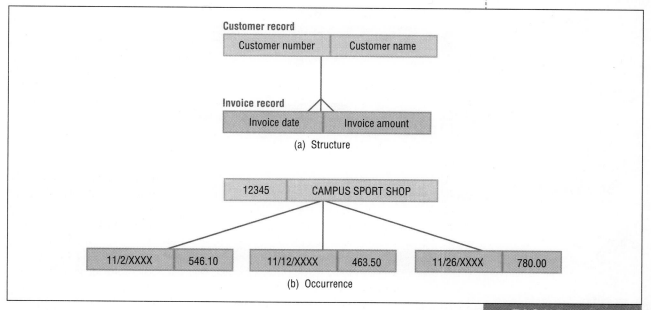

Customer record

Customer number	Customer name

Invoice record

Invoice date	Invoice amount

(a) Structure

12345	CAMPUS SPORT SHOP

11/2/XXXX	546.10		11/12/XXXX	463.50		11/26/XXXX	780.00

(b) Occurrence

FIGURE 7.7

A one-to-many relationship ▲

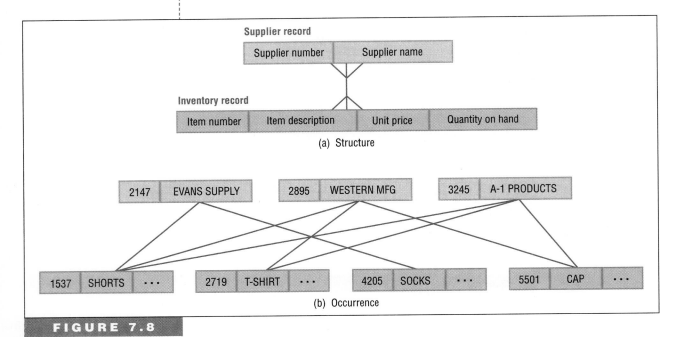

FIGURE 7.8

▲ A many-to-many relationship

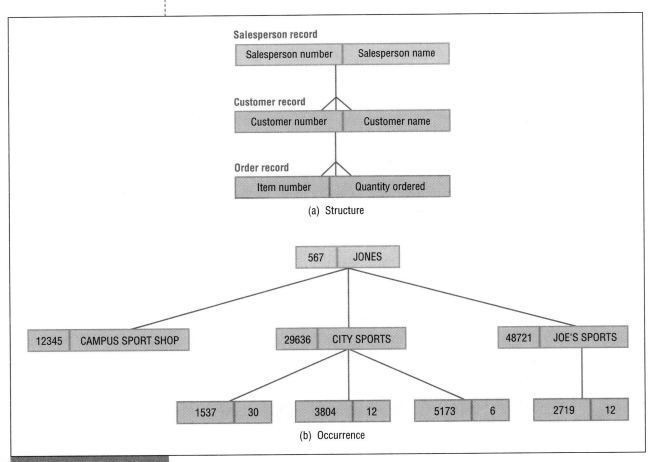

FIGURE 7.9

▲ A hierarchical database

Figure 7.8a shows the structure of the inventory and supplier records and the many-to-many relationship between them. In this figure, the boxes for the records are connected by a line that spreads out at each end, signifying a many-to-many relationship between the records. Figure 7.8b gives an occurrence of these records and the relationship between them. Notice in this occurrence that supplier number 2147 can supply items number 1537 and 4205, and that item number 1537 can be supplied by all three suppliers.

Early Databases

The data in a database should be organized in a way that is easy for people to understand. Early databases used approaches for organizing data that by today's standards are considered complex. They are still in use in many businesses today, however.

The first database software, developed in the 1960s, used an approach for organizing data in which all relationships between groups of data must be one-to-one or one-to-many, but no group of data can be on the "many" side of more than one relationship. A database organized in this way is called a **hierarchical database**. Figure 7.9 shows an example of a hierarchical database. Notice that only one-to-many relationships are used in this database and that all the relationships go in the same direc-

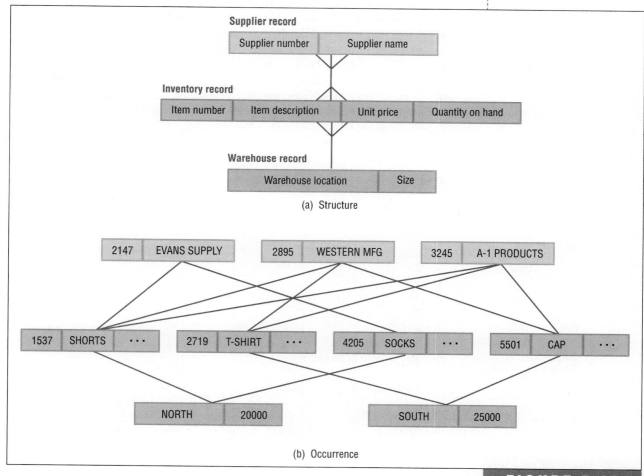

(a) Structure

(b) Occurrence

FIGURE 7.10

A network database

tion. (One-to-one relationships could also be used, but many-to-many relationships cannot.) The meaning of the database is that each salesperson has any number of customers, and each customer can place any number of orders.

In the 1970s, database software became available that allowed data to be organized with all types of relationships—one-to-one, one-to-many, and many-to-many relationships. A database organized in this way is called a **network database**. Figure 7.10 shows an example of a network database. This database has one many-to-many relationship, which is interpreted as meaning that each supplier can supply many inventory items and that each item can be supplied by many suppliers. The database also has one one-to-many relationship, which is interpreted as meaning that each warehouse can store any number of inventory items, but each item can be stored in only one warehouse.

Relational Databases

Early databases and database software were considered complex to use; only professional programmers where trained in their use. In the 1980s, with the increased popularity of personal computers, a simpler approach that users could more easily understand and use became available. This approach uses a **relational database**. It is the most common form of database today.

In a relational database, data is arranged in tables that have rows and columns. For example, Figure 7.11 shows a table with 10 rows and 4 columns. To be absolutely correct, a table in a relational database is called a *relation* (not to be confused with a *relationship*), a row is called a *tuple* (which rhymes with *couple*), and a column is called an *attribute*. These terms are not commonly used, however. Instead, relational databases usually use the terms *table*, *row*, and *column*, or the terms *file*, *record*, and *field*, or a combination of these. This book uses the terms *table*, *row*, and *column*.

A relational database is a group of related tables. Figure 7.12 shows an example of a relational database with three tables. The structure of the database is indicated by

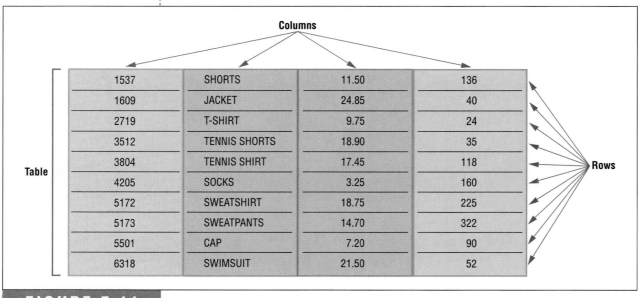

Columns

1537	SHORTS	11.50	136
1609	JACKET	24.85	40
2719	T-SHIRT	9.75	24
3512	TENNIS SHORTS	18.90	35
3804	TENNIS SHIRT	17.45	118
4205	SOCKS	3.25	160
5172	SWEATSHIRT	18.75	225
5173	SWEATPANTS	14.70	322
5501	CAP	7.20	90
6318	SWIMSUIT	21.50	52

Table   Rows

FIGURE 7.11

A table in a relational database

identifying the tables and their columns. A name is given to each table and to each column in each table. These names are listed at the top of the tables in Figure 7.12.

Each table in a relational database must have a column or combination of columns, called the **primary key**, that uniquely identifies the row in the table. The primary key is similar to the key field in the records of a file. Given the value of the primary key of a table, the corresponding row can be located in the table. In Figure 7.12, the primary key of the Inventory table is Item Number and the primary key of

Inventory Table

Item Number	Item Description	Unit Price	Quantity on Hand
1537	SHORTS	11.50	136
1609	JACKET	24.85	40
2719	T-SHIRT	9.75	24
3512	TENNIS SHORTS	18.90	35
3804	TENNIS SHIRT	17.45	118
4205	SOCKS	3.25	160
5172	SWEATSHIRT	18.75	225
5173	SWEATPANTS	14.70	322
5501	CAP	7.20	90
6318	SWIMSUIT	21.50	52

Order Table

Customer Number	Item Number	Quantity Ordered
48721	2719	8
48721	5501	6
29636	3804	5
12345	1537	10
12345	2719	12
12345	3804	18
51387	2719	2
51387	5501	4

Billing Table

Customer Number	Customer Name	Total Due
12345	CAMPUS SPORT SHOP	546.10
29636	CITY SPORTS	87.25
34074	SMITH'S SPORT SHOP	0.00
48721	JOE'S SPORTS	121.20
51387	ABC SPORTING GOODS	48.30

FIGURE 7.12

A relational database

the Billing table is Customer Number. In both of these tables, the primary key is a single column. The primary key can also be the combination of several columns. Thus, in the Order table the primary key is the combination of two columns, the Customer Number and the Item Number, because it is necessary to have both of these to uniquely identify a row in the table.

The reason relationships in relational databases exist is different from the reason relationships exist in hierarchical and network databases. In hierarchical and network databases, relationships exist because connections between records are stored as part of the database. (In other words, the lines in Figure 7.9b and 7.10b between records are actually part of the database, although they are stored in a special way.) In a relational database, however, relationships are not stored this way. Instead, a relationship exists between two tables because there is a common column in the tables. The common column normally is the primary key of one of the tables. For example, there is a relationship between the Inventory table and the Order table in Figure 7.12 because the Item Number column, which is the primary key of the Inventory table, is also in the Order table. Similarly, there is a relationship between the Billing table and the Order table because the Customer Number column, the primary key of the Billing table, appears in both tables. Any type of relationship—one-to-one, one-to-many, and many-to-many—can be represented in a relational database, although the details of how each is represented are beyond the scope of this book.

Object-oriented Databases

Hierarchical, network, and relational databases all store only data (and relationships) in the database. Instructions for processing the data are stored in the application program, separate from the database. Another approach to database organization is to store the data and instructions together in the database. Such a combination of data and instructions is called an *object*, and databases organized around objects are called **object-oriented databases**.

Object-oriented databases are based on the object-oriented programming concepts described in Chapter 5. In both object-oriented databases and object-oriented programming, objects are the basic elements used for representing data and instructions (see Figure 5.17). The difference is that with object-oriented programming, the objects are present only while the program is executing (we say they are *transient*), whereas with object-oriented databases, the objects are stored between executions of a program (we say the objects are *persistent*). Thus, the objects in an object-oriented program cannot be used to store data permanently, whereas the objects in an object-oriented database do store data permanently.

Although object-oriented databases have attracted a lot of attention, they are not in widespread use; there are only a few object-oriented DBMSs. Most databases in use are relational, although some older ones are hierarchical or network databases. Recently, however, object-oriented capabilities have been incorporated into relational databases to create hybrid **object-relational databases**. This approach to databases may become common in the future because it combines the best features of the relational and object-oriented approaches.

Common Database Software

As you know, a DBMS is a program that provides capabilities for manipulating data in a database. The DBMS handles all interaction between the user or application program and the database. It provides capabilities for storing data in the database,

The Affinity Database for the Carolina Mudcats

Minor league baseball's Carolina Mudcats boosted attendance in 1999 by 40%, thanks in part to a fan-loyalty database. Bill Gunger, who oversees information technology for the Mudcats (the AA affiliate of the Colorado Rockies, based in Zebulon, North Carolina), said the new Top Cat Club fan appreciation/loyalty program entices people back to the team's new park and draws in sponsors wanting to target ads.

The Mudcats is one of a growing number of teams that are overcoming the difficulties of customer affinity programs at large-crowd events by using up-to-date database and scan-card technology. Now, they can instantly sign up fans and provide them with coupons to learn who's going to games and how to keep fans coming back.

The Top Cat Club rewards fans for attending games—free T-shirts for three games, and more attractive prizes for more. "We're getting 300 to 500 new sign-ups per night," Gunger says. Personal and demographic data from sign-up sheets enters the system each night, and more is captured from questionnaires on kiosks when Top Cat Club members scan their cards at the park.

The Mudcats bought a $75,000 system that runs on three new IBM Netfinity servers and an IBM DB2 database that also runs its ticketing, accounting, and mail-order operations. The built-in query tools in DB2 let Gunger look up data for targeted mailings and statistics to entice advertisers. "Our biggest challenge will be to figure out how to best use all the data we're collecting," Gunger says.

Ten other professional teams have similar programs, due to the help of AIM Technologies in Austin, Texas.

The Oakland A's counted a 15% reduction in game no-shows, thanks to its FanCard program, says Dave Alioto, director of sales and marketing for the team. Dave Lozow, the A's director of business services, says FanCard helped increase revenue by $200,000 in 1998 just by converting single-game ticket buyers into season-ticket holders.

"We've had great attendance, but people have plenty of options for entertainment," says Charlie Vascellaro, public relations director at Maryland Baseball LLC, which is the owner of three minor league teams that use FanCard. "We want to make sure we don't take them for granted," Vascellaro says.

Questions

1. What data is stored in the Mudcats's affinity database?
2. What database software is used for the Mudcats's affinity database, and what type of DBMS is it?
3. What benefits have the Mudcats received from the affinity database system?

Web Site

Carolina Mudcats:
www.gomudcats.com

Source: *Adapted from* Stewart Deck, "Affinity System Keeps Fans Coming Back," *Computerworld*, July 26, 1999, p. 38.

retrieving data from the database, and updating data in the database. Without the DBMS, the manipulation of a database would be very complex.

Each DBMS is based on one of the database approaches described previously. Thus, a DBMS may be a hierarchical, network, relational, or object-oriented DBMS. The first DBMSs were developed for mainframe computers in the late 1960s. In the 1970s, DBMSs were developed for minicomputers, and in the 1980s personal computer DBMSs appeared. In the 1990s, DBMSs for networked computer systems became common.

Personal Computer Database Software

Personal computer database software is the simplest form of DBMS. This software is designed to be used by one person at a time. Almost all common personal computer database programs use the relational approach. Most of the programs not only provide the ability to create, access, and update databases, but also allow the user to print reports based on data in the database, design forms for input and output of data on the screen, and develop entire computer applications around a database. Most also include a programming language for developing complex applications. Some personal computer database programs for IBM clones are Access, FoxPro, Approach, and dBASE. Fourth Dimension is a database program for the Macintosh. Database programs for personal computers usually cost between $100 and $500.

Multiple-user Computer Database Software

Database management systems for multiple-user computers are large, complex programs that are designed to be used by multiple users at one time. They are expensive, typically costing $25,000 to over $100,000. Because of their complexity, specially trained computer professionals are usually needed to utilize them. Most multiple-user computer DBMSs in use are relational, but some hierarchical DBMSs and network DBMSs are still used. A few of the more widely used mainframe and minicomputer DBMSs are IMS (hierarchical) for IBM mainframe computers; IDMS (network) for IBM and some other mainframe computers and some minicomputers; DB2 (relational) for IBM mainframe computers; and Oracle (relational) for a wide range of mainframe and minicomputers.

Networked Computer Database Software

Networked computer systems use database software that runs on a database server, manipulating data in a database stored on the server. The software for data processing and the user interface, on the other hand, runs on client computers in the network. This is the idea of client/server computing, as discussed in Chapter 6. (Refer to Figure 6.14.) The database software handles the creation, accessing, and updating of the data in the database. It receives instructions from multiple client computers over the network and sends the results of database processing to the clients.

Examples of database programs for networked computer systems are Oracle, Sybase, SQL Server, and Informix. These programs are all relational DBMSs for use on database servers. The client computers use other software for data processing and user interface control. An example of the software used for these purposes on client computers is PowerBuilder. The cost of database and client software depends on how many computers are in the network, but can be as expensive as multiple-user computer database software. Most object-oriented DBMSs are also designed for use on server computers in networks. Examples are GemStone, ObjectStore, and Versant ODBMS.

Networked computer systems also allow the creation of a **distributed database**. In this approach, the database is divided into parts, and each part is stored on a different computer in a network. The database is manipulated through a distributed *DBMS*. Each computer in the network has a copy of the distributed DBMS. Using the distributed DBMS, a user at any computer can access data from any part of the database, no matter where it is stored. The user, however, is unaware of where the data is stored. The advantage of distributed databases is that each user has control over the part of the database stored on his or her computer, but all users may have access to all parts of the database.

Using Database Software

Two main approaches for manipulating a database using database software are summarized in Figure 7.13. In the first approach, the user interacts directly with the DBMS by using a special language called a *query language*. In the second approach, an application program sends instructions to the DBMS, which carries out the actions requested by the program. The user interacts with the application program by supplying input and receiving output.

Query Languages

A **query language** is a language that allows the user to *query* a database—that is, to retrieve data from a database. This type of language also allows the user to update the database. The user uses a query language by entering an instruction, usually called a *command*, at the keyboard. The instruction goes directly to the DBMS, which reviews it and performs the requested processing. Depending on the command, the DBMS may display data on the screen or perform an update. Thus, with a query language, the user interacts directly with the database software to process the data in the database.

The most widely used query languages is **SQL**, which stands for Structured Query Language. SQL is used with relational DBMSs (not with hierarchical or network DBMSs). Recall that a relational database consists of tables with rows and columns. In SQL, a user can retrieve selected rows and columns from a single table or several related tables in a database. A user can also update data in one or more tables.

In a relational database, each table and each column has a name. To query a table, the user gives the name of the table, a condition that indicates the rows to be displayed from the table, and the names of the columns the user wants to display from those rows. The form of a query in SQL is

SELECT *column names*
FROM *table name*
WHERE *condition*

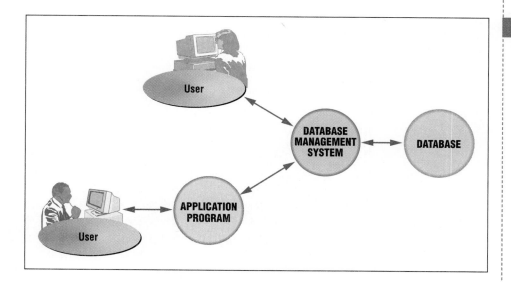

FIGURE 7.13

Using database software ▲

As an example, assume that a user wants to query the inventory/order/billing relational database shown in Figure 7.12. If the user wants to know the item number and description of all items in inventory with a quantity on hand of fewer than 100, he or she would use the following query in SQL:

SELECT Item Number, Item Description
FROM Inventory
WHERE Quantity on Hand < 100

Figure 7.14 shows the screen display after executing this command. Notice that several lines are displayed because several items in the Inventory table in Figure 7.12 satisfy the condition that the quantity on hand is less than 100.

As another example, assume that a user wants to know the names of the customers who ordered item 2719 and the quantity that each customer ordered. The item number and the quantity ordered are in the Order table, and the names of the customers are in the Billing table. The two tables are linked together by the customer number, which is in both the Order table and the Billing table. Hence there is a relationship between these tables. The following SQL command accomplishes what the user wants:

SELECT Billing.Customer Name, Order.Quantity Ordered
FROM Billing, Order
WHERE Billing.Customer Number = Order.Customer Number
 AND Order.Item Number = 2719

This command retrieves the Customer Name column from the Billing table (Billing.Customer Name) and the Quantity Ordered column from the Order table (Order.Quantity Ordered), where Customer Number in the Billing table is the same as Customer Number in the Order table, and Item Number in the Order table is 2719. Figure 7.15 shows the screen display after executing this command. The operation performed by this query is called a *join* because it brings together data from two tables based on a relationship. It is the main way of using relationships between data in a relational database.

FIGURE 7.14

▲ **Executing an SQL command**

SELECT Item Number, Item Description
FROM Inventory
WHERE Quality on Hand < 100

SQL command

Item Number	Item Description
1609	JACKET
2719	T-SHIRT
3512	TENNIS SHORTS
5501	CAP
6318	SWIMSUIT

Screen display

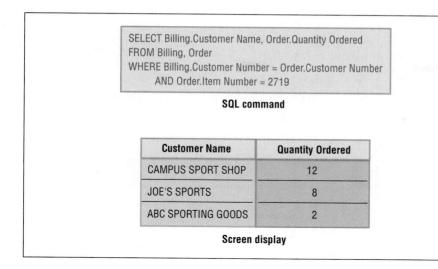

```
SELECT Billing.Customer Name, Order.Quantity Ordered
FROM Billing, Order
WHERE Billing.Customer Number = Order.Customer Number
    AND Order.Item Number = 2719
```

SQL command

Customer Name	Quantity Ordered
CAMPUS SPORT SHOP	12
JOE'S SPORTS	8
ABC SPORTING GOODS	2

Screen display

FIGURE 7.15

Executing an SQL command ▲

The examples given here show how SQL can be used to query a relational database. SQL also has commands to update a relational database. With these commands a user can add rows to a table, delete rows from a table, and change data in rows in a table.

SQL is used with most relational database management systems. In fact, it has become the standard query language for relational databases. Some relational database software also uses a graphical approach called **query-by-example (QBE)** (Figure 7.16). In this approach, the user makes entries into a grid pattern, indicating the columns he or she wants to display and the conditions that determine which rows are to be displayed.

Application Programs

An application program can be developed by writing the program in a programming language or by using special software to develop the program. A **host language** is a programming language for writing application programs containing commands from a query language. A host language may be a general-purpose programming language

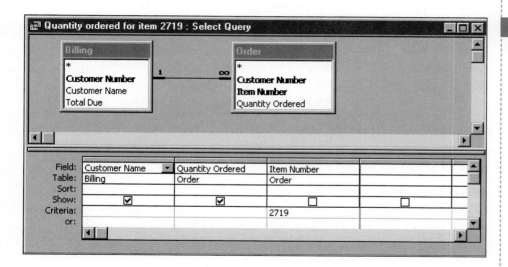

FIGURE 7.16

A query-by-example ▲

FIGURE 7.17

Part of a COBOL program with
▲ an SQL query

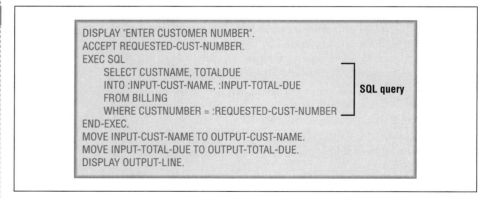

```
DISPLAY "ENTER CUSTOMER NUMBER".
ACCEPT REQUESTED-CUST-NUMBER.
EXEC SQL
     SELECT CUSTNAME, TOTALDUE
     INTO :INPUT-CUST-NAME, :INPUT-TOTAL-DUE          SQL query
     FROM BILLING
     WHERE CUSTNUMBER = :REQUESTED-CUST-NUMBER
END-EXEC.
MOVE INPUT-CUST-NAME TO OUTPUT-CUST-NAME.
MOVE INPUT-TOTAL-DUE TO OUTPUT-TOTAL-DUE.
DISPLAY OUTPUT-LINE.
```

that is used for other types of data processing. For example, COBOL, C, and C++ are commonly used host languages in business. When a programmer uses a host language for database processing, commands from a query language, such as SQL, are placed within a program written in the host language. For example, Figure 7.17 shows part of a COBOL program containing an SQL query. Usually, a programmer can use a host language with several different database management systems. Thus, a programmer can query several databases by using the query languages of different DBMSs. To use a general-purpose programming language as a host language requires special training in computer programming and is only done by computer professionals.

A host language may also be a special-purpose programming language that can be used only with a particular database management system. In this case, queries are contained within the host language program, but the program can be used only with the DBMS for which it is designed. This is the most common approach used with personal computer database software.

An **application generator** is a special software system that makes it easy to develop a computer application. With an application generator, the user does not write a program in a programming language, but instead specifies input and output form layouts, report formats, menus, and calculations. The user also specifies the database queries needed to complete the forms and reports and do the calculations. Then the application generator prepares an application program that accomplishes the required processing. The application program may be in a general-purpose programming language such as COBOL, C, or C++; in a special-purpose language; or in some other form. After the program has been prepared, it can be executed on the computer to perform the required processing. Application generators are a type of 4GL, as discussed in Chapter 5.

Application generators are very convenient for developing computer applications. They are included in most personal computer database software and are used by professional computer personnel and end users. They have limits, however, because not all types of processing that can be done with a host language can be done with an application generator. Still, their ease of use makes them very popular.

Web Access

Many Web sites are designed to give users access to a database by means of a browser. For example, a business may have a Web site that lets customers check a product specification database through the Internet. As another example, a business may let suppliers access its inventory database through an extranet so that they can check inventory quantities for automatic replenishment.

In order to provide Web access to a database, additional software capabilities are needed between the user's browser and the database software. These capabilities, which may be provided by software on a Web server (see Chapter 6), take the user's request for data from the browser on the user's computer and convert it to a form that the database software on a database server can understand. When the data is sent back to the user's browser from the database software, these capabilities convert the data into a form that can be displayed by the browser.

Database Use in Information Systems

Databases used in individual information systems are often called **personal databases** because they are used by only one person. Usually, these databases are stored on a personal computer and processed with personal computer database software. Typically, they are simple databases, with a relatively small amount of data, and are used for only one application. An example is a database of customer and sales data used by only one salesperson. The salesperson creates the database, updates data in it as needed, and accesses data in it to help make sales. It is a personal database for that salesperson.

Workgroup, organizational, and other multiple-user information systems often require large, complex databases. These databases are used by many users at one time, so they are called **shared databases**. Such databases are stored on multiple-user computer systems or servers in networked computer systems. Networks with shared databases may be local area networks (LANs), wide area networks (WANs), or internetworks, including interorganizational networks. Usually, shared databases are used for several applications. For example, the inventory/order/billing database described earlier could be used for inventory control, order entry, and billing.

Often, with a shared database, each user needs only a part of the database. For example, in processing the inventory/order/billing database, one user may need only inventory and order data, and another user may need only order and billing data. To prevent users from processing data that they do not need, the database is divided into **views**, which are parts of the database (Figure 7.18). Each user is given access only to

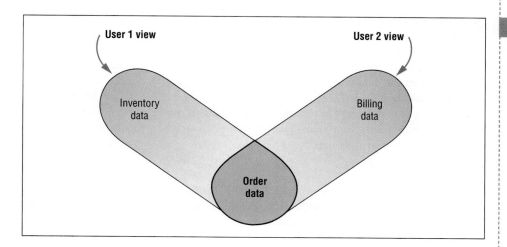

FIGURE 7.18

User views of a database

his or her view of the database. The database software prevents a user with access to one view from processing data in another view.

Sometimes a user with a personal database on a personal computer needs data from a large, shared database on another computer. To get the data, the user can use data communications techniques (discussed in Chapter 6) to communicate with the other computer. Then the user can use the communications software to download the needed data from the large database to his or her personal database.

Data Warehouses

Most databases are used to store current data about a business. For example, the inventory/order/billing database shown in Figure 7.12 contains data about current orders, bills due now, and items presently in inventory. When an order is filled, a bill is paid, or an item is dropped from stock, data about the order, bill, or item is deleted from the database. Sometimes, it is useful to be able to analyze old, historical data. For example, a business could look at older orders to see what items were ordered, in what quantities, and by which customers. Most databases, however, are not designed to retain historical data.

Data in one database, whether current or historical, may be related to data in another database. For example, customer data in a customer database is related to order data in the inventory/order/billing database because customers place orders. Supplier data in a supplier database is related to inventory data in the inventory/order/billing database because different suppliers provide different inventory items. Accessing data from different but related databases can be useful. For example, accessing inventory and supplier data from different databases can help a business decide from which supplier to purchase certain inventory items. Most databases, however, are not designed to be accessed along with other databases.

To make historical data and data from multiple databases available, many businesses use a **data warehouse**. A data warehouse is a collection of data drawn from other databases used by the business. The data warehouse contains data extracted over time from other databases so that historical data is included in the warehouse. The data warehouse includes data taken from multiple databases within the organization. The idea is to bring together data from all sources within the business. The data in the data warehouse is analyzed to provide users with information to help in the management of the business (Figure 7.19).

A data warehouse can contain vast quantities of data—so much data that users have difficulty analyzing it. To solve this problem, data related to specific areas can be separated from the data warehouse and made available to specific users. The specific data from the data warehouse is called a **data mart**. For example, data only used in human resource management can be put in one data mart, data used in production can be put in another data mart, and data used in marketing can be put in a different data mart. This approach makes it easier for users in separate areas to have access to just the data they need.

Data Mining

Analysis of data in a data warehouse or a data mart often uses a technique called **data mining**. This technique involves searching for patterns in the data that are not immediately obvious. For example, a data warehouse of customer purchasing data could be mined to find buying patterns, such as which products are likely to be purchased with which other products.

FIGURE 7.19

Creating and using a data warehouse

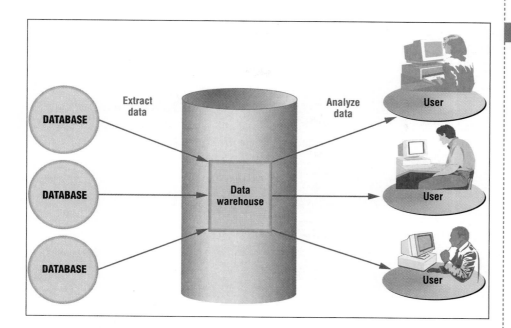

Data mining is different from querying a database. When querying a database, the user has to determine the conditions to be included in the query in advance. For example, to find buying patterns from customer purchasing data using querying, the user would have to try all combinations of patterns. Thus, for grocery purchases, the user would need queries such as "What percentage of customers buy apples and peaches together?" and "What percentage of customers buy apples and oranges together?" Thousands of combinations would have to be checked. With data mining, on the other hand, the user just asks one question to find all patterns. It is not necessary for the user to check each combination separately. Thus data mining is better for discovering patterns in large amounts of data.

Multidimensional Databases

Data in a relational database is viewed in rows of a table; each row represents all the important characteristics about one thing. This view of the data is one dimensional. For example, assume that we have sales data for different sales regions. For each sales region, the sales data is broken down by season, and for each season it is broken down by product line. Figure 7.20 shows how this data could be represented in a relational table. Notice that there is one row for each sales region, season, and product line combination with its sales.

The problem with viewing the data as it's shown in Figure 7.20 is that it can be difficult to visualize how the data could be analyzed. For example, assume that we want the total spring sales of all product lines and all sales regions. Imagining how to extract this total from the data in the form shown in Figure 7.20 is difficult.

In situations such as this one it is helpful to view the data in more than one dimension. A **multidimensional database** presents the data to the user in several dimensions. For example, Figure 7.21 shows the data from Figure 7.20 in a three-dimensional database that looks like a cube. One dimension of this database is

FIGURE 7.20

Sales data in a relational
▲ table

Sales Region	Season	Product Line	Sales
West	WINTER	A	$125,000
West	WINTER	B	$52,000
West	SPRING	A	$158,000
West	SPRING	B	$74,000
West	SUMMER	A	$91,000
West	SUMMER	B	$37,000
West	FALL	A	$112,000
West	FALL	B	$47,000
East	WINTER	A	$41,000
East	WINTER	B	$78,000
East	SPRING	A	$92,000
East	SPRING	B	$67,000
East	SUMMER	A	$45,000
East	SUMMER	B	$32,000
East	FALL	A	$91,000
East	FALL	B	$116,000
South	WINTER	A	$131,000
South	WINTER	B	$114,000
South	SPRING	A	$151,000
South	SPRING	B	$139,000
South	SUMMER	A	$89,000
South	SUMMER	B	$114,000
South	FALL	A	$78,000
South	FALL	B	$97,000

the sales region, another dimension is the season, and the third dimension is the product line. The sales are at the intersections of these three dimensions.

Visualizing the data in this way makes it easier to see how to answer questions about the data. For example, we can think of the total sales in the spring season as the sum of all the data in the part of the database found by "slicing" the cube through the Spring plane (Figure 7.22). To get a more detailed answer about spring sales, such as the sales of Product Line A in the spring, we can cut the spring data again, a process we can think of as "dicing." Because we think of answering questions from multidimensional databases in this way, this approach is often called "slice and dice."

A multidimensional database can be created using special multidimensional database software. The data in the database is stored in a multidimensional form that makes it easy for the software to manipulate the data. The data can have any number of dimensions, although when we get beyond three dimensions we cannot visualize the data. Alternatively, data can be stored in a relational database, and then the multidimensional software can be used to extract data and present it to the user as if it were arranged in a multidimensional way. In either case, the user views the data as multidimensional and can slice and dice the data to find answers to questions.

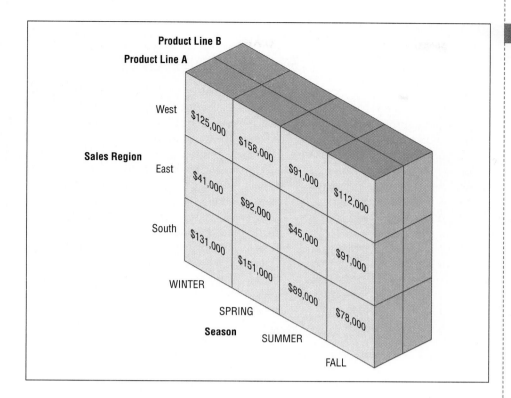

FIGURE 7.21

Sales data in a multidimensional database

On-line Analytical Processing

Analysis of multidimensional databases using a slice-and-dice approach is part of a category of techniques for database and data warehouse analysis called **on-line analytical processing (OLAP)**. The idea of OLAP is to make analysis of large amounts of data stored in databases, data warehouses, and multidimensional databases easy for users. OLAP software tools allow users to interactively extract data from databases in various patterns and to analyze the data, often using statistical techniques. For exam-

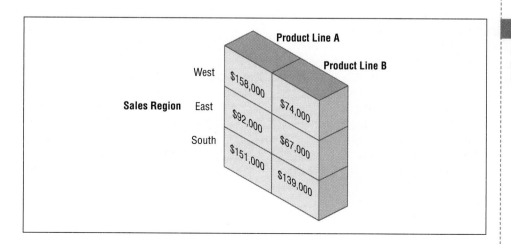

FIGURE 7.22

A slice of the multidimensional sales database for spring

Multidimensional Data Analysis at Aqua-Chem

"If it ain't broke, don't fix it" is the guiding principle at Milwaukee-based Aqua-Chem, a leading boiler manufacturer. The company runs old mainframe-based financial software packages in conjunction with a host-based Computer Associates (CA) International CA-Datacom database management system. Generally satisfied with the performance of the mainframe system, Aqua-Chem is reluctant to change.

The company's only complaint with the software is its inability to perform multidimensional financial analysis—viewing data from a variety of angles to uncover otherwise overlooked trends—but that wasn't enough to make the company switch to a new database.

"We looked at new financial packages and client/server tools," recalls Chuck Norris, Aqua-Chem vice president and CIO, but the company stuck with the legacy systems. "We liked the security, functionality, and reliability of the old system," Norris says.

Instead of changing systems, Aqua-Chem augmented its core financial systems with a new database and business intelligence tools. It opted for Microsoft's SQL Server DBMS to create a financial server running Cognos's business intelligence tools. Manufacturing, sales, and other data are regularly extracted, transformed, transferred, and loaded into SQL Server using Informatica data warehouse products. With the SQL Server database, Aqua-Chem managers access, analyze, and manipulate the data through online analytical processing (OLAP) cubes (three-dimensional databases) created with Cognos tools.

"People now access the financial server over the intranet, go to their particular cubes and do what they need to do," Norris explains. Using the Cognos tools, managers can analyze products or customers. The mainframe system continues to handle all the core financial processing.

The business intelligence system has enabled Aqua-Chem to virtually eliminate paper. In the past, the company generated dozens of greenbar reports, split them up for distribution to various managers, and sent them to its 11 plants across the United States and Canada. "Now, we do not have even one report," Norris boasts. Managers who want a printed report access their OLAP cubes and print out the parts they want.

Norris is so comfortable with the mainframe and the older applications that the company recently ordered a new IBM OS/390 mainframe. Norris says he doesn't mind the old CA-Datacom database. IBM is wooing him with low pricing and flexible terms for DB2, and it's tempting. "I'd love to convert from Datacom to DB2," Norris says, but his 18-person information technology staff isn't large enough to handle a database migration, at least not until something breaks.

Questions

1. How did Aqua-Chem solve the problem of doing multidimensional data analysis with its old database?
2. Why has Aqua-Chem not replaced its old mainframe DBMS with a new system?

Web Site

Aqua-Chem:
www.aqua-chem.com

Source: *Adapted from* Alan Radding "New Life for Old Databases," *Computerworld,* July 12, 1999, pp. 70–72.

ple, using the appropriate OLAP software, a user could extract historical sales data from a data warehouse and then use a statistical technique to project future sales trends. The OLAP software could then present the results of the analysis in a graph for easy viewing. Techniques such as this make OLAP very useful for users.

Database Administration

Data is an important resource for an organization. With the right data available at the right time, an organization can operate better and be managed more effectively. To accomplish this goal, organizational data must be managed, just as people and money are managed. As data increases in volume and complexity, the management of the data becomes more difficult. With large, complicated databases, the problem of data management is the most severe.

To solve this problem, an organization with large databases often has a person called a **database administrator (DBA)** who is responsible for managing the organization's databases. Some organizations have several DBAs or people with other titles performing the database administration function. As the number, size, and complexity of databases increase, the number of people needed to manage the databases increases.

The DBA is responsible for the databases. The DBA designs the databases based on the needs of the users. If necessary, he or she changes the databases to meet new requirements. The DBA selects the DBMS to process each database. He or she controls the use of the database by giving permission only to specific users to access data in the databases. The DBA performs these tasks and others to manage the database.

CHAPTER SUMMARY

1 The main advantage of file processing is that it is simple to use. Many information systems do not need anything more complex. Disadvantages appear when it is necessary to process data in more than one related file. One disadvantage in this situation is that data may be duplicated in several files, making it difficult to ensure that changed data is updated every place it is stored. Another disadvantage is that it is difficult to access data from more than one file at a time. A final disadvantage of file processing is that there is a dependency between programs and data, which means programs may have to be modified if a file's organization is changed. (pp. 201–205)

2 A **database** is a collection of data and relationships between data. A **relationship** is a way in which one group of data in a database relates to another group. Unlike in file processing, in which separate files are needed to store the data for each application, in a database all data is stored together. A **database management system**

(DBMS), is a program that provides capabilities for creating, accessing, and updating a database. (pp. 206–207)

3 One advantage of database processing over file processing is that duplication of data is reduced. Another advantage is that with database processing, it is easier to process different groups of data than with file processing. A third advantage is that programs that perform database processing are not dependent on the organization of the data in the database. One disadvantage of database processing is that certain costs are greater than with file processing. Another disadvantage is that data is more vulnerable with database processing than with file processing. A third disadvantage is that information systems that use database processing can be more complex to develop than those that use file processing. (pp. 209–210)

4 Relationships are important in databases because related data is processed through relationships. The three main types of relationships are **one-to-**

one relationships, in which one group of data is related to only one other group of data, and vice versa; **one-to-many relationships**, in which one group of data is related to many other groups of data, but not vice versa; and **many-to-many relationships**, in which many groups of data are related to many other groups of data, and vice versa. (pp. 210–213)

5 A **relational database** is a group of related tables. Each table consists of data arranged in rows and columns. The column or combination of columns in a table that uniquely identifies the rows in the table is called the **primary key**. A relationship exists between two tables when there are common columns in the tables. (pp. 214–216)

6 Database software for personal computers is the simplest form of DBMS and is designed to be used by one person at a time. Almost all personal computer database programs are relational. Database management systems for multiple-user computers are large, complex programs designed to be used by many users at a time. A few multiple-user hierarchical or network DBMSs are still used, but most are relational. Database software for networked computers runs on database servers and communicates with client computers in a network. Most DBMSs for networked computers are relational, but some are object oriented. (pp. 216–218)

7 Database software can be used through a **query language**, which allows the user to query a database—that is, to retrieve data from a database. Database software can also be used through an application program written in a **host language**, which is a programming language containing commands in a query language. A host language may be a general-purpose programming language that can be used with several database management systems, or it can be a special-purpose programming language that can be used with only one database management system. Databases can also be accessed through a browser and the Web, provided that the necessary software capabilities are available. (pp. 219–222)

8 Databases used in individual information systems are often called **personal databases**. These databases usually are stored on personal computers and used by only one person. Databases used in workgroup, organizational, and other multiple-user information systems are called **shared databases**. These databases are stored on multiple-user computer systems or on servers in networks. Often, with a shared database, each user needs only a part of the database, called a **view**. Sometimes a user with a personal database uses data communications techniques to transfer data from a shared database to a personal database. (pp. 223–224)

9 A **data warehouse** is a collection of data drawn from other databases used by the business. The data warehouse contains historical data extracted over time from another database. It also contains data taken from multiple databases within the organization. **Data mining** is the process of searching for patterns that are not immediately obvious in the data in a data warehouse. (pp. 224–225)

10 A **multidimensional database** is a database that the user views as organized into several dimensions, like a cube. The user can extract information from a multidimensional database by using software to "slice and dice" the data. **On-line analytical processing (OLAP)** involves analysis of large amounts of data stored in databases, data warehouses, and multidimensional databases by users using special interactive techniques and tools. (pp. 225–227)

K E Y   T E R M S

Application Generator (p. 222)
Database (p. 207)
Database Administrator (DBA) (p. 229)
Database Management System (DBMS) (p. 206)
Data Mart (p. 224)
Data Mining (p. 224)
Data Validation (p. 204)

Data Warehouse (p. 224)
Direct (Random) File (p. 202)
Distributed Database (p. 218)
Hierarchical Database (p. 213)
Host Language (p. 221)
Indexed File (p. 204)
Key Field (p. 202)
Many-to-Many Relationship (p. 211)

Multidimensional Database (p. 225)
Network Database (p. 214)
Object-Oriented Database (p. 216)
Object-Relational Database (p. 216)
One-to-Many Relationship (p. 210)
One-to-One Relationship (p. 210)
On-Line Analytical Processing (OLAP) (p. 227)

Personal Database (p. 223)   Relational Database (p. 214)   Shared Database (p. 223)
Primary Key (p. 215)   Relationship (p. 207)   SQL (p. 219)
Query-By-Example (QBE) (p. 221)   Sequential File (p. 202)   View (p. 223)
Query Language (p. 219)

REVIEW QUESTIONS

1 What is the field that uniquely identifies a record in a data file called? Why is it usually a code field rather than a name or description field?

2 What are the differences between the organization of a sequential file, a direct file, and an indexed file?

3 What three activities are involved in updating a data file? a database?

4 How is the accuracy of the data in a file or database ensured? What is the process called?

5 How is data in a file or database secured against loss or destruction?

6 What is a database?

7 What does a database management system do?

8 What is the main difference between file processing and database processing?

9 What are several advantages of database processing?

10 What are several disadvantages of database processing?

11 Why are relationships important in database processing?

12 What type of relationship does each of the following situations describe?

   a Each student can have at most one car, and each car can be owned by only one student.

   b Each advisor has many students, and each student has only one advisor.

   c Each student can belong to several clubs, and each club can have many student members.

13 How is a relational database organized?

14 What is a primary key?

15 What is an object-oriented database?

16 How does database software function in a network?

17 What are two ways a user can use a database?

18 What is SQL?

19 What type of databases do individual users use, and what type do multiple users use?

20 What is a view of a database?

21 What is a data warehouse?

22 What is data mining used for?

23 What is on-line analytical processing?

24 What is a database administrator?

DISCUSSION QUESTIONS

1 Will file processing eventually be entirely replaced by database processing? Why or why not?

2 Think of a computer application in a business with which you are familiar. Would this application be better using file processing or database processing? Why?

3 Pick several relationships at your college or university, and determine whether each is a one-to-one, one-to-many, or many-to-many relationship. Some relationships you could consider are student/professor, professor/class, student/major, professor/department, and student/dorm.

4 Sometimes a relationship is supposed to be one type, but in reality is another type. For example, at a college or university a student is supposed to have one advisor, meaning that there is supposed to be a one-to-many relationship between advisor and student, but may, in fact, talk to several advisors, meaning that there is actually a many-to-many relationship. Identify several relationships in your experience that you think might be like this.

5 Many people who work in a business need to access data in a database. Should they all have to learn a query language such as SQL to do this?

6 Why does a business have separate databases and a data warehouse? Why does it not have just one large database for all its data, both current and historical?

E T H I C S   Q U E S T I O N S

1 Views are used to keep users from accessing data that they are not supposed to see in a database. To access data in a view, a user needs a special password or code. Assume that one of your coworkers has access to a view that contains personnel data that you are not supposed to see. Your coworker is very busy one day and asks if you would retrieve some personnel data from his view. He says he will give you his password so you can see the data in his view. What would you do in this situation?

2 Data in a data warehouse is only as accurate as the data in the databases from which the data is taken. Assume that you suspect, but are not sure, that the data in one of the databases used for a data warehouse in your business has a number of errors in it. The data in the data warehouse is used to make decisions on how to advertise some of the business's products. What would you do in this case? If the data were used to determine employee raises, would your answer be different? Why or why not?

P R O B L E M - S O L V I N G   P R O J E C T S

1 Find out how an organization or a business to which you have access uses data files or databases. What data files or databases does the organization have? For what information systems is each data file or database used? Which data files or databases are used by individual users, and which by multiple users? Write a summary of your findings.

2 Think of the database that would be used for class registration at your college or university. What data and relationships do you think would be in the database? Draw a diagram similar to Figure 7.9 or 7.10 of how you think the database is organized. Use graphics software to prepare your diagram.

3 Using appropriate software, set up a table that includes information about different personal computer database software. Include columns for the name of the software, the current version, the price, what type of computer the software runs on, and characteristics of the software, such as whether it uses SQL, has a programming language, or can generate complete applications. Fill in the table with information about software listed in the chapter, as well as other software. Use the Web to find more information to complete the table. As new software or new versions of existing software become available, update the table.

4 Using personal computer database software, set up the inventory/order/billing database discussed in the chapter, with the data shown in Figure 7.12. Then use the software to complete the queries shown in Figures 7.14 and 7.15. Finally, use the software to answer the following queries:

a What are the names of the customers who owe more than $100?

b What are the descriptions, prices, and quantities ordered of all items ordered by customer 12345?

5 Human resource management information systems often include a personnel database. The data in such a database usually includes employee data (name, address, Social Security number, pay rate, etc.), skills data (skill, training, years of experience, etc.), and work history (previous positions, dates, pay rates, etc.). Each employee can have one or more skills and can have any number of previous positions. Set up a personnel database with these and other data that you think would be appropriate. Enter data for 10 to 20 fictitious employees in the database. Then design queries that you think would be useful to a personnel manager. Test your queries to be sure they work correctly.

6 Spreadsheet software can sometimes be used for small two- and three-dimensional databases. Use spreadsheet software to set up the multidimensional database shown in Figure 7.21. (Look at Figure 7.20 for the data not shown in Figure 7.21.) You will have to use more than one worksheet for the database. Then use the spreadsheet software to find the total sales for all sales regions and all product lines for the spring season. Also find the total sales for Product Line A for all sales regions for the spring season.

INTERNET AND ELECTRONIC COMMERCE PROJECTS

1 Use the Web to gather information about several DBMSs that are used on database servers in networks. Prepare a brief description of each system.

2 Use the Web to locate information about data mining tools. Prepare a table listing the tools you identify and their characteristics.

3 Locate an e-commerce Web site that you think uses a database to provide information about a company's products. (One possibility is the Web site for a mail order company.) Prepare a list of the data items that you think are stored in the database. Organize the data items into tables of related items.

real world case

Procter & Gamble

Pow, right in the kisser! Being the chair of a $38 billion company didn't earn John E. Pepper any respect from members of the People for the Ethical Treatment of Animals (PETA).

In fact, twice in 1998 PETA heaved pies into the face of the Procter & Gamble (P&G) chief, protesting his company's use of animals in product safety tests.

But PETA has put its pies back in the fridge and now hails P&G's use of information technology to eliminate much of its animal testing. In June 1999 the giant maker of Tide, Crest, Crisco, Pampers, Oil of Olay, and some 300 other products announced it was immediately ending the use of animals for testing several hundred beauty, fabric, home-care, and paper products.

"That was a big step forward for that company, although it didn't by any means cover all our concerns," says Mary Beth Sweetland, director of research investigations and rescue at PETA in Norfolk, Virginia. "They deserve a pat on the back but still need a shove forward," she adds.

Cincinnati-based P&G has eliminated approximately 80% of its animal testing since 1984, while tripling in size. Some of the reduction is due to the substitution of human and animal cell cultures. But most of it, especially in recent years, is due to the use of data mining, analysis, and modeling.

The key is to use huge databases of information about existing chemicals and past tests to predict whether a new product ingredient will be safe—that is, testing it in software instead of on animals.

In a computer demonstration at P&G's secretive research laboratory near Cincinnati, a toxicology and bio-infomatics specialist keys in the molecular structure of a new and untested chemical. The structure—in essence a map of how atoms join to form the molecule—is tested against the structures of 450,000 known and previously tested chemicals in a 2 GB Oracle database.

Because the demonstration uses a new chemical, no match is found. But sophisticated search and display software from Oxford Molecular Group in Campbell, California, does find 43 near matches, similar chemicals called *structural analogues*. The closer the match, the more likely that the untested chemical will have the same properties as the previously tested analogue.

Edward D. Thompson, a cancer specialist by training "but now a database expert," explains how he might present the results to a P&G product developer: "I would say, 'Well, we have a nitro group here, which in my experience says it's going to be a carcinogen, so I wouldn't use it.'"

P&G has added to the structures database information from external sources—such as the U.S. Environmental Protection Agency (EPA) and the National Cancer Institute—about the harmful effects of some 120,000 chemicals. Included are the results of more than 1 million tests on those chemicals. This toxicology data is attached to the results of structures searches, put into spreadsheets, and sent to P&G scientists around the world who request it.

If a significant number of the analogues found in a search are known carcinogens, the new chemical is simply dropped from further consideration, and no animals are exposed to it. Previously, the substance would have gone straight to the animal lab. "You tested, you got the positive (result for cancer) and you lost six months of product development," Thompson says. "Basically, you tested everything."

It gets a little harder when the analogues are known to be safe. "You have to make a decision—am I smart enough to expose a lot of people to this chemical based on what I know? That's a tough decision, and one we don't take lightly," Thompson says. Often, the answer is still to test the new substance on animals.

Although the impetus for this work originally was to reduce research on animals, Thompson says it now also gives P&G better results at a lower cost. "If you do this right, you can do it in three days," he says. "You can't fill out the paperwork for an animal study in that time."

Now P&G is funding development of a computer model that holds promise for reducing or eliminating eye-inflammation tests—the ones that animal welfare groups often illustrate with photographs of a caustic substance dripping into a rabbit's eye. In tests of 130 chemical structures so far, a simulated eye membrane has in most cases mirrored the reaction of a real eye, Thompson says. P&G has decided not to patent the model so it will be available to all companies.

Katherine A. Stitzel, a veterinarian and an associate director of P&G's Human & Environmental Safety Division, heads the P&G's search for testing alternatives and is a leader in the international animal welfare movement as well. She says she's hopeful that models will help reduce the number of animals used in acute toxicity tests, in which rats are fed a chemical until half have died from it. "We are working to see if we can predict most of that with computers," she says.

Not all of the information technology that is leading to animal testing alternatives is that sophisticated, however. P&G has combined the results of all its animal and environmental tests from three decades with the structures and toxicology data into one 40 GB database. "We can often go back now and see that we've already tested something very similar and so we may not have to do it again," Stitzel says.

And P&G is able to apply statistical methods to this huge store of historical data in order to refine future tests. That can allow a test to use fewer animals or lower chemical doses and still produce reliable results, Stitzel says.

Stitzel is leading an initiative involving 15 to 20 companies to find a way they can share test data with one another without giving away proprietary information. That could involve each company giving its data to a trusted third party. "We'd let them watch over it and search it and tell us the results," she says. "With enough data from enough different kinds of companies, any one company's data would be hidden."

P&G has invested $120 million since 1984—$28 million in 1998 alone—to develop nonanimal tests. "Of all major corporations, they are perhaps the biggest funders of alternative methods," says Martin Stephens, vice president for animal research issues at the Humane Society in Washington. "P&G is part of the IT solution to the problem of animal testing."

Stitzel says information technology will eventually allow P&G to eliminate all animal testing, but she can't say just when. "People say to us, 'That's not possible,' but when my grandmother was born in 1884, no one would have thought you could fly an airplane, much less go to the moon."

Questions

1 What information technology techniques does P&G use to eliminate much of its animal testing?

2 What data is stored in the database used in the P&G system?

3 What happens if no match is found for a new chemical in the database?

4 What benefits, other than a reduction of animal testing, does P&G receive from using the system?

5 What ethical issues are raised in this case?

Web Site
Procter & Gamble: www.pg.com

Source: *Adapted from* Gary Anthes, "P&G Uses Data Mining to Cut Animal Testing," *Computerworld*, December 6, 1999, pp. 44–45.

]Part
three

Business
Information
Systems

Personal Productivity
A N D   P R O B L E M
S O L V I N G

C H A P T E R   O U T L I N E

Improving Personal Productivity

Managing Stored Data

Analyzing Data

Presenting Information

Locating and Retrieving Information Using the Internet

Solving Problems with Personal Applications

The Problem-solving Process

After completing this chapter, you should be able to

1. Explain how individual information systems can improve personal productivity.

2. Explain how stored data is managed with database software.

3. Describe how data is analyzed in a spreadsheet and why spreadsheet software makes the analysis easier.

4. Describe several types of software used to prepare information for presentation to others.

5. Explain how data management, data analysis, and information presentation applications can be combined.

6. Describe how the Internet can be used to locate and retrieve information.

7. Explain how personal computer applications are used to help individuals solve problems.

8. Explain the meaning of end-user computing.

9. Describe the activities in the problem-solving process.

ndividuals in a business use a variety of personal information systems, including word processing, spreadsheet, and database systems. These systems do not affect a workgroup or an entire business—only individuals in an organization. As you learned in Chapter 1, a system that affects the work of a single personal is called an *individual information system*.

This chapter examines the common computer applications found in individual information systems, and shows how these applications are used in businesses. The chapter also describes how individuals solve business problems by using these applications. First, the chapter explains how productivity is improved by individual information systems. Then it examines computer applications for data management, data analysis, and information presentation. Next, it describes how the Internet is used to locate and retrieve information. Finally, the chapter discusses problem solving and the problem-solving process used with personal computer applications.

Improving Personal Productivity

Businesses use individual information systems to improve personal productivity. *Productivity* has to do with how much a person contributes to a business in a period of time. For example, if a salesperson can make six sales calls in a day instead of five, with just as good a chance of making a sale on each call, then that salesperson is more productive than one who makes only five calls. If a person can write a new advertising brochure in three weeks instead of four, and the new brochure is just as effective, then the person is more productive.

Businesses are always looking for ways to improve the productivity of employees. The more an individual contributes to the business, the greater will be the business's revenues or the lower will be its expenses. Thus, improving personal productivity can affect the profitability of the business. Individual information systems are one way of improving personal productivity.

Individual information systems include computer applications that assist individuals in storing and analyzing data, in presenting information, and in locating and retrieving information on the Internet. These systems, which typically use personal computers, include database software to manage stored data, spreadsheet software to analyze data, and word processing and graphics software to present information. They also include browsers and search software to locate and retrieve information on the Internet. By using an individual information system a person can be more productive because information that the person uses in his or her job is easier to locate, retrieve, manage, analyze, and present.

An individual information system can use just one type of software. For example, an individual financial analysis system may use spreadsheet software. Alternatively, an individual information system can use several types of software, with data being transferred between programs. For example, Figure 8.1 shows one pattern used in

Using software in an individual information system

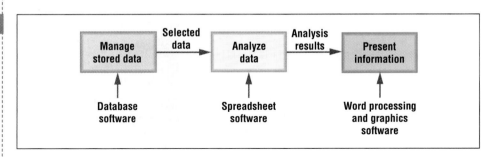

some individual information systems. In this pattern, stored data is managed by database software. Selected stored data is retrieved and then analyzed by using spreadsheet software. Finally, the results of the analysis are presented, using word processing and graphics software. You will see how this pattern is applied in a case study that runs through much of this chapter.

Managing Stored Data

Individual information systems often require that data be stored in secondary storage so that it can be easily accessed for processing. As you know, data can be stored in secondary storage in *data files* or *databases*. Recall that a data file consists of a group of *records*, each record contains several *fields*, and each field has several *characters*. A database consists of groups of data with *relationships* between the groups. With the proper software, the user can store data in a data file or a database, access the stored data, and update the data. These tasks are needed in many individual information systems.

Although an individual information system can store data in a data file, usually the data in such a system is stored in a database. The database is managed by *database software*. Recall from Chapter 7 that with this type of software, which is also called a *database management system* (*DBMS*), the user can simultaneously process related data from different groups of data in a database. Examples of personal computer database software are Access, Approach, Paradox, FoxPro, and dBASE. All these programs are relational DBMSs in which the data is organized into tables consisting of rows and columns. Using database software can increase an individual's productivity in managing data.

Using Database Software to Manage Data

Three main functions that the user can perform to manage stored data with database software are creating a database, accessing a database, and updating a database (Figure 8.2). Before a database can be used, it must be *created* by using the database software, a process that involves two steps. First, the user must enter a description of the structure of the data and relationships in the database. The database software must be told what fields are in each record, what type of data is in each field, what records are in the database, and what types of relationships exist between the records. With this information the database software initializes the database, which means it reserves space for the data in secondary storage and stores the description of the database in this space. Second, the user must enter the initial data into the database, a process sometimes called *populating* the database. Data for each field in each record must be entered. The database software stores the entered data in secondary storage.

After a database has been created, a user can use the database software to *access* data in the database. Accessing data means retrieving the data from the database in secondary storage and bringing it into primary storage. The user may access all the data in a database, or he or she may access only certain data. With database software, the user can use relationships to access data from several related records simultaneously. After the data has been brought into primary storage, it can be processed, displayed on the screen, printed on paper, or used in others ways.

The third main function a user can perform to manage stored data with database software is to *update* data in a database. Updating includes three tasks. One is to *add* new data to a database, which usually involves adding one or more records. Another task is to *delete* old data in a database, which normally involves deleting one or more

FIGURE 8.2**

Using database software to manage stored data

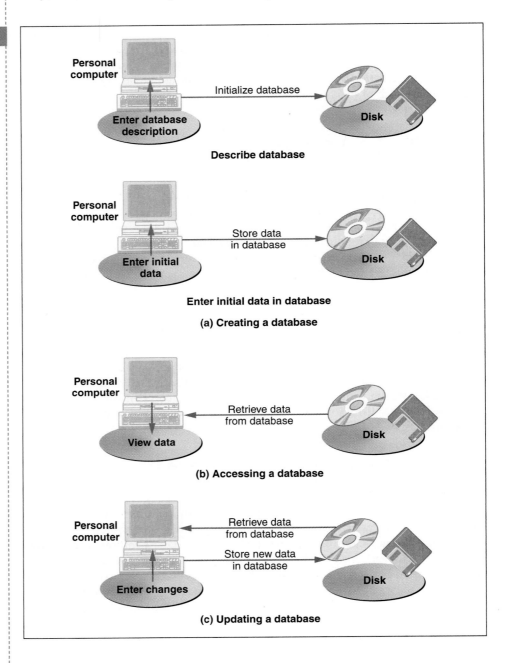

records. A final task is to *change* the data in the database, which typically involves changing the data in one or more fields of a record.

When a database is updated in any of these ways, changes are made in the data stored in secondary storage. The updating process usually involves three steps. First, the user enters information about what changes he or she wants to make. Then the database software retrieves the old data—that is, the record that is to be changed. Finally, the software makes changes in the old data and stores the new data in secondary storage. (If new records are to be added or old records deleted, the process is slightly different.)

A Case Study of Data Management

To illustrate how data management using database software is used in an individual information system, assume that you are the national sales manager of an athletic-clothing wholesaler. As part of your job, you need to keep track of data about each salesperson you manage. You must be able to quickly look up the month's sales for any salesperson, the region in which the person works, and the person's address. Every month, you have to update each salesperson's sales and, occasionally, you have to change a salesperson's address because the person has moved. Also, sometimes you have to delete all information about a salesperson because the person has left the company, and sometimes you must add information about a new salesperson who has been hired.

You could keep the information for all the salespeople on paper. For example, you could store the information about each salesperson on a separate card. If there are many salespeople, however, looking up information stored this way can be time-consuming, and updating data can involve much erasing and rewriting. Therefore, you decide to develop an individual information system with a database containing the data about all salespeople. The system will allow you to retrieve the required information and do the necessary updating more easily than you could by using a paper system. Thus, you will be more productive in your job.

Your first step is to determine what data is to be stored in the database and how the database is to be organized. You have decided to use Access, a personal computer relational DBMS. In Access, data is stored in tables. Each row in a table is called a record and each column is called a field. You have to determine what fields and records make up the tables in the database. You decide that you need the following fields for each salesperson:

Salesperson number

Salesperson name

Salesperson address

Region name

Salesperson sales

Because all these fields apply to a salesperson, they can be in the same record. Hence, you decide that the database should have one record for each salesperson with these five fields. The records for all salespeople can be in one table in the database.

First, you must create the database. You select the software function to create a new table in a new database. You enter a name for each field in the records in the table and specify the type of data in each field (e.g., number, text, currency, date). For example, you call the salesperson number field Salesperson Number, and you indicate that this field contains a number. You also give a name to the table—Salesperson. Figure 8.3 shows the screen after all the required information has been entered. The database software uses this information to reserve space for the database in secondary storage.

With information about the fields and records in a table in the database specified, you can store the initial data in the records. You enter the data for each field in each record. Figure 8.4 shows the screen after you have entered the data for several records. After you enter the data for each record, the database software stores the record in the table in secondary storage; you do not have to tell the software to save the data, as in some other types of software. After all the data has been entered and stored in secondary storage, the database creation process is complete.

FIGURE 8.3

Creating a database: Describing the fields in the records of the Salesperson table

Field Name	Data Type	Description
Salesperson Number	Number	
Salesperson Name	Text	
Salesperson Address	Text	
Region Name	Text	
Salesperson Sales	Currency	

Sometime after creating the database, you need to access data in it to help you with your job. First, you want a complete list of all the data in the database. You select a software option that retrieves all the data in the Salesperson table and displays it on the screen. You also print a copy of this list. Figure 8.5 shows the printed output. Notice that the data is displayed in rows and columns. Each row is a record in the table, and each column is a field. The name of the field is displayed above its column.

Next, you want to analyze the sales for each of the four sales regions that you manage. You create a query that retrieves just the records for the salespeople in the northern region and lists the salesperson number, name, and sales from these records. You display the result of this query in a special form on the screen. Figure 8.6 shows the screen output. Notice that only five rows are displayed because only five salespeople work in the northern region. From this display you can see which of the salespeople in the northern region are the best and which are not doing well. You do the same thing for the southern, eastern, and western regions.

Periodically you have to update the data in the Salesperson table. When a new salesperson is hired, you have to add a record for that salesperson. You enter the data for the salesperson in the same way that you enter data when creating the database, and the database software stores the new record in the table. If a salesperson leaves the business, that person's record must be deleted from the table, which you can do easily with the software. At the end of each month, you have to change the sales figure in each record in the table to reflect the current month's sales. You enter the new sales figure for each record, and the database software changes the data in the records. Also, you sometimes have to change a salesperson's address in the table because the person has moved. All updating involves making changes in data stored in secondary storage.

After you have used the Salesperson table for a while, you decide you would like to create another table to keep track of data about each region. You need the following fields for each region:

Region name

Region total sales

Number of salespeople in region

FIGURE 8.4

Creating a database: Entering initial data in the records of the Salesperson table

Salesperson Number	Salesperson Name	Salesperson Address	Region Name	Salesperson Sales
10421	John Smith	San Francisco, CA	Western	$29,500
12307	Alan Wood	Atlanta, GA	Southern	$1,050
15096	Susan Jenson	Cincinnati, OH	Northern	$42,800
17228	Frank Fuller	Flint, MI	Northern	$12,050

Salesperson Number	Salesperson Name	Salesperson Address	Region Name	Salesperson Sales
10421	John Smith	San Francisco, CA	Western	$29,500
12307	Alan Wood	Atlanta, GA	Southern	$1,050
15096	Susan Jenson	Cincinnati, OH	Northern	$42,800
17228	Frank Fuller	Flint, MI	Northern	$12,050
22751	Joyce McAdams	Newark, NJ	Eastern	$10,250
23105	James Bennett	Eugene, OR	Western	$18,050
28625	Francis Benton	Birmingham, AL	Southern	$3,675
28733	Andrew Lee	New York, NY	Eastern	$14,700
31970	Mary Wong	Seattle, WA	Western	$37,025
34582	Fred Parks	Philadelphia, PA	Eastern	$14,800
39377	Robert Marshall	Minneapolis, MN	Northern	$31,500
46068	Susan Brown	Boston, MA	Eastern	$8,525
47216	Paul Napier	New Orleans, LA	Southern	$12,100
51927	Olivia Lock	Chicago, IL	Northern	$40,550
58114	Jose Sanchez	Miami, FL	Southern	$21,415
63725	Martha Young	Indianapolis, IN	Northern	$25,900

FIGURE 8.5

A list of the data in the Salesperson table

You could create a Region table by describing these fields and entering data into the table. An easier approach, however, is to set up a special operation that retrieves data from the Salesperson table, computes each region's total sales, counts the number of salespeople in each region, and stores the required data in a Region table. Figure 8.7 shows a printed list of the data in the Region table after this operation has been performed.

You now have two tables: the Salesperson table and the Region table. Because each table contains a field for the region name, there is a *relationship* between these tables. Hence, the database consists of two related tables.

Now you can retrieve related data from the two tables at the same time. You decide that you need a list of the salesperson name and sales data for each salesperson from the Salesperson table, as well as all the data for the region in which the salesperson works from the Region table. You create a query to retrieve the required data and a form to display the data on the screen. The database software retrieves each salesperson's record and related region record, and displays the required data. Figure 8.8 shows the screen output. With this information you can determine, among other things, how much each salesperson is contributing to the region's total sales.

At the end of each month, you need to update the database with each region's total sales. After changing each salesperson's sales in the Salesperson table, you perform a series of operations to modify the data in the Region table, using the new data in the Salesperson table. Then you print a report from the data in the Region table, giving the total sales for each region and the total sales for all regions (Figure 8.9).

Northern Region Sales

Salesperson Number	Salesperson Name	Salesperson Sales
15096	Susan Jenson	$42,800
17228	Frank Fuller	$12,050
39377	Robert Marshall	$31,500
51927	Olivia Lock	$40,550
63725	Martha Young	$25,900

FIGURE 8.6

A form with the result of a query of data from the Salesperson table

FIGURE 8.7

FIGURE 8.7

A list of the data in the Region
▲ table

Region Name	Region Total Sales	Number of Salespeople
Eastern	$48,275	4
Northern	$152,800	5
Southern	$38,240	4
Western	$84,575	3

FIGURE 8.8

A form with the result of a
query of related data from the
Salesperson and Region
▲ tables

Salesperson Name	Salesperson Sales	Region Name	Region Total Sales	Number of Salespeople
John Smith	$29,500	Western	$84,575	3
Alan Wood	$1,050	Southern	$38,240	4
Susan Jenson	$42,800	Northern	$152,800	5
Frank Fuller	$12,050	Northern	$152,800	5
Joyce McAdams	$10,250	Eastern	$48,275	4
James Bennett	$18,050	Western	$84,575	3
Francis Benton	$3,675	Southern	$38,240	4
Andrew Lee	$14,700	Eastern	$48,275	4
Mary Wong	$37,025	Western	$84,575	3
Fred Parks	$14,800	Eastern	$48,275	4
Robert Marshall	$31,500	Northern	$152,800	5
Susan Brown	$8,525	Eastern	$48,275	4
Paul Napier	$12,100	Southern	$38,240	4
Olivia Lock	$40,550	Northern	$152,800	5
Jose Sanchez	$21,415	Southern	$38,240	4
Martha Young	$25,900	Northern	$152,800	5

FIGURE 8.9

A report of data from the
Region table

▲

Sales by Region

Region Name	Region Total Sales	Number of Salespeople
Eastern	$48,275	4
Northern	$152,800	5
Southern	$38,240	4
Western	$84,575	3
	$323,890	**16**

Notice in this example how you have taken advantage of the database software's capability to store, retrieve, and update data. These capabilities allow you to manipulate data in a database more easily than if you kept the same data on paper. The advantages are especially great when there is a large amount of related data in a database.

Analyzing Data

Many individual information systems analyze data to get information that can help in the operations or management of the business. The analysis can involve various calculations, such as those used in finance, accounting, and statistics. Although data can be analyzed with many types of software, the most widely used is *spreadsheet software*. Examples of spreadsheet software used in individual information systems are Excel, 1-2-3, and Quattro Pro.

A **spreadsheet** is an arrangement of data into rows and columns that is used to analyze the data. In the past, accountants and financial analysts prepared paper spreadsheets by hand. With spreadsheet software, however, an individual creates an *electronic spreadsheet*, or **worksheet**, in the computer's primary storage. For example, Figure 8.10 shows a worksheet with revenue, expense, and net income figures for a business for three years.

Using Spreadsheet Software to Analyze Data

To analyze data using spreadsheet software, the user must first create a worksheet with the necessary data and calculations. When the spreadsheet software is first loaded, a blank worksheet appears on the screen. To create a worksheet, the user enters numbers, text, and formulas for the calculations into the worksheet.

After a worksheet is created, it can be changed easily. Each time data or formulas in a worksheet are changed, the spreadsheet software automatically recalculates any affected values in the worksheet. This capability gives spreadsheet software a great advantage over hand-prepared spreadsheets. With a hand-prepared spreadsheet all recalculations must be done manually, which can be very time-consuming. With spreadsheet software, however, the computer does the recalculations, thus saving the user considerable time. Because of this capability, using spreadsheet software increases the individual's productivity in analyzing data.

FIGURE 8.10

A worksheet

	A	B	C	D
1		PROJECTED NET INCOME		
2				
3		Year 1	Year 2	Year 3
4				
5	Revenue	$ 2,784,500	$ 3,062,950	$ 3,369,245
6				
7	Expenses			
8	Cost of goods sold	$ 1,058,700	$ 1,164,570	$ 1,281,027
9	Salaries	483,600	531,960	585,156
10	Rent	399,000	438,900	482,790
11	Advertising	181,000	199,100	219,010
12	Delivery	162,200	178,420	196,262
13	Supplies	18,300	20,130	22,143
14	Depreciation	148,200	163,020	179,322
15	Total expenses	$ 2,451,000	$ 2,696,100	$ 2,965,710
16				
17	Net Income	$ 333,500	$ 366,850	$ 403,535

One of the main reasons for making changes in a worksheet is to see what would happen to other figures when changes are made. This technique is called **what-if analysis** because someone usually asks a question that begins with the words *what if*. For example, with the worksheet in Figure 8.10, a person might ask, "What if revenue increases 10% each year, and salaries increase 15%?" Answering this question involves using new numbers in the spreadsheet and recalculating the total expenses and net income for each year. This recalculation can be a lot of work for a large spreadsheet and is especially tedious if someone decides to ask several what-if questions. With spreadsheet software, all the work is done by the computer.

The result of a spreadsheet analysis is often used to help in decision making. For example, the worksheet in Figure 8.10 could be used to help in making a decision about purchasing a new office building by showing whether there is likely to be sufficient income each year to cover the expense of the building. Many decisions involve trying different alternatives to see what effect each alternative might have. Spreadsheet software makes this process easier.

A Case Study of Data Analysis

To illustrate how data analysis using spreadsheet software is used in an individual information system, assume, as in the data management case study earlier, that you are the national sales manager of an athletic-clothing wholesaler. You want to do an analysis each month of the sales in the four regions that you manage. You are interested in how the sales for the current month compare with the sales for the previous month, and you would like to know the percentage increase or decrease in the sales for each region and in the total sales of all four regions. You could calculate the values by hand, but you plan to do the analysis each month. Therefore, you decide to develop an individual information system that uses spreadsheet software to do the analysis for you in a worksheet. Because the software will do the analysis more easily than you could by hand, you will be more productive in your job.

Your first step is to enter into a worksheet the numbers, text, and formulas needed for your analysis. You have decided to use Excel as your spreadsheet software. You start by entering the text for the column headings and row labels. Next, you enter numbers for the sales data for each region. You enter the data for last month and for this month, but you do not enter the totals or percentages because these values will be calculated by the spreadsheet software. After the headings, labels, and sales data have been entered, the screen looks like the one shown in Figure 8.11.

The final step is to enter formulas for the calculations. You enter a formula for the total sales last month and the total this month. Then you enter formulas for the per-

FIGURE 8.11

The sales analysis worksheet after the headings, labels, and sales data are entered

	A	B	C	D
1		SALES ANALYSIS		
2				
3		Last Month	This Month	Pct Change
4				
5	Region:			
6	Eastern	$ 48,275	$ 121,400	
7	Northern	152,800	72,325	
8	Southern	38,240	39,500	
9	Western	84,575	85,525	
10				
11	Total:			

FIGURE 8.12

The sales analysis worksheet
after the formulas are entered ▲

	A	B	C	D
1		SALES ANALYSIS		
2				
3		Last Month	This Month	Pct Change
4				
5	Region:			
6	Eastern	$ 48,275	$ 121,400	151.48%
7	Northern	152,800	72,325	-52.67%
8	Southern	38,240	39,500	3.29%
9	Western	84,575	85,525	1.12%
10				
11	Total:	$ 323,890	$ 318,750	-1.59%

centage changes—one for each region and one for the total. As each formula is entered, its value is calculated and displayed in the worksheet. Figure 8.12 shows the final worksheet, with all values calculated. At this point you save your worksheet in secondary storage and print a copy so that you can refer to it later.

The next month, you need to perform the same analysis with new data. You start by retrieving the previous month's worksheet from secondary storage. You change the worksheet by copying the sales data in the column labeled This Month to the Last Month column. Then you enter new sales figures for the This Month column. The formulas automatically recalculate the totals and the percentages as the changes are made. The result is shown in Figure 8.13. You save the revised worksheet in secondary storage and print a copy for use later.

Notice in this example how you have taken advantage of the fact that the worksheet already contains the text, formulas, and some of the numbers you needed. Although setting up the worksheet in the first month can be time-consuming, using the worksheet each of the following months makes the analysis much easier.

Combining Data Management and Data Analysis

It is often possible to use the results of one application in another application. Essentially, this means that an *output* from one application becomes an *input* to another. With the proper software, data can be transferred from a database to a worksheet or vice versa, thus saving the effort of having to key in input.

FIGURE 8.13

The sales analysis worksheet
after the sales data is
changed for the next month ▲

	A	B	C	D
1		SALES ANALYSIS		
2				
3		Last Month	This Month	Pct Change
4				
5	Region:			
6	Eastern	$ 121,400	$ 103,500	-14.74%
7	Northern	72,325	94,550	30.73%
8	Southern	39,500	42,725	8.16%
9	Western	85,525	96,730	13.10%
10				
11	Total:	$ 318,750	$ 337,505	5.88%

To illustrate this approach, consider the data management and data analysis case studies. One of the results of the data management case was the total sales for each region, which was recomputed from salesperson sales data entered into the database each month (Figure 8.7). The region totals are used in the worksheet in the data analysis case (Figure 8.12). Using the software, you can retrieve the region total sales from the database and transfer them to the worksheet.

Transferring data between applications reduces the time needed to complete the work. Thus, productivity is improved. Accuracy is also improved because no keying mistakes will be made in entering the data. When developing an individual information system, you should always consider how applications could fit together and whether data can be transferred between applications. We will see other examples of this approach in the next section.

Presenting Information

One of the most common tasks performed by individuals in a business is to prepare information for presentation to others. The information may be presented in a text form such as a memo, letter, or report; in a graphical form such as a diagram or chart; in a published form that includes text and graphics such as a pamphlet or brochure; or in a multimedia form that includes pictures and sound such as a sales presentation. Individual information systems often present information in one or more of these forms. This section examines each of these forms and shows how they can be part of an individual information system.

Presenting Information in Text Form

Information is prepared for presentation in a text form by using **word processing**, which is the use of a computer to prepare documents containing characters, words, paragraphs, and other types of text. Documents such as memos, letters, and reports are often used to present information to others, and word processing makes the preparation of such documents easier and faster. Sometimes, very short documents that are used only once, such as a brief memo or letter, can be prepared just as easily with a typewriter, and preprinted forms are usually easier to complete using a typewriter. But for long reports and documents that may require changes in the future, word processing is much more efficient. The principle advantage of word processing is that a person's productivity is improved. Most organizations no longer use typewriters, but instead use computers for preparing all memos, letters, reports, and other documents.

Word processing software provides the functions needed to accomplish word processing with a personal computer. These functions include the ability to enter text into a document; format the text of the document by selecting the font (character form), font size, and font style (e.g., boldface, italics); edit (change) the text in the document; and print the document. Examples of word processing software are Word, WordPerfect, and Word Pro.

A Case Study of Text Information Presentation

To illustrate how text information presentation using word processing software is used in an individual information system, assume, as in the data management and data analysis case studies given earlier, that you are the national sales manager of an athletic-clothing wholesaler. Each month you have to send a memo to the vice president of marketing, summarizing the company's sales for the month. You could type a new sales memo each month, but with word processing you can reduce the amount

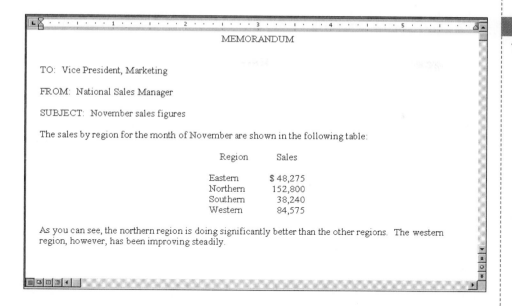

FIGURE 8.14

The sales memo

of typing required and save time. Preparing the first month's memo will take you about the same amount of time using word processing as it would take using a typewriter, but preparing the memo for each subsequent month will take less time.

At the end of your first month—November—you need to enter the text for your sales memo. You have decided to use Word as your word processing software. You start by keying in the text of the sales memo. After entering the text, you read it over and decide to make several wording changes. You also use the spell-checking feature of the software to locate and correct spelling errors. Figure 8.14 shows how the memo looks on the screen after the memo is completed. Then you save the text of the memo in secondary storage and print a copy to send to the vice president of marketing.

At the end of the next month—December—you need to send a similar memo with the sales figures for that month. Instead of rekeying the entire sales memo, you decide to edit the current one. You start by retrieving the text of the previous month's memo from secondary storage. At this point the memo on the screen is the same as the one in Figure 8.14. You change the month in the SUBJECT line from November to December. You do the same with the month in the first paragraph. Next, you key in new sales figures for the four regions for December. Then you decide that you need an entirely new final paragraph, so you delete the existing paragraph and enter a new one. After making these changes, the memo on the screen will look like Figure 8.15. After reading it over to be sure there are no errors and checking the spelling, you save the text of the memo in secondary storage and print a copy.

Notice in this example how you have taken advantage of the editing capabilities of the word processing software. These capabilities let you reuse work that you have done previously instead of redoing everything from scratch. By reusing previous work, you can greatly increase your productivity in preparing memos, letters, reports, and other documents.

Presenting Information in Graphical Form

Information is prepared for presentation in a graphical or pictorial form by using computer graphics. With computer graphics the user can create a variety of types of images (Figure 8.16). One is *charts* or *graphs*, which are often used by business people,

FIGURE 8.15

The sales memo after it is edited for the next month

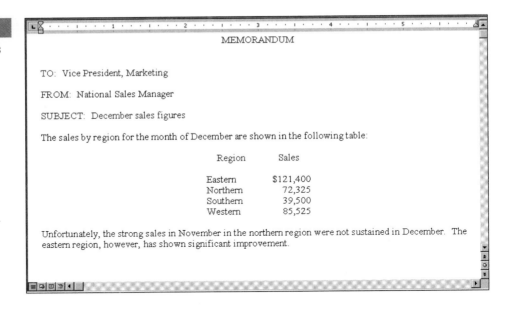

MEMORANDUM

TO: Vice President, Marketing

FROM: National Sales Manager

SUBJECT: December sales figures

The sales by region for the month of December are shown in the following table:

Region	Sales
Eastern	$121,400
Northern	72,325
Southern	39,500
Western	85,525

Unfortunately, the strong sales in November in the northern region were not sustained in December. The eastern region, however, has shown significant improvement.

scientists, and others to summarize data in an easily understood form. Another is *diagrams* showing outlines or designs of objects. These are used by architects and engineers when designing buildings, automobiles, and other objects. *Graphic designs* are another type of computer graphics. These are used in advertisements in magazines and on television, and often include movement or animation. Another type of computer graphics is a *realistic image* of an object, such as a car or an airplane. One use of this type of image, which may be three dimensional and include movement, is in machines that simulate real-world situations, such as airplane simulators. Another use is in motion picture production. A final type of computer graphics is *computer art*. Many artists use computers to create unique works of art.

Computer graphic output is produced by *graphics software*. With this type of software the user can create charts, graphs, diagrams, designs, images, art, and other forms of graphic output on a screen or on paper. Some graphics software is very specialized and is used only by certain types of people, such as graphic designers and artists. Other graphics software is more general and can be used by almost anyone.

Several common types of graphics software are used in businesses (Figure 8.17). **Charting software** is used to create charts and graphs that summarize business data. The data charted using this type of software usually comes from a worksheet, database, or data file. Spreadsheet programs such as Excel, 1-2-3, and Quattro Pro have the ability to produce charts and graphs from data in a worksheet. Other charting programs can produce charts and graphs from other sources.

Drawing software allows the user to draw pictures and diagrams on the screen by providing the user with many standard shapes and symbols that can be used to create the drawing. Boxes, circles, and other shapes are provided. The user selects shapes, positions them on the screen, changes their sizes, rotates them, and fills them with shades and colors to create complex drawings. Examples of drawing programs are Visio and CorelDRAW.

Graphic output is often used in presentations given to groups of people. To create high-quality graphic output for such presentations, **presentation graphics software** is used. This type of software is usually a combination of a charting program and a drawing program, with additional capabilities. The output produced by a pre-

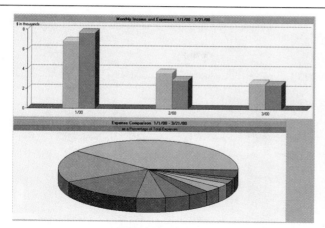

(a) Chart or graph

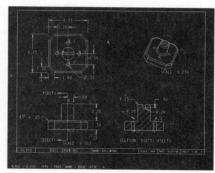

(b) Diagram

(c) Graphic design

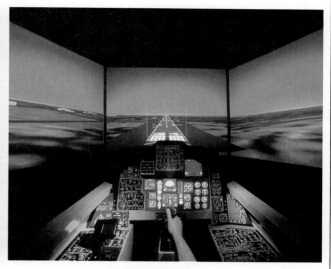

(d) Realistic image

(e) Computer art

FIGURE 8.16

Computer graphics

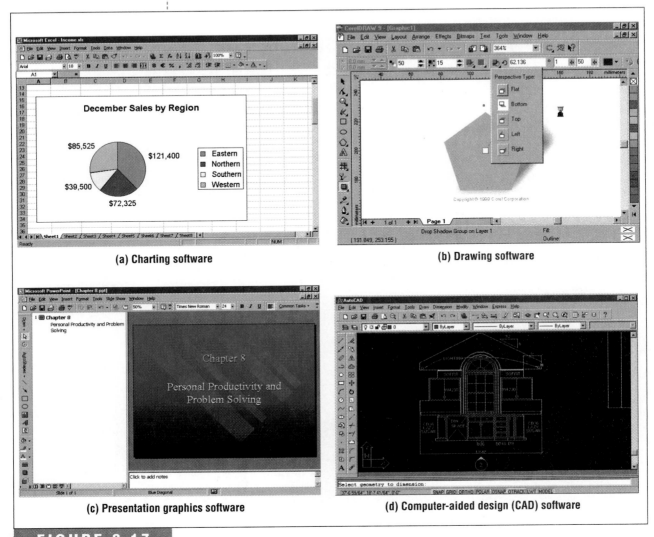

(a) Charting software

(b) Drawing software

(c) Presentation graphics software

(d) Computer-aided design (CAD) software

FIGURE 8.17

▲ Graphics software

sentation graphics program can be displayed on a large computer screen or projected, using special hardware, on a film screen for viewing by an audience. A laser or ink-jet printer can produce presentation graphics output on transparency sheets for projection on a film screen. Special hardware is available that records graphic output on photographic slide film for use with a slide projector. Examples of presentation graphics software are PowerPoint and Harvard Graphics.

Graphics software used for designing objects such as buildings and machines is called **computer-aided design (CAD) software.** Using CAD software, a person can draw the design of an object with a computer, modify the design, try different designs, and perform other design functions. For example, an automotive engineer can use CAD software to design an automobile. Using the graphics capability of the software, the engineer draws the design of a car on the screen, analyzes characteristics of the design, changes the design, and analyzes the new design. When a design is finalized, it can be drawn on paper with a plotter. Other people who commonly use CAD are aircraft engineers, computer circuit designers, ship builders, and architects. AutoCAD is an example of a CAD program.

A Case Study of Graphical Information Presentation

To illustrate how graphical information presentation using graphics software is used in an individual information system, assume, as in the previous cases studies, that you are the national sales manager of an athletic-clothing wholesaler. Each month you analyze the sales in the four regions you manage, using spreadsheet software. (See Figure 8.12). You decide that you would like a chart of the sales last month and the sales this month for each region. Such a chart will help you analyze the sales when you prepare your sales memo.

The data for the chart will come from the sales analysis worksheet you created earlier, so you decide to use spreadsheet software to create the chart. You start by retrieving the worksheet from secondary storage using your spreadsheet software. Then you select the data in the worksheet to be charted. For this example, you want a chart of the sales in each region for both last month and this month. You decide to display the output in a column chart, and you indicate this to the software. Finally, you enter titles and legends to make the graphic output easier to read. When these tasks have been done, you display the sales analysis chart on the screen and print a copy. Figure 8.18 shows the graphic output that is produced by the spreadsheet program.

Combining Other Applications and Information Presentation

The results produced by other applications such as data management and data analysis are often used in text and graphical information presentation. With text information presentation, data from a worksheet or a database can be transferred into a document without the need to rekey the data. For example, consider the data analysis case study discussed previously. The total sales for each region can be transferred from the sales analysis worksheet. (See Figure 8.12). directly to the sales memo. (See Figure 8.15). This process saves time in preparing the sales memo and reduces the chances of making an error.

When graphic output is produced by spreadsheet software from data in a worksheet, it is not necessary to transfer data between programs; the data that already existed in the worksheet is used to produce the graphic output. If graphic output is to be produced by a different program, then the data to be graphed can often be copied from a worksheet or database into the graphics software.

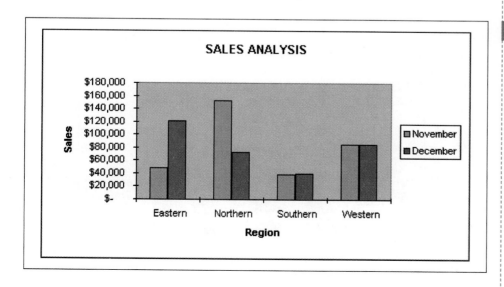

FIGURE 8.18

The sales analysis chart ▲

Graphic output can normally be incorporated into a text document. Word processing software has the ability to include diagrams, charts, and other graphic images in a document. For example, the sales analysis chart created in the case study earlier (see Figure 8.18) can be transferred from the worksheet to the sales memo document (see Figure 8.15). Then the memo can be edited and printed with the chart. Figure 8.19 shows how the printed sales memo would look with the chart included.

Combining applications can greatly improve productivity and reduce errors. The data management, data analysis, text information presentation, and graphical information presentation case studies in this chapter illustrate how applications can be combined (Figure 8.20). In the data management case, individual salesperson sales are entered into the Salesperson table and totaled for each region in the Region table (see Figure 8.7). Then the region total sales are transferred from the database to the sales analysis worksheet (see Figure 8.12) and used to analyze changes in sales in the data analysis case. The sales data in the worksheet is also used to produce the sales analysis chart in the graphical information presentation case (see Figure 8.18). Next, the region total sales are transferred from the worksheet to the sales memo in the text information presentation case (see Figure 8.15). Finally, the sales analysis chart is

FIGURE 8.19

▲ **The sales memo with a chart**

MEMORANDUM

TO: Vice President, Marketing

FROM: National Sales Manager

SUBJECT: December sales figures

The sales by region for the month of December are shown in the following table:

Region	Sales
Eastern	$121,400
Northern	72,325
Southern	39,500
Western	85,525

Unfortunately, the strong sales in November in the northern region were not sustained in December. The eastern region, however, has shown significant improvement. The following graph shows the sales trend for the past two months.

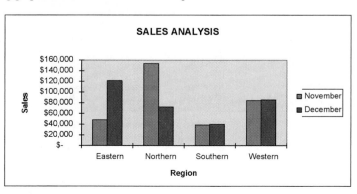

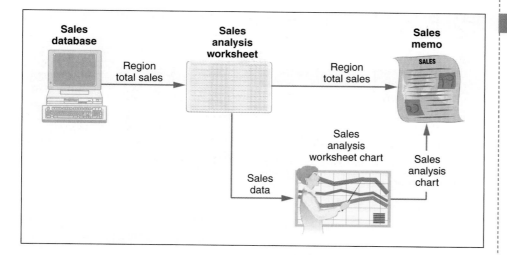

FIGURE 8.20

Transferring data between applications

transferred to the sales memo (see Figure 8.19). All these applications can be combined in an individual information system that provides capabilities for managing data, analyzing data, and presenting information in text and graphical form.

Because of the benefits of combining applications, individual programs are often sold together in a software **suite**. A suite usually includes a word processing program, a spreadsheet program, a presentation graphics program, and a database program. The programs in the suite are designed so that data can be transferred between them easily. Examples of suites are Office, WordPerfect Office, and SmartSuite.

An alternative to a suite of separate programs is **integrated software**, which is a single program containing word processing, spreadsheet, database, and graphics capabilities. The capabilities of integrated software are not as sophisticated as those in the programs of a software suite, but they are sufficient for many applications and their combination in a single program makes them easy to use. An example of integrated software is Works.

Presenting Information in Published Form

Information can be prepared for presentation in a published form by using **desktop publishing**. With desktop publishing, professional-looking reports, newsletters, pamphlets, brochures, and other high-quality printed materials similar to those produced by a printing company can be prepared by the user.

To do desktop publishing, a user must have **desktop publishing software** designed specifically for this use. This type of software has many word processing capabilities. More importantly, it has the capability to incorporate complex design features, such as graphic images, various type styles, and different column widths, into the printed output. Examples of desktop publishing programs are PageMaker and Publisher.

The functions of desktop publishing software are similar to those of word processing programs, except that some capabilities are more sophisticated. A user can enter text using the desktop publishing program, or he or she can retrieve text created by a separate word processing program. In addition, the user can insert graphic images created by other software using the desktop publishing program. After text and graphic images are entered, editing can be done, as with a word processing program.

The most powerful function of desktop publishing software, however, is its formatting capabilities. The text and graphic images can be formatted in numerous

FIGURE 8.21

▲ **Desktop publishing software**

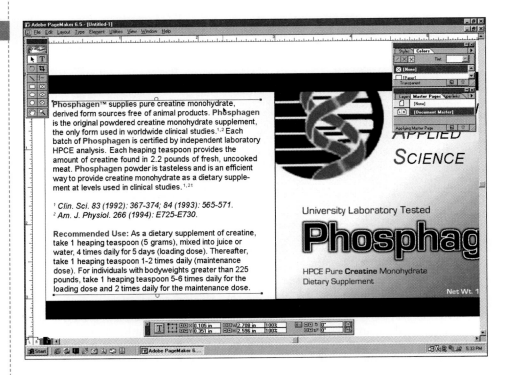

ways. This process is called *page layout* because it involves preparing pages of the document in the format in which they will be printed. In doing page layout, text can be arranged in one or several columns, graphic images can be enlarged or reduced to fit with the text, and the text can be rearranged to conform to the shape of the graphics. Horizontal and vertical lines can be included to set off text and graphics, and boxes can be drawn around text and graphic images. Practically any formatting feature seen in a book, newspaper, or magazine can be incorporated into the document. After the document is prepared with the software it can be printed on a high-quality printer for reproduction by a copier, or multiple copies can be printed by a printing company with special printing capabilities. Figure 8.21 shows the screen of a desktop publishing program.

Presenting Information in Multimedia Form

Information can be prepared for presentation in a multimedia form, using special software. Recall from Chapter 4 that *multimedia* refers to the use of a computer to present information in more than one way. Word processing software presents information in a text form (sometimes incorporating graphical images), graphics software presents information in a graphical form, and desktop publishing software presents information in a high-quality text and graphical form. Multimedia presentations include text, graphics, animation, video, sound, voice, music, and other forms.

The parts of a multimedia presentation are prepared by using a variety of techniques. Text can be prepared by using word processing software. Graphic images can be prepared with graphics software or scanned into the computer by using a scanner. Video can be converted to a digital form and stored in secondary storage, using special hardware and software. Sound can be recorded and stored by using other hardware and software.

After all the parts of the multimedia presentation have been prepared, they are brought together by using **authoring software**. This type of software lets the user link

Multimedia Presentation at Orient-Express Trains & Cruises

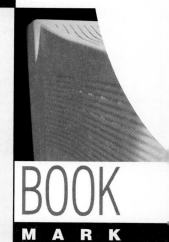

BOOK

M A R K

Orient-Express Trains & Cruises offers international luxury travel on four trains and a cruise ship. But until recently, this high-end travel service was using an unwieldy combination of slides and videos to sell itself. "When you have 80 to 120 slides, plus videos, organizing a presentation gets to be cumbersome and time-consuming," says Annette Kishon-Pines, the company's director of sales administration for North America. The time for a change had come.

Kishon-Pines thought her video sections were sufficiently impressive, but felt that the transitions between the slides and the video were often clunky. Furthermore, if she wanted to talk about only one train or exclusively about the ship, she would have to either rearrange the slides or quickly advance through slides of the other three trains.

She had heard of the Atlanta-based company Interactive, and decided to take her material to the company for a new presentation. Her request was simple: "I asked for a presentation that would pull all the slides and the video into one." But the end product also needed to be flexible, easy to navigate through, and easy to use.

Gary White, president of Interactive, decided to convert Kishon-Pines's pitch into a Microsoft PowerPoint presentation, with the videos converted into MPEG-2 (a video file format) files. "To do that, we had to equip the client with a laptop that could handle full-screen MPEG-2 video," says White, who eventually went with a Sony PCG-F190 VAIO notebook.

For built-in flexibility, Interactive created an opening navigation screen with separate modules that could be clicked on to reach different areas of the presentation. Interactive also added a customization feature, allowing Kishon-Pines to type in the name of her client on the first screen for automatic placement throughout the presentation.

According to White, the package was built in PowerPoint, with some extra touches thrown in from Adobe's Photoshop and After Effects, and the tweaking of some Microsoft Visual Basic development code. Both Macintosh- and Windows-compatible systems were used to put the final presentation package together, which was then burned onto a CD-ROM.

According to Kishon-Pines, the end result was well worth the effort. A first-time PowerPoint user, her initial presentation using the new CD took place in front of 100 incentive buyers and corporate end users. "I was using my new laptop and a projector," she says. Afterward, people came up to me and said, 'Wow, you're really a pro at this.'"

Another added bonus is that Kishon-Pines no longer has to lug around her slide projector and an armful of videos. Now, all she carries to meetings are her notebook computer and, occasionally, a projector. If fewer than three people are involved, she simply shows the presentation on her laptop.

The folks at Interactive were equally pleased with the project because it convinced them that quality digital video can be used effectively in laptop presentations. "Gone are the days of watching a grainy little video in the corner of the screen," White says. With MPEG-2 and ever-faster computers, he notes, the prospects for effective, high-quality video have never been better.

Questions

1. What media are used in the Orient-Express Trains & Cruises presentation, and what other media could be used?
2. Why did Orient-Express Trains & Cruises want a multimedia presentation?
3. What special features were included in the Orient-Express Trains & Cruises presentation?

Web Site

Orient-Express Trains & Cruises: www.orient-expresstrains.com

Source: *Adapted from* Julie Hill, "A Travel Company in the Laptop of Luxury," *Presentations*, August 1999, p. 16.

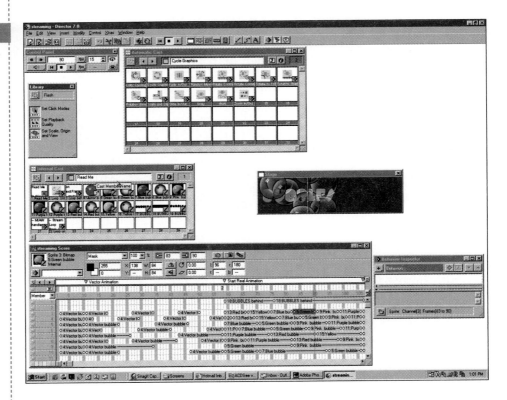

FIGURE 8.22

Multimedia authoring software

together the different parts to create a multimedia presentation (Figure 8.22). After the presentation has been prepared, a person can read, view, or hear the information in the presentation as he or she chooses. Examples of authoring software are Director and Authorware.

Locating and Retrieving Information by Using the Internet

The case studies presented in this chapter have shown how individual applications can be used to manage, analyze, and present business data and information. The data used in these applications often comes from within a business. For example, the sales data entered into the Salesperson database described in the data management case study comes from salespeople who work for the business. In some situations, however, a user needs data and information from outside the business. For example, a sales manager may need to know what the business's competitors are selling and how they are promoting their products.

A number of sources of external data and information exist. Databases are available with demographic data, company financial data, and consumer buying-habit data. Information about a company's products is readily available from the company, and data about sales can sometimes be obtained from other sources. Some of this data must be purchased from businesses that specialize in gathering the data, but much data is free.

The Internet makes much of the free data easily accessible. Using a personal computer connected to the Internet and the appropriate software, an individual can access Web pages to search for useful information. A *browser* lets a user follow links from one Web page to another to locate information. Each time the user selects a new link, the browser retrieves the requested Web page and displays it on the screen. Thus, a browser allows a user to locate and retrieve information from the Web.

When a user displays the desired information on the screen with a browser, the information can easily be transferred to other individual applications. For example, information can be transferred from a browser to a database, a worksheet, or a word processing document for storage, analysis, or presentation. Examples of browsers are Microsoft Internet Explorer and Netscape Navigator.

Searching the World Wide Web

A browser provides a way to retrieve and view Web pages, and to follow links to other Web pages. Locating information on the Web using only a browser, however, can be hit and miss. A better approach is to use a **search engine**, which is software on the Web that lets users search for specific types of information. If a user enters a word or phrase—such as the name of an organization, a type of product, or almost anything—into a search engine, the search engine locates Web pages that refer to the word or phrase (Figure 8.23). Then the user can retrieve and display the located Web pages by using a browser.

There are three main types of search engines. The first type has a directory that contains references to Web pages. Employees of the company providing the directory identify Web pages and classify them into different categories for entry in the directory. An example of this type of search engine is Yahoo!. (This type of service is not really a search engine because the software does not search for pages on the Web. It is more correctly called a *subject directory*, but people commonly refer to it as a search engine.) Another type of search engine locates pages on the Web by periodically sending programs, sometimes called *spiders*, over the Web to look for new pages. An example of this type of search engine is AltaVista. The third type of search engine, sometimes called a *meta-search engine*, does not search the Web, but instead

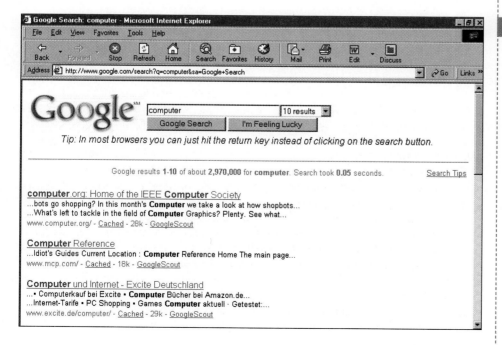

FIGURE 8.23

A search engine

BOOK
MARK

Web Searching at Sparks.com

With thousands of items in its inventory, Web greeting card retailer Sparks.com can easily outdo its brick-and-mortar competitors in sheer size of selection. When it comes to helping customers choose cards, though, Sparks.com may be at a disadvantage: It has to create an online equivalent to the real world's nearly perfect search interface.

"If you walk into a physical card store, it's really easy just to scan this broad range," says Jason Monberg, Sparks.com's chief technology officer. "You can take in a lot of data really quickly, and you see things you aren't necessarily looking for." So Sparks.com has invested heavily in building search features that help shoppers find the cards they want as quickly as possible. It has found that effective search features depend not just on superior technology, but also on careful design and a lot of human labor.

Users searching content sites often make do with brute-force searches of raw text. From e-commerce sites, though, users often expect more sophisticated searching, based on specific product characteristics and other data. This is all well and good for computer products, which have discrete and easily defined characteristics such as processor speed and memory, or for books, for which there is an accepted set of cataloging characteristics such as title, author, and publisher.

It's not so easy for greeting cards. A search of raw text isn't much help, as many cards consist only of pictures and a short, common phrase like "Happy Birthday." And there is no industrywide greeting card cataloging system that would be much help to the consumer.

Sparks.com's solution was to come up with its own cataloging system of 50 to 100 characteristics that describe greeting cards. Monberg says the full list is considered a company secret, but it includes items ranging from the physical dimensions of the card, to its manufacturer, to the emotion it aims to convey.

Employees personally examine each greeting card in Sparks.com's inventory and hand enter the card's characteristics into the company database. The process, Monberg says, takes three to five minutes for an average card—not a big deal, until you consider that Sparks.com has 10,000 cards in its database and has plans to scale up to about 30,000.

The enriched catalog data, together with the LexiQuest thesaurus software hooked into Sparks.com's Fulcrum search engine, lets users perform creative, highly specialized searches. A search for "beach" brings up cards with pictures of seaside scenes. "Kiss photograph" will turn up cards showing smooching couples.

Sparks.com also periodically reviews its search logs to gain insights into how visitors are using the site's search features and adjusts the site's behavior to match. As a simple example, if customers searching for the word "funny" and the word "golf" frequently end up buying cartoon cards, Sparks.com will reconfigure its software to make sure customers looking for funny cards see more cartoon cards among their search results, and not just golf-themed cards.

The point, Monberg says, is that while it's certainly important that the site return results relevant to the user's search terms, it's sometimes just as important to lead visitors away from their specific search terms.

"The whole goal is to get them the cards that really mean something to them, and unfortunately, it's not always what they type in," he says. "You want to bring back a few results that are maybe going to take them down a slightly different path." Sparks.com's other challenge is to get users to type in enough search terms to begin with. With an inventory as large as Sparks.com's, a search for "my boyfriend's birthday" won't narrow the results nearly enough, and customers might leave the site empty-handed.

Part of Sparks.com's solution to the problem is a fill-in search that asks a customer to specify five characteristics with a set of pull-down menus: the recipient's age, gender, and relation to the sender, as well as the occasion and the desired tone for the card.

All this aims at getting around one of the toughest problems of running e-commerce sites: Customers often have high expectations, but they may give very little consideration to constructing accurate searches. Monberg isn't complaining, though. "I think that's totally fair," he says, "because that's really our job."

Questions
1. Why is searching for greeting cards on a Web site different from searching for other items, such as computers or books?
2. How does Sparks.com make searching for greeting cards on its Web site easier?

Web Site
Sparks.com: www.sparks.com

Source: *Adapted from* James C. Luh, "A System Devised for Fine-Tune Search," *Internet World*, July 15, 1999, p. 59.

BOOK
M A R K

searches other search engines. An example of this type of search engine is MetaCrawler.

The Web sites for some search engines include more than just the ability to search the Web. These sites may provide electronic mail (e-mail) capabilities, news bulletins, access to electronic commerce (e-commerce) Web sites, chat features, and other facilities for which users would normally have to go to other Web sites. This type of Web site is an example of a *portal*. In general a **portal** is a Web site that provides multiple services for its users. Portals with search engines are popular, but portals are used in other situations. For example, a company may have a *corporate portal* for its employees that provides access to all the Web-based information and services, both inside and outside the company, that the employees need in their jobs.

Searching the Web for information using a browser or a search engine can be thought of as *pulling* information into the user's computer because the user actively selects the information. An alternative to this "pull" approach is to use a special Internet service to have certain types of information sent automatically to the user's computer. This process uses a technique called **push technology** to find information for the user and send, or "push," it to the user's computer, where it can be displayed with a browser. For example, a sales manager may be interested in news articles that refer to products sold by the business's competitors. The manager can use a service to search for appropriate articles periodically, such as every day, and have them sent to the manager's computer automatically. The manager must enter information into the service, indicating what types of articles he or she wants, but after that the service identifies and sends articles regularly without the manager having to search for them. An example of a service that uses push technology is EntryPoint.

Evaluating Information from the World Wide Web

Although a tremendous amount of information is available on the Web, it is important for the user to recognize that some information may be inaccurate or misleading. Almost anyone can put almost anything on the Web. The user must carefully analyze the credibility of the source of the information to ensure that what is received is accurate and relevant.

With this warning in mind, using the Web can greatly improve a user's productivity in locating information. Often it is not necessary to go to a library, contact a government agency, or call a business to get information. A user can easily and quickly search for information by using a search engine and a browser, or receive information automatically by using push technology.

Solving Problems with Personal Applications

Personal computer applications are used to help individuals solve problems in businesses. The case studies presented earlier in this chapter illustrate this idea. For example, the data analysis case study shows how a spreadsheet application can help an individual solve the problem of identifying sales regions that have had large changes in sales. Although the solution to this problem could be worked out by hand, using personal application software makes the analysis much easier.

Problems, Solutions, and Solution Procedures

To understand problem solving, it is necessary to know what we mean by a problem, a solution, and a solution procedure. A **problem** is a question to which someone does not know the answer, or a statement of something to be done. For example, a problem in sales management could be in the form of a question: What is the commission for each salesperson? A problem in finance could be in the form of a statement: Calculate the expected return on a certain investment. Both these examples are problems because the people involved do not know their solutions.

The **solution** to a problem is the answer to the problem question or the result of doing what is required by the problem statement. The solution to the sales management problem is the commission for each salesperson. The solution to the finance problem is the expected return on the investment. A computer application is designed to solve one or more problems for someone.

In business, people want to know solutions to problems because it helps them do their jobs. A sales manager needs to know the answer to a commission calculation problem, and a finance manager wants to know the result of an investment return calculation. To find the solution requires a sequence of steps that may involve calculations, decision making, and other forms of data manipulation. These steps form a solution procedure for the problem.

In general, a **solution procedure** is a set of steps that, if carried out, results in the solution of a problem.[1] For example, consider the "problem" of starting a car. Figure 8.24 shows a solution procedure for this problem. If a driver carries out this procedure, the problem will be solved; that is, the car will be started. Another example of a solution procedure is a recipe for baking a cake; if a cook follows the solution procedure—the recipe—he or she solves the problem of baking a cake.

A computer application is an implementation of a solution procedure or, more often, several procedures combined. Each procedure in an application solves a particular problem; the application uses the procedures together to solve a complex problem. For example, spreadsheet software has many built-in *functions* for calculating different values, such as a function for calculating the return on an investment. Each function is a procedure that solves a particular problem. A user can create a solution procedure for a complex data analysis problem in a worksheet by combining spreadsheet functions in different ways. Similarly, database software has many solution procedures for manipulating stored data. A user can select individual procedures

---

[1]Computer professionals often use the term *algorithm* for *solution procedure*.

```
1. Insert key in ignition
2. Put car in neutral
3. Repeat the following until car starts, or at most 3 times:
      a. Turn key to start position
      b. Press accelerator pedal
      c. Release key after car starts or after 5 seconds
4. If car does not start
      a. Put car in park
      b. Take key out of ignition
      c. Call service station to have car started
```

FIGURE 8.24

A solution procedure for starting a car ▲

to create a solution procedure for a complex data management problem by using database software.

One of the main tasks in computer problem solving is determining the solution procedure needed to solve the problem. This task can be stated as follows: Given a problem, a person must figure out what steps the computer has to go through to solve the problem. Only after these steps have been determined can someone set up the software to solve the problem. This task of developing a solution procedure can be one of the most difficult in computer problem solving; more will be said about it later.

End-user Computing

When a user develops procedures to solve problems using personal computer software, he or she is using the computer to the fullest extent. Often, people use the term **end-user computing** when referring to the development and use of personal computer applications by end users. In end-user computing, the user identifies problems that need to be solved, decides what software he or she will use to solve the problems, determines the procedures that the software must follow to solve the problems, customizes the software for the solution procedures, and uses the customized software to determine the solutions to the problems.

End users can use personal computer software to solve problems with little formal training other than that required to operate the software. Often, however, untrained users spend considerable time developing solution procedures that are incorrect or that do not fully meet their needs. With an understanding of how problems should be solved using personal computer software, end users can be more effective in their use of computers. The next section describes the personal computer problem-solving process.

The Problem-solving Process

Several tasks must be performed to prepare a computer solution to a problem. One of these tasks is to set up the software to solve the problem. This task, however, is only one activity in the problem-solving process. The five main activities in the process are

- Understand and define the problem.
- Design the solution procedure.

FIGURE 8.25

▲ **The problem-solving process**

> **Problem definition**
>   Define output
>   Define input
>   Define calculations
>   Define other processing
>
> **Solution procedure design**
>   Design procedure to solve problem
>
> **Software implementation**
>   Implement solution procedure in software
>
> **Implementation testing**
>   Test software implementation
>   Debug software implementation
>
> **Documentation**
>   Prepare user documentation
>   Prepare developer documentation

- Implement the solution procedure, using the selected software.
- Test the software implementation and correct any errors.
- Document the result.

These activities are summarized in Figure 8.25.

The five activities in the problem-solving process are not necessarily performed in sequence. In fact, several activities usually take place at the same time. For example, documenting begins while trying to understand and define the problem. Similarly, testing part of the solution procedure can begin while implementing the rest of the procedure. Often, it is necessary to return to a previous activity. For example, when designing the solution procedure, it may be necessary to go back to the first step to understand more about the problem. The activities are listed not in the order in which they are *started*, but in the order in which they are *finished*. For example, designing the solution procedure cannot be finished until the problem is completely understood and defined. Nevertheless, the designing activity may be started before the first activity is completed. Similarly, the solution procedure cannot be completely implemented until the design is finished; all testing cannot be completed until implementation is entirely finished; and certain documentation cannot be put into final form until all other activities have been completed.

Problem Definition

The first activity in the problem-solving process involves completely understanding and carefully defining the problem to be solved. Frequently, the most difficult step is recognizing that a problem exists for which a computer solution is appropriate. Normally this step starts when the user finds a situation in his or her work that requires careful analysis. Often in this case one or more problems exist for which solutions are needed to help resolve the situation.

At first the user should try to understand the problem as a whole. What are the requirements of the problem? Usually this involves determining what output is to be produced. What data is available? Answering this question often involves determining what input is to be processed. What calculations and other processing needs to be done? It is best to get a general understanding of the problem as a whole, without going into details about the input, output, calculations, and other processing.

After gaining a general understanding of the problem, the user can refine the problem definition to include specific information about the output, such as its layout; the input, such as how it will be entered; the calculations, such as what formulas are needed; and other processing, such as what conditions affect the results. The refinement of the problem definition should continue until there is sufficient detail to begin designing a solution procedure. At a minimum the problem definition should include descriptions of the following:

- The output to be produced and its layout.
- The input data available and how it will be entered.
- The calculations to be performed.
- Other processing to be done.

Sometimes it is difficult to understand a problem. When this happens, it often helps to isolate parts of the problem and work with each part separately. Another approach is to think of a simpler but similar problem and understand it first. Insight from the simpler problem can help explain the more complex problem.

Software Selection.   At this stage, or perhaps earlier, the user must select the type of software that will be used to implement the solution procedure. The most common alternatives are database, spreadsheet, word processing, and graphics software, but other software, such as statistical software, is also used. Often, the type of software needed for implementing the solution procedure is obvious, but at other times it is not. For example, a problem may require storage and retrieval of data, plus analysis of the data. Should database or spreadsheet software be used, or should both be used together?

In general, database software is best for situations in which a large amount of data needs to be stored, updated, and retrieved. It is especially appropriate when several different groups of data are related. Spreadsheet software is best when data needs to be analyzed using sets of formulas. It is very good for what-if situations, but not appropriate for storage and retrieval of large amounts of data. Word processing, graphics, and desktop publishing software are best for presenting the results of analysis. As shown in this chapter, an individual application often requires the use of several types of software, with data transferred from one program to another. Thus, more than one type of software may be needed to solve a problem.

The selection of the appropriate software must be based on the characteristics of the problem. It is not necessary to identify the specific software at this point, however, only what type of software will be used. The selection is necessary so that the design of the solution procedure can proceed.

Solution Procedure Design

With an understanding of the problem, the user can design the procedure to solve the problem. The steps necessary to solve the problem must be carefully planned. As explained earlier, these steps form the solution procedure for the problem. Written notes should be made of the solution procedure. Professional programmers have various ways of writing a procedure, but for an end user a list or an outline is usually easiest. (Figure 8.24 shows a procedure for starting a car in an outline form.) The designing activity does *not* involve setting up the software to solve the problem. Before the software can be prepared, the procedure to solve the problem must be determined.

Designing a solution procedure is usually the most difficult task in the problem-solving process, and there are many strategies to help. It is useful to know common solution procedures so that when a problem or a part of a problem requires a known procedure, it can be quickly supplied. When the solution procedure is not known, one must be devised, which can be difficult to do. One approach that may help is to think first of a related problem and develop a procedure to solve it. Another approach is to simplify the problem by discarding some of the conditions and then develop a solution procedure to solve the simpler version. Sometimes it is necessary to return to the problem definition to determine whether anything has been omitted. Any of these approaches may help in designing a procedure for solving the problem.

Software Implementation

After the solution procedure for the problem has been designed, the user can implement it by using the selected software. How this is done depends on the software being used. With spreadsheet software, numbers, text, and formulas for the solution procedure are entered into a worksheet. With database software, it is necessary to enter the description of the database, the specifications of the queries, and the formats of the forms and reports, all of which together form the solution procedure for the problem.

Doing the implementation requires knowing how to use the software. With this knowledge, an understanding of the problem to be solved, and the solution procedure designed previously, the implementation can be completed. Various documents are helpful in the implementation, including sheets with layouts of the input and output; an outline of the solution procedure; and a list of formulas to be used in calculations. With this information the software can be set up to solve the problem.

Occasionally, during the implementation activity an error in the design is discovered. For example, steps may be done in the wrong sequence. When this happens, it is necessary to redesign part of the solution procedure. It may even be necessary to return to the problem definition and work forward again if a serious error is discovered.

Implementation Testing

Although the solution procedure may be carefully designed and implemented in the software, the implementation may not be correct. Computer problem solving is a complex activity, and it is easy to make mistakes. Thus, the next step in the process is for the user to *test* the software implementation to see if it has any errors.

Types of Errors.   Three types of errors can occur in a software implementation: syntax errors, execution errors, and logic errors. A *syntax error* is an error in the form of a command and other entry given to the software. For example, misspelling a command or incorrectly entering a formula results in syntax errors. These errors are detected by the software. Usually when such an error is detected, a message describing the error is displayed on the screen. Even though the software has detected a syntax error, it cannot figure out what the user wants. If there are any syntax errors, the software cannot proceed. The user must locate and correct any incorrect entries that cause syntax errors.

If there are no syntax errors, the software can execute the commands and instructions given to it. During execution, however, other errors may appear. These are called *execution errors*. For example, an attempt to divide a number by zero causes an execution error. These errors are detected by the software as it performs the steps required to solve the problem. When such an error is detected, a message describing the error is displayed on the screen. Still, the software cannot correct the error. The user must determine the cause of the error and correct it.

The final type of error is detected only after the software has finished processing. If the output is not correct, there is a *logic error*. For example, if the solution procedure requires that two numbers be added, but instead the software implementation mistakenly uses an instruction that subtracts the numbers, then no syntax or execution error will be detected. The final output will be incorrect, however, because the logic of the implementation is wrong. The software cannot detect such an error because it does not know what the logic should be. The user must detect and correct any logic errors.

The Testing Process.   The process used to find logic errors in a software implementation is called **testing**. The steps the user goes through in testing are as follows:

1 Make up input test data.
2 Determine by hand what output is expected from the test data.
3 Run the software implementation with the test data to get the actual output.
4 Compare the actual output with the expected output. If the outputs are not the same, there is a logic error in the software implementation.

A software implementation must be tested thoroughly before being put to use. Typical sets of input data should be tested first to be sure the software works in the usual cases, and then unusual sets of input data should be tested. The objective of testing is to reveal as many errors as possible in the software implementation.

After a logic error has been detected through testing, the cause of the error must be located and corrected. An error in a software implementation is called a **bug**, and the process of locating and correcting errors is called **debugging**. *Testing* involves determining whether errors are present; *debugging* involves finding and correcting errors.

Debugging logic errors in a software implementation can be difficult. Various strategies are used to try to find the causes of errors, but they can be very time-consuming. In fact, testing and debugging often takes as much time as all the other activities of the problem-solving process put together. To minimize the time spent testing and debugging a software implementation, the problem must be thoroughly understood and defined, and the solution procedure must be carefully designed. The more time spent on these first two activities, the less time will be needed for testing and debugging.

Documentation

In the last step of the problem-solving process the user brings together all the material that describes the problem, its solution procedure, its software implementation, and the implementation testing. This step results in the **documentation**, which is a general term used for any written description of a computer application. Two types of documentation are user documentation and developer documentation.

User documentation provides information so that the user can understand how to utilize the software implementation. This type of documentation gives instructions for running the software on the computer, including what input to enter and what output to expect. It describes the keys to press and the mouse selections to make to get the software implementation to perform its functions. It also describes the meanings of any messages displayed on the screen and what to do if the software does not work.

Developer documentation is not designed for users, but rather for the person who developed the software implementation. It describes how the software implementation works so that it is easier to correct errors and make modifications in the future. This type of documentation includes any written information about the problem definition, the solution procedure design, the software implementation, and the implementation testing. Typically, this documentation contains a brief summary stating the purpose of the software implementation; detailed descriptions of the input and output data; an outline or other description of the solution procedure; a list of input test data and the resulting output; and a printed listing of the commands, instructions, and formulas used in the software implementation.

It is important that software be thoroughly documented. The user must know how to use the software, and the developer must know how the software functions so that changes can be made. Only after all documentation is finished is the problem-solving process complete.

CHAPTER SUMMARY

1 Productivity has to do with how much a person contributes to a business in a period of time. Individual information systems can improve personal productivity by making it easier for individuals to locate, retrieve, manage, analyze, and present information related to their jobs. (pp. 238–239)

2 Users manage stored data with database software by creating a database, accessing a database, and updating a database. To create a database, a user must first describe the fields and records in the database, and then enter data for the database, which is stored in secondary storage. Accessing a database involves retrieving data from the database in secondary storage. Updating a database includes adding new data, deleting old data, and modifying existing data. (pp. 239–245)

3 Users analyze data in a **spreadsheet** by organizing the data in rows and columns, and performing calculations with the data. Spreadsheet software makes the data analysis easier because the user can create an electronic spreadsheet, or **worksheet**. Users can make changes in data or formulas in the worksheet, and the computer automatically recalculates values in the worksheet—a procedure called **what-if analysis**. (pp. 245–246)

4 Several types of software are used to prepare information for presentation to others. Word processing software is used to prepare information in text form, and graphics software is used to prepare information in graphical form. Types of graphics software include **charting software, drawing software, presentation graphics software**, and **computer-aided design (CAD) software**. **Desktop**

publishing software is used to prepare information in a published form such as a newsletter, pamphlet, or brochure. **Authoring software** is used to prepare information for presentation in a multimedia form that includes text, graphics, animation, video, sound, and other forms. (pp. 248–258)

5 Data management, data analysis, and information presentation applications can be combined by transferring data from one application to another. The output from one application becomes the input to another application. Data from a database can be transferred to a worksheet or document, or it can be used in a graph. Data in a worksheet can be graphed, or it can be transferred to a document or database. A graph can be transferred to a document. Combining applications improves productivity and increases accuracy. (pp. 258–259)

6 Much information is available on the Internet. Using a browser, an individual can locate and retrieve useful information from the Web. When the desired information is displayed on the screen, it can be incorporated into other individual applications. A **search engine** allows a user to search for specific types of information on the Web. Information can also be sent to the user's computer automatically by using **push technology**. Some information found on the Web may not be correct or useful, and the user must evaluate the credibility of the source of the information. (pp. 259–261)

7 Personal computer applications are used to help individuals solve problems in business. A **problem**

is a question to which someone does not know the answer, or a statement of something to be done. The **solution** to a problem is the answer to the problem question or the result of doing what is required by the problem statement. A **solution procedure** is a set of steps that, if carried out, results in the solution of a problem. A personal computer application implements a solution procedure to find the solution to a problem for an individual. One of the main tasks in computer problem solving is determining the solution procedure needed to solve a problem. (pp. 262–263)

8 **End-user computing** is the development and use of personal computer applications by end users. In end-user computing, the user identifies problems that need to be solved, decides what software he or she will use to solve the problems, determines the procedures that the software must follow to solve the problems, customizes the software for the solution procedures, and uses the customized software to determine the solutions to the problems. (p. 263)

9 There are five main activities in the problem-solving process. First, the user must completely understand and carefully define the problem to be solved. As part of this activity, the user may also select the type of software to be used for the implementation. Next, the user must design the procedure to solve the problem. Then the user can implement the solution procedure, using the selected software. Next, the user must detect and correct any errors in the software implementation. **Testing** involves determining whether there are errors in the software implementation; **debugging** involves locating and correcting any errors, or **bugs**, that are detected. Finally, the user must prepare **documentation** of the result of the process. (pp. 263–268)

KEY TERMS

Authoring Software (p. 256)
Bug (pp. 267)
Charting Software (p. 250)
Computer-Aided Design (CAD) Software (p. 252)
Debugging (p. 267)
Desktop Publishing (p. 255)
Desktop Publishing Software (p. 255)

Documentation (p. 267)
Drawing Software (p. 250)
End-User Computing (p. 263)
Integrated Software (p. 255)
Portal (p. 261)
Presentation Graphics Software (p. 250)
Problem (p. 262)
Push Technology (p. 261)

Search Engine (p. 259)
Solution (p. 262)
Solution Procedure (p. 262)
Spreadsheet (p. 245)
Suite (p. 255)
Testing (p. 267)
What-If Analysis (p. 246)
Word Processing (p. 248)
Worksheet (p. 245)

REVIEW QUESTIONS

1 How can individual information systems improve personal productivity?

2 What two steps are required to create a database?

3 What three tasks can a user perform in updating a database?

4 In what situation is data analysis with a spreadsheet used?

5 Why does spreadsheet software make data analysis easier?

6 Give the formula for each of the following cells in the worksheet in Figure 8.10:

Cell	Formula
B15	=B8+B9+B10+B11+B12+B13+B14
B17	=B5−B15
C15	
C17	
D15	
D17	

7 Give the formulas needed to complete the worksheet in Figure 8.11. Be sure to indicate the cell in which each formula belongs.

8 In what situations might it be better to use a typewriter instead of a computer with word processing software?

9 What are several types of graphics software?

10 How can data management, data analysis, and information presentation applications be combined?

11 What is desktop publishing?

12 What software is used to prepare multimedia presentations?

13 What software is used to locate information on the Web?

14 How are personal computer applications used to help individuals solve problems?

15 What is end-user computing?

16 In what order are the activities of the problem-solving process performed?

17 What should be included in a problem definition?

18 During which activity of the problem-solving process are the steps in the solution procedure determined?

19 What types of errors can occur in a software implementation?

20 What is the difference between testing and debugging?

DISCUSSION QUESTIONS

1 Sometimes setting up and using a computer application takes more time than doing the work some other way. When this happens, is there still an improvement in personal productivity when using the computer application?

2 What ways can information be presented besides those discussed in this chapter? What ways might information be presented in the future?

3 This chapter shows how data management, data analysis, and information presentation can be combined in a sales analysis system. Think of another system in which these applications can be combined, and describe how it would work.

4 The Internet provides access to information around the world. What problems might be encountered when using Web information from other countries?

5 As software becomes easier to use, will it become unnecessary for end users to develop computer applications? Why or why not?

6 How can the problem-solving process be adapted for solving problems without using computers?

ETHICS QUESTIONS

1 Assume that a coworker has developed a spreadsheet application for calculating bonuses for employees in your company. You ask him if he has tested the spreadsheet, and he says he did not have to because he knows it is correct. What would you do in this situation?

2 You are browsing the Web, and find some information at an obscure site that one of your company's competitors has been involved in sexual harassment of several female employees. You know the women involved, and you know that the allegations are completely false. If the information were to become widely known, however, it could damage your competitor. What would you do in this situation?

3 At a meeting, an executive in your company says that he has been surfing the Web and found some information that supports his plan for a new product line. The information seems a little unusual to you, and you ask the executive about the source of the information. He replies that he doesn't recall, but that he got it from the Web. What would you do in this situation?

PROBLEM-SOLVING PROJECTS

1 Using database software, set up the database described in this chapter. Include the Salesperson table and the Region table. You can use the data shown in the figures in the chapter or make up your own data. Then develop the following:

   a A query giving the names and addresses of salespeople who had sales of $25,000 or more. Also develop a form to display the result of the query.

   b A query that, for each salesperson, gives the name of the region in which the salesperson works, the number of salespeople in the region, the salesperson's name, and the salesperson's address. The query should display the output in order, by region name. Also develop a form to display the result of the query.

   c A report giving each salesperson number, name, address, and sales, along with the total sales for all salespeople.

2 Using spreadsheet software, create the sales analysis worksheet described in the chapter. Add another column for the projected sales next month. The projected sales should be the average of the sales last month and the sales this month, plus a 15% increase. Transfer data from the database you created in Problem-solving Project 1 to your worksheet.

3 Using the charting capabilities of your spreadsheet software, develop a graph of the data in the worksheet you created in Problem-solving Project 2. The graph should show the sales last month, the sales this month, and the projected sales next month.

4 Using word processing software, prepare a memo to the finance department explaining the projected sales for next month. (The finance department needs to plan for the availability of funds in the future.) Include in your memo the data for all three months from the spreadsheet you created in Problem-solving Project 2 and the graph you created in Problem-solving Project 3. Explain in your memo how the projected sales were computed.

5 Interview several end users in a business to which you have access to find out how they developed the computer applications they are using. If there are a lot of users, you can develop a questionnaire to ask the same questions of all users. Find out what process the users followed in developing their applications. Which steps in the problem-solving process described in this chapter did they follow? How successful were they in developing their applications? Write a summary of your findings.

6 Using database software, develop a computer application to keep track of sales contacts. The data stored in the application should include the customer number, customer name, customer address, customer phone number, and date of the last sales contact. The application should produce the following outputs:

   a A list of the data for all customers.

   b A display of a specific customer's name, address, and phone number, given the customer number.

   c A list of all customers who have not been contacted since a given date.

   Supply data for 15 to 20 customers to test the application.

7 Using spreadsheet software, develop a computer application to compare your expenses each month with your budget for various items (e.g., rent, food, transportation). Enter the amount that you budget for each item and the amount you actually spent on each item for a recent month. Have the application calculate the difference between each budgeted amount and the amount spent. Also have the application calculate the percentage differences.

8 Using spreadsheet software, prepare charts of the data in the spreadsheet you developed in Problem-solving Project 7. Prepare a bar chart that shows how the amount budgeted and the amount spent compare for all items. Also prepare pie charts for the budgeted amounts and amounts spent.

INTERNET AND ELECTRONIC COMMERCE PROJECTS

1   Assume that you are the national sales manager of an athletic-clothing wholesaler, as described in this chapter. Use the Web to find at least one other company that also sells athletic clothes wholesale. What types of products does the company sell? Select one product that the company sells and analyze how the company promotes it on its Web site. Write a summary of what you find.

2   Assume that you are the national sales manager of an athletic-clothing wholesaler, as described in this chapter. You have decided to have an e-commerce Web site set up to sell your products directly to retail stores. Locate one or more sites similar to what you want on the Web. After evaluating the sites you locate, decide what capabilities you want your Web site to have. Write a description of your Web site's capabilities.

3   The user interface is a critical part of a computer application. Using the Web, locate information on how to design a good user interface. Prepare a brief summary of recommendations for user interface design that you find on the Web.

4   Use several search engines to find information about search engines. Identify as many search engines as you can, and determine their characteristics. Try to find Web sites that have comparisons of different search engines. Write a report listing all search engines that you identify and their characteristics.

Haworth Inc.

Dilbert would not be a fan of Haworth's corporate mission. That's because Haworth manufactures office cubicles. It is a company drowning in a sea of 21 million disparate and untracked inventory parts that make up its products.

The answer for Haworth, based in Holland, Michigan, has been to equip sales representatives with computer-visualization software from Trilogy Development Group, in Austin, Texas. The software lets sales representatives with laptop computers show a customer exactly what's being ordered and how it will look.

Today, the baffling array of possible Haworth furniture combinations is so complex that many customers don't know exactly what they've bought until it's delivered, according to Ward Smith, Haworth's senior sales-automation consultant.

For example, an office chair alone could be assembled in 200 different ways. And the 21 million inventory parts don't even include the many possible color combinations.

Software visualization gives sales representatives the ability to assemble on a laptop's screen the pieces of Haworth's cubicles at the customers' premises. This augments the company's sales process, in which the sales representative must shuttle back and forth between the customer and an office-equipment dealership, allowing a CAD operator at the dealership to create a mock-up based on the parts being ordered, Smith says.

"We can give the laptop to a salesperson who knows nothing about how to configure our product, because the software is programmed to know how our products go together," Smith says.

Smith likes to compare his complicated sales problem to the relatively easy sales approach taken in the automobile industry.

"You can look at a red Corvette, drive it, kick the tires, and then buy it," Smith says. "But with us, you can fly to Michigan headquarters to look at a close facsimile of our product that is not exactly what you are buying. Then you can work with our dealer on ordering 21 million parts. Then the dealer's CAD operator will try to visualize what

you're buying; you'll see a two-dimensional blue-print and maybe a 3-D rendering of one of the several workstations you're probably buying. We make it and deliver it in 15 million parts with instructions on how to put it together. And until you put it together, you will not know if the order is right."

Haworth's executives hope that the Trilogy application, called the Sales Builder Engine, will shorten the company's sales cycle, make its huge parts catalog more easily understood, and increase order accuracy. According to Smith, that would be a significant competitive advantage for the 9,000-employee company, which is the world's second-largest seller of office cubicles and had $1.2 billion in sales in 1995. Smith says Haworth spent more than $1 million on the Trilogy software.

The software is expected to speed up Haworth's sales cycle and improve accuracy by eliminating some of the repetitive CAD work and sales representative trips to the customers' sites.

The salesperson and CAD operator typically have to go through the CAD mock-up process several times—with the sales representative returning each time to the customer to show the mock-up—to complete an order. Only after the last CAD mock-up is approved is the CAD workstation software used to create a bill of materials that goes to Haworth's factory for manufacturing. What's more, having the sales representative relay information from the customer to the CAD operator sometimes allows errors to creep into the CAD mock-up.

The Trilogy visualization software should eliminate some of the sales representatives' trips back and forth between the customer and CAD operator, while reducing the number of errors, Smith says.

Sales representatives who use the laptops equipped with Trilogy software should be able to configure clusters of as many as 10 cubicles and give the customer approximate prices for what has been created on the laptop screen—all without returning to the dealership.

"The result is that the salesperson can do 'what ifs' with the client all day long," Smith says.

One additional reason the Trilogy software will be useful in eliminating errors is that, besides assembling the Haworth product on-screen, it provides a virtual walkthrough of a group of assembled work cubicles.

"We have a user group that says it now usually takes five discussions between the customer and the dealer before an order goes to manufacturing. I hope to eliminate two of those discussions by collecting the customer requirements accurately the first time," Smith says. "That's important, because the tightest piece of the funnel in the sales process is the CAD-operator design function; for every 10 salespeople there are only two or three CAD operators."

The CAD operator still has a role, however. After the sales representative and customer have agreed on a configuration for the cubicles, the CAD operator takes the configuration file from the laptop, matches it against the architecture of the customer's building, and checks that the parts of the cubicles fit together properly.

But the Trilogy software simplifies the CAD operator's job, Smith says. "The laptop CAD file has the information about exactly how everything is configured, right down to the fabric and the finish. The CAD operator takes that same file, overlays it on a diagram of the customer's building, then hits the configure button. The CAD system, using the Trilogy model, makes sure that the operator doesn't put workstations in the middle of a wall, and that parts are configured correctly, Smith says.

Smith says that the Trilogy application shouldn't be confused with traditional sales-force automa-tion, which typically means giving a worker a laptop computer and software tools for expense reporting, sales tracking, and e-mail.

With the Trilogy software, Haworth is reengineering its sales by shifting detailed parts-assembly information from the corporate level to the customer level.

"We're going to empower the salesperson with everything the CAD operator could do, in effect, moving those capabilities to the point of sale," Smith says. "We're automating something they couldn't do before, instead of automating what they were doing before."

Questions

1 For what application do Haworth sales representatives use laptop computers?
2 How does the use of a laptop computer application improve a sales representative's productivity?
3 How can a Haworth sales representative do what-if analysis?
4 Why is it important to have CAD support at the dealership, even though sales representatives have laptop computers?
5 What benefits does Haworth expect to receive from the use of laptop computers by its sales representatives?

Web Site
Haworth Inc.: www.haworth.com

Source: *Adapted from* Steve Alexander, "Trilogy helps Haworth get through a maze of cubicles," *InfoWorld*, January 27, 1997, p. 92.

Group
COLLABORATION

NINE

CHAPTER OUTLINE

Encouraging Group Collaboration
Characteristics of Group Collaboration
Types of Workgroup Applications
Office Automation
The Virtual Work Environment

After completing this chapter, you should be able to

1 Explain why group collaboration is difficult in businesses and how workgroup information systems encourage group collaboration.

2 Describe the main characteristics of group collaboration.

3 Explain what groupware is.

4 List and briefly describe the main types of workgroup applications.

5 Summarize the group collaboration characteristics of the main types of workgroup applications.

6 Explain what office automation is.

7 Describe the changes in the work environment that can take place as a result of the use of workgroup applications.

ndividuals in a business usually do not work entirely alone, but instead in teams, committees, departments, and other types of workgroups. To collaborate on common tasks, workgroup members can have meetings, talk on the telephone, send faxes, and distribute memos. Group members can also use *workgroup information systems* to help them collaborate. As you learned in Chapter 1, a workgroup information system is one that affects a group of people who work together. This type of system is also called a **group support system (GSS)** because it supports the work of people in a group.

This chapter looks at applications used in workgroup information systems, and shows how these applications affect group collaboration in businesses. First, the chapter explains how workgroup information systems encourage group collaboration. Then it examines the characteristics of group collaboration. Next, it describes common workgroup applications and the software used for these applications. Finally, the chapter discusses office automation and the virtual work environment.

Encouraging Group Collaboration

Businesses use workgroup information systems to encourage group collaboration. Collaborating with others is an essential part of business. People need to discuss ideas, share thoughts, coordinate plans, and comment on the work of others. Employees have to exchange documents, transmit designs, send images, and communicate with different people. Group members need to solve problems together and make collective decisions. When done well, these activities can improve the effectiveness and productivity of the group beyond what individuals can do separately.

The principal difficulty with group collaboration is that group members often are not in the same place at the same time. If everyone in a workgroup can get together in one room at one time for a meeting, then much can be accomplished. But often meetings are difficult to arrange, especially when individuals work at distant locations. In addition, meetings can be very expensive and time-consuming when people travel significant distances to get together.

Group collaboration is also difficult because groups often change. Individuals come into a workgroup, work for a while, and then leave for another workgroup or job. Some people may be in several workgroups at the same time, and shift between groups from time to time. Workgroups can also cross departmental boundaries. Individuals from several departments, and in some cases several businesses, may be in a workgroup. All these situations make group collaboration complex.

Telephones play an important role in group collaboration. Much communication takes place between individuals by telephone, and conference calls, which involve three or more people in a group, are common. But when employees have varying schedules or are located across many time zones, finding a time when everyone is available to talk by telephone can be difficult.

Telephones are also deficient because they provide only verbal communication; text, graphics, and images cannot be seen through a telephone. As a consequence, fax machines are used extensively. A fax of a document, diagram, or picture can be sent and received within a few minutes. Then, if necessary, the faxed image can be discussed on the telephone. This approach is not ideal either because any time the document, diagram, or picture changes, a new fax must be sent.

To solve many of the problems of telephones and faxes, workgroup information systems have been developed. These systems make it easier for members of a group to collaborate over distance and time. They typically use personal computers connected to local area networks (LANs) or wide area networks (WANs). The Internet, intranets, and extranets (discussed in Chapter 6) are also used. Workgroup information systems use many types of software, including electronic mail software so that individuals in the group can communicate easily, database software so that the group can share information, and electronic conferencing software so that group members can discuss problems and reach decisions. By making these and other group applications available, a business encourages group collaboration.

Characteristics of Group Collaboration

Group collaboration can be characterized by *when* and *where* the collaboration takes place, and by *what* is communicated during the collaboration. This section examines these characteristics to provide a basis for understanding workgroup information systems.

The Time and Place of Collaboration

Two of the basic characteristics of group collaboration are *time* and *place*—the when and where of collaboration. Figure 9.1 shows these characteristics in two dimensions. If two or more people collaborate, they may do so at the same time or at different times. To work together at the same time, they could be in a room together or talk by telephone. To collaborate at different times, they could leave voice messages, send faxes, use overnight delivery, or send regular mail.

People may also work together at the same place or at different places. They may be in the same room or building, making it possible for them to have direct contact. Alternatively, they may be at widely separated locations, in which case they cannot have direct contact without extensive travel.

Figure 9.1 shows four possible combinations of these characteristics. People working at the same time and place can collaborate directly. A face-to-face meeting is an example of this type of collaboration. People working at the same time but in differ-

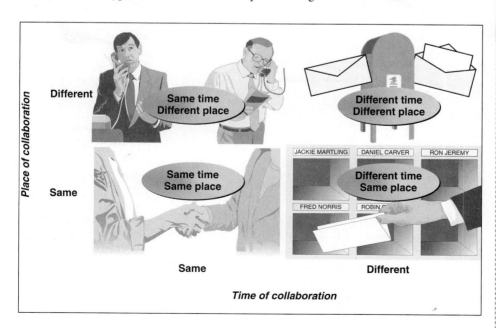

FIGURE 9.1

Time and place of group collaboration

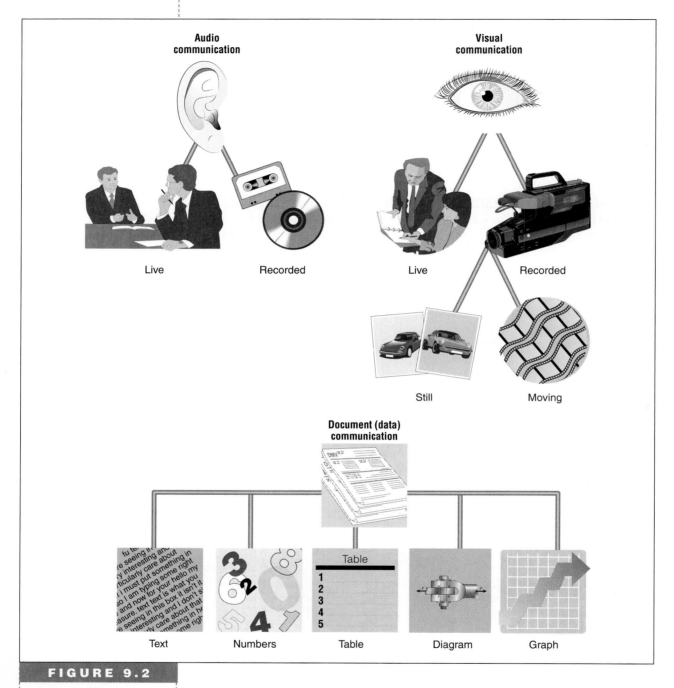

FIGURE 9.2

Forms of communication in
▲ group collaboration

ent places often use the telephone for collaboration. Conference calls are also common in this situation. When people work at different times but at the same place, they collaborate by leaving messages, either on the telephone or in paper notes. Putting written messages in mailboxes in staff mail rooms is a common way of communicating in this situation. A complex situation is when people working at different times and places need to collaborate. Voice messages, faxes, overnight deliveries, and regular mail are used in this situation.

The Form of Communication

Another characteristic of group collaboration is the *form* that the communication between people takes—the what of collaboration. Figure 9.2 summarizes some of the forms. Perhaps the most often used form of communication in business is *audio communication*; people talk to each other, either in person or on the telephone. Audio communication is not only what is said, but also how it is said. Tone, inflection, and other characteristics of speech often express information. In addition to live, verbal communication, recorded sound is used in group collaboration. Voice mail, taped sound, and other recorded sound are part of audio communication.

A second form of communication in group collaboration is *visual communication*, specifically sights of people or other real things. When groups meet in person, the members of the group can see each other. Their facial expressions and body language give visual clues that provide information about what they are saying and thinking. Recorded sights are also used in some collaborative situations. Still pictures or moving images on videotape may be shown to groups for discussion.

A final form of communication used in group collaboration is *document* (or *data*) *communication*. Documents may contain text, numbers, tables, diagrams, graphs, and other written representations of information. Examples are a report sent to members of a team, a table of data examined by committee members, a diagram of a design examined by several people, and a graph of data discussed by a group.

Types of Workgroup Applications

The previous section discusses the when, where, and what of group collaboration. The how has to do with the mechanisms used for group work. Without computers, face-to-face meetings, telephones, faxes, and mail are typically used for collaboration. With networked computers, however, various types of group collaborative software can be used. In general, these types of software are called **groupware**. The use of groupware by members of a workgroup for collaboration is sometimes referred to as **group**, or **collaborative**, **computing**.

People working in groups can use personal computer software, such as spreadsheet software, to assist in workgroup tasks. For example, a worksheet may be used by several people in a workgroup to analyze data. The worksheet could be stored on a server in a LAN, and different individuals, using spreadsheet software on personal computers connected to the network, could use the worksheet at different times.

Although personal computer software can be beneficial in workgroup tasks, these programs are not designed specifically for group work. Groupware, on the other hand, is intended only for workgroup information systems. These programs are used on networks, either LANs or WANs, and group members use the programs through personal computers connected to the network.

Increasingly, groupware is being designed for use through a Web browser. The Internet, or an intranet or extranet, provides the communication link between users. Called *Web-based groupware*, this software makes it easy for individuals at distant locations to collaborate.

This section takes a look at the main types of workgroup applications and examines the time (when), place (where), and form (what) characteristics of each type. It also introduces common groupware used for each type of application. It is important to note, however, that many workgroup programs encompass several types of applications.

Electronic Messaging

One of the most common forms of collaboration in workgroups is simple document communication; written notes, memos, task lists, notices, and other messages are commonly sent between members of a group. This form of communication is essential for all aspects of business, and software designed to facilitate it is at the heart of most workgroup information systems. In general, this type of application is called **electronic messaging**.

Electronic messaging allows *document communication* to take place between group members at *different times* from *different places*. Individuals can send written messages to others at any time of the day or night, and from any place in the world. A disadvantage of electronic messaging, however, is that an important message may not be read immediately. In fact, it could be several days before a message is read. In addition, communication in written form has limitations. Tone, inflection, facial expression, and other nonwritten forms of communication do not come through in an electronic message.

A basic form of electronic messaging is **electronic mail (e-mail)** in which simple text messages are sent between people. *Electronic mail software* is needed to send and receive e-mail. When sending e-mail, the sender identifies the receiver by his or her *electronic mail address*, and the e-mail software stores the mail in the receiver's *electronic mailbox*, which is a space on a disk in the network reserved for e-mail. The receiver can review the mail in the mailbox at any time.

A number of e-mail programs are in use. Some common ones are QUALCOMM Eudora, Microsoft Outlook, and Lotus cc:Mail. Figure 9.3 shows the screen of an e-mail program.

E-mail is designed mainly for document communication. It is possible, however, to send various types of files, including non-document files, along with an e-mail message. The file that is sent is called an *attachment*, and it could contain sound, a

FIGURE 9.3

▲ **An e-mail program screen**

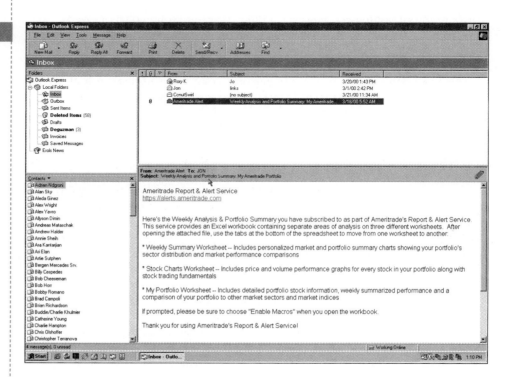

photographic image, a video image, or just about anything that can be stored in the computer. Using attachments, e-mail becomes audio and visual communication, as well as document communication.

More sophisticated *electronic messaging software* is also available. Such software allows users to send special types of messages to individuals or groups. For example, some electronic messaging software lets a user assign tasks to another person or group of people. Thus, a department manager can assign specific jobs to an employee in the department. When the employee completes each job, he or she can report this fact to the department manager, using the messaging software.

An example of a program that includes electronic messaging is Novell Group-Wise. GroupWise has e-mail capabilities plus electronic messaging features such as the ability to assign tasks. Another example of electronic messaging software is Microsoft Exchange. Figure 9.4 shows an electronic messaging groupware screen.

Because electronic messaging is different-time collaboration, a message may not be read immediately upon receipt. Some messaging software uses a technique called **instant messaging** to overcome this problem. With this technique, the sender uses the messaging software to determine whether the intended receiver is currently connected to the network. If the receiver is connected, the sender can send a message that appears almost immediately on the receiver's screen. The receiver can then read the message and reply, using instant messaging. An example of software that provides instant messaging is Lotus Sametime.

With instant messaging, individuals can send electronic messages back and forth quickly. An alternative to this approach is to use **chat**, which is an application that allows two or more individuals to have an electronic "conversation." Using chat, each person's screen shows all messages entered by each chat user in sequence, along with the name of the person who entered the message. When someone enters a new mes-

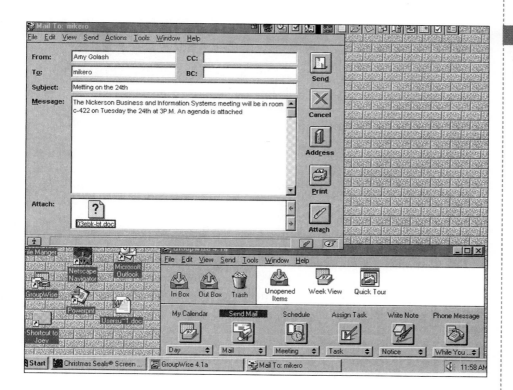

FIGURE 9.4

An electronic messaging groupware screen

FIGURE 9.5

▲ **A chat screen**

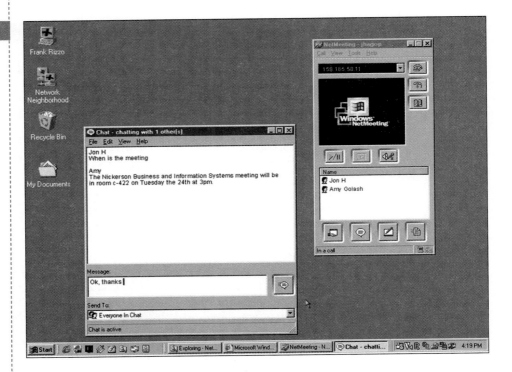

sage, it is added to the list of messages for all others to see immediately on their screens (Figure 9.5). Chat extends electronic messaging to *same-time* communication. It does not, however, provide all the capabilities of electronic messaging software.

Information Sharing

In addition to being able to send messages to each other, members of a workgroup need to be able to share information in other ways. Although information to be shared could be sent from one person to another by using e-mail, it often is easier to put the shared information in a single location and let each group member access it as needed. One way of accomplishing this is with database software. A database of shared information can be created, and each person can use database software to access the database.

The difficulty with using database software to share information is that often the information does not fit the database approach. For example, members of a product design group might want to share information, including diagrams, graphs, video, and sound, about a new product being developed. Group members might also want to share a spreadsheet analysis, a written report, and data extracted from an outside source. Common database software does not provide the capabilities for this type of information sharing.

Information sharing is a workgroup application that involves sharing different types of information among members of a group. With *information sharing software*, many different types of information, including text, graphics, spreadsheets, databases, video, and sound, can be shared. Users can access the information, change it, comment on it, and add new information.

Information sharing allows *audio, visual, and document communication* to take place between group members at *different times* from *different places*. The advantage of information sharing is that individuals in a workgroup can access the shared information

Group Collaboration for the Sable Offshore Energy Project

BOOK MARK

When you're about to step off a boat onto an oil rig platform in the Atlantic Ocean, 120 miles from land, this is the last thought you want to pop into your head: "Did the rig engineers have the latest specs when they built this thing?"

Engineers at the Sable Offshore Energy Project (SOEP) certainly didn't want to have to worry about that. Building oil rigs using incorrect or outdated specifications means, at the very least, wasted time and money. It could even mean disaster.

When they took on a major natural gas development project, managers at SOEP knew it wasn't going to be easy to keep project designers on the same page, however. That's because SOEP is not a single company, but a consortium of dozens of international best-in-class experts brought together to extract and deliver gas from Sable Island, Nova Scotia, the site of one of the largest known deposits in North America.

So, to ensure that all members of the SOEP project development chain were kept up-to-date on project specs 24 hours per day, the project's information technology team set up an extranet based on the Salvo Web-based collaboration software from Simware, of Ottawa. The site acted as an online collaboration portal, making all current project information available at every desktop, whether that desktop was at the fabrication plant of Kvaerner, in Teesside, England, or in the Houston office of engineering management company Brown & Root. Officials said the project management collaboration extranet helped SOEP cut what would have been a two-year effort to just one year.

A growing number of enterprises are latching on to a new crop of extranet software products and Web portals that allow for online collaborative product design. Enterprises such as SOEP are finding that these products can help them think faster and get products to market sooner and with less expense.

Online real-time collaboration represents a profound change in traditional product engineering processes. Most product design and development today is done in a sequential way that can waste large chunks of time. Engineers often work separately on portions of a design, and then pass the work on to another engineer when it is completed. If at any point a problem arises, the engineer stops work on the job until the whole team can meet and decide what to do next. Because teams are often physically separated and sometimes in different companies, there's historically been no chance for continual collaboration.

"In the past, contractors have worked in considerable isolation from each other," says Stacey Darragh, a quality assurance associate for SOEP, in Halifax, Nova Scotia. "But with this project, partners have made every effort to get together, whether by teleconference or data link or through Salvo."

Online design collaboration also cuts the need for expensive, time-consuming travel on the part of engineers. Before turning to Salvo, the SOEP consortium was forced to temporarily locate six experts from one partner, Kvaerner, at the Houston office of Brown & Root, one of the engineering management companies in the consortium. Commuting from England to Texas may sound drastic, but it was essential for the project to be sure the critical design specifications were being accurately communicated, according to Hugh MacIntyre, finance and administration manager at Agra Monenco, in Halifax. "[We had] to make sure that what was engineered could be handled in plant," MacIntyre says. "If [manufacturing experts are] involved directly in design, it makes their lives during fabrication easier."

"It's a multinational issue," says Hadley Reynolds, director of research at The Delphi

Group, in Boston. "Larger organizations are almost all geographically scattered all over the country, all over the globe. What was your company yesterday isn't your company today. You're working with people on the other coast, and you have to learn how to work with them." This is particularly true if the people on the other coast are the ones who designed the drilling platform you're about to step on, 120 miles out in the Atlantic.

Questions

1. What information was shared using the SOEP system, and among whom was it shared?

2. What form of group collaboration was involved in the SOEP system?

3. In addition to information sharing, what benefits did SOEP receive from the use of collaborative software?

Web Site
SOEP: www.soep.com

Source: *Adapted from* Lisa Vaas, "Shipshape Design," *PC Week*, August 23, 1999, pp. 75–78.

at any time from any place. A disadvantage of information sharing is that a person may not access relevant information immediately. Using information sharing effectively requires that all members of a workgroup examine the shared information on a regular basis.

Perhaps the best-known information sharing program is Lotus Notes.[1] With Notes, users can create "document databases" to share information. Each database can contain text, numbers, graphs, images, sound, and video. Users can comment on information in a database and add new information.[2] Other examples of information sharing software are SoftArc's FirstClass and Accentuate Systems' SamePage. Figure 9.6 shows an information sharing groupware screen.

Document Conferencing

Information sharing lets members of a workgroup collaborate at different times. Often, however, group members want to confer at the same time. **Document conferencing**, also called **data conferencing**, is a workgroup application that provides this form of collaboration on documents. Group members at different locations can simultaneously view a document containing text, numbers, graphs, and other forms of information. Individuals can add comments to the document for others to see and can make changes in the document.

Document conferencing provides for *document communication* between group members at the *same time* from *different places*. It is useful in situations where individuals cannot meet face-to-face to discuss a document. A disadvantage, though, is that group members must be available at the same time to confer on the document.

Two main types of document conferencing are whiteboard conferencing and application conferencing. With **whiteboard conferencing**, each user sees the same document on an *electronic whiteboard*, which is a white area on the screen containing the document (Figure 9.7). Any user can write comments on the whiteboard, and all

---

[1] Lotus Notes is software used on a client computer in a client server/system. To use all the features of Notes, the server computer must run a program called Lotus Domino. The combination is sometimes identified as Lotus Notes/Domino, but many people just refer to it as Lotus Notes.

[2] Lotus Notes includes a number of applications besides information sharing.

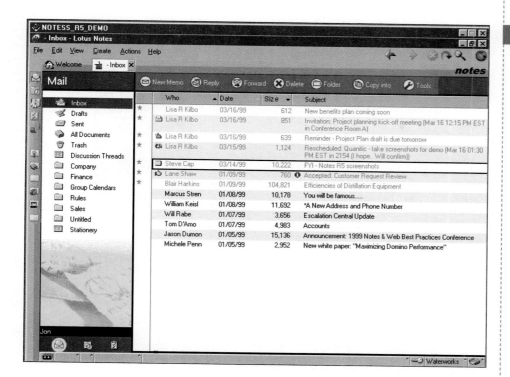

FIGURE 9.6

An information sharing
groupware screen ▲

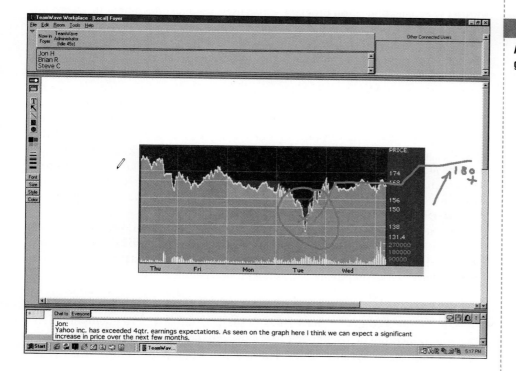

FIGURE 9.7

A whiteboard conferencing
groupware screen ▲

FIGURE 9.8

An application conferencing
▲ groupware screen

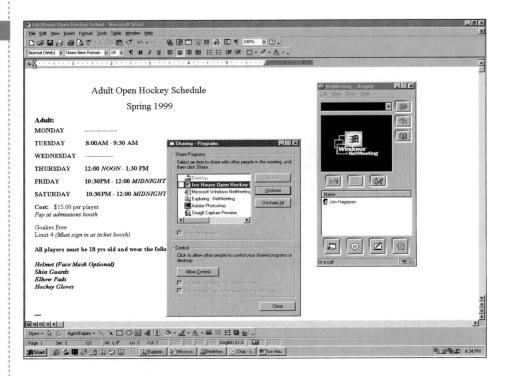

users see the comments simultaneously on their whiteboards. An example of *white-board conferencing software* is TeamWave Workplace.

With **application conferencing**, each user also sees the same document on his or her screen. But instead of seeing the document on a whiteboard, the user sees it within the actual application program. Thus, users see a text document in a word processing program screen and a worksheet in the spreadsheet software screen. The document is displayed by one user for all users to see, but any user can comment on the document on the screen. In addition, any user can make changes in the document by using the software, and all users will see the changes. An example of *application conferencing software* is Microsoft NetMeeting. Figure 9.8 shows an application conferencing groupware screen.

Although document conferencing is primarily for simultaneous collaboration, it is also possible with some software for a user to work on a document alone and then send the document to other users so that they can work on it at other times. This *store-and-forward* capability makes it unnecessary in some situations for all users to be connected at the same time.

Audioconferencing

Perhaps the most common way in which people in a workgroup communicate is by telephone. Telephones are universal and easy to use, so people find them very convenient for discussing group work. The telephone can also be used to communicate when working with computers. For example, two people can talk on the telephone about a document that is displayed on both their computer screens. Although not ideal, this form of collaboration is used often.

Many personal computers have speakers (or headphones) and a microphone, so it is natural to incorporate telephone capabilities into computers. Some personal computers come with telephone circuitry that allows communication over telephone lines. Another approach, called **computer telephony**, uses a network, usually the Internet, for audio communication, thus bypassing the regular telephone lines.

For computer telephony to work, each computer needs special *computer telephony software*, as well as the appropriate audio input (microphone) and output (speaker or headphone) devices. Many computer telephony programs are available. An example is VocalTec's Internet Phone.

With computer telephony, audioconferencing with computers is possible. In general, **audioconferencing** is a workgroup application in which two or more members of a group at different locations communicate with each other at the same time by voice over a computer network. It is not necessary to set up a telephone conference call or to use standard telephone lines. All communication takes place using computers and networks.

As with telephone communication, audioconferencing provides *audio communication* between group members at the *same time* from *different places*. Its advantage over a telephone is that it uses a computer network for communication, which may be less expensive than a telephone line. Its main disadvantage is the same as that of a telephone: Group members can only communicate verbally; visual and document communication is not provided in audioconferencing. In addition, group members must be available at the same time in order to have an audioconference.

Videoconferencing

During an audioconference, people often want to see who they are talking to. Facial expressions and body language can sometimes convey information as much as the words that are spoken. **Videoconferencing** is a workgroup application in which members of a group at different locations can see each other at the same time that they talk to each other. Videoconferencing always includes audio, although audioconferencing can be done without video.

Videoconferencing allows *audio and visual communication* between group members at the *same time* from *different places*. It overcomes one of the disadvantages of audioconferencing by providing visual communication. It is especially beneficial as a replacement for face-to-face meetings that would require expensive travel by meeting participants. Some businesses use videoconferencing extensively instead of face-to-face meetings in this situation. Videoconferencing does have some disadvantages, however. Documents cannot be communicated in a videoconference, and conference participants must be available at the same time.

To have a videoconference, each user location needs a video camera, monitor, microphone, and speaker. Audio and video signals are transmitted from one location to another. Video images are displayed on distant monitors, and sound is projected through a speaker. Some videoconferencing systems, called *point-to-point* systems, allow users at only two locations to communicate. Other videoconferencing systems, called *multipoint* systems, allow users at more than two locations to participate in a conference simultaneously.

Two types of videoconferencing systems are room systems and desktop systems. A **room** (or **group**) **videoconferencing system** is designed for use by several people in a room. These systems have a large, special-purpose monitor, often 32 inches across. Some room systems come with several monitors. Room systems also include a high-quality video camera that can be pointed at different parts of the room and can zoom in on the person speaking. Room videoconferencing systems can cost up to $50,000. Figure 9.9 shows a room videoconferencing system.

Unlike a room system, a **desktop videoconferencing system** is designed for use by an individual. It uses a personal computer for processing and sending video and

FIGURE 9.9

A room or group videocon-
ferencing system

audio signals. A desktop system requires a small video camera connected to the computer. Usually the camera is mounted on top of the computer monitor, although a separate camera also may be used. Video images are displayed on computer monitors, not on separate monitors, as with room systems. The desktop system also needs a microphone and speaker (or headphone) connected to the computer. Finally, desktop systems need *desktop videoconferencing software* to provide the video and audio processing and transmission. Examples of desktop videoconferencing systems are Intel's ProShare system and PictureTel's Live system. Figure 9.10 shows a desktop videoconferencing system.

One difficulty with videoconferencing is that video signals require a large number of bits when transmitted over a digital channel. Because of this characteristic, special processing called *video compression* is used to code the video signal in such a way that

FIGURE 9.10

A desktop videoconferencing
system

Collaborative Applications for a Web Site at Reebok International

Reebok International has turned to collaboration software to transform its Web site into an interactive experience and keep its customers coming back. Along the way, it has reduced the hassles involved in updating the ever-changing contents of the site.

The Stoughton, Massachusetts-based sneaker and sports apparel manufacturer redesigned Reebok.com using Radnet's WebShare, a Web-based groupware system. Reebok is using the built-in e-mail hooks, discussion groups, bulletin boards, and e-mail postcards to make the site far more interactive than when it debuted in 1994, according to Marvin Chow, Reebok's director of interactive marketing.

The goal was to create a Web site that fostered a community of users, Chow says. "If you just try and use the Web to sell them products, something is missing," he says. Reebok.com gets about 800,000 hits per day, and the company has signed up about 25,000 site members.

Reebok offers several microsites, each devoted to a particular fitness category, where customers can get profiles of athletes and training tips from coaches. Visitors who fill out a profile form in which they list their favorite sports get customized workout tips, news updates about their sport, and other information on future visits. Site members can also send e-mail postcards to their favorite athletes.

"Delivering customized content via Web sites is still pretty rare but extremely valuable to companies like Reebok that sell to a mass market," says Mark Cecere, an analyst at Giga Information Group in Cambridge, Massachusetts. It is particularly key for Reebok, "which is probably marketing to a younger audience that is looking for a fair amount of glitz," Cecere says.

Although Chow envisions customers chatting online with the large stable of athletes who have endorsed Reebok's products, built-in groupware isn't the primary reason WebShare got the nod. Instead, it was the capability for Reebok employees to update the contents of a Web page—for example, modifying the address of a distributor or adding a recent interview with a sports figure—by using a Web browser. The workflow features in WebShare help Reebok manage the contents of its site, explains Jim Burke, president of Mindseye Technology, the Boston-based consultancy firm that designed the site. Reebok's marketers can update information and pass those changes to the appropriate people automatically, using a workflow engine. Previously, updates to the site had to be coordinated through Reebok's Internet service provider.

The kind of do-it-yourself updating that Reebok now enjoys is one of the main advantages of using a Web-based collaboration platform such as WebShare or Lotus Development's Domino as the basis of a Web site, Burke says. WebShare better fit Reebok's needs than Domino because Reebok wanted to integrate its site with existing databases, which house information on products and retail outlets. WebShare works in conjunction with an SQL database, whereas Domino uses its own proprietary object store.

Questions

1. What collaborative applications are available at the Reebok Web site?
2. What capability of the groupware used for the Web site is most important for Reebok employees?
3. How are the workflow features of the groupware used by Reebok?

Web Site
Reebok: www.reebok.com

Source: *Adapted from* Barb Cole-Gomolski, "Groupware Gives Lift to Reebok Site," *Computerworld*, January 19, 1998, p. 50.

it takes fewer bits for transmission. Then, *video decompression* is used to decode the signal after it is received for display on a monitor. Desktop videoconferencing systems often have a separate circuit board for compression and decompression purposes, although with some high-speed personal computers it is possible to do the required compression and decompression by using software in the main computer rather than with a separate board.

Desktop videoconferencing systems are much less expensive than room systems. Typical prices for the hardware and software that must be added to a personal computer for desktop videoconferencing are $1,500 to $3,000, although some systems are less than $1,000. Desktop videoconferencing systems have the disadvantage of being able to show only a small image, such as a single person. The video camera usually can be moved, however, to show someone else in the room or even to show an object. In addition, the video image is often jerky because of the slow speed at which most desktop systems operate. Still, as the price of these systems decreases, it is likely that their use will increase. Someday, all personal computers may be equipped with desktop videoconferencing capabilities.

Electronic Conferencing

Videoconferencing systems let members of a workgroup at different locations have audio and visual communication with each other. Combining document conferencing with videoconferencing creates a system with which workgroup members can also have document communication. This combination forms a workgroup application called **electronic conferencing**.

Some desktop videoconferencing software can be combined with separate whiteboard or application conferencing software to create electronic conferencing systems. More often, however, *electronic conferencing software*, which integrates whiteboard or application conferencing with desktop videoconferencing, is used. Such integrated software offers the most versatility in electronic conferencing.

An example of electronic conferencing software is InPerson from Silicon Graphics. Figure 9.11 shows an InPerson screen. With InPerson, users at any location can talk to and see each other while sharing images on an electronic whiteboard. Several people can confer at one time, with all their video images showing on each person's screen. Each participant in the conference has a different-shape cursor for marking the whiteboard so that all users know whose comments are appearing on the screen. Electronic conferencing software such as InPerson lets users talk to each other, see each other, view objects that are in front of the camera, hear recorded sound, view recorded video, and see and comment on text, graphics, and other images on the whiteboard.

Electronic conferencing provides *audio, visual, and document communication* between group members at the *same time* from *different places*. Because all forms of communication can be used, it is a very useful tool for group collaboration. It requires powerful computers and networks, however, to handle the software and data, thus making it an expensive form of group computing.

Although electronic conferencing is designed primarily for users to confer at the same time, some systems let users work at different times, storing information and then forwarding it to other users. For example, a user can work on text or a diagram on his or her whiteboard, record video images and sound, and then send everything to other users for later review and additional work. With this type of system, all participants in an electronic conference do not have to be available at the same time.

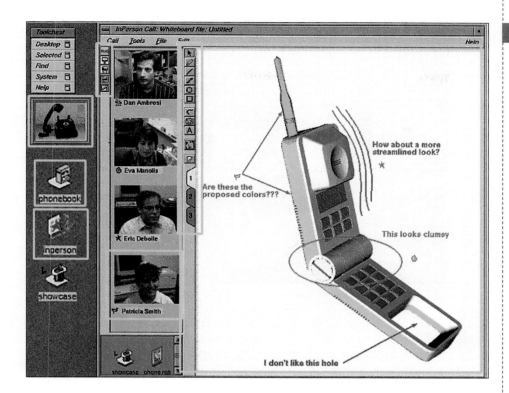

FIGURE 9.11

An electronic conferencing groupware screen ▲

Electronic Meeting Support

Members of a group work together in various ways, some informal and some formal. Informal collaboration includes everything from casual conversations to in-depth discussions. More formal collaboration often takes the form of a meeting, which we usually think of as a group of people discussing specific topics from an agenda and reaching conclusions about those topics. When computer systems are used to facilitate the meeting, the result is often called an **electronic meeting**. A workgroup application that is designed to support electronic meetings is called an **electronic meeting system** (**EMS**).

Electronic meeting systems come in two main forms: room systems and desktop systems. With a room electronic meeting system, a separate *electronic meeting room* is set up with special hardware and software (Figure 9.12). This type of room is also called a *decision room* because it is used for making group decisions.

An electronic meeting room includes individual workstations for the participants in the meeting. Each workstation has a personal computer that is connected by a network to the other personal computers in the room. In addition, there is a special workstation for the meeting leader or facilitator. This workstation has a personal computer connected to the network and to a large screen, which can be seen by everyone in the room. Finally, special *electronic meeting software* is used to link the workstations and to coordinate the electronic meeting. This software includes a variety of features, including a common whiteboard.

The electronic meeting begins when the leader presents the topic for discussion. Participants in the meeting can key in ideas and comments about the topic at their workstations. Anything entered by a participant is anonymous so that no one knows who made which comments. The comments are summarized by the meeting leader

FIGURE 9.12

▲ **An electronic meeting room**

and displayed on the large screen, without identifying who made each comment. For example, the topic of a meeting of the marketing group may be a new advertising campaign. Each participant can enter ideas for the campaign, and all participants see the ideas on the large screen. Each participant can enter comments on any idea, and again the comments are seen by all on the screen. The fact that the ideas and comments are anonymous means the meeting participants can concentrate on what people write, and not be influenced by who is writing. The meeting leader can summarize the ideas, and then an *electronic vote* can be taken to rank the ideas and decide what actions should be taken.

Room electronic meeting systems are designed for collaboration to take place at the same time and in the same place. Desktop electronic meeting systems, on the other hand, allow collaboration to take place at the same time among users located at different places. These systems provide capabilities similar to those of room systems, but for participants in a geographically dispersed meeting. Users of a desktop electronic meeting system use personal computers connected by a LAN or WAN. An example of electronic meeting software that can be used for both room systems and desktop systems is Ventana's GroupSystems.

Electronic meeting systems provide *document communication* between group members at the *same time* from the *same place* for room systems, or from *different places* for desktop systems. They go beyond basic document conferencing by providing special support needed in meetings. Room systems are very expensive, however, because of the cost of setting up the room. In addition, all group members must be available at the same time for an electronic meeting.

Electronic meeting systems often are used to help groups make decisions. In general, any workgroup application that facilitates group decision making is called a **group decision support system (GDSS)**. Chapter 11 has more to say about information system support for decision making in businesses.

Group Calendaring and Scheduling

When people in a workgroup need to collaborate at the same time, conflicts often arise because of differences in schedules. People work various hours and have numerous time commitments because of work and other responsibilities. Finding a time when everyone can get together for a conference or meeting, whether face-to-face or electronic, can be difficult. The problem is even more complex when members of a workgroup are located in different time zones.

Group calendaring and scheduling is a workgroup application that helps workgroup members coordinate their time. *Group calendaring and scheduling software* includes calendaring capabilities that let users keep individual calendars of appointments and meetings. The software also includes scheduling capabilities to set up meetings. With these capabilities, a user who needs to schedule a meeting indicates in the software who must attend the meeting, and then the software searches the individual calendars for times that would be acceptable to all participants. The software can then notify the individuals about the meeting.

This application allows a specific type of *document communication* between group members at *different times* and *different places*. The documents communicated deal with calendars and schedules. For the application to be effective, users must keep their individual calendars up-to-date. Examples of group calendaring and scheduling software are Open Text's OnTime, ON Technology's Meeting Maker, and CrossWind Technologies's Synchronize. Figure 9.13 shows a screen of this type of program.

Workflow Management

Group work sometimes involves sequences of tasks that are done by different members of a group. For example, in a marketing department, the design of a new catalog must go through steps such as writing advertising copy, selecting product photographs, laying out the pages in the catalog, and proofreading the pages. Group work may also require that documents be passed from one person in a group to another for processing. For example, in a human resource management department, a prospective employee's application must be passed to several people for review and

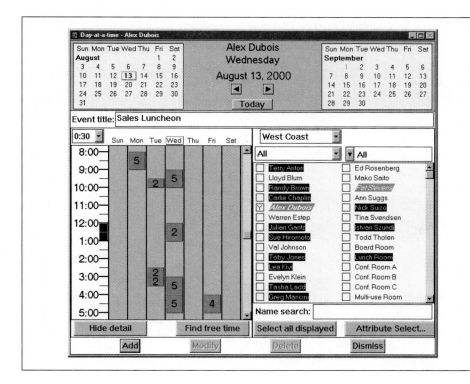

FIGURE 9.13

A group calendaring and scheduling groupware screen ▲

approval. In both examples, different people are involved in performing tasks or processing documents, with the work flowing from one person to the next. To make the work flow more smoothly, a workgroup application called **workflow management** can be used.

Workflow management software coordinates the tasks performed by different individuals in a workgroup and the flow of documents between people. Some workflow software is oriented toward tasks. These programs ensure that each task in the workflow is performed by the right person and in the right sequence. This type of software could be used to coordinate the work of the people designing the new catalog described in the previous paragraph. Other workflow software is oriented toward documents. This type of program ensures that the right documents flow from one person to the next, a process called *document routing*. The processing of the job application described in the previous paragraph could be coordinated by this type of software.

Workflow management allows *document communication* between group members working at *different times* and *different places*. The document communicated might indicate the tasks to be performed on some other document, or it might be the actual document being worked on. In any case, the software is used to coordinate the flow of work between group members. Users, however, must check the system regularly to see if they have received work. Examples of this type of software are FileNET's Visual WorkFlo and JetForm's InTempo. Figure 9.14 shows a screen of this type of program. Information sharing software such as Lotus Notes as well as other types of groupware also have workflow capabilities.

Summary of Workgroup Applications

Table 9.1 summarizes the main types of workgroup applications discussed in this section in terms of their time, place, and form characteristics. Some applications are designed for same-time collaboration, and some are designed for collaborating at different times. Most group applications are designed for different-place collaboration, although electronic meeting systems are used in the same place (room systems) or

FIGURE 9.14

A workflow management groupware screen

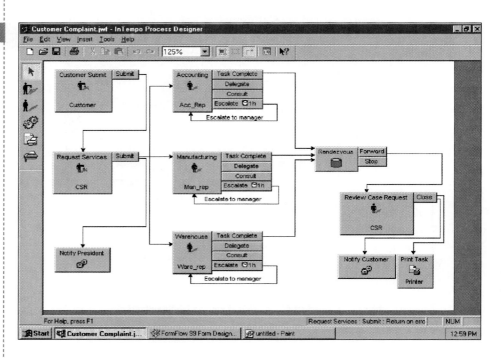

Table 9.1 Summary of types of workgroup applications	Time of collaboration		Place of collaboration		Form of communication			
Type of workgroup application	Same	Different	Same	Different	Document	Audio	Visual	Example of software
Electronic messaging		X		X	X			Novell GroupWise
Information sharing		X		X	X	X	X	Lotus Notes
Document conferencing	X	X*		X	X			Microsoft NetMeeting
Audioconferencing	X			X		X		VocalTec Internet Phone
Videoconferencing	X			X		X	X	Intel ProShare
Electronic conferencing	X	X*		X	X	X	X	Silicon Graphics Inperson
Electronic meeting support	X		X	X	X			Ventana GroupSystems
Group calendaring and scheduling		X		X	X			Open Text OnTime
Workflow management		X		X	X			FileNET Visual WorkFlo

*With store-and-forward capability.

different places (desktop systems). Document communication is the main form of communication used in group applications, although some applications provide audio and visual communication. As you can see from the table, many combinations of time, place, and form characteristics are found in workgroup applications.

Some groupware provides only the capability of a single type of workgroup application. For example, basic e-mail programs provide only simple electronic messaging features. Many programs, however, provide capabilities of several types of workgroup applications. For example, Lotus Notes, which provides information sharing, also has electronic messaging, workflow management, and group calendaring and scheduling features. Another example is Microsoft NetMeeting, which has videoconferencing, document conference (whiteboard and application conferencing), and chat capabilities. New programs that overlap different categories of workgroup applications or even create new categories are likely to be developed in the future.

Workgroup software often requires customization by the user to create a group application. Some software, such as Lotus Notes, is not ready to use until it has been customized. Programs such as these are really frameworks for developing group applications. Other programs, such as Microsoft NetMeeting, are ready to be used as soon as the software is installed. There are many shades between these extremes.

Workgroup applications are designed to be used on networks. LANs are used for collaboration among nearby group members, and WANs are used for collaboration among group members spread over considerable distances. International WANs are used when group members are located in different countries. Many groupware programs are designed to use the Internet or intranets, and in the future, most workgroup applications may use Internet technology for communication.

As you can see from the discussion in this section, many workgroup applications and many types of groupware exist. In the future, it is likely that there will be even more applications and software for workgroup collaboration. Personal computer software, such as word processing and spreadsheet software, will take on more groupware characteristics. In the future, most software used by individual users is likely to be some form of groupware

Office Automation

Workgroup applications are often used together with individual applications, such as word processing, and other applications to provide support for a variety of office functions in an organization. The use of these applications together is sometimes called **office automation**. People at all levels of an organization need office support to do their jobs. Secretarial and clerical personnel are not the only ones who do office work. Managers throughout an organization perform office functions to assist them in their managerial activities. Office automation is used in almost all areas of a business.

Historically, office tasks have been done mainly by secretarial personnel. For example, a manager would dictate a memo to a secretary, who would type, copy, mail, and file it. With the introduction of personal computers, managers and other personnel began doing more of their own office work. For example, a manager would use word processing to prepare a memo. Still, a secretary would copy, mail, and file the memo. The next step was to link the office personal computers to a LAN that included special hardware and software to perform office functions. The result was office automation.

Office automation may include individual applications such as word processing, desktop publishing, and presentation graphics. It may also include workgroup applications such as e-mail, information sharing, calendaring and scheduling, and workflow management. In addition, office automation may provide special applications such as

- *Voice processing.* With voice processing, voice messages can be recorded and stored in secondary storage. Then, a stored message can be sent to another person who has access to the system. The person can listen to the voice message by playing it back.
- *Facsimile.* A fax modem can be connected to the network so that users can fax documents from their personal computers.
- *Unified messaging.* With *unified messaging*, common forms of messaging—including e-mail, voice mail, paging, and fax—are combined into one system.
- *Electronic filing.* Instead of filing a paper copy of a document in order to save it, a copy can be filed electronically in secondary storage. The document can be retrieved in the future and printed if necessary.
- *Image processing.* In image processing, copies of graphs, charts, photographs, and other images can be stored in secondary storage. The images can be viewed by people who have access to the system, or they can be graphed or printed.
- *Document management.* Image processing and electronic filing are often combined to form a *document management* application that stores and keeps track of documents.

Office automation can support almost any function in an office. In the future, the distinction between individual applications, workgroup applications, and office automation applications may diminish, until they all converge into one common type of application.

The Virtual Work Environment

Workgroup applications make it possible for people to collaborate in many ways, at any time, and from any place. As a result, it is no longer necessary for everyone in an organization to be at a central office at the same time. People can work in remote offices, at home, in a hotel room, or even in a car. People can work during the day, in the evening, late at night, and in different time zones. The result is that the work environment no longer has to be a real place where everyone comes at the same time. Instead, for many types of work, the workplace can be a **virtual work environment** consisting of wherever and whenever people work.

Telecommuting

The first step toward a virtual work environment came when some employees of businesses began working at home, using personal computers with modems to communicate with their companies' computer systems. This way of working is called **telecommuting** because instead of commuting by car or public transit, the employees "commute" over the telephone. Initially, mainly computer professionals such as programmers telecommuted, but now many types of employees work this way.

Telecommuting offers several advantages to individuals and businesses. Individuals do not have the expense of commuting to work, and businesses do not have to provide office space. Employees can work whenever they find it convenient, and can watch after their children while they work. Businesses often find that telecommuting increases productivity and decreases absenteeism. Disadvantages of telecommuting for individuals include the expense of setting up a home office, although some companies provide the necessary computer systems and telephone lines. Another disadvantage for individuals is the lack of face-to-face contact with coworkers and the feeling of isolation. For businesses, disadvantages include difficulty supervising employee work. Despite the disadvantages, telecommuting continues to become more popular.

Virtual Offices

When a large number of employees in a group work at home or at other nontraditional locations, using computers to telecommute and to collaborate with others, the result is a **virtual office**. Employees may receive work through electronic messaging and information sharing systems. Workflow management systems may be used to coordinate the work. Electronic conferencing systems may be used to allow employees to collaborate on ideas. Employees can work wherever they happen to be; the office exists where the employees are.

Virtual offices compound the advantages and disadvantages of telecommuting because the number of people involved tends to be greater. In addition, more sophisticated software is needed so that electronic conferences and meetings can be held. Still, so many employees telecommute that virtual offices are becoming increasingly common.

Virtual Meetings

Using electronic conferencing and meeting systems allows people at different locations to confer and meet at the same time. Sometimes, however, an electronic meeting occurs in which not everyone is available simultaneously. For example, an electronic meeting may be held between research and development people to discuss a product design, but the participants do not communicate simultaneously. Instead, different people contribute ideas at different times. The meeting may last several days, until all involved have had a chance to comment and a conclusion is reached. This type of meeting is sometimes called a **virtual meeting**.

Virtual meetings are possible because of the store-and-forward capabilities of some groupware. One participant in a virtual meeting can enter his comments and forward them to another participant, who enters her comments and then forwards everything to the next participant. When the meeting participants are located around the world, the virtual meeting can take place during daytime working hours in many time zones. Such global virtual meetings are becoming increasingly common in international businesses.

Virtual Companies

Sometimes a company is set up in such a way that it does not have any regular place of business or an office. Each employee works at his or her home, or uses a rented space near where the employee lives. When an employee is traveling, he or she may work out of a hotel room, or from a client's or customer's office. Employees of the company communicate and collaborate using groupware. This type of company is sometimes called a **virtual company**. Virtual companies are especially common among new, startup businesses.

Workgroup applications and groupware make it possible for a business to operate in nontraditional ways. Telecommuting, virtual offices, virtual meetings, and virtual companies are the result of workgroup systems. In the future, you can expect even more businesses to have virtual work environments.

C H A P T E R   S U M M A R Y

1 Businesses use workgroup information systems to encourage group collaboration because collaborating with others is an essential part of business. The main difficulty with workgroup collaboration is that people often are not in the same place at the same time. Group collaboration is also difficult because groups often change. Workgroup information systems encourage group collaboration by making it easier for members of a workgroup to communicate, share information, and collaborate over distance and time. (pp. 276–277)

2 Group collaboration has several characteristics. One characteristic is the time when the collaboration takes place. People can collaborate at the same time or at different times. Another characteristic is the place where the collaboration takes place. People can work together at the same place or at different places. A third characteristic is the form the communication takes. Audio, visual, and document communication may be used between people. (pp. 277–279)

3 In addition to the time, place, and form characteristics of group collaboration, another characteristic

is the mechanisms used for the group work. Without computers, people may collaborate in face-to-face meetings, by telephone, by fax, by regular mail, and by other means. With networked computers, people can work together using software that allows users to communicate, share information, and collaborate in other ways. This type of software is called **groupware**. (p. 279)

4 The main types of workgroup applications are
- **Electronic messaging**. This application involves sending messages between members of a workgroup. (pp. 280–282)
- **Information sharing**. This application involves sharing information in different forms between members of a workgroup. (pp. 282–284)
- **Document conferencing**. This application involves simultaneous collaboration on a document by members of a workgroup. (pp. 284–286)
- **Audioconferencing**. This application involves voice communication between members of a workgroup, using **computer telephony**. (pp. 286–287)

- **Videoconferencing**. This application involves visual and audio communication between members of a workgroup over a network. (pp. 287–290)
- **Electronic conferencing**. This application involves a combination of videoconferencing and document conferencing. (p. 290)
- **Electronic meeting support**. This application provides computer support for **electronic meetings** of members of a workgroup. (pp. 291–292)
- **Group calendaring and scheduling**. This application involves coordinating calendars and scheduling meetings of members of a workgroup. (pp. 292–293)
- **Workflow management**. This application involves coordinating the flow of work between members of a workgroup. (pp. 293–294)

5 Workgroup applications can be distinguished by their time, place, and form characteristics. Some applications are designed for same-time collaboration and some for collaborating at different times. Most applications are designed for different-place collaboration, but electronic meeting systems can be used in the same or different places. Document communication is the most common form of communication used in workgroup applications,

although some applications provide audio and visual communication. Table 9.1 summarizes these characteristics for the main types of workgroup applications. (pp. 294–296)

6 **Office automation** is the use of various applications to support a variety of office functions at all levels of an organization. It may include individual applications as well as workgroup applications. In addition, it may provide other applications, such as voice processing, facsimile, unified messaging, electronic filing, image processing, and document management. (p. 296)

7 Workgroup applications make it possible for people to collaborate in many ways, at any time, and from any place. As a result, many people no longer always have to work at a central office, but, instead, can have a **virtual work environment** wherever and whenever they work. The first step toward a virtual work environment came with **telecommuting**. When a large number of employees work in nontraditional locations, and telecommute and collaborate using computers, the result is a **virtual office**. **Virtual meetings**, which can last several days, also take place in the virtual work environment. Some companies, called **virtual companies**, do not have a regular place of work or an office, but exist wherever employees are located. (pp. 297–298)

KEY TERMS

Application Conferencing (p. 286)
Audioconferencing (p. 287)
Chat (p. 287)
Computer Telephony (p. 287)
Desktop Videoconferencing System (p. 287)
Document (Data) Conferencing (p. 284)
Electronic Conferencing (p. 290)
Electronic Mail (E-Mail) (p. 280)
Electronic Meeting (p. 291)
Electronic Meeting System (EMS) (p. 291)

Electronic Messaging (p. 280)
Group Calendaring and Scheduling (p. 293)
Group (Collaborative) Computing (p. 279)
Group Decision Support System (GDSS) (p. 292)
Group Support System (GSS) (p. 276)
Groupware (p. 279)
Information Sharing (p. 282)
Instant Messaging (p. 281)
Office Automation (p. 296)

Room (Group) Videoconferencing System (p. 287)
Telecommuting (p. 297)
Videoconferencing (p. 287)
Virtual Company (p. 298)
Virtual Meeting (p. 298)
Virtual Office (p. 297)
Virtual Work Environment (p. 297)
Whiteboard Conferencing (p. 284)
Workflow Management (p. 294)

REVIEW QUESTIONS

1 Why is group collaboration difficult?

2 How do workgroup information systems encourage group collaboration?

3 What are some of the deficiencies in the use of telephones for group collaboration?

4 If you put a note on a bulletin board for other

workgroup members to read, what would be the characteristics of the group collaboration?

5 What is groupware?

6 What are the disadvantages of electronic messaging?

7 What is the difference between e-mail and chat?

8 What is the main advantage of information sharing?

9 What are two types of document conferencing?

10 What is the difference between using a telephone and using computer telephony for audio communication?

11 What forms of communication are used in videoconferencing?

12 How can videoconferencing save money for a business?

13 What workgroup applications are combined in electronic conferencing?

14 What capabilities other than document communication are provided by an electronic meeting system?

15 What workgroup application would be helpful to set up a meeting between five people with different schedules?

16 What workgroup application would be used to route a contract through the legal department of a business?

17 What applications are often used in office automation?

18 What is telecommuting?

19 What is a virtual meeting?

20 What is a virtual company?

D I S C U S S I O N   Q U E S T I O N S

1 Think of a situation in a business or an organization with which you are familiar where a workgroup information system would be useful. Describe how that system would work.

2 In the future, most software used by individuals will be groupware. Do you agree or disagree with this statement? Why?

3 Most of the workgroup applications discussed in this chapter involve document communication. Why do you think this is the case?

4 With electronic conferencing software at international locations in many time zones, it is possible to get 24 hours of work per day from knowledge workers without anyone having to work at night. Explain how this can happen.

5 What type of employee, in terms of job function and work habits, would be best suited for telecommuting?

6 What are the advantages and disadvantages of a virtual company?

E T H I C S   Q U E S T I O N S

1 Some businesses read their employees' e-mail, arguing that e-mail is like any other correspondence for the business produced by the employee. Other businesses do not read their employees' e-mail, saying that to do so would be a violation of the employee's right to privacy. If you were in a position in a company to make a decision on this issue, what would you do and why?

2 A new groupware system has been installed in the department you manage. Most of the employees

in the department are enthusiastic about using it, but two employees have refused to use it, saying that face-to-face meetings and telephone conversations are a better way to collaborate. To provide the most benefit to the department, however, everyone in the department must use the system. What options do you have for dealing with the two employees who do not use the system? What ethical issues are involved? What would you do and why?

PROBLEM-SOLVING PROJECTS

1 Find out how an organization or a business to which you have access uses groupware. What groupware does the organization use? For what does the organization use the groupware? How has the use of groupware affected group collaboration in the organization? Write a summary of your findings.

2 Using appropriate software, set up a table that includes information about groupware. Have columns for the name of the software, the vendor, and the types of applications in the software. Start with the software listed in Table 9.1. Remember that many of these programs include several applications. Use the Internet to research these programs and find out what types of applications are in each program. Then locate several more group programs and add information about them to your table.

3 Imagine that you have to organize a meeting of three high-ranking executives in a business. One of the executives works where you work, and the other two are located in two different parts of the country. The meeting will last three to four hours. You have to decide whether to recommend a face-to-face meeting, with two of the executives flying to the third executive's location, or a videoconference involving all three executives. Assume that your company does not own videoconferencing equipment and would have to use a commercial service that rents room videoconferencing facilities for this purpose. Making any other assumptions you need, determine the approximate costs of a face-to-face meeting and a videoconference meeting. Using spreadsheet software, prepare a spreadsheet with your cost figures. Write a memo summarizing your analysis and stating your conclusion.

4 Form a team of three or four students and think of a business you would like to start. After you have had your first face-to-face meeting, agree not to talk in person or over the telephone with your team members about your startup business. All communication should take place through e-mail and other workgroup software that you have available. Using these methods of communication, prepare a written plan for your new business. The plan should describe the product or service of the business, the potential market for the product or service, and how the business will be organized and financed. After you have completed the plan, write a summary of the advantages and disadvantages of using groupware alone for this type of activity.

INTERNET AND ELECTRONIC COMMERCE PROJECTS

1 Check the Web sites of the groupware vendors mentioned in this chapter, or of other groupware vendors. Some of these sites have demonstrations of the software. Find a site with a complete demonstration, and go through the demonstration until you understand the software and how it is used. Write a memo to your supervisor (real or hypothetical) evaluating the software. What is good about the program? What is bad about it? Would you recommend it for your organization? Why or why not?

2 Find the Web site of a groupware vendor that provides a demonstration of its software as in Internet and Electronic Commerce Project 1. Also find the Web site of a vendor of the same type of groupware that does not provide a demonstration. Thoroughly evaluate each site in terms of how effective it is in explaining the vendor's groupware. Does one type of site have a clear advantage over the other? Write a summary of your conclusions.

Saab

When Loren Morris joined Saab Cars USA in April 1996, he was amazed at the degree of automation Saab provided mobile field workers like himself. But he was just seeing the early stages of a sophisticated remote access strategy Saab plans to have.

As district service sales and parts manager at Saab, Morris is in charge of all Saab independent dealerships in a four-state district, encompassing Wisconsin, Minnesota, and the Dakotas. Morris's "official" office is in Minnesota, at his home in Marine on St. Croix. But he's on the road visiting dealers at least 75% of his working life. To complicate matters, Saab USA's national office is in Atlanta, but Morris reports to a supervisor at his district's regional office in San Francisco. To say remote access is important to Morris is perhaps the understatement of the year. "I couldn't live without it," he says.

Although Morris has spent his entire professional life in the automotive industry and the past 11 years on the road in various field sales and support positions, he'd never before worked for a company that didn't "drown [him] in paper." Morris's previous job had been with a leading Japanese automaker, but until he joined the Saab team, he had never been offered anything but barebones technology support. Most employers gave him only the most rudimentary dial-up capabilities.

So the laptop Saab provided, which gave him access to e-mail as well as the ability to send and receive files from any hotel room in his region, was a major step forward, as were the many incremental applications and accessories Saab has gradually put in his hands. For example, Morris was issued a CD-ROM player for his laptop that gave him instant access to Saab's massive parts and service library. "It takes me about three minutes to answer just about any question a dealer might have," he says. "Before, it would take hours or days to comb through all the paper manuals."

But today, Morris beams as he considers the technology that will be in his hands soon. Called the Intranet-Based Retailer Information System,

the technology will enable him to get immediate online snapshots of all sales, parts, warranty, and financial data that affects dealerships in his district. "Since JJ has taken over, we are moving ahead by quantum leaps," Morris says.

"JJ" is John Jacobs, Saab's retailer and field information manager. Based in Atlanta, Jacobs is responsible for all technology that supports Saab remote workers and affiliated retail dealers. Currently, that includes approximately 90 Saab employees and 250-plus retailers spread throughout three geographic regions, each of which comprises 24 districts.

Jacobs has several major remote access initiatives under way, which he hopes to have completed soon. The one he and Morris are most excited about is a complete overhaul of Saab's dealer information system. Currently, each dealer uses a DOS-based system that allows it to order cars and parts and submit warranty claims, but otherwise provides for very little interaction.

That's the bad news. The good news is that Jacobs was able to start with a clean slate. Using Lotus Notes, Domino, and Java, the new system will offer dealers a satellite link between local Windows systems that run Netscape and the legacy AS/400 systems in Atlanta. Web pages will be distributed via the satellite link, providing dealers with up-to-the-minute data on everything from current sales to inventory status, parts availability, and warranty claims.

"We looked at frame relay, but it was three times the cost of satellite," Jacobs says of his choice of communications technology. Now, instead of dialing in to the Saab modem bank in Atlanta, each dealer will have a continuous online, high-bandwidth connection to a plethora of rich information systems.

"The beautiful thing is that the system refreshes itself continuously," Morris says. For example, the dealer doesn't have to wait for the next update issued via paper reports. Also, the system immediately verifies items such as part number, price, and availability. If the dealer has made a mistake in entering a part number or if a part is out of stock, the system catches it on the spot.

Morris, as district manager, will be able to log in to the Saab intranet using the satellite link from any dealer he visits or through phone lines. In either case, he will be able to get to all internal Saab intranet applications as well as to dealership information for his area.

Morris says he believes the technology will make him and his dealers much more productive. But Jacobs says the real benefits will be reaped in more strategic ways. When you advance from merely moving data back and forth to actually sharing what you know, "you acquire not only information, but knowledge. Then, if you're lucky, you might even get to wisdom," he says.

Questions

1 Why is remote access important for a Saab district manager?

2 What applications does a Saab district manager currently use?

3 What will the Intranet-Based Retailer Information System do?

4 Why is this case an example of a virtual office?

5 Why does sharing what is known— as opposed to just moving data back and forth—allow people to acquire knowledge, and not just information?

Web Site
Saab: www.saab.com

Source: *Adapted from* Alice LaPlante, "When the Road Is Increasingly Well-Traveled," *Computerworld*, July 20, 1998, p. 54.

Business
OPERATIONS

After completing this chapter, you should be able to

1 Give an example of a computer information system that increases the efficiency of business operations.

2 Explain the purpose and structure of transaction processing systems.

3 Describe the functions of transaction processing systems.

4 Describe several ways of controlling transaction processing systems.

5 Explain the difference between batch processing and on-line transaction processing.

6 Summarize the characteristics of basic business information systems.

7 List several examples of accounting, financial, marketing, manufacturing, and human resource information systems.

8 Explain what an enterprise resource planning system is.

CHAPTER OUTLINE

Increasing Business Operations Efficiency
Transaction Processing Systems
Basic Business Information Systems
Other Business Information Systems
Enterprise Resource Planning Systems

The basic operations of a business are those activities that help the business function on a daily basis. These activities provide goods and services for the business's customers; ensure payment for those goods and services; keep track of the business's products; acquire goods and services needed by the business; pay the business's obligations; and report on the business's profitability. Information systems support business operations by processing data related to these activities and by providing information to assist in their management.

This chapter examines the structure and functions of information systems for operational support of a business. First, the chapter explains how computer information systems can increase the efficiency of business operations. Then it presents the main type of information system, the *transaction processing system*, used to support business operations. Next, the chapter examines examples of basic information systems used in business operations. Then it describes other examples of information systems in different areas of business. Finally, the chapter discusses integrated systems that link together the functions of many separate systems.

Increasing Business Operations Efficiency

Computer information systems increase the efficiency of business operations. Efficiency has to do with how much a system produces relative to the resources, such as people and money, used by the system. For example, consider a system for processing customer orders in a business (Figure 10.1). Such a system would receive a customer's request for products, check to see if the desired products were available, check the customer's credit, and, if all checks were satisfactory, produce a sales order describing what is to be sold to the customer.

Customer order processing could be handled entirely manually. A salesperson could write the customer request by hand, a warehouse clerk could check the shelves for the desired product's availability, another clerk could look in a credit file or call the customer's bank to check the customer's credit record, and, finally, a typist could type the sales order. This manual approach would require considerable personnel resources to produce the sales order. It would also require a great deal of time to complete the order, with the possible result that the customer might look elsewhere for the product.

Now consider a computer information system for customer order processing. In such a system the customer's request would be keyed into a computer by a salesperson or, in some cases, by the customer. The system would look up the product availability in an inventory file and the customer's credit rating in a customer file. The system would then produce the sales order without further keying being required. The

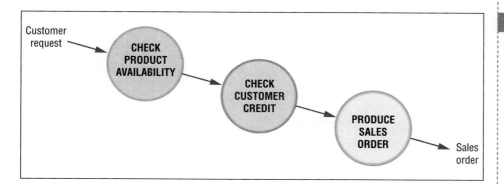

FIGURE 10.1

Customer order processing

computer information system would be more efficient than the manual system because it would produce the sales order with fewer resources and in less time.

This example illustrates the idea of increasing the efficiency of business operations. Many information systems that support business operations have a similar benefit for the business. To be competitive today, most businesses require some form of computer information system for their basic operations.

Transaction Processing Systems

The main type of information system used for operational support in a business is the **transaction processing system** (**TPS**). This type of system processes data about **transactions**, which are events that occur that affect the business in some way. For example, the sale of a product is a transaction; it affects the business by reducing inventory and increasing revenue. An example of a transaction processing system is an inventory control system. This system processes data about transactions that affect a business's inventory.

Transaction Processing System Structure

The general purpose of a transaction processing system is threefold: (1) to keep records about the state of the organization; (2) to process transactions that affect these records; and (3) to produce outputs that report on transactions that have occurred, that report on the state of the organization, and that cause other transactions to occur.

An inventory control system keeps a file of records about the stock of goods that a business has on hand—the inventory—which is one aspect of the state of the business. When items are shipped or received, the state of the business is affected, and the inventory control system makes changes about the inventory in the stored records. Periodically, the system prints a list of the shipments and receipts—that is, the transactions—that have occurred. It also prints a report giving the quantity on hand for each item in inventory, which is a characteristic of the state of the business. Finally, when inventory is low, the system produces output that causes more inventory to be ordered, which is another type of business transaction.

Figure 10.2 shows the general structure of transaction processing systems. The users of a transaction processing system typically are personnel who deal with business transactions, such as salespeople, accounting clerks, and inventory personnel. Input, which includes data about transactions, comes from users and other transaction processing systems. Output, which includes screen displays and printed reports, goes to users and to other systems. The stored data in the transaction processing system consists of files or a database with data about the state of the organization. The transaction processing system software is application software that accepts the input

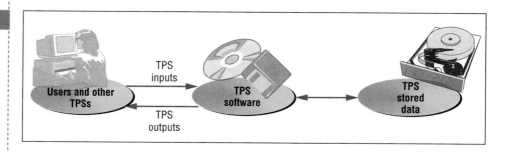

data about transactions, processes it, makes changes in the stored data, and produces the outputs.

Transaction processing systems exist in all areas of an organization. Examples include systems for entering customer orders, billing customers, keeping track of inventory, and other basic systems, as discussed later in this chapter. Transaction processing systems exist in all types of businesses. As one example, a system in a bank for keeping track of customer deposits and withdrawals is a transaction processing system. Transaction processing systems are used for the daily data processing in practically all organizations. As you will see in Chapter 11, they form the foundation for other information systems.

Transaction Processing System Functions

Transaction processing systems, as well as other types of information systems, perform four main functions to accomplish their purposes. As noted in Chapter 1, these are the input function, the storage function, the processing function, and the output function. The *input function* accepts data from outside the system so that the data can be processed in the system. The *storage function* stores and retrieves data in the system so that it is available for processing. The *processing function* manipulates the input and stored data within the system. The *output function* makes the results of processing available outside the system. Next we discuss the characteristics of these functions in transaction processing systems. Figure 10.3 summarizes these functions.

The Input Function.   Before transaction data can be brought into a transaction processing system, it must be acquired from its source—a step called *data capture*. Often, the data is captured by a person who writes the data on a piece of paper or on a form called a **source document**. Once the data is captured, it must be put into the system—a step called *data entry*. Usually, the data is entered by a person who keys in the data on a keyboard.

An athletic shoe store's inventory control system illustrates data capture and entry. For one part of this system, data about the receipt of merchandise from a supplier must be captured and entered into the system. The data capture occurs when a stock clerk prepares a receiving report, which is a source document indicating that certain items have been received (Figure 10.4a). This document is then sent to a data-

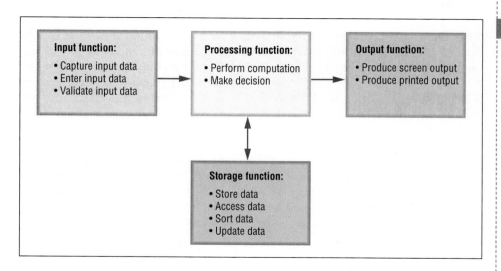

FIGURE 10.3

The functions of a transaction processing system

FIGURE 10.4

▲ **Data capture and entry**

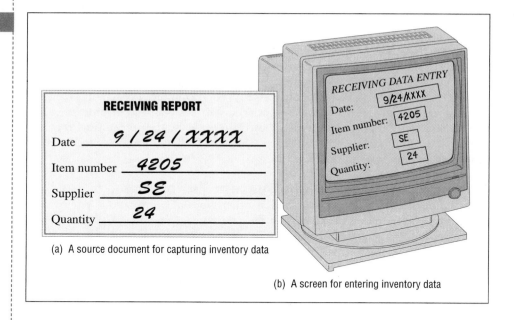

RECEIVING REPORT

Date ___9 / 24 / XXXX___

Item number ___4205___

Supplier ___SE___

Quantity ___24___

(a) A source document for capturing inventory data

RECEIVING DATA ENTRY

Date: 9/24/XXXX

Item number: 4205

Supplier: SE

Quantity: 24

(b) A screen for entering inventory data

entry person, who keys the data into a computer, thus entering the data into the system (Figure 10.4b).

As data is entered into the system, a program must check it for errors, which is called **data validation**. Incorrect data must not be allowed to go beyond the data-entry step. Data validation involves checking input data for all possible errors. Every value entered should be checked. Values that are supposed to be numbers, such as item numbers in the inventory control system, should be checked to be sure they contain only digits. Names, such as customer names, should be checked to be sure they contain only letters. Codes, such as codes indicating the type of payment, should be checked to be sure they are correct. Quantities, such as the quantity sold, should be checked to be sure they are in appropriate ranges. All possible data validation checks should be done to ensure that the data is correct. If the data passes all validation checks, then the system accepts the data and passes it on for processing; otherwise, the system rejects the data.

The Output Function.   Output from a transaction processing system can be displayed on a screen or printed on paper. Much transaction processing system output is in the form of **reports**, which are lists of output data on a screen or on paper. Several types of reports are commonly produced by a transaction processing system. A **detail report** lists detailed information about the results of processing and may contain totals for some of the data. For example, Figure 10.5a shows a detail report produced by the athletic shoe store's inventory control system that lists inventory transactions for a particular item that have occurred in the last week and gives the total sold and received for the week. A **summary report** contains totals that summarize groups of data but has no detail data. Figure 10.5b shows a summary report that gives the total inventory value for each line of products stocked by the shoe store. An **exception report** contains data that is an exception to some rule or standard. Figure 10.5c shows a report about items that have a quantity on hand below a certain level and thus should be reordered. Other items with sufficient quantity are not listed in

FIGURE 10.5

Types of reports ▲

INVENTORY TRANSACTIONS
Item number 4205
Week of 9/19/XXXX

DATE	QUANTITY SOLD	QUANTITY RECEIVED
9/19	14	
9/20	16	
9/21	21	120
9/22	18	
9/23	12	
9/24	35	24
9/25	16	
TOTAL	132	144

(a) A detail report

**INVENTORY VALUE
BY PRODUCT LINE**
Week of 9/30/XXXX

PRODUCT LINE	TOTAL VALUE
Running shoes	$24,368.00
Tennis shoes	10,852.00
Sport shoes	8,147.50
Clothing	12,255.75
Accessories	3,604.00
TOTAL	$59,227.25

(b) A summary report

INVENTORY REORDER REPORT

ITEM NUMBER	ITEM DESCRIPTION	QUANTITY ON HAND
1681	RUNNING SHOE	11
1945	TENNIS SHOE	8
3347	TRACK SHOE	3
4205	SOCKS	20
5172	SWEATSHIRT	15

(c) An exception report

this report. This last report would cause other transactions to occur, namely the ordering of more stock.

The Storage Function.   Data in a transaction processing system is stored in data files and databases. Two types of stored data are commonly found in transaction processing systems: master data and transaction data. **Master data** is the main data used by the system. For example, an inventory control system for an athletic shoe store could have an inventory master file with one record for each item in inventory. Each record would contain fields for the item number, item description, unit cost, unit price, and quantity on hand. Master data usually is permanent data that remains with the system as long as the system is in use.

Transaction data is data about transactions that have occurred. For example, in an inventory control system for an athletic shoe store, an inventory transaction file could be used to store data about additions to and removals from stock. Each record would contain fields for the item number, the quantity added to stock, and the quantity removed from stock. Transaction data usually remains with the system only until the transactions are processed. The transaction data is then replaced with other transaction data for new transactions.

Master and transaction data may be stored in data files or databases. The only difference is the organization of the data; the concept of master data and transaction data is the same no matter how the data is stored. In either case, the data files or databases would form the stored data component of the system.

Before a transaction processing system can do anything with stored data it must *create* the file or database containing the data. That is, it must *store* data in the file or database. Thus, the athletic shoe store must create the inventory master file before it can be used in the inventory control system. To create this file, someone would enter the data for each item currently in inventory, and the system would store the data in the inventory file. Usually, files or databases with master data are created only once. Transaction data, however, is stored in a file or database whenever transactions need to be processed.

After the file or database is created, the transaction processing system can retrieve data from the file or database, a process called **accessing** the data. The data that is retrieved is processed to produce output such as a report or, sometimes, to create a new file or database. For the inventory control system, the inventory transaction file would have to be accessed to produce the inventory transactions report shown in Figure 10.5a; the inventory master file would have to be accessed to produce the inventory value report in Figure 10.5b and the inventory reorder report in Figure 10.5c.

Sometimes, before a transaction processing system can access stored data, it must arrange the data in a different way. The process of arranging data into a particular order is called **sorting**. In the inventory control system, sorting would be needed if the records in the inventory master file were not in the order in which a user wanted to see them. For example, the user might want the inventory reorder report to give the items in alphabetical order by their descriptions. If the records were not in this order to begin with, they would have to be sorted into the proper order before the report could be prepared.

The data put into a file or database when it is created will become out of date over time. Therefore, the transaction processing system will have to modify the data periodically, a process called **updating** the data. Updating may involve *changing* existing data, *adding* new data, or *deleting* old data. In the athletic shoe store's inventory control system, whenever stock is added to or removed from inventory, the quantity on hand for each item affected must be changed in the inventory master file. If a new item—one not currently stocked by the store—is added to the inventory, the number, name, unit cost, unit price, and quantity on hand for that item must be added to the inventory master file. Finally, if an old item is dropped from the inventory, all data about that item must be deleted from the inventory master file.

Updating often is performed by using transaction data to make changes in master data. Thus, the inventory transaction file's data can be used to update the quantity on hand in the inventory master file. After the master file has been updated, it can be processed to produce various reports.

The Processing Function. Processing involves manipulating data within the system. In a sense, all the functions already described involve data processing in a transaction processing system. One function that involves just data processing and does not involve any of the other functions is *computation*, which means doing calculations with data. Before a transaction processing system can produce output, the system typically must perform some computations. Input data and stored data are used in the computations to produce the required results that go into the output.

Another processing function is *decision making*. Often, other functions in a transaction processing system depend on a condition that needs to be checked during processing. When a system checks a condition, it makes a decision that causes processing to continue in different ways depending on the result of the decision.

Computation and decision making are needed in the athletic shoe store's inventory control system. For example, to produce the total value in the inventory value report shown in Figure 10.5b, arithmetic computations must be performed with the inventory data. To determine whether an item needs to be reordered so that the item's information can be printed in the inventory reorder report shown in Figure 10.5c, a decision must be made by the system.

Controlling Transaction Processing Systems

Transaction processing systems must have procedures to ensure the completeness of the data processing and to minimize the chance of errors. In general, these procedures are called **controls**. Many types of controls are used in information systems. We discuss several types here, but others are also used.

Control Totals. All data may not be processed in a transaction processing system for various reasons. A source document may be misplaced or a data-entry person may forget to key some data. Sometimes hardware fails or a program has an error that causes data to be lost. An information system should have controls to check for these types of errors.

One way that a transaction processing system checks that all data is processed is to use **control totals**. A control total is a number that is computed when data enters a system and then computed again after the system has processed the data. For example, in the athletic shoe store's inventory control system discussed in the previous section, assume that data from the receiving report (Figure 10.4a) is used to update the inventory master file. Each day a batch of receiving reports is sent in by the stock clerk for entry into the system. The person who receives the receiving reports would count the number of reports sent in. This count would be the control total. As the data was entered and processed, the system would produce a similar count or control total. Then the two control totals would be compared. If the counts were not equal, then not all data was entered and processed by the system. The cause of the error would have to be located and corrected.

This example uses just one type of control total—a count of the number of documents. Other types of control totals are also used, including totals of data on documents. Sometimes, several control totals are calculated and checked in the system to be sure all data has been processed.

Audit Trails.   An **audit trail** is a way of tracing the effect of data through a system. A good audit trail is one in which someone can start with the output and go back through the system to the source document, or vice versa. For example, in the athletic shoe store's inventory control system, one source document is the receiving report prepared by a stock clerk. If one output is a list of all stock received during a month, an audit trail would provide a way of tracing back to the actual receiving report for any shipment listed in the output, or of starting with a receiving report and tracing through the system to a shipment listed in the output. This audit trail would make it possible to randomly check that the system worked correctly, and thus that data was properly processed by the system.

Backup and Recovery Procedures.   Computer systems sometimes fail. (We say the system "crashes.") The failure may be because of a malfunction in the hardware or software, or because of some outside factor such as an electric power interruption. When a failure occurs, data stored in the computer can be damaged or lost. In such a circumstance, there must be a way of restoring the data.

The main way of ensuring against loss of stored data is to use a **backup procedure**. Backing up means that the data is copied periodically to another storage media. For example, in the inventory control system, the inventory master file, which is stored on magnetic disk, would be copied to another disk or to a magnetic tape. How often the data should be backed up depends on how frequently the data is changed. The more often changes are made in the data, the more often it should be backed up. Usually data files and databases are backed up every day or every week, although sometimes backup occurs more or less frequently.

The backup copy of the stored data should be stored away from the computer system in case of fire or other physical disaster. If a system failure occurs, the backup copy can be used to re-create the original stored data by means of a **recovery procedure**. Without adequate backup and recovery procedures, there is a great risk of losing data permanently.

Processing Data in Transaction Processing Systems

Data in a transaction processing system can be processed by using two basic approaches: batch processing and on-line transaction processing. In **batch processing**, the data for all transactions to be processed is prepared in a form that is understandable to the computer before the actual processing begins. Then, the batch of data is processed by the computer, and the resulting output is received in a batch. An example of batch processing is the preparation of the weekly payroll for an organization. At the end of the week, each employee turns in a time sheet. The data from each sheet is keyed into the computer and stored in a payroll file. When all the data is ready, it is processed in a batch by the payroll program to produce the paychecks.

With **on-line transaction processing (OLTP)**, often just called *on-line processing*, a person uses a keyboard and screen or other I/O devices connected to the computer at the time the processing is done. Each set of data for a transaction is entered directly into the computer, where it is processed, and the output is received before the next input data is supplied. Airline reservation processing is an example of this approach. When a customer requests a ticket for a particular flight, the reservation clerk enters the data directly into the computer by using a keyboard. The reservation system checks the data in a flight database and determines whether a seat is available on the requested flight. The output goes immediately to the screen so that the customer will know whether the reservation is confirmed.

A transaction processing system may use batch processing, on-line processing, or, most commonly, both. For example, the athletic shoe store's inventory control system, discussed in the previous sections, uses both batch and on-line processing. Batch processing is used to prepare the reports. The data in the inventory file is processed in a batch when each report is printed. On-line processing is used by a salesperson to check inventory availability. The salesperson enters a request for information at a keyboard and receives the response on a screen.

Sometimes you hear the term **interactive processing** instead of on-line processing. Interactive processing means the user interacts with the computer system while the processing takes place, as opposed to batch processing, in which there is no user interaction. For interactive processing, the user must be *on-line*, that is, connected to the computer at the time, so that input can be entered directly into the computer and the output can be received from the computer. Either term can be used, although on-line is heard more frequently than interactive. Sometimes data for batch processing is prepared *off-line*—that is, with the use of equipment not connected to the computer— and then transferred to the computer. For example, data may be keyed onto a magnetic disk with the use of special data preparation equipment. The data on the disk can then be processed in a batch by the computer.

Occasionally, people use the term **real-time processing** instead of on-line processing. *Real-time* means the processing is done immediately after the input is received. This description is not quite accurate for on-line processing. If there are many users of an on-line system, processing may not begin for some time after the input is received. The amount of time, which can be several seconds to several minutes, depends on how many users there are and the type of computer being used. In real-time processing, a delay is not acceptable. Real-time processing is used when an immediate response is essential. An example is a system that monitors a process in a chemical plant. The system must respond immediately—that is, in real time—to any significant change in temperature, pressure, and other critical factors in the chemical process.

Basic Business Information Systems

Chapter 2 introduces eight basic information processing activities carried out in businesses:

- Entering customer orders
- Billing customers
- Collecting customer payments
- Keeping track of inventory
- Purchasing stock and materials
- Paying bills
- Paying employees
- Reporting financial information

These activities are needed to support the operations of most businesses. They are often performed by computer information systems, which include hardware, soft-

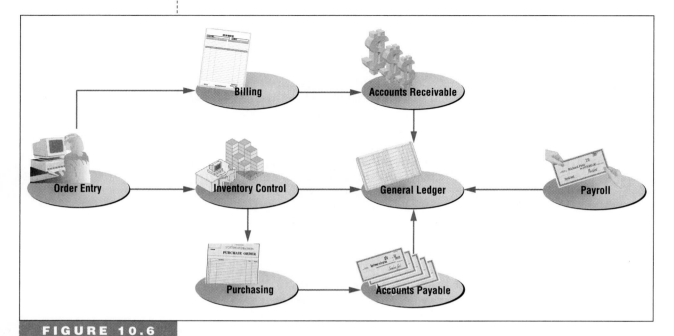

▲ Basic business information systems

ware, stored data, personnel, and procedure components. The systems perform the input, storage, processing, and output functions needed to accomplish these information processing activities. This section describes a computer information system for each of these activities.

Figure 10.6 shows the relationships between the systems described in this section. In the figure, an arrow connects two systems if information flows from one to the other. These systems are mainly transaction processing systems, and the flow of information from one system to another often causes another transaction to take place.

Each of the systems described here processes one or more types of master data. Sometimes the same master data is used by several systems, and sometimes the data is used by only one system. Transaction data is also used by many of these systems. These systems may process master and transaction data stored in data files or in a database.

Each system involves several computer programs and manual procedures performed over a period of time. Each system also includes numerous controls to check for errors and has backup and recovery procedures. Some systems may involve batch processing, some may involve on-line processing, and some involve both types of processing. These details would be needed for a complete explanation of a system.

Although each system is described separately, it is common for several systems to be combined into one, larger system. For example, order entry, billing, and inventory control often form one integrated information system. It is important to understand each system separately, but it is also important to remember that various combinations of systems are common.

Order Entry System

The purpose of an **order entry system** is to accept customer orders for goods or services and to prepare the orders in a form that can be used by the business. The functions of this system are summarized in Figure 10.7. The input to the system is the cus-

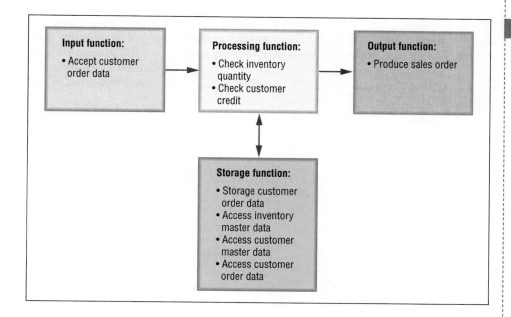

FIGURE 10.7

The order entry system

tomer order data, which could be received on an order entry form or over the telephone. The output is the sales order.

In some businesses, customer orders are entered into the system as they are received, and in others, orders are collected and entered periodically in batches. Orders may also be received electronically using electronic data interchange (EDI). As an order is entered, the data in it is validated by a program. Invalid orders are displayed on a screen for manual correction and reentry. Valid orders, which form the transaction data for the system, are stored by the system. This customer order data contains one record for each item ordered by a customer, with fields for the customer number, item number, and quantity ordered.

After the customer order data is stored, the orders can be processed. The following questions must be answered:

1 Does the business have sufficient inventory to fill the order?

2 Should the business extend credit to this customer or require that the customer pay in advance?

To answer the first question, another program accesses the inventory master data and decides whether the quantity on hand for the item ordered is adequate. There is one record in the inventory master data for each item stocked by the business, with fields for the item number, item description, and quantity on hand. The answer to the second question is found by accessing the customer master data and deciding if the customer's credit rating is acceptable. There is one record in this customer master data for each customer, with fields for the customer number, customer name, shipping address, and credit rating.

If sufficient inventory is on hand and the customer's credit rating is acceptable, a sales order, which is the output from the system, is produced by the program. This document contains the customer number, name, and shipping address from the customer master data; the item and the description from the inventory master data; and the quantity ordered from the customer order data.

This system involves two programs and a manual procedure. One program is needed for data entry, data validation, and storage of the customer order data. Another program is needed to access the inventory master data, the customer master data, and the customer order data; and to produce the sales order. These programs are executed in sequence. A manual procedure is needed to correct errors in the customer order.

The data-entry program involves on-line processing. The program interacts with the person entering the data to allow errors to be corrected. The sales order preparation program involves batch processing. The stored customer order data is processed in a batch, and the sales orders are printed in a batch.

The customer order data is transaction data used only by this system. It is kept for a time for backup purposes but deleted eventually. The inventory master and customer master data are permanent, stored data that are used repeatedly.

Billing System

The purpose of a **billing system** is to prepare the customer's bill or invoice. Figure 10.8 summarizes the functions of this system. The sales order data from the order entry system is the input to the billing system. The output is the invoice, which contains the information about how much the customer owes for the items ordered.

To prepare the invoice from the sales order data, two types of master data are needed. The first is the customer master data, which is also used in the order entry system. For the billing system, records in this data must have fields for the customer number, customer name, and billing address so that this information can be printed on the invoice. The second type is the inventory master data, which is also used in the order entry system. For the billing system, the records in this data must have fields for the item number, item description, and unit price. The system looks up the unit price of each item shipped in this data and computes the order amount by multiplying the quantity shipped by the unit price. This information is printed on the invoice, along with the item description. The system also computes the total amount for all items purchased and prints this amount on the invoice.

With computerized order entry and billing systems, data can be passed electronically from one system to the other. Data from the sales order, including the customer number, item number, and quantity ordered, could be put in a sales order file by the

▲ The billing system

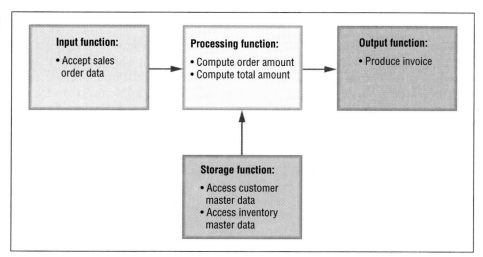

order entry system. The billing system could then use this transaction file along with the customer master and inventory master data, to prepare the invoice.

Accounts Receivable System

The purpose of an **accounts receivable system** is to keep track of money owed to the business by its customers and to record customer payments for invoices. In addition, the system reminds customers of overdue invoices, sends summaries of invoice charges and payments to customers, and provides reports of accounts receivable to other functions of the business.

The functions of the accounts receivable system are summarized in Figure 10.9. The inputs to the system are the invoice data and data about the customer payment. The outputs include statements that summarize the invoice charges and payments made recently and give the current balance due for each customer; overdue notices that are sent to the customers who have not paid their invoices; and an accounts receivable report summarizing charges and payments for the month. This report contains the total invoice charges and total customer payments for all customers.

To produce the outputs, two types of stored data are used. One is accounts receivable data consisting of one record for each customer, with fields for the customer number, previous balance due, invoice date, invoice amount, payment date, and payment amount. The previous balance due is the balance due at the beginning of the current month. The invoice date and amount fields are repeated for each invoice for the current month. The payment date and amount fields are also repeated for each payment made during the current month. The other stored data that is used is the customer master data, which is also used in the order entry and billing systems. For the accounts receivable system, the records of this data need fields for the customer number, customer name, and billing address.

Processing in the accounts receivable system involves several activities. Data from new invoices and customer payments are used to update the accounts receivable data. Each month, statements are printed from this data. The new balance due on each statement is computed by adding the customer's previous balance due and the

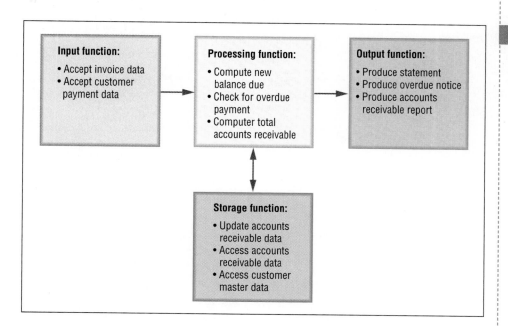

FIGURE 10.9

The accounts receivable system ▲

total of the current month's invoices, and subtracting the total of the current month's payments. The customer name and address on the statements come from the customer master data. Overdue notices are printed for customers who have not paid their bills recently. Also each month, the total accounts receivable is computed and printed in the accounts receivable report, along with other accounts receivable data.

With computerized billing and accounts receivable systems, data can be passed electronically from one system to the other. Data about each invoice, including the customer number, the invoice date, and the invoice amount, could be put in an invoice file by the billing system. Then the accounts receivable system could use this file to update the accounts receivable data.

Inventory Control System

The purpose of an **inventory control system** is to keep track of the business's inventory, to indicate when inventory should be reordered, and to compute the value of the inventory. Figure 10.10 summarizes the functions of this system. The inputs to the system are the sales order data and the receiving notice data giving the quantity of items received from suppliers. The outputs from the system are the inventory reorder report, which lists the items that should be reordered, and the inventory value report, which gives the value of the items in stock.

The stored data needed in this system is the inventory master data, which is also used in the order entry and billing systems. For the inventory control system, the fields needed in each record of this data are the item number, item description, unit cost, quantity on hand, reorder point, and reorder quantity. These fields are used to produce the output in the reports. The unit cost, which is the cost per item, and the quantity on hand are multiplied to compute the inventory value for the inventory value report. The reorder point is the quantity below which the business does not want the inventory to fall. If the quantity on hand is less than or equal to the reorder point, the item should be reordered, and this fact is printed in the inventory reorder

FIGURE 10.10

▲ **The inventory control system**

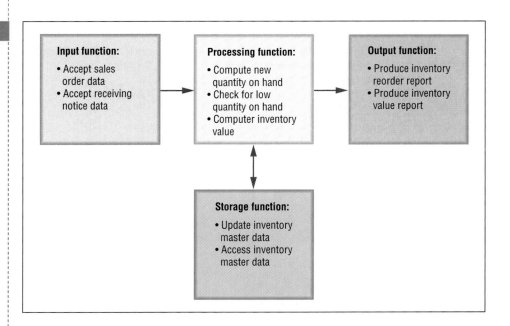

Input function:
- Accept sales order data
- Accept receiving notice data

Processing function:
- Compute new quantity on hand
- Check for low quantity on hand
- Computer inventory value

Output function:
- Produce inventory reorder report
- Produce inventory value report

Storage function:
- Update inventory master data
- Access inventory master data

Warehouse Management at Owens & Minor

BOOK
M A R K

Owens & Minor, a $3.05 billion wholesale distributor of medical and surgical supplies, already runs a tight ship, according to Wall Street analysts. It keeps its costs down, does a good job of keeping track of inventory, and doesn't lose its merchandise, they say.

But thanks to a new $5 million warehouse management system it recently rolled out to its 39 U.S. warehouses, the Glen Allen, Virginia based company is about to become even more efficient.

Owens & Minor, the nation's leading medical supplies distributor, says it expects the new warehouse management system from Cambar Software in Charleston, South Carolina, to help improve its inventory accuracy from about 89% today to a percentage in the mid-90s, said Pat Caine, project director for warehouse management systems at Owens & Minor.

"There's not a point in time [from] when the product arrives at our door that we don't know where it is," Caine says. The anticipated increases in inventory accuracy should reduce the amount of inventory the company carries, thereby reducing costs even further. Caine says the company's projection is that the $5 million investment will pay for itself in two years, at a cost of roughly $128,500 per warehouse location.

The new system is already paying dividends. Since the company finished installing it, its warehouse staffs have been able to pick (sort and itemize) through 10% more products per hour than they could prior to the new system, says Craig Smith, Owens & Minor's president and chief operating officer. This increase "should reduce our overtime and temporary help" costs, says Smith. The first quantifiable cost savings should become evident by mid-December, he adds.

The new system gives Owens & Minor a greater variety of pick methods to choose from when putting together a customer's shipment. As a result, it lets the company's warehouse workers fill orders for several customers at the same time, reducing the number of trips they need to make to gather products in the warehouse, says Caine.

The deployment of a more efficient warehouse management system is a major benefit for a company like Owens & Minor, which ships 90% of its syringes, sutures, and 140,000 other products to hospitals. As hospital profits are squeezed by managed care companies, profit margins for suppliers like Owens & Minor become razor thin. Net income as a percentage of sales last year was a meager 1% at the company, said Bob Willoughby, a health care analyst at Credit Suisse First Boston Corp. in New York.

Owens & Minor took an arguably circuitous route to selecting and installing the Cambar system. The company had been using a mainframe-based warehousing system from Cambar since the mid-1980s. But by the early 1990s, the system was becoming expensive to maintain and difficult to customize to meet the needs of its decentralized operations, says Caine.

The company wanted to select a distributed warehouse system that could be tweaked to meet specific workflow requirements at each site. For example, a warehouse in Dallas might have to separate orders for 75% of its hospital customers, and another warehouse in San Francisco might ship 75% of those orders in bulk.

The company's year 2000 review team—pushing to replace the mainframe system that represented one quarter of the company's computing environment—recommended a client/server system from Cambar because of its flexibility in both technical and business functions.

Questions

1. What is the principal benefit that Owens & Minor expects to receive from its new warehouse management system?

2. What benefits has Owens & Minor already received from its warehouse management system?

3. Why did Owens & Minor select a client/server system for its warehouse management system?

Web Site
Owens & Minor:
www.owens-minor.com

Source: *Adapted from* Thomas Hoffman, "Warehouse Overhaul to Fatten Supplier's Slim Margins," *Computerworld*, October 25, 1999, p. 41.

report. The reorder quantity for the item is also printed in the report and indicates the quantity of the item that should be ordered.

Processing in the inventory control system first involves updating the quantity on hand in the inventory master data from data in the sales orders and receiving notices. The quantity shipped of an item from each sales order is subtracted from the item's quantity on hand, and the quantity received for the item from each receiving notice is added to determine the new quantity on hand. Once a month, or perhaps more often, the inventory reorder report is prepared from the inventory master data, listing all items that should be reordered. Also once a month, the inventory value report is prepared.

With computerized shipping, receiving, and inventory control, updating of the inventory master data can be done by shipping and receiving personnel. As items are shipped, the quantity removed from inventory is entered into the system and subtracted from the quantity on hand at that time. Similarly, as items are received, the quantity added to the inventory is entered and added to the quantity on hand.

Purchasing System

The purpose of a **purchasing system** is to determine the best suppliers (also called vendors) from which to purchase items and to prepare purchase orders, which indicate to the supplier what items are wanted. Figure 10.11 shows the functions of the purchasing system. The input is the data from the inventory reorder report indicating what items are to be reordered and what quantity of each should be ordered. The output is the purchase order, which lists the items the business wants to purchase.

FIGURE 10.11

▲ **The purchasing system**

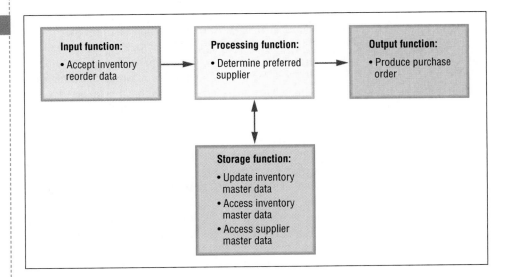

To produce the purchase order, the preferred supplier for the item to be purchased must be determined. The inventory master data, which is used in several other systems, provides this information. The fields in the records of this data that are needed for the purchasing system are the item number, item description, and preferred supplier number. Supplier master data is also needed. There is one record in this data for each supplier, with fields for the supplier number, supplier name, and supplier address. In addition, there may be fields that give information about the supplier's sales policy and performance, such as the payment terms, the average delivery time, the quality of items sold, and so forth.

The purchasing system analyzes the supplier's sales policy and performance information to determine the best supplier for each item. The selection of the best supplier may be based on sales terms, delivery time, or other factors that the business considers important. The preferred supplier number is updated in the inventory master data, based on the analysis of the suppliers. When purchase orders are to be prepared, the preferred supplier number is determined from the inventory master data, and then that supplier's name and address are found in the supplier master data. This information is printed on the purchase order, along with the item number, item description, and quantity ordered.

With computerized inventory control and purchasing systems, reordering data can be passed electronically from one system to another. The data about what items are to be reordered and the quantity to order could be put in an inventory reorder file by the inventory control system. Then the purchasing system could use this file, along with the inventory master and supplier master data, to prepare the purchase orders.

Accounts Payable System

The purpose of an **accounts payable system** is to keep track of money owed by the business for purchases, to pay suppliers for the items purchased, and to provide reports of accounts payable to other functions of the business. The functions of the accounts payable system are summarized in Figure 10.12. The inputs to the system are the purchase order data indicating what items were ordered, the invoice data from the supplier showing what items the supplier shipped and the charges for the items, and

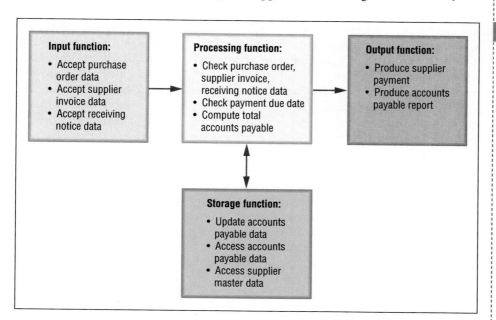

Input function:
- Accept purchase order data
- Accept supplier invoice data
- Accept receiving notice data

Processing function:
- Check purchase order, supplier invoice, receiving notice data
- Check payment due date
- Compute total accounts payable

Output function:
- Produce supplier payment
- Produce accounts payable report

Storage function:
- Update accounts payable data
- Access accounts payable data
- Access supplier master data

FIGURE 10.12

The accounts payable system ▲

the receiving notice data indicating what items were received by the business. The outputs from the system include the supplier payment, which is a check sent to the supplier, and the accounts payable report summarizing the supplier charges and payments for the month. This report contains the total charges and payments for all suppliers.

To produce the outputs, two types of stored data are used. One is accounts payable data consisting of one record for each supplier, with fields for the supplier number, supplier invoice date, supplier invoice amount, supplier payment due date, supplier payment date, and supplier payment amount. All fields in this data, except the supplier number, are repeated for each supplier invoice. The other stored data used is the supplier master data, which is also used in the purchasing system. For the accounts payable system, the fields needed in the records of this data are the supplier number, supplier name, and supplier address.

Processing in the accounts payable system includes several activities. The purchase order is compared with the supplier invoice to determine whether the items ordered were shipped by the supplier. The supplier invoice is compared with the receiving notice to see whether the items shipped were received. If the supplier invoice correctly states what items were ordered and received, then the data from the invoice is used to update the accounts payable data. Included in the updated data is the due date for the payment of the invoice sent by the supplier. Frequently, perhaps every day, the accounts payable data is checked to see whether any invoice payments are due soon. When a payment is almost due, a check is prepared. The supplier master data is used to find the supplier's name and address. As the checks are prepared, the accounts payable data is updated to indicate that the invoice has been paid. Once a month, the total accounts payable is computed from the accounts payable data, and the accounts payable report is printed.

With computerized purchasing and accounts payable, data can be passed electronically from one system to the other. Data about each purchase order, such as the supplier number, item number, and quantity ordered, could be put in a purchase order file by the purchasing system. Then the accounts payable system could use this file to update the accounts payable data.

Payroll System

The purpose of a **payroll system** is to prepare paychecks for employees and to provide reports of payroll. Figure 10.13 summarizes the functions of the payroll system. The input to the system is the employee work report data, which indicates how much the employee has worked. For an employee who is paid on an hourly basis, this report is a time sheet that shows how many hours the employee has worked each day. For an employee who is paid a fixed salary, the report indicates whether the employee was present for all work days, and, if absent, for what reason. The outputs from the system include the paycheck, giving the amount the employee is paid; and the payroll report, listing for each employee the gross pay, the amount deducted for taxes and for other reasons, and the net pay. The report also gives the total of the gross pay, deductions, and net pay for all employees.

To produce the outputs, the system first stores employee work data from the employee work reports. For hourly employees, there is one record in this data for each employee who worked, with fields for the employee number and hours worked. For salaried employees, each record indicates whether the employee has worked the entire pay period or only part of the pay period. Also needed by the system is employee master data. This data has one record for each employee, with fields for the employee number, employee name, employee address, and pay rate or salary.

Payroll processing involves using the employee work data and the employee master data to calculate the payroll data for each employee. If the employee is paid on an

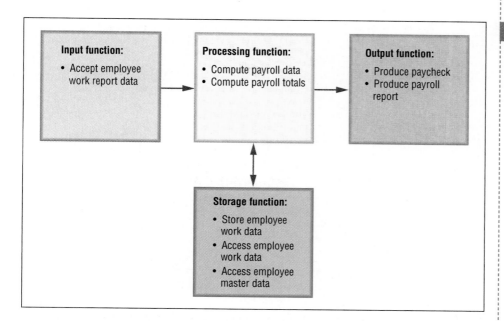

FIGURE 10.13

The payroll system

hourly basis, the hours worked from the employee work data is multiplied by the pay rate from the employee master data to determine the gross pay. For a salaried employee, the gross pay is the employee's salary from the employee master data, unless he or she worked less than a full pay period. Next, the deductions and net pay are calculated and the paycheck is printed with the employee name, address, and net pay. Finally, the total gross pay, deductions, and net pay are calculated for all employees, and the payroll report is printed.

General Ledger System

The last basic business information system is a **general ledger system**, the purpose of which is to maintain the business's financial accounts and to prepare financial statements. The functions of the general ledger system are summarized in Figure 10.14. The inputs are data on revenues, expenses, assets, and liabilities. We have discussed several reports that contain such data, including the accounts receivable report, the inventory value report, the accounts payable report, and the payroll report. The outputs from the general ledger system are financial statements such as the income statement and the balance sheet.

To produce the financial statements, the general ledger system uses stored general ledger data. There is one record in this data for each financial account the business maintains. Thus, there is one record each for sales revenue, for salary expense, for inventory, and for accounts payable, among others. Each record has fields for the account number, account description, and account balance.

Processing in the general ledger system first involves updating the general ledger data with data about current revenues and expenses, and changes in assets and liabilities. After all accounts have been updated, the general ledger data is used in various financial computations, and the financial statements are printed.

If other systems are computerized, data can be passed electronically to the general ledger system. For example, the accounts receivable data could be put in a file by the accounts receivable system, and payroll expense data could be put in a file by the payroll system. These and other files could be used to update the general ledger data.

FIGURE 10.14

▲ **The general ledger system**

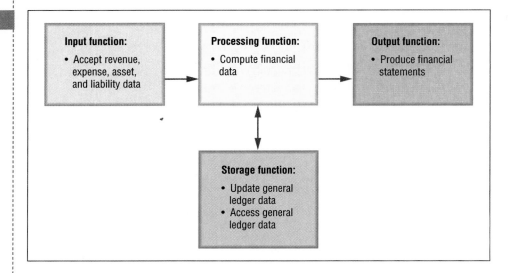

Other Business Information Systems

The eight information systems discussed in the previous section are the basic ones found in many businesses. Other systems, however, are used. Here we describe systems often found in the main functions of a business.

Accounting Information Systems

Recall from Chapter 2 that the accounting function of a business is responsible for recording and reporting financial information about the business. **Accounting information systems** support the accounting function. Of the information systems discussed previously, billing, accounts receivable, accounts payable, payroll, and general ledger are usually considered to be accounting information systems. In some businesses, order entry, inventory control, and purchasing are also thought of as accounting information systems. Several other common accounting information systems are

- *Fixed asset accounting.* The purpose of this system is to account for business assets such as buildings, land, and equipment.
- *Budgeting.* This system prepares projections of revenues and expenses, and compares actual figures with the projected ones.
- *Tax accounting.* The purpose of this system is to prepare business tax reports and to pay taxes.

Financial Information Systems

The finance function of a business is responsible for obtaining money needed by the business and for planning the use of that money. **Financial information systems** provide the necessary support for the finance function. None of the systems discussed previously are considered financial information systems, although accounting and financial information systems often are grouped together. Some common financial information systems are

- *Cash management.* This system balances the needs of the business for cash with the expected cash availability.
- *Capital expenditure analysis.* The purpose of this system is to analyze the effect on

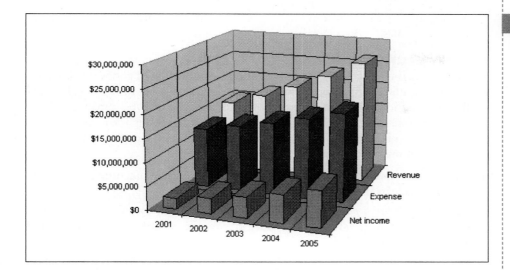

FIGURE 10.15

Financial forecasting

the business of large expenditures such as those associated with building a new factory or replacing major equipment.

- *Financial forecasting*. This system forecasts financial information, such as revenues and expenses, for the future (Figure 10.15).
- *Portfolio management*. This system analyzes alternative investment strategies for the business's cash and keeps track of investments.
- *Credit analysis*. Businesses that extend credit to customers need to determine which customers should receive credit, which is the purpose of this system.

Marketing Information Systems

The marketing function of a business is responsible for selling goods and services. **Marketing information systems** assist in the marketing function. Of the systems discussed previously, order entry usually is considered a marketing information system because customer orders are procured by salespeople working in the marketing function. Billing and inventory control are also sometimes considered marketing information systems. Other common marketing information systems are

- *Sales analysis*. This system determines which products are selling well and poorly, which sales regions have the best and worst sales, which salespeople are selling the most and the least, and so forth.
- *Sales forecasting*. The purpose of this system is to project future sales.
- *Marketing research*. This system analyzes information gathered about consumers and products in order to identify trends.
- *Direct mail advertising*. This system prepares advertising pieces for mailing directly to potential customers.
- *Electronic commerce*. This system uses the World Wide Web to advertise and sell a business's goods and services. (Chapter 12 covers electronic commerce systems in detail.)
- *Sales force automation*. This system, which is also called *customer relationship management (CRM)*, provides information, usually through notebook computers that can

be connected to a central computer, to help sales representatives keep track of customers and sales.

Manufacturing Information Systems

The manufacturing function is concerned with the production of goods that the business sells. **Manufacturing information systems** provide services to support the manufacturing function. Inventory control is often considered to be a manufacturing information system because manufacturing produces the goods for inventory. Purchasing may also be a manufacturing information system in some businesses. Some other common manufacturing information systems are

- *Production scheduling*. This system schedules the use of manufacturing facilities to produce products most efficiently.

- *Material requirements planning* (*MRP*). The purpose of this system is to determine what parts and materials will be needed during the manufacturing process and when they will be needed.

- *Manufacturing resource planning* (*MRP II*). This system is called MRP II to distinguish it from materials requirements planning. It combines MRP with production scheduling and other functions in a comprehensive manufacturing information system.

- *Just-in-time* (*JIT*) *inventory management*. This system is a form of inventory control in which parts and materials are scheduled to arrive from suppliers just before they are needed in the manufacturing process.

- *Computer-aided design* (*CAD*). This system involves using computers to assist in the design of products to be manufactured.

- *Computer-aided manufacturing* (*CAM*). This system involves using computers to control machines in the manufacturing process.

- *Robotics*. This system uses computer-controlled robots in the manufacturing process (Figure 10.16).

- *Computer-integrated manufacturing* (*CIM*). This system combines many of the other manufacturing systems into a single system.

- *Supply-chain management*. This system manages the movement of materials and products from suppliers through manufacturing and distribution to retailers.

FIGURE 10.16

▲ **Robotics**

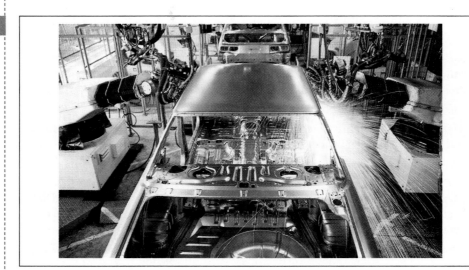

Supply Chain Management at Miller SQA

BOOK
M A R K

If they could get order information any faster, the suppliers for Miller SQA, an office furniture maker, wouldn't know what to do with it.

Miller SQA cut its order-to-ship cycle in half—to five days—by using an Internet-based supply chain application that tells suppliers exactly what materials and parts are needed and precisely when.

The technology allows Miller SQA to send the data instantaneously, says Jim Von Ins, director of information systems for Miller SQA, a young business unit of the 76-year-old furniture firm Herman Miller. Miller SQA's suppliers said they only need a few snapshots daily, so Miller SQA refreshes the information three times per day and alerts users to changes by color-coding new information.

A couple of years ago, Miller SQA's two-week cycle time was already half the industry average. The Internet application, called SupplyNet, cut the cycle time in half again. "We take the order, build, and ship within five days," says Von Ins.

Once an order is entered into the Miller SQA system, the data about the needed screws, hanger frames, laminates, cloth, electrical parts, wooden cores, and other parts are made available to the 80 suppliers that account for 95% of Miller SQA's buying. These daily demand statements make quarterly forecast meetings with Miller SQA nearly irrelevant now, says Geno Plitt, executive vice president of Bay View Industries. Bay View, with $25 million in annual revenue, is a supplier of work surfaces and table tops to Miller SQA and other furniture makers. Says Plitt, "The only thing that matters is the daily demand."

Short-term demand forecasting, especially for components, is the most common form of supply chain management activity being done over the Internet, according to Sandy McCullough, an analyst at Forrester Research. Order management is a more visible Web-based activity than supply management, but behind a successful customer order management application is most likely some kind of supply chain application to reconcile supply and demand, McCullough says.

For 15 years, Miller SQA (SQA stands for "simple, quick, and affordable") has been on a quest to speed up delivery of its office furniture products to corporate customers. The business unit was founded to offer a less costly product line that could be delivered more quickly than the parent company's products, which include custom furnishings. By offering fewer choices in styles and colors, and by capitalizing on technology, Miller SQA grew quickly. Today it accounts for 18% of the parent's $1.8 billion in annual revenue. Miller SQA's customer base includes small, emerging companies looking for quality furnishing at a good price, and fast-growing larger companies that need speedy delivery.

SupplyNet uses a combination of Lotus Domino, Progress Software's Web Speed (which takes data from the ERP system and publishes it as HTML), and Symix ERP from Symix Computer Systems. Von Ins says Miller SQA found no single tool that would offer the supply chain management application it needed. SupplyNet, which incorporates user IDs and passwords for access control, delivers the information to suppliers in files they can channel into their ERP systems with a minimum of keystrokes. Using browsers, the suppliers can see only their slices of the information.

Bay View, for example, built an interface that pumps the order information directly into its system, thus eliminating the time-consuming rekeying of data. Plitt says it saves him from hiring at least two staffers who would do nothing but spend hours rekeying data and, perhaps more importantly, reduces the error rate to zero. Bay View has used EDI systems for years, but the Internet offers far more flexibility, Plitt says.

Questions

1. What is the principal benefit of SupplyNet for Miller SQA?

327

BOOK

M A R K

2. What data does SupplyNet provide to Miller SQA's suppliers after an order is entered?

3. How does SupplyNet provide data for Miller SQA's suppliers' ERP systems?

Web Site
Miller SQA: www.sqa.net

Source: *Adapted from* Bill Roberts, "Live-wire Supply Line," *Internet World*, September 15, 1999, p. 60.

Human Resource Information Systems

The human resource management function is responsible for hiring, training, compensating, and terminating employees. **Human resource information systems (HRISs)** support this function. The only system discussed previously that is sometimes considered to be a human resource information system is payroll. Some common human resource information systems are

- *Performance appraisal.* This system analyzes employee performance on the job.
- *Skills inventory.* This system keeps track of employee skills and matches employees with specific jobs.
- *Benefits administration.* This system manages employee fringe benefit packages.
- *Job applicant tracking.* This system keeps track of applicants for jobs with the business.

Enterprise Resource Planning Systems

Each of the information systems described so far in this chapter deals with a single activity or function of a business. Although several of these systems, such as order entry, billing, and inventory control, may be combined in one system, often the systems are used separately, possibly with data passed between them. For many businesses this approach is acceptable, but increasingly businesses find it advantageous to closely link many systems and to have common data shared among them. These systems integrate many applications to support different aspects of the business.

An **enterprise resource planning (ERP)** system is an information system that supports several areas of a business by combining a number of applications with a single database that stores all the data used by the applications. ERP systems originally evolved from manufacturing resource planning systems. To these systems were added applications in other functions of the business, such as accounting and finance. Over time, the applications found in ERP systems have increased, until today they include many of the applications essential for the operation of a business. Figure 10.17 shows some of the applications found in ERP systems.

ERP systems are designed for applications that encompass a large portion of the business, hence the word *enterprise* in the name. Although they include features that help with planning for enterprise resources, such as materials, money, and people, they have many transaction processing features.

Software for ERP systems is available from a number of companies, including SAP, Oracle, Baan, and PeopleSoft. ERP software, however, is very expensive to purchase. In addition, the software requires considerable effort to set up for an organiza-

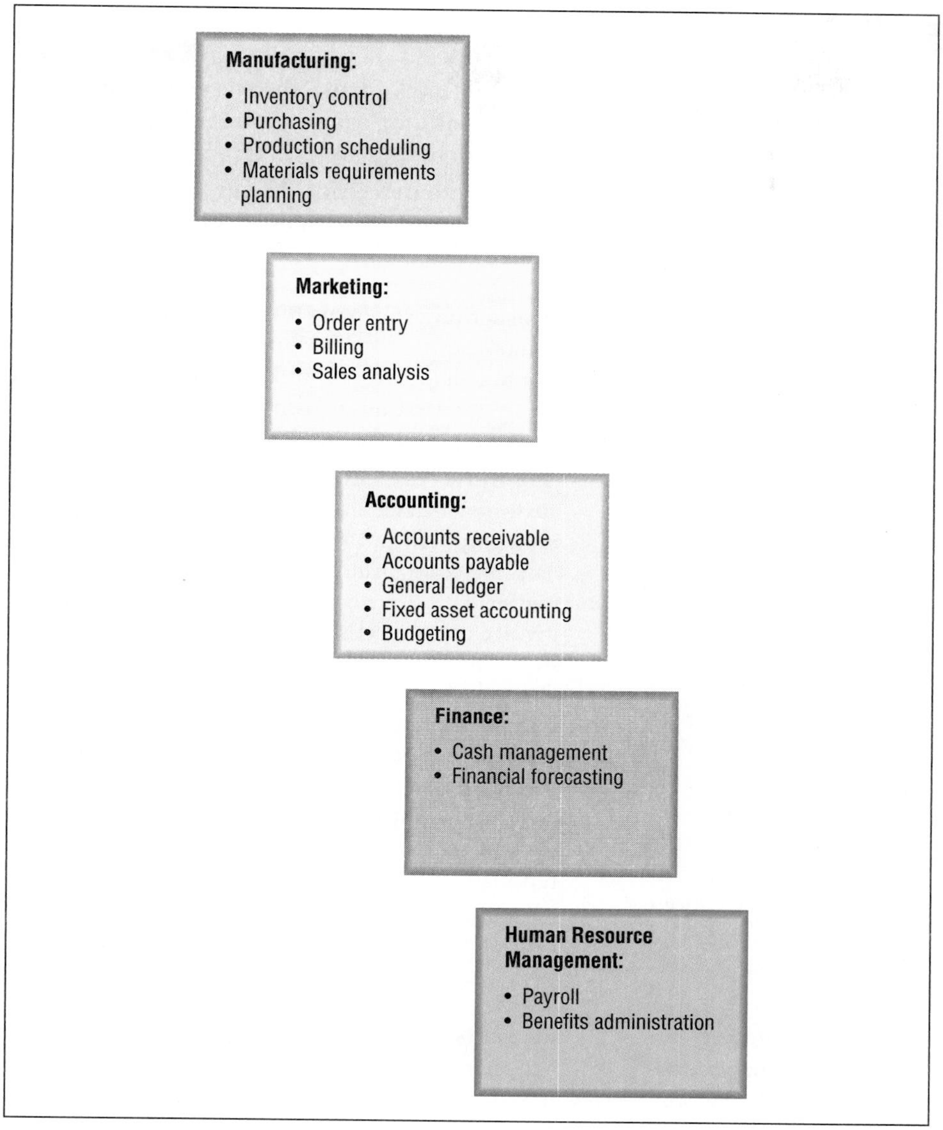

FIGURE 10.17

Enteprise resource planning
applications ▲

Manufacturing:

- Inventory control
- Purchasing
- Production scheduling
- Materials requirements
  planning

Marketing:

- Order entry
- Billing
- Sales analysis

Accounting:

- Accounts receivable
- Accounts payable
- General ledger
- Fixed asset accounting
- Budgeting

Finance:

- Cash management
- Financial forecasting

**Human Resource
Management:**

- Payroll
- Benefits administration

tion. Businesses have spent millions and even hundreds of millions of dollars to con-figure their ERP software for their specific needs. Often the business has to change the way it functions to fit the way the software works.

In addition to the cost of software, businesses may need to upgrade their hard-ware to set up an ERP system. ERP systems typically use a client/server approach with sophisticated servers. Businesses often have to acquire new computer and net-work hardware in order to implement ERP systems.

Even though ERP systems can be expensive, the fact that they integrate many common applications into one system makes them desirable for many businesses. You can expect to see an increasing use of ERP systems in all types of businesses in the future.

CHAPTER SUMMARY

1 An example of a computer information system that increases the efficiency of business operations is customer order processing. When done manually, customer orders are written out by hand, shelves are checked for product availability, a credit file is checked for the customer's credit record, and a sales order is typed. With a computer information system, customer orders are keyed into the system, product availability and customer credit rating are looked up by the system, and the sales order is produced by the system. The computer information system is more efficient than the manual system because it produces the sales order with fewer resources and in less time. (pp. 305–306)

2 The purpose of a **transaction processing system (TPS)** is to keep records about the state of the organization, to process **transactions**, which are events that have occurred that affect the organization, and to produce output that reports on transactions, reports on the state of the organization, and causes other transactions to occur. Inputs to a transaction processing system come from users and other transaction processing systems. Outputs go to users and other transaction processing systems. Transaction processing system files and databases store data about the state of the organization. Transaction processing system software accepts data about transactions, processes it, makes changes in stored data, and produces the outputs. (pp. 306–307)

3 Transaction processing systems perform input, output, storage, and processing functions. Input functions include capturing data on a **source document**, entering the input data into the system, and checking input data for errors, a process called **data validation**. Output functions include producing screen or paper **reports,** such as **detail reports, summary reports**, and **exception reports**. Storage functions include storing data in files and databases, **accessing** stored data, **sorting** stored data, and **updating** stored data. Processing functions involve the manipulation of data, including computation and decision making. (pp. 307–311)

4 Transaction processing systems use procedures, called **controls**, to ensure the completeness of the data processing and to minimize the chance of errors. One type of control is the use of a **control total**, which is a number used to check for errors in the processing. Another control is an **audit trail**, which is a way of tracing the effect of data through

a system. **Backup** and **recovery procedures** are ways of ensuring against loss of data in case of a malfunction of the system. (pp. 311–312)

5 Two ways of processing data in a transaction processing system are **batch processing**, in which data for all transactions to be processed is brought together and processed in a group, and **on-line transaction processing** (**OLTP**), in which a person enters the data for a transaction into a system, where it is processed and the output is received before the next input is entered. (pp. 312–313)

6 An **order entry system** accepts customer order data and accesses stored inventory master data and customer master data to produce sales orders. A **billing system** produces invoices from sales order data and from customer master data and inventory master data. An **accounts receivable system** uses invoice data and customer payment data to update stored accounts receivable data, and it accesses this data, along with a customer master data, to produce statements, overdue notices, and accounts receivable reports. An **inventory control system** accepts customer order data and receiving notice data, updates inventory master data, and produces inventory reorder reports and inventory value reports from inventory master data. A **purchasing system** updates inventory master data with the preferred supplier, and then uses this data and stored supplier master data, along with inventory reorder data, to produce purchase orders. An **accounts payable system** accepts purchase order, supplier invoice, and receiving notice data; updates stored accounts payable data; and then accesses this data and supplier master data to produce supplier payments and accounts payable reports. A **payroll system** produces paychecks and payroll reports from employee work data and stored employee master data. A **general ledger system** uses revenue, expense, asset, and liability data to update stored general ledger data, and then accesses this data to produce financial statements. (pp. 314–323)

7 Examples of **accounting information systems** include billing, accounts receivable, accounts payable, payroll, general ledger, fixed asset accounting, budgeting, and tax accounting. Examples of **financial information systems** include cash management, capital expenditure analysis, financial forecasting, and credit analysis. Some

examples of **marketing information systems** are sales analysis, sales forecasting, marketing research, direct mail advertising, electronic commerce, and sales force automation. **Manufacturing information systems** include production scheduling, material requirements planning, manufacturing resource planning, just-in-time inventory management, computer-integrated manufacturing, and supply-chain management. Examples of **human**

resource information systems (**HRISs**) are performance appraisal, skills inventory, benefits administration, and job applicant tracking. (pp. 324–328)

8 An **enterprise resource planning** (**ERP**) system is an information system that supports several areas of a business by combining a number of applications with a single database that stores all the data used by the applications. (pp. 328–329)

KEY TERMS

Accessing (p. 310)
Accounting Information System (p. 324)
Accounts Payable System (p. 321)
Accounts Receivable System (p. 317)
Audit Trail (p. 312)
Backup Procedure (p. 312)
Batch Processing (p. 312)
Billing System (p. 316)
Control (p. 311)
Control Total (p. 311)
Data Validation (p. 308)
Detail Report (p. 308)
Enterprise Resource Planning (ERP) (p. 328)

Exception Report (p. 308)
Financial Information System (p. 324)
General Ledger System (p. 323)
Human Resource Information System (HRIS) (p. 328)
Interactive Processing (p. 313)
Inventory Control System (p. 318)
Manufacturing Information System (p. 326)
Marketing Information System (p. 325)
Master Data (p. 310)
On-Line Transaction Processing (OLTP) (p. 312)

Order Entry System (p. 314)
Payroll System (p. 322)
Purchasing System (p. 320)
Real-Time Processing (p. 313)
Recovery Procedure (p. 312)
Report (p. 308)
Sorting (p. 310)
Source Document (p. 307)
Summary Report (p. 308)
Transaction (p. 306)
Transaction Data (p. 310)
Transaction Processing System (TPS) (p. 306)
Updating (p. 310)

REVIEW QUESTIONS

1 How can a computer information system increase the efficiency of business operations?

2 What is a transaction?

3 What is the purpose of a transaction processing system?

4 Where do the inputs for a transaction processing system come from?

5 What do the outputs of a transaction processing system do?

6 Why is data validation important?

7 What is an exception report?

8 What is the difference between master data and transaction data?

9 What three things can be done when a file or database is updated?

10 What is a control total?

11 Explain the difference between batch processing and on-line transaction processing.

12 What is the input to an order entry system?

13 For what system(s) is the sales order an input, and for what system(s) is it an output?

14 What is the output from a billing system?

15 What is the purpose of an accounts receivable system?

16 What updating is done in an inventory control system?

17 What is the output from a purchasing system?

18 What stored data is used in an accounts payable system?

19 What computation is done in a payroll system?

20 What is the purpose of a general ledger system?

21 What are examples of an accounting information system, a financial information system, a marketing information system, a manufacturing information system, and a human resource information system?

22 What is an enterprise resource planning system?

DISCUSSION QUESTIONS

1 Think of the course registration system at your college or university. Would a new or changed computer information system improve its efficiency? How would it do so?

2 Identify several transaction processing systems not described in the chapter. What are the input, output, processing, and storage functions of each system?

3 Think of an information system with which you are familiar and identify the controls used in the system.

4 In what types of information systems would batch processing be preferred over on-line transaction processing? Why?

5 Many information systems cannot easily be classified as accounting, financial, marketing, manufacturing, or human resource information systems. Think of several information systems not discussed in the chapter, and try to identify in which area or areas they would be classified. Do any fall into several categories?

6 Are enterprise resource planning systems a good choice for all businesses? Why or why not?

ETHICS QUESTIONS

1 Because of the increased efficiency resulting from the use of computer information systems, some employees may lose their jobs when a business starts using a new system. What ethical issues does this situation raise, and how would you handle them if you were in a decision making position in a business?

2 Transaction processing systems, although only supporting the basic operations of a business, can be used unethically. Pick several of the systems discussed in this chapter and describe how they could be used unethically.

PROBLEM-SOLVING PROJECTS

1 The system used by banks with automated teller machines is a transaction processing system. Identify the input, output, processing, and storage functions of the system. Draw a diagram like Figure 10.7 that shows these functions. Use graphics software to draw the diagram.

2 The eight basic business information systems described in the chapter use stored data containing different types of records, with many fields in each record. Some types of records are used in only one system and some are used in several systems. In records used in several systems, some fields may be used in one system and others may be used in another system. Prepare a table in which the rows list the fields in each type of record used in the eight basic business information systems. Organize the rows by record; in other words, identify the first type of record, then the fields in that record, then the second type of record, then the fields in that record, and so forth. The columns of the table should list the eight basic business information systems. At the intersection of a row and column, put a mark if the field in the row is used in the system identified in the column. Use appropriate software to prepare your table.

3 Using database software, create a simple order entry system like that described in the chapter.

4 Investigate a transaction processing system in an organization or a business to which you have access. Find out as much as you can about the system. What are the functions of the system? What controls are used in the system? Is the processing batch or on-line? In what business area does the system fall? Prepare a report of your findings.

5 Inventory master data in an inventory control system includes the reorder point and the reorder quantity. These can be calculated as follows items:

$$\text{Reorder point} = \text{Demand rate} \times \text{Delivery time}$$

$$\text{Reorder quantity} = \sqrt{\frac{2 \times \text{Demand rate} \times \text{Set-up cost}}{\text{Holding cost}}}$$

Using spreadsheet software, create a spreadsheet to calculate the reorder point and reorder quantity. Test the spreadsheet for the following items:

Item	Demand rate	Delivery time	Set-up cost	Holding cost
1	1025	.25	$75	$2
2	500	.08	$250	$12
3	2250	.04	$35	$1
4	125	.17	$450	$50

INTERNET AND ELECTRONIC COMMERCE PROJECTS

1 Locate a Web site for a mail-order company such as L.L. Bean, Lands' End, or REI. Be sure the site has an on-line ordering system that allows the customer to order items using the Internet. How are customer orders entered? In what ways can the customer pay for the order? Does the system tell the customer if the item ordered is available in stock? What special features does the ordering system have? What master data do you think the company is keeping to support the ordering system? What information systems discussed in this chapter are found in the company's on-line ordering system? Write a summary of what you find.

2 Use the Web to investigate ERP software. Go to the Web sites of major ERP software providers, such as SAP, Oracle, Baan, and PeopleSoft. (Search the Web for other ERP software companies.) Find out what applications the ERP software of each company provides. Prepare a table in which you list the different applications and which company includes it in its software.

Kozmo.com

With legs pumping hard on icy pedals, the spandex-clad rider weaves through traffic, cabbies cursing as he passes. He eyes his destination and cuts over, dismounting to lock the bike and head upstairs. When the apartment door opens, an arm reaches out from a bathrobe, takes a sack from the rider, and pulls back.

E-mission accomplished.

In the past few years, Kozmo.com has managed to create a new face for e-commerce. The city might be New York, Boston, San Francisco, or Washington. From 10 a.m. to 1 a.m., people can go to www.kozmo.com to order CDs, event tickets, videos to rent or buy, snacks, and takeout food. They pay by credit card and request a delivery time. The catch for Kozmo.com is that it offers delivery—an expensive service—free of charge, and promises to make most deliveries within an hour after the order is placed. That means the company needs business processes—and systems—to make this logistical madness work. Such demands raise information technology from a supporting position to a starring role, where decisions could make or break the company.

Kozmo.com has all the characteristics of a dot-com operation. Started in 1997, the company launched its New York service in 1998. It's now in 5 cities and has announced plans to expand to 30 markets. Its growth to date has been funded with $28 million in first-round venture financing. According to knowledgeable sources, the company is expecting to complete a substantial second round of financing. And recently Kozmo announced a five-year comarketing agreement with Starbucks. The deal will bring Starbucks $150 million from Kozmo and give Kozmo publicity in Starbucks coffee shops. In return, Kozmo will sell Starbucks coffee on its site.

Although dot-coms have a reputation for putting stock price before profits, making money is the ultimate goal and proving ground for every business. Kozmo prices goods comparably to what local convenience stores ask, and then offers gratis delivery. The combination can seem disastrous to observers.

"Certainly, there will be people who use it. Nobody ever went broke banking on laziness," says Malcolm Maclachlan, an e-commerce analyst at International Data in Framingham, Massachusetts. "Whether they can make a profit doing this? Gosh, it's not a business I'd want to be in."

Kozmo managers—and investors—seem confident that the company can drive to profits. Delivery services may be expensive, but the bet is that cost savings from serving an entire city from a few locations can take up the slack. To get to the black, the company is focusing on selling high-margin products and offering an assortment of goods that will increase the average order size.

But even with orders growing at a rate of 20% to 30% per month, Kozmo won't see daylight without efficient processing. First and foremost, that has meant finding solutions to business problems and developing systems to implement those solutions.

"All you have to do is look at the traditional types of problems that a retail business is going to have, that an e-commerce business is going to have," says Skip Trevathan, Kozmo.com's chief operating officer and former managing director of North American logistics at Memphis-based FDX, parent of FedEx.

The solution: Divide a city into delivery districts, each with a warehouse ranging in size from 2,500 to 10,000 square feet or more. Warehouses typically hold a couple thousand items and are replenished several times a day by local distributors. It's a logistical nightmare. Customers have to see what products are available at the local warehouse. Orders must travel to the right warehouse, be readied for delivery, and end up at the customer's door within an hour.

Kozmo.com uses a three-tiered computing infrastructure. Each warehouse has a server and PCs. The server handles such tasks as scheduling deliveries and managing inventory reorders. Employees use the PCs when receiving goods, picking orders, and sending deliveries.

The warehouse servers connect through a wide area network to redundant Sun Microsystems Enterprise 4500 machines, which act as servers for an Oracle database. The Sun 4500s are maintained and run by Exodus Communications at its New York facilities. Customer orders go to Web servers at the same site.

The choice of hardware was economically important. "You can put a lot more power in [the 4500s], and they're space-efficient," says Chris Siragusa, Kozmo.com's chief technology officer. According to Siragusa, 50 square feet in a co-location facility costs a few thousand dollars per month, and peak Internet bandwidth of 5M bps. usually costs between $4,000 and $5,000 per month. Yet Siragusa says the expenses are justified. Kozmo.com can focus on its core strengths—building systems and attracting customers—while the colocation facility manages network traffic and provides additional bandwidth as customer demand increases.

By outsourcing host and network tuning, Siragusa's department is able to concentrate on its core competencies, such as writing software for warehousing and dispatching systems. Kozmo.com considered using third-party systems, but decided that would leave too many unsatisfied requirements.

Flexibility and openness are vital to the company. Not only do customers have to see custom Web pages that show only the products available in their areas, but dispatching systems must also account for the transportation mix in a particular city, based on existing traffic characteristics. For example, New York relies heavily on bicycle messengers, but San Francisco uses motorized delivery, which comes in handy when delivery people face the city's famously steep hills.

To avoid disappointing customers, Kozmo.com needs systems that alert the user when meeting a delivery deadline is impossible. "We can create a huge amount of demand," says Trevathan. "We just have to make sure we do not create demand faster than we have the facility to fulfill [it]." The systems use a scheduling technique to measure product availability and delivery capacity. In unusual conditions, such as a heavy January snowstorm in the Northeast, a Web page might warn customers to expect delays.

Questions

1 Why is information technology important to Kozmo.com?

2 Which of the eight basic business information systems discussed in the chapter are most important in this case, and why are they important?

3 What other information systems are used in this case?

4 Why are custom Web pages needed for Kozmo.com customers?

5 What information system notifies the customer if a delivery deadline cannot be met?

Web Site
Kozmo.com: www.kozmo.com

Source: *Adapted from* Erik Sherman, "Web Delivery—In an Hour," *Computerworld*, March 6, 2000, pp. 54–56.

Management Decision
MAKING

E L E V E N 11

1 Explain how information systems can improve management decision-making effectiveness.

2 Describe the characteristics of information needed by managers for decision making at different levels of an organization.

3 Describe the structure of management information systems.

4 Describe the structure of decision support systems.

5 Explain the purpose of executive support systems.

6 Explain how an expert system can provide expert advice.

7 Describe what organizational knowledge is and what knowledge management systems do.

CHAPTER OUTLINE

Improving Management Decision-making Effectiveness

Management Decisions

Management Information Systems

Decision Support Systems

Executive Support Systems

Expert Systems

Knowledge Management Systems

nformation systems support the *operations* and *management* of an organization. Chapter 10 describes information systems that assist business operations, principally by processing data about business transactions. This chapter examines systems that help with the management of a business. Management involves making decisions, and the systems discussed in this chapter provide information to assist in management decision making.

This chapter first explains how information systems can improve the effectiveness of management decision making. Then it looks at management decisions, and explains the information needed for different types of decisions. Next the chapter describes the structure and functions of common types of information systems that provide management support. These systems include management information systems, decision support systems, expert systems, and executive support systems. Finally, the chapter looks at organizational knowledge and knowledge management systems.

Improving Management Decision-making Effectiveness

People make decisions all the time. Some decisions are personal and some are business related. For example, you make a decision when you buy a new car. The decision answers the question "What car should I buy?" A business manager in an athletic shoe store makes a decision when he or she selects new products to sell. In this case, the question answered by the decision might be "What style shoes should we stock next winter?"

A *decision* is a selection among several courses of action. For the car-buying decision, you have to decide whether to buy a Ford, a Toyota, a Volkswagen, or some other make of car. For the product-selection decision, the business manager has to decide whether to stock running shoes, tennis shoes, or walking shoes. Almost always when making a decision, there is uncertainty about what will happen with each alternative. Will the car require a lot of repair? Will customers want to buy the types of shoes stocked by the store?

Information helps reduce uncertainty. With better information, a decision maker is more certain about the outcome from the decision. If you have information about the repair records of the models of cars you are considering, you can be more certain about the reliability of the car you buy. If the business manager has information about the buying public's interest in athletic shoes, he or she can be more certain about what types of shoes will sell. You cannot eliminate uncertainty entirely, however. Thus, the car you buy may still need repair and the shoes stocked may not sell. With good information, however, uncertainty can be reduced and the outcome from the decision is more likely to be satisfactory.

Information systems improve decision-making effectiveness by providing decision makers with information related to the decisions for which they are responsible. Such information systems can be used for personal as well as business decisions. For example, if you are making a car purchasing decision, you can use a computerized library information system to search for articles and reviews of the cars in which you are interested. A business manager making a product-selection decision can use a sales analysis information system to examine sales trends and a marketing information system to look at marketing research data. In these cases, the effectiveness of the decision making is improved by the information systems.

Chapter 1 explains the difference between data and information. *Data* is a representation of a fact, number, word, image, picture, or sound. *Information*, on the other hand, is data that is meaningful or useful to someone. An information system accepts, stores, and processes data, and produces information. The information is used in the management of the business to help in decision making. To be competitive today, businesses must have information systems that provide information to support their management decision making.

Management Decisions

Before examining information systems that support management decision making, you need to know some things about management decisions. You need to understand the different levels of management decisions, the characteristics of management decisions, and the information needs for management decisions.

Levels of Management Decisions

Management decisions are made at several levels in an organization. Figure 11.1 shows the hierarchy of management decisions. Starting at the bottom, *operational decisions* are day-to-day decisions needed in the operation of the organization. These decisions affect the organization for a short period of time, such as several days or weeks. For example, in an athletic shoe store, an operational decision is whether to order more running shoes today. This decision affects the business for the next few weeks. Operational decisions are made by lower-level managers.

The next level of decisions are *tactical decisions*, which are those that involve implementing policies of the organization. They affect the organization for a longer period of time than operational decisions, usually for several months or a few years, and are made by middle-level managers. For example, deciding whether to sell running shoes next winter is a tactical decision; it has an effect on the organization for a long period of time.

At the highest level of decisions are *strategic decisions*, which are made by top-level managers. These decisions involve setting organization policies, goals, and long-term plans, and they affect the organization for many years. For example, a strategic decision for an athletic shoe store is whether the store should stop selling athletic shoes and start selling some other product. This decision has a long-term effect on the business.

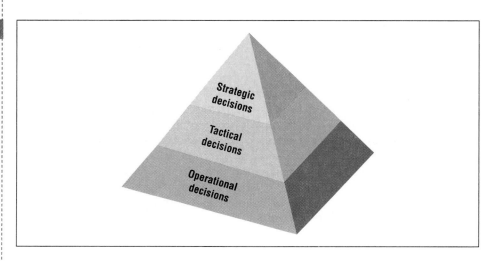

Characteristics of Management Decisions

Management decisions at different levels have different characteristics, as summarized in Figure 11.2. The first characteristic, already described, is the time horizon affected by the decision. As shown in Figure 11.2a, operational decisions affect the business for the short term, tactical decisions affect the business for the intermediate term, and strategic decisions affect the business for the long term.

A second characteristic of management decisions, shown in Figure 11.2b, is the frequency of repeating the same type of decision. Operational decisions are made frequently. For example, deciding whether to order more running shoes is made every day or every week. Tactical decisions are made less frequently. Thus, the decision of whether to sell running shoes next winter is made only once each year. Strategic decisions are made very infrequently. Deciding what business to be in may only be made every 10 or 20 years.

A final characteristic of management decisions, shown in Figure 11.2c, is the degree of structure in the decision process. By this we mean the degree with which

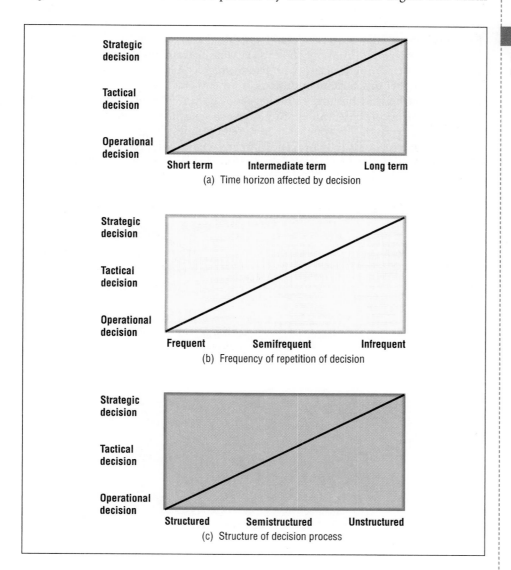

(a) Time horizon affected by decision

(b) Frequency of repetition of decision

(c) Structure of decision process

FIGURE 11.2

Characteristics of management decisions

someone can specify a procedure or formula to help make the decision. Operational decisions tend to be very structured. For example, deciding whether to order more stock is a well-structured decision; there are mathematical formulas to help make such a decision. Tactical decisions are semistructured. Thus, the procedure for deciding what to stock next winter is not so well formulated, although there are methods, such as statistical methods, to help in the decision making. Finally, strategic decisions are unstructured. For example, there are few good procedures for deciding what business to be in.

Information Needs for Management Decisions

As you know, information helps reduce uncertainty about the outcome of a decision. The information needs are different, however, for different levels of decision making. Figure 11.3 summarizes two characteristics of information needed for management decision making. The first characteristic is the source of information, which means where the information comes from. As shown in Figure 11.3a, most information for operational decisions comes from inside the organization, whereas most information for strategic decisions comes from outside the organization. Information for tactical decisions comes from both inside and outside the organization. Thus, to decide whether to order more running shoes today (an operational decision), a manager needs to know the current quantity on hand, which comes from inside the business. To decide whether to sell running shoes next winter (a tactical decision), the manager needs to know how the business's running shoes are selling, which comes from inside the business, and consumer interest in running shoes, which comes from outside the business. Finally, to decide whether to stop selling shoes altogether (a strategic decision), the manager needs to know general trends in shoe sales compared to trends in sales of other products, which is information that comes from outside the business.

FIGURE 11.3

Characteristics of information
▲ for management decisions

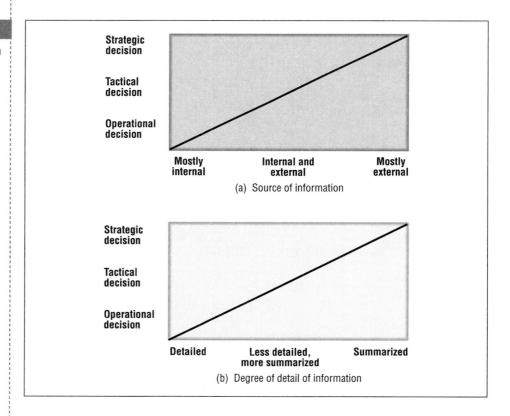

(a)   Source of information

(b)   Degree of detail of information

The second characteristic of information needed for management decision making, shown in Figure 11.3b, is the degree of detail or summarization required in the information. Operational decisions require detailed information, tactical decisions require less detailed and more summarized information, and strategic decisions need summarized information. Information is detailed if it pertains to individual entities, such as items in inventory, or events, such as sales. Information is summarized if it presents totals or other figures derived from groups of entities or events. For example, to make the operational decision of whether to order running shoes today, the manager may need to know how many pairs of running shoes were sold yesterday, which is very detailed information. To make the tactical decision of whether to sell running shoes next winter, the manager may need to know the total sales of running shoes for each month of the past two years, which is less detailed and more summarized information than daily sales. Finally, to make the strategic decision of whether to stop selling shoes altogether, the manager may need to know the total sales of all shoes for each of the past five years, which is even more summarized information.

Information Systems for Management Support

With this background on management decision characteristics and information needs, you can understand how information systems support management. Information systems provide information to help managers make decisions at each of the three levels of decision making. The information is derived from a number of internal and external sources and presented at different levels of detail or summarization. The information helps the manager make decisions, but does not make the decision for the manager.

Information systems support management in all the functions of a business and at all levels (Figure 11.4). Accounting information systems provide accounting information at operational, tactical, and strategic levels. Financial information systems

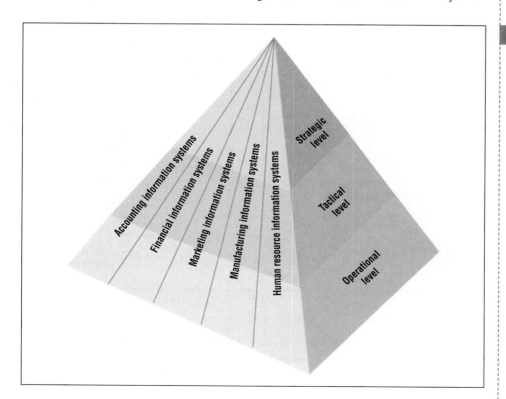

FIGURE 11.4

Information system support for management ▲

help in financial decision making at all levels. Marketing information systems provide information to marketing managers at different levels. Manufacturing information systems assist in making decisions related to manufacturing and production at all levels. Finally, human resource information systems support personnel decision making at operational, tactical, and strategic levels.

Several general types of information systems for management support are found in organizations. The next sections of this chapter look at four types. *Management information systems* provide information to managers in the form of reports and query responses. *Decision support systems* provide analysis of information to managers. *Executive support systems* provide special support for the highest level of management. Finally, *expert systems* provide information to managers in the form of expert advice.

Management Information Systems

A **management information system (MIS)** supports management decision making by providing information in the form of reports and responses to queries to managers at different levels of an organization. This type of system is sometimes called an *information reporting system*, or a *management reporting system*. The term *management information system* is also used to refer to all types of information systems, including transaction processing systems (TPSs), although in this book we use it only for the type of system described in this section.

Management Information System Structure

Figure 11.5 shows the general structure of management information systems and their relationship to transaction processing systems. The users of an MIS are managers at each of the three levels of decision making. The users request information

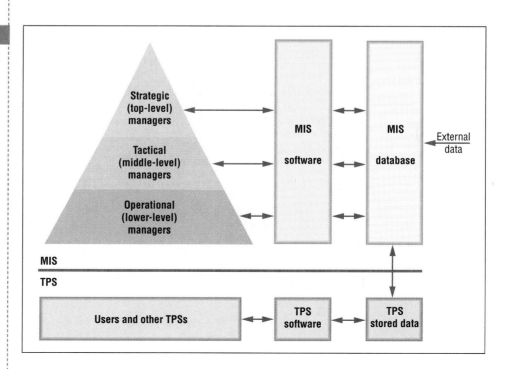

from the system, and the information is returned in the form of reports and query responses. The MIS database contains data that is processed to provide the information to the managers. The MIS software consists of application software to manipulate the data in the database. The software accepts requests for information from the managers, accesses data in the database, processes the data, and produces output. The software also updates the data in the database as needed.

The data in the MIS database comes from both inside and outside the organization. Some internal data may be entered by managers, but most comes directly from the stored data of transaction processing systems, as shown in Figure 11.5. For example, consider a business that has a transaction processing system for inventory control. Assume that this system keeps track of the quantity on hand for each item in inventory in an inventory master file. Each day the quantity data in this file is passed to the MIS database. Then, the MIS software uses the data to help make the operational decision of whether to order more inventory that day. Data at lower levels in the MIS database is passed up through the database, where it is summarized for higher-level decisions. Thus, daily inventory quantities used for operational decisions are summarized to get weekly and monthly figures for tactical decisions and summarized again to get yearly figures for strategic decisions.

Data from outside the organization comes from many sources. Periodicals, government publications, and research company reports often contain data that is useful in management decision making. This type of data may be entered into the MIS database by managers or their assistants, or downloaded from external databases. Useful data can also be found on the Internet. The data can be retrieved from the Internet and stored in the MIS database. Push technology, discussed in Chapter 8, can automatically provide important data found on the Internet for storing in the MIS database. Some companies, such as Dow Jones, provide business-related data to customers for a fee. The data can be downloaded to the MIS database.

As an example of a management information system, consider one that supports inventory decisions at all three levels in an athletic shoe store. This system would contain a database of daily inventory data for each item the store sells. The inventory control system, a transaction processing system, would supply the data. At the operational level, MIS software would produce output with inventory figures for each item. These figures would help a decision maker determine whether to order more of certain items. The inventory data would be summarized by the MIS for the tactical-level decision makers. This data would be used to decide what types of items were overstocked so that appropriate actions, such as dropping them from the product line, could be taken. Finally, inventory data would be summarized further for strategic managers to help determine policies, such as whether another store should be opened.

Management Information System Functions

Management information systems perform the four main functions of an information system: the input function, the output function, the storage function, and the processing function. The functions together provide the capabilities of the system for the user.

The Input Function. Little data entry is required for an MIS. As noted earlier, the internal data for the system comes mainly from transaction processing systems. Those systems provide the data capture, data entry, and data validation steps necessary to get the data into the organization's information systems. External data is often transferred into the MIS by using data communications techniques. For example, data may be downloaded from an external database and stored directly in the MIS database.

After data is in the MIS, a user may want to inquire about the data. A **query**, or an **inquiry**, is a request for information from a system. Before a system can respond to a query, the query must be entered into the system. Often, the user enters the query directly into a computer. For example, consider an information system that helps manage the inventory for an athletic shoe store. A manager may use the system to inquire about the availability of stock for a particular item in order to decide if more of the item should be ordered. The manager enters the query by keying the number of the item for which the available inventory is needed (Figure 11.6).

The Output Function.   The output function of an MIS produces reports and responses to queries. Reports can be *detail reports* or *summary reports*, two types of reports introduced in Chapter 10. MISs that support operational decision making require mainly detail reports. Those that support strategic decision making require mostly summary reports. Systems that affect tactical decision making need some detail reports and some summary reports.

Exception reports, described in Chapter 10, are also produced by MISs. They are very common because they provide information for an approach to management called *management by exception*, which involves taking action only if the business is not functioning as expected. An exception report provides information about exceptions to some rule or standard. A manager who receives such a report can then take the necessary steps to correct the situation and return the business to normal functioning.

An inventory reorder report is an example of an exception report (Figure 11.7). This report gives a list of the items whose inventory on hand has fallen below an acceptable level. Based on this exception information, a manager can decide whether to order more inventory. Note that the manager may, after reviewing the report, decide not to order more stock because of other information the manager has. For example, the manager may know that a new product line is coming out (this is exter-

FIGURE 11.6

▲ **Query entry**

FIGURE 11.7

An exception report ▲

INVENTORY REORDER REPORT

ITEM NUMBER	ITEM DESCRIPTION	QUANTITY ON HAND
1681	RUNNING SHOE	11
1945	TENNIS SHOE	8
3347	TRACK SHOE	3
4205	SOCKS	20
5172	SWEAT SHIRT	15

nal information from the supplier), and therefore the business does not want to replenish stock of the old item. Thus, just because an exception has occurred does not necessarily mean that a certain action should be taken.

Reports are prepared by an MIS at different times. Some reports are prepared periodically and are called **scheduled reports**. For example, a scheduled report may be prepared every month or every week. Other reports are prepared only when requested. These are called **demand reports** because someone must request that the report be prepared. A final type of report is one that is prepared only once, for a specific purpose. This is called an **ad hoc report**.

In addition to report output, an MIS provides responses to queries. The response is an output from the system and is usually displayed on a screen, although it may be printed on paper. The response may be just a few lines, or it could be a lengthy report. For example, in an inventory management system, a manager could enter a query about the available stock for a particular item. After determining the stock on hand, the system would respond to the query by displaying the information on the screen (Figure 11.8).

FIGURE 11.8

Query response ▲

STOCK AVAILABILITY QUERY

Item Number	Item Description	Quantity on Hand
1945	TENNIS SHOE	8

The Storage Function.   Data for an MIS may be stored in files, which are usually master files, but more often the MIS data is stored in a database. Storing data in a database makes it easier to access related data and to produce ad hoc reports and query responses.

The data for the MIS database comes from the transaction processing system and from external sources. This data is used to *create* and *update* the database. The database can then be *accessed* to provide information for the decision makers. The relationships between the data in the database can be used to join related data to produce reports or responses to the queries. A database management system makes it easy to enter queries, view the responses, and produce ad hoc or other types of reports.

**INVENTORY VALUE
BY PRODUCT LINE
9/30/XXXX**

PRODUCT LINE	TOTAL VALUE
Running shoes	$24,368.00
Tennis shoes	10,852.00
Sport shoes	8,147.50
Total shoes	43,367.50*
Running clothing	6,025.00
Tennis clothing	5,410.50
Misc clothing	820.25
Total clothing	12,255.75*
Sport bags	2,268.25
Other items	1,335.75
Total accessories	3,604.00*
TOTAL	**$59,227.25****

(a) A report with group and subgroup totals

**INVENTORY VALUE
BY PRODUCT LINE
9/30/XXXX**

PRODUCT CATEGORY	TOTAL VALUE
Shoes	$43,367.50
Clothing	12,255.75
Accessories	3,604.00
TOTAL	**$59,227.25***

(b) A report with group totals

The Processing Function. Processing in an MIS normally involves simple computations. For example, a report may give the value of an item in inventory. This value is found by simply multiplying the quantity on hand by the price per item. Most computations in an MIS are not much more complex than this one.

The main computation that is performed by an MIS involves accumulating totals for reporting at different levels of decision making. Totals of groups of data may be computed for one level, and totals of all data may be produced for a higher level. For example, Figure 11.9a shows a report with group and subgroup totals and Figure 11.9b shows a report with only main group totals. The latter report, which is more summarized and less detailed than the former report, would be used for higher-level decision making.

Management Information System Software

Software for management information systems is often custom written using business programming languages. (See Chapter 5.) Such software may use a database management system to provide access to the MIS database. Users may also use a *query language*, such as SQL (discussed in Chapter 7), to access the database for queries and ad hoc reports. Special *report generator* software may also be used to prepare reports from data in the database.

When client/server computing is used, the software that provides the report and query response output executes in each user's client computer, and the database software executes in the server computer. The client computer software in this case may provide a graphical user interface for easy access to the database (Figure 11.10). Queries and reports can easily be created in the graphical user interface on the client computer, with data for the query response and report output being supplied by the database software on the server.

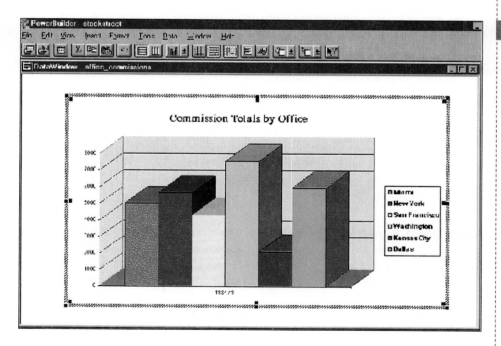

FIGURE 11.10

The graphical user interface for a client computer in a management information system ▲

Decision Support Systems

A management information system helps managers make decisions by providing information from a database with little or no analysis. A **decision support system (DSS)**, on the other hand, helps managers make decisions by analyzing data from a database and providing the results of the analysis to the manager. An MIS supports all three levels of management decision making with reports and query responses. A DSS, on the other hand, is usually best for decisions at the middle and top levels of management. As with an MIS, a DSS helps with making decisions but does not actually make decisions; only managers make decisions.

Management Decision Support

To understand decision support systems you need to know how data can be analyzed to help make management decisions. A DSS includes several ways of analyzing data. Usually, the manager can select the form of analysis he or she wants. The system performs the calculations required for the analysis and displays or prints the results.

One form of analysis is *statistical calculations*. In these calculations, data is manipulated to determine characteristics of the data or to draw conclusions from the data. For example, assume that a manager in an athletic-clothing store has data about the sales of different types of shoes for each of the past five years. He or she can calculate the average yearly sales for each type, which is one way of characterizing this data. The manager can also use this data to forecast sales in future years. Both of these examples are types of statistical calculations.

Another form of analysis is *mathematical modeling*. A *model* is a representation of reality. For example, a model airplane is a representation of a real airplane. Models used for decision making are not physical things like airplanes, but sets of mathematical equations. A model can be used to help predict what will happen with different decisions. In effect, the model uses mathematical equations to *simulate* the real world.

An example of a model is one used to simulate inventory flow so that a manager can try different inventory reordering decisions. The following equation is a simple inventory model that might be used to simulate the inventory of running shoes in an athletic shoe store:

$$\text{Inventory today} = \text{Inventory yesterday} - 5$$

This model says, in equation form, that each day the store sells five pairs of running shoes. The manager can also write an equation that calculates the cost of keeping items in inventory. With these equations a manager can compare the cost of ordering a small amount of inventory frequently with the cost of ordering a large amount of inventory less frequently. By trying different strategies, a manager can use the model to determine the least expensive inventory reordering policy.

Decision Support System Structure

Figure 11.11 shows the general structure of decision support systems. The users of a DSS are managers, usually at the tactical and strategic levels in the organization. The user requests analysis of data from the system, and the results of the analysis are displayed on the user's screen or printed in a report. The DSS database contains data that is analyzed to produce the output. The DSS **model base** (analogous to a database) contains the mathematical models and statistical calculation routines that are used to analyze data from the database.

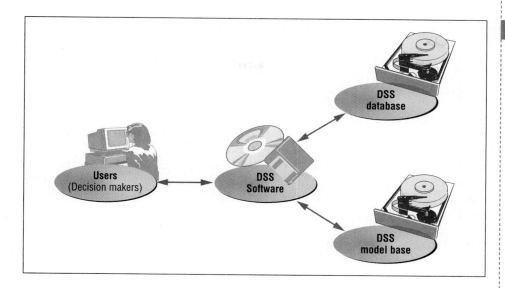

FIGURE 11.11

The structure of decision support systems (DSSs) ▲

The DSS software provides capabilities for the user to access data in the database and to use models from the model base to analyze the data. The software also displays the result of the analysis on the screen or prints it on paper. Often, the output from a DSS is given in a graphic form, although other forms of output are used. Using the software, the user can try different models and data to see what happens.

The data for the DSS database comes from several sources. The user may enter data into the database, or data may be retrieved from the MIS database or the transaction processing system stored data. In addition, the results of a previous analysis by the DSS may be stored in the database for use in later analysis. External sources may also be used to supply data for the DSS database.

An example of a DSS is one that helps a manager in an athletic shoe store decide what types of shoes to advertise. The system would use data from a database containing past sales of different types of shoes. The sales data would be analyzed by statistical calculation routines to project sales trends. Then, a mathematical model would be used to simulate the effect of advertising on sales. The manager would try different advertising strategies until he or she found the one that was most likely to increase sales.

Decision support systems are best used for situations in which decisions are semistructured or unstructured. The nature of these decisions often involves trying different approaches, asking what-if questions, finding input values that produce a specific output (a process called *goal seeking*), and checking the result to see how it might change if the input were slightly different (a process called *sensitivity analysis*.) The types of decisions that fit this situation are not made very frequently and often affect the business for some time. All these characteristics point to the use of decision support systems at the tactical and strategic decision-making levels.

Decision Support System Functions

The capabilities of a decision support system are provided by the four information system functions performed by the system.

The Input Function.   User input to a DSS is mainly in the form of requests for analysis of data. The user may enter some input data, but as noted earlier, most of the data used in the DSS comes from the databases and files of other systems. The user may also enter instructions to tell the software to use certain models from the model base or to combine models for different forms of analysis. The main input, however, is in the form of specifying what type of analysis is to be done with what data. For example, the user may request that a particular statistical routine be used to analyze a set of data from the database or that a certain model be used to simulate a decision.

The Output Function.   The output function of a DSS produces the results of analysis on screens and in printed reports. Screens usually display the output in a table or graphical form. Graphs may be printed on paper or displayed on a large screen using presentation graphics software for group discussion. Reports typically are summary or exception reports. Because of the level of decision making a DSS supports, detail reports are rarely produced. Reports are usually created on demand or on an ad hoc basis; scheduled reports are not as common in a DSS.

The Storage Function.   Data in a DSS is usually stored in a database. The database may be managed by the DSS software or by separate database management software. The software allows the database to be created and updated using input data from various sources, both internal and external to the business. The software also allows the data to be accessed for analysis by a model.

The storage function of a DSS also provides capabilities for managing the model base. Software, sometimes called *model base management software*, allows models to be created and modified. This software also lets the user combine models to form more complex models. Finally, with this software the user can use models to analyze data retrieved from the database.

The Processing Function.   Processing in a DSS can be very complex. Some statistical analysis routines require sophisticated computations. Models in DSSs often involve complex calculations. When several models or statistical procedures are combined, the processing is even more involved. Such processing can be time-consuming, and DSSs can take several minutes or longer to compute the results.

Decision Support System Software

A decision support system is usually developed using general software that is adapted for a specific decision. An example of simple DSS software is spreadsheet software. This type of software usually includes limited data management capabilities, built-in statistical calculation routines, and simple mathematical models. A user can use the software to access data, do calculations, use and develop models, and display the results in either a table or a graph. The capabilities of spreadsheet software are limited; nevertheless, this type of software can be used to create a DSS for some types of decision problems.

More sophisticated DSS software is available for personal computers, multiple-user computers, and networks. Some DSS software is like spreadsheet software but with more complete database and modeling capabilities. Other DSS software is statistical calculation software with limited database capabilities. Still other software is modeling software, which is used to simulate decision situations. Using the appropriate software, a DSS can be created to help managers make many types of decisions. Figure 11.12 shows the screen of a decision support system.

A DSS can also be used to analyze the data in a data warehouse. Recall from Chapter 7 that a *data warehouse* is a collection of data drawn from other databases used in a business. Analysis of data in a data warehouse often requires searching for patterns in the data, which is the process of *data mining*, as discussed in Chapter 7. For

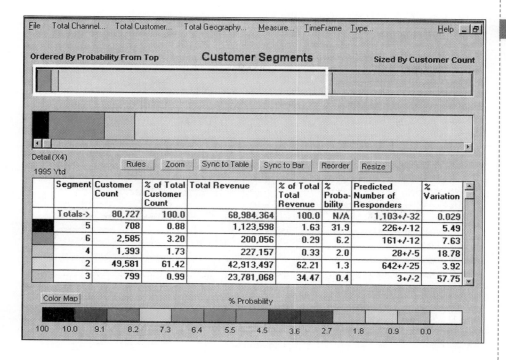

FIGURE 11.12

Decision support system software

example, a data warehouse of customer purchasing data can be mined to find buying patterns, such as what products are more likely to be purchased on what days. The result of data mining in a data warehouse can support decision making, such as deciding when certain products should be put on sale or when special advertising should be done.

Group Decision Support Systems

Decision support systems can be used for individual decision making or for group decision making. A **group decision support system** (**GDSS**) is a system designed to support group decision making. A GDSS is an example of a workgroup information system, as discussed in Chapter 9.

A GDSS is typically used in a network. The GDSS provides information and analysis of data to users at personal computers connected to the network. The users can then collaborate through the network to reach a group decision. Many of the workgroup applications discussed in Chapter 9, such as information sharing and electronic meeting support, are used in GDSSs.

Geographic Information Systems

A **geographic information system** (**GIS**) is an information system that provides information for decision making based on geographic location. Certain information depends on where it originates. For example, demographic data, such as population and income levels, is based on geographic location. Similarly, sales data can be gathered by the geographic locations where the sales were made.

A geographic information system includes a database in which all data is organized by geographic location. Thus, a database may contain average household income levels, average resident age, product sales figures, and similar data, organized by location. Almost any type of data can be stored in such a database. You can think

FIGURE 11.13

A geographic information
system (GIS)

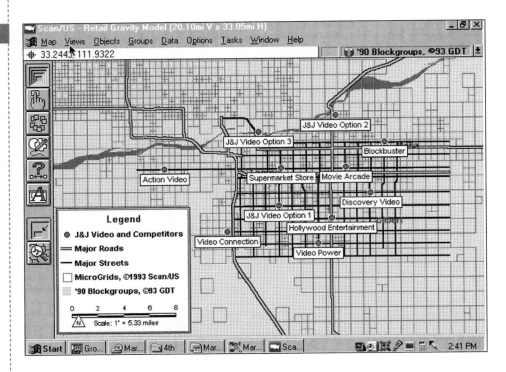

of the data as being stored in layers tied together only by geographic location (Figure 11.13).

Using the data in such a database, a geographic information system can provide information to support decision making. For example, a database of demographic and sales data can be used to look for demographic patterns that result in higher sales. This information can be used to target areas for special advertising and increased product availability.

Executive Support Systems

The top-level managers of a business have information system needs that are different from those of other managers. Although management information and decision support systems can meet some of those needs, these systems are not commonly used by executives, but rather by managers and staff members below the highest level. An **executive support system (ESS)**, on the other hand, is designed specifically for the information needs of strategic managers. This type of system, which is also called an **executive information system (EIS)**, provides information and support that is most appropriate and useful for top-level managers.

Executive Information Needs

As discussed earlier, managers at the strategic level generally need summarized and not detailed information. Sometimes, however, a manager needs to focus on the details of a particular aspect of the information. For example, a manager may notice that the sales in a certain region have fallen off dramatically. Is this fall off the result

Geographic Information System at the City of Oakland

A dozen years ago, Frank Kliewer began working for the City of Oakland, California, and it wasn't long before someone slapped him with the dreaded B-word. "The first time someone called me a bureaucrat, I froze," Kliewer recalls. "I just hated the concept."

Kliewer, who ran the Permits Department, sought to throw off that label by changing the way he and his department dealt with the community and provided information. Bureaucracy not being synonymous with good customer service, it has been a struggle, but Kliewer believes the Internet, a modest Pentium-based server, and a sophisticated bit of software have finally given him a fighting chance.

"The way bureaucrats maintain power and position is to have a bunch of information that they control and parse out as they see fit," says Kliewer, now manager of the city's Internet Working Division. "When the Web came along, it seemed like a wonderful place to really get the public into the government area of information, documents, and so forth."

The result of Kliewer's vision is the map-driven Oakland Web site, which uses geographic information system (GIS) software to serve up multilayered, on-the-fly maps, zoning reports, emergency response data, and more to the public and to city employees. Users can instantly access information—the zoning status of a particular parcel of land or the location of fallout shelters, for example—instead of wait in line for hours at City Hall or get tied up in a call center.

Kliewer's work on the project began in October 1991, after the Oakland Hills fire devastated thousands of homes. Using GIS software from ESRI, he started mapping the recovery effort. Eventually, he began to see Internet-based GIS as a way to aid emergency response, enabling those in command to see where assets and problems lie.

"It dawned on me that if we could publish some of these layers, the public could muck around with the data and make decisions," says Kliewer. "I wanted to get information to the public so they could determine for themselves any time of day, from anywhere, what parcels might be appropriate for development or understand what's going on next door." With $350,000 in funding from the city and a staff of programmers, Kliewer put up a GIS site that displayed a few hundred downtown parcels. But the application was slow, and data was churned out on HTML pages, not on the fly.

"It became clear it was going to be a headache to maintain," says Kliewer. "I needed a programmer to make changes every time there was a change in the city." So Kliewer turned to Autodesk's MapGuide, which accesses multiple layers of data to create vector-based maps, thus eliminating the expense of calling on a programmer each time a change occurs. With this system, for example, a real estate developer in Chicago can search for one-acre commercial sites near transit lines, zoom down to photo level, and find out the property's owner's name and zoning status. Accessing other data sets, the fire chief can see hydrant locations, measure distances between hydrants and fires, and calculate how much hose is needed—all before arriving at the scene.

The site doesn't track individual users, but Kliewer says the maps get 20,000 to 50,000 hits per week, usually from architects, engineers, designers, and developers, as well as community activists trying to understand the dynamics of their neighborhoods. One woman, Kliewer recounts, identified a "crack house" and, using the map's zoning record data, found the building's owner and made him aware of the situation. Emergency personnel, meanwhile, have not taken full advantage of the site, but Oakland's city manager has shown a keen interest. He wants crime statistics loaded onto the site so

BOOK
M A R K

he can request dynamic maps, pinpointing the locations of robberies, drug arrests, and the like for use at community meetings.

"I really believe this is the way you're going to access government information in the future," says Kliewer.

Questions

1. What type of information can be accessed using the City of Oakland's geographic information system?

2. Why is it important that the City of Oakland's geographic information system be accessible over the Web?

Web Site
City of Oakland:
www.oaklandnet.com

Source: *Adapted from* Andrew Marlatt, "Dynamic Data Saves Time, Money—and Lives," *Internet World*, June 15, 1998, p. 27.

of poor sales at a particular sales office, or is it a general loss of sales in the region? To answer the question, the manager must get more detailed information through a process called **drilling down**. The manager starts with the region's sales and drills down to the sales in each sales office in the region, trying to locate the source of the lost sales (Figure 11.14). When the source is found (in Figure 11.14, a problem appears at the Miami office), the manager can drill down even more to try to identify

FIGURE 11.14

▲ Drilling down for detailed information

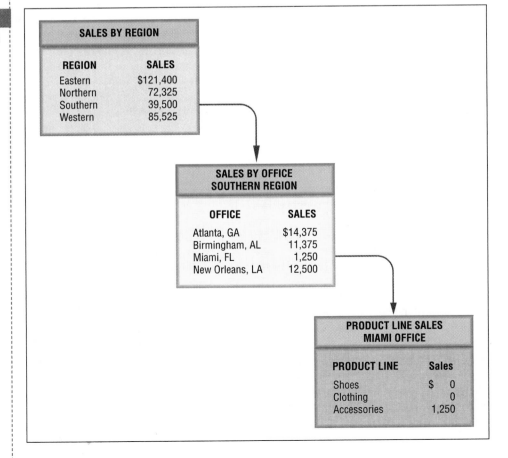

more detailed causes of the problem (in Figure 11.14, the Miami office sold no shoes or clothing). When the problem has been fully identified, the manager can concentrate his or her effort on trying to correct the problem.

Managers at the highest level need external information as well as internal information. External information provides executives with an understanding of the environment within which the business functions. For example, managers need to know about general economic trends to make decisions about business expansion in the future. They need to know about consumer likes and dislikes to decide which products to produce or which services to provide. Managers need to know about financial markets to make decisions about where to borrow or invest money. All this information is external to the organization.

Executives often work in an unstructured way, not knowing in advance what information they will need or what computer functions they will use. They need extremely flexible systems that they can easily adapt to their own requirements. They need to be able to access summarized internal and external information on the spur of the moment and to drill down to more detailed information as needed. All these functions are necessary to support the information needs of top executives.

Executive Support System Structure

The capabilities of executive support systems vary. Some of the capabilities are similar to those found in MISs and some are similar to those found in DSSs. Individual and workgroup applications may also be found in ESSs. An ESS may include any of the following capabilities:

- On-line access to reports.
- The ability to query the MIS database for information not usually received in reports.
- The ability to access external databases.
- The ability to analyze and summarize data from reports and queries, and to view the results of the analysis graphically.
- The ability to drill down to detailed information.
- Electronic mail (e-mail) to communicate with employees.
- An electronic appointment calendar.
- Basic word processing capabilities for writing notes, memos, and other simple communications.

Figure 11.15 shows the general structure of executive support systems. The users of an ESS are top-level, strategic managers. The user uses the ESS software to access a variety of databases, which may include the MIS database (for reports and queries), external databases, special databases created just for the ESS, personal databases created by the user, and electronic mailboxes. The ESS software provides capabilities for analyzing and summarizing data as well as other capabilities listed previously. The user can select the functions to be performed based on his or her needs.

An example of an ESS is one that helps the owner of an athletic shoe store make top-level decisions. Such a system may provide summarized sales information for different categories of products sold by the store. The system would allow the owner to drill down to detailed sales figures in each category. The system would also provide access to other information stored in various internal databases as well as to external databases containing general economic and consumer trend information. The system

FIGURE 11.15

The structure of executive
▲ support systems (ESSs)

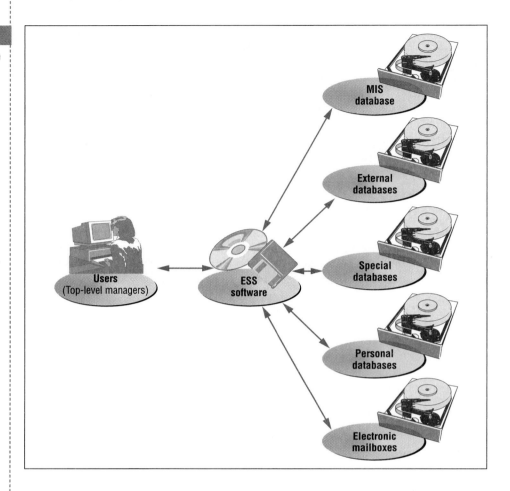

would provide e-mail for communication with employees and an electronic calendar for keeping track of the owner's appointments.

Executive Support System Functions

An executive support system provides its capabilities through the four information system functions.

The Input Function.   Executives usually do not enter input data into an ESS, although they may key in e-mail, notes and memos, and appointment information. Most of the input to an ESS is in the form of selecting functions for the software to perform. The user can select the reports he or she wants to see, the data to retrieve from a database, the analysis to perform on the data, and so on. ESSs are very flexible so as to allow the executive to select exactly the information needed.

The Output Function.   Most of the output produced by an ESS is displayed on a screen, although the user may select to have some output printed on paper. Data is usually displayed in a table or presented in graphical form. Reports are not scheduled but produced on demand or on an ad hoc basis.

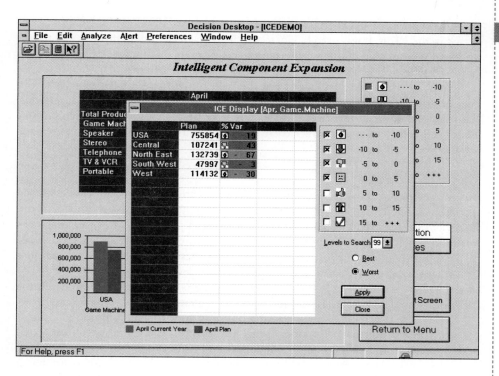

FIGURE 11.16

Executive support system
software ▲

The Storage Function. The principal storage function provided by an ESS is access to various databases. The ESS software or separate database management software provides the database access capabilities. Executives do not normally create or update databases, but they do need to access data in a variety of ways. The ability to drill down to more detailed information in the database is an important storage function provided by the ESS.

The Processing Function. Any processing functions provided by MISs and DSSs may be included in an ESS. Simple total calculations, sophisticated statistical analysis, and complex model calculations may be used in an ESS. The processing functions depend on the capabilities provided by the ESS.

Executive Support System Software

An executive support system is developed using software that is customized for the specific executive information needs. Figure 11.16 shows the screen of an executive support system.

Expert Systems

Management information, decision support, and executive support systems help managers make decisions by providing and analyzing information. They do not, however, advise the decision maker on what to do. An **expert system (ES)**, on the other hand, is a type of information system that gives expert advice to the decision maker. An expert system mimics the way a human expert would analyze a situation and then recommends a course of action. The system accomplishes this task by incorporating human expert knowledge and by using this knowledge to analyze specific problems.

An early example of an expert system is Mycin, which was developed at Stanford University in the 1970s. It was used by doctors to help diagnose certain diseases and to recommend treatment. A more recent example is an expert system developed by American Express to decide whether to issue a credit card to a customer.

Expert systems use techniques from the field of **artificial intelligence** (**AI**). The goal of artificial intelligence is to mimic human intelligence by using a computer. For example, artificial intelligence programs have been developed to play complex games of strategy such as chess. Expert systems are just one application of artificial intelligence.

Expert Advice

Business managers rely on advice from experts in many situations. When a technical question arises, managers call on engineers or scientists for expert advice. Many financial decisions require the help of an expert in a particular area of finance. The health care field uses medical experts; the computer field relies on computer experts.

People are experts in a particular area for many reasons. Some are experts because of formal education or specialized training. Others develop expertise through job or other practical experience. Still others become experts by self-study. In all cases, the individual can demonstrate his or her expertise in a tangible way.

Expert advice is used in all levels of a business, but is most commonly required for structured problems at the operational and tactical levels. Problems in research and development, engineering, production, finance, computer systems, accounting, and other areas use expert advice. There is practically no area of a business in which experts and expert advice are not used.

Expert System Structure

Figure 11.17 shows the general structure of expert systems. The users of an expert system are decision makers who are not experts in the types of problems that the expert system is designed to solve. A user uses the system interactively by requesting advice from the expert system and answering questions asked by the system. The expert system responds to the user's request with advice and recommendations.

The **knowledge base** is a database of expert knowledge. Different types of expert systems use different techniques for storing knowledge. One technique is to use **rules**. A rule is an *if-then* structure: *If* something is true, *then* something else is true. For example, Figure 11.18 shows five rules that might be used in a simple expert system for deciding whether to hire an applicant for a job. All the rules form the knowledge base for the expert system.

The expert system software consists of a user interface and an inference engine. The user interface receives input from the user and displays output. The **inference engine** analyzes rules in the knowledge base to draw conclusions.

FIGURE 11.17

The structure of expert systems (ESs)

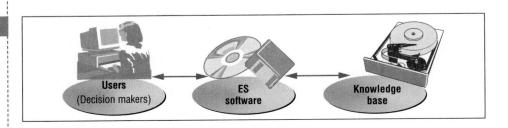

FIGURE 11.18

Rules in a knowledge base ▲

Rule 1: *If* applicant has required education
and applicant has required experience,
then hire applicant

Rule 2: *If* applicant has BA in business,
then applicant has required education

Rule 3: *If* applicant has BA in non-business field
and applicant has an MBA,
then applicant has required education

Rule 4: *If* applicant has two or more years experience in sales position,
then applicant has required experience

Rule 5: *If* applicant has four or more years experience in any position,
then applicant has required experience

An example of an expert system is one that evaluates a job applicant with the knowledge base given in Figure 11.18. Figure 11.19 shows how the interaction with the user of this system might appear on the screen. The user enters the applicant's name, education, and work experience. Then, the inference engine uses the knowledge base to evaluate this data. The inference engine does the evaluation by deciding which rules apply and by linking the rules together to draw a conclusion. In this example, the inference engine determines that John Doe has the required education because of Rule 2 and the required experience because of Rule 5. Therefore, because of Rule 1, he should be hired. This recommendation is displayed on the screen.

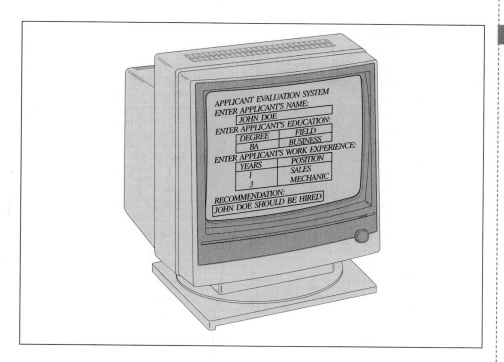

FIGURE 11.19

Expert system use ▲

Expert System Functions

Expert system capabilities are provided by the four information system functions.

The Input Function.　User input to an expert system is in the form of basic information needed by the system to provide the expert advice. In the example in Figure 11.19, the input is the applicant's name, education, and work experience. Normally, only a small amount of input is required from the user.

The Output Function.　The output from an expert system is the advice of the system. Thus, in the example in Figure 11.19, the output is the recommendation about whether the applicant should be hired. Sometimes, several options are given by the system, with an indication of the likelihood that each option is best. For example, a financial investment expert system may indicate that one investment has a 60% chance of making a particular profit and another investment has a 70% chance of making a lesser profit.

The Storage Function.　The storage function of an expert system involves managing the knowledge base. Although the example in Figure 11.18 has only five rules, most expert systems have hundreds or even thousands of rules. Storing, updating, and accessing the rules are the main activities of the storage function of an expert system.

The Processing Function.　The processing function of an expert system is very complex. Determining which rules apply and how they interact require sophisticated processing. This function is the role of the inference engine in the expert system. Different techniques are used, depending on the inference engine. When there are many rules, the evaluation of the rules can be time-consuming.

Expert System Software

Expert systems are much more complex than the example shown in Figures 11.18 and 11.19. Their knowledge base may contain hundreds or thousands of rules, and the inference engine may be very complex. Development of such systems is difficult. Specialists called *knowledge engineers* usually do the development. The knowledge engineer must first contact experts in the problem that the system is trying to solve, and determine what rules the experts use. For example, the rules in a personnel expert system would be determined by asking experienced personnel managers in the business how they make hiring decisions. This process can be extremely time-consuming.

After the rules have been determined, the knowledge engineer must construct the knowledge base and the inference engine to evaluate the rules. One way of doing this is to prepare a program in a programming language designed for artificial intelligence. Examples of such languages are LISP and PROLOG. Most often, however, a program is used that provides the skeleton of an expert system. This type of program, called an *expert system shell*, contains an inference engine and a user interface (Figure 11.20). The knowledge engineer has to enter the rules in the knowledge base into the program to form a complete expert system. Expert system shells are available for all types of computers, including personal computers.

Other Artificial Intelligence Applications

Expert systems are only one application of artificial intelligence in business. Several other applications are becoming common.

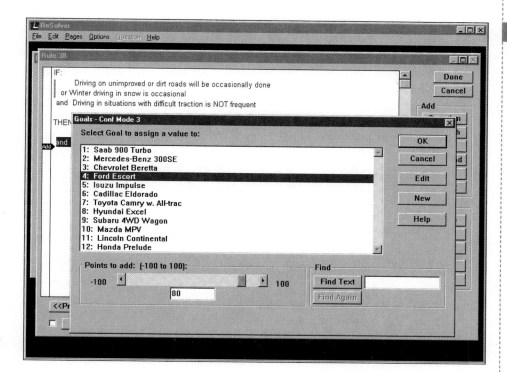

FIGURE 11.20

An expert system shell ▲

Neural Networks. One application of artificial intelligence in business is **neural networks**. A neural network is a program that mimics the way humans learn and think by creating a model of the human brain. The brain is made up of cells, called *neurons*, that are interconnected in complex patterns. (There are about 100 billion neurons in the human brain.) A neuron receives signals from other neurons and sends signals to certain other neurons based on those signals.

A neural network functions in a similar way. It consists of artificial neurons, which are software elements that act like human neurons. The artificial neurons are interconnected in various patterns. Each artificial neuron receives inputs from other neurons and sends outputs to certain other neurons. Unlike the human brain, however, a neural network may have only a few hundred artificial neurons.

A neural network can learn from experience. By entering inputs into the network and having the network compare its outputs with known outputs, the network can modify itself over time to respond correctly. After the neural network has learned how to respond to different inputs, it can be used for situations where the outputs are not known. Uses of neural networks in business include detecting credit card fraud, making financial forecasts, and identifying trends in the stock market.

Intelligent Agents. Another use of artificial intelligence in business is for **intelligent agents**. An intelligent agent is a program that acts on behalf of an individual, based on preferences that are given to the agent. For example, an intelligent agent can be used to identify useful information on the Internet. The user can give the intelligent agent his or her preferences for the types of information to find. Then the agent can locate that information on the Internet and return it to the user's computer.

Some intelligent agents use techniques from artificial intelligence to learn the user's preferences. For example, an intelligent agent can keep track of the types of information that a user requests from the Internet. Then the agent can adjust its behavior based on what it has learned. Examples of intelligent agents include agents that find the best prices for products offered for sale on the Internet, ones that put together custom on-line editions of newspapers, and agents that watch for Internet postings for specific types of employment opportunities.

Expert systems, neural networks, and intelligent agents are three applications of artificial intelligence. A number of other applications are found in business and new uses of artificial intelligence are likely to appear in the future.

Knowledge Management Systems

This chapter has concentrated on systems that provide *information* to support management decision making. Increasingly, business managers have come to realize that information is not all that is needed for decision making; *knowledge* is also needed. But what is knowledge and how can an information system provide knowledge in an organization?

Organizational Knowledge

As you know, information is data that is meaningful or useful to someone. **Knowledge**, on the other hand, is the understanding that a person has gained through education, experience, discovery, intuition, and insight. It is the whole of what someone knows about a particular area.

There are many types of knowledge, but as one example, consider knowledge about what to do when certain information is received. For instance, assume that a manager in an athletic shoe store receives the information that there are five pairs of a particular type of shoe left in inventory. What the manager does with this information depends on his or her knowledge about shoe sales and reorder policies. Thus, the manager may have knowledge about the sales of this type of shoe and may know that this quantity is too low to meet expected demand. Therefore, more shoes need to be ordered. The manager may also know that he or she should check to see whether more shoes of this type are currently on order before placing an order for more.

Knowledge takes on two main forms. It can be *explicit*, meaning that it can be stated or written in a form that someone else can understand. For example, the athletic shoe store manager's knowledge of what to do when the quantity of shoes is too low is explicit knowledge; the manager can state that before ordering more shoes, he or she should check for an existing order for the shoes. Knowledge can also be *implicit*, which means that it cannot be expressed easily but is understood by the individual. The athletic shoe store manager's knowledge that a certain quantity of a particular type of shoe is too low is implicit knowledge; the manager cannot state this knowledge because it is based on his or her understanding of which types of shoes are likely to sell well, and thus need more stock, and which types are not likely to sell well. Making decisions involves the use of both explicit and implicit knowledge.

Knowledge is individual. That is, each person has his or her own knowledge. The knowledge of a business or other type of organization is made up of the knowledge of the people who work for the organization. This **organizational knowledge** is an important asset of the organization, and it needs to be managed like other assets.

Knowledge Management

Knowledge management is the process of managing organizational knowledge. It involves several activities. First, an organization must determine what knowledge it has and acquire the knowledge that it is lacking. Discovering existing knowledge in

A Knowledge Management System at Shell Oil

Knowledge management tries to resolve a troublesome paradox: Information is becoming ever more important in the economy, and most companies say knowledge can confer competitive advantage. But corporations are already flooded with information, and most of us have more of it than we can handle.

Different companies approach that dilemma in different ways, but all try to increase the value of information by making it more timely and better targeted.

Whereas some companies see knowledge management in terms of communications and collaboration, Shell Oil views it as a knowledge multiplier. The "best practice" of a single person has the potential for tremendous leverage in a company with 21,000 employees, says Marc Davidson, associate director of the Shell Learning Center.

The center employs 10 subject matter specialists who scour Shell sources—and external sources including universities, consultants, other companies, and the literature—for leading-edge practices and ideas. Its Knowledge Management System (KMS) repository contains 1,000 documents and 50 best practices, Davidson says. For example, Shell has included in its repository a model developed by a university professor that helps an organization meet its business goals. The model has already been adopted by all four of Shell's major operating units, Davidson says.

The custom system was developed by Shell and a systems integrator. It holds knowledge in three general areas: business models, leadership, and engagement (also called human interactions). Other groups at Shell, such as geologists, have similar knowledge management systems, Davidson says.

Shell calls the knowledge repository, which is a SQL database, the "convergent" part of the KMS. The other major component, the "divergent" part, is a Lotus Domino groupware application for carrying out dialogues among employees via the company intranet. For example, the author of a best practice in the repository might talk with colleagues about his experiences with it.

In 1991 Shell reported the worst financial results in its history, and it was a wake-up call for the need to fundamentally change the way the oil giant did business, Davidson says.

"It became obvious that focusing on just the technical aspects of the business was not enough," he says. The Learning Center and the KMS are intended to "get every employee to maximize his or her contribution," he says.

One user of the KMS is Sandi Fitch, a senior executive at Shell Services International. Fitch says the KMS is helping the company undergo a systemic transformation to excellence mandated by a new CEO in the early 1990s. It's also helping Fitch, a member of a corporate leadership group, mentor technical subordinates in the ways of business leadership. "I can go into [the KMS], and we can walk through the business model, look at concepts, do some exercises together and then look at the best practices of others," Fitch says.

Davidson wouldn't say what the KMS cost, and he says Shell is just starting to analyze its benefits. Initially, benefits will be measured in terms of usage and the number of best practices posted to the database. Later, the company will seek to track ideas that are actually put into practice from the system.

Questions

1. What organizational knowledge is contained in the Shell Oil knowledge management system?
2. What is the divergent part of the Shell Oil knowledge management system?
3. How does Shell Oil plan to determine the benefits of its knowledge management system?

Web Site

Shell Oil: www.countonshell.com

Source: *Adapted from* Gary H. Anthes, "Learning How to Share," *Computerworld*, February 23, 1998, pp. 75–77.

BOOK

M A R K

an organization is difficult because it is based on what individuals know. Acquiring new knowledge can be done by hiring employees with the required knowledge or by having existing employees educated in the needed knowledge.

Next, explicit knowledge needs to be organized and recorded in a way that makes it usable by others in the organization who do not have that knowledge. Much explicit knowledge is documented in policies and procedures manuals or other forms of written documentation maintained by the organization. Organizing and recording explicit knowledge is a major task for many organizations. Implicit knowledge is very difficult, if not impossible, to record.

Finally, knowledge needs to be communicated to those who need it and shared among the employees in an organization. Making written manuals available to employees is one way of communicating explicit knowledge. Explicit as well as implicit knowledge can be shared among individuals through meetings, teamwork, varying job assignments, and similar activities.

Knowledge Management Systems

To facilitate knowledge management many organizations use knowledge management systems. A **knowledge management system (KMS)** is an information system that provides capabilities for organizing, storing, accessing, and sharing organizational knowledge. These types of systems may organize and store documents with explicit knowledge, such as procedures manuals, that can be accessed over an intranet by employees of a business. They may also provide collaborative capabilities, using groupware to facilitate sharing of explicit and implicit knowledge among employees. Knowledge management systems may use expert systems to provide expert knowledge, and they may use other techniques from artificial intelligence, such as intelligent agents, to acquire knowledge. These systems may also use data mining tools to search data warehouses for information that can serve as the basis for organizational knowledge. Any of these techniques can be used in knowledge management systems.

FIGURE 11.21

Knowledge management soft-
▲ **ware**

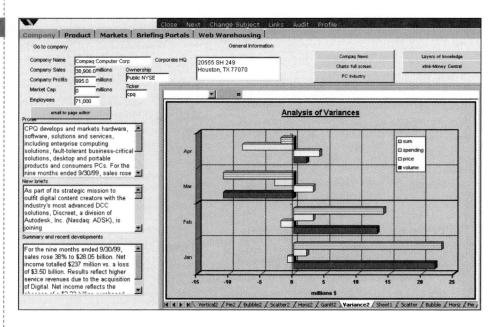

Many knowledge management systems use software designed for other purposes. For example, groupware is often used in knowledge management systems. Some systems, however, use software designed specifically for knowledge management. Examples of knowledge management software are Wincite, grapeVine, and KnowledgeX. Figure 11.21 shows a knowledge management software screen.

Knowledge management systems are new, and the concept is still evolving. It is hard to define precisely what is or is not a knowledge management system. As more experience is gained in the use of these systems, a better understanding of them will develop. You can expect to see an increase in the use of knowledge management systems in organizations in the future.

C H A P T E R   S U M M A R Y

1 Information systems improve management decision-making effectiveness by providing decision makers with information related to the decisions for which they are responsible. The information helps reduce the uncertainty about what will happen after the decision is made. Although it is not possible to eliminate all uncertainty, with good information uncertainty can be reduced and the outcome from the decision is more likely to be satisfactory. (pp. 337–338)

2 A manager needs detailed information, mainly from inside the organization, to make operational decisions related to the day-to-day running of the organization. To make tactical decisions that involve implementing policies of the organization, a manager needs less detailed, more summarized information from both inside and outside the organization. To make strategic decisions that involve setting organizational policies, goals, and long-term plans, a manager needs summarized information, much of which comes from outside the organization. (pp. 338–342)

3 A **management information system (MIS)** provides information in the form of reports and query responses to meet managers' needs at different levels of an organization. An MIS maintains a database of internal and external data, and processes the data to produce the information at the required level of detail. Transaction processing system stored data provides most of the internal data for the MIS databases. (pp. 342–347)

4 A **decision support system or (DSS)** helps managers make decisions by analyzing data from a database and providing the results of the analysis to the manager. The data is analyzed using statistical calculations and mathematical models. A DSS consists of a database, a **model base**, and software that lets the user access data in the database and use models from the model base to analyze the data. (pp. 348–352)

5 An **executive support system (ESS)** provides top-level managers with support for the functions they perform. This support includes on-line access to reports, the MIS database, and external databases; the ability to analyze and summarize data and view the results graphically; the ability to **drill down** to detailed information; and personal and workgroup applications such as e-mail, an electronic appointment calendar, and basic word processing. (pp. 352–355)

6 An **expert system (ES)** provides expert advice by storing human expert knowledge in a **knowledge base** and then using the knowledge to draw conclusions about specific problems. The knowledge is stored as **rules**, which are *if-then* structures. The expert system software consists of a user interface and an **inference engine**, which analyzes the rules in the knowledge base to draw conclusions. (pp. 357–359)

7 **Knowledge** is the understanding that a person has gained through education, discovery, intuition, and insight. **Organizational knowledge** is the total of the knowledge of the people who work for an organization. **Knowledge management** is the process of managing organizational knowledge and involves discovering, acquiring, organizing, storing, communicating, and sharing organizational knowledge. **A knowledge management systems (KMS)** provides capabilities for organizing, storing, accessing, and sharing organizational knowledge. (pp. 362–365)

KEY TERMS

Ad Hoc Report (p. 345)
Artificial Intelligence (AI) (p. 358)
Decision Support System (DSS) (p. 348)
Demand Report (p. 345)
Drilling Down (p. 354)
Executive Information System (EIS) (p. 352)
Executive Support System (ESS) (p. 352)

Expert System (ES) (p. 357)
Geographic Information System (GIS) (p. 351)
Group Decision Support System (GDSS) (p. 351)
Inference Engine (p. 358)
Intelligent Agent (p. 361)
Knowledge (p. 362)
Knowledge Base (p. 358)
Knowledge Management (p. 362)

Knowledge Management System (KMS) (p. 364)
Management Information System (MIS) (p. 342)
Model Base (p. 348)
Neural Network (p. 361)
Organizational Knowledge (p. 362)
Query (Inquiry) (p. 344)
Rule (p. 358)
Scheduled Report (p. 345)

REVIEW QUESTIONS

1 Why is information important in decision making?

2 How can information systems improve management decision-making effectiveness?

3 What are the levels of management decisions in an organization?

4 What is meant by the degree of structure of a decision, and how does it apply to decisions at different levels of an organization?

5 What are the characteristics of information needed at different levels of management decision making in an organization?

6 How does a management information system meet the information needs of managers in an organization?

7 From where does the data in the database of a management information system come?

8 What is a decision support system?

9 What ways of analyzing data may be included in a decision support system?

10 In what decision-making situations are decision support systems most appropriate?

11 What type of information system is used to support decision making among members of a workgroup?

12 How is the data in the database of a geographic information system organized?

13 What capability of an executive support system can be used to find the detailed information that produces summary information?

14 What types of databases are used in an executive support system?

15 What is an expert system?

16 Consider an expert system with the knowledge base shown in Figure 11.18. If Mary Roe is a job applicant with a BA in psychology, an MBA, and three years of experience as a teacher, what would the expert system recommend?

17 What is a neural network?

18 What is an intelligent agent?

19 What is organizational knowledge?

20 What does a knowledge management system do?

DISCUSSION QUESTIONS

1 What types of management information systems would be found at a college or university?

2 What limitations of spreadsheet software make it difficult to create sophisticated decision support systems?

3 As more computer- and information systems-literate employees move into executive positions, will

executive support systems be needed? Why or why not?

4 For an international business, management decision-making styles may be different in different parts of the world. As one example, in some countries the emphasis is on individual decision making, and in others it is on group decision making. What impact would decision-making styles have on the design of information systems that support decision making in international businesses?

5 Will computers ever be able to think like humans do? Why or why not?

6 What special knowledge, other than that found in a college catalog, is needed to advise students about course and degree requirements in a college or university? Is it explicit or implicit knowledge? Could this knowledge be made available through a knowledge management system? Why or why not?

ETHICS QUESTIONS

---

1 Information systems that support management decision making are not designed to replace managers, but to assist them. Still, some managers may rely heavily on an information system in making their decisions. What ethical problems could arise by relying too much on an information system for making a decision?

2 Assume that you are an expert in some area, and the business you work for has decided to create an expert system based on your knowledge. You have been asked to help in creating the expert system, but when it is finished, you may no longer be needed by the business. What ethical problems could this create for you?

PROBLEM-SOLVING PROJECTS

---

1 Investigate the management of an organization or a business to which you have access. Who are the managers of that organization? At what levels of the organization do they make decisions? What types of decisions do they make? What information do they need to make their decisions? Write a summary of your findings.

2 Investigate an information system that supports management decision making in an organization or a business to which you have access. (This can be the same organization or business you investigate in Problem-Solving Project 1.) Find out as much as you can about the system. Is it an MIS, a DSS, an ESS, an ES, or a KMS? (Many information systems are combinations of these.) What levels of management decision making does it support? What are its input, output, storage, and processing functions? What software does it use? What database, model base, or knowledge base does it use? Write a summary of your findings.

3 Using database software, create a simple management information system to supply information about different types of cars that a business is considering purchasing for its employees to use. The internal data that goes into the database should be data about employees and their needs for company-supplied cars. (You can use a real business or think of a hypothetical business for this data.) The external data that goes into the database should be data about cars that you gather from the Internet and other sources. Supply data for 5 to 10 employees and 20 to 30 cars of different makes and models. Develop reports that provide information to management to help in making their decision about what cars should be purchased for what employees.

4 This chapter presents the input, output, storage, and processing functions of management information, decision support, executive support, and expert systems. Chapter 10 presents these functions for transaction processing systems. Using appropriate software, prepare a table with columns for the four functions and rows for the five types of information systems. Then, fill in the table with brief summaries of each function for each type of system. Identify where the functions of the systems are similar and where they are different. Use the color capabilities of the software to mark common characteristics with the same color.

5 Prepare a spreadsheet to help a business decide how much to charge for a new product it is developing based on the following assumptions:

a The business expects to sell 12,000 units per year.

b The fixed expenses (i.e., the expenses that do not depend on how much is sold) are expected to be $45,000 per year.

c The variable expenses (i.e., the expenses that depend on how much is sold) are expected to be $8.75 per unit.

There should be rows in the spreadsheet for the revenue, the fixed expenses, the variable expenses, the total expenses, the net income (revenue minus total expenses), and any other items that might be helpful. The product price, which should be rounded to the nearest cent, should be in a separate cell. Enter different prices into this cell until you find the price for the product, based on the above assumptions, such that the net income is at least 12% of the revenue. What would be the price if the business thought it could sell 15,000 units per year?

6 Pick a course at your college or university that is optional and has a number of prerequisite courses. The course should be appropriate for some students but not for others. Develop the rules for an expert system that advises students about whether to take this course. Test the rules on several students. If available, use expert system software to create the expert system, using the rules you develop.

INTERNET AND ELECTRONIC COMMERCE PROJECTS

1 Assume that you are going to purchase a new car. Think of three or four cars that are similar in size and price that you would consider buying. Set up a table with the cars in the columns, and five or six characteristics of the cars in the rows. Assume that the specifications of the cars, such as the size of the engine and the mileage, are all about the same, so do not include these characteristics in the table. Instead, include characteristics of the cars that are important to you, but about which you cannot be certain. Examples of these characteristics are reliability, cost of maintenance, and crash-worthiness, but there are many others. Use the Web to gather information about these characteristics of the cars. Go to various Web sites to find out about each characteristic for each car, and record this information in the table. Finally, evaluate how your uncertainty about the characteristics has changed with the information you gathered. Write a summary of your conclusions.

2 Locate a Web site for a mail-order company such as L.L. Bean, Lands' End, or REI. Be sure that the site has an on-line ordering system that allows the customer to order items by using the Internet. What information does the company gather from its site that it can use for decision making? What types of decisions would be affected by this information? What types of information systems discussed in this chapter might use the information? Write a summary of your conclusions.

Grand & Toy, Canada

As Canada's largest office-supplies company, Grand & Toy sells the pens, the printers, the sticky notes, and the filing cabinets that keep the country's businesses organized and productive. But until recently, Grand & Toy, which has about $257 million in annual sales, had trouble keeping track of its own products' profitability.

In fact, when it was time to figure out which products were selling or bombing, the office-supplies giant was relying a little too much on one of its own oldies but goodies: paper. Millions of records boiled down to hundreds of sheets of paper, which somewhere contained the critical information Grand & Toy needed to analyze its business.

Toronto-based Grand & Toy is a wholly owned subsidiary of Boise Cascade Office Products. At any given time, the company has about 6,000 active SKUs (i.e., merchandise numbers), with a history that includes as many as 20,000. In addition to its own retail stores, Grand & Toy sells to more than 50,000 business clients throughout Canada. Keeping track of product and customer profitability is of critical importance. But before switching its 70 million–line sales history to a database, Grand & Toy's merchandising and marketing departments had little access to information on profitability and cost.

The company's relatively new IBM AS/400 computer was a good source for data already waiting to be mined. But when department heads went looking for an analysis of how a particular product line was doing, a glacial reporting system didn't give up answers easily. Instead, people had to rely on estimates or a feeling for how something sold in the past. Or they had to search through paper records.

"Lots of data, no information," says John Melodysta, Grand & Toy's director of information technology, describing the situation. "Anyone who wanted information had to write a query to the company's AS/400 and hope that it would run some time that month. Some queries could run for a whole weekend to produce data on a category of products. That information is available literally at the click of a mouse now."

Working with Clarity Systems, a Toronto consulting company that specializes in data warehousing, Grand & Toy went looking for a tool that would turn its sales-history data into information.

Essbase, the leading product for online analytical processing from Arbor Software, in Sunnyvale, California, soon emerged as a front-runner.

"Essbase seemed to be the most open with the current technology," says Mark Nashman, Clarity Systems's president, and it provided a nice interface for Microsoft Excel, which Grand & Toy already used. Customized spreadsheets for the merchandising department were created for Microsoft Excel.

Currently, Grand & Toy has two Essbase applications: One contains 7 GB of data on profitability for about 20,000 products. The other deals with customer profitability. It contains 4 GB of data about Grand & Toy's 60,000 customers.

Grand & Toy's merchandising department is a key user of the new system, relying on it to decide which products to list or take off the list. With information from Essbase, merchandising can find out which products are selling well in the space of a mouse click.

"Now, in a real-time environment, as the salespersons sitting there, we can say, 'Oh, yeah, it was a great seller, we sold x number last year. We'll buy a whole bunch more from you this year.' So we use it to make decisions on product," Melodysta says. "With help from Essbase, an individual product manager is able to oversee more than 1,000 SKUs. They've been able to streamline their product offerings so much better by having this tool."

Essbase has also helped Grand & Toy remain flexible and quick on its feet when it comes to sales promotions, Melodysta says. "Throughout a promotion, we want to be able to judge the effectiveness of the item that's being sold. Are we selling a lot of it?" Melodysta says. "If we need to adjust the price downward, we want to know how to react to it quickly."

"The customer-profitability [database] lets Essbase's customer-sales reps identify which customers are doing well and lets them fine-tune product mix for them," Nashman says. "We've taken the dollars per customer, sales dollars, profit dollars, as well as variable costs per customer, to come up with the true contribution of that customer."

Grand & Toy allocates the costs of delivery, selling, and warehousing on an order-by-order basis. That information lets sales representatives know which customers might have to increase order size or find a different mix of products to be profitable.

Although it currently has fewer users, a Sybase database complements Essbase by letting Grand & Toy employees drill down to an even finer level of detail.

"We use Essbase to identify what products are hot or not or what customers are hot or not, then we can look at finer detail in the Sybase world, once you've limited the data that you want to look at," Nashman says.

"Using Cognos Impromptu as a front end, the marketing department can target customers whose profitability is not what it should be. Maybe their mix of products is not that profitable," Nashman says. "You want to drill down and find out what products they're buying and rank those from high-gross profit to low-gross profit."

Grand & Toy plans to add new views of data in the future and expand Essbase access to other departments. A customer-sales view is in the works that Grand & Toy will make available to its branch offices throughout Canada.

Another project is designed primarily for the company's more than 80 retail stores. "That'll be for the district sales managers and eventually right down to the retail-store managers' level," Melodysta says.

A purchasing database has been built that lets Grand & Toy look at product vendors. "We can sort of look at what 3M is doing for us, as opposed to Acco or some of these other vendors," Melodysta says.

With so many people at Grand & Toy gaining access to Essbase, user reaction remains on a high. Of course, this is information that the business community has been dying for, Melodysta adds, so it's embraced very quickly.

Questions

1 Why did Grand & Toy have "lots of data, no information" before developing the applications described in this case?

2 What data does Grand & Toy use in its applications?

3 Why do Grand & Toy employees make use of drilling down?

4 What decisions at Grand & Toy are supported by the applications described in this case?

5 What type of information system is described in this case?

Web Site

Grand & Toy: www.grandandtoy.com

Source: *Adapted from* Heather Mackey, "One office-supplies company put an end to its paper trail," *InfoWorld*, March 24, 1997, p. 76.

Electronic Commerce
AND THE STRATEGIC IMPACT OF INFORMATION SYSTEMS

T W E L V E

12

CHAPTER OUTLINE

Providing a Strategic Impact
Electronic Commerce Systems
Interorganizational Information Systems
Global Information Systems
Strategic Information Systems

After completing this chapter, you should be able to

1 Describe how information systems can have a strategic impact on a business.

2 Describe the main types of electronic commerce.

3 List the functions provided by electronic commerce systems.

4 Explain why interorganizational systems are used in business alliances.

5 Describe several ways that a business can participate in an interorganizational system.

6 Explain how an electronic data interchange system functions.

7 Explain what global information systems are.

8 Describe different forms global information systems can take and how each form relates to international business strategy.

9 Explain what a strategic information system is and what types of information systems are strategic.

10 Describe how strategic information system opportunities can be identified in a business.

nformation systems provide many benefits to an organization. Systems that are used by individuals, such as personal database management and spreadsheet analysis systems, improve personal productivity. Systems that help members of a group work together, such as information sharing and electronic conferencing systems, encourage group collaboration. Systems that support business operations, such as transaction processing systems, increase the efficiency of the operations. Systems that provide information for management decision making, such as management information and decision support systems, improve the effectiveness of the decision making. To be competitive today, businesses must have a number of computer information systems so that they will be as productive and effective as their competitors.

Even with the necessary computer information systems, some businesses are not as competitive as others because their information systems do not have a *strategic impact* on the businesses. A strategic impact provides a business with an advantage over its competitors. This chapter looks at information systems that can have a strategic impact on a business.

The chapter first explains how an information system can have a strategic impact on a business. Then it looks at systems that are having a significant strategic impact on many businesses today—those that support electronic commerce. Next the chapter examines other information systems that can have a strategic impact, including interorganizational information systems and global information systems. Finally, the chapter discusses strategic information systems in general.[1]

Providing a Strategic Impact

Information systems that have a strategic impact on a business help create a **competitive advantage** for the business. This advantage, which puts the business in a stronger position to compete than other businesses, can be gained in several ways. Figure 12.1 summarizes the main approaches for gaining a competitive advantage and how information systems can help in each approach.

Cost Leadership

One way a business can gain a competitive advantage is through *cost leadership*, which means having the lowest production or operating costs among the business's competitors. Information systems can help create cost leadership by providing unique operational and managerial support that reduces costs. For example, consider an athletic shoe manufacturer. With special types of manufacturing information systems, such as computer-integrated manufacturing (CIM), the shoe manufacturer could have the lowest production costs in the athletic shoe industry. Its shoes would sell for less than its competitors' shoes, thus giving the business a competitive advantage.

Differentiation

Another way a business can gain a competitive advantage is through *differentiation*, which means providing goods or services that are unique so that the customer wants to purchase from the business. Information systems can help create differentiation by providing the tools to identify and develop unique goods or services. For example, the athletic shoe manufacturer could use a marketing research information system to

---

[1] Many of the ideas about strategic impact and strategic information systems presented in this chapter are based on Seev Neumann's book *Strategic Information Systems* (New York: Macmillan College Publishing, 1994).

FIGURE 12.1

Gaining a competitive advantage

Approach	How Business Can Achieve	How Information Systems Can Help
Cost leadership	Have lowest production or operating costs among competitors	Provide unique operational and managerial support that reduces costs
Differentiation	Provide goods or services that are unique	Provide tools to identify and develop unique goods or services
Focus	Provide goods or services that are designed for a specific segment of the market (niche)	Provide information to identify niche markets
Innovation	Develop new ways of operating or managing the business	Provide the technology necessary for innovation in a business
Growth	Expand goods or services provided by the business	Provide capabilities to handle increased volume of business
Business alliances	Form groups of businesses that work together	Provide the technology for businesses in alliance to work effectively together

identify consumer interest in a new type of shoe, a computer-aided design (CAD) system to design the shoe quickly, and a computer-aided manufacturing (CAM) system to produce the shoe rapidly. If the business could identify and produce a new product before its competitors did, the business would have a competitive advantage, at least until other businesses caught up.

Focus

A third way competitive advantage can be gained by a business is to *focus on a niche*, which means to provide goods or services that are designed for a specific segment of the market. For example, the athletic shoe manufacturer might decide to focus on track shoes and gain a competitive advantage by becoming the principal producer of such shoes. Information systems can help a business focus on a niche by providing information to identify niche markets. For example, the athletic shoe manufacturer could use a decision support system to analyze the data in a data warehouse by using data mining techniques to help identify potential market niches. (Data warehouses and data mining are discussed in Chapter 7.)

Innovation

Another way of gaining a competitive advantage is through *innovation*, which means developing new ways of operating or managing the business. Information systems can provide the technology necessary for innovation in a business. For example, the athletic shoe manufacturer could use an innovative approach to inventory control that requires a special information system to function. The innovative approach, which would not be possible without the information system, would provide better inventory management than the approach used by competitors, thus giving the business a competitive advantage.

Growth

A fifth way a business can gain a competitive advantage is by *growth*, which means expanding the goods or services provided by the business. Such expansion could be into new goods or services or into new geographic regions. (This approach is the opposite of the focus approach.) Information systems are essential for businesses to grow because they provide the capabilities to handle the increased volume of business. For example, if the athletic shoe manufacturer wants to grow by expanding into new lines of shoes, it needs the appropriate information systems (order entry, inventory control, and others) for the increase in transactions.

Business Alliances

A sixth way a business can gain a competitive advantage is through *business alliances*, which means forming groups of businesses that work together. For example, the athletic shoe manufacturer could form an alliance with a shoe distributor to exclusively distribute its shoes. Information systems can help create alliances by providing the technology for the businesses in the alliance to work effectively together. Thus, the shoe manufacturer and the distributor could link their information systems so that the manufacturer could check the distributor's inventory to decide when to increase production, and the distributor could electronically place orders with the manufacturer. (Business alliances are discussed in detail later in this chapter.)

Helping a business gain a competitive advantage through cost leadership, differentiation, focus, innovation, growth, and business alliances are just some of the ways that information systems can have a strategic impact on a business. As you read about different types of information systems in this chapter, you will see other ways these systems can have a strategic impact.

Electronic Commerce Systems

The information systems that are currently having a significant strategic impact on many businesses and other types of organizations are those that support electronic commerce. **Electronic commerce (e-commerce)** is the use of networks, especially the Internet, to promote and sell goods and services. An **electronic commerce (e-commerce), system** is an information system that provides e-commerce capabilities for an organization. Chapter 6 describes the hardware and software needed for e-commerce. This section discusses the business uses of e-commerce and the characteristics of electronic commerce systems.

The Strategic Impact of Electronic Commerce

Electronic commerce can have a strategic impact on businesses in several ways. One way is by providing an innovative approach for conducting business. The promotion and sale of goods and services using networks is a new and unique way of doing business. Businesses that have developed e-commerce capabilities have an advantage over their competitors that only use traditional commerce methods because of the innovation in e-commerce.

Another strategic impact of e-commerce on businesses is a reduction in the cost of transactions, which can create a cost-leadership advantage. The cost of transactions is lower with e-commerce because electronic commerce systems handle much of the work done manually in traditional commerce; selling, ordering, billing, and related activities are all done electronically, thus reducing costs.

Still another way e-commerce can have a strategic impact on businesses is through differentiation. E-commerce allows a business to provide unique, customized products for its customers. Because an e-commerce business does not have to stock standard products on the shelves of a store, it can offer customized products to its customers. This ability provides a competitive advantage over traditional commerce.

E-commerce also has a strategic impact on businesses because with it a business can provide its goods and services 24 hours per day, 7 days per week, in almost any part of the world. A business no longer closes for two-thirds of the day and on weekends and holidays. Customers in different time zones do not have to wait until the business opens to purchase goods or services. Geographic distance no longer matters because all transactions take place at electronic speed.

E-commerce has several disadvantages over traditional commerce. One is that customers cannot see or touch the actual product; only pictures or other images of the product are provided. This disadvantage is most significant for retail customers, but less important for business customers. Another disadvantage is that the product is not received immediately, but delivered after some time. Again, this disadvantage is more important for retail customers than for others.

Types of Electronic Commerce

Electronic commerce can be characterized by the parties that are involved in the transaction, resulting in two main types of e-commerce: business-to-consumer and business-to-business electronic commerce. Several other types of electronic commerce are also used.

Business-to-Consumer Electronic Commerce. **Business-to-consumer (B2C) electronic commerce** involves a business selling its goods or services electronically to the final consumer, which is usually an individual. B2C e-commerce is retail sales done electronically, and businesses that engage in B2C e-commerce are sometimes called **e-tailers**. B2C e-commerce is the type most recognizable to end users. Figure 12.2 lists examples of companies that engage in B2C e-commerce.

B2C e-commerce companies operate in several ways.[2] Some e-tailers (called *direct marketers*) sell the products they produce, and some (called *indirect marketers*) use other

Company	Product	Web Site URL
Amazon.com	Books, music, videos	www.amazon.com
Lands' End	Apparel	www.landsend.com
United Airlines	Airline travel	www.ual.com
Dell Computer	Computers	www.dell.com
Egghead.com	Software	www.egghead.com
Charles Schwab	Stock brokerage services	www.charlesschwab.com
eToys	Toys and games	www.etoys.com
drugstore.com	Health and beauty items	www.drugstore.com
FTD	Flowers	www.ftd.com
Hallmark	Greeting cards	www.hallmark.com
Wal-Mart	General merchandise	www.walmart.com
E*TRADE	On-line investing	www.etrade.com

FIGURE 12.2

Companies engaging in business-to-consumer electronic commerce ▲

[2] Efraim Turban, Jae Lee, David King, and H. Michael Chung, *Electronic Commerce: A Managerial Perspective* (Upper Saddle River, New Jersey: Prentice Hall, 2000), pp. 44–46.

e-commerce companies to sell their products. Some companies (called *full cybermarketers*) only sell their products electronically, and others (called *partial cybermarketers*) sell through traditional means as well as electronically. Some companies (called *electronic distributors*) fill the orders they take from their own stock, and other companies (called *electronic brokers*) send the orders they receive to manufacturers or wholesalers that fill the orders. Some e-tailers specialize in a certain type of product, and others provide a wide range of products for their customers. Finally, some e-commerce companies operate only in a limited geographic region, and others provide their products nationally or globally.

B2C e-commerce normally involves the use of the Internet and the World Wide Web. Consumers connect to an e-tailer's Web site, review product information, make a selection, fill out an order form on the screen, and provide payment information. The product is generally delivered after several days. E-tailers also provide after-sales service information as well as return and exchange options.

Business-to-Business Electronic Commerce.   **Business-to-business (B2B) electronic commerce** involves one business selling its goods or services electronically to other businesses. Although not as well known to end users, more B2B e-commerce takes place than B2C e-commerce. Figure 12.3 lists some examples of companies that engage in B2B e-commerce.

There are three main types of B2B e-commerce, depending on what type of business is in control of the market.[3] In the first type (called a *supplier-oriented marketplace*), a supplier company provides e-commerce capabilities for other businesses to order its products. The other businesses place orders electronically from the supplier, much in the same way that consumers place orders in B2C e-commerce. In the second type of B2B e-commerce (called a *buyer-oriented marketplace*), the business that wants to purchase products requests quotations or bids from other companies electronically. Each supplier company that is interested places a bid electronically, and the buyer selects the winning supplier from the submitted bids. In the final type of B2B e-commerce

FIGURE 12.3

Companies engaging in business-to-business ▲ electronic commerce

Company	Product	Web Site URL
Cisco Systems	Network equipment	www.cisco.com
eFueloil	Fuel oil	www.efueloil.com
GE Information Services	Industrial goods and services trading	www.tpn.geis.com
Ingram Micro	Computer products	www.ingrammicro.com
Boeing	Aircraft parts	www.boeing.com
FedEx	Package delivery	www.fedex.com
RE/MAX	Real estate	www.remax.net
ProcureNet	Maintenance, repair, and operations goods procurement	www.procurenet.com
Boise Cascade Office Products	Office products	www.bcop.com

[3] Ibid., pp. 203–209.

(called an *intermediary-oriented marketplace*), a third business acts as an intermediary between the supplier and the buyer. The intermediary business provides e-commerce capabilities for suppliers and buyers to identify each other and to electronically transact business. The intermediary may also provide facilities for businesses to auction products to the highest bidder using an **electronic auction**. Some businesses may provide just one type of B2B e-commerce, but many businesses provide several types. For example, a business could be an e-commerce supplier for some types of products and an e-commerce intermediary for others.

B2B e-commerce may use the public Internet or it may use a private extranet set up by a company. An extranet, which links the intranets of two businesses, provides more security than the Internet. This added security is important for many business-to-business transactions.

Other Types of Electronic Commerce.   In addition to business-to-consumer and business-to-business electronic commerce, several other types of e-commerce exist. One is **consumer-to-consumer (C2C) electronic commerce**. In this form of e-commerce one consumer sells a product or service to another consumer, usually through an intermediary e-commerce business. The intermediary provides a Web site for consumers to advertise their products and may also provide for completion of the sales transaction, including payment. In one approach, the intermediary acts as an electronic classified-ad section of a newspaper and advertises products for consumers. In another approach, consumers put up items for *electronic auction* through the intermediary.

Another type of e-commerce is **intrabusiness** (or **organizational**) **electronic commerce**. This form of e-commerce involves transactions between departments, regions, subsidiaries, or other units of a business. For example, the manufacturing unit of a computer company may sell its computers to administrative units of the company by means of intrabusiness e-commerce. The electronic transactions in intrabusiness e-commerce usually take place over the business's intranet.

In these descriptions of the types of e-commerce, the word *business* refers not just to for-profit businesses, but to any type of organization. Thus, the business in B2C or B2B e-commerce could be a school, a not-for-profit organization, a government agency, or almost any other type of organization. E-commerce is not limited to just businesses, but is used by most types of organizations.

Characteristics of Electronic Commerce Systems

Information systems that support electronic commerce provide a number of functions. Some of these functions are similar to those found in traditional information systems, and some are unique to electronic commerce systems. Figure 12.4 summarizes the functions that electronic commerce systems provide.

Product Presentation.   An electronic commerce system should provide a way for customers, which can be individual consumers or businesses, to identify products they want to purchase. Products need to be promoted electronically to attract the attention of customers. E-commerce Web sites should provide easily accessible information about the characteristics and features of the company's products. Web sites should also make pricing information readily available to the customer. Many e-commerce Web sites have an **electronic catalog**, which is a list of products with descriptions, pictures, and prices. The data in the catalog is derived from a product database maintained by the business's inventory control system. Customers can browse the catalog or use a search tool provided by the e-commerce

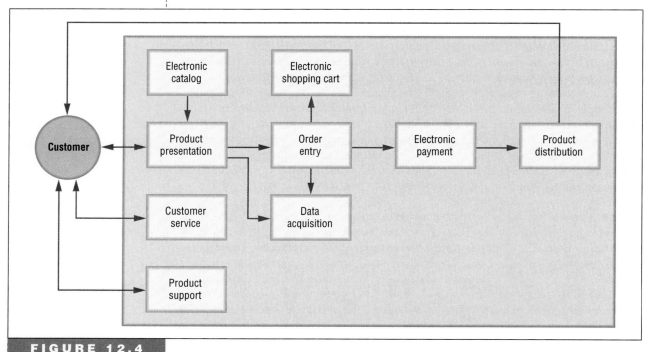

FIGURE 12.4

Functions of electronic commerce systems

system to locate desired items quickly. Often the customer can click on an item to obtain more detailed information about it.

Order Entry.   After a customer has selected the desired product, he or she needs to enter an order for the product into the electronic commerce system. Order entry is often accomplished by allowing the customer to add items to an **electronic shopping cart**, which is a list of the products the customer wants to purchase. Before an item is added to the shopping cart, the e-commerce system should have the inventory control system check the product database to see if there is adequate stock on hand or if the product needs to be ordered from a manufacturer. When the customer has finished selecting all the items needed, he or she can complete the order by providing name and address information, as well as information for payment (described next). After all these steps are completed, the customer's order is processed by the e-commerce system. Processing involves providing data to the inventory control system to update the product database to reflect the sales. Processing also involves providing for distribution of the product to the customer (discussed later in this chapter).

Payment.   To allow customers to pay for the items purchased, an electronic commerce system should have an **electronic payment** capability. Various approaches are used for electronic payment. For individual consumers, the most common approach is payment by a credit or debit card. The customer enters the card number and expiration date, and the e-commerce system checks the customer's credit with the bank's information system and then charges the customer's card with the total amount of the purchase. To ensure the security of the card information sent over the Internet, special protocols that provide data encryption are used. For business customers, the seller can bill the customer, if the customer's credit rating is satisfactory, or the customer can provide for automatic payment through electronic funds transfer (EFT) between the customer's and seller's bank accounts.

Product Distribution. Product distribution in electronic commerce systems depends on the type of product the business sells. If the product is a physical item such as an item of clothing or a truck load of spare parts, then the e-commerce information system needs to notify the shipping department or other distribution center that the product should be shipped. Many items sold over the Internet, however, can be distributed electronically. These include software, music, and information. In this case, the e-commerce system can send the item to the customer's computer over a network as soon as the purchase is completed.

Customer Service. At any time before, during, or after purchasing an item, the customer may need special services. For example, a customer may have a question about how a particular item of clothing fits before purchasing it. During the ordering process, the customer may have difficulty using the electronic commerce system. After receiving an item, the customer may decide to exchange or return the item. Many of these customer service situations can be dealt with by providing detailed information and answers to questions electronically. A well-designed e-commerce system should provide capabilities for customer service. It should also give a toll-free telephone number for the customer to call or an e-mail address to contact if the answers to the questions cannot be found on the Web site.

Product Support. After a customer has purchased a product, he or she may need additional support from the business. For example, a purchaser of software may need help installing or using the software. Product support can be provided by the electronic commerce system by including detailed information about the product on the Web site. A common technique is to include a list of frequently asked questions (FAQs) and their answers. Customers can browse through the information and, in many cases, find the answers to their questions. The e-commerce system may also provide an e-mail system so that the customer can send a question to the business and receive the answer through e-mail, usually several days later. There may also be a chat system to allow the customer to interact with a customer service representative. If a question cannot be answered by using one of these approaches, the customer can usually call a toll-free number for help.

Data Acquisition. The final function provided by an electronic commerce system is data acquisition. Important data can be acquired from an e-commerce Web site and used for various purposes, especially market research. For example, data about customer preferences can be recorded electronically each time a customer searches the e-commerce site. Additional market research data can be obtained when the customer makes a selection and enters an order. In all data acquisition, provisions should be provided to ensure the privacy of the individual customer. The data that is acquired is stored in a data warehouse for later analysis using data mining tools.

Throughout this description of electronic commerce systems we have focused on systems that sell products. Many e-commerce systems, however, provide services. For example, e-commerce is used for electronic banking, making hotel and other travel reservations, trading stocks, and taking college courses on-line. Many of the same functions are needed in these types of e-commerce systems. The system should provide capabilities for identifying the service the customer wants, entering an order for the service, paying for the service, distributing the service to the customer, providing customer service, providing support on the service, and gathering market research data.

Business-to-Business E-Commerce at Adolph Coors

When Adolph Coors in Golden, Colorado, rolled out its merchandise catalog to beer distributors via an extranet, it looked just like a regular merchandise store on the front end. But on the back end, pieces of the orders stream from a shopper's cart to some 60 vendors, each responsible for providing specific products, such as t-shirts or hats.

Routing the orders to separate vendors for drop shipment to customers is handled by a bridging technology developed by Digital River. The Minneapolis-based firm also hosts Coors's new catalog site. Dave Reid, manager of CoorsNet, the network that links distributors to the corporation, says Coors chose to outsource the site because Digital River's business-to-business order system was ready to go, and it simply didn't make sense to reinvent it.

Coors had been using an expensive printed catalog to sell branded merchandise to distributors, Reid says. He adds, "If someone [had] to order three hats, three shirts, and a golf bag, they probably [had] to make three phone calls. With the online catalog, they can put them in one shopping basket. Digital River splits them out."

Matt Voda, senior director of marketing at Digital River, says the company's proprietary licensed vendor system treats each of the Coors merchandise vendors as a single store and then displays all the vendors as a collective on the catalog site. "There's one shopping cart, one set of order management tools, one shipping engine, and one taxation engine," Voda says. The shipping engine can be configured to ship from multiple warehouses or different warehouses for the same vendor to reduce shipping times and cost, Voda adds.

Coors's decision to outsource follows a trend that Ted Schadler, group director for business-to-business strategy at Forrester Research in Cambridge, Massachusetts, calls exIT, or external IT. "It's where the technology is external and can be shared (by different companies)," Schadler says.

For Coors, selling commercial merchandise makes good business sense. It reinforces the Coors name, Reid says, and could turn a break-even business unit into a better profit center.

Coors will offer merchandise both online and through the printed catalog throughout the year, Reid says. But he said he plans to cut the usage of the printed piece. "Hopefully, we'll be able to cut the number (of catalogs printed) in half next year," he says.

Reid says he anticipates that Coors will increase merchandise sales through the online catalog by adding promotions on the fly—an approach that isn't cost-effective in print.

Questions

1. How does the Coors electronic catalog handle merchandise from multiple vendors?
2. Why does it not matter to a beer distributor using the Coors e-commerce system that merchandise comes from multiple vendors?
3. How does the Coors e-commerce system handle merchandise distribution?

Web Site

Adolph Coors: www.coors.com

Source: *Adapted from* James Cope, "Coors Moves Branded Merchandise Online," *Computerworld,* March 13, 2000, p. 14.

Electronic Business

Electronic commerce is one element of a broader concept of using computers and networks in all aspects of a business; this concept is called **electronic business (e-business)**. In e-business, many of the functions of the business are performed electronically. These functions do not just include product promotion and selling, but also product development, materials purchasing, production, and other business activities. Some companies use the term *e-business* instead of *e-commerce* to emphasize the fact that they go beyond commerce in their use of electronic technology. The use of technology in business is expanding rapidly, and in the future all business may be e-business.

Interorganizational Information Systems

Business-to-business electronic commerce is a way for two or more organizations to transact business over a network. Much B2B e-commerce is for a specific purpose, such as to purchase repair parts or schedule delivery of an item. The business may not know in advance who the supplier of the product will be and only selects the supplier after investigating several sources. This type of e-commerce uses the public Internet because it is readily available and easy to use.

In many B2B e-commerce situations, however, a business uses the same supplier repeatedly. Because the business knows who the supplier will be, it can establish a relationship in advance with the supplier. In this case, the two businesses may create an information system that they share. This type of B2B e-commerce system is called an **interorganizational information system**, or, for short, an **interorganizational system (IOS)**.

Traditionally, interorganizational systems have used value added networks (VANs) to connect the information systems of two or more organizations. Recall from Chapter 6 that a VAN is a wide area network supplied by a communications company for the exclusive use of the business contracting for the VAN. The VAN provides the communications link between businesses for the IOS. Although VANs are still used for IOSs, increasingly these systems use the Internet to transmit data between organizations. In this case, an extranet links the intranets of two or more organizations over the Internet. Special protocols and data encryption are used to ensure the security of the transmitted data.

Unlike other B2B e-commerce systems, IOSs transmit data in standardized formats. The particular format used depends on the type of IOS, but the businesses using the system must agree on the format.

The most familiar examples of IOSs are electronic data interchange (EDI) systems, which provide for the transfer of data between businesses, and electronic funds transfer (EFT) systems, which provide for the transfer of funds between financial institutions. Other types of IOSs also are used. Before examining the characteristics of IOSs, however, you need to understand business alliances.

Business Alliances

Businesses compete with other businesses, so it would seem that two businesses, especially if they were direct competitors, would not want to cooperate with each other. This is not always the situation, however, because many businesses find it to their mutual benefit to cooperate. These businesses coordinate some of their operations or link some of their resources to form **business alliances**, which serve the interests of all businesses in the alliance.

There are several types of business alliances (Figure 12.5). Some alliances involve businesses that compete directly with each other. For example, computer companies sometimes work together to develop software for use on each companies' hardware. Banks work together to provide automated teller machine access for each other's customers. Insurance companies work together to share the risks of large insurance

FIGURE 12.5

▲ Business alliances

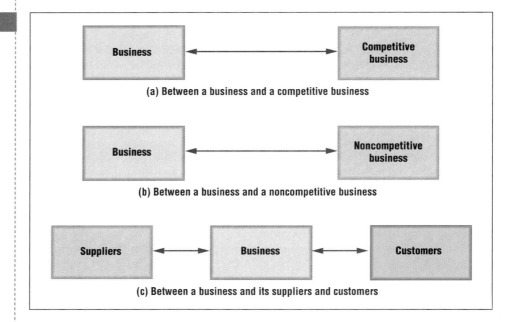

(a) Between a business and a competitive business

(b) Between a business and a noncompetitive business

(c) Between a business and its suppliers and customers

losses. All these businesses continue to compete; their alliances help them provide their products to their customers.

Direct competitors are not the only businesses that form alliances. Many alliances involve promoting and selling the products of two businesses that do not compete directly. For example, a bank might form an alliance with an airline company to promote the bank's credit card along with the airline's frequent flyer program. A software company might form an alliance with a publisher to provide software to be packaged with books and manuals. In these situations the businesses in the alliance benefit from promoting and selling their products together.

Alliances also exist between a business and its suppliers and customers. A business may form an alliance with its suppliers to provide for favorable delivery and pricing of raw materials. The business may also form an alliance with its customers to provide for easy ordering of finished products. These alliances are to the benefit of the business as well as to its suppliers and customers.

The Strategic Impact of Interorganizational Systems

Interorganizational systems provide for the sharing of information and processing between businesses in a business alliance. Such systems are essential for many alliances to function efficiently. For example, banks could not provide ATM access for other banks' customers without an extensive interbank network. An airline could not link its frequent flyer program to a bank's credit card without the necessary system to provide for the transfer of data between the companies. A business could not provide other businesses with easy ordering of its products without an EDI system. All these examples illustrate IOSs that make it possible for the business alliances to operate smoothly and efficiently.

IOSs can have a strategic impact on the businesses in an alliance. This impact affects the way the businesses in the alliance compete with other businesses and thus provides them with a competitive advantage. The advantage can come from reduced costs because of the alliance. For example, ordering products electronically with an EDI system is less expensive than ordering other ways. The advantage can also come from unique products provided through the alliance, such as when a bank's credit card is linked with products from other businesses. Without the appropriate IOSs, many business alliances would not function efficiently, and no competitive advantage would be gained.

Characteristics of Interorganizational Systems

Businesses are involved in interorganizational systems as either sponsors or participants. An IOS *sponsor* is a business that sets up and maintains an IOS. For example, an airline that sets up an airline reservation system is an IOS sponsor. So is a communications company that sets up a network to be used by banks for ATM communication. The sponsor develops the IOS and makes it available to other businesses.

An IOS *participant* is a business that uses an IOS. For example, a travel agent uses an airline reservation system and thus is a participant in the IOS created by the airline. A bank attaches its ATMs to a network and thus is a participant in the IOS created by the communications company.

Businesses can participate in an IOS in several ways (Figure 12.6). In one approach, the business simply enters input and receives output by using an IOS sponsored by another business. The example of a travel agent making reservations through an airline reservation system illustrates this approach. EDI systems also illustrate this approach.

In another approach, a business accesses data storage or processing capabilities of another business in the IOS. For example, a supplier may be able to check the inventory levels in the inventory database of its customers through the IOS. With this information, the supplier can automatically restock the customer when inventory levels are too low. (This technique is called *supplier-* or *vendor-managed inventory*.) Another example is a system that allows a business to check the status of its shipment in a freight company's database.

A third way a business can participate in an IOS is to use capabilities of the IOS received from the sponsor for managing internal operations. The business also par-

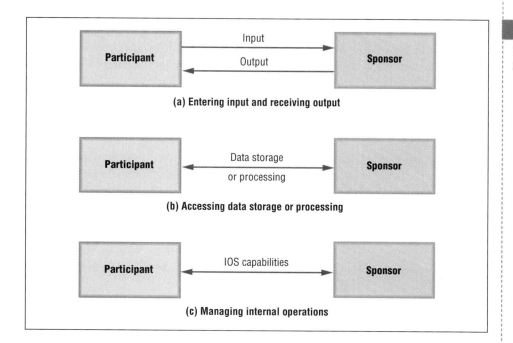

(a) Entering input and receiving output

(b) Accessing data storage or processing

(c) Managing internal operations

FIGURE 12.6

Participation in interorganizational systems

ticipates in ways described previously, but in addition uses the IOS for other functions. For example, an IOS for a pharmacy can be used to order drugs from a supplier, manage the pharmacy's inventory, and prepare financial statements for the pharmacy. This last function does not require transmitting data to the supplier; it only involves the internal operations of the business.

An athletic shoe manufacturer may be a sponsor or a participant in various IOSs. It might sponsor an EDI system so its customers can order products more easily. It might also use an IOS to check customer inventory levels and automatically resupply certain customers when stocks fall too low. The shoe manufacturer might also participate in various IOSs with its suppliers to order raw materials. It might also participate in systems with transportation companies for scheduling shipment of materials or finished products.

Electronic Data Interchange Systems

Because electronic data interchange (EDI) systems are so common, we take a separate look at these IOSs. An EDI system provides for electronic communication of data between businesses. Purchase order data, shipping data, invoice data, product description data, price list data, and insurance data are some of the types of data sent using EDI systems.

EDI Data.   The data a business sends by using an EDI system often represents a transaction. The data is an output of one business's transaction processing systems and an input to another business's transaction processing system (Figure 12.7). For example, purchase order data may be sent electronically to order products. The purchase order data is an output of one business's purchasing system and an input to the other business's order entry system. As another example, invoice data may be sent to bill for the products sold. The invoice data is produced by the billing system in one business and received by the accounts payable system in the other business. In effect, the transaction processing systems of two businesses communicate with each other by using the EDI system.

Not all data sent by EDI systems represents transactions. For example, Figure 12.8 shows several ways that EDI systems can be used between a business and its suppliers and customers. A business can send specifications for a product to a supplier, along with a request for a quotation for supplying the product. The supplier can then send back the requested quotation, which the business can use to make a purchasing decision. At that point the business can send a purchase order, which the supplier can acknowledge. When the product is ready for shipping, the supplier can send a notification to the business. After shipment, the supplier can send an invoice to the business.

A customer can send a price request to the business, and the business can send back a price list. Then the customer can send an order, which the business can acknowledge. Eventually, after the order is sent, the business can send a bill to the customer. All this data can be transmitted between the business and its suppliers and customers electronically by using EDI.

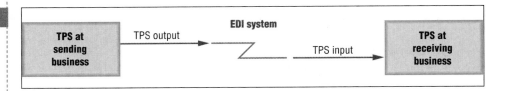

FIGURE 12.8

Electronic data interchange ▲

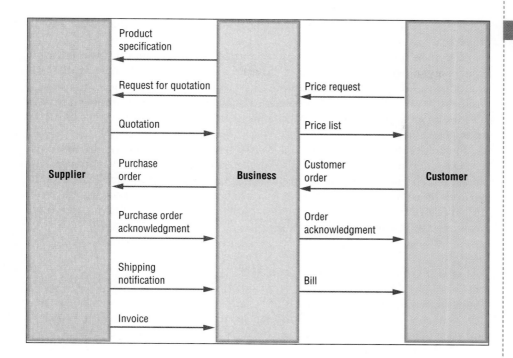

Traditional Versus Internet EDI. An EDI system, like all IOSs, requires a data communications link between businesses. Traditionally, this communications link has been a VAN or a special network set up by the sponsor of the EDI system. To use EDI over the network, each business participating in an EDI system needs communications hardware to connect to the network and special EDI software to transmit and receive electronic data over the network. The data is sent in a standardized format agreed to by the businesses participating in the EDI system.

The Internet can also be used for EDI communications. In this case, special Internet EDI software is needed that sends and receives standardized EDI data over the Internet. In addition, the software provides data encryption capabilities to ensure the security of the EDI data. In the future, the Internet may become the principal means for EDI communication.

Data sent by EDI is not the same as a fax or electronic mail. A fax document is received and read on paper or on a screen by a person. Similarly, e-mail is read on a screen by a person. EDI data, on the other hand, is, in general, input to a system used by the receiving businesses. For example, EDI purchase order data is input to an order entry system and starts the process of shipping a product. EDI invoice data is input to an accounts payable system that generates a payment. Some EDI data may be read by people, but for the most part, this data is entered into other systems.

EDI Benefits and Problems. There are several benefits of EDI. One is speed. Electronic data can be transmitted faster than paper documents, so EDI saves time. Another benefit is that data entry errors are reduced. When a paper document, such as a purchase order, is sent from one business to another, the data from the document must be keyed into the system used by the receiving business. Any time data is keyed, errors are possible. With EDI data, however, the data is entered electronically, thus eliminating keying errors at the receiving business. Thus, with EDI, data is transmitted faster and more accurately. These benefits can reduce the cost of transactions for a business.

The main problems with EDI are organizational and technical. First, organizations have to agree to participate in the EDI system. If one business proposes to sponsor an EDI system, other businesses must agree to participate. Second, technical problems must be solved. Appropriate hardware and software must be available to all businesses participating in the system, and the necessary communications link must be in place.

In addition to the organizational and technical problems, EDI can be expensive. The expense is not only in special hardware and software that must be purchased and set up, but also in the communications costs, which can be considerable for a private network or a VAN, although lower if the Internet is used. Even though EDI can be difficult to set up and expensive, once established, the system can provide significant benefits to the businesses participating in it.

Global Information Systems

Some businesses operate entirely within a single country. All the business's product development, production, sales, and management take place in the same country, and all suppliers and customers of the business are located in that country. Increasingly, however, businesses engage in activities that extend beyond national borders. An *international business* may produce its products in several countries and sell them in many countries. Its suppliers and customers may be located anywhere in the world. It may employ engineers and designers in a number of countries to develop new products. The managers of the business may be spread among a number of countries.

The information systems of a business that operate only in a single country are confined to that country. These systems can be called *domestic information systems*. Some of the information systems of an international business may also be confined to a single country and thus are domestic information systems. For example, the payroll system for the business's operations in each country may be specific to the country. Many information systems for international businesses, however, span national borders. These systems, called **global (international) information systems**, provide communication between business locations around the world, transfer of data between international locations, and use of system functions (input, output, processing, and storage) at different locations worldwide.

An example of a global information system is an order entry system that allows customer orders to be entered in the different countries in which an international business sells its products. The orders are then transferred to a single location for storage and processing. After processing, the sales orders are transmitted to distribution points located in other countries for shipment of products to customers. Because the components and functions of this system span national borders, it is a global information system.

International Business

Businesses engage in international activities for several reasons (Figure 12.9). One is for *international sales*. That is, businesses want to be able to sell their products in many countries. For example, consider an athletic shoe manufacturer. Athletic shoes are sold all over the world, and a shoe manufacturer might want to sell its shoes in many countries to increase its sales.

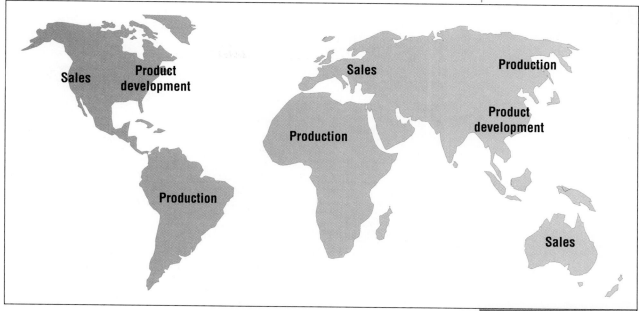

FIGURE 12.9

International business activities ▲

Another reason that businesses engage in international activities is for *international production*. That is, businesses want to be able to produce or manufacture their products in many countries. Thus, the athletic shoe manufacturer might want to produce its shoes in various countries. The decision of where to manufacture a product depends on production costs in different countries and where the product will be sold.

A third reason that businesses engage in international activities is to take advantage of *international product development*. Research and development activities can take place anywhere in the world, depending on where the best development personnel are located. Thus, an athletic shoe manufacturer might use shoe designers in many countries to design its shoes.

International businesses generally follow one of several basic strategies[4] (Figure 12.10). In the *multinational* strategy, the business allows its foreign operations to function largely independently of each other and of the central headquarters. In effect, each foreign operation is a separate business that makes its own decisions regarding product development, production, and selling. For example, an athletic shoe manufacturer that follows this strategy would allow each foreign production facility to decide independently what and how many shoes to make. This strategy is very responsive to local needs. The central headquarters exercises only loose control over the foreign operations, and the foreign operations mainly report only financial results to the headquarters.

In the *global* strategy, the central headquarters coordinates the activities of the foreign operations closely. The headquarters standardizes products for sale in foreign locations and determines how the products will be sold. Product development takes place at the central location, and production may also be centralized. For example, the central headquarters of an athletic shoe manufacturer that follows the global strategy would determine what and how many shoes to produce at each foreign facil-

---

[4] Jahangir Karimi and Benn R. Konsynski, "Globalization and Information Management Strategies," *Journal of Management Information Systems*, Spring 1991, pp. 7–26.

FIGURE 12.10

International business strategies

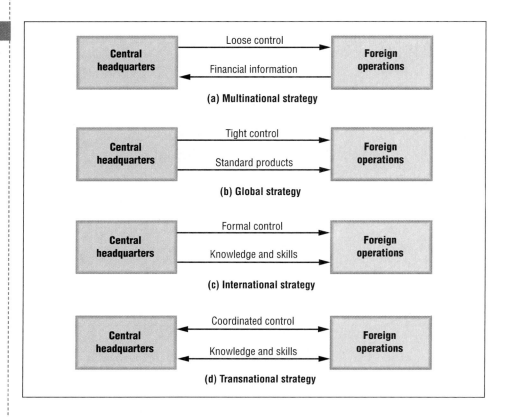

(a) Multinational strategy

(b) Global strategy

(c) International strategy

(d) Transnational strategy

ity. This strategy is less responsive to local needs than the multinational strategy. The central headquarters exercises tight control over the foreign operations.

The *international* strategy involves transferring knowledge and skills from the central headquarters to the foreign operations. Product development is centralized, but the foreign operations use the knowledge and skills they receive to determine how best to produce and sell products for their markets. An athletic shoe manufacturer that follows this strategy would provide special knowledge and skills to each foreign facility to help the facility determine the best type and quantity of shoes to produce. This strategy is different from the global strategy in which the central headquarters determines how products will be produced and sold. Still, formal control of foreign operations is needed in the international strategy.

The *transnational* strategy involves using knowledge and skills from both the central headquarters and the foreign operations. Knowledge and skills flow between different locations of the business, depending on where the greatest expertise lies. Thus, the different parts of the business learn and gain from each other, and they coordinate product development, production, and marketing decisions. For example, if an athletic shoe manufacturer follows this strategy, the central headquarters and the foreign operations would share knowledge and skills to decide what and how many shoes to produce. With this strategy, control must be carefully coordinated between the central headquarters and different foreign operations.

The Strategic Impact of Global Information Systems

Global information systems are needed to operate and manage the international activities of a business. For example, an international athletic shoe manufacturer would need a global order entry system to allow its customers around the world to place orders and a global distribution system to plan shipments to the customers. It would also need a global manufacturing information system to schedule and coordinate production in a number of countries. Finally, it would need a global product design system to allow designers in a number of locations around the world to work together on shoe design.

Global information systems can have a strategic impact on international businesses. This impact comes from several sources. One is the ability of the system to compress time and space. International businesses operate in many different time zones and across considerable distances. Global information systems allow distant operations of a business to transmit data nearly instantaneously across any number of time zones and over any distance. This characteristic helps the business function as if its operations were nearby, in the same time zone. This ability of global information systems to compress time and space gives an international business a competitive advantage over businesses without this capability.

Another source of strategic impact from global information systems is the capability for sharing business resources over long distances. With global information systems, business operations and management do not have to be in the same location. For example, engineers working on the design of a new product can be in different locations and share design ideas and details through a global information system. Information for management decision making can come from many locations around the world and be distributed to managers in different locations through a global information system. The business gains a competitive advantage over other businesses without these capabilities because of its global information systems.

Characteristics of Global Information Systems

Global information systems differ from domestic information systems in a number of ways. One source of difference is in data communications technology. Domestic information systems generally require shorter-distance data communication than global information systems, in which data communications between countries is necessary. Long-distance data communications in global information systems may require special technology such as satellites, which may not be needed in domestic information systems. In addition, domestic information systems only have to deal with the telecommunication (telephone) system in a single country. Global information systems, on the other hand, must deal with telecommunication systems in many countries that can vary in technical details and quality. Connecting to these systems as part of an international network can create significant technical problems. Finally, the cost of data communications for domestic information systems is lower than for global information systems. Data communications with global information systems is more costly not only because the distances are greater, but also because charges for the use of telecommunication systems for international communications in some countries can be very high.

Another difference between domestic and global information systems is the concern for cultural differences between countries. Domestic information systems only have to be concerned with the culture of a single country, whereas global information systems must take into consideration the many cultural differences between countries. These considerations involve not only language differences, but also differences in values, norms, and other societal characteristics. For example, a business with a global information system that links operations in many countries must take into consideration such differences as working hours, religious holidays, and the importance of group versus individual work.

Finally, political and legal factors can create differences between domestic and global information systems. Domestic information systems only have to deal with the rules and laws in a single country, whereas global information systems must take into consideration the rules and laws in several countries. In addition, many countries have laws that affect transactions that take place over their borders. For global information systems, these laws often affect the flow of data between countries, commonly called **transborder data flow (TDF)**. For example, some countries do not allow personal data about employees to leave the country.

The form that a global information system takes can depend on the basic strategy the business follows[5] (Figure 12.11). Businesses that follow a *multinational* strategy tend to have *decentralized*, or independent, information systems for their central headquarters and different foreign operations. Because the multinational strategy allows foreign operations to function independently, separate information systems are usually used by each operation, with no link between these systems and the systems at the headquarters. Each foreign operation is allowed to select its own hardware and software, and develop its own information systems. In effect, the business does not have a global information system, but rather a set of independent domestic systems.

Businesses that follow the *global* strategy have a tendency to have highly *centralized* global information systems determined by the central headquarters. The global strategy involves considerable control of foreign operations by the headquarters. Hence, information systems in businesses that use this strategy are centrally developed and controlled. Such systems are located in the central headquarters, with the foreign operations having no information systems or minimal systems determined by the headquarters.

When the *international* strategy is followed, businesses tend to have *distributed* global information systems in which systems in the central headquarters are connected to those in the foreign operations. Because the international strategy involves transferring of information from the central headquarters to the foreign operations, information systems in businesses that use this strategy must have the necessary communication capability. In addition, the systems in the central headquarters and foreign operations must be able to coordinate their processing and databases. The result is information systems in which the systems at the central headquarters are linked to those at the foreign operations.

Finally, businesses that follow the *transnational* strategy require complex, *integrated* global information systems in which the central headquarters and all the foreign operations participate equally. The transnational strategy involves transferring information between all locations of the business and using the best expertise, wherever it lies in the organization. Hence, businesses that follow this strategy must have information systems that communicate between *all* offices and operations of the business, not just between headquarters and foreign operations. These systems must be able to share databases and processing worldwide in a highly cooperative way.

Figure 12.12 summarizes two characteristics of the different forms that global information systems can take. One characteristic is the amount of control of the system exercised by the central headquarters. Distributed and centralized global information systems require the most central control, whereas integrated and decentralized systems require the least. The other characteristic is the amount of interconnectivity required by the system, which means how much the systems in the business's different locations must be connected. Centralized and decentralized global information systems require the least interconnectivity, whereas distributed and integrated systems require the most.

[5] Ibid.

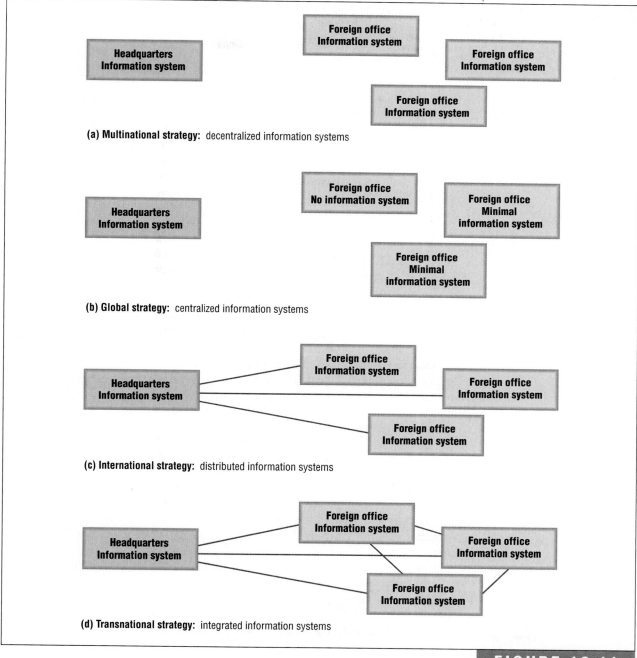

(a) Multinational strategy: decentralized information systems

(b) Global strategy: centralized information systems

(c) International strategy: distributed information systems

(d) Transnational strategy: integrated information systems

FIGURE 12.11

International business strategies and global information
systems

Global information systems can be almost any type of system. Transaction processing, management information, decision support, executive support, expert, and
knowledge management systems can all be global. Workgroup information systems
can also be global systems. Business transactions can be transmitted internationally
by a global transaction processing system. Information can be made available to
managers worldwide with a global management information system. Decision support can be provided for international managers by a global decision support system.

FIGURE 12.12

Characteristics of global information systems ▲

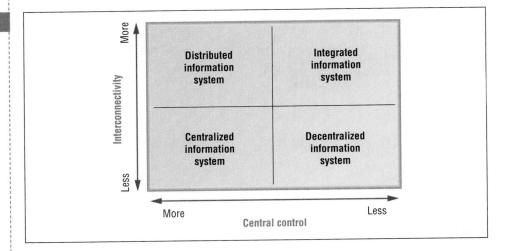

Executives can gain access to global information through a global executive support system. Expert advice can be made available throughout the world with a global expert system. Organizational knowledge around the work can be managed with a global knowledge management system. Employees around the world can collaborate by using a global workgroup information system.

Global Electronic Commerce

Electronic commerce is not limited to a single country, but takes place globally. Information systems that support global electronic commerce need to have special capabilities. One is the ability to display screens in multiple languages. Although English is widely understood around the world, not everyone knows it. In addition, many people who know English prefer to use their native language. Consequently, global e-commerce systems should offer sites in several languages, with a feature that allows the user to select the preferred language.

Another capability needed by global electronic commerce systems is the ability to deal with different currencies. Although a product price might be given in one currency (such as U.S. dollars), the e-commerce system should allow a customer to pay in another currency (such as European euros) and provide conversion between the currencies.

In addition to language and currency differences, global electronic commerce systems need to take into consideration other differences between countries. Global e-commerce systems need to be sensitive to cultural differences in various countries. For example, certain types of products should not be promoted in certain countries because they are not acceptable in the culture. Global e-commerce systems must deal with different laws in various countries. For example, it might not be legal to import certain products into some countries. In addition, tax and tariff laws must be adhered to. All these factors, as well as others, must be considered in global e-commerce systems.

Global information systems can be interorganizational systems. Many international businesses use global IOSs for sharing information and processing in international business alliances. For example, global EDI systems link businesses with international suppliers and customers. Global EFT systems are used to transfer funds internationally. An international business may be a sponsor or a participant in a global IOS.

A Global Information System at Avon

BOOK

MARK

The new chief information officer of Avon Products, Sateesh Lele, knew he had a Herculean problem on his hands after finishing a 10-week, 10-country tour of the beauty products company's top revenue-producing regions.

Some of those operations—in South America, Asia, the United Kingdom, and Puerto Rico—are riddled with myriad, outdated hardware platforms; dozens of incompatible, homegrown order-processing and financial software systems; and hundreds of information technology staffers with 15 to 20 years of mainframe experience.

Worldwide, "we wound up with 700 [disparate] local systems, despite the fact we were spending a significant amount on IT," says Charles Perrin, chief executive officer of Avon. Even in the United States, the order system the New York–based company uses is 20 years old. Most of Avon's field representatives still write orders on carbon paper forms and mail them to headquarters, where they have to be manually keyed in to a mainframe computer. Yet they still manage to send out 4 million orders every two weeks.

"It's kind of like revisiting the mid-'80s—like the world stood still," says Lele, who was formerly the chief information officer at General Motors in Europe. He joined Avon to spearhead the overhaul, after helping GM with its reengineering projects. Lele also led similar projects at Network Equipment Technologies and Telogy, both in California.

The good news is that Avon has still managed to grow into a $5.3 billion empire, with 2.8 million sales representatives in 135 countries. Earnings rose 40% in the first quarter this year from the same quarter a year ago. But 1998 revenue was up just 3% over 1997.

Industry dynamics are changing, and e-commerce has become the focal point. Although Avon's field representatives continue to be the company's strongest sales link, the increase in two-income families means that nobody is home when Avon pays a call.

"The direct sales industry in general is having a hard time" reaching its audience, says Brian Hume, president of retail consulting firm Martec International in Atlanta. So Avon has created additional channels, including more catalog offerings, a Web site—which Lele acknowledges is in a nascent stage—and 40 new retail stores nationwide. Lele says he wants to link those entities through common systems sharing information over the Internet. So he has outlined an aggressive plan for a massive information technology overhaul.

Lele says he plans to standardize all hardware on UNIX platforms and Oracle relational databases; choose a common enterprisewide system for financials and supply-chain and human resources; consolidate 35 data centers into about 10; and replace or retrain Avon's 1,300 information technology employees on client/server systems, e-commerce, and supply-chain technologies.

He also plans to develop a worldwide intranet for sharing information among countries and an extranet to tie in with suppliers, allow sales representatives to place orders quickly and directly, check product availability in real time, and track order delivery.

Lele says he plans to finance the new information technology initiatives with the money saved by cutting inefficiencies such as manual order entry and maintenance on too many systems. The effort should take three to five years.

Perrin says the overhaul is critical to Avon's competitiveness. "We're not an easy company to do business with. We're still a paper-based company, we're not flexible enough, we don't offer the representative as much information as she should have in running her business. We see the role of technology [in changing that]," he says.

Some industry observers say Avon is making a timely move. "Now that Avon has

got its [channels] in place, now's the time to improve the behind-the-scenes function," says William Steele, an analyst at Banc of America Securities LLC in San Francisco.

Questions

1. What type of global information system does Avon currently have?

2. What type of global information system is Avon moving toward?

Web Site

Avon Products: www.avon.com

Source: *Adapted from* Stacy Collett, "Avon Calls for Revamp of Its Worldwide IT," *Computerworld*, July 12, 1999, p. 38.

Information systems in international businesses can be organized in many ways and provide many different functions. As businesses expand into global sales, production, and product development, global information systems will become increasingly important.

Strategic Information Systems

This chapter has described several types of systems that can have a strategic impact on a business. In general, such a system is called a **strategic information system (SIS).** A strategic information system affects the way a business competes with other businesses, thus giving it an advantage over its competitors. As explained in the first section of this chapter, this advantage can take several forms, including cost leadership, differentiation, focus, innovation, growth, or business alliances.

Characteristics of Strategic Information Systems

Any type of information system can be a strategic information system. Transaction processing, management information, decision support, executive support, expert, and knowledge management systems can all have a strategic impact. Electronic commerce, interorganizational, and global information systems can be strategic systems. Even workgroup and individual information systems can be strategic. The word *strategic* in its name does *not* mean that a strategic information system only supports strategic decision making. A strategic information system can provide information for decision making at all levels of an organization. An SIS can also support the basic operations of a business, as well as workgroups and individuals (Figure 12.13).

An order entry system, which is a basic transaction processing system, can be a strategic information system for a business if it allows the business to take orders faster than its competitors. A management information system that provides marketing information to managers can be a strategic information system if the information is unique to the business. A decision support system that includes a special model for analyzing data is a strategic information system if the model is not used by other businesses. An executive support system can be a strategic information system if the system provides the executives with the ability to make decisions more quickly than the business's competitors. An expert system is a strategic information system when it incorporates expert advice available only to the business. A knowledge management system can be a strategic information system if it provides capabilities for organizing, storing, accessing, and sharing organizational knowledge that are unique to the business.

An electronic commerce system often is a strategic information system because it provides an innovative approach for doing businesses. An e-commerce system can

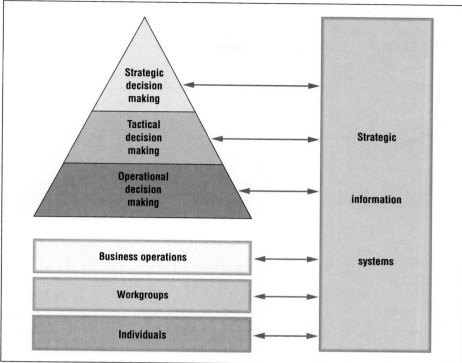

FIGURE 12.13

Strategic information systems (SIS) support for all levels of a business ▲

also be strategic if it reduces costs below those of competitors or provides a product that is unique to the industry. An interorganizational system is a strategic information system when it provides an advantage for the businesses in an alliance over other businesses. A global information system that helps a business share resources over long distances can be a strategic information system.

A workgroup information system is a strategic information system if it allows employees of a business to collaborate in unique ways. For example, a system that lets engineers in different locations around the world participate in the design of a new product without having to travel can have a strategic impact on the business. The advantage can come from quicker, less expensive development of new products. In some business, an individual information system can have a strategic impact if it increases personal productivity significantly over that of competitors.

A strategic information system can provide support in all areas of a business (Figure 12.14). Information systems in accounting, finance, marketing, production, and human resource management can have a strategic impact. For example, a budgeting system in accounting is a strategic information system when it provides more accurate control over costs than do similar systems used by competitors. A credit analysis system in finance is a strategic information system when it reduces credit losses below those of competitors. A marketing research system is a strategic information system if it provides marketing data to the business that is not available to competitors. A computer-integrated manufacturing system is a strategic information system when it reduces production costs below those of competitors. A job applicant tracking system used in human resource management is a strategic information system if it lets the business hire better employees than its competitors. The point is that any information system in an organization can be a strategic information system if it provides an advantage for the business over its competitors.

FIGURE 12.14

Strategic information systems support in all areas of a
▲ business

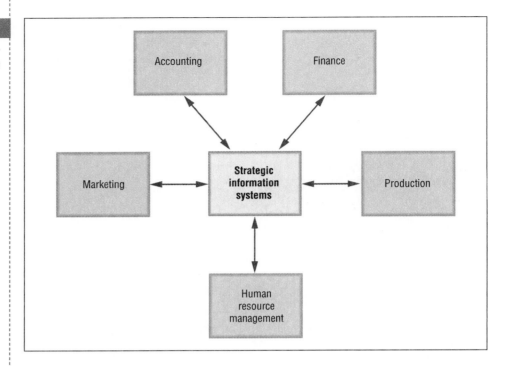

Strategic information systems do not remain strategic forever. Such systems give a business an advantage for a period of time, until the competition catches up. For example, the first banks to have ATM systems had an advantage over other banks, and thus these systems were strategic information systems. Eventually though, all banks implemented ATM systems and so the advantage was lost. Thus, the systems were no longer strategic information systems but a necessary part of the banking business. Electronic commerce systems, which are currently having a significant strategic impact on many businesses, will no longer be strategic when most businesses have such systems.

A strategic information system is specific to a particular business. A system is not strategic if all competitors use it and it performs the same function in each business. The type of information system does not make it strategic; the uniqueness of the use of the system is strategic.

Some strategic information systems can create barriers to entry for competitors. In general, a *barrier to entry* is something that makes it difficult for a new business to enter the market and compete. A strategic information system can require expensive information technology and costly development. To compete, a new business may have to make such a substantial investment in information technology and systems that it becomes too expensive to enter the market. An example of a barrier to entry provided by a strategic information system is an airline reservation system such as the American Airlines SABRE system or the United Airlines Apollo system. These systems are so expensive to develop that it is almost impossible for a new business to enter this market.

Strategic information systems can also make it expensive for the customers of a business to change to another business. The expense arises because of high *switching costs*, which are the costs associated with switching to another business. For example, EDI systems used by some businesses require the customer to make a substantial investment in information technology. Switching to another business becomes too costly for the customer because new technology would be required.

Sometimes a business develops a strategic information system that can provide a source of revenue for the business. When the SIS is sufficiently unique, other businesses may be willing to purchase the system or pay to make use of the system. Airline reservation systems are an example of this situation. American Airlines developed the SABRE system and now it is used by many other airlines. Thus, SABRE has become a major source of revenue for American Airlines.

Identifying Strategic Information System Opportunities

It is sometimes difficult to identify situations in which information systems can have a strategic impact. One approach is to look at the business's **value chain**. The value chain is the series of activities that add value to the product provided by the business.

Figure 12.15 summarizes the activities in the value chain.[6] There are two types of activities: primary activities and support activities. The *primary activities* involve creating, selling, and servicing the business's product:

■ *Inbound logistics.* This activity involves acquiring the materials needed for production from suppliers.

■ *Operations.* This activity involves manufacturing the product of the firm.

■ *Outbound logistics.* This activity involves distributing the finished product to the customers.

■ *Marketing and sales.* This activity involves selling the product.

■ *Service.* This activity involves servicing the product after sale.

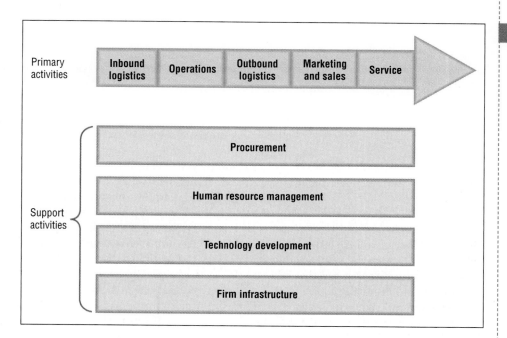

FIGURE 12.15

The activities in the value chain ▲

[6] Michael E. Porter and Victor E. Millar, "How Information Gives You Competitive Advantage," *Harvard Business Review*, July–August 1985, pp. 149–160.

The *support activities* provide the resources and infrastructure needed by the primary activities:

- *Procurement*. This activity involves purchasing resources needed by the business.
- *Human resource management*. This activity involves hiring and training employees.
- *Technology development*. This activity includes improving products and business processes.
- *Firm infrastructure*. This activity supports the entire chain with general management and other functions.

The value chain can be used to identify information systems that can have a strategic impact on the business. The idea is that a business can gain a competitive advantage when it can perform some activities in the value chain in such a way that the value to the customer of a product is increased or the cost of performing the activities is decreased. An information system that adds value or reduces cost can have a strategic impact on the business.

Information systems for all nine of the activities shown in Figure 12.15 can have an impact. The following are examples of potential strategic information systems for the primary activities in the value chain:

Inbound logistics: Just-in-time inventory management system

Operations: Computer-integrated manufacturing system

Outbound logistics: Delivery scheduling system

Marketing and sales: Electronic commerce system

Service: Problem diagnosis expert system

Some possible strategic information systems for the support activities include the following:

Procurement: Purchasing system

Human resource management: Employee skills analysis system

Technology development: Computer-aided design system

Firm infrastructure: Business planning system

Any of the systems listed here, as well as many others, can have a strategic impact on a business.

The value chain can be useful to help identify strategic information system opportunities. Often, however, strategic information systems are not planned, but rather evolve over time. Many times a business develops an information system and enhances it over the years. Eventually, the system has a strategic impact on the business. An example of this phenomenon is airline reservation systems, which were not planned as strategic information systems, but developed into such systems for the airlines. Thus, although the value chain is a useful way to identify strategic information system opportunities, it is not the only way that such systems are created.

Businesses continually look for ways to gain advantages over their competitors. By examining the value chain and looking for information systems that can have a strategic impact, the business may gain such an advantage. If accomplished, the business will get the greatest benefit from its use of information technology and its information systems.

CHAPTER SUMMARY

1 Information systems can have a strategic impact on a business by creating a **competitive advantage** for the business over others. This advantage can be gained through cost leadership, differentiation, focus, innovation, growth, or business alliances. A special manufacturing information system can help a business become a cost leader. A marketing research information system can help a business differentiate products. A decision support system that analyzes data in a data warehouse can provide information so a business can identify market niches. A special information system can use an innovative approach to inventory control. Certain information systems can provide the capabilities to handle the increase in transactions that result when a business grows. An information system that links companies can be used in a business alliance. (pp. 372–374)

2 The two main types of **electronic commerce (e-commerce)** are **business-to-consumer (B2C)** and **business-to-business (B2B)** electronic commerce. In B2C e-commerce, a business or other type of organization promotes and sells its goods or services to individual consumers. In B2B e-commerce, a business promotes and sells its goods and services to other businesses. Other types of e-commerce are **consumer-to-consumer (C2C) electronic commerce**, in which a consumer sells to another consumer, and **intrabusiness (organizational) electronic commerce**, in which transactions take place between units of a business or organization. (pp. 374–377)

3 The functions provided by an **electronic commerce (e-commerce) system** include product presentation, order entry, payment, product distribution, customer service, product support, and data acquisition. Product presentation helps a customer identify products he or she wants to purchase, often by browsing an **electronic catalog**. Order entry allows a customer to enter an order for a product into the e-commerce system, usually by adding it to an **electronic shopping cart**. Payment by the customer takes place with the aid of an **electronic payment** capability. Product distribution may be accomplished by notifying a distribution center that the product should be shipped or by sending the product electronically over a net-

work. Customer service provides special services for customers before, during, and after purchasing an item. Product support makes available additional information about and help with the use of a purchased product. Finally, data acquisition lets the business gather data that can be used for market research. (pp. 377–379)

4 Many businesses coordinate their operations or link their resources to form **business alliances**. An **interorganizational system (IOS)**, which is a type of business-to-business electronic commerce system, is an information system that is shared by two or more businesses in an alliance. Such systems are essential for many business alliances to function because information or processing needs to be shared between businesses in the alliance. Without the necessary IOSs, many business alliances would not operate smoothly or efficiently. (pp. 381–383)

5 A business can participate in an interorganizational system in several ways. One way is by entering input and receiving output by using an IOS sponsored by another business. Another approach is to use an IOS to access data storage or processing capabilities of another business. A third way a business can participate in an IOS is to use capabilities of the IOS received from the sponsor for internal operations. (pp. 383–384)

6 An electronic data interchange (EDI) system provides electronic communication of data between businesses. The data often represents transactions that are output from one business's transaction processing system and input to another business's transaction processing system. An EDI system can use a value added network (VAN), a special network set up by the business sponsoring the EDI system, or the Internet. Each participating business needs communications hardware to connect to the network and EDI software for transmitting and receiving electronic data in a standardized format over the network. (pp. 384–386)

7 An international business develops, produces, and sells products in more than one country. Such a business may have domestic information systems confined to a single country in which it operates and **global (international) information**

systems that span national borders. The global information systems provide communication between business locations around the world, transfer of data between international locations, and use of system functions at many locations. These capabilities are needed to operate and manage the international activities of the business. (p. 386)

8   Some international businesses follow a multinational strategy in which foreign operations function largely independently. These businesses tend to have decentralized information systems for their various foreign operations. Other international businesses follow a global strategy in which the central headquarters standardizes products and marketing. These businesses often have centralized global information systems. Still other international businesses follow an international strategy in which knowledge and skills are transferred from the headquarters to the foreign operations. These businesses tend to have distributed global information systems. Finally, some international businesses follow a transnational strategy in which knowledge and skills are transferred between all locations of the business. These businesses usually have complex, integrated global information systems. (pp. 386–388)

9   A **strategic information system** (**SIS**) is an information system that has a strategic impact on a business. This impact affects the way the business competes with other businesses, thus giving it an advantage over its competitors. Any type of information system can be a strategic information system, including transaction processing, management information, decision support, executive support, expert, and knowledge management systems. In addition, electronic commerce, interorganizational, and global information systems can be strategic information systems as can workgroup and individual information systems. Systems in all areas of a business—including accounting information systems, financial information systems, marketing information systems, manufacturing information systems, and human resource information systems—can be strategic. The type of information system does not make it strategic; the uniqueness of the use of the system is strategic. (pp. 394–396)

10   Strategic information system opportunities can be identified by looking at the business's **value chain**. This is the series of activities that add value to the product provided by the business. A business can gain a competitive advantage when it can perform some activities in the value chain in such a way that the value to the customer of the product is increased or the cost of performing the activity is decreased. An information system that adds value or reduces cost can have a strategic impact on the business. (p. 397)

KEY TERMS

Business Alliance (p. 381)
Business-to-Business (B2B) Electronic Commerce (p. 376)
Business-to-Consumer (B2C) Electronic Commerce (p. 375)
Competitive Advantage (p. 372)
Consumer-to-Consumer (C2C) Electronic Commerce (p. 377)

Electronic Auction (p. 377)
Electronic Business (E-business) (p. 380)
Electronic Catalog (p. 377)
Electronic Commerce (E-commerce) (p. 374)
Electronic Commerce (E-commerce) System (p. 374)
Electronic Payment (p. 378)
Electronic Shopping Cart (p. 378)
E-tailer (p. 375)

Global (International) Information System (p. 386)
Interorganizational (Information) System (IOS) (p. 381)
Intrabusiness (Organizational) Electronic Commerce (p. 377)
Strategic Information System (SIS) (p. 394)
Transborder Data Flow (TDF) (p. 390)
Value Chain (p. 397)

R E V I E W   Q U E S T I O N S

1 How can an information system have a strategic impact on a business?

2 What are several ways a business can gain a competitive advantage over other businesses?

3 What is an example, other than the one in the chapter, of an information system creating a cost leadership advantage for a business?

4 How can an electronic commerce system have a strategic impact on a business?

5 What are the main types of electronic commerce?

6 What functions are provided by an electronic commerce system?

7 What is e-business?

8 What characteristics distinguish interorganizational systems from other types of business-to-business electronic commerce systems?

9 Why are interorganizational systems needed for many business alliances to function?

10 How can an interorganizational system have a strategic impact on businesses in an alliance?

11 In what ways can a business participate in an interorganizational system?

12 What type of data is commonly sent by using an EDI system?

13 What are the main advantages of EDI?

14 Why do international businesses need global information systems?

15 What are the four basic business strategies international businesses follow?

16 If an international business operates in several countries, must it have a global information system? Why or why not?

17 What are some of the differences between global and domestic information systems?

18 What are the different forms global information systems can take, and how do they relate to international business strategies?

19 Can only certain types of information systems be strategic systems? Explain your answer.

20 What types of decisions can a strategic information system support in a business?

21 Do strategic information systems remain strategic forever? Why or why not?

22 How can the value chain be used to identify strategic information system opportunities?

D I S C U S S I O N   Q U E S T I O N S

1 What information systems could give a college or university a strategic advantage over similar institutions?

2 What are some other types of electronic commerce besides those listed in the chapter? Give an example of each type you identify.

3 Will all business be e-business eventually? Why or why not?

4 What problems can arise when using the Internet for interorganizational systems?

5 As more and more businesses become international, will all information systems eventually be global systems? Why or why not?

6 How can the value chain be used to identify strategic information systems opportunities in a service business?

E T H I C S   Q U E S T I O N S

1 Assume that an executive in your company has proposed a new information system that may provide a strategic impact on the business by gathering data on competitors' customers. What ethical problems could this system create? Does it matter whether the customers are individuals or businesses?

2 What ethical issues can arise in electronic commerce? Are they different for business-to-consumer and business-to-business electronic commerce?

3 Some electronic auction Web sites allow sellers to put almost anything up for auction, even though an auction item may offend some people. What controls should be placed on the products sold in electronic auctions? What ethical issues can arise in electronic auctions?

4 Are ethical questions different for global information systems than for domestic systems? Why or why not?

PROBLEM·SOLVING PROJECTS

1 A way of selecting among alternatives in a decision is to compute the expected monetary value of each alternative. This calculation involves multiplying the value of each outcome of an alternative by the probability of that outcome, and summing the results. For example, if one alternative has a .6 probability of making $1,000 and a .4 probability of losing $500 (that is, of making −$500), the expected monetary value of that alternative is

$$.6 \times 1000 + .4 \times (-500) = \$400$$

The best alternative is the one with the greatest expected monetary value.

Assume that a business has to determine which of two new products—A and B—to develop. The time required to develop the product is critical because the business thinks that its competitors are developing similar products. If the business can get its product to market before its competitors finish their products, then the business can gain a competitive advantage.

The business estimates that it will cost $2 million to develop either product. The development time in years, the probability of taking that amount of time, and the expected revenue in millions of dollars if the product is brought to market in that amount of time for each product are estimated by the business to be as follows:

	Product A		Product B	
Development Time (Years)	Probability	Expected Revenue (Millions of Dollars)	Probability	Expected Revenue (Millions of Dollars)
1	.4	5	.2	10
2	.4	3	.5	3
3	.2	2	.3	0

Prepare a spreadsheet to calculate the expected monetary value of developing each product. Design the spreadsheet so that the development cost, the probabilities, and the expected revenues can be changed easily. Based on the data given so far, which product should be developed? Next, adjust the data to see how sensitive your answer to this question is to different values. What if the product costs $3 million to develop? What if the expected revenue for Product B is $12 million if the development time is one year? What if the probabilities are different? (Be sure that the probabilities for each product sum to 1.0.) Try different values and combinations of values to see if the preferred alternative changes. What conclusions can you reach?

2 Prepare the general design of a business-to-consumer Web site for a hypothetical business. The design should summarize, in outline form, what each page of the Web site will display. Also outline the functions that the Web site should provide.

3 Form two teams of three to four students each. Assume that one team works for a supplier and the other team works for a customer. Decide on the types of products the customer buys from the supplier. Then, using database software, the supplier team should develop a simple order entry system and the customer team should develop a simple purchasing system. During the development of these systems, the teams should not talk to each other. After the systems are developed, develop a simple interorganizational information system that will allow purchase orders from the customer's purchasing system to be entered into the supplier's order entry system. What problems arose in developing the interorganizational system?

4 Investigate an international business to which you have access. Does it follow a multinational, a global, an international, or a transnational strategy? Are its global information systems predominantly decentralized, centralized, distributed, or integrated? Write a summary of your findings.

INTERNET AND ELECTRONIC COMMERCE PROJECTS

1 Examine the business-to-consumer electronic commerce Web sites listed in Figure 12.2. Identify which of these are for full cybermarketers and which are for partial cybermarketers. Write a summary of what you find.

2 Investigate several business-to-consumer electronic commerce Web sites. (Use the list in Figure 12.2 for a start, but try to find others.) Identify how in each Web site the functions of product presentation, order entry, payment, and product distribution are provided. Write a summary of what you find.

3 Examine the business-to-business electronic commerce Web sites listed in Figure 12.3. Identify which of these provide a supplier-oriented marketplace, a buyer-oriented marketplace, or an intermediary-oriented marketplace. Note that some sites may provide several types of marketplaces. Write a summary of what you find.

5 Using the value chain, identify one or more information systems that could have a strategic impact on a business or an organization to which you have access. Write an analysis of your conclusions.

4 Investigate several business-to-business electronic commerce Web sites. (Use the list in Figure 12.3 for a start, but try to find others.) How do these Web sites differ from business-to-consumer Web sites? Write a summary of the differences you observe.

5 Use the Web to find information about an international business not headquartered in the United States. What products does the business sell, and where does it sell them? Where does it develop and produce its products? What problems do you think the business would have setting up global information systems? Write a report that answers these questions.

real world case

1-800-Flowers

Cultivating a successful Internet-based business is a skill—much like gardening—where all the conditions must be balanced just right for it to thrive. For Norman Dee, network director at 1-800-Flowers, the right mix comes in the form of secure, scalable, user-friendly technology that will extend the reach of the company's online order capability as well as prune costs.

Dee has achieved this with BloomLink, an Internet-based order system that relies on digital certificates for security and the most basic of Internet connections.

The Westbury, New York, company embraced the Internet several years ago, with its consumer-oriented Web site, which enables individuals to place orders online. But when it came time to fulfill those orders across the country, the process was impaired. A crop of the local florists on which 1-800-Flowers relied, in cities such as Milwaukee, Wisconsin, and Boise, Idaho, were decidedly unsophisticated, relying on telephones, faxes, or first-generation dedicated-line ordering systems such as FTD's Mercury Network.

Dee changed that, using the Web. To make it work, however, the back-end solution had to be robust, and the user side had to be easy to use and low cost, allowing the most horticulturally astute but technically illiterate local florists to get online—inexpensively.

"It's an industry that is fairly [nontechnical], and we are dragging it kicking and screaming into the 21st century," Dee says. But it's time, he adds. "The average truck driver knows about the Internet. Why can't our florists?" They can. Dee convinced the florists that the Internet was just the thing for them. After working out some problems with BloomLink in the beginning, local florists are finding that now they can save time, which translates into more money in their pockets.

When BloomLink first launched in early 1997 with about 200 florists—it now has more than 700—it had, in the words of one florist, "a few bugs."

"Two years ago, we went up with it and it didn't do so well," says Jeff Kerber, owner of the

House of Flowers, in Milwaukee. "But this year—this past Valentine's Day—it's like night and day."

Since the initial launch, BloomLink has improved in both performance and the manner in which it presents information, Kerber says. As a result, this past Valentine's Day, he processed hundreds of out-of-town orders through Bloom-Link. There were no glitches, and he believes that the reports he was able to receive online, more than anything, saved him time.

"Last year [on Valentine's Day], I still had drivers out at 9 [p.m.] making deliveries. This year, they were back in by 5," Kerber says. "And anywhere that I can save time I can save money." Dee expects that BloomLink will do the same for many other florists.

BloomLink, which took about 7 months to build, replaced the Mercury system, a 14-year-old store-and-forward system, much like the electronic data interchange technology used in other industries. Similarly, Teleflora has Dove, which is a messaging system comparable to Mercury. The problem with these systems, however, is that they are expensive to implement and difficult to maintain.

Using BloomLink, florists need only use the Web, a ubiquitous tool, to log in to a private Web site as many times as they want during the day to gather their orders and start their deliveries.

On the florists' end, all that is required is a Pentium-based PC; in Kerber's case, it is a Dell Computer OptiPlex PC. Desktops must be equipped with the Netscape Navigator or Microsoft Internet Explorer browser and some form of Internet access from an Internet service provider (ISP).

On the other end, the 1-800-Flowers computer systems, which are housed and managed at Fry Multimedia, in Ann Arbor, Michigan, are built to handle an influx of orders on flower-heavy holidays. Fry relies on AT&T's network backbone, but also has arrangements with UUNet Technologies and ANS Communications for redundancy in ISP connections.

1-800-Flowers also uses front-end Windows NT–based servers for customers, which are actually customized versions of Microsoft's Site Server

Enterprise. Typically 15 to 20 NT servers are in use, but they can be pumped up to 50 during busy holidays.

From there, the orders are transferred into two Oracle databases running on Sun Microsystems 6500 servers that work in conjunction with a storage network from EMC.

1-800-Flowers takes all its orders and turns them into HTML pages stored on the Sun servers. To ensure that local florists get the orders during busy holiday times, 1-800-Flowers developers wrote a basic JavaScript command that allows the retailers to access their customer data. The florists, in turn, are authenticated by digital certificates issued and managed by VeriSign, based in Mountain View, California.

The cornucopia of technology is enabling the flower giant to work with small retail shops all over the country. "We've had our blips here and there, but I think we're doing well at this point," Dee says.

Continued success will mean that Dee will look to harvest more technology to help grow the business. In fact, he's talking to Hughes Network Systems about a satellite ordering system that will work hand in hand with the BloomLink network, he says.

Whatever Dee and 1-800-Flowers do, Kerber, at least, is a convert. "I think anybody who doesn't get involved with [the Internet]," he says, "is going to get left behind in the business world." But that won't be the case for Kerber, who is getting ready for the next big flower opportunity: Mother's Day.

Questions

1 What is the B2C e-commerce system in this case?
2 What is the B2B e-commerce system in this case?
3 How are customer orders transferred from the B2C e-commerce system to the B2B e-commerce system?
4 How is security handled in BloomLink?
5 Why does BloomLink give 1-800-Flowers a competitive advantage over companies that use older systems to place orders with florists?

Web Site

1-800-Flowers:
www.1800flowers.com

Source: *Adapted from* Jim Kerstetter, "Business Is Blooming on the Net." *PCWeek*, April 12, 1999, pp. 35, 40.

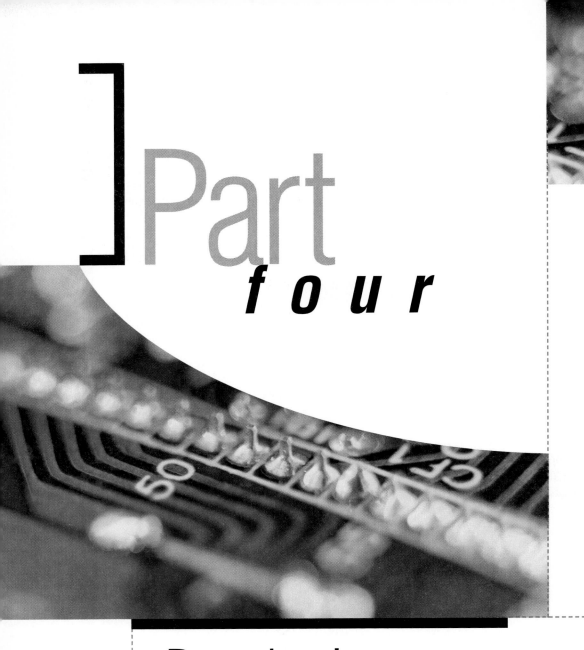

Part
four

Developing
and Managing
Information
Systems

Information System
DEVELOPMENT

CHAPTER OUTLINE

People in Information System Development
The System Development Process
System Development Tools
A Case Study of Information System Development
Other System Development Approaches
Individual Information System Development
Electronic Commerce System Development
Business Process Reengineering

After completing this chapter, you should be able to

1 Explain the roles of the people who are involved in information system development.

2 Outline the phases and steps in the information system development process.

3 Describe the user's involvement in each phase of the system development process.

4 Explain the purpose of common tools used for system development.

5 Explain the use of prototyping and rapid application development in system development.

6 Explain how the system development process can be adapted to the development of individual information systems.

7 Describe the process of developing electronic commerce systems.

8 Describe the purpose of business process reengineering.

nformation systems, whether they are individual, workgroup, organizational, interorganizational, or global, are developed by people who have an understanding of how to apply information technology to meet business needs. Individual information systems are often developed by end users to solve specific business problems, as described in Chapter 8. Multiple-user information systems used by workgroups, organizations, several organizations, or international businesses, are developed by specialists who are knowledgeable in system development techniques. These specialists often follow a detailed system development process that involves many steps and may take a few days to several years to complete. End users are involved in this process in a number of ways.

This chapter discusses the process of developing multiple-user information systems, emphasizing user involvement in the process. First, the chapter explains the roles of the various people who participate in information system development. Then it describes the system development process and shows when and how users participate in the process. It also explains some of the tools used in system development. Then the chapter describes a case study of system development from a user's perspective. Next it explains several other approaches to system development. Then the chapter discusses how the system development process can be adapted by end users for developing individual information systems and for developing electronic commerce applications. Finally, the chapter discusses the reengineering of business processes.

People in Information System Development

The people who are primarily responsible for developing information systems are called **systems analysts**. Systems analysts follow a step-by-step process, described later in this chapter, to develop information systems. Other people, such as computer programmers, may also be involved in the process. Programming, however, is just part of system development.

Users of the system are another important group of people involved in the system development process. An information system is designed to meet the needs of its users. To accomplish this goal, the users must explain their needs to the systems analysts. In addition, the users must determine whether the system that is developed meets their needs. As will be explained later in this chapter, users are involved in many steps of the system development process.

Usually, information systems are developed by a group of people who form a **project team**. The team may consist of several systems analysts, programmers, and users. One person, usually an experienced systems analyst, is the team leader. Some system development teams are made up of just a few people, such as one systems analyst, a programmer, and a user, but other teams consist of hundreds of people.

The System Development Process

The system development process, which is also called the **system development life cycle (SDLC)**, can be described in many ways. This book divides the process into five main phases:

- System planning
- System analysis

FIGURE 13.1

The system development process ▲

SYSTEM DEVELOPMENT STEPS	USER INVOLVEMENT
System planning	
Problem recognition and definition	High
Feasibility analysis	Low
System analysis	
Current system analysis	High
User requirements analysis	Very high
Conceptual design	Low
Alternative identification and evaluation	Low
System design	
Input and output design	High
File or database design	None
Program design	None
Procedure design	High
System implementation	
System acquisition	Low
System testing	Moderate
System installation	Very high
System maintenance	Varies

- System design
- System implementation
- System maintenance

Each phase involves several steps, which are summarized in Figure 13.1 and discussed later. Figure 13.1 also summarizes the user involvement in each step.

System planning is the phase in which the systems analyst decides whether a new information system should be developed. During **system analysis**, the analyst studies the existing system and determines what the new system must do. Then, during **system design**, the analyst specifies how the new system will function. In the next phase, **system implementation**, the systems analyst acquires the components of the system—such as programs—tests the system, and changes over to the new system. Finally, **system maintenance** involves modifying the system during its life to meet new requirements.

The phases of the system development process are supposed to be performed in sequence. Planning is done before analysis, which comes before design, followed by implementation. Often, however, it is necessary to return to previous phases. For example, during design it may be discovered that further analysis is needed or that the planning was not adequate. Thus, the system development process is really an iterative, or repetitive, process.

System Planning

In the first phase of the system development process the systems analyst plans what information systems will be developed. To start the planning phase, someone must recognize the need for a new information system. Usually, some type of system already exists in the organization. The existing system may be manual or computerized; it may be formal, with written procedures, or informal, remembered by a few people. In any case, someone must recognize a problem with the existing system and recommend that a new system be developed.

Often, the user of an existing system recognizes the problem. For example, a salesperson using an order entry system may sense a problem with the system when customers complain that orders are being lost. A user might also determine that an entirely new system is needed—one that does things that are not done by any existing system. Even in this case there still is a problem: What is wrong with the existing system that it cannot do everything required? When the user recognizes the problem, he or she must report it to the person responsible for system development.

Next, someone, usually a systems analyst, must carefully define the problem, distinguishing it from its symptoms. For example, lost orders are a symptom of a problem in an order entry system. The actual problem may be inadequate checks for errors in the system, unreliable hardware, or a poorly designed user interface. The systems analyst must prepare written documentation of the problem. This documentation establishes the need for the information system.

After the need for an information system has been recognized, the systems analyst must determine whether it is feasible to develop the system, a process called **feasibility analysis** (Figure 13.2). In this process, the analyst must determine whether the system is technically feasible, operationally feasible, and economically feasible. An information system is *technically feasible* if it is possible to develop it using existing technology. For example, a system that requires unrestricted voice input is not yet technically feasible. A system is *operationally feasible* if the people in the business will use it. For example, a system to be used by people who do not want it is not operationally feasible. Finally, an information system is *economically feasible* if it makes sense economically. For example, a system that costs more than it provides in benefits for the organization is not economically feasible.

To evaluate the economic feasibility of the system, the expected costs of developing and operating the system are compared with the expected benefits, in a process called **cost/benefit analysis**. If the total benefits over the life of the system are greater than the total costs over its life, then the system is economically feasible.

For an information system to be *feasible*, it must be technically, operationally, and economically feasible. The analyst should prepare written documentation of the feasibility analysis that examines these three forms of feasibility. If the system is not feasible, the development process ends at this point. If the system is feasible, the analyst goes on to the next phase.

User Involvement in System Planning. The user is often very involved in the first stages of system planning. As noted, the user is likely to be the one who recognizes the problem. The analyst may talk to the user extensively about the prob-

FIGURE 13.2

▲ **Feasibility analysis**

Type of Feasibility	Analysis
Technical	Determine whether the system can be developed using existing technology.
Operational	Decide whether the people in the organization will use the system.
Economic	Evaluate the costs and benefits of the system and determine whether the total benefits are greater than the total costs over the life of the system.

lem to define it completely. The user typically is not involved in feasibility analysis, although the analyst may discuss some aspects of feasibility with the user.

System Analysis

After the systems analyst has decided that a new system is feasible, he or she must analyze the system to determine *what* it must do. The analyst starts by analyzing the current system. He or she gathers any written documentation about the current system and collects copies of all forms and documents used in the system. If the current system is computerized, the analyst determines the output (screens and reports) produced by the system, the files or databases used by the system, the input entered into the system, and the processing done by the system. The systems analyst must interview the user to determine what the system actually does. Finally, the analyst prepares written documentation that describes the current system.

Next, the analyst determines what the user requires in the new system. The analyst talks to the user extensively about the user's needs and prepares written **user requirements**, which state what the system will do to help the user in his or her job. The requirements should be such that the new system will solve the problems identified earlier. The following is an example of a requirement for an order processing system:

> *The system will allow a salesperson to determine the current status of any sales order at any time.*

In the user requirements analysis, the analyst determines what the user needs. Next, the analyst determines what the new system must do to meet the user's needs. The result of this step is called the **conceptual design**[1] of the system. For example, to satisfy the requirement for the order processing system just given, the systems analyst may decide that the system will process a query from the salesperson regarding the status of a sales order. To do so, the system will access stored data about sales orders and will supply a response to the salesperson. The systems analyst determines what the system will do to meet each of the user's requirements, and prepares written documentation of these functions. The analyst may review this documentation with the user.

Now that the analyst has an understanding of the functions of the new system, he or she needs to examine alternatives for performing the functions. The alternatives mainly revolve around the hardware and software components of the system, although the other components (stored data, personnel, and procedures) may be considered. The analyst identifies alternatives and estimates the costs and benefits of each alternative. Then, using cost/benefit analysis, the analyst selects the best alternative for the system and prepares written documentation to justify the choice.

Hardware and Software Alternatives.   Figure 13.3 summarizes the common hardware and software alternatives for an information system. If the organization already has a computer system in-house, then the decision often is to continue to use it. If the decision is to acquire a new computer, then the choice must be made between a personal computer system, a multiple-user computer system, and a networked computer system. An alternative to in-house hardware is to use hardware operated by a separate company that does computer processing for various organizations. This approach is called **outsourcing** because it involves using resources outside the organization.

---

[1] This step is also called *logical system design*, and the system design phase later in the process is called *physical system design*.

FIGURE 13.3

Information system hardware
▲ and software alternatives

Hardware:

Use in-house hardware:
      Personal computer system
      Multiple-user computer system
      Networked computer system
Use outsourced hardware

Software:

Develop custom software using in-house programmers
Have custom software developed by contract programmers
Purchase packaged software
Purchase packaged software and modify
Use outsourced software

The software alternatives depend on the hardware choice. If in-house hardware is used, the organization can develop custom software using its own in-house programmers. This approach yields software that is designed for the exact needs of the organization, but it can be very time-consuming and expensive to develop the software. In addition, the organization must have its own programming staff for this approach. Alternatively, the organization can contract with a separate company for programmers, called *contract programmers*, to develop the software. (Sometimes using contract programmers is called *outsourcing* software development.) This approach also provides for highly customized software, but it may be more expensive than using in-house programmers. Still, the organization is not left with a programming staff after the software has been developed.

The next alternative is to purchase prewritten software called **packaged software**. This alternative is usually the least expensive, but the software may not be exactly what the organization needs. Another alternative is to purchase packaged software and modify the programs to more closely meet the organization's needs. This approach produces software that is closer to the organization's needs than just the packaged programs; it is more expensive than packaged software but less expensive than custom software.

When outsourcing is used for hardware, it can also be used for software. In this case, the company supplying the hardware usually supplies the software. Sometimes, however, the organization provides its own software. Then the software can be acquired by any of the methods discussed previously.

User Involvement in System Analysis.   The user is very involved in the first two steps of system analysis. The user will likely provide the analyst with much of the information about the current system. The user's greatest involvement in the entire system development process, however, comes in the user requirements analysis. Because the information system must meet the user's needs, the user must describe in detail those needs to the systems analyst. This process can involve many long hours of meetings with the systems analyst. The user usually is not involved in the remaining two steps of the system analysis phase, although the analyst may discuss the results of these steps with the user.

System Design

After the analyst has an understanding of *what* the new system must do, he or she can design *how* the system will do it. The steps in this process depend on which alternative is selected. If the software will be developed by in-house programmers, one approach is followed. The result of this approach is a system design that specifies how the information system will work. If a different alternative is selected, another approach is needed.

System Design for In-house Development.

When the software will be developed in-house, the first step in the system design process is to decide how the functions of the information system will be performed. At this stage the analyst selects the form of the input and output. For example, the analyst decides how input will be entered—by keyboard, by mouse, or by some other method. He or she decides in what form the output will be returned—on a screen, on paper, or in some other form. The analyst also selects the type of secondary storage—magnetic disk, optical disk, magnetic tape—and decides whether files or a database will be used. Finally, the analyst identifies the programs and manual procedures that will be involved in the processing and the personnel that will be needed.

Next, the analyst specifies the details of the design. These details include the following:

- Layouts of all screens, reports, and forms.
- Organization of all records, files, and databases.
- Descriptions of all programs.
- Descriptions of all manual procedures.
- Specifications for all hardware.
- Descriptions of all personnel.

The systems analyst will consult with the user while designing some parts of the system. For example, the analyst will ask the user about screen, report, and form layouts. In addition, the user may be involved in identifying what procedures are needed. The systems analyst, however, will develop other parts of the system without the help of the user. When the design is complete, the systems analyst prepares written documentation of the design.

Alternative Approaches.

When an alternative other than in-house software development is selected, the system design phase may be modified. If an external company is to develop the software, the system design may proceed as described using the organization's analysts, or analysts from the external company may design the system following this process. When packaged software is to be purchased, a detailed system design is not needed because the software usually determines how the system will function. Instead, requirements that specify what the software packages should do are prepared at this time. If packaged software is to be modified, then software requirements are prepared and a system design that specifies what modifications are needed is developed. When the decision is to have an outside company do the processing with its own software, a system design is not necessary. Instead, requirements for processing are prepared so that outside companies can prepare estimates and bids.

User Involvement in System Design.

The user will be involved in the aspects of the system design that affect him or her directly. These include the input and output, or user interface design, and the design of procedures that the user must follow. The user normally will not be involved in other aspects of system design such as file, database, and program design.

System Implementation

In the next phase of the system development process, the analyst puts together the components of the new system, tests them, and changes over to using the new system. The steps in this phase may vary somewhat, depending on which hardware and software alternatives are selected.

Acquiring System Components.   The first step in the system implementation phase is to acquire the components of the new system. Recall from Chapter 1 that an information system has five components: hardware, software, stored data, personnel, and procedures. Some of the components may already exist in the organization, some may have to be acquired from outside the organization, and some are constructed within the organization.

For the hardware component, if the system will use existing in-house hardware, then usually nothing needs to be done. If new hardware is to be purchased, however, then alternative equipment that meets the hardware specifications is evaluated and a selection is made. When outsourcing is to be used for hardware, different businesses supplying the hardware are evaluated and one is selected.

For the software component, if in-house programmers are to be used to develop the software, then the programming is done at this time. The programming process can be complex, involving many activities, and can take considerable time. When contract programmers are to develop the software, the system implementation is turned over to the company doing the programming. If packaged software is to be purchased, then software alternatives are evaluated and a selection is made at this time. Any modifications to the software are done after the software has been acquired.

The stored data component is not completely constructed at this time. Instead, files or databases are created with sample data that can be used to test the software and the system. The actual data is stored later.

Employees are selected for the personnel component during this step. The personnel may already work for the organization, or they may have to be hired from outside the organization. Training usually takes place later.

Finally, the manual procedures that make up the procedures component are written at this time. Although the type of procedures needed are identified earlier, during system design, the detailed writing of these procedures does not take place until implementation. Written documentation of any manual procedures required in the system is prepared by technical writers.

Testing the System.   The next step in system implementation is to make sure the system works as required, which involves testing the system. Before this step is undertaken, the parts of the system are tested individually as they are acquired. For example, all programs are thoroughly tested as they are prepared. During the system testing step, the parts are brought together, and the system is tested as a whole. This process involves running the system through all its phases, using sample input data and sample data in files and databases. All system functions are checked with what is expected, and any differences mean that there are errors in the system. When an error is detected, the part of the system that caused the error must be modified and tested again. This process continues until no errors are detected in the system.

Installing the System. The last step in the system implementation phase is to install the new system in the business. It is usually at this time that the personnel, including the users, receive training in the operation and use of the system. In addition, the actual data to be used by the system is stored in the files or databases.

The final activity of this step is to convert from the old system to the new system. The conversion usually is done in one of four ways:

- *Plunge.* The old system is stopped one day, and the new system is started the next day.
- *Phased.* The new system is divided into parts, sometimes called modules, and one part is phased in at a time.
- *Pilot.* The new system is installed in part of the organization, such as a single office, as a pilot test before it is used in the rest of the organization.
- *Parallel.* The old and the new systems are used simultaneously for a period of time.

The plunge approach usually is the most dangerous because if the new system fails, there may be no way of returning to the old system. This approach is the least expensive, however, if the new system does not fail. The parallel approach is the safest because if the new system fails, the old system is still operating. This approach is the most expensive, however, because both systems must be in operation at the same time. Between these two extremes are the pilot and phased approaches, which can be effective ways of converting to a new system.

The steps in the implementation phase are performed under the direction of the systems analyst, although other personnel may do much of the work. Hardware specialists may be involved in acquiring any hardware. Programmers develop the software, create files or databases, and assist with the testing. Managers usually hire personnel, and technical writers prepare written procedures. The training staff trains personnel, including users. After the system is finished, the user is usually asked to compare the system with the user's requirements and accept or reject it.

User Involvement in System Implementation. The user involvement in system implementation starts off low but ends very high. The user normally is not involved in system acquisition, although the user may be contacted by programmers to clarify aspects of the requirements. During testing, the user may be asked to supply data to test the system, and to check the results produced by the system with what is expected. The user's greatest involvement comes during system installation. At this time the user is trained in the use of the new system. The user is also greatly involved in the conversion to the new system.

System Maintenance

After an information system has been in use for a while, it may need to be modified, which is the process of system maintenance. Maintenance is required for three reasons. The first is that errors are found that were not detected when the system was tested. Even though the system was thoroughly tested, errors often appear after the system has been in use for a while. The second reason is that a new function is to be added to the system. For example, the preparation of a new report may be needed. The final reason for system maintenance is that requirements change. For example, programs that produce income tax returns have to be modified almost every year because of changing tax laws.

Whenever maintenance is needed, an abbreviated version of the previous four phases is followed. First, the problem that requires system maintenance must be rec-

BOOK
MARK

System Conversion at Carlson Hospitality Worldwide

A hotel chain can lose tens of thousands of dollars in revenue for every minute a reservation system is down, industry experts say. So most reservations centers would rather keep an old system than break in a new one.

"Once you've adopted a technology and paid the horrible price of assimilating it into your culture, you don't want to give up on it until you absolutely have to," says Steve Medina, director of application development for Carlson Hospitality Worldwide's international reservation call center in Omaha, Nebraska, which handles reservations for 500 Radisson, Regent International, and Country Inns and Suites hotels.

But with calls to Carlson's reservation system numbering 130,000 per day, the system had reached the end of the road. After 13 years of upgrades and patches, the mainframe system, with homegrown applications written in a nearly extinct Action language, wasn't scalable enough to quickly update reservations around the globe or handle files with a million records on customer preferences.

So in 1996, Carlson waded into a four-year, $15 million revamp of its reservation call center system. To reduce the risk, the company took the expensive step of keeping the new system backward compatible with its legacy system. The results, officials say, are less downtime, an easier training schedule, and the ability to build confidence in the new technology.

To link the two systems, Carlson first traded its homegrown, nonrelational database for an Oracle distributed database. Then the company programmed the legacy application and the new system to talk directly to the Oracle database, using C++

development tools from Forte Software in Oakland, California.

"At any time, people can fall back to the old system during the transition period," says Medina, who recalled a glitch that took the new reservation system down for five hours. Reservationists simply booted up the old system on their terminals. "It's a much more controlled [situation]," he adds.

There are cheaper ways to link old and new systems, according to Greg Nyberg, senior architect at Born Information Services Group in Minneapolis, which has helped Carlson and many hotels bridge old and new reservation systems. A method called "rapporting," where queries search the old database, rather than the reservationists connecting directly with it, is half the cost of the direct-access method. But in the long run, "you are continuing to be dependent on the old system," Nyberg says.

About 50% of Carlson users are on the new system, according to Medina, who says he expects Carlson to stay linked to its legacy system until all users are trained and fully confident with the new system. According to Nyberg, that could take up to two years.

Questions
1. Why did Carlson make its new reservation system compatible with its legacy system?
2. What conversion method did Carlson use for its reservation system?

Web Site
Carlson Hospitality Worldwide:
www.chwpg.com

Source: *Adapted from* Stacy Collett, "Upgrade? Sure. But Keep the Old System, Just in Case," *Computerworld*, September 27, 1999, p. 42.

ognized and defined. Then, the feasibility of performing the maintenance must be examined. In some cases, such as in correcting an error in the system or in meeting new legal requirements, feasibility is not an issue, but in other cases, such as when new functions are requested, a feasibility analysis should be done.

Next, the current system needs to be examined to determine how the change should be made. If not already stated, the user's requirements for the change need to be specified, and the specific system function affected by the change must be analyzed. Sometimes alternatives to modifying the existing system are examined. For example, it may be less costly to purchase a new program than to modify an existing one.

System design for the modification should be performed. Then, the programming or other activity necessary to make the change is done. Next, the system is tested with the modification. Finally, the modified system is installed.

Any of the people associated with the development of an information system may be involved in system maintenance. Systems analysts and programmers usually do most of the work, but hardware specialists, managers, technical writers, and trainers may also be involved. The user, too, is included in the process to ensure that the modified system meets the user requirements.

Legacy Systems.   Many businesses have older information systems that have been in use for many years. These systems, called **legacy systems**, often require regular maintenance. For example, a business could have a 20-year-old payroll system that functions well but requires periodic modification because of changes in payroll laws.

When a business has a legacy system that needs maintenance, it has to decide whether to modify the system or develop an entirely new one. The extent of the changes needed often determine which approach the business takes. For example, if only 5% of a system needs to be changed, it usually makes sense to modify it; but if 25% of the system must be modified, it may be better to develop an entirely new system. A business might also decide to develop a new system rather than modify an old one because of a change in the basic approach to computing in the organization, such as a change from a multiple-user mainframe approach to a networked, client/server approach.

One of the biggest problems in maintaining legacy systems occurred before the year 2000. Many older systems stored the year in a date as two digits. For example, 1998 was stored as 98. Using this approach, the year 2000 would be stored as 00. As a result, any system that relied on the years increasing would no longer function correctly after the year 2000. For example, interest calculation programs in banking systems or accounts receivable systems could fail to calculate interest correctly. This situation was called the *Y2K problem*.

Modifying legacy systems to correct the Y2K problem was an enormous job. Hundreds of billions of dollars were spent making the modifications. As a result of this effort, very few problems occurred after the year 2000. Those that did occur were mainly minor nuisances and were fixed fairly quickly.

System Development Tools

Several tools are used during the system development process to help in the analysis and design of the system. These tools provide a way for the systems analyst to organize his or her thinking about the system and to examine alternative designs. They also serve as documentation of certain steps in the process. The user may have to review some of this documentation during the system development process. A description of several of the most commonly used tools follows.

Data Flow Diagrams

A tool that many analysts use to show the flow of data in an information system is a **data flow diagram (DFD)**. This diagram uses symbols with different shapes to indicate how data flows in the system. Figure 13.4 shows the symbols used in a data flow

FIGURE 13.4

▲ **Data flow diagram symbols**

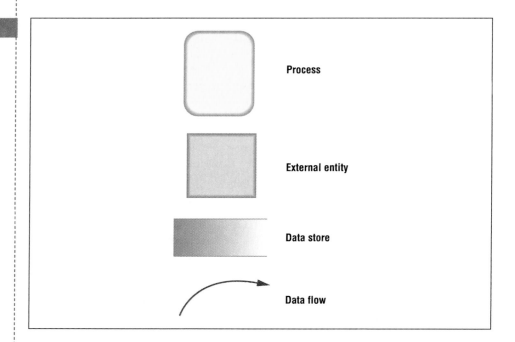

diagram, and Figure 13.5 gives an example of a DFD using these symbols. In a DFD, a rectangle with rounded corners is used for a *process*, which is any step that involves manipulating data. The words inside the symbol briefly state what the process does. A square is used for an *external entity*, which is a person, an organization, or another system that sends input data (*data source*) or receives output data (*data destination*). A descriptive name for the person, organization, or system is written inside the symbol. A rectangle open at one end is used for a *data store*, which is a collection of data kept by the system in any form, such as in a file or database. A name that describes the data store is written in the symbol. Finally, lines with arrowheads are used for *data flows*. Data may flow from an external entity to a process, between processes, from a process to an external entity, and between a process and a data store. The arrowhead indicates the direction of the data flow. Each data flow line has a name written next to it that describes the data that flows.

The DFD in Figure 13.5 is for an order entry system. In this diagram, a customer is an external entity that sends in a customer order. The order is received by a process that checks the order data for errors. This process sends invalid orders to another process for correction and stores valid orders in an order data store. The process to prepare sales orders produces sales orders from data in the order data store, the inventory data store, and the customer data store. The sales order is sent to the shipping department, which is an external entity.

DFDs are used in several steps of the system development process. They are used in the analysis of the current system to document what the existing system does. In addition, they are used in conceptual design to describe what the new system will do.

Entity-Relationship Diagrams

Many information systems process data stored in a database. Recall from Chapter 7 that a database consists of data and relationships between data. To show the design of a database, many systems analysts use a tool called an **entity-relationship (ER) diagram**. An *entity* is something about which data is stored in a database, such as a cus-

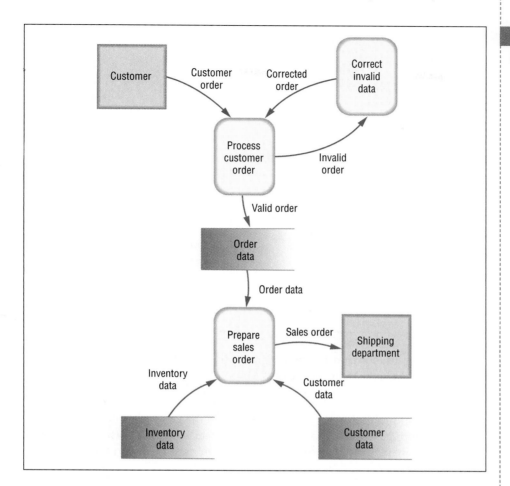

FIGURE 13.5

A data flow diagram ▲

tomer, an item in inventory, or an order.[2] A *relationship* is an association between entities. An entity-relationship diagram shows the entities and the relationships between entities in a database.

An entity-relationship diagram uses the symbols shown in Figure 13.6. Figure 13.7 gives an example of an entity-relationship diagram using these symbols. A rectangle is used for an entity. The name of the entity is written inside the rectangle. A diamond-shape symbol is used for a relationship. A word or phrase that describes the relationship is written inside this symbol. The lines leaving the relationship symbol extend to the entities that are related. The notations on the lines indicate whether the relationship is one-to-one, one-to-many, or many-to-many. (Types of relationships are discussed in Chapter 7.)

The entity-relationship diagram in Figure 13.7 is for a database used in an order entry system. This diagram indicates that the database stores data about three entities: customers, orders, and items in inventory. Customers are related to orders by a one-to-many relationship, which means that each customer places many orders, but each order is placed by only one customer. Orders are related to items by a many-to-many relationship, which means that each order contains many items from inventory and that each item can be contained in many orders.

---

[2] Do not confuse an *entity* in an entity-relationship diagram with an *external entity* in a data flow diagram. The former is something about which data is stored, and the latter is a sender or receiver of data.

FIGURE 13.6

▲ Entity-relationship diagram
  symbols

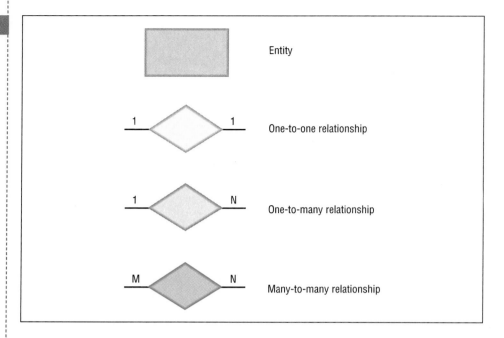

Entity

One-to-one relationship

One-to-many relationship

Many-to-many relationship

Although not shown in Figure 13.7, an entity-relationship diagram can also list the type of data stored about each entity. Thus, the diagram could show that the customer number, name, and address are stored for each customer. This information could be written on the diagram or on separate paper.

Entity-relationship diagrams are used mainly in the conceptual design step of the system development process to describe how a database of the new system will be organized. They may also be used to document an existing database design during the analysis of the current system.

CASE Tools

Some of the tools that are used in system development are available in computer software. For example, software is available that allows the systems analyst to draw data flow and entity-relationship diagrams on a screen (Figure 13.8). Using computer-based

FIGURE 13.7

▲ An entity-relationship diagram

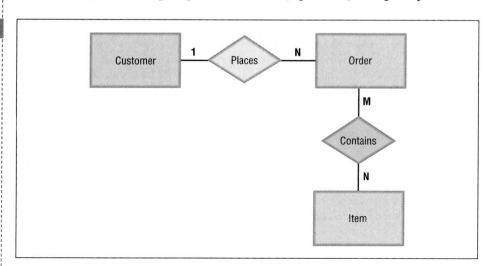

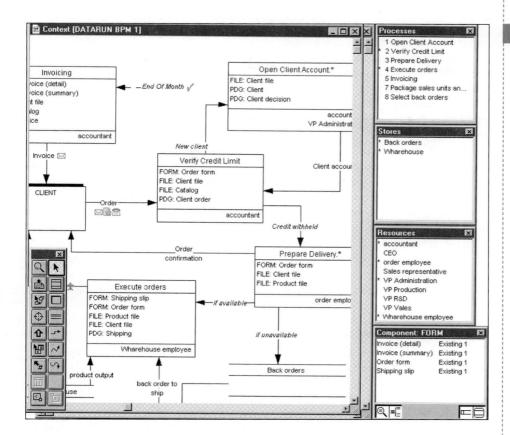

FIGURE 13.8

The screen of a CASE tool ▲

tools such as these for system development is called **CASE**, which stands for computer-aided software engineering. (The term *software engineering* is sometimes used for the process of developing systems of computer programs.) CASE tools are available to help in many other tasks in system development.

A Case Study of Information System Development

To illustrate the ideas examined in this chapter, this section presents a case study of the development of an information system. Sportswear Enterprises sells and distributes athletic clothing to retail stores throughout the United States. It currently has basic information systems for order entry, billing, and so forth. The sales manager, Pat Nichols, feels that the business is not doing the best job it can in selling athletic clothing because she and other sales personnel do not have good information about how well different items are selling and which regions of the country have high sales and which have low sales. Therefore, Pat has requested a sales analysis system.

System Planning

Pat has started the system development process by recognizing the need for a new system. She has identified a problem with the existing system. The problem, as she sees it, is that inadequate sales information is available. She has requested that a new system be developed to help solve the problem. She will be the user of the system, as will other sales personnel.

A systems analyst, Brad Johnson, is then assigned to the project. Brad talks to Pat about the problem and about the idea of a computerized sales analysis system. After a little research into the existing systems, Brad realizes that the problem is not that sales information is unavailable; the necessary data is stored in a database. The real problem is that no system exists for retrieving the data and making it available for use by sales personnel.

Next, Brad does a feasibility analysis of the proposed system. He talks to Pat again and to the sales personnel to get a general idea of their requirements for the new system. He realizes that the system involves retrieving data from an existing database and preparing appropriate reports. The system is within the technical sophistication of the computer personnel in the business, and the people are likely to use the system because the sales manager has requested it and the sales personnel are enthusiastic about it. Brad does a cost/benefit analysis to determine the economic feasibility of the new system. He estimates the costs of developing and operating the system and the benefits from increased sales. Because the benefits exceed the costs, the system is economically feasible and the decision is made to proceed with the development of the system.

System Analysis

Now Brad looks at how sales analysis is currently done. He knows there is no computerized sales analysis system, but there may be a manual system in use. In talking to Pat and the sales personnel, he discovers that sheets are prepared by hand each month, listing the best-selling items and the sales regions that have the most sales (Figure 13.9). No information, however, is kept on poor-selling items or on regions with low sales. The current system is very informal and inaccurate. Each month someone in the sales department goes through copies of sales orders for that month and counts the number of orders on which each item appears. This person also determines from the address on each sales order which sales region the customer is in, and counts the number of sales orders in each region. Finally, he or she prepares a list of the five best-selling items and the three top sales regions.

Brad notices immediately that these lists do not take into consideration the quantity sold or the selling price, and that only the best-selling items and top sales regions are listed. He talks to Pat about the current system. Together they prepare the user requirements for the new system (Figure 13.10). Brad then discusses these requirements with the other sales personnel to be sure they correctly state what is needed.

FIGURE 13.9

▲ Sales analysis sheets

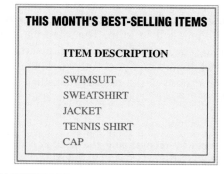

THIS MONTH'S BEST-SELLING ITEMS

ITEM DESCRIPTION

SWIMSUIT
SWEATSHIRT
JACKET
TENNIS SHIRT
CAP

THIS MONTH'S TOP SALES REGIONS

SALES REGION

NORTHWEST
ATLANTIC
SOUTHEAST

FIGURE 13.10

The user requirements for the new system ▲

SALES ANALYSIS SYSTEM USER REQUIREMENTS

1. The system will produce a report each month, listing the month's total dollar sales for each item. The items will be listed in decreasing order of sales.
2. The system will produce a report each month, listing the month's total dollar sales for each sales region. The regions will be listed in alphabetical order.

Next, Brad prepares the conceptual design of the new system. He knows that order data, item data, and customer data are available in a customer order database. This database has the organization shown previously, in the entity-relationship diagram in Figure 13.7. By using this database, the data needed for sales analysis can be retrieved. After the sales analysis data is retrieved, it can be analyzed in different ways to prepare reports listing the total sales of each item (sales by item) and the total sales for each sales region (sales by region). Brad draws a data flow diagram for the system (Figure 13.11). He does not have to draw an entity-relationship diagram because one already exists for the database (Figure 13.7). He goes over the conceptual design with Pat to be sure the new system will meet the users' needs.

The business has adequate computer hardware for the new system. Brad thinks briefly about using packaged software, but decides that the system must be customized for the business and that packaged software therefore will not work. The

FIGURE 13.11

The data flow diagram for the new system ▲

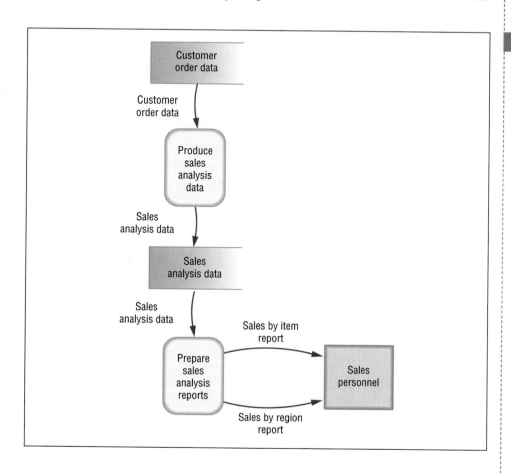

business has in-house programmers who are capable of preparing the programs, so Brad decides to develop the software using the existing programming staff.

System Design

Now Brad prepares the system design. The order data, item data, and customer data already exist in a database on magnetic disk. Brad decides that the sales analysis data should be a file on magnetic disk. Three programs will be needed in the system: one to produce the sales analysis data from the customer order database, one to prepare the sales by item, and one to prepare the sales by region report.

Next, Brad designs the layout of each report with word processing software (Figure 13.12). Before a programmer writes a program to prepare a report, Brad wants to be sure of the layout. He determines the headings and column titles that will appear on each report, and where variable output (indicated by Xs) will be printed. He shows the layouts to Pat for her approval. The organization of the database with the order, item, and customer data is known, but Brad must decide what data will be in the sales analysis file and how the file will be organized. He also documents what each program must do and notes that a manual procedure will be needed to tell the computer operator how to run the programs and what to do with the output.

System Implementation

Next, a programmer is assigned to prepare the programs for the system. While the programmer works on the programs, Brad arranges the other components of the system. The hardware is available, so nothing needs to be done about it. The database already exists, but Brad decides to make a copy of part of it for testing purposes. The computer operator who will run the programs and deliver the output is identified. Finally, Brad prepares the operator's procedures.

After the programs and other components have been completed, Brad tests the

FIGURE 13.12

The layouts of the sales
▲ analysis reports

SALES BY ITEM REPORT

ITEM NUMBER	ITEM DESCRIPTION	TOTAL SALES
XXXX	XXXXXXXXXXXXXXX	XX,XXX.XX
XXXX	XXXXXXXXXXXXXXX	XX,XXX.XX
XXXX	XXXXXXXXXXXXXXX	XX,XXX.XX

SALES BY REGION REPORT

SALES REGION	TOTAL SALES
XXXXXXXXXXXXXXX	XX,XXX.XX
XXXXXXXXXXXXXXX	XX,XXX.XX
XXXXXXXXXXXXXXX	XX,XXX.XX

FIGURE 13.13

The sales analysis reports ▲

SALES BY ITEM REPORT

ITEM NUMBER	ITEM DESCRIPTION	TOTAL SALES
5172	SWEATSHIRT	15,147.50
6318	SWIMSUIT	12,370.65
1609	JACKET	11,094.00
3804	TENNIS SHIRT	10,755.25
1537	SHORTS	9,208.00
5501	CAP	8,541.75
5173	SWEATPANTS	6,468.50
3512	TENNIS SHORTS	2,370.40
2719	T-SHIRT	512.00
4205	SOCKS	498.75

SALES BY REGION REPORT

SALES REGION	TOTAL SALES
ATLANTIC	15,342.50
NORTH CENTRAL	6,850.20
NORTHWEST	18,678.00
PACIFIC COAST	12,287.00
SOUTHEAST	14,134.50
SOUTHWEST/CENTRAL	9,674.60

system with the sample database. He carefully checks the output for errors and has to have some corrections made by the programmer. When he has determined that the system is working correctly, he takes the sample output to Pat for her approval (Figure 13.13). Pat brings in sales personnel who will be using the output. After they discuss the output and how the system works, Pat approves the system.

Next, Brad trains the computer operator in the operation of the new system. He also makes sure that all sales personnel understand their role in the system. He replaces the sample database with the actual database. Finally, he decides to phase in the new system. The first month, the system will produce the sales by item report. If all goes well, then during the second month the system will produce both reports.

System Maintenance

The conversion goes smoothly, and after several months of operation Brad checks with Pat to see if there are any problems. Pat feels that, for the time being, the system is functioning well, but she thinks that modifications may be needed in the future. She wonders if it is possible to display the reports on her computer screen, rather than having them printed on paper. Brad assures her that this and other modifications can be handled when requested.

Other System Development Approaches

The system development process described so far in this chapter is the traditional approach used for developing information systems. Other approaches are used, however, either alone or along with this approach. Here we describe three other approaches: prototyping, rapid application development, and object-oriented analysis and design.

Prototyping

One of the biggest problems in information system development is understanding the user's requirements. Often, the user cannot state clearly what he or she needs. Many times, after a system has been developed, the user says that the system is not what he or she wanted. All the steps that follow the user requirements analysis step depend on accurate requirements. If the requirements are not accurate, the system will not meet the user's needs.

An approach that attempts to solve this problem is called **prototyping**. In prototyping, the systems analyst obtains informal and incomplete requirements from the user. He or she then develops a **prototype** of the system, which is a partial version of the system that acts like the real system but that does not perform all the required functions of the system. The prototype is developed very quickly, using special prototyping software. The prototype includes sample screens and reports so that the user can see what the system will do. The user then has a chance to change his or her requirements, and the analyst modifies the prototype to reflect the changes. After several such modifications, the prototype reaches a point at which the user is satisfied with it.

Prototyping replaces the user requirements analysis and conceptual design steps of the system analysis phase of the information system development process. The other steps in the process are still necessary, including identifying and evaluating alternatives, but one of the alternatives now is to continue to develop the prototype into the final system. If this alternative is selected, then prototyping also replaces the system design and part of the implementation phases.

Rapid Application Development

The system development process can take years to complete. After such a time, system requirements may change, new users may be hired, or the system may no longer be feasible. Finding ways to shorten the development time has been an ongoing goal of systems analysts.

One approach to shortening system development time is called **rapid application development** (**RAD**). This approach uses some of the techniques already discussed. Prototyping is used to determine user requirements. In addition, the prototype is often developed into the final system. CASE tools are used to speed up the analysis and design process. Some of these tools can produce database and program implementations that may be satisfactory for the final system. Other specialized rapid application development software tools may also be used.

Most importantly, rapid application development requires significant user involvement in the development process. The user is involved in requirements analysis, prototype development, system design, and implementation. As a result, the system is more likely to meet the users' needs and require fewer changes because of misunderstandings between users and systems analysts. In addition, the system is developed faster than it would be by using other approaches.

Object-oriented Analysis and Design

In the system development process discussed earlier, the data and the methods for processing the data are separated. The data organization is specified in the entity-relationship diagram. The methods for processing the data are given in the descriptions of the processes in the data flow diagram. An alternative approach is to combine the data and processing methods. This approach is called **object-oriented analysis and design**.

Object-oriented programming is described in Chapter 5, and object-oriented databases are discussed in Chapter 7. Recall that in object-oriented approaches, data and instructions for processing the data are combined to form an *object*. Object-oriented analysis and design involves analyzing the objects that are important in the system and designing the system based on these objects.

Figure 13.14 shows a diagram that could be used in the object-oriented analysis and design of a system in a bank. The boxes represent objects; the name of each object is given above the top line. In the middle of each box are the names of the data items in the object. Below the bottom line are the names for the processing (called *methods*) that the object can perform on the data in the object. The lines connecting the boxes mean that a customer account is a checking account or a savings account.

Object-oriented analysis and design replaces much of the system development process. System planning, current system analysis, and user requirements analysis are still needed. Object-oriented analysis and design then takes over, replacing the remainder of the system analysis phase and the system design phase. The system is usually implemented by using an object-oriented programming language.

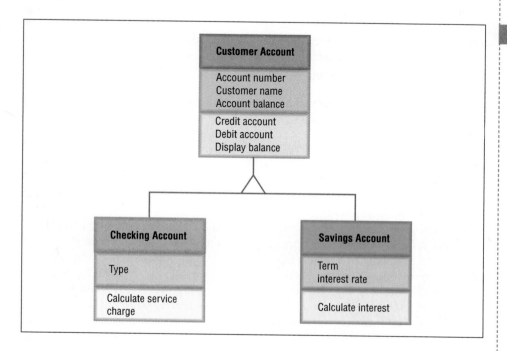

FIGURE 13.14

A diagram used in object-oriented analysis and design

Individual Information System Development

Many of the techniques used in multiple-user information system development described in this chapter can be adapted by end users to develop individual information systems. Chapter 8 discusses *end-user computing*, which is the development and use of personal computer applications by end users. End-user computing can involve sophisticated individual information systems that require careful planning, analysis, design, and implementation to develop.

The phases of the system development process can serve as a guide for end users developing their own information systems. The steps of each phase are not carried out as formally or completely as would be done in a large, multiple-user information system development project. But many steps can be done informally to help the end user develop the best system for his or her use.

Individual information system planning starts when the user recognizes a problem in his or her work that might be solved with the aid of an individual system. As with larger systems, it is important for the user to distinguish between symptoms and problems. After the user has defined the problem, he or she should think about whether it is feasible to develop an individual information system to solve the problem. Does the user have the technical skill to develop the system, will he or she use it when it is completed, and do the benefits of the system outweigh the costs? Users often assume that a computer information system is the best alternative, but sometimes a new manual procedure is better. The user has to realize that developing an individual system can be time-consuming, and that time will be taken away from other job-related activities.

System analysis for individual information systems begins with the user looking at how things are currently done. If the user does not understand the current procedures well, he or she cannot develop a new system to replace them. Then the user should outline the requirements for the new system. The requirements should be such that the problem identified earlier is solved by the system. The user should also evaluate alternative approaches. Is the problem best solved with a database application, a spreadsheet application, some other type of application, or several applications used together?

In designing an individual information system, the user needs to determine how the system will function. The user must decide what the user interface will be like, perhaps laying out the arrangement of input and output data for screens and reports. The user has to decide what data will be stored in the system, and how it will be organized. Finally, the user needs to determine what business procedures and policies (often called *business rules*) will be included in the system. The user should write down formulas needed for calculations, descriptions of any other data processing, and conditions under which different processing is done.

To implement an individual information system, the user creates the system by using the selected software. This process may involve creating one or more applications by using database, spreadsheet, or other types of personal computer software. After the system has been put together, the user needs to test it thoroughly to ensure that it works correctly. Finally, the user can start using the new system, perhaps in parallel with the old system for a while or phased in over a period of time.

Individual information systems, like larger systems, need to be maintained. Errors may have to be corrected, new features may need to be added, or requirements may change. Whenever maintenance needs to be done, the user must go through a careful process to plan, analyze, design, and implement any changes in the system.

System development by end users follows similar steps to those used by systems analysts for larger systems. In fact, when an end user develops an individual information system, he or she is acting as a systems analyst (and perhaps a programmer). The user may not use the same tools as the systems analyst, and the analysis may not be as formal, but the user must follow a systematic approach to ensure that the resulting system meets his or her needs.

Electronic Commerce System Development

The development of information systems for electronic commerce may use some of the steps in the system development process described in this chapter. Enough is unique, however, about e-commerce systems that the process needs to be modified.

One of the major differences in e-commerce systems is the user. In e-commerce systems, the main user is the customer, which may be an individual or a business. Determining the user's requirements, then, is not the same as in other types of information systems, where the systems analyst can talk directly to the user. In e-commerce systems the developer may have to make an educated guess at what will best meet the user's needs. For example, designing a business-to-consumer e-commerce system involves, among other things, deciding how the products of the business will be presented to the user on a Web site. Although concepts from marketing can provide some guidelines, e-commerce is so new that there is not yet a clear understanding of the best approach for product presentation.

Another major difference in e-commerce system development is the software that is used to implement the system. Other types of information systems are often implemented using traditional or object-oriented programming languages. E-commerce systems, on the other hand, are typically implemented using special e-commerce development software. This software is in some ways like rapid application development software that allows the developer to quickly implement the system. In the fast-changing world of e-commerce, such rapid system development is essential.

The process for developing an e-commerce system is not as formal as that used for developing other types of information systems. Figure 13.15 shows the phases and steps. The phases follow a similar pattern to that of the information system development process, but the steps are not all the same.

Planning for an e-commerce system involves first recognizing that such a system is needed by the business. Recognizing need is not an issue in many businesses because they know that they should have e-commerce capabilities to compete. Some businesses, however, may be slow at seeing the importance of e-commerce. After recognizing the need, the business must make sure that the proposed e-commerce system is consistent with the business's overall strategy and objectives. For example, if the business's plan is to become a premier seller of expensive, rare books, then setting up an e-commerce system to market low-cost self-help books is not in keeping with that plan.

Analysis for an e-commerce system starts with determining the requirements for the system. The requirements are not user requirements in the usual sense, but requirements for the functions provided by the system. How will the system present products to customers? Will the system take orders electronically and provide for

FIGURE 13.15

▲ The electronic commerce system development process

```
┌──────────────────────────────────┐
│    DEVELOPMENT STEPS             │
│                                  │
│  Planning                        │
│      Needs recognition           │
│      Strategic analysis          │
│                                  │
│  Analysis                        │
│      Requirements analysis       │
│      Alternative evaluation      │
│                                  │
│  Design                          │
│      Front-end (Web site) design │
│      Back-end design             │
│                                  │
│  Implementation                  │
│      Building                    │
│      Testing                     │
│      Publishing                  │
│                                  │
│  Enhancement                     │
└──────────────────────────────────┘
```

secure electronic payments? What sort of product distribution will be included in the system? How will customer service and product support be handled? Will data be gathered for market research? After the requirements have been determined, design and implementation alternatives must be evaluated. Will the system be designed by in-house staff or by an outside company specializing in e-commerce site design? Will it be implemented using company personnel, or will the implementation be outsourced?

The design of an e-commerce system involves two main parts. One part is the Web site that includes the product presentation, order entry, and electronic payment capabilities of the system. We call this the *front end* of the system because it is what the customer sees when using the system. The other part can be thought of as the *back end* of the system because it provides the capabilities necessary for completing the customer's order, including inventory control and product distribution. Front-end design often involves considerable creative talent in graphics and multimedia, whereas back-end design involves an understanding of information technology such as database systems.

Implementation requires building, testing, and publishing the e-commerce system. *Building* involves using software to create the various parts of the system. As mentioned earlier, e-commerce systems are usually implemented using special software, such a Microsoft Visual InterDev, which is designed specifically for this purpose. Internet programming languages such as HTML and Java are also used. The objective is to get the system up and running as quickly as possible, so software tools that expedite the process are used. *Testing* must be done carefully because e-commerce systems with errors will affect customer relations. *Publishing* the system is the process of setting up the system on a server and making it available through the Internet.

E-commerce systems, like all information systems, need to be maintained. Maintenance of e-commerce systems, however, can involve more than small modifications. Significant enhancement or even radical redesign of e-commerce Web sites is often necessary when the original design does not attract customers as expected or results in customer problems or complaints. In the rapidly changing world of e-commerce, e-commerce systems are constantly being enhanced.

E-commerce System Development at AutoNation

Building a cutting-edge, far-reaching e-commerce infrastructure for a company doesn't have to be a long-term, bank-breaking undertaking, according to car retailer AutoNation.

In 18 months, working from scratch, a four-person information technology team at the nation's largest auto seller teamed with several vendors to create what experts have called the auto industry's most robust and advanced e-commerce site.

AutoNation's Web site will eventually enable customers to buy vehicles from all of its more than 400 new- and used-car stores without setting foot in a dealership.

AutoNation started its e-commerce initiative by contracting Fusive.com to build a prospect management system it had designed. The Boca Raton, Florida–based software company wrote the code for a standalone server. That move, which took roughly six weeks, was forced when AutoNation couldn't find an off-the-shelf prospect management package for the auto industry.

Next, AutoNation contracted with Seattle-based Cobalt Group to create Web sites for 270 of its dealers. That took only a few weeks, says Art DeLaurier, vice president of e-commerce technology.

Leads that come in to the dealers' individual Web sites are first sent to the prospect management system, where the customer data is time-stamped and recorded. Leads are then sent back to the linked dealer. That way, online sales specialists can track the progress of leads, and AutoNation can alert customers about service, recalls, and special promotions.

Leads that come to the central site are sent through the prospect management system and on to the nearest dealer. The AutoNation site offers features not available at the dealers' individual sites, such as online financing, insurance procurement, and a chat line.

The company also integrated the prospect system with SkyTel's paging services, which cut AutoNation's response time from 48 hours to two. "This [has] had a dramatic impact on customer service," DeLaurier says.

And to keep people on the site, AutoNation added a product from WebLine Communications in Burlington, Massachusetts, that supports a chat line feature whereby shoppers with questions can get answers from a call center agent in real time. AutoNation chose the WebLine technology over e-mail because of its immediacy.

AutoNation agents will eventually be able to help consumers trying to decide between two sizes of sports utility vehicles, for example, by "pushing" information on them to the consumers while they are logged on to the site, DeLaurier says.

BOOK

M A R K

Questions

1. How did AutoNation develop its e-commerce system?
2. What is the back end of the AutoNation e-commerce system, and why was it developed before the front end was developed?

Web Site

AutoNation:
www.autonationdirect.com

Source: *Adapted from* Bob Wallace, "Car Retailer Builds Site the Fast Way," *Computerworld*, July 12, 1999, p. 62.

Business Process Reengineering

The system development process described in this chapter is a framework for developing information systems. Many of the ideas in this process, along with some of the tools used in it, can be incorporated into the development of other types of systems in an organization. For example, a production system can be developed by using some of the ideas presented in this chapter, along with other ideas from production management.

Another approach to business system development is called **business process reengineering** (**BPR**). (Sometimes it is called *business process redesign*.) The goal of this approach is to completely redesign **business processes**, which are groups of activities or tasks that accomplish things for the business. For example, completing an order for a customer is a business process. Similarly, authorizing credit, purchasing materials, and developing a new product are business processes.

The goal of business process reengineering is to completely redesign one or more business processes in order to dramatically improve the way the organization functions. For example, reengineering a customer ordering process may result in customers receiving their orders in 3 days instead of 10. Attempting to achieve such a dramatic improvement is the goal of business process reengineering.

Business process reengineering often involves starting from scratch. The question is sometimes asked: "If we could design this business process any way we wanted, what would be the result?" This approach is different from starting with the current system and modifying it, as described earlier in this chapter. Business process reengineering is *not* gradual improvement, but rather radical redesign of business processes.

The approach to business process reengineering may involve some of the ideas and tools used in information system development. A team of analysts and users is usually formed to perform the redesign. The team follows a sequence of steps in their efforts. First, the processes in the organization must be identified, and those to be redesigned must be selected. Then the existing processes must be understood. Next the new processes must be designed from scratch. Finally, the new processes must be implemented. During the analysis and design, the team may use tools such as data flow diagrams to document their work.

Information technology plays a fundamental role in business process reengineering. Information technology allows business processes to be radically redesigned. For example, an existing process for customer ordering may involve clerks entering customer order data into an ordering system. In this process, the clerks may have to explain prices, credit terms, delivery schedules, and other details to customers. In a reengineered ordering process, the customers can check the business database directly for details such as prices, terms, and schedules, and place orders electronically using electronic data interchange. Thus, information technology provides a way to redesign the process to dramatically improve customer service.

Business process reengineering is a new approach to redesigning business processes. Although it has had many successes, it has also failed at times. How much of a role it will play in the future is not certain.

CHAPTER SUMMARY

1 The people who are primarily involved in information system development are **systems analysts**. They follow a step-by-step process to develop the system. In addition, programmers are involved because they write and modify the programs that are part of the system. Users are also involved in system development because the system must be

designed to meet the needs of its users. Systems analysts, programmers, and users often work together in a **project team** that is responsible for developing the information system. (p. 408)

2 The first phase in the information system development process, also called the **system development life cycle** (**SDLC**), is **system planning**, in which the systems analyst decides whether a new information system should be developed. In this phase, the analyst defines the problem to be solved by the system and performs **feasibility analysis** to determine whether it is feasible to develop a system to solve the problem. The next phase is **system analysis**, in which the analyst determines what the new system must do. In this phase, the analyst analyzes the current system, determines the **user requirements**, prepares the **conceptual design**, and identifies and evaluates alternative ways of meeting the requirements. In the next phase, **system design**, the analyst specifies how the new system will function. The result of this phase is the design of the new system. The next phase is **system implementation**, in which the analyst acquires the components of the system, tests the system, and changes over to the new system. The last phase, called **system maintenance**, involves modifying the system during its life to meet new requirements. (pp. 408–409)

3   The user is often the one who recognizes the need for a new information system by identifying a problem with the existing system. The user should report the problem to the person responsible for system development, thus beginning the system planning phase. During system analysis, the user is interviewed about how the current system functions. In addition, the user provides detailed information about his or her requirements for the new system. The user's involvement in system design is mainly in reviewing screen, report, and form layouts and helping to describe procedures. The user may be involved with system testing during system implementation. When the system is finished, the user is trained in the use of the system and is asked to compare the system with his or her requirements. Finally, the user is involved in system maintenance to ensure that the modified system meets the user's requirements. (pp. 410–417)

4   A **data flow diagram** (**DFD**) shows the flow of data in an information system. It uses symbols of different shapes to show processes, external entities, and data stores, connected by data flow lines. An **entity-relationship** (**ER diagram**) shows the design of a database. It uses symbols for entities and relationships between entities. **CASE** (computer-aided software engineering) tools provide computerized versions of other tools. (pp. 417–421)

5   **Prototyping** is an alternative approach to system development that attempts to overcome some of the problems of identifying and describing user requirements. In this approach, a **prototype** of the system is developed very quickly, using special prototyping software. The prototype is a partial version of the system that acts like the real system for the user but that does not perform all the required functions of the system. The user can change his or her requirements, and the systems analyst can modify the prototype to reflect the changes. **Rapid application development** (**RAD**) is an approach to information system development that shortens the development time. It involves significant user involvement, along with prototyping, CASE, and other software tools. (pp. 426–427)

6   The system development process can serve as a guide for developing individual information systems. Individual information system planning involves the user recognizing a problem and determining whether it would be feasible for him or her to develop an individual system to solve the problem. In system analysis for individual information systems the user looks at how things are currently done, outlines the requirements for the new system, and evaluates alternative approaches. In designing an individual information system, the user determines what the user interface will be like, what data will be stored in the system, and what business procedures and policies will be included in the system. Implementation of an individual information system involves creating the system by using the selected software. In individual information system maintenance, the user must plan, analyze, design, and implement changes in the system. (pp. 428–429)

7   The process of developing electronic commerce systems is similar to the information system development process. Planning for an e-commerce system involves recognizing that such a system is needed and making sure the proposed system is consistent with the business's strategy and objectives. E-commerce system analysis involves determining the system requirements and evaluating alternatives for designing and implementing the system. To design an e-commerce system, both the front end (i.e., Web site) and the back end (i.e., order completion capabilities) of the system must be designed. Implementation of an e-commerce

system requires building, testing, and publishing the system. After an e-commerce system has been developed, it may have to be significantly enhanced or redesigned. (pp. 429–430)

8 The purpose of **business process reengineering (BPR)** is to completely redesign **business**

processes, which are groups of activities or tasks that accomplish things for the business. In business process reengineering, one or more business processes are redesigned so that the organization realizes a dramatic improvement in the way it functions. (pp. 431–432)

K E Y   T E R M S

Business Process (p. 432)
Business Process Reengineering
  (BPR) (p. 432)
CASE (p. 421)
Conceptual Design (p. 411)
Cost/Benefit Analysis (p. 410)
Data Flow Diagram (DFD) (p. 417)
Entity-Relationship (ER) Diagram
  (p. 418)
Feasibility Analysis (p. 410)

Legacy System (p. 417)
Object-Oriented Analysis and
  Design (p. 427)
Outsourcing (p. 411)
Packaged Software (p. 412)
Project Team (p. 408)
Prototype (p. 426)
Prototyping (p. 426)
Rapid Application Development
  (RAD) (p. 426)

System Analysis (p. 409)
System Design (p. 409)
System Development Life Cycle
  (SDLC) (p. 408)
System Implementation (p. 409)
System Maintenance (p. 409)
System Planning (p. 409)
Systems Analyst (p. 408)
User Requirements (p. 411)

R E V I E W   Q U E S T I O N S

1 What people are usually on an information system development project team?

2 What are the five main phases of the system development process?

3 How is the user involved in system planning?

4 What types of feasibility must the systems analyst evaluate?

5 What steps are involved in system analysis?

6 How is the user involved in system analysis?

7 What are the main software alternatives for an information system?

8 What system details does the systems analyst specify during system design?

9 What steps are involved in system implementation?

10 What approaches can a business use to convert from an old information system to a new one?

11 Why do information systems need to be maintained?

12 What is a data flow diagram used for?

13 In the case study in this chapter, why did Pat Nichols want a new information system?

14 During which phases of the system development process in the case study in this chapter was Pat Nichols most involved, and during which phase was she least involved?

15 Why is prototyping used?

16 Can the system development process be used by end users in developing individual information systems? Explain your answer.

17 How is an electronic commerce system developed?

18 What is business process reengineering?

DISCUSSION QUESTIONS

1. The users of many information systems in a college or university (e.g., course registration system, library catalog system) are students. Are students ever consulted at your college or university about user requirements? If not, why?

2. Think of an information system that you might use in your career. What would you want that system to do for you? That is, what would be your requirements for the system?

3. As more and more computer-based tools used to develop information systems (e.g., CASE tools, rapid application development tools) become available in the future, will user involvement in information system development increase or decrease? Why?

4. Workgroup information systems are sometimes developed by members of the group. What steps in the system development process might be different in this situation?

5. What difficulties could arise in developing an information system for an international business?

6. What are some difficulties that an untrained end user can have in trying to develop an individual information system?

7. Sometimes an individual information system is developed for use by several users on different computers. What additional factors need to be considered in developing such a system?

8. What differences are there in the development process for business-to-consumer and business-to-business electronic commerce systems?

ETHICS QUESTIONS

1. Should ethical issues be considered as part of the planning phase of an information system? Why or why not?

2. Assume that you use a technique to help you with your job that no one else in the organization knows about. The technique helps you do your work very well, and you receive excellent work reports. The organization has decided to develop an information system to assist you and others in the organizations who do work that is similar to yours. A systems analyst has come to your office to ask you questions about how you do your job, including the techniques you use. What would you do in this situation? What ethical issues arise?

3. What ethical issues arise in the design of a Web site for an electronic commerce system?

PROBLEM-SOLVING PROJECTS

1. Interview a systems analyst to find out what he or she does when developing an information system. What steps does the analyst follow in developing an information system? What tools does the analyst use to help in developing a system? Write a summary of your interview.

2. Some departments and offices in your college or university may need new information systems. For example, a computer lab may need an information system to keep track of hardware and software, and an academic department office may need an information system to keep track of its students. Locate a department or an office at your college or university that needs a new information system. Identify the users of the system. Then, interview the users to determine their requirements for the new system. Prepare a written description of the requirements and show the written requirements to the users to get their reaction. Make any changes in the requirements that the users feel are necessary.

3. Think about how the course registration system at your college or university functions. Draw a data flow diagram of how you think the system works. Use graphics software to prepare your diagram.

4. A college bookstore has a large inventory of books that are used in many courses taught by many pro-

fessors. Draw an entity-relationship diagram of how you think a database for such a bookstore would be designed. Use graphics software to prepare your diagram.

5 A technique used to analyze a project, such as a new information system, is to find the net present value of the difference between the project's benefits and costs over the life of the project. The net present value can be found by using the net present value function in spreadsheet software. Use the help system of your spreadsheet software to find out how to use this function.

Assume that a new information system will cost $500,000 to develop, and it will have an expected life of five years. During the first year the system will cost $150,000 to operate, during the second year it will cost $125,000 to operate, and during the third, fourth, and fifth years it will cost $100,000 per year to operate. The business expects an economic benefit of $50,000 the first year, $100,000 the second year, $250,000 the third year, and $500,000 each of the fourth and fifth years.

Develop a spreadsheet to determine the net present value of the differences between the benefits and operating costs of this information system over its five-year life. Assume a discount rate of 8%. If the net present value is greater than the initial development cost, the system is economically feasible. What can you conclude about this information system?

INTERNET AND ELECTRONIC COMMERCE PROJECTS

1 Locate information about several CASE tools on the Web. What features do the tools offer? How can they be used in developing information systems? Write a summary of your findings.

2 Use the Web to investigate any lingering effects of the Y2K problem. Have all related problems been solved? Are there likely to be new problems that appear in the future? Write a summary of what you find.

3 Use the Web to investigate several companies that provide electronic commerce system consulting services. These companies could do anything from designing Web sites to developing complete e-commerce systems for their clients. Find out the processes that these companies go through in providing their services. How do their processes compare with the e-commerce system development process described in this chapter? Write a summary of what you find.

Pinnacol Assurance

Rob Norris had reached rock bottom. "I sat in a meeting thinking: 'We can't do this project. We tried, and it went to hell. What went wrong?' " In a word, everything. Twelve months into a six-month project to develop a crucial new medical payments system, the team at Pinnacol Assurance had just concluded that it would have to start over. The project was a morass. Nothing had been delivered. The businesspeople were angry. The information technology team was drowning in depression. Company executives were seething, and Norris's job was on the line.

It had all started a year before when Norris, the new chief information officer at the Denver-based medical insurance provider, discovered that the recently acquired PC-based claims payments system was a disaster. It was building up huge backlogs while overpaying claimants to the tune of more than $5,000 per day. The company needed a new system that could translate thousands of rules, regulations, fee schedules, and billing guidelines into 2,000 accurate payments to insureds per day while enabling Pinnacol to strike creative deals with individual providers and networks. Norris, who had built complex systems before, decided his development staff of two dozen would build it. The MedPay project began with a six-month time line.

Right off the bat, the project team made some critical errors. "We succumbed to the lure of new technology," Norris admits. "We felt that Oracle Forms and PL/SQL, which were the meat and potatoes of how we did things here, were just not going to cut it."

Anecdotal evidence had led them to believe that Forms couldn't handle the fine control required over the user interface. Java, on the other hand, was enticing. Norris and project leader Duane Hitz had used it in a couple simple e-commerce applications and liked it. "It seemed like the natural choice," Norris says.

Norris and Hitz also chose a rapid application development/joint application development (RAD/JAD) approach that sidestepped formal project-management disciplines. The plan was to work closely with users. "[We thought we could] just talk about something, and the next day we'd show them some screens and go back and forth and get it done very quickly," Norris says.

It soon became obvious that problems with Java were sabotaging the RAD approach. Instead of coming back a day later to show users a screen, developers would struggle with Java for two or three weeks. By the time they returned, no one was sure what had been agreed upon. "It became frustrating, and you tended to push the onus on the other side," says Bonnie Cahoon, medical payments manager. "We'd go home shaking our heads."

After months of failure, even RAD champion Norris admitted that the approach wasn't working, and he demanded more formal requirements and sign-offs. But it was too little, too late.

Meanwhile, problems remained on the business side, where the existing payment system continued to spew out errors. Steeped in that turmoil, the business team members had little patience for a project that was clearly running amok.

In the information technology trenches, depression had settled in like mustard gas. Hitz had lost most of his programmers and was the only one left who knew anything about Java. So besides leading the project, he was also doing all the Java development.

About six months into the project, the team decided to seek some relief by outsourcing the existing payment system, which was causing much anxiety on the business side. But trying to get that relationship under control ate up six more months.

And just when it seemed things couldn't get any worse, they did. Almost a year into the project, Hitz programmed for 105 hours straight in a last-ditch effort to get the graphical user interface and database connections in Java to work. He failed. "It was one of the low points for me," he recalls.

Giving up on Java was "devastating for everyone," Hitz says. "Rob announced it to the group, and you could see the eyes roll."

If information technology had any credibility left among the business team members, dropping

Java killed it. "You heard all of these great things about Java, and all of a sudden we make the change back to Oracle," says Cahoon.

As MedPay came unglued, two things kept Norris sane. One was the knowledge that, for all its ugliness, the foundering project was an aberration. All the other projects in information technology—from data marts to online service centers—were coming in on time and on budget, leaving a trail of happy customers.

The other ray of hope was the dawning of a new strategy. Norris realized that the same few people were doing all the work, as well as managing the outsourcing and dealing with other issues that came along. He delegated management of the outsourcer, and then he saw the light: The key to MedPay was to break up the whole thing.

They would break MedPay into nearly two-dozen discrete modules, each of which could be managed as a RAD project. The modules wouldn't need formal requirements or heavy documentation, because each would be a real RAD project: small and quick.

Each module would be assigned to a programmer who would work directly with the businesspeople. Norris hired from a short list of programming superstars who had good rapport with users, could work independently, and wouldn't be discouraged by the past.

Deciding on the size of the modules was another eureka moment. Norris had come upon some studies that concluded that regardless of size or complexity, projects are almost never identified as late until three weeks before deadline. "I had seen that happen so many times I practically wept when I read it," he recalls. "I said, 'That's it!'"

Norris decided that no module should take longer than three weeks to complete. That would mean that if there was trouble, he would know almost immediately and could act. He asked module managers every day whether they were going to meet their deadlines. "As soon as there was any hesitation, I'd find out why," he says.

The three-week schedules gave programmers permission to refuse other work. "When you have months, you have slack, and you know it," Norris says. "But when you've got three weeks, and

somebody asks for something else, you know the answer is no."

Upon completion, each module would be integrated into existing systems and put to work to the extent possible. That would lessen the complexity of final integration. The combination of all the modules—the overall project—would be managed formally by Norris, who took over that role to allow Hitz to focus on providing technical leadership.

The team began to deliver completed modules almost immediately, but it took a while for the mood to lighten. "Things started to ease up a bit as a firmer picture of the system started to develop," Hitz says. "But it took a long time to gain back that credibility."

Finally, the project was completed on schedule and went live. "We're very, very proud of the system we built," Norris says. MedPay has virtually eradicated duplicate payments. Billing turnaround time has improved from about a month to days, and where there used to be a backlog of tens of thousands of bills, now there is no backlog. The system is enabling millions of dollars a year in further savings because it allows flexible contacting and discounting with providers, Norris says.

Questions

1. What business problem led to the development of MedPay?
2. What were the main errors made by the project team at Pinnacol in the MedPay project?
3. Why did outsourcing the existing payment system not solve the MedPay project problems?
4. What development strategy helped save the MedPay project?
5. Why did limiting the size of modules so that none should take longer than three weeks to complete help in the project development?
6. What role did users play in the development of the MedPay system?

Web Site

Pinnacol Assurance:
www.pinnacol.com

Source: *Adapted from* Kathleen Melymuka, "Turning Around the Project from Hell," *Computerworld*, November 22, 1999, pp. 42–46.

Managing Information
SYSTEMS AND
TECHNOLOGY

CHAPTER OUTLINE

Planning for Information Systems and Technology

Acquiring Information Technology

Organizing Information Systems Activities

Controlling and Securing Information Systems

The Effects of Information Technology on Employment

Ethical Management of Information Systems and Technology

After completing this chapter, you should be able to

1 Identify several factors that should be considered in planning for information systems and technology.

2 Describe common sources for acquiring information technology.

3 Describe the traditional organizational structure of a information systems department.

4 List the specialized personnel needed for World Wide Web and electronic commerce support.

5 Identify methods used by organizations to control and secure their information systems.

6 Describe different forms of computer crime and ways of preventing them.

7 List several effects of information technology on employment.

nformation systems are an important part of an organization. As you have seen throughout this book, businesses need information systems to support their operations and management. But like other parts of a business, information systems must themselves be managed. The information systems in an organization must be carefully planned; the technologies used in information systems must be thoughtfully acquired; the development, operation, and use of the information systems must be appropriately organized; and the functioning of the information systems must be precisely controlled. All these activities are part of managing information systems and technology.

This chapter covers topics related to the management of information systems and technology. The chapter first explains how planning for information systems and technology can be done in an organization. Then it looks at ways a business can acquire information technology. Next the chapter describes the organization of information system activities in a business. Then it explains how to control and secure information systems, including preventing computer crime. Next it discusses the effect of information technology on employment. Finally, the chapter takes another look at ethics and information systems.

Planning for Information Systems and Technology

One of the fundamental activities that managers do is *planning*. This activity involves determining *what* should be done. For example, a manager plans when he or she determines what products a business will produce or what form an advertising campaign will take. Planning is always future directed: What will the business do next month? next year? in five years?

Planning for information systems and technology involves determining what systems will be developed and what technology will be used in the future. Will the business develop a new order entry system, or will it develop a new customer support system? Will the new system involve transaction processing, or will it provide expert advice? Will it use keyboard input and screen output, or will it have voice input and multimedia output? These are the types of questions managers ask as part of information systems and technology planning.

Determining the Planning Horizon

Planning can involve varying amounts of time in the future, called **planning horizons** (Figure 14.1). *Operational planning* involves a planning horizon of a few weeks to a few months. For example, planning what system modification will be done in the next three months is operational planning. In *tactical planning*, the planning horizon is several months to a few years. For example, planning what new systems will be

FIGURE 14.1

▲ **Planning horizons**

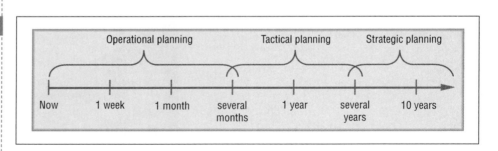

developed and what technology will be used with those systems in the next two years is tactical planning. Finally, *strategic planning* involves a planning horizon of several years to a decade or more. For example, planning the use of global information systems in five years is strategic planning.

Determining the planning horizon is an important part of planning for information systems and technology. How far into the future do we plan? Information *technology* changes rapidly, so it is often difficult to plan for specific technology more than a few years into the future. But information *systems* often stay with a business for many years. For example, some businesses have legacy systems that are more than 20 years old. These older systems most likely use updated information technology, but they still function essentially the same as when they were first developed. Thus, the planning horizon for information systems can be many years, but the planning horizon for information technology is usually only a few years.

Evaluating Risk

Planning can involve varying amounts of *risk*. Whenever you make plans for the future, you cannot be certain of the result or outcome. For example, you may plan to take a vacation in August because the weather is likely to be best that time of year, but then it might rain your entire trip. There are many risks in information systems and technology. A system may take longer to develop than was planned, or it may not work correctly when completed. New technology that is less expensive and better than current technology may become available soon after the current technology is implemented. Another business may develop a better system that reduces that business's costs, thus giving it a competitive advantage, just as your business installs its new system. All these risks make information systems and technology planning difficult.

Risk is often related to three factors that should be considered when planning new information systems.[1] The first is the size of the system development project. In general, larger projects have more risk than smaller projects. Developing a new on-line inventory control system is riskier than developing a spreadsheet application. The second factor is the familiarity of the business with the information technology used in the new system. Systems that use low technology relative to the business, that is, technology with which the business is already familiar, are less risky than those that use high technology that is unfamiliar to the business. The final factor is the amount of structure in the system development project, which means how accurately the system's characteristics, such as its outputs, can be described in advance. Projects with high structure are, in general, less risky than those with low structure.

Figure 14.2 summarizes the risk associated with information system development when these three factors are combined. The most risky systems to develop involve large projects that have low structure and use high technology. An example might be an expert system for financial analysis in a national stock brokerage. The least risky systems to develop involve small projects that have high structure and use low technology. An example might be a spreadsheet application used for simple budgeting. In between are many other types of systems, with varying degrees of risk.

Selecting the Application Portfolio

Planning what information systems should be developed and what technology should be used involves selecting an **application portfolio**. An application portfolio is a description of what systems will be developed and when, as well as an assessment of the risk associated with each system. For example, Figure 14.3 shows an applica-

---

[1] Lynda A. Applegate, F. Warren McFarlan, and James L. McKenney, *Corporate Information Systems Management* (Chicago: Irwin, 1996) pp. 266–267.

FIGURE 14.2

Information system and tech-
▲ nology risk

		Low Structure	High Structure
Low Technology	**Large Project**	Low risk	Low risk
	Small Project	Very low risk	Very low risk
High Technology	**Large Project**	Very high risk	Medium risk
	Small Project	High risk	Medium low risk

Source: Lynda M. Applegate, F. Warren McFarlan, and James L. McKenney, *Corporate Information Systems Management* (Chicago: Irwin, 1996), p. 267.

tion portfolio for planning information systems in a hypothetical business. The port-folio allows the business to balance the risks associated with different projects. For example, if the portfolio contains only low-risk projects, then consideration should be given to higher-risk projects that might provide a strategic impact for the business. Similarly, a portfolio of primarily high-risk projects may cause problems for the busi-ness if too many projects fail.

In summary, a business needs to plan for information systems and technology with varying time horizons and risk levels. A business needs to consider all types of systems, from short-term, low-risk transaction processing systems, to long-term, high-risk management information systems. The factors discussed in this section need to be taken into consideration in developing an application portfolio for information systems planning in a business.

FIGURE 14.3

An information system appli-
▲ cation portfolio

PROJECT	DEVELOPMENT TIME FRAME	SIZE	TECHNOLOGY	STRUCTURE	RISK
E-commerce	2002–2003	Large	High	Low	Very high
Budgeting	2002	Small	Low	High	Very low
Inventory control	2003–2004	Large	Low	High	Low
Workgroup support	2004–2005	Large	High	High	Medium
Executive support	2006	Small	High	Low	High

Acquiring Information Technology

Managers often need to make decisions about how to acquire the technology used in information systems. Hardware needs to be purchased; software has to be developed or bought; networks must be acquired; and data management systems need to be selected. In addition, managers need to make decisions about hiring and training personnel to operate and use the information systems. All these decisions are part of managing information systems and technology. Figure 14.4 summarizes some of the sources of information technology.

Hardware

Computer hardware can be purchased from a number of sources. Servers and multiple-user computer systems (minicomputers, mainframe computers, and supercomputers) are usually purchased directly from computer manufacturers. Companies such as IBM, Unisys, Hewlett-Packard, and Cray Research sell their computers directly to businesses. Sometimes larger computer systems are not purchased, but rather leased from the manufacturers.

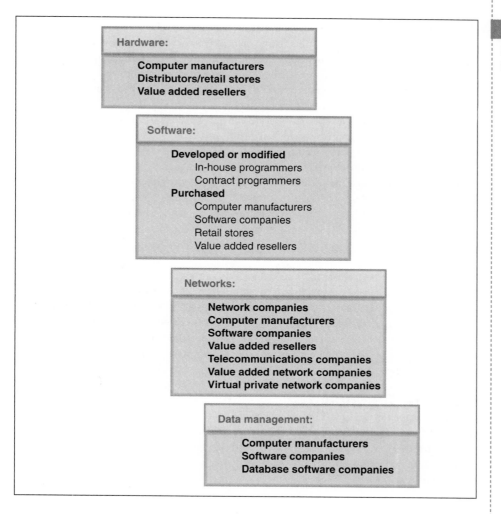

FIGURE 14.4

Sources of information technology

Hardware:
Computer manufacturers
Distributors/retail stores
Value added resellers

Software:
Developed or modified
In-house programmers
Contract programmers
Purchased
Computer manufacturers
Software companies
Retail stores
Value added resellers

Networks:
Network companies
Computer manufacturers
Software companies
Value added resellers
Telecommunications companies
Value added network companies
Virtual private network companies

Data management:
Computer manufacturers
Software companies
Database software companies

Personal computer systems are sometimes purchased directly from manufacturers. IBM, Apple, Compaq, Dell, and many other companies sell their microcomputers directly to businesses. Alternatively, many microcomputer manufacturers sell their computers to distributors, computer stores, or other businesses that resell them to businesses and individuals. Businesses called **value added resellers (VARs)** purchase computers from manufacturers, add other hardware, software, and services, and then resell the complete package to businesses and individuals. IBM clones can be purchased from numerous businesses and computer stores that assemble the computers from parts purchased from other sources.

Software

As discussed in Chapter 13, computer software can be developed from scratch, purchased as a package, or purchased and then modified. Often, one of the biggest management decisions a business must make is whether to custom develop software or purchase a software package. Sometimes this is called the "make or buy" decision. Custom-developed software usually fits the organization's requirements better than packaged software, but it is also usually much more expensive. Purchasing software and then modifying it is sometimes a good compromise between custom-developed software and packaged software. For personal computers, software is usually purchased; for multiple-user and networked computer systems, software may be purchased, purchased and modified, or developed from scratch.

If software is going to be developed from scratch, or purchased and modified, then managers must decide whether to use in-house programmers or contract programmers from an outside source. The advantage of using in-house programmers is that they are usually less expensive than contract programmers and they may be more loyal to the business. Contract programmers, on the other hand, may be more experienced in developing the type of software needed by the business or have specializations the in-house programmers do not have, and they do not remain on the business's payroll after the work is completed.

Software can be purchased from a variety of sources. Computer manufacturers sell many software packages directly to businesses, as do general software companies such as Microsoft. Many specialty software companies also sell software packages to businesses. For example, a company may develop an accounting package for the hospitality industry that it sells directly to hotels. Individuals and some businesses purchase software packages from retail stores or e-tailers. Value added resellers usually sell software with hardware.

An alternative to operating its own hardware and software for its information systems is for a business to contract with an outside company to handle some or all processing. This approach is *outsourcing*, which is discussed in Chapter 13. The advantage of outsourcing is that the business can sometimes reduce expenses and get specialized services. One disadvantage is that the contracts for outsourcing are often very long—as long as 10 years. Not only will technology change significantly during the contract, but the business's needs will often change considerably as well.

Network Technology

Technology for networks can be acquired from a number of sources. Local area network hardware and software can be purchased from companies specializing in network technology, such as Novell, Cisco, and 3Com; from computer manufacturers, such as IBM; or from software companies, such as Microsoft. Value added resellers also provide complete LANs constructed from hardware and software from several sources.

Much of the hardware and software for wide area networks can be acquired from companies specializing in communications technology. Long-distance channels, however, are often provided by telecommunications companies such as AT&T, Sprint, and MCI. These companies are called *common carriers* because anyone who pays the necessary fees can use them. They provide two types of telephone lines. The first, called *switched* or *dial-up* lines, are the standard lines used by business and residential telephone customers for everyday telephone calls. The second, called *leased* or *dedicated* lines, can be used only by customers who lease them. These lines are better quality and provide faster and more accurate transmission. Other alternatives for WAN communication are a *value added network* (*VAN*) and a *virtual private network* (*VPN*). Recall from Chapter 6 that a VAN is a network provided by a communications company that leases communications lines from common carriers and adds special services for long-distance data communication, and a VPN is a network that uses the Internet for communications.

Data Management Technology

Acquiring data management technology first requires that a decision be made about the basic approach to data management: Will databases be stored on a server in a network? Will large multiple-user computers such as mainframe computers be used for databases? Will data be distributed among different computers? After this decision has been made, the necessary software can be selected. Many companies supply database software, including computer manufacturers such as IBM, general software companies such as Microsoft, and specialized database software companies such as Oracle, Sybase, and Informix.

Personnel and Training

Although they are not a form of information technology, personnel are needed to operate and use an information system. Managers can select the personnel from inside the organization or hire from outside. In either case, the personnel must be trained. Some businesses have training departments with full-time instructors to provide courses and other forms of computer and information systems training. Sometimes special **computer-based training** (**CBT**) software is used to train personnel on-line. Some businesses use outside services to provide training on a contract basis. In any case, personnel must be carefully trained before they can use and operate the system.

Organizing Information Systems Activities

The activities associated with developing, operating, and using information systems must be carefully organized in a business. Personnel who work in these activities need to be part of an organizational structure that provides appropriate direction and control. Businesses use a variety of organizational structures for their information systems activities. This section takes a look at some of the common elements of these structures.

Centralized Versus Decentralized Management

One of the fundamental questions in information systems management is whether to have a centralized or decentralized management structure (Figure 14.5). In a *centralized* management structure, decisions related to information systems and technology are made for the entire organization by a single, centrally located group of managers. Information systems are developed by specialists working at a central location, and

FIGURE 14.5

Centralized versus decen-
tralized information system
▲ management structure

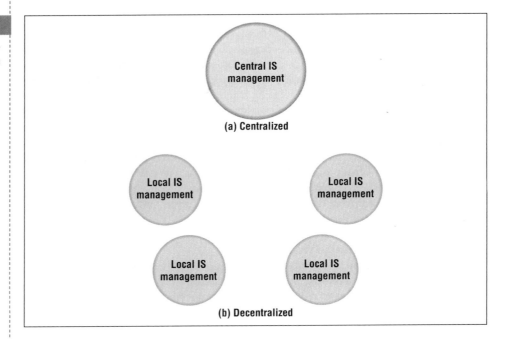

(a) Centralized

(b) Decentralized

then deployed throughout the organization. The resulting systems may use centralized computers connected by networks to computers at other locations. For example,
a business using a centralized information systems management structure might
decide to develop a new sales reporting system that, after development, is distributed
to its sales offices around the country.

In a *decentralized* management structure, information systems and technology
decisions are made by managers working in local departments or groups. Systems are
developed by specialists in those groups. The resulting systems use computers and
networks that are located at the local site. For example, in a business using a decentralized information systems management structure, a regional office may decide to
develop a new information system to keep track of its own sales. The system is developed and implemented at the regional office.

Both of these management structures have advantages. Centralized information
systems management can be more economical than decentralized management
because there is less duplication of personnel. With the decentralized approach,
information systems specialists are needed throughout the organization, possibly
resulting in duplication of effort. Centralized management also provides more control of system development than the decentralized approach. Managers can keep
track of systems development projects more easily when the development effort is
centralized, and costs can be controlled more closely.

Decentralized information systems management provides better response to user
needs than centralized management. When information system decisions are made
at the department or workgroup level, the users' needs usually are more carefully considered. The system development effort is closer to the users, and the users feel more
a part of the process, often resulting in greater satisfaction with the system.

The debate over centralized versus decentralized information systems management
has gone on for years. The pendulum swings back and forth between these approaches.
Both have advantages and disadvantages. Some businesses may find the centralized
approach better for their needs, and others may prefer the decentralized approach.

Information Systems Organizational Structure

Many organizations and businesses have a department that is responsible for the development and operation of computer information systems. This department may be called information systems (IS), management information systems (MIS), information technology (IT), or something similar. It is headed by an **information systems manager** who is responsible for the management of the department. A business that follows the centralized information systems management approach usually has a single such department for the entire business. In a business that follows the decentralized approach, information systems departments or similar groups may exist in a number of areas throughout the organization. Many organizations have a single person, called the **chief information officer** (**CIO**), who is responsible for all information systems and technology in the organization, not just that done by a single information systems department. The CIO usually reports to the chief executive officer (CEO) of the company.

Figure 14.6 shows the traditional way that an information systems department is organized. This department has four areas: systems development, operations, technical support, and end-user support. Each area has its own manager.

Systems Development.   The systems development area is concerned with developing and maintaining information systems. *Systems analysts*, as discussed in Chapter 13, and *programmers*, as discussed in Chapter 5, work in this area. The programmers are often called **application programmers** because they develop applica-

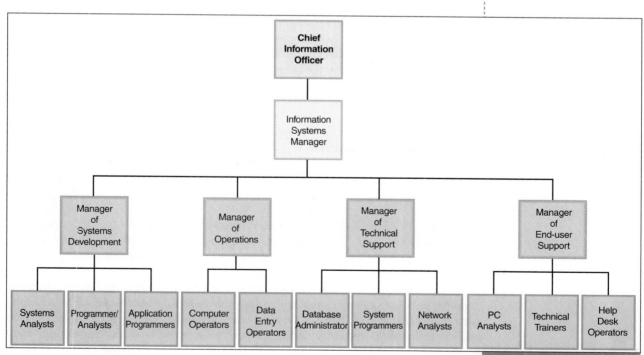

FIGURE 14.6

Traditional organization of an information systems department

tion programs. Sometimes a person does both system analysis and application programming and is called a **programmer/analyst**.

Operations.   The operations area is concerned with operating the computer and network equipment needed in information systems. **Computer operators** run the equipment. They put disks and tapes into the appropriate drives, load paper in printers, start and stop programs, remove output from printers, and monitor the hardware and software for errors and malfunctions. **Data entry operators** key input data, verify that data has been correctly keyed, and correct errors.

Technical Support.   The technical support area provides assistance in technical specialties to the other areas. The *database administrator* (*DBA*), discussed in Chapter 7, is responsible for managing the organization's databases. This person (or group of people) designs databases for the organization, selects database management software, and controls the use of databases by giving permission to specific users to access data in the databases. **System programmers** are responsible for setting up and maintaining system software such as operating systems and compilers. **Network analysts** (or **administrators**) are responsible for the organization's data communications hardware and software used in LANs and WANs.

End-user Support.   The end-user support area has **personal computer analysts** who are responsible for evaluating and selecting personal computer hardware and software for use in the organization. In addition, they help users set up personal computers, develop applications for end users, and assist users in utilizing application software. For example, a personal computer analyst may help a user select and install a personal computer or set up a graphics application on the user's personal computer. The analyst also may show a user how to access data in a company database or may develop a spreadsheet application for several users. Often, personal computer assistance is provided over the telephone from a **help desk**, which is staffed by special **help desk operators**. The end-user support area also has **technical trainers** who provide users with in-house training courses on personal computer hardware and software.

Some organizations have a separate department for end-user support. Sometimes called an **information center**, this department helps end users develop and use computer applications, mainly on personal computers. It is staffed by personal computer analysts, computer trainers, and other personnel, and usually provides a help desk for end-user assistance.

World Wide Web and Electronic Commerce Support

The traditional organization of an information systems department shown in Figure 14.6 does not take into consideration the specialized personnel who are needed for World Wide Web and electronic commerce support. Increasingly businesses are finding that a number of specially trained employees are needed for this activity. In many cases these employees require skills from several areas. For example, Web designers who also understand marketing concepts are needed to design e-commerce sites. As another example, graphic artists with special software skills are needed to implement multimedia Web sites. Individuals with the necessary expertise are often difficult to find.

Businesses have created a number of positions for those involved in Web and e-commerce applications. A **Webmaster** is responsible for developing and managing Web sites for an organization. This person needs skills in various types of Internet

Internet Technology Strategist at Sprint Paranet

BOOK
MARK

Day two has dawned in the world of e-commerce. On this day, companies want their Web efforts to generate profits and blow away the competition. Rising to the occasion is the Internet technology strategist, a new breed of techie who can take responsibility for end-to-end development of competitive electronic-business processes and applications. This job isn't for the weakhearted, but if done right, it could lead to the richest position of all: chief technology officer.

Diplomacy and strong analytical skills are paramount. In one instance, Patrick Wilson, Internet technology strategist at Sprint Paranet, an information technology consulting firm in Houston, Texas, stepped into a Web development project midstream. The client had just bought a retail store and wanted to build a grandiose Web site. "I had to come up with the Web site business flow from the consumers' and the business's perspective," Wilson says.

Before he proceeded, Wilson backed up and asked the client some tough questions: What must happen from a buyer standpoint? How does the user find, check out, and buy products? How do we as a business want to process these orders? How do we want to tie these into a back-office system and fully automate it? How do we want to handle customer relationship management?

Wilson's biggest challenge is customers changing their minds midstream. "Every client thinks they know what they want," he says. "But the life of a Web site is a moving target. I often hear, 'Wait. We changed our minds.' Web projects are constantly evolving. That's the problem with the Web stuff—you know it can always be better. But you have to draw a line in the sand and roll out the project in versions by asking the client, 'What are the requirements you'd accept to get the product out by this date?'"

Often, clients say they want certain changes "no matter what it takes," Wilson says. These changes often push deadlines back. When deadlines aren't met, the clients conveniently forget the changes they ordered.

Wilson handles it this way: When a client comes to him with new ideas, he mirrors back to the customer: "This is what you want. This is what's involved in making this change. This is how long it will take. Would you like it now or in the next version?"

Wilson's current project is with a dot-com startup. But dot-coms don't have any business processes, so they build them on the fly. And they change—a lot—which means Web development starts and stops in fits. "Right now, our client's business processes are changing a lot in the middle of the project. We thought we were going to have x amount on this side of the business, but we found out we had y, so now we have to redesign the business process to interact with y," Wilson says.

While developing a site for the largest model-train store in the world, Wilson had to rebuild some archaic internal processes. The company wanted to put its entire catalog on the Web, for which Wilson did the coding while at the same time setting up the business rules. "It was hard to build a calculator for shipping costs when no one knew how much a train model weighed," Wilson says. He later helped the company change its shipping and weighing processes, as well as other business processes, into a fully automated system. "Now the company uses more advanced technology, and their Web site is truly dynamic," he says.

Barring the demise of the Internet, the still-evolving job of the Internet technology strategist will be in high demand for many years to come. Marketers like The GAP in San Francisco and Ann Taylor Stores in New York need to get their sites running competitively online, says Lina Fafard, a contract technical recruiter in Redondo Beach, California. The next evolution of the position, Fafard says, is "support for the front-end cus-

tomer. Whatever you do, support that front-end customer. That's the next technical critical edge."

Questions

1. What does an Internet technology strategist at Sprint Paranet do?
2. What are the most important characteristics of an Internet technology strategist?
3. What is the biggest challenge an Internet technology strategist faces?

Web Site
Sprint Paranet:
www.sprintparanet.com

Source: *Adapted from* Deborah Radcliff, "Strategist of the Net," *Computerworld*, January 10, 2000, p. 74.

software tools such as HTML, as well as an understanding of Web site design principles. **Web programmers** develop sophisticated Web applications for the Internet, intranets, and extranets, using Internet programming languages such as XML and Java. **Multimedia developers** develop multimedia applications for Web sites. They must be familiar with multimedia software and often have backgrounds in graphic arts. An **e-commerce project manager** is responsible for managing the development of e-commerce systems.

The people involved in Web and e-commerce support are often part of the system development area in the information systems department. Alternatively, in some businesses these specialists may form their own group or department, separate from the information systems department.

Controlling and Securing Information Systems

One of the biggest concerns managers have with information systems is ensuring that the systems function properly and securely. Many questions arise related to these concerns. Is all data being processed correctly? What will happen if the hardware malfunctions? Is the system secure from damage or failure? Is the system safe from criminal activity? Answering these questions and more is part of controlling and securing information systems.

Information System Controls

Information system controls deal with ensuring that the system functions correctly. These controls fall into three main categories: application controls, hardware controls, and failure recovery procedures. Figure 14.7 summarizes these controls.

Application Controls.   Application controls are designed to ensure that the application processes all data correctly and produces the desired output. These controls are implemented in the software and procedures of the information system. They involve the four main functions of the system: input, output, storage, and processing.

Input controls are concerned with ensuring that input data is correctly entered into the system. An example is *data validation*. As discussed in Chapter 10, this technique involves checking input data for possible errors. All input data should be validated as it is entered into the system. Invalid data must not be allowed into an information system.

FIGURE 14.7

Information system controls ▲

Control Category	Type of Control	Example
Application controls	Input controls Output controls Storage controls Processing controls	Data validation Control total Data access control Redundant processing
Hardware controls	Error-checking hardware Redundant hardware Uninterruptible power	Parity-checking memory Fault-tolerant computer system UPS
Failure recovery procedures	Backup and recovery procedures Disaster recovery plan	Disk backup with safe storage Computer system failure service

Output controls deal with ensuring that all required output is produced. An example of an output control is a *control total*, described in Chapter 10. For instance, a count of the number of output documents is a control total. This control total can be compared with a similar total produced from the input data to indicate whether all output has been produced.

Storage controls are designed to ensure that the correct data is stored and accessed. An example is a *data access control*. Anyone needing access to stored data must go through the database administrator (DBA). The DBA provides information on how to access the data, including file or database names and special access codes. The file or database software checks the names and codes to be sure the correct data is being accessed.

Processing controls ensure that computations are performed correctly. An example is *redundant processing*, which means performing a particular computation several ways and comparing the results. In critical systems, where it is essential that the results are correct, computations are sometimes done differently on different computers, and then the results are compared on another computer. Computer systems that control the flight of airplanes and spacecraft often work this way.

Hardware Controls. Hardware controls are features in hardware that reduce the chance of failure. One type of hardware control is *error-checking hardware*, which automatically checks for errors in hardware. An example of error checking hardware is primary storage with *parity bits*, as discussed in Chapter 4, to check for errors in the memory of the computer. This technique, called *parity checking*, is a feature of many business computers.

Another type of hardware control is *duplicate*, or *redundant*, *hardware*. For example, some businesses use a *RAID* (redundant array of inexpensive disks) system, as discussed in Chapter 4, with their computers. This system includes multiple magnetic disks with data duplicated on different disks. Thus, if one disk is damaged, the data is not lost. Sometimes many components of a computer system are duplicated to create a **fault-tolerant computer system**. All input, output, storage, and processing is done on two computers simultaneously. If any component fails, the system continues processing, using other components.

So that computers will not stop when power is interrupted, many organizations use equipment that provides an *uninterruptible power source* for the system. An example is a **UPS**, which stands for uninterruptible power supply. A UPS is a device that includes a battery that takes over when the main power is cut off. The programs running on the computer at the time can then be terminated and the computer turned off without damaging the system. Alternatively, the UPS can take over until a generator is started to supply continuous power and keep the computer running. Uninterrupted power is essential for a fault-tolerant computer system.

Failure Recovery Procedures.   Information systems do not always work correctly. Hardware can fail, software can have bugs, amd people can make mistakes. Control procedures need to be in place to recover the system in case of a failure.

One of the most common system failures is loss of data on a magnetic disk or other secondary storage medium. Data can be accidentally erased, a disk drive can fail, a magnetic tape can be damaged, and many other things can happen to lose data. The most common type of procedures for dealing with this situation are *backup and recovery procedures*, as discussed in Chapter 10. Secondary storage data needs to be backed up periodically and stored in a safe location. Procedures need to be in place to back up data and to recover the stored data if the original is lost.

A computer system can fail completely, or it can be damaged by a natural or other disaster. In this case, the business needs a *disaster recovery plan*, which is a plan for dealing with a disaster. For example, a business can contract with special companies that provide computer services in case of a complete system failure. Sometimes these companies have computer systems in trucks that they can take to the business's location and use to continue the business's processing (Figure 14.8).

Information System Security

Information systems must be secure from damage due to unauthorized access or use. Security for information systems falls into two categories: physical security and electronic security.

Physical Security.   Physical security involves methods that prevent physical access or damage to components of an information system. Major hardware systems, such as multiple-user computers and network database servers, are often isolated with limited access. Employees may require special identification cards or codes to gain entry to computer rooms (Figure 14.9). Secondary storage data is secured by storing backup copies in a fireproof vault or at a site away from the business.

FIGURE 14.8

A computer disaster recovery
▲ truck

FIGURE 14.9

Computer room access control ▲

Electronic Security. More complex than physical security is electronic security, which involves preventing access to the information system or system components through communications links. With the extensive use of networks and data communications, especially the Internet, electronic security has become very important. Data sent over a communications channel can be intercepted, unauthorized access to a system can be gained through a terminal or a personal computer, and even the Internet can be used for intercepting data or accessing a business's computer system. Electronic commerce systems are especially vulnerable because of the storage and transmission of payment information, such as credit card numbers.

As discussed in Chapter 6, *data encryption* is a common technique for preventing intercepted data from being interpreted. Encrypted data is unintelligible unless a special number called a *key* is known. Unauthorized access to a system can be reduced by having *account names* and *passwords* for all authorized users. Some systems are designed so that when a user connects to the system, the computer breaks the connection and then calls the user back to reestablish the connection.

The Internet and e-commerce cause special security problems for businesses. Many businesses have one or more computers connected to the Internet to provide information and advertising, or for e-commerce transactions. These businesses want potential customers to gain access to these computers through the Internet. When a connection is made, however, it may be possible to access other business information in these or other computers. To prevent this from happening, a *firewall*, as discussed in Chapter 6, is used. The firewall consists of special hardware and software that creates an electronic barrier between the Internet site and the rest of the business's computer systems.

Preventing Computer Crime

Information systems must be protected from criminal activities. With computers and other technology, many crimes are possible that were not possible in the past. To guard against these activities, special forms of security are needed. Figure 14.10

FIGURE 14.10

▲ Computer crimes

Type of Crime	Examples of Preventive Measures
Theft of money	Regular financial audits Independent software checks
Theft of data	Password access to data Data encryption Removable storage media policies
Theft and destruction of hardware	Computer room access control PC security cable
Illegal copying of software	Software copying policies
Destruction of data and software	Backup and recovery procedures Virus-checking software

lists common computer crimes and some measures that can be taken to prevent them.

Theft of Money.   Information technology can be used to steal money from organizations and businesses. Computers are used extensively in banks and other financial institutions. Networks are used to transfer billions of dollars electronically all over the world every day, using electronic funds transfer (EFT). There are many opportunities for electronic theft of money in the complex systems needed by financial institutions.

Some examples of the use of computers to steal money are

■ A consultant taps into the electronic funds transfer system of a bank and transfers money to a secret account.

■ A computer programmer modifies the interest calculation program for a savings and loan so that fractions of a cent are not rounded correctly, but instead are put into a special account. Over time, the fractions build up to thousands of dollars.

■ A manager at a credit union modifies computer records of loans to a friend so that the loans appear to have been repaid.

To prevent such crimes, organizations need procedures that detect discrepancies in transactions and files. Financial records should be audited regularly for any inconsistencies. Software should be independently checked to be sure it performs correctly. For example, some organizations have one programmer develop a program and another programmer test it. The programmers would have to be in collusion to illegally modify the program. Most importantly, the organization should hire trustworthy employees.

Theft of Data.   Data is a valuable resource of an organization. Businesses store data about their operations in computer systems, and the data is often of interest to competitors. For example, a business might store data about prices of a new product. A competitor would be interested in the prices so that it would know what to charge in order to undersell the business. This type of data must be protected so that others cannot obtain it.

Security at MasterCard International

Credit-card firm MasterCard International has gone well beyond the use of firewalls to ensure the security of data shared among 2,400 internal users and 23,000 financial institutions worldwide. MasterCard, based in Purchase, New York, uses a variety of security approaches, from traditional passwords to secure ID cards that generate ever-changing passwords. Sam Alkhalaf, St. Louis–based senior vice president of technology and strategic architecture, explains the security strategy.

MasterCard uses passwords but has problems with people forgetting them or using obvious passwords. Some users have ID cards that can be read by card readers. In addition, about 2,000 users who need greater security use secure ID, which has a little window with password digits that change every two minutes and are synchronized to an algorithm in the computer system.

The firm also uses an internally developed piece of security software called MasterCard Online, which resides on its own server and interacts with a separate secure ID server and Cisco Systems routers. All extranet applications ride on top of MasterCard Online, which provides common communications, security, and encryption.

Applications servers are on protected network segments, with applications invoked only through the MasterCard Online desktop icon. Users must be authenticated to gain access to applications, and additional levels of security can be added at the screen or field level.

Benefits include a consistent security policy across all kinds of different applications; applications that can leverage MasterCard Online's security strength with little or no incremental investment; and side processes such as managing user IDs, which are handled for the user and are well defined and proven.

MasterCard is looking at new ways to use passwords. From a cost perspective, the combination of a password and the secure ID card is extremely effective for the level of security it provides. The company has looked at biometric technology, which recognizes fingerprints, faces, or the iris of the eye—but those methods are expensive. MasterCard has also taken a preliminary look at using an adaptive firewall, which identifies potential threats by looking at patterns of use.

Security places a burden on users, who might not use an application if they perceive the security procedures as too difficult. As a result, the secure ID cards are used only for very sensitive applications.

Every firewall comes with its own audit trail logs. MasterCard may add its own alerts. MasterCard Online is a custom-developed application. The secure ID cards come from Security Dynamics Technologies in Bedford, Massachusetts.

The firm believes MasterCard Online allows it to bring new applications to market more quickly by answering about 90% of security concerns.

Questions

1. What physical security technology does MasterCard International use?
2. What electronic security technology does MasterCard International use?
3. What new security technology is MasterCard International looking into?

Web Site

MasterCard International: www.mastercard.com

Source: *Adapted from* Steve Alexander, "Project: MasterCard International, Inc., Going Above and Beyond the Firewall", *Computerworld Intranets*, July 27, 1998, p. 7.

Electronic commerce systems contain much valuable data about individuals. Personal information, purchasing histories, and credit card numbers are just some of the data that is stored in such systems. This data must be safeguarded so that individuals will feel secure in their use of e-commerce systems.

To prevent the improper use of data, data security measures need to be taken. One measure is to use passwords to access the computer system. Whenever someone attempts to retrieve or change data, the system asks for the person's password. If the person cannot supply the correct password, the system does not perform the requested processing. Passwords should be changed frequently to prevent a person with an old password from using the system without authorization. In addition, passwords must be kept secret so that an unauthorized person cannot discover them.

Some people enjoy gaining access to computer systems not to steal data, but just for the challenge of breaking in. Often the term **hacker** is used for this type of person, although this term is also used for computer programmers in general. Many hackers use personal computers at home to gain access to remote computers operated by businesses and organizations. Most hackers are not interested in doing anything malicious, but just want to investigate other computer systems. To prevent hackers from accessing their computers, many organizations use sophisticated security procedures. In addition, various laws provide penalties for illegally accessing a computer system.

Another data security measure is to use data encryption to change the data on a disk to an unintelligible form. Then, even if someone knows the password, he or she cannot understand the data because it is encrypted. Data encryption is also used when data is sent over a communications channel. Because channels can be tapped for illegal purposes, data can be intercepted as it is transmitted. If the data is encrypted, however, the person intercepting the data cannot interpret it without the encryption key.

Data stored on removable storage media such as floppy disks and rewritable compact disks poses an especially difficult security problem for a business or an organization. Often, important data is stored on removable storage media, and stealing such media is relatively easy. For example, if a floppy disk is left on a desk, someone can take it, with little chance of detection. Many organizations have a policy that removable storage media may not be taken from the organization's property and that all such media must be stored in a locked case when not in use. Also, data encryption can be used for data stored on removable media so that only the person with the key can view the data.

Theft and Destruction of Hardware.   Hardware can be physically damaged or stolen. An unhappy former employee or another person may try to destroy hardware. An unscrupulous employee may steal equipment to use elsewhere or to sell. Security procedures need to be taken to prevent occurrences such as these.

Multiple-user computer systems, servers, and network equipment are usually kept in locked rooms, and only authorized personnel are allowed access. Computer rooms often have special fire-extinguishing equipment to protect the hardware in case of fire. Precautions such as these are necessary to protect the equipment from physical damage.

Personal computers in an office environment are sometimes easy to steal. To prevent theft, personal computers are often attached to a desk with a security cable. Use by unauthorized personnel is also a potential problem with personal computers. Consequently, some personal computer systems require a password before they can be used. Security procedures such as these are used to protect personal computer equipment.

Illegal Copying of Software.   Most software is *copyrighted*, just as books, movies, and recordings are copyrighted. This means that it is illegal to make a copy of the software without the permission of the owner of the copyright, which is usually the person or company that developed the software. When someone works hard developing a program, he or she should be rewarded for the effort. Just as you should not make a copy of someone else's book, movie, or recording, you should also not make a copy of someone else's software.

An individual who purchases a program purchases the right to use the program, but not the right to give away or sell copies of it. Most programs come with a written **software license agreement**, which states what the purchaser can legally do with the software. Most software license agreements allow the purchaser to use the program on only one computer at a time and to make copies only for backup purposes.

When a business or an organization purchases a program, it purchases the right for its employees to use the program. Usually, however, only one employee can legally use the program at a time. Making copies of the program so that more than one employee in the organization can use it is usually illegal. If several people need to use the program, multiple copies must be purchased. Alternatively, most software vendors sell a **site license** for an additional fee, which allows more than one person in the organization to use the program at a time.

To prevent the illegal copying of software, many organizations have policies stating that employees who copy software illegally will be disciplined or fired. As an additional measure, employees are usually not allowed to take software disks away from the organization's property.

Some software is not copyrighted. This software, called **public domain software**, can be legally copied and used by anyone. Another kind of software, called **shareware**, is copyrighted, but is given away or sold for a small fee and includes permission to use the software and to make copies for others for evaluation purposes. If, after evaluating the software, the business or individual decides to continue to use it, the full price for the software must be paid. If the business or individual decides not to use the software, however, nothing is owed. Because shareware is copyrighted and is not public domain software, the terms specified by the developer must be followed. The shareware concept is, however, an inexpensive way of evaluating many programs to decide which is the best for the business's or individual's needs.

An individual or a business that makes an illegal copy of a program and tries to sell it is performing an illegal act often called **software piracy**. The software developer may sue the individual or the business. The purchaser of software should always be sure to buy a legal copy of any program.

Destruction of Data and Software.   Some people do not want to steal data or illegally copy software, but instead want to destroy or otherwise vandalize it. A disgruntled employee might try to physically damage disks or tapes. A hacker might try to erase programs or data electronically. In addition, data may be destroyed by fire or natural disaster. To help prevent the permanent destruction of data and programs, a business should make backup copies and store them in a fireproof vault or at a location away from the business.

A particularly dangerous form of data and program destruction is caused by a computer program called a **virus**. A virus is created by a hacker who puts the virus on floppy disks or on a hard disk on a computer used by several people. Usually, the virus does not do any damage for some period of time, such as several months. During this time people may unknowingly copy the virus to other disks, or the virus may

FIGURE 14.11

▲ **A virus-checking program**

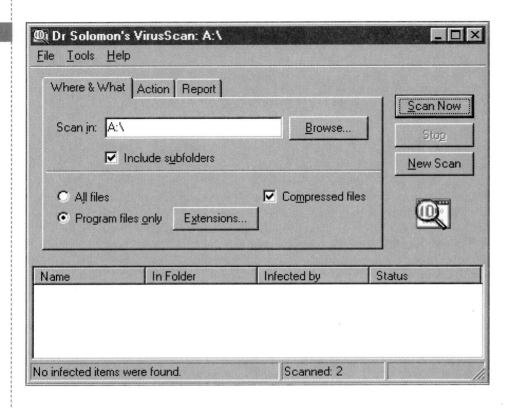

copy itself. At a certain time all the copies of the virus activate themselves and destroy programs and data in many computers.

Sometimes a hacker will put a virus on a computer in a LAN or WAN. Then the virus will copy itself to other computers in the network. This type of virus is sometimes called a *worm* because of the way it moves through the network. After a while, all the copies of the virus in the network begin destroying programs or data in the network.

To prevent viruses, no one should copy a disk from an unreliable source. Backup copies of original software disks should always be kept in case of a virus attack. Virus-checking programs can be used to search disks for the presence of viruses (Figure 14.11). Some of these programs are designed so that they check for viruses whenever a new program is executed. Detecting viruses in a network is especially difficult because there are many computers in the network. Special virus-checking software is needed to detect viruses on networks.

The Effects of Information Technology on Employment

Information systems and technology have had significant efforts on employment. Some people have lost their jobs to computers, and others have obtained new jobs as a result of computerization. Many, if not most, people's jobs have changed because of information technology. Overall, people's work lives have been affected by information systems and technology. Businesses and organizations need to be aware of these changes and consider them in their management of employees.

Displaced Employees

Information technology sometimes replaces employees. When an organization installs a computer information system for some function, the people who previously performed that function are displaced. Some of these people may lose their jobs, and others may be shifted to different jobs in the organization.

What should a business or an organization do with workers who are displaced by computers? If people lose their jobs because of information technology, they just add to society's social and economic problems. Many organizations offer the option of retraining to the affected workers. People have to adapt in a changing society, and retraining should be expected in life. Retrained employees continue as productive members of the organization and of society. Another option is early retirement for older employees. Some workers who are close to retirement may prefer this option to retraining.

It may seem like many jobs have been lost to computers, but that is not the case. Although some jobs have been lost, new jobs have been created. Many of these new jobs have been in the computer hardware and software industries, including jobs in the manufacturing, sales, and repair of computers, and in software development. Other new jobs have been created in businesses and other organizations. For example, programming, information systems analysis, and Web site development were not needed before computers, but are common jobs today.

Changing Patterns of Work

Many people's jobs have changed as a result of information technology. The typist uses a computer for word processing rather than a typewriter for typing. The office manager communicates with electronic mail rather than with paper memos. The factory worker checks on the operation of computerized robots rather than working on the assembly line. The jobs are still there; what the employees do is different.

Where and when people work have also changed. With personal computers, data communications, and workgroup applications, it is possible for some people to regularly work away from their office or business. Many people *telecommute*, a topic discussed in Chapter 9. They use computers in their home or elsewhere to communicate with an organization's computer systems. In addition, people can work at almost any time of the day or night on almost any day of the week because computer systems usually operate 24 hours a day, 7 days a week. Thus, some employees may choose to work in the evenings or on weekends rather than during the regular 9-to-5 workday. The effect is to create a *virtual office* of employees, another topic discussed in Chapter 9. Businesses need to adjust their management styles to accommodate these changing work patterns.

Employee Health

In addition to changes in employment patterns, information technology may affect the physical and mental health of employees. In the past, people have thought that prolonged use of computer screens may cause cataracts, birth defects, miscarriages, and other serious problems. Most of these concerns have not proven to be true, although the evidence is not conclusive in all cases. Until final proof of safety has been established, some people recommend against prolonged use of computer screens, especially by pregnant women.

Other physical problems, however, definitely occur in some computer users. Eyestrain, headaches, backaches, neck pain, wrist pain, and similar conditions are common among people who use computers extensively. One way a business can reduce these problems is through good *ergonomic* design of both the computer and the employee's work environment. (Ergonomics is discussed in Chapter 4.) In some areas, legislation requiring employers to provide ergonomically sound environments has been enacted.

In addition to physical health, there is concern that computer use can affect employees' mental health. Because computers work fast, some people feel pressured to work faster than normal just to keep up with the computer. This situation can create stress for the employee. In addition, people who work with computers often work alone, which can create a feeling of isolation. One potential problem with telecommuting is that the employee does not have the social interaction common in an office environment, again contributing to a feeling of isolation. These concerns need to be considered by businesses when managing employees who work extensively with computers.

Ethical Management of Information Systems and Technology

Management of information systems and technology must include ethical considerations. Recall from Chapter 1 that *ethics* are the standards of behavior that people follow. Chapter 3 discusses four ethical issues that can arise in information systems: privacy, accuracy, property, and access. Many of the management topics discussed in this chapter involve these or other ethical issues.

When planning for information systems and technology, ethical issues may have to be considered. For example, when deciding which information system to develop next, a business might have a choice between a system that increases profits and one that supports employee health. The first system will provide benefits to the owners of the company, and the second system will provide benefits to the employees. Which system the business develops first depends on the ethical approach the business takes.

Acquiring information technology may also involve ethical considerations. For example, deciding whether to purchase hardware with or without error-checking capabilities can raise ethical questions involving accuracy of information. As another example, deciding whether to develop software using in-house personnel or using contract programmers can involve ethical concerns about the responsibility of the business to its existing programmers.

How a business organizes its information system activities may bring up ethical issues. For example, changing from a decentralized to a centralized information system management structure can affect how easily employees can access information. Decentralized management is often more responsive to users' needs than centralized management, and thus a change to centralization may make it harder for users to have systems that provide them with the information they need.

Controlling and securing information systems may also involve ethical issues. Security measures are important for information systems, but they make it harder for legitimate users to access the systems they need. Similarly, the measures needed to combat computer crime can interfere with the rightful use of information and technology by employees. In some cases, these measures may invade the privacy of employees, such as when personnel files are searched to try to identify employees with the potential for criminal activity.

Evaluating the effect of information technology on the employees of a business requires careful consideration of ethical questions. What obligations does a business have to employees who are displaced by information technology? What special responsibilities does telecommuting impose on employees? Who is responsible for health issues related to computer use—the employee or the company?

Businesses may confront a number of ethical issues and questions in their management of information systems and technology. Only by understanding and addressing these issues and questions will businesses be able to ensure the ethical use of information systems and technology.

CHAPTER SUMMARY

1 Factors that should be considered in planning for information systems and technology include **planning horizon** and risk. Operational planning involves a planning horizon of a few weeks to a few months. In tactical planning, the planning horizon is several months to a few years. Strategic planning involves a planning horizon of several years to 10 years or more. Risk in information systems and technology is often related to three factors. The first factor is the size of the system development project; smaller projects are less risky than larger projects. The second factor is the familiarity of the business with the information technology; low (familiar) technology is less risky than high (unfamiliar) technology. The third factor is the amount of structure in the system development project; high-structure projects are less risky than low-structure projects. An **application portfolio** describes what systems should be developed and when, and assesses risk associated with each system. (pp. 440–442)

2 Information technology can be acquired from a number of sources. Computer hardware can be purchased from computer manufacturers, distributors, retail stores, and **value added resellers (VARs)**. Software can be developed using in-house programmers or contract programmers, or purchased from computer manufacturers, software companies, retail stores, and VARs. Network technology can be acquired from network companies, computer manufactures, software companies, VARs, telecommunications companies, value added network (VAN) companies, and virtual private network (VPN) companies. Data management technology can be acquired from computer manufacturers, general software companies, and specialized database software companies. (pp. 443–445)

3 An information systems department traditionally is organized into four areas: systems development, operations, technical support, and end-user support. The systems development area includes systems analysts, **application programmers**, and **programmer/analysts**. The operations area includes **computer operators** and **data-entry operators**. The technical support area consists of a database administrator, **system programmers**, and **network analysts**. The end-user support area includes **personal computer analysts**, **technical trainers**, and **help desk operators**. The information systems department is headed by an **information systems manager**. There is often a **chief information officer (CIO)** who is responsible for all information systems and technology in the organization. (pp. 445–448)

4 Specialized personnel are needed for World Wide Web and electronic commerce support. A **Webmaster** develops and manages Web sites for an organization. **Web programmers** develop Web applications for the Internet, intranets, and extranets, using Internet programming languages. **Multimedia developers** develop multimedia applications for Web sites. An **e-commerce project manager** manages the development of e-commerce systems. (pp. 448–450)

5 Information systems controls include application controls, hardware controls, and failure recovery procedures. Application controls are designed to ensure that all data is correctly processed and that the desired output is produced. They include input controls, output controls, storage controls, and processing controls. Hardware controls are features built into hardware to reduce the chance of failure. They include error-checking hardware, redundant hardware, and an uninterrupted power source. Failure recovery procedures are designed to recover the system in case of failure. They include backup and recovery procedures, and a disaster recovery plan. Information system security includes physical security and electronic security. Physical security involves methods that prevent physical access and damage to components of an information system. It includes computer room access control and off-site storage of backup data. Electronic security involves preventing access to the information system or system components through communication links. It includes data encryption and firewalls. (pp. 450–452)

6 One form of computer crime is theft of money. Regular financial audits and independent software checks can help prevent this type of crime. Another form of computer crime is theft of data. Some ways of preventing this type of crime are password access to data, data encryption, and policies against taking removable storage media away from the business. A third form of computer crime is theft and destruction of hardware. Keeping large computer and network equipment in locked rooms with controlled access and using security cables on personal computers can help prevent this type of crime. Illegal copying of software is another form of computer crime. Policies against copying software can help prevent it from happening. A final form of computer crime is destruction of data and software. To help prevent this crime, backup and recovery procedures should be followed and **virus** checking software should be used. (pp. 452–458)

7 Information systems and technology have had a significant effort on employment. Information technology sometimes displaces employees in an organization. Many people's jobs have changed as a result of information technology. The physical and mental health of employees can be affected by computer use. (pp. 458–460)

KEY TERMS

Application Portfolio (p. 441)
Application Programmer (p. 447)
Chief Information Officer (CIO) (p. 447)
Computer-Based Training (CBT) (p. 445)
Computer Operator (p. 448)
Data Entry Operator (p. 448)
E-commerce Project Manager (p. 450)
Fault-Tolerant Computer System (p. 451)
Hacker (p. 456)

Help Desk (p. 448)
Help Desk Operator (p. 448)
Information Center (p. 448)
Information Systems Manager (p. 447)
Multimedia Developer (p. 450)
Network Analyst (Administrator) (p. 448)
Personal Computer Analyst (p. 448)
Planning Horizon (p. 440)
Programmer/Analyst (p. 448)
Public Domain Software (p. 457)

Shareware (p. 457)
Site License (p. 457)
Software License Agreement (p. 457)
Software Piracy (p. 457)
System Programmer (p. 448)
Technical Trainer (p. 448)
UPS (p. 452)
Value Added Reseller (VAR) (p. 444)
Virus (p. 457)
Webmaster (p. 448)
Web Programmer (p. 450)

REVIEW QUESTIONS

1 What are the differences in the planning horizons of operational, tactical, and strategic planning?

2 What factors affect the risk associated with a new information system?

3 What is an application portfolio?

4 What are the main sources for acquiring computer hardware and software for an information system?

5 What is a VAR?

6 What are the advantages of centralized and decentralized information system management?

7 Who is the highest-ranking information systems and technology employee of an organization?

8 How is an information system department traditionally organized?

9 What specialized personnel are needed for World Wide Web and electronic commerce support?

10 What are application controls?

11 What are some forms of hardware controls?

12 What type of computer can keep processing after a component fails?

13 How can an information system be secured from damage due to unauthorized access or use?

14 What can be done to help prevent the theft of money by using information technology?

15 What is a software license agreement? What is a site license?

16 What is the difference between public domain software and shareware?

17 What can be done to help prevent the permanent destruction of data and programs?

18 What are some of the effects of information systems and technology on employment?

DISCUSSION QUESTIONS

1 Think of several new information systems for your college or university. How much risk would be involved in developing each system?

2 What additional factors, besides those given in this chapter, should an international business consider in planning its global information systems?

3 What information systems management structure—centralized or decentralized—would be best for a college or university? Why?

4 Consider the course registration system at your college or university. What controls should be included in that system to ensure that students are enrolled in the classes they request? What security should be included in the system to prevent inappropriate use of it?

5 Think of the jobs that you have had in the past or may have in the future. What effects has information technology had on these jobs?

6 Some viruses do not do any damage to a computer system. They may play a song on a speaker, display an image on a screen, or do some other benign thing that is simply a nuisance. Why would a business be concerned about these viruses?

ETHICS QUESTIONS

1 Assume, as in the chapter, that your company must decide between developing an information system that increases profits and one that supports employee health. Which system would you recommend the company develop first and why?

2 How much should a business look into the background of employees to try to identify those with the potential for criminal activity? What ethical issues arise in this situation?

3 Assume that a new information system has been installed in the department that you manage in your business. The system is such that 20% fewer employees will be needed in your department. You have been told by your superior to determine which employees will be terminated. How will you make this decision?

PROBLEM-SOLVING PROJECTS

1 Develop an application portfolio for information system projects for a business with which you are familiar. Use spreadsheet software to prepare the portfolio. Design the spreadsheet so that the projects can be sorted by different factors. Sort the projects by development time frame and by risk.

2 Investigate the organization of the information systems department of a business with which you are familiar. Draw a diagram, similar to Figure 14.6, that shows the organizational structure. Use graphics software to prepare your diagram.

3 Interview a computer professional about his or her career in the computer field. How did the person get started? What education does the person have? What was his or her first job in the computer field? What promotions has the person had in his or her career? What does the person do now? Write a summary of your interview.

INTERNET AND ELECTRONIC COMMERCE PROJECTS

1   Use the Web to find information on several value added resellers. What products or services do they provide? What do they add to the computer hardware they purchase? Write a report summarizing what you find.

2   Use the Web to find surveys of salaries in the information systems and technology field. Try to find a survey that categorizes salaries not only by job, but also by location and by industry. What are the typical salaries for the various jobs described in this chapter in your area? (Note that the job titles may not be exactly the same as those used in this chapter.) How do the salaries vary by industry? Write a summary of what you find.

3   A number of e-commerce sites advertise jobs that are available. Locate at least one such site and examine how employers post jobs on the site. Then search for jobs in your field of interest. Write an evaluation of the site from the employer's point of view and from the job seeker's point of view.

4   A number of reported viruses have actually been hoaxes. Use the Web to find information about several virus hoaxes. Write a report describing common virus hoaxes and how to identify them.

eBay

"This is in trouble. You'd better get down here. The guys aren't moving fast enough." The call was from eBay Chief Executive Officer (CEO) Meg Whitman to the new president of eBay Technologies, Maynard Webb. Not only had Whitman spotted impending trouble while monitoring the operations center, but she had diagnosed it. "She said, 'That's a hardware issue. This is what you'll see, and this is how long it will take,' " Webb recalls. "And she was right."

Whitman brings new meaning to the concept of a hands-on CEO. She literally lived in the information technology operations center through much of the summer after a catastrophic 22-hour outage in June convinced her she was battling for San Jose–based eBay's life. "We put in cots, and I was just there," she says. "I lived it."

The massive outage, hard on the heels of a flurry of shorter crashes that year, was a trial by fire for Whitman. Her information technology department had been unable to keep up with the company's phenomenal growth and was already stretched to the breaking point, the volatile and vocal eBay community was screaming bloody murder, and the stock price was plummeting.

Whitman's credentials were among the best American education and business could offer, but her technical savvy was that of a casual user. All she had was instinct, but it had to be enough. "Without technology, we don't have a company," she explains. "It was very clear that I had to step in and provide the leadership to get us through this."

Whitman came out of the experience a technically astute CEO with a visceral understanding of what technology means to the company. "I am a far better executive than I was," she says, "and I have a deep understanding of the technology challenges and what the options are."

eBay came out of the summer with a beefed-up information technology department, a strong new information technology executive in Webb (formerly chief information officer at San Diego–based Gateway), and a commitment to build the kind of e-commerce system that the world has literally never seen.

Whitman grew up on New York's Long Island and topped off an economics degree from Princeton University with an MBA from Harvard. Following that were stints as brand manager at Procter & Gamble; consultant at Boston-based Bain & Co.; marketing executive at The Walt Disney Company; division president at Stride Rite in Lexington, Massachusetts; CEO of FTD, the flower delivery service in Downers Grove, Illinois; and general manager at Pawtucket, Rhode Island–based Hasbro's preschool division, from which she was lured to eBay in May 1998.

What makes an up-and-coming executive with a blue-chip business background take a leap of faith to a funky online auction site specializing in rummage-sale treasures like Pez dispensers and Beanie Babies? "It was funny," she says. "Sometimes in life you just have an instinct about things."

Whitman says her instinct told her the Internet was going to change everything and that something was going on with the trading community coalescing around eBay that gave it a leg up on other businesses. Whitman saw eBay as a perfect Internet company because it did something unique that couldn't be done without the Internet. "There's no substitute in the land-based world for eBay," she says. "I just had an overwhelming instinct that this thing was going to be huge."

Whitman's willingness to trust her instincts may be the key to her success in the frantic world of the Internet. "In this space, the price of inaction is higher than the price of making a mistake," she says. She figures that she makes 20 decisions a day that would occur over a two- or three-month period at another company. For example, in the second quarter of 1999 alone, eBay acquired Butterfield & Butterfield Auctioneers in San Francisco; Kruse International, an Auburn, Indiana, firm dealing in collectible autos; Alando.de AG, Europe's largest online auction; and Billpoint, a Redwood City, California, company enabling person-to-person credit-card transactions.

Because things move so fast at eBay, her experience counts, Whitman says, particularly since most of the staff are twentysomething Web kids. "There's no shortage of energy, brilliance, drive, but they just don't know because they haven't done it before," she says. "There have been many times when I've said, 'I know what's going to happen here,' because I've seen it unfold before."

But no one foresaw the June crash, even though it was eventually attributed to an operating system bug that Sun Microsystems had previously alerted eBay about but that eBay hadn't yet fixed. Clearly, seat-of-the-pants technology management was no longer adequate for eBay's mission.

The site had been growing a minimum of 30% to 40% each quarter. It serves up to 90 million interactive bidding pages per day. It has the transactional volume of Charles Schwab & Co. in San Francisco, but unlike Schwab, it lacks a back-end legacy system painstakingly developed over years. And unlike Schwab, eBay virtually never closes.

Whitman acknowledges that she made a costly error by waiting too long to hire key senior managers, especially Webb. But in June, she had to play catch-up, imposing stringent discipline and conducting top-level technical diplomacy to dig eBay out of the technology hole it was in. "This was about putting very specific procedures and processes in place and marshalling Sun, Oracle, and Veritas Software and really figuring out how we were going to get quickly to far more redundancy and recoverability than we had," she explains.

Whitman's learning curve was steep. "I remember for the first few meetings I really didn't understand what people were saying," she says. But that didn't last long. "It's sort of like learning French," she laughs. "If you immerse yourself, after a week you can actually speak French."

Again, instinct played heavily. "I can just tell the way people are talking about something that it's not right," she says. "They don't even know it's not right, but I know."

Once Whitman had the lingo down, she was able to coax options out of her technical staff and vendors, and then build consensus about what to do. But there's no simple way out of eBay's technical difficulties. "We are absolutely pioneering a technical infrastructure that does not exist," Whitman states.

The need to build in nearly infinite scalability is keeping Webb busy. "We've got this Ferrari screaming down the highway and I'm kind of standing on the hood, throwing asphalt down in front of it as we go," he says. eBay raced to great complexity in record time, he says. "Last year at this time, we had no E10Ks (Sun's largest servers). Today I have seven. It gives you an idea of the dynamics of growth."

Webb's strategy is to split up eBay's huge, maxed-out database into more manageable, distributed chunks. Functions such as customer feedback, accounting, and some product categories will be moved to separate machines. This will provide vastly more room for growth and less catastrophic consequences when one server goes down. But the cost is a lot more management complexity, and a lot more discipline. And imposing traditional management discipline is difficult in a freewheeling dot-com environment where "folks, in many cases, have never done any of that before and don't want to," Webb says.

His other concern is reliability. Shortly after another spate of outages in November, Webb moved eBay from a "warm backup" system—in which a copy of the database resides on another machine and operations can be switched over—to a high-availability cluster, where live data and the backup copy share a disk. Theoretically, this will cut recovery time from hours to minutes in most cases. Webb is also working toward better early warnings of impending crashes.

Questions

1 Why is instinct important for the CEO of eBay?
2 Why does the CEO of eBay have to make decisions quickly?
3 What was the CEO of eBay able to do after she became familiar with the technology used in the eBay system?
4 How did the president of eBay Technologies reduce the consequences of system failure and improve system reliability?
5 Is it important that all CEOs understand information technology?

Web Site
eBay: www.ebay.com

Source: *Adapted from* Kathleen Melymuka, "Internet Intuition," *Computerworld*, January 10, 2000, pp. 48–50.

The number following each entry indicates the chapter in which the term is defined.

A

accessing The process of retrieving stored data. (10)

accounting The function of a business that records and reports financial information about the business. (2)

accounting information system An information system that supports the accounting function of a business. (10)

accounts payable system A system that keeps track of money owed by the business, pays the business's bills, and provides reports of money owed by the business. (10)

accounts receivable system A system that keeps track of money owed to the business by its customers, records customer payments, and provides reports of money owed to the business. (10)

ad hoc report A report that is prepared only once, for a specific purpose. (11)

address A unique number that identifies a storage location in primary storage. (4)

AI Artificial intelligence. (11)

ALU Arithmetic-logic unit. (4)

analog signal A signal that transmits data by a wave pattern that varies continuously. (6)

application conferencing A form of document conferencing in which each user sees the same document within an application program. (9)

application generator A program that is used to develop a computer application including input and output forms, reports, menus, calculations, and database queries. (7)

application portfolio A description of the information systems an organization should develop and when, as well as an assessment of the risk associated with each system. (14)

application programmer A programmer who develops application programs. (14)

application software Programs designed for specific computer applications. (3)

arithmetic-logic unit (ALU) The unit of the CPU that does arithmetic and performs logical operations. (4)

artificial intelligence (AI) The use of computers to mimic human intelligence. (11)

ASCII An industry-standard code for representing characters using 7 bits per character, although commonly extended to 8 bits per character. Stands for American Standard Code for Information Interchange. (4)

assembler A program that translates assembly language programs into equivalent machine language programs. (5)

assembly language A programming language in which each instruction consists of a symbolic operation code and one or more symbolic operands. (5)

audioconferencing A workgroup application that involves voice communication by members of a group located at different places using a computer network. (9)

audit trail A way of tracing the effect of data through an information system. (10)

authoring software Software used to create multimedia presentations. (8)

auxiliary storage Secondary storage. (4)

B

B2B electronic commerce Business-to-business electronic commerce. (12)

B2C electronic commerce Business-to-consumer electronic commerce. (12)

backup copy A copy of data stored separately in case the original data is lost or destroyed. (4)

backup procedure A procedure for making a copy of stored data in order to ensure against loss. (10)

bandwidth The capacity of a channel to transmit data. (6)

bar-code scanner A device that recognizes a bar code, which is a series of bars of different widths. (4)

BASIC A programming language used mainly for simple programs. Stands for Beginner's All-purpose Symbolic Instruction Code. (5)

batch processing A form of data processing in which all the data to be processed is prepared in a form understandable to the computer before processing, and is then processed in a batch to produce the output. (10)

baud rate The rate at which a signal on a communications channel changes. (6)

billing system A system that prepares customer bills or invoices. (10)

binary digit A 1 or 0. (4)

bit Binary digit. (4)

booting The process of loading the supervisor of an operating system. (5)

BPR Business process reengineering. (13)

browser A program that lets a user locate information on the World Wide Web by following links between Web pages. (5)

bug An error in software. (3, 8)

bus network A network in which each node is connected to a single, common communications channel. (6)

business alliance A group of businesses that coordinate some of their operations or link some of their resources. (12)

business process A group of activities or tasks that accomplishes something for a business. (13)

business process reengineering (BPR) The complete redesign of one or more business processes in an organization. (13)

business-to-business (B2B) electronic commerce Electronic commerce in which a business or other type of organization promotes and sells its products or services to another business or organization. (12)

business-to-consumer (B2C) electronic commerce Electronic commerce in which a business or other type of organization promotes and sells its products or services to a consumer. (12)

button An icon or other symbol on a screen enclosed in a shape that looks like a key on a keyboard. (5)

byte A group of bits used to store a character. (4)

C A programming language used for system programs and for complex application programs. (5)

C2C electronic commerce Consumer-to-consumer electronic commerce. (12)

cable modem A modem for a cable television channel. (6)

CAD Computer-aided design. (8)

CASE The use of computer-based tools to help in the development of an information system. Stands for computer-aided software engineering. (13)

CBT Computer-based training. (14)

CD Compact disk. (4)

CD-R A type of optical disk drive that can record data on a compact disk but cannot erase data. Stands for compact disk-recordable. (4)

CD-ROM A type of optical disk drive that can retrieve data from compact disks but cannot store data on compact disks. Stands for compact disk–read-only memory. (4)

CD-RW A type of optical disk drive that can erase data on a compact disk and record new data on the disk. Stands for compact disk–rewritable. (4)

central processing unit (CPU) The central component of a computer that carries out instructions in the program. Sometimes called the processor. (4)

channel interface device A device, such as a modem, that provides a connection between a computer and a communications channel. (6)

character A symbol such as a digit, letter, or special symbol. (3)

charting software Software used to create charts and graphs. (8)

chat A computer application that allows several users to communicate in such a way that each user immediately sees messages entered by other users. (9)

chief information officer (CIO) The person responsible for all information systems and technology in an organization. (14)

chip A common term for an integrated circuit, which is a piece of silicon containing millions of electronic circuits. (4)

CIO Chief information officer. (14)

CIS Computer information system. (1)

client A computer in a network with which the user interacts and that provides access to a server in the network. (3)

client/server computing The use of a network in which some computers are client computers running application software that provides data processing and a user interface, and one or more other computers are database servers providing database storage and database software. (3)

client software Software used on a client computer to process and display data. (6)

COBOL A programming language used mainly for business application programs. Stands for COmmon Business Oriented Language. (5)

code of ethics A set of standards or rules for ethical behavior in a business, an organization, or a profession. (3)

collaborative computing Group computing. (9)

command A word or phrase entered into a computer that tells a program to perform a function. (5)

communications channel A link between computer devices used for data communications. (6)

communications control unit A device that controls communications traffic over a channel. Includes multiplexers, controllers, and front-end processors. (6)

communications hardware Equipment that provides for communication between computers and computer devices. (3)

communications processor A device that provides communication processing capabilities, usually between a computer and a communications channel. (6)

communications software Software used to control communication between computers. (3)

compact disk (CD) A small optical disk. (4)

competitive advantage An advantage that puts a business in a stronger position to compete than other businesses. (12)

compiler A program that translates third-generation language programs into equivalent machine language programs. (5)

computer An electronic device that stores and processes data by following the instructions in a program. (4)

computer-aided design (CAD) software Software used to design objects such as buildings and machines. (8)

computer application A use of a computer. (1)

computer-based training (CBT) The use of computers to train employees. (14)

computer hardware The physical equipment that makes up a computer. (3)

computer information system (CIS) An information system that includes one or more computers. (1)

computer operator A person who operates computer equipment. (14)

computer telephony The use of a computer network for audio communication. (9)

conceptual design A description of what a new system must do to satisfy the user's requirements. (13)

consumer-to-consumer (C2C) electronic commerce Electronic commerce in which a consumer sells a product or service to another consumer. (12)

control A procedure for ensuring the completeness of data processing and for minimizing errors in an information system. (10)

control total A number, computed when data enters a system and again after the system has processed the data, that is used to check for errors during the processing. (10)

control unit The unit of the CPU that analyzes and executes instructions. (4)

cost/benefit analysis The process of comparing the expected costs and benefits of an information system to determine its economic feasibility. (13)

C++ A version of the programming language C with additional features for object-oriented programming. (5)

CPU Central processing unit. (4)

CRT A tube similar to that used in a television. Stands for cathode ray tube. (4)

cursor A mark on a screen that indicates where the next output will be displayed or the next input will be entered. (4)

custom software Programs that are prepared from scratch for a specific person, business, or organization. (3)

D

data A representation of a fact, a number, a word, an image, a picture, or a sound. (1)

database A collection of data and relationships between the data, stored in secondary storage. (3, 7)

database administrator (DBA) A person responsible for managing an organization's databases. (7)

database management system (DBMS) Software that provides capabilities for creating, accessing, and updating data in a database. (7)

database server A server with a secondary storage device, usually a large hard disk drive, that is used for database processing by other computers in the network. (6)

database software Software used to create, access, and update a database. (5)

data conferencing Document conferencing. (9)

data encryption The process of changing data to a form that is unintelligible unless a special key is known. (6)

data entry operator A person who keys input data into an information system. (14)

data file A collection of related records stored in secondary storage. Also just called a file. (3)

data flow diagram (DFD) A diagram of the flow of data in an information system. (13)

data mart A part of a data warehouse containing just the data needed by a group of users. (7)

data mining The process of searching for patterns in the data of a data warehouse. (7)

data validation The process of checking data entered into a system for errors. (7, 10)

data warehouse A collection of current and historical data extracted from databases used in an organization. (7)

DBA Database administrator. (7)

DBMS Database management system. (7)

debugging The process of locating and correcting errors in software. (8)

decision support system (DSS) An information system that helps managers make decisions by analyzing data from a database and providing the results of the analysis to the manager. (11)

demand report A report that is prepared only when requested. (11)

department A group of people in a business who have specific responsibilities related to a business function. (2)

desktop computer A microcomputer designed to sit on a desk and not be moved. (3)

desktop publishing The use of a personal computer to prepare high-quality printed output similar to that produced by a printing company. (8)

desktop publishing software Software used for desktop publishing. (8)

desktop videoconferencing system A videoconferencing system designed for use by individuals with personal computers. (9)

detail report A report that lists detailed information about the results of processing. (10)

DFD Data flow diagram. (13)

dialog box A box on a screen in which the user provides input requested by software. (5)

digital signal A signal that transmits bits as high and low pulses. (6)

direct access Random access. (4)

direct file A data file in which each record is stored at a location determined directly from the record's key field. (7)

disk pack A stack of several hard disks, with spaces between the disks. (4)

distributed database A database that is divided into parts, with each part stored on a different computer in a network. (7)

distributor Wholesaler. (2)

document conferencing A workgroup application that involves simultaneous collaboration on a document by members of a group. (9)

documentation Written descriptions of an information system or a computer application. (3, 8)

dot-matrix printer A printer that prints each character by striking a ribbon and the paper with a group of pins that cause dots, arranged in a rectangular pattern or matrix, to be printed on the paper. (4)

downloading Transferring data from a remote computer to a local computer. (6)

draft-quality printer A printer that produces output that is of low to medium quality. (4)

drawing software Software used to draw pictures and diagrams. (8)

drilling down The process of finding detailed information that is used to produce summary information. (11)

DSL A digital telephone line communications system. Stands for Digital Subscriber Line. (6)

DSS Decision support system. (11)

DVD A large-capacity optical disk. Stands for digital video (or versatile) disk. (4)

DVD-ROM A type of optical disk drive that can retrieve data from DVDs but cannot store data on DVDs. Stands for digital video (or versatile) disk–read-only memory. (4)

E

EBCDIC A code developed by IBM for representing characters, using 8 bits per character. Stands for Extended Binary Coded Decimal Interchange Code. (4)

e-business Electronic business. (12)

e-commerce Electronic commerce (1, 6, 12)

e-commerce project manager A person who manages the development of electronic commerce systems. (14)

e-commerce system Electronic commerce system. (12)

EDI Electronic data interchange. (1)

EFT Electronic funds transfer. (1)

EIS Executive information system. (11)

electronic auction A form of electronic commerce in which products or services are auctioned to the highest bidder. (12)

electronic business The use of computers and networks to perform many functions of a business electronically. (12)

electronic catalog A list of products with descriptions, pictures, and prices used in an electronic commerce system. (12)

electronic commerce The use of networks, especially the Internet and the World Wide Web, to promote and sell products and services. (1, 6, 12)

electronic commerce system An information system that provides electronic commerce capabilities for an organization. (12)

electronic conferencing A workgroup application that combines video- and document conferencing. (9)

electronic conferencing software Software that lets members of a group talk to and see each other while also viewing a common document on a computer screen. (5)

electronic data interchange (EDI) The use of computers to exchange data electronically between businesses. (1)

electronic funds transfer (EFT) The use of computers to transfer funds electronically between financial institutions. (1)

electronic mail A computer application that involves transmitting messages electronically between users. Also refers to the messages that are transmitted. (1, 6, 9)

electronic meeting The use of a computer system to facilitate a meeting among members of a group. (9)

electronic meeting system (EMS) A workgroup application designed to support electronic meetings. (9)

electronic messaging A workgroup application that involves sending different types of messages between members of a group. (9)

electronic messaging software Software used to send different types of messages between members of a group. (5)

electronic payment An electronic commerce system capability that allows customers to pay for purchases electronically. (12)

electronic shopping cart A list of the products a customer wants to purchase used in an electronic commerce system. (12)

e-mail Electronic mail. (1, 6, 9)

EMS Electronic meeting system. (9)

end user User. (1)

end-user computing The development and use of personal computer applications by end users. (8)

enterprise information system Organizational information system. (1)

enterprise resource planning (ERP) A type of information system or software that supports several areas of a business by combining a number of applications that use a single database to store all the data used by the applications. (10)

entity-relationship (ER) diagram A diagram of the design of a database. (13)

ER diagram Entity-relationship diagram. (13)

ergonomics The study of how to design machines for effective human use. (4)

ERP Enterprise resource planning. (10)

ES Expert system. (11)

ESS Executive support system. (11)

e-tailer A business that engages in business-to-consumer electronic commerce. (12)

ethics The principles, rules, or standards that govern right and wrong behavior. (1)

exception report A report that contains data that is an exception to some rule or standard. (10)

executive information system (EIS) Executive support system. (11)

executive support system (ESS) An information system that provides support for the information needs of strategic managers. (11)

expert system (ES) An information system that provides expert advice. (11)

extranet An intranet that is accessible from outside an organization by companies or individuals that have special codes or passwords. (6)

F

fault-tolerant computer system A computer system designed with duplicate components so that if any component fails, the system will continue to function. (14)

feasibility analysis The process of determining whether it is feasible to develop an information system. (13)

field A group of related characters. (3)

file A collection of related items stored in secondary storage. Also refers specifically to a data file. (3)

file server A server with a secondary storage device, usually a hard disk drive, that is used for file storage by other computers in the network. (6)

file transfer A function provided by communications software that allows files to be transferred between computers. (6)

finance The function of a business that obtains money needed by a business and plans the use of that money. (2)

financial information system An information system that supports the finance function of a business. (10)

firewall A hardware and software system to prevent access to an organization's private computer data from outside the organization. (6)

flat-panel screen A screen that is thin and lightweight. (4)

floppy disk A magnetic disk made of flexible plastic with a metallic coating. (4)

FORTRAN A programming language used mainly for scientific application programs. Stands for FORmula TRANslation. (5)

4GL Fourth-generation language. (5)

fourth-generation language (4GL) A programming language that requires significantly fewer instructions to accomplish a particular task than does a third-generation language. (5)

G

GB Gigabyte. (4)

G byte Gigabyte. (4)

GDSS Group decision support system. (9, 11)

general ledger system A system that maintains the business's financial accounts and prepares financial statements. (10)

geographic information system (GIS) An information system that provides information based on geographic location. (11)

GHz Gigahertz. (4)

gigabyte (G byte, GB) 2^{30} bytes. Commonly thought of as one billion bytes. (4)

gigahertz (GHz) The units used to measure the internal clock speed of some computers. One gigahertz is one billion cycles per second. (4)

GIS Geographic information system. (11)

global information system An information system that spans national borders. (1, 12)

graphical user interface (GUI) A user interface that usually includes icons, menus, and windows. (5)

graphics software Software used to create graphic output. (5)

group calendaring and scheduling A workgroup application that involves coordinating appointment calendars and scheduling meetings of members of a group. (9)

group computing The use of groupware by members of a workgroup for collaboration. (9)

group decision support system (GDSS) A workgroup information system that supports decision making among members of a group. (9, 11)

group information system Workgroup information system. (1)

group support system (GSS) Workgroup information system. (9)

group videoconferencing system Room videoconferencing system. (9)

groupware Software used for group collaboration. (5, 9)

GSS Group support system. (9)

GUI Graphical user interface. (5)

H

hacker A person who gains access to a computer system mainly for the challenge of breaking in and investigating the system. Also a term for a computer programmer. (14)

handheld computer A small microcomputer designed to be held in the hand. (3)

hard disk A magnetic disk made of rigid metal. (4)

hardware The computer, communications, and related equipment used in an information system. (1)

help desk A group in an organization that provides personal computer assistance to end users, usually over the telephone. (14)

help desk operator A person who provides personal assistance to end users. (14)

hierarchical database A database in which all relationships are one-to-one or one-to-many, but no group of data can be on the "many" side of more that one relationship. (7)

hierarchical network   A network in which the nodes are organized in a hierarchical fashion, like a family tree. (6)

host language   A programming language for preparing application programs in which commands from a query language are embedded. (7)

HRIS   Human resource information system. (10)

HTML   A language used to create pages on the World Wide Web. Stands for Hypertext Markup Language. (5)

human resource information system (HRIS)   An information system that supports the human resource management function of a business. (10)

human resource management   The function of a business that hires, trains, compensates, and terminates employees. (2)

hybrid network   A network that is a combination of star, hierarchical, bus, ring, and other network organizations. (6)

I

icon   A small picture, displayed on a screen, that represents a function that a program can perform. (5)

impact printer   A printer that makes an image by striking paper with a metal or plastic mechanism. (4)

indexed file   A system of two files, one a sequential data file and the other an index file containing the key field of each record in the data file and the location of the corresponding record in the data file. (7)

individual information system   An information system that affects a single person. (1)

inference engine   Software that analyzes rules in a knowledge base to draw conclusions. (11)

information   Data that is meaningful or useful to someone. (1)

information center   A department or group in an organization that helps end users develop and use computer applications, mainly on personal computers. (14)

information services   The function of a business that provides computer information system support for the business. (2)

information sharing   A workgroup application that involves sharing different types of information among members of a group. (9)

information sharing software   Software used for sharing different types of information among members of a group. (5)

information superhighway   A concept for allowing any computer to be connected to a national or an international network. (6)

information system (IS)   A collection of components that work together to provide information to help in the operations and management of an organization. (1)

information systems manager   The person responsible for the management of the information systems department in an organization. (14)

information technology (IT)   Computers and technology used in information systems. (1)

ink-jet printer   A printer that prints each character by spraying drops of ink on paper. (4)

input data   Data that goes into an information system. (1)

input device   A device that accepts data from outside the computer and converts it into an electronic form that the computer can understand. (4)

input function   The actions of an information system that accept data from outside the system. (1)

inquiry   Query. (11)

instant messaging   A form of electronic messaging in which a message is sent and immediately displayed at the receiver's computer. (9)

integrated software   Software that provides multiple applications. (8)

intelligent agent   A program that acts on behalf of an individual, based on preferences given to it. (11)

interactive processing   A form of data processing in which the user interacts with the computer as the processing takes place. (10)

internal storage   Primary storage. (4)

international information system   Global information system. (1, 12)

Internet   A public, international collection of interconnected wide area and local area networks offering a variety of services for users. (1, 6)

Internet service provider (ISP)   A company that provides Internet access and e-mail services. (6)

internetwork   A collection of networks that are interconnected. (6)

interorganizational information system   An information system that functions between several organizations. (1, 12)

interorganizational system (IOS)   Interorganizational information system. (12)

interpreter   A program that translates and immediately executes program instructions. (5)

intrabusiness electronic commerce   Electronic commerce that involves transactions between units of a business or organization. (12)

intranet   An Internet-type network accessible only from within an organization. (6)

inventory control system   A system that keeps track of a business's inventory, indicates when inventory should be reordered, and computes the value of the inventory. (10)

IOS   Interorganizational system. (12)

IS   Information system. (1)

ISDN   A digital telephone line communications system. Stands for Integrated Services Digital Network. (6)

ISP   Internet service provider. (6)

IT   Information technology (1)

J

Java A programming language that allows a World Wide Web page developer to create programs for applications that can be used through a browser. (5)

K

KB Kilobyte. (4)

K byte Kilobyte. (4)

keyboard An input device that accepts keyed data. (4)

key field A field that uniquely identifies a record in a data file. (7)

kilobyte (K byte, KB) 1,024 bytes. Commonly thought of as 1,000 bytes. (4)

KMS Knowledge management system. (11)

knowledge The understanding that a person has gained through education, experience, discovery, intuition, and insight. (11)

knowledge base A collection of expert knowledge stored in a computer. (11)

knowledge management The process of managing organizational knowledge. (11)

knowledge management system (KMS) An information system that provides capabilities for organizing, storing, accessing, and sharing organizational knowledge. (11)

L

LAN Local area network. (6)

laptop computer Notebook computer. (3)

laser printer A printer that prints each page by recording an image of the page on the surface of a metal drum with a laser, and then transferring the image to paper. (4)

legacy system An information system that has been used in an organization for many years. (13)

letter-quality printer A printer that produces output that is the quality expected in a business letter. (4)

line printer A printer that prints one line at a time. (4)

local area network (LAN) A network that covers a small area such as a single building or several nearby buildings. (6)

M

machine language The basic language of a computer. (4)

magnetic disk A form of secondary storage that consists of a disk with a metallic coating on which data is recorded magnetically. (4)

magnetic disk drive A device for recording data on and retrieving data from magnetic disks. (4)

magnetic ink character recognition (MICR) A technique used by the banking industry for processing checks imprinted with special characters. (4)

magnetic strip reader A device that can recognize data recorded in a magnetic strip. (4)

magnetic tape A form of secondary storage that consists of a tape similar to audio recording tape on which data is recorded magnetically. (4)

magnetic tape drive A device for storing data on and retrieving data from a magnetic tape. (4)

mainframe computer A large, multiple-user computer. (3)

management information system (MIS) An information system that supports management decision making by providing information to managers at different levels of an organization. (11)

manufacturer A business that produces goods sold to other businesses or to individual customers. (2)

manufacturing information system An information system that supports the manufacturing function of a business. (10)

many-to-many relationship A relationship in which many groups of data are related to many other groups of data. (7)

marketing The function of a business that sells the goods and services of the business. (2)

marketing information system An information system that supports the marketing function of a business. (10)

massively parallel processing The use of hundreds to thousands of CPUs in a computer simultaneously to increase speed. (4)

master data The main data used by an information system. Usually permanent data that stays with the system. (10)

matching The process of comparing data in several files or databases for the purpose of locating common data. (3)

MB Megabyte. (4)

M byte Megabyte. (4)

megabyte (M byte, MB) 1,048,576 bytes. Commonly thought of as one million bytes. (4)

megahertz (MHz) The units used to measure the internal clock speed of a computer. One megahertz is one million cycles per second. (4)

menu A list of options for a program displayed on a screen. (5)

MHz Megahertz. (4)

MICR Magnetic ink character recognition. (4)

microcomputer A small, single-user computer. Also called a personal computer or PC. (3)

microprocessor A CPU contained on a single chip. (4)

microsecond One-millionth of a second. (4)

millisecond One-thousandth of a second. (4)

minicomputer A medium-sized, multiple-user computer. (3)

MIS Management information system. (11)

model base A collection of mathematical models and statistical calculation routines stored in a computer. (11)

modem A device that converts digital signals to analog signals (modulation) and analog signals to digital signals (demodulation). (6)

monitor A CRT designed for computer use. (4)

mouse A handheld device that is rolled on a table top and that is used to enter input by pressing buttons on its top. (4)

multidimensional database A database that the user views as organized in several dimensions. (7)

multifunction printer A printer that can perform other functions, including sending and receiving faxes, scanning, and copying. (4)

multimedia Using a computer to store data and present information in more than one form. (3, 4)

multimedia developer A person who develops multimedia applications for Web sites. (14)

multiprocessing The use of several CPUs simultaneously in a computer to increase speed. (4)

multitasking The process of executing more than one program at a time by switching between programs. (5)

N

nanosecond One-billionth of a second. (4)

network A collection of computers and related equipment connected electronically so that they can communicate with each other. (1)

network administrator Network analyst. (14)

network analyst A person who is responsible for an organization's local area and wide area networks. (14)

network computer An inexpensive computer with capabilities limited to Internet access. (6)

network database A database in which any type of relationship is allowed. (7)

network interface card (NIC) A device for connecting a computer to a local area network channel. (6)

network operating system (NOS) Software, used on server computers in a network, that manages multiple client computers, and provides communication between clients and servers. (5)

neural network A program that mimics the way humans learn and think by creating a model of the human brain. (11)

NIC Network interface card. (6)

nonimpact printer A printer that makes an image in some way other than by striking the paper. (4)

nonvolatile storage A storage medium that does not lose its contents when the power to the computer is turned off. (4)

NOS Network operating system. (5)

notebook computer A small microcomputer that folds to the size of a notebook. (3)

O

object A combination of data and instructions for processing the data. (5)

object-oriented analysis and design The analysis and design of information systems based on objects. (13)

object-oriented database A database that stores objects. (7)

object-oriented programming A form of programming that uses programming languages in which the data and the instructions for processing the data are combined to form an object. (5)

object-relational database A database that includes object-oriented and relational database capabilities. (7)

office automation The use of various applications, including individual and workgroup applications, to support a variety of office functions at all levels of an organization. (9)

OLAP On-line analytical processing. (7)

OLTP On-line transaction processing. (10)

one-to-many relationship A relationship in which one group of data is related to many other groups of data, but not vice versa. (7)

one-to-one relationship A relationship in which one group of data is related to only one other group of data. (7)

on-line analytical processing (OLAP) Analysis of large amounts of data stored in relational databases, data warehouses, and multidimensional databases by users using special interactive techniques and tools. (7)

on-line transaction processing (OLTP) A form of data processing in which a person enters the data for a transaction into a computer, where it is processed and the output is received before the next input is entered. (10)

operating environment A program that provides a special interface between the user and the operating system. (5)

operating system A set of programs that controls the basic operation of a computer. (3)

operations The function of a business that performs the main activities of the business. (2)

optical disk A form of secondary storage in which data is recorded and retrieved by using a laser. (4)

optical disk drive A device for recording data on and retrieving data from an optical disk. (4)

order entry system A system that accepts customer orders for goods and services, and prepares them in a form that can be used by the business. (10)

organization chart A diagram that shows the arrangement of people who work for a business. (2)

organizational electronic commerce Intrabusiness electronic commerce. (12)

organizational information system An information system that affects people throughout a business or organization. (1)

organizational knowledge The total knowledge of the people who work for an organization. (11)

output data Data that comes out of an information system. (1)

output device   A device that converts data from an electronic form inside the computer to a form that can be used outside the computer. (4)

output function   The actions of an information system that produce information resulting from processing. (1)

outsourcing   Using hardware, software, and personnel resources from an outside company for information systems. (13)

P

packaged software   Programs that are purchased. (3, 13)

page   A screen on the World Wide Web. (5)

page printer   A printer that prints one page at a time. (4)

palmtop computer   Handheld computer. (3)

payroll system   A system that prepares paychecks for employees and provides reports of payroll. (10)

PC   Personal computer. Also used to refer specifically to an IBM-type personal computer. (3)

PDA   Personal digital assistant. (3)

pen input   An input method involving a screen that is sensitive to the touch of a special pen. (4)

peripheral equipment   A device used with a computer other than primary storage and the CPU, such as secondary storage and input and output devices. (4)

personal computer (PC)   A computer used by one person at a time. (3)

personal computer analyst   A person responsible for evaluating and selecting personal computer hardware and software in an organization, and helping end users utilize personal computers. (14)

personal database   A database used by only one user. (7)

personal digital assistant (PDA)   A handheld microcomputer with capabilities to assist an individual in his or her work. (3)

personal information system   Individual information system. (1)

personnel   People who use and operate an information system. (1)

pixel   The smallest mark or dot on a screen. Short for picture element. (4)

planning horizon   The time span for which planning is done. (14)

platform   The computer and communications hardware and operating system on which the application software of an information system runs. (3)

plotter   A device that creates graphic output on paper. (4)

portal   A World Wide Web site that provides multiple services for users. (8)

presentation graphics software   Software used to create graphic output for presentations. (8)

primary key   A column or combination of columns that uniquely identifies a row in a table of a relational database. (7)

primary storage   The part of a computer that stores data currently being processed and instructions in the program currently being performed. (4)

print server   A server with a printer that can be used for printing by other computers in the network. (6)

printer   An output device that produces output data on paper. (4)

problem   An unanswered question or a statement of something to be done. (8)

procedures   Instructions that tell personnel how to use and operate an information system. (1)

processing function   The actions of an information system that manipulate the data in the system. (1)

processor   Central processing unit. (4)

production   The function of a business that produces or manufactures the goods sold by the business. (2)

program   A set of instructions that tells a computer what to do. (4)

programmer   A person who prepares computer programs. (5)

programmer/analyst   A person who functions as both a systems analyst and an application programmer. (14)

programming   The process of preparing a computer program. (5)

programming language   A set of rules for the form and meaning of instructions in computer programs. (5)

project team   A group of systems analysts, programmers, and users that work together to develop an information system. (13)

prompt   A word or symbol, displayed on a screen, indicating that the software is ready for input. (5)

protocol   A rule that describes how computer devices communicate. (6)

protocol converter   A device that converts the protocols of one computer device to those of another computer device. (6)

prototype   A partial version of an information system that acts like the system for the user but does not perform all the system's functions. (13)

prototyping   The process of developing a prototype of an information system. (13)

public domain software   Software that is not copyrighted. (14)

purchasing system   A system that determines the best suppliers from which to purchase items and prepares purchase orders. (10)

push technology   A technique for identifying on-line information that is of interest to a user and sending the information to the user's computer. (8)

Q

QBE   Query-by-example. (7)

query   A request for information from an information system. (11)

query-by-example (QBE) A graphical approach for querying a relational database. (7)

query language A language that is used to query a database, that is, to retrieve data from a database. May also be used to update a database. (7)

R

RAD Rapid application development. (13)

RAID A system of magnetic disks on which data is duplicated or stored such that data can be recovered if a disk is damaged. Stands for redundant array of inexpensive disks. (4)

RAM Random access memory. (4)

random access The process of reading or writing data in secondary storage in any order. (4)

random access memory (RAM) A type of primary storage in which programs and data can be stored and retrieved in any order. (4)

random file Direct file. (7)

rapid application development (RAD) An approach to the development of information systems that involves significant user involvement, prototyping, and the use of CASE and other tools in order to reduce the development time. (13)

read-only memory (ROM) A type of primary storage in which programs and data, stored once by the manufacturer, can be retrieved as many times as needed, but in which new programs and data cannot be stored. (4)

real-time processing A form of data processing in which the processing is done immediately after the input is received rather than possibly being delayed while other processing is completed. (10)

record A group of related fields. (3)

recovery procedure A procedure for re-creating original stored data from a backup copy. (10)

relational database A database that consists of one or more related tables. (7)

relationship A way in which groups of data in a database are related. (7)

report A list of output data printed on paper or displayed on a screen. (10)

research and development The function of a business that develops new products to be manufactured by the business. (2)

retailer A business that purchases quantities of goods from wholesalers or manufacturers, and resells them one at a time or in small quantities to individual customers. (2)

ring network A network in which the nodes are connected to form a loop. (6)

ROM Read-only memory. (4)

room videoconferencing system A videoconferencing system designed for use in a room with several people. (9)

rule An *if-then* structure that is used in a knowledge base. (11)

S

scanner A device that senses the image on a page for input to a computer. Also called an image scanner or a page scanner. (4)

scheduled report A report that is prepared at regular intervals. (11)

screen An output device that displays output data as video images. (4)

screen projector A device for projecting a screen image on a viewing screen some distance away. (4)

screen resolution The number of pixels that can be displayed on a screen at one time. (4)

SDLC System development life cycle. (13)

search engine A program on the World Wide Web that lets a user search for specific types of information. (8)

secondary storage A device that stores data not currently being processed by the computer and programs not currently being performed. (4)

sequential access The process of reading or writing data in secondary storage in sequence. (4)

sequential file A data file in which the records are organized in sequence one after the other, in the order in which they are stored in the file. (7)

serial printer A printer that prints one character at a time. (4)

server A computer in a network that provides services, such as data storage and printing, to other computers in the network. (3)

service business A business that provides services to other businesses or to individuals. (2)

shared database A database used by many users. (7)

shareware Inexpensive or free copyrighted software that comes with permission to use and make copies for evaluation purposes, but that must be paid for in full if the user wants to use it after evaluating it. (14)

SIS Strategic information system. (12)

site license A software license agreement that allows the use of software by more than one person at a time within an organization. (14)

software Instructions that tell computer hardware what to do. (1)

software license agreement A written statement of what the purchaser of certain software can legally do with the software. (14)

software piracy The process of making illegal copies of software in order to sell the copies. (14)

solution The answer to a problem question or the result of doing what is required by a problem statement. (8)

solution procedure A set of steps that, if carried out, results in the solution of a problem. (8)

sorting   The process of arranging data in a particular order. (10)

source document   A document in which data is captured at its source. (10)

spreadsheet   An arrangement of data into rows and columns used for data analysis. (8)

spreadsheet software   Software used to create, modify, and print electronic spreadsheets. (5)

SQL   A commonly used query language. Stands for Structured Query Language. (7)

star network   A network in which each node is connected to a central computer. (6)

storage function   The actions of an information system that store and retrieve data in the system. (1)

storage location   A group of bits in primary storage used to store a certain amount of data. (4)

stored data   Data that is kept in an information system. (1)

strategic information system (SIS)   An information system that has a strategic impact on a business. (12)

suite   A group of programs sold together as a package. (8)

summary report   A report that contains totals that summarize groups of data but that has no detail data. (10)

supercomputer   A computer designed for very fast processing. (3)

system analysis   The phase in the system development process in which the systems analyst studies the existing system and determines what the new system must do. (13)

system design   The phase in the system development process in which the systems analyst specifies how the new system will function. (13)

system development life cycle (SDLC)   The process of developing an information system. (13)

system implementation   The phase in the system development process in which the systems analyst acquires the system components, tests the system, and changes over to the new system. (13)

system maintenance   The process of modifying an information system. (13)

system planning   The phase in the system development process in which the systems analyst decides whether a new information system should be developed. (13)

system programmer   A programmer who sets up and maintains system software. (14)

system software   General programs designed to make a computer usable. (3)

systems analyst   A person who develops an information system. (13)

T

TB   Terabyte. (4)

T byte   Terabyte. (4)

TDF   Transborder data flow. (12)

technical trainer   A person who trains end users in the use of personal computer hardware and software. (14)

telecommuting   Working with a computer away from an office or business and communicating with the organization's computer systems electronically. (9)

terabyte (T byte, TB) 2^{40} bytes. Commonly thought of as one trillion bytes. (4)

terminal   A device that is a combination of an input device and an output device. Often a keyboard combined with a screen. (4)

terminal adapter   A device used to connect a computer to an ISDN line. (6)

terminal emulation software   Communications software that makes a personal computer appear to another computer as if it is a terminal. (6)

testing   The process of determining whether there are any errors in software by executing the software with test data and comparing the result with what was expected. (8)

time-sharing   A technique used by an operating system for allowing multiple users to use a computer by giving each user a small amount of time to execute his or her program before going on to the next user. (5)

touch screen   A screen that can sense where it is touched by a person's finger. (4)

TPS   Transaction processing system. (10)

track   A concentric circle on a magnetic disk, a spiral line on an optical disk, or a straight line on a magnetic tape, along which bits are recorded. (4)

trackball   A device with a ball on top to move the cursor on the screen and buttons to select program functions. (4)

trackpad   A small, touch-sensitive pad for moving the cursor on the screen. (4)

trackpoint   A small stick for moving the cursor on the screen. (4)

transaction   An event that has occurred that affects a business. (10)

transaction data   Data about transactions that have occurred. (10)

transaction processing system (TPS)   An information system that keeps records of the state of an organization, processes transactions, and produces outputs that report on transactions, report on the state of the organization, and cause other transactions to occur. (10)

transborder data flow (TDF)   The flow of data between countries. (12)

U

unicode   A code for representing characters using 16 bits per character. Stands for Universal Code. (4)

uniform resource locator (URL)   An identifier used to locate a page on the World Wide Web. (6)

updating The process of modifying data. Includes changing existing data, adding new data, and deleting old data. (10)

uploading Transferring data from a local computer to a remote computer. (6)

UPS A device containing a battery that takes over supplying power to a computer system when the main power is cut. Stands for uninterruptible power supply. (14)

URL Uniform resource locator. (6)

user A person who gains some benefit from using a computer information system in his or her personal or work life. (1)

user interface The part of a computer application that forms the link between the user and the other parts of the application. (5)

user requirements A description of what an information system will do to help a user in his or her job. (13)

utility program A program that provides additional capabilities beyond those of an operating system, such as sorting and merging. (5)

V

value added network (VAN) A network provided by a company that leases communications lines from common carriers and adds special hardware, software, and services for data communication. (6)

value added reseller (VAR) A business that purchases computers from manufacturers; adds other hardware, software, and services; and resells the complete package to businesses and individuals. (14)

value chain The series of activities in a business that add value to the business's product or service. (12)

VAN Value added network. (6)

VAR Value added reseller. (14)

VDT Video display terminal. (4)

videoconferencing A workgroup application that involves visual and audio communication between members of a group at different locations. (9)

video display terminal (VDT) A terminal consisting of a keyboard and a screen. (4)

view Part of a database to which a user has access. (7)

virtual company A company that does not have a regular place of business or an office, and in which employees work at home or other places not operated by the company. (9)

virtual meeting An electronic meeting between members of a workgroup that does not involve simultaneous communication, and typically takes place over several days. (9)

virtual memory The memory that a computer appears to have, consisting of primary storage and some secondary storage. It is created by the operating system so that programs that are too large for primary storage can be executed. (5)

virtual office A group of employees who work at different locations and use computers to collaborate with other employees. (9)

virtual private network (VPN) A network that uses the Internet for communications. (6)

virtual reality The use of a computer to produce realistic images and sounds in such a way that the user senses that he or she is part of the scene. (4)

virtual work environment A work environment consisting of wherever people are at whatever time they work. (9)

virus A computer program that copies itself from one disk to another and that activates itself after a period of time, usually destroying programs and data in many computer systems. (14)

volatile storage A storage medium that loses its contents when the power to the computer is turned off. (4)

VPN Virtual private network. (6)

W

WAN Wide area network. (6)

Web World Wide Web. (1, 6)

Web programmer A person who develops World Wide Web applications for the Internet, intranets, and extranets by using Internet programming languages. (14)

Web server A server used to store an organization's World Wide Web pages. (6)

Web site A set of World Wide Web pages with information about a business or organization. (6)

Webmaster A person who develops and manages World Wide Web sites for an organization. (14)

what-if analysis The process of changing certain data in a spreadsheet to see the effect on other data in the spreadsheet. (8)

whiteboard conferencing A form of document conferencing in which each user sees the same document on an electronic whiteboard on a screen. (9)

wholesaler A business that purchases large quantities of goods, and then sells smaller quantities to retailers and ships or distributes the goods to the retailers. (2)

wide area network (WAN) A network that covers a large geographic area. (6)

window A section of a screen surrounded by a border and containing one type of display. (5)

wireless LAN A local area network that uses a wireless system such as radio waves or infrared beams for communication. (6)

word processing The use of a computer to prepare documents containing text. (8)

word processing software Software used to enter, edit, and print documents. (5)

workflow management A workgroup application that involves coordinating the flow of work between members of a group. (9)

workgroup   A group of people working together in a business to perform specific tasks or activities. (2)

workgroup information system   An information system that affects a group of people who work together in a business or organization. (1)

worksheet   A spreadsheet created by spreadsheet software. (8)

workstation   A powerful microcomputer. (3)

World Wide Web (WWW)   A service on the Internet that links information so that the user can easily go from one piece of information to another, related piece. (1, 6)

WWW   World Wide Web. (1, 6)

X

XML   A language used to define other languages for describing documents for the Internet and the World Wide Web. Stands for Extensible Markup Language. (5)

PHOTO CREDITS

1.8   Reprinted by permission of Microsoft Corporation.

1.9   Reprinted by permission of Microsoft Corporation.

1.11   Reprinted by permission of Microsoft Corporation.

1.16   Reprinted by permission of Eddie Bauer, Inc.

3.3   From The Computer Ethics Institute Website. Reprinted with permission from Brookings Institution Press.

4.3b   Courtesy of International Business Machines Corporation.

4.8a   ViewSonic.

4.8b   Sony Multiscan SDM-N50LCD.

4.10   Courtesy of International Business Machines Corporation.

4.12   Courtesy of Ventana Corporation. Group Systems is a registered trademark of Ventana.

5.5   Reprinted by permission of Microsoft Corporation.

5.6   Reprinted by permission of Microsoft Corporation.

5.18   Fom *Building Business Applications Using C++* by Lucy Garnett © 1997 Addison-Wesley Longman Inc. Reprinted by permission.

5.19   Microsoft Corporation 1999, Microsoft Visual Basic.

6.19   Reprinted by permission of Eddie Bauer.

7.16   Reprinted by permission of Microsoft Corporation.

8.3   Reprinted by permission of Microsoft Corporation.

8.4   Reprinted by permission of Microsoft Corporaiton.

8.5   Reprinted by permission of Microsoft Corporation.

8.6   Reprinted by permission of Microsoft Corporation.

8.7   Reprinted by permission of Microsoft Corporation.

8.8   Reprinted by permission of Microsoft Corporation.

8.9   Reprinted by permission of Microsoft Corporation.

8.10   Reprinted by permission of Microsoft Corporation.

8.11   Reprinted by permission of Microsoft Corporation.

8.12   Adobe Inc. 1999/EAS, Inc. 1999, 2000.

8.13   Reprinted by permission of Microsoft Corporation.

8.14   Reprinted by permission of Microsoft Corporation.

8.15   Reprinted by permission of Microsoft Corporation.

8.16a Quicken 1998.

8.16b Autodesk, Autocad CAD.

8.16c Montes de Oca/FPG International.

8.16d Greg Pease/Stone.

8.16e Lois and Bob Schlows/Stone.

8.17a Microsoft Excel, Microsoft Corporation.

8.17b Microsoft Paint, Microsoft Corporation.

8.17c Microsoft PowerPoint, Microsoft Corporation.

8.17d AutoCAD AutoDesk Corporation.

8.22   Macromedia Director, Macromedia, Inc.

9.3   Microsoft Corporation 1999.

9.4   Courtesy of Novell.

9.5   Microsoft Corporation 1999, Microsoft Netmeeting, Microsoft Windows 98.

9.6   Lotus Notes, Lotus Development Corporation.

9.7   Teamware.

9.8   Reprinted by permission of Microsoft Corporation.

9.11   Image courtesy of Silicon Graphics, Inc.

9.14   Form Flow 1999, Intemp Process Designer.

10.15 Reprinted by permission of Microsoft Corporation.

11.10 Courtesy of Sybase Inc.

11.12 Courtesy of Pilot Software.

11.13 Courtesy of MicroGrids, © 1993 San/US.

13.8   Courtesy of Silverrun Technologies, Inc.

14.11 Permission to reproduce the screen shot from the Gauntlet Firewall product, has been provided by Network Associates, Inc.

Network Associates and Dr. Solomon's are registered trademarks of Network Associates, Inc. and/or its affiliates in the US and/or other countries. © 2000 Networks Associates Technology, Inc.

ACKNOWLEDGMENTS

Chapter 1

Bookmark: *Inventory Management at 7-Eleven* From "Sales Data Helps 7-Eleven Maximize Space, Selection" by David Orenstein from *Computerworld*, July 5, 1999. Copyright © 1999 *Computerworld, Inc.* Reprinted with the permission of *Computerworld Magazine.*

Bookmark: *Electronic Commerce at Michelin North America* From "Michelin Links Dealers" by Carol Sliwa from *Computerworld*, November 30, 1998. Copyright © 1998 *Computerworld, Inc.* Reprinted with the permission of *Computerworld Magazine.*

Real-world Case: *The Benetton Group, Italy* From "Millennium Bug": Benetton Case History from the Benetton Web Site. Reprinted by permission.

Chapter 2

Bookmark: *Internet Connections for Native Canadian Tribes* From "Canada Hooks Native Tribes to Internet" by Carol Sliwa from *Computerworld*, September 7, 1998. Copyright (1998 *Computerworld, Inc.* Reprinted with the permission of *Computerworld Magazine.*

Bookmark: *Order Processing at the Sharper Image* From "The Sharper Image Hones in on I-Commerce" by Stephanie Sanborn from *InfoWorld*, January 24, 2000. Reprinted by permission.

Real-world Case: *Coca-Cola* From "Coca Cola: Marketing Partner" by Kathleen Melymuka from *Computerworld*, June 21, 1999. Copyright © 1999 *Computerworld, Inc.* Reprinted with the permission of *Computerworld Magazine.*

Chapter 3

Bookmark: *Handheld Computers at Sodexho Marriott Services* From "Smaller Isn't Better for Some Handheld Users" by Matt Hamblen from *Computerworld*, August 2, 1999. Copyright © 1999 *Computerworld, Inc.* Reprinted with the permission of *Computerworld Magazine.*

Bookmark: *Web Site for HarlemLive* From "Unsung Heroes" by Kathleen Melymuka from *Computerworld*, June 7, 1999. Copyright © 1999 *Computerworld, Inc.* Reprinted with the permission of *Computerworld Magazine.*

Real-world Case: *Beamscope Canada* "Beamscope Canada, Inc." by Chris Staiti, from *Computerworld: Client/Server Journal*, August, 1996, pp. 49–50. Copyright © 1996 *Computerworld, Inc.* Reprinted with the permission of *Computerworld Magazine.*

Chapter 4

Bookmark: *Virtual Reality at the Education Center in Alvdalen, Sweden* From "Virtual Reality Saves on Training" by David Orenstein from *Computerworld*, March 8, 1999. Copyright © 1999 *Computerworld, Inc.* Reprinted with the permission of *Computerworld Magazine.*

Bookmark: *Massively Parallel Processing at United Airlines* From "United Taps Massively Parallel Application" by Stewart Deck from *Computerworld*, June 28, 1999. Copyright © 1999 *Computerworld, Inc.* Reprinted with the permission of *Computerworld Magazine.*

Real-world Case: *Chevron* From "Chevron Hits the Gas on PC Standardization" by Kristina B. Sullivan from *PC Week*, June 21, 1999. Reprinted by permission of author.

Chapter 5

Bookmark: *Linux at the City of Medina, Washington* From "Linux in a Three Piece Suit?' by Barry Nance from *Computerworld*, September 6, 1999. Copyright © 1999 *Computerworld, Inc.* Reprinted with the permission of *Computerworld Magazine.*

Bookmark: *A Java Inventory Ordering System at Motor Spares & Staff* From "Motor Spares" www.4.ibm.com/software/developer/casestudies/stony-motor-spares.html. Reproduced by permission from IBM Copyright © 2000 by International Business Machines Corporation.

Real-world Case: *BMG* From "BMG Site Hits the Right Notes" by Ilan Greenberg from *InfoWorld*, May 4, 1998. Reprinted with permission.

Chapter 6

Bookmark: *Wireless Communications at Illinois Power* From "Wireless Net Helps Utility Improve Customer Service" by Matt Hamblen from *Computerworld*, January 24, 2000, p. 36. Copyright © 2000 *Computerworld, Inc.* Reprinted with the permission of *Computerworld Magazine.*

Bookmark: *A Wide Area Network for Designer Shoe Warehouse* From "Shoe Chain Likes Fit of Dial-Up For its VPN" by Bob Wallace from *Computerworld*, May 3, 1999, p. 66. Copyright © 1999 *Computerworld, Inc.* Reprinted with the permission of *Computerworld Magazine.*

Real-world Case: *CDNOW* From "When Sales are Tied to a Site's Capacity" by Sarah L. Roberts-Witt, from *Internet Week*, June 1, 1998, pp. 28–29. Reprinted by permission.

Chapter 7

Bookmark: ***The Affinity Database for the Carolina Mudcats*** From "Affinity System Keeps Fans Coming Back" by Stewart Deck from *Computerworld*, July 26, 1999, p. 38. Copyright © 1999 *Computerworld, Inc.* Reprinted with the permission of *Computerworld Magazine*.

Bookmark: ***Multidimensional Data Analysis at Aqua-Chem*** From "New Life for Old Database" by Alan Radding from *Computerworld*, July 12, 1999, pp. 70–72. Copyright © 1999 *Computerworld, Inc.* Reprinted with the permission of *Computerworld Magazine*.

Real-world Case: ***Procter & Gamble*** From "P&G Uses Data Mining to Cut Animal Testing" by Gary Anthes, from *Computerworld*, December 6, 1999, pp. 44–45. Copyright © 1999 *Computerworld, Inc.* Reprinted with the permission of *Computerworld Magazine*.

Chapter 8

Bookmark: ***Multimedia Presentation at Orient Express Trains & Cruises*** From "A Travel Company in the Lap of Luxury" by Julie Hill from *Presentations*, August 1999, p. 16. Reprinted by permission.

Bookmark: ***Web Searching at Sparks.com*** From "A System Devised for Fine-Tune Search" by James C. Luh from *Internet World*, July 15, 1999, p. 59. Reprinted by permission.

Real-world Case: ***Haworth Inc.*** From "Trilogy helps Haworth get through a Maze of Cubicles" by Steve Alexander from *InfoWorld*, January 27, 1997, p. 92. Reprinted with permission.

Chapter 9

Bookmark: ***9–1 Group Collaboration for the Sable Offshore Energy Project*** From "Shipshape Design" by Lisa Vaas. Reprinted from *PC Week*, August 23, 1999, with permission. Copyright © 1999, Ziff Davis Media, Inc. All rights reserved. Note for Web reuse: Reprinted from *PC Week*, August 23, 1999, with permission. Copyright © 1999, Ziff Davis Media, Inc. All rights reserved.

Bookmark: ***Collaborative Applications for a Web Site at Reebok International*** From "Groupware Gives Lift to Reebok Site" by Barb Cole-Gomoloski from *Computerworld*, January 19, 1998, p. 50. Copyright © 1998 *Computerworld, Inc.* Reprinted with the permission of *Computerworld Magazine*.

Real-world Case: ***Saab*** From "When the Road is Increasingly Well-Traveled" by Alice LaPlante from *Computerworld*, July 20, 1999, p. 54. Copyright © 1999 Computerworld, Inc. Reprinted with the permission of *Computerworld Magazine*.

Chapter 10

Bookmark: ***Warehouse Management at Owens & Minor*** From "Warehouse Overhaul to Fatten Supplier's Slim Margins" by Thomas Hoffman from *Computerworld*, October 25, 1999, p. 41. Copyright © 1999 *Computerworld, Inc.* Reprinted with the permission of *Computerworld Magazine*.

Bookmark: ***Supply Chain Management at Miller SQA*** From "Live Wire Supply Line" by Bill Roberts from *Internet World*, September 15, 1999. Reprinted by permission.

Real-world Case: ***Kozmo.com*** From "Web Delivery in an Hour" by Erik Sherman from *Computerworld*, March 6, 2000, pp. 54, 56. Copyright © 2000 *Computerworld, Inc.* Reprinted with the permission of *Computerworld Magazine*.

Chapter 11

Bookmark: ***Geographic Information System at the City of Oakland*** From "Dynamic Data Saves Time, Money—and Lives" by Andrew Marlatt from *Internet World*, pp. 27, 29. Reprinted by permission.

Bookmark: ***A Knowledge Management System at Shell Oil*** From "Learning How to Share" by Gary Anthes from *Computerworld*, February 23, 1998, pp. 75–77. Copyright © 1999 *Computerworld, Inc.* Reprinted with the permission of *Computerworld Magazine*.

Real-world Case: ***Grand & Toy, Canada*** From "One Office-Supplies Company Put an End to its Paper Trail" by Heather Mackey from *InfoWorld*, March 24, 1997, p. 76. Reprinted with permission.

Chapter 12

Bookmark: ***Business-to-Business E-commerce at Adolph Coors*** From "Coors Moves Branded Merchandise Online" by James Cope from *Computerworld*, March 13, 2000. Copyright © 2000 *Computerworld, Inc.* Reprinted with the permission of *Computerworld Magazine*.

Bookmark: ***A Global Information System at Avon*** Adaptation of "Avon Calls for Revamp of its Worldwide IT" by Stacy Collett from *Computerworld*, July 12, 1998. Reprinted by permission.

Real-world Case: ***1-800-FLOWERS*** From "Business is Blooming on the Net" by Jim Kerstetter reprinted from *PC Week*, April 12, 1999, with permission. Copyright © 1999, Ziff Davis Media, Inc. All rights reserved. Note for Web reuse: Reprinted from *PC Week*, April 12, 1999, with permission. Copyright © 1999, Ziff Davis Media, Inc. All rights reserved.

Chapter 13

Bookmark: *System Conversion at Carlson Hospitality World Wide* From "Upgrade? Sure. But Keep Old System, Just in Case" by Stacy Collett from *Computerworld*, September 27, 1999. Copyright © 1999 *Computerworld, Inc.* Reprinted with the permission of *Computerworld Magazine*.

Bookmark: *E-commerce System Development at Auto-Nation* From "Car Retailer Builds Site the Fast Way" by Bob Wallace from *Computerworld*, July 12, 1999. Copyright © 1999 *Computerworld, Inc.* Reprinted with the permission of *Computerworld Magazine*.

Real-world Case: *Pinnacol Assurance* From "Turning Around the Project from Hell" by Kathleen Melymuka from *Computerworld* from November 22, 1999. Copyright © 1999 *Computerworld, Inc.* Reprinted with the permission of *Computerworld Magazine*.

Chapter 14

Bookmark: *Internet Technology Strategist at Sprint Paranet* From "Strategist of the Net" by Deborah Radcliff from *Computerworld*, January 10, 2000. Copyright © 2000 *Computerworld, Inc.* Reprinted with the permission of *Computerworld Magazine*.

Bookmark: *Security at MasterCard International* "Project MasterCard International, Inc., Going Above and Beyond the Firewall" by Steve Alexander from Computerword Intranets, July 27, 1998, p. 7.

Real-world Case: *eBay* From "CEO Meg Whitman powers eBay on instinct and experience and gains an education in technology" by Kathleen Melymuka from *Computerworld*, January 10, 2000. Copyright © 2000 *Computerworld, Inc.* Reprinted with the permission of *Computerworld Magazine*.

INDEX

A

Access. *See* Random access; Sequential access
Access (software), 218, 239
Access to information, 82–83
Accessing data, 310
Accentuate Systems, 284
Accounting, 37, 324
Accounting information system, 324
Account name, 453
Accounts payable, 52
   data, 322
   report, 52, 322
   system, 321–322, 324
Accounts receivable, 48
   data, 317
   report, 48, 317
   system, 317–318, 324
Accuracy, 80–81
ACM. *See* Association for Computing Machinery
Address, 112
Ad hoc report, 345
Adolph Coors, 380
AI. *See* Artificial intelligence
AITP. *See* Association of Information Technology Professional
Algorithm, 262n
Alta Vista, 260
ALU. *See* Arithmetic-logic unit
Amdahl, 70
American Airlines, 396–397
American Standard Code for Information Interchange. *See* ASCII
Analog signal, 169
Analysis. *See* System analysis
Apple Computer, 67, 69, 111, 117, 147, 444
Apple Macintosh, 67, 117, 147, 218
Applet, 159
Apple II, 67
Application. *See* Computer application
Application conferencing, 286
   software, 286
Application control, 450–451
Application generator, 153, 222
Application portfolio, 441–442
Application program. *See* Application software
Application programmer, 447–448
Application software, 71, 135–136
   individual, 136–137
   interorganizational, 138

organizational, 137–138
   workgroup, 137
Apollo, 396
Approach, 218, 239
Aqua-Chem, 228
Arithmetic-logic unit (ALU), 113–115
Artificial intelligence (AI), 358, 360–362
ASCII, 111
Assembler, 151
Assembly, 151
Assembly language, 151
Asset, 55
Association for Computing Machinery, 78
Association of Information Technology Professionals, 78
AT&T, 174, 445
ATM. *See* Automated teller machine system
Attachment, 280–281
Attribute, 214
Audio communication, 279
Audioconferencing, 286–287
Audit trail, 312
Authoring software, 256–258
Authorware, 258
AutoCAD, 252
Automated teller machine (ATM) system, 16
AutoNation, 431
Auxiliary storage. *See* Secondary storage
Avon, 393–394

B

Baan, 328
Backbone, 188
Back end, 430
Backup and recovery procedure, 452
Backup copy, 126
Backup procedure, 312
Balance sheet, 55, 323
Bandwidth, 170
Bar code, 97
Bar code scanner, 97
Barrier to entry, 396
BASIC, 154
Batch operating system, 144
Batch processing, 312
Baud rate, 170
Beamscope Canada, 88–89
Beginner's All-purpose Symbolic Instruction Code. *See* BASIC

Bell Laboratories, 147, 154
Benefits administration, 328
Benefits of information systems, 22–24
Benetton Group, 29–30
Billing, 45–47
   system, 316–317, 324, 325
Binary digit, 111
Binary representation, 110–111
Bit, 111
Bits per second (bps), 169–170
BMG, 165–166
Booting, 141
BPR. *See* Business process reengineering
Bps. *See* Bits per second
Braille display device, 105
Bridge, 188
Browser, 137, 158, 238, 260
B2B electronic commerce. *See* Business-to-business electronic commerce
B2C electronic commerce. *See* Business-to-consumer electronic commerce
Budgeting, 324
Bug, 81, 267
Bus, 116, 180
Business, 32–33
   basic information processing, 44–45
   environment, 32–33
   functions, 37–39
   and information systems, 55–57
   international, 16, 33, 386–388
   management, 43–44, 338–341
   operations, 38, 40–43, 305–306, 337, 397, 398
   organization, 39
   purpose, 32
   trends, 37–39
   types, 33–36
Business alliance, 374, 381–382
Business process, 432
Business process redesign, 432
Business process reengineering (BPR), 431–432
Business rule, 428
Business-to-business (B2B) electronic commerce, 376–377
Business-to-consumer (B2C) electronic commerce, 375–376
Bus network, 180–181
Button, 141

Buyer-oriented marketplace, 376
Byte, 112

C

C, 152, 154–156, 157, 222
Cable modem, 175
Cable television communication, 174–175
CAD. *See* Computer-aided design
CAD software. *See* Computer-aided design software
CAM. *See* Computer-aided manufacturing
Camera input device, 99
Capital expenditure analysis, 324–325
Carlson Hospitality Worldwide, 416
Carolina Mudcats, 217
Carpal tunnel syndrome, 94
CASE, 420–421, 426
Cash management, 324
Categorical imperative, 77
Cathode Ray Tube. *See* CRT
CBT. *See* Computer-based training
cc:Mail, 280
CD, 123
CDNOW, 198–199
CD-R, 124
CD-ROM, 124
CD-RW, 125
Centralized information system
  international, 390
  management, 445
Central processing unit (CPU), 63, 93, 113
  common, 116–119
  compatibility, 115–116
  speed, 116
  structure, 113–115
CEO. *See* Chief executive officer
Channel. *See* Communications channel
Channel interface device, 175–176
Chat, 189, 281–282
Chevron, 132–133
Character, 73, 201, 239
Characters per second (cps), 101
Chart, 249–250
Charting software, 250
Chief executive officer (CEO), 39
Chief information officer (CIO), 447
Chip, 109
CIM. *See* Computer-integrated manufacturing
CIO. *See* Chief information officer
CIS. *See* Computer information system
CISC, 116
Cisco, 444
City of Oakland, 353–354
City of Medina, 146

Client, 71, 148, 178, 184, 218
Client/server computing, 71, 178, 184–185, 218
Client software, 178–179
Clock speed, 116
Clone. *See* IBM clone
Coaxial cable, 171
COBOL, 152, 154, 222
Coca-Cola, 60–61
Codec, 173
Code of ethics, 78
Collaboration. *See* Group collaboration
Collaborative computing. *See* Group computing
Column, 214
Command, 141
COmmon Business Oriented Language. *See* COBOL
Common carrier, 174, 445
Communications, 168–169
Communications channel, 168
  characteristics, 169–170
  media, 170–174
  sources, 174
Communications control unit, 176
Communications hardware, 63
  channel, 169–174
  need for, 65
Communications processor, 168, 175–176
Communications protocol. *See* Protocol
Communications software, 72, 148
  multiple-user computer, 178–179
  network, 179
  personal computer, 178–179
Compact disk. *See* CD
Compact Disk-Read Only Memory. *See* CD-ROM
Compact disk recordable. *See* CD-R
Compact disk rewritable. *See* CD-RW
Compaq Computer, 67, 118, 444
Competitive advantage, 24, 372–374
Compilation, 152
Compiler, 92, 152
Compiler language, 152
Complex instruction set computer. *See* CISC
Components
  of a computer, 92–94
  of an information system, 9–11, 63
  of a system, 4, 63
Computation, 311
Computer, 94
Computer-aided design (CAD), 326
  software, 252
Computer-aided manufacturing (CAM), 326
Computer-aided software engineering. *See* CASE

Computer application, 4
Computer art, 250
Computer-based training (CBT), 445
Computer crime, 453–454
  destruction of data and software, 457–458
  illegal copying of software, 457
  theft and destruction of hardware, 456
  theft of data, 454–456
  theft of money, 454
Computer hardware, 63–71
  acquiring, 443–444
  alternatives, 411–412
  central processing unit, 93, 113–119
  input devices, 92, 94–99
  need for, 64
  output devices, 92, 99–104
  primary storage, 92–93, 109–113
  secondary storage, 94, 119–126
Computer information system (CIS), 4
Computer-integrated manufacturing (CIM), 326
Computer operator, 448
Computer system, 94
  multiple-user, 69–70
  networked, 70–71
  personal, 65–69
Computer telephony, 287
  software, 287
Conceptual design, 411, 422
Consumer-to-consumer (C2C) electronic commerce, 377
Contract programmer, 412
Control, 311, 450. *See also* Information system control
Controller, 176
Control total, 311–312, 451
Control unit, 113–115
Copyright, 457
Copy utility, 148
CorelDraw, 250
Corporate portal, 261
Cost/benefit analysis, 410, 411, 422
Cost leadership, 372
C++, 152, 157, 159, 222
Cps. *See* Characters per second
CPU. *See* Central processing unit
Cray Research, 70, 443
Credit analysis, 325
Crime. *See* Computer crime
CRM. *See* Customer relationship management
CrossWind Technologies, 293
CRT, 99, 100
C2C electronic commerce. *See* Consumer-to-consumer electronic commerce
Cursor, 95

Customer database system, 13
Customer master data, 315, 316, 317
Customer order, 7, 45, 314
Customer relationship management (CRM), 325–326
Customer service, 379
Custom software, 72, 73

D

Dartmouth College, 154
Data, 8, 11, 207, 338. *See also* Stored data; Input data; Output data
  organization, 73–74
  representation, 110–112
  versus information, 11
Data access control, 451
Data acquisition, 379
Database, 12–13, 73, 201, 207, 239
  management, 207–209
  object-oriented, 216
  organization, 210–216
  relational, 214–216
  types, 213–216
  use, 223–224
Database administrator (DBA), 229, 448
Database management system (DBMS), 148–149, 206–207, 216–218, 239
Database processing, 206–207, 209–210
  advantages, 209
  disadvantages, 209–210
Database server, 183
Database software, 12, 137, 206, 216–218, 238, 239. *See also* Database management system
  case study, 241–245
  multiple-user computer, 218
  networked computer, 218
  personal computer, 218
  using, 219–223, 239–240
Data capture, 307
Data communication. *See* Communications; Document communication
Data conferencing. *See* Document conferencing
Data destination, 418
Data encryption, 178, 378, 453
Data entry, 307
Data entry operator, 448
Data file, 73, 201, 204, 239. *See also* File
Data flow, 418
Data flow diagram (DFD), 417–418, 422

Data management
  acquiring technology for, 445
  combining with other applications, 253–256
  combining with spreadsheet analysis, 247–248
  in information systems, 201
  in individual information systems, 239–240
  operating system function, 140
Data mart, 224
Data mining, 224–225, 350–351, 379
Data rate, 169–170
Data relationship. *See* Relationship
Data source, 418
Data store, 418
Data validation, 204, 308, 450
Data warehouse, 224–225, 350–351, 379
DBA. *See* Database administrator
dBASE, 218, 239
DBMS. *See* Database management system
DB2, 218
Debugging, 267
Decentralized information system
  international, 390
  management, 446
Decision, 43–44, 135, 337. *See also* Management decision
Decision making, 311
Decision room, 291
Decision support system (DSS), 342, 348, 391, 394
  functions, 349–350
  group, 351
  software, 350–351
  structure, 348–349
Dedicated line, 445
Dell Computer, 67, 444
Demand report, 345
Demodulation, 175
Department, 39
Design. *See* System design
Designer Shoe Warehouse, 186
Desktop computer, 67–69
Desktop printer, 100, 101–102
Desktop publishing, 255
  software, 255–256
Desktop videoconferencing
  software, 288
  system, 287–288
Detail report, 308, 344
Developer documentation, 267–268
DFD. *See* Data flow diagram
Diagram, 250
Dialog box, 141
Dial-up line, 445
Differentiation, 372–373
Digital signal, 169
Digital subscriber line. *See* DSL

Digital versatile disk. *See* DVD
Digital versatile disk-read only memory. *See* DVD-ROM
Digital video disk. *See* DVD
Digital video disk-read only memory. *See* DVD-ROM
Digitizer tablet, 96
Direct access. *See* Random access
Direct file, 202–204
Direct mail advertising, 325
Direct marketer, 375
Director, 258
Disaster recovery plan, 452
Disk. *See* Magnetic disk; Optical disk
Disk drive. *See* Magnetic disk drive; Optical disk drive
Disk operating system. *See* DOS
Disk pack, 120
Distributed database, 218
Distributed database management system, 218
Distributed information system, 390
Distributor. *See* Wholesaler
Documentation, 76–77, 267–268
Document communication, 168, 279
Document conferencing, 284–286
Document management, 296
Document routing, 294
Domestic information system, 386
Domino, 284*n*
DOS, 145–147
Dot-matrix printer, 102
Downloading data, 179
Draft-quality printer, 101
Drawing software, 250
Drilling down, 354–355
DSL, 174
DSL terminal adapter, 176
DSS. *See* Decision support system
Dumb terminal, 104
Duplicate hardware, 451
DVD, 123
DVD-ROM, 124

E

eBay, 465–466
EBCDIC, 111
E-business. *See* Electronic business
E-commerce. *See* Electronic commerce
E-commerce project manager, 450
E-commerce system. *See* Electronic commerce system
Economic feasibility, 410
EDI. *See* Electronic data interchange
Efficiency, 305–306
EFT. *See* Electronic funds transfer
EIS. *See* Executive information system

Electronic auction, 377
Electronic broker, 376
Electronic business, 380–381
Electronic catalog, 377
Electronic commerce, 21, 192, 325, 374, 448–450
  global, 392–394
  hardware and software, 192
  strategic impact, 374–375
  types, 375–377
  use, 193
Electronic commerce system, 374, 394–395
  characteristics, 377–380
  development, 429–430
  strategic impact, 374–375
Electronic conferencing, 290
  software, 137, 290
Electronic data interchange (EDI), 16, 381
  benefits and problems, 385–386
  data, 384
  Internet, 385
  software, 138
  system, 384–386
Electronic distributor, 376
Electronic filing, 290
Electronic funds transfer (EFT), 16, 381
Electronic mail, 13, 137, 189, 280
  software, 280
Electronic mail address, 189, 280
Electronic mailbox, 280
Electronic meeting, 291
  software, 291
  support, 291–292
Electronic meeting room, 291
Electronic meeting system (EMS), 291
Electronic messaging, 280–282
  software, 137, 281
Electronic payment, 378
Electronic shopping cart, 378
Electronic spreadsheet, 136, 245
Electronic vote, 292
Electronic whiteboard, 284–286
E-mail. See Electronic mail
Employee master data, 322
Employment, 458–460
EMS. See Electronic meeting system
Encryption. See Data encryption
End-user. See User
End-user computing, 263
End-user support, 448
Enterprise information system. See Organizational information system
Enterprise resource planning (ERP), 328–329
Entity, 418–419, 419n
Entity-relationship (ER) diagram, 418–420, 422

ER diagram. See Entity-relationship diagram
Ergonomics, 94–95, 459, 460
ERP. See Enterprise resource planning
Error, 266–267
Error-checking hardware, 451
ES. See Expert system
ESS. See Executive support system
E-tailer, 375
Ethernet, 183
Ethical dilemma, 18
Ethical egoism, 77
Ethics, 18–19, 77
  applying, 83–84
  decision making, 77–78
  issues, 78–83
  and management of information systems, 460–461
Eudora, 280
Exchange, 281
Excel, 245, 250
Exception report, 308–310, 341
Executing a program, 114–115
Execution error, 266
Executive information system (EIS), 352
Executive support system (ESS), 342, 352, 392, 394
  functions, 356–357
  software, 357
  structure, 355–356
Expense, 32, 55
Expert system (ES), 342, 357–358, 392, 394
  functions, 360
  software, 360
  structure, 358–359
Expert system shell, 360
Explicit knowledge, 362
Explorer. See Internet Explorer
Exporter, 34
Extended Binary Code Decimal Interchange Code. See EBCDIC
Extensible Markup Language. See XML
External entity, 418, 419n
External modem, 175
Extranet, 191–192

F

Facsimile, 296
Failure recovery procedures, 452
FAQs. See Frequently asked questions
Fault tolerant computer system, 451
Fax modem, 175
Feasibility analysis, 410, 422

Fiber-optic cable, 171–173
Field, 73, 201, 239
Fifth-generation language, 153
File, 73, 201, 239
  management, 204–205
  organization, 202–204
FileNET, 294
File processing, 201–202
  advantages, 205
  disadvantages, 205
File server, 183
File transfer, 178
File-transfer protocol (FTP), 189
Finance, 37–38, 324
Financial analysis system, 12
Financial forecasting, 325
Financial information system, 324–325
Financial statement, 55, 323
Finished goods inventory, 51
Firewall, 191, 453
Firm infrastructure, 398
FirstClass, 284
First-generation language, 150
Fixed asset accounting, 324
Flat panel screen, 99–100
Floppy disk, 120
Focus on a niche, 373
Forms designer, 153
FORmula TRANslation. See FORTRAN
FORTRAN, 152, 153, 154
4GL. See Fourth-generation language
Fourth Dimension, 218
Fourth-generation language (4GL), 152–153, 222
FoxPro, 218, 239
Frequently asked questions, 379
Front end, 430
Front-end processor, 176
FTP. See File transfer protocol
Full cybermarketer, 376
Functional area, 37
Functions
  of a business, 37–39
  of information systems, 8–9, 72

G

Gateway, 67, 188
GB. See Gigabyte
G byte. See Gigabyte
GDSS. See Group decision support system
GemStone, 218
General ledger
  data, 323
  system, 3, 323, 324
Generations of programming languages, 150–153

Geographic information system (GIS), 351–352
GHz. See Gigahertz
Gigabyte, 113
Gigahertz, 116
GIGO, 75, 81
GIS. See Geographic information system
Global information system, 16–17, 386
  characteristics, 389–392
  strategic impact, 388–389
Global strategy, 387–388, 390
Goal seeking, 349
Golden Rule, 77
Gopher, 189
Government, 36
Grand & Toy, 369–370
GrapeVine, 365
Graph, 249–250
Graphical user interface (GUI), 141
Graphic design, 250
Graphics, 13, 249
  case study, 253
  combining with other applications, 253–256
  software, 136–137, 238, 250–252
  system, 13
Graphics tablet, 96
Group calendaring and scheduling, 292–293
  software, 293
Group collaboration, 276–277
  characteristics, 277–279
Group computing, 279
Group decision support system (GDSS), 292, 351
Group information system. See Workgroup information system
Group support system (GSS), 276
Group Systems, 292
Group videoconferencing system. See Room video conferencing system
Groupware, 137, 279
GroupWise, 281
Growth, 374
GSS. See Group support system
GUI. See Graphical user interface

H

Hacker, 456
Handheld computer, 69
Hard disk, 120
Hard drive, 122n
Hardware, 9–10, 92. See also Computer hardware; Communications hardware
  types, 63

Hardware control, 451–452
HarlemLive, 79–80
Harvard Graphics, 252
Haworth, 273–274
Health, 459–460
Help desk, 448
Help desk operator, 448
Hewlett-Packard (HP), 69, 118, 148, 443
Hierarchical database, 213–214
Hierarchical database management system, 217, 218
Hierarchical network, 180
High-volume printer, 100, 102, 103
Home page, 193
Host language, 176, 221–222
HP. See Hewlett-Packard
HRIS. See Human resource information system
HTML, 158, 159, 430
Human resource, 9
Human resource information system (HRIS), 328
Human resource management, 38, 328, 398
Hybrid network, 181–182
Hyperlink, 158
Hypertext, 189
Hypertext markup language. See HTML

I

IBM, 67, 69, 70, 111, 117, 118, 147, 148, 153, 183, 218, 443, 444, 445
IBM clone, 67, 117
IBM PC, 67, 116, 117, 120
IBM Personal Computer. See IBM PC
IBM System/390, 118
Icon, 141
IDMS, 218
Illinois Power, 172–173
Image processing, 296
Image scanner. See Scanner
Impact printer, 100
Implementation. See System implementation
Implicit knowledge, 362
Importer, 34
IMS, 218
Inbound logistics, 397, 398
Income statement, 55, 323
Indexed file, 204
Indexed sequential access method, 204n
Index file, 204
Indirect marketer, 375–376
Individual application software, 135–138

Individual information system, 12–13, 238, 395
  development, 428–429
Inference engine, 358–359
Information, 8, 11, 23, 362
  and business management, 43–44
  and business operations, 40–43
  executive needs, 352–355
  management decision needs, 340–341
  versus data, 11
Information center, 448
Information processing, 44–55
Information reporting system, 442
Information services, 39
Information sharing, 65, 282–284
  software, 137
  system, 13–15
Information superhighway, 188
Information system (IS), 3, 4, 63
  benefits, 22–24
  and business, 55–57
  components, 9–11, 63
  development. See System development
  ethics, 18–19, 77–84, 460–461
  examples, 4–8
  functions, 8–9, 72
  organizational structure, 447–448
  types, 12–17
  users, 17–19
Information system control, 450
  application control, 450–451
  failure recovery procedure, 452
  hardware control, 451–452
Information system security, 452
  electronic security, 453
  physical security, 452
Information systems manager, 447
Information technology (IT), 4, 9
  acquiring, 443–445
  connecting users to, 19–21
Informix, 218
Ink-jet printer, 101
Innovation, 373
InPerson, 290
Input control, 450
Input data, 8
Input device, 63
  camera, 99
  keyboard, 94–95
  magnetic scanning, 97–98
  multimedia, 106–107
  optical scanning, 97
  for people with disabilities, 105–106
  pointing, 95–96
  touch, 96
  visual reality, 107–109
  voice, 98–99

Input function, 8, 72, 307
  decision support system, 349–350
  executive support system, 356
  expert system, 360
  management information system, 343–344
  transaction processing system, 307–308
Inquiry, 344
Instant messaging, 281
Integrated information system, 390
Integrated services digital network. *See* ISDN
Integrated software, 255
Intel, 117, 288
Intelligent agent, 361–362
Intelligent terminal, 104
InTempo, 294
Interactive operating system, 144
Interactive processing, 313
Intermediary marketplace, 377
Internal modem, 175
Internal storage. *See* Primary storage
International business, 16, 33, 386–387
  and global information systems, 386, 388–389
  strategies, 387–388
International Business Machines. *See* IBM
International information system. *See* Global information system
International network, 188
International product development, 387
International production, 387
International sales, 386
International strategy, 388, 390
Internet, 19–21, 158, 238, 258. *See also* World Wide Web
  communication, 188–189
  locating and retrieving information, 258–260
  services, 189
Internet Explorer, 260
Internet Phone, 287
Internet programming language, 158–161
Internet Protocol. *See* IP
Internet service provider (ISP), 189
Internet II, 189
Internetwork, 182, 187–188
Interorganizational application software, 138
Interorganizational communication, 65
Interorganizational information system, 16, 381. *See also* Interorganizational system
Interorganizational network, 16, 188

Interorganizational system (IOS), 381
  business alliance and, 381–382
  characteristics, 383–384
  participant, 383
  sponsor, 383
  strategy impact, 382–383
Interpretation, 152
Interpreter, 152
Intrabusiness electronic commerce, 377
Intranet, 191
Inventory, 6, 51
Inventory control, 48–51
  information flow in, 41–42
  system, 3, 6, 8–9, 318–320, 325, 326
Inventory master data, 315, 316, 318, 321
Inventory reorder report, 49, 318
Inventory value report, 49, 318
Invoice, 45, 316
I/O device, 92
IOS. *See* Interorganizational system
IP, 188–189
IS. *See* Information system
ISAM. *See* Indexed sequential access method
ISDN, 174
ISDN terminal adapter, 176
ISP. *See* Internet service provider
IT. *See* Information technology
Item, 6

J

Java, 159, 430
JetForm, 294
JIT. *See* Just-in-time inventory management
Job applicant tracking, 328
Join, 220
Just-in-time (JIT) inventory management, 326

K

KB. *See* Kilobyte
K byte. *See* Kilobyte
Key, 178, 453. *See also* Key field; Primary key
Keyboard, 94–95
Key field, 202, 204
Kilobyte, 112
KMS. *See* Knowledge management system
Knowledge, 362
Knowledge base, 358–359
Knowledge engineer, 360
Knowledge management, 362–364
Knowledge management system (KMS), 364–365, 392, 394

KnowledgeX, 365
Kozmo.com, 335–336

L

LAN. *See* Local area network
Laptop computer, 69
Laser printer, 101–102
LCD, 100
Leased line, 445
Legacy system, 417
Letter-quality printer, 101
Liability, 55
Light pen, 96
Line printer, 101, 102–103
Lines per minute (lpm), 101
LINUX, 148
Liquid crystal display. *See* LCD
LISP, 360
Loading a program, 114
Local area network (LAN), 13, 19, 182
  business uses, 183–184
  structure, 183
Logging in, 141
Logging out, 141
Logical system design, 411*n*
Logic error, 267
Loop, 135
Lotus, 280, 281, 284*n*, 294, 295
Lpm. *See* Lines per minute

M

Mac. *See* Apple Macintosh
Machine dependent language, 150
Machine independent language, 152
Machine language, 115–116, 150
Macintosh. *See* Apple Macintosh
Mac OS, 71, 147, 148
Mainframe computer, 15, 70
  CPU, 117–118
Magnetic disk, 119–120
  access, 122–123
  drive, 121–122
  usage, 123
Magnetic ink character recognition (MICR), 98
Magneto-optical disk. *See* MO disk
Magnetic scanning input device, 97–98
Magnetic strip reader, 97–98
Magnetic tape, 125
  access, 126
  drive, 125–126
  usage, 126
Maintenance. *See* System maintenance
MAN. *See* Metropolitan area network
Management. *See* Business management

Management by exception, 344
Management decision. *See also*
    Decision making
    characteristics, 339–340
    information needs for, 340–341
    levels, 338
    support, 341–342, 348
Management information system
    (MIS), 342, 391, 394
    functions, 343–347
    software, 347
    structure, 342–343
Management reporting system, 342
Manager, 39
Manufacturer, 33–34
Manufacturing, 38, 326
Manufacturing information system,
    326
Manufacturing resource planning
    (MRP II), 326, 328
Many-to-many relationship, 211–213
Marketing, 38, 325, 397, 398
Marketing information system,
    325–326
Marketing research, 325
Mark-sense reader, 97
Massively parallel processing, 119
MasterCard International, 455
Master data, 310
Matching, 80
Material requirements planning
    (MRP), 326
Mathematical modeling, 348
MB. *See* Megabyte
M byte. *See* Megabyte
MCI, 174, 445
Meeting Maker, 293
Megabyte, 112–113
Megahertz, 116
Memory. *See* Primary storage
Menu, 141
Merge utility, 148
Mesh, 180
MetaCrawler, 260
Meta-search engine, 261
Method, 427
Metropolitan area network (MAN),
    182
MHz. *See* Megahertz
Michelin North America, 22
MICR. *See* Magnetic ink character
    recognition
Microcomputer, 65–67, 104. *See also*
    Personal computer
    CPU, 117
Microprocessor, 117
Microsecond, 116
Microsoft, 145, 280, 281, 286, 295,
    430, 444, 445
Microwave, 173
Midrange computer, 70

Miller SQA, 327–328
Millisecond, 116
Minicomputer, 69–70
    CPU, 117–118
MIS. *See* Management information
    system
Mobile computing, 174
Model base management system,
    350
Model, 348
Model base, 348–349
Modem, 168, 175
MO disk, 125
Modulation, 175
Monitor, 99
Monochrome monitor, 99
Motorola, 117
Mouse, 95
MPE, 148
MRP. *See* Material requirements
    planning
MRP II. *See* Manufacturing resource
    planning
Multidimensional database, 225–226
Multifunction printer, 102
Multimedia, 74, 106, 256–258
    input and output, 106–107
Multimedia developer, 450
Multinational strategy, 387, 390
Multiple-user computer system,
    69–70
    communications software, 179
    database software, 218
    operating system, 148
Multiple-user operating system, 144
Multiplexer, 176
Multipoint videoconferencing, 287
Multiprocessing, 119
Multitasking, 142–144

N

Nanosecond, 116
Natural language, 149, 153
Navigator. *See* Netscape Navigator
Net income, 32
NetMeeting, 286, 295
NetNews, 189
Netscape Navigator, 260
NetWare, 148
Network, 19, 63, 70–71, 179–180.
    See also Local area network;
    Wide area network;
    Internetwork
    acquiring technology, 444–445
    communications, 169
    communications software, 179
    organization, 180–182
    types, 182
Network administrator, 448
Network analyst, 448

Network computer, 191
Network database, 214
Network database management
    system, 217, 218
Networked computer system, 70–71
    database software, 218
    operating system, 148
Network interface card (NIC), 183
Network operating system (NOS),
    148, 179
Neural network, 361
Neuron, 361
NIC. *See* Network interface card
Niche, 373
Node, 180
Nonimpact printer, 100–101
Nonvolatile storage, 110
NOS. *See* Network operating system
Notebook computer, 69
Notes, 284, 284*n*, 295
Not-for-profit organization, 36
Novell, 148, 281, 444

O

Object, 156, 216, 427
Object-oriented analysis and
    design, 427
Object-oriented database, 216
Object-oriented database
    management system, 216,
    217, 218
Object-oriented programming, 156
Object-oriented programming
    language, 156–158
Object program, 151, 152
Object-relational database, 216
ObjectStore, 218
OCR. *See* Optical character
    recognition device
Office, 255
Office automation, 296
Off-line, 313
OLAP. *See* On-line analytical
    processing
OLTP. *See* On-line transaction
    processing
1–800-flowers, 404–405
One-to-many relationship, 210–211
One-to-one relationship, 210
1–2–3, 245, 250
On-line, 313
On-line analytical processing
    (OLAP), 227–229
On-line processing. *See* On-line
    transaction processing
On-line transaction processing
    (OLTP), 312–313
On Technology, 293
OnTime, 293
Open Text, 293

Operand, 150
Operating environment, 145
Operating personnel, 76
Operating system, 71, 139
    capabilities, 142–145
    common, 145–148
    functions, 140
    organization, 140–141
    using, 141
Operational decision, 44, 338
Operational feasibility, 410
Operational planning, 440
Operation code, 150
Operations. *See also* Business
        operations
    information system, 448
Optical character recognition (OCR)
        device, 97
Optical disk, 123
    access, 124
    drive, 124
    rewritable, 125
    usage, 124–125
Optical scanning input device, 97
Oracle, 218, 328
Order entry, 45, 378
    system, 7, 314–316, 328
Order processing, 305–306
Organizational electronic commerce,
        377
Organizational information system,
        15–16, 137–138
Organizational knowledge, 362
Organization chart, 39
Organization of a business, 39
Orient-Express Trains & Cruises,
        257
OS/390, 148
OS/2, 147, 148
Outbound logistics, 397–398
Outlook, 280
Output control, 451
Output data, 8, 11
Output device, 63
    multimedia, 106–107
    for people with disabilities,
        105–106
    plotter, 103
    printer, 100–103
    screen, 99–100
    sound, 104
    virtual reality, 107–109
    voice, 103–104
Output function, 8, 72, 307
    decision support system, 350
    executive support system, 356
    expert system, 360
    management information system,
        344–345
    transaction processing system,
        308, 310

Outsourcing, 411, 412, 444
Owens & Minor, 319–320

P

Pacific Bell, 174
Packaged software, 72, 73, 412
Page, 137
Page layout, 256
PageMaker, 256
Page printer, 101, 103
Page scanner. *See* Scanner
Pages per minute (ppm), 101
Palmtop computer, 69
PAPA, 78
Paradox, 239
Parallel processing. *See* Massively
        parallel processing
Parallel system installation, 415
Parity bit, 112, 451
Parity check, 451
Partial cybermarketer, 376
Password, 453
Payroll, 53–54
    system, 16, 322–323, 324, 328
Payroll report, 53
PC. *See* IBM clone; IBM PC;
        Personal computer
PDA. *See* Personal digital assistant
Pen input, 96
Pentium, 117
PeopleSoft, 328
Performance appraisal, 328
Peripheral equipment, 94
Personal computer (PC), 67. *See
        also* Apple Macintosh; IBM
        clone; IBM PC
    communications software,
        178–179
    database software, 218
    operating system, 145–148
Personal computer analyst, 448
Personal computer system, 65–69
Personal database, 223
Personal digital assistant (PDA), 69
Personal information system. *See*
        Individual information system
Personnel, 11, 75, 445. *See also*
        Human resource
        management
    need for, 76
    types, 75–76
Phased system installation, 415, 425
Physical system design, 411*n*
PictureTel, 288
Pilot system implementation, 415
Pinnacol Assurance, 437–438
Pixel, 99
Planning. *See* System planning
Planning horizon, 440–441
Platform, 72

Plotter, 103
Plunge system implementation, 415
Pointing device, 95–96
Point-of-sale (POS) system, 3
Point-to-point communication, 169
Point-to-point videoconferencing,
        287
Populating, 239
Portal, 261
Portfolio management, 325
POS. *See* Point-of-sale system
PowerBuilder, 218
PowerPC, 117
PowerPoint, 252
Ppm. *See* Pages per minute
Presentation graphics software, 13,
        250–252
President, 39
Primary activity, 397
Primary key, 215–216
Primary storage, 63, 92–93
    capacity, 112–113
    data representation, 110–112
    organization, 112
    structure, 109–110
Printer, 100
    classifications, 100–101
    desktop, 101–102
    high-volume, 102–103
Print server, 183
Print utility, 148
Privacy, 78–80
Private communications system, 74
Problem, 262
    solution. *See* Solution
Problem solving, 262, 263
    documentation, 267–268
    implementation testing, 266–267
    problem definition, 264–265
    process, 263–264
    software implementation, 266
    solution procedure design,
        265–266
Procedures, 11, 76
    need for, 77
    types, 76–77
Process, 418. *See also* Business
        process
Processing control, 451
Processing function, 8, 72
    decision support system, 350
    executive support system, 357
    expert system, 360
    management information system,
        347
    transaction processing system,
        311
Process management, 140
Processor. *See* Central processing
        unit
Proctor & Gamble, 234–235

Procurement, 398
Product differentiation, 372–373
Product distribution, 379
Production. *See* Manufacturing
Production printer. *See* High-volume printer
Production scheduling system, 7–8, 16, 326
Productivity, 23, 238–239
Product presentation, 377–378
Product support, 379
Profit, 32
Program, 92, 135. *See also* Software
    execution, 114–115
    loading, 114
Programmer, 149, 447–448
Programmer/analyst, 448
Programming, 149
Programming language, 149
    concepts, 149–150
    Internet, 158–161
    object-oriented, 153–156
    selection, 150
    traditional, 156–158
    types, 150–153
Project team, 408
PROLOG, 360
Prompt, 141
Property, 82
ProShare, 288
Protocol, 176–178
Protocol converter, 177–178
Prototype, 426
Prototyping, 426
Public communications system, 174
Public domain software, 457
Publisher, 256
Publishing, 430
Purchase order, 51
Purchasing, 51–52
    information flow in, 42
    system, 320–321, 326
Push technology, 261

Q

QBasic, 154
QBE. *See* Query-by-example
QUALCOMM, 280
Quattro Pro, 245, 250
Query, 344
Query-by-example (QBE), 221
Query language, 153, 219, 347
QuickBASIC, 154

R

RAD. *See* Rapid application development
RAID, 122, 451
RAM. *See* Random access memory
Random access, 110, 123, 124, 202

Random access memory (RAM), 110
Random file. *See* Direct file
Rapid application development (RAD), 426–427
Raw materials inventory, 51
Read only memory (ROM), 110
Read/write head, 121
Realistic image, 250
Real memory, 144
Real-time, 313
Real-time operating system, 144
Real-time processing, 313
Receiving notice, 49
Record, 73, 201, 239
Recovery procedure, 312
Reduced instruction set computer. *See* RISC
Redundant array of inexpensive disks. *See* RAID
Redundant hardware, 451
Redundant processing, 451
Reebok International, 289
Relation, 214
Relational database, 214–216
Relational database management system, 217, 218, 219
Relationship, 207, 239, 419
    many-to-many, 211–213
    one-to-many, 210–211
    one-to-one, 210
Remote access, 65
Repetitive strain injury, 94
Report, 308–310, 344
Report generator, 153, 347
Requirements. *See* User requirements
Research and development, 39
Resolution. *See* Screen resolution
Resource management, 140
Resource sharing, 65
Retailer, 34
Retail sales, 33
Revenue, 32, 55
Rewritable optical disk, 125
Ring network, 181
RISC, 116
Risk, 441
Robotics, 326
ROM. *See* Read only memory
Room videoconferencing system, 287
Router, 188
Row, 214
Rule, 358–359

S

Saab, 302–303
Sable Offshore Energy Project, 283–284

SABRE, 396, 397
Sales analysis, 325
    system, 3
Sales force automation, 325–326
Sales forecasting, 325
Sales information flow, 40–41
Sales order, 44, 315
SamePage, 284
SAP, 328
Scanner, 97
Scheduled report, 345
Screen, 99–100
Screen projector, 100
Screen resolution, 9, 100
SDLC. *See* System development life cycle
Search engine, 260
Secondary storage, 63, 94
    magnetic disk, 119–123
    magnetic tape, 123–125
    optical disk, 125–126
Second-generation language, 151
Security. *See* System security
Sensitivity analysis, 349
Sequential access, 123, 124, 126, 202
Sequential file, 202
Serial printer, 101
Server, 71, 148, 183
    CPU, 119
Service, 397, 398
Service business, 34–36
7-eleven, 5
Shared database, 223–224
Shareware, 457
Sharper Image, 46
Shell Oil, 363
Shipping order, 45
Signal type, 169
Silicon Graphics, 69, 290
Simulation, 348
Single-tasking, 142
Single-user operating system, 144
SIS. *See* Strategic information system
Site. *See* Web site
Site license, 457
Skills inventory, 328
Slice and dice, 226
Smalltalk, 157
SmartSuite, 255
Sodexho Marriott Services, 68
SoftArc, 284
Software, 10, 71, 92, 135
    acquiring, 444
    alternatives, 411–412
    application, 135–138
    development, 145–161
    implementation, 266

need for, 72
selection, 265
sources, 72–73
system, 139–149
types, 71–72
Software engineering, 421
Software license agreement, 457
Software piracy, 457
Solution, 262
Solution procedure, 262–263
design, 265–266
Sorting, 310
Sort utility, 148
Sound output device, 104
Source document, 307
Source program, 151, 152
Sparks.com, 259–260
Speech synthesis, 104
Spider, 261
Spreadsheet, 12, 136, 245
Spreadsheet analysis, 245–246
case study, 246–247
combining with database
management, 247–248
combining with other applications,
253–256
Spreadsheet software, 12, 136, 238,
245
using, 245–246
Sprint, 174, 445
Sprint Paranet, 449–450
SQL, 219–221, 222, 347
SQL Server, 218
Star network, 180
Statement, 48, 317
Statistical calculation, 348
Storage control, 451
Storage function, 8, 72, 307
decision support system, 350
executive support system, 357
expert system, 360
management information system,
346
transaction processing system,
310–311
Storage location, 112
Store-and-forward, 286, 290
Stored data, 10–11, 73
need for, 75
organization, 73–74
Strategic advantage. See Strategic
impact
Strategic decision, 44, 338
Strategic impact, 372–374, 394,
397
electronic commerce system,
374–375
global information system,
388–389
interorganizational system,
382–383

Strategic information system (SIS),
394
characteristics, 394–397
opportunities, 397–398
Strategic planning, 441
Structured Query Language. See
SQL
Subject directory, 261
Suite, 255
Summary report, 308, 344–345
Sun Microsystems, 69
Supercomputer, 70
CPU, 118–119
Supervisor, 140
Supplier-managed inventory, 383
Supplier master data, 321, 322
Supplier-oriented marketplace,
376
Supply chain, 33n
Supply-chain management, 328
Support activity, 398
Switched line, 445
Switching cost, 396–397
Sybase, 218
Synchronize, 293
Syntax, 149
Syntax error, 266
System acquisition, 414, 424
System analysis, 409, 411, 412
case study, 422–424
user involvement in, 412
System design, 409, 413
case study, 424
user involvement in, 413–414
System development, 408–409,
447–448
case study, 421–425
other approaches, 426–427
people in, 408
process, 409–417
tools, 417–421
System development life cycle
(SDLC), 408
System implementation, 409,
414–415
case study, 424–425
user involvement in, 415
System installation, 414, 425
System maintenance, 409,
415–417
case study, 425
System planning, 409–410,
440–442
case study, 421–422
user involvement in, 410–411
System programmer, 448
Systems analyst, 408, 447
System software, 71–72, 139
operating system, 139–148
other, 148–149
System testing, 414, 425

T

Table, 214
Tactical decision, 44, 338
Tactical planning, 440–441
Tag, 158
Tape. See Magnetic tape
Tape drive. See Magnetic tape
drive
Tape library, 126
Tax accounting, 324
TB. See Terabyte
T byte. See Terabyte
TCP, 188–189
TCP/IP, 189
TDF. See Transborder data flow
TeamWave, 286
Technical feasibility, 410
Technical support, 448
Technical trainer, 448
Technology development, 398
Telecommunications, 168
Telecommunications monitor, 179
Telecommuting, 297, 459
Telnet, 189
Terabyte, 113
Terminal, 103–105
Terminal adapter, 176
Terminal emulation, 178–179
Testing, 266–267, 414, 430
Thin client, 191
Third-generation language,
151–152
3Com, 69, 147, 444
Three-tiered client/server computing,
192n
Time-sharing, 141
Token Ring, 184
Touch input device, 96
Touchpad, 95
Touch screen, 96
TPS. See Transaction processing
system
Track, 120, 123, 125
Trackball, 92
Trackpoint, 95
Training, 448
Transaction, 306
Transaction data, 410
Transaction processing system
(TPS), 305, 306, 342, 343,
384, 391, 394
controlling, 311–312
functions, 307–311
processing data in, 312–313
structure, 306–307
Transborder data flow (TDF), 390
Transmission control protocol. See
TCP
Transnational strategy, 388, 390
Tuple, 214

Twisted-pair wiring, 171
Two-tiered client/server computing, 192*n*

U

Unicode, 112
Unified messaging, 296
Uniform resource locator (URL), 189
Uninterruptible power source, 451–452
Uninterruptible power supply. *See* UPS
Unisys, 70, 443
United Airlines, 118, 396
Universal Code. *See* Unicode
Universal product code (UPC), 97
UNIX, 71, 147, 148, 156
UPC. *See* Universal product code
Updating data, 204, 239–240, 310, 311
Uploading data, 179
UPS, 452
URL. *See* Uniform resource locator
Usenet, 189
User, 17–19, 75
  in decision support systems, 348, 349
  direct versus indirect, 17–18
  effective, 25
  in electronic commerce systems, 429
  in executive support systems, 355
  in expert systems, 358
  in management information systems, 342–343
  problem solving, 262–268
  in system development, 410–411, 412, 413–414, 415, 417, 428–429
  in transaction processing systems, 306–307
User documentation, 267
User interface, 141
User requirements, 411, 422
Utilitarianism, 77
Utility program, 148

V

Value added network (VAN), 182, 381, 385, 445
Value added reseller (VAR), 444
Value chain, 397–398
VAN. *See* Value added network
VAR. *See* Value added reseller
VDT. *See* Video display terminal

Vendor-managed inventory, 385
Ventana, 292
Versant ODBMS, 218
Vice president, 39
Video compression, 288–290
Videoconferencing, 287–290
Video decompression, 290
Video display terminal (VDT), 104
View, 223–224
Virtual company, 298
Virtual meeting, 297–298
Virtual memory, 144–145
Virtual office, 297, 459
Virtual private network (VPN), 187, 445
Virtual reality, 107
  input and output, 107–109
Virtual work environment, 297–298
Virus, 457–458
Visio, 250
Visual Basic, 152, 154, 158
Visual communication, 279
Visual InterDev, 430
Visual programming language, 157–158
Visual WorkFlo, 294
VocalTec, 287
Voice input device, 98–99
Voice output device, 103–104
Voice processing, 296
Voice recognition, 98
Volatile storage, 110
VPN. *See* Virtual private network

W

WAN. *See* Wide area network
Web. *See* World Wide Web
Web-based groupware, 279
Web browser. *See* Browser
Webmaster, 448–450
Web programmer, 450
Web server, 192
Web site, 192
What-if analysis, 246, 349
Whiteboard conferencing, 284–286
  software, 286
Wholesaler, 34
Wholesale sales, 33
Wide area network (WAN), 15, 19, 182
  business use of, 187
  structure, 185–187
Wincite, 365
Window, 141
Windows, 71, 145–147
Windows CE, 147

Windows 98, 147, 148
Windows NT. *See* Windows 2000 Professional; Windows 2000 Server
Windows 2000 Professional, 147, 148
Windows 2000 Server, 148
Wire cable, 170–171
Wireless communication, 173
Wireless LAN, 183
Word, 248
WordPerfect, 248
WordPerfect Office, 255
Word Pro, 248
Word processing, 238, 248
  case study, 253, 256
  combining with other applications, 253–256
  system, 12
Word processing software, 12, 136, 248
Workflow management, 293–294
  software 294
Workgroup, 39
Workgroup application
  software, 137
  summary, 294–296
  types, 279–294
Workgroup information system, 13–15, 276, 392, 394
Work-in-process inventory, 51
Workplace, 286
Works, 256
Worksheet, 245. *See also* Spreadsheet
Workstation, 69
World Wide Web (WWW), 19–21, 158, 189, 260–262, 448, 450
  database access, 222–223
  evaluating information from, 261–262
  searching, 260–261
Worm, 458
WORM drive, 124
Write once, read many drive. *See* WORM drive
WWW. *See* World Wide Web

X

Xerox, 157, 183
XML, 159

Y

Yahoo!, 260
Y2K problem, 417